The Mystery of the Wooden Rose

Before the Rose

The Wooden Rose

After the Rose

By Soraya

Copyright © 2017 Soraya

All rights reserved.

ISBN-13: 978-1544719573

ISBN-10: 1544719574

Table of Contents

Copyright © 2017 Soraya _____ 2

Chapter 1 Before the Rose, the Gypsy's Curse _____ 13

Chapter 2 _____ 17

Chapter 3 _____ 22

Chapter 4 _____ 25

Chapter 5 _____ 29

Chapter 6 _____ 32

Chapter 7 _____ 36

Chapter 8 _____ 40

Chapter 9 _____ 46

Chapter 10 _____ 51

Chapter 11 _____ 56

Chapter 12 _____ 61

Chapter 13 _____ 66

Chapter 14 _____ 70

Chapter 15 _____ 75

Chapter 16	79
Chapter 17	83
Chapter 18	88
Chapter 19	92
Chapter 20	96
Chapter 21	99
Chapter 22	104
Chapter 23 Before the Rose, Mary's Story	108
Chapter 24	112
Chapter 25	117
Chapter 26	121
Chapter 27	125
Chapter 28	130
Chapter 29	135
Chapter 30	140
Chapter 31	143
Chapter 32	149
Chapter 33	155

Chapter 34 _____ 160

Chapter 35 _____ 165

Chapter 36 _____ 170

Chapter 37 _____ 175

Chapter 38_____ 179

Chapter 39 _____ 185

Chapter 40 _____ 188

Chapter 41_____ 191

Chapter 42 _____ 195

Chapter 43 _____ 199

Chapter 44 _____ 203

Chapter 45 _____ 207

The Wooden Rose, 1889 _____ 210

Chapter 1_____ 210

Chapter 2 _____ 213

Chapter 3 _____ 218

Chapter 4 _____ 224

Chapter 5 _____ 229

Chapter 6	234
Chapter 7	239
Chapter 8	246
Chapter 9	251
Chapter 10	256
Chapter 11	262
Chapter 12 Present Day	267
Chapter 13	271
Chapter 14	279
Chapter 15	284
Chapter 16	289
Chapter 17	294
Chapter 18	298
Chapter 19	305
Chapter 20	311
Chapter 21	314
Chapter 22	318
Chapter 23	323

Chapter 24	327
Chapter 25	332
Chapter 26	337
Chapter 27	341
Chapter 28	345
Chapter 29	350
Chapter 30	356
Chapter 31	362
Chapter 32	369
Chapter 33	372
Chapter 34	376
Chapter 35	381
Chapter 36	386
Chapter 37	392
Chapter 38	396
Chapter 39	401
Chapter 40	406
Chapter 41	412

Chapter 42	418
Chapter 43	423
Chapter 44	427
Chapter 45	433
Chapter 46	439
Chapter 47	444
After the Rose, breaking the curse	449
Chapter 1	449
Chapter 2	453
Chapter 3	458
Chapter 4	462
Chapter 5	466
Chapter 6	470
Chapter 7	476
Chapter 8	481
Chapter 9	488
Chapter 10	492
Chapter 11	497

Chapter 12 _____ 503

Chapter 13 _____ 507

Chapter 14 _____ 511

Chapter 15 _____ 517

Chapter 16 Fabiana _____ 522

Chapter 17 _____ 527

Chapter 18 _____ 531

Chapter 19 _____ 535

Chapter 20 _____ 540

Chapter 21 _____ 546

Chapter 22 _____ 550

Chapter 23 _____ 553

Chapter 24 _____ 557

Chapter 25 _____ 564

Chapter 26 _____ 568

Chapter 27 _____ 571

Chapter 28 _____ 576

Chapter 29 _____ 579

Chapter 30	583
Chapter 31	588
Chapter 32 Alina	593
Chapter 33	598
Chapter 34	606
Chapter 35	617
Chapter 36	623
Chapter 37	627
Chapter 38	631
Chapter 39	636
Chapter 40	640
Chapter 41	644
Chapter 42	652
Chapter 43	660
Chapter 44	664
Chapter 45	670
Chapter 46	674
Chapter 47	679

Chapter 48	684
Chapter 49	689
Chapter 50	694
Chapter 51	698
Chapter 52	703
Chapter 53	708
Chapter 54	713
Chapter 55	716
Chapter 56	720
Other Books by Soraya	725
Dedication	725
Coincidences	726

Chapter 1 Before the Rose, the Gypsy's Curse

Coralina's Story February 1873

Coralina Kelly sat on the padded bench beside the thick brown woollen curtain that closed off the sleeping area in the wagon, and she listened to her mother's feeble cries. She was sitting on her hands, because she knew that if she didn't keep them under her legs, she would have bitten her nails down until they bled. She rocked backwards and forward in her space; she was scared. She was the only child to have survived birthing, all the others had come away before their time, and she could remember when two boys had been born, but they were blue when they came out. She hadn't seen them but she had heard the aunties talking. They would have been her brothers, and she was sad that they hadn't lived. She was sad for her Mam too, because she cried whenever anyone in the camp birthed a new baby.

"Push, push, try harder lass," she heard old Mither Morrison saying.

The men were outside leaving the women to look after things, and she was alone in the wagon, separated from the others only by the curtain. She wanted to pee so badly, but she was afraid to leave, not that she was any help, but still, she didn't want to run through the dark to the toilet tent to relieve herself of her full bladder, just in case she was needed. Finally, when she could hold it no longer, she left the wagon at a run.

"Where ye goin' lass?" her father John called as she scooted past him. He and the others were sitting around the campfire patiently, if worriedly, waiting for the birth of the next child, sharing a bottle of whisky, and silently praying that all would be well.

"Ah'm goin' tae the dunny Da."

"Straight back Coralina, mind now, straight back."

The Gypsies' camp was set in a clearing surrounded by trees near Glasgow Green and close to the River Clyde. There was a narrow road close by, but no one could see the camp from there, and that was fine because their privacy was important. Eight wagons were on this camp, nearly forty Gypsies in all, and they were relatives of each other by birth, marriage, or close kinship. This location gave them access to all the places that they would travel to, selling their wares or services, whether they were heading to the Ayrshire coast or to villages and towns further afield. The wagons were in a semi circle, with a campfire in the middle. Over the fire stood a Chitty Prop, a three legged cast iron frame for suspending a large kettle for boiling water. At meal times, the kettle would be replaced with a heavy iron pot for cooking soups and stews.

Off she ran to the space that had been prepared, which contained a large galvanised steel bin. A lid with a hole in the centre, forming a seat, had been fashioned out of wood so that anyone who needed to use it could sit without touching the cold hard steel. A hap made of canvas was fastened to the wooden frame of the dunny and gave some privacy when it was in use. Coralina hitched up her thick woollen skirt and dragged at her knickers, pulling them down as far as her thighs, and then she squatted over the seat. She sighed with relief as she emptied her bladder; she had held it in for so long that she thought she would never stop. She paused when she had finished, hoping the last drips had fallen before she hitched up her knickers, and hurried back to the wagon.

She could smell the wood smoke from the fire and as she came through the trees, the light from the fire guided her. She could see the shadows of the men sitting around the fire, wearing their thick jackets, caps, and scarves to keep themselves warm in the cold February air. She could hear their whispered conversations but couldn't make out what they were saying. The heat from the fire warmed her face as she ran past it, and quietly crept back into the wagon. She was shivering now, and grabbing a blanket, she threw it over her shoulders. Once more, she took her place on the bench in the sitting area. She didn't know what time it was but she knew that it had been hours and hours. It would be morning soon and still she sat.

Mither Morrison had been in and out several times demanding more hot water as she tried to help Mary Ellen, her daughter-in-law, deliver her baby. Coralina didn't know what all the hot water was for, but Mither Morrison needed plenty of it. Just as the day was breaking she heard a funny little noise, a squeak almost, and then loud lusty cries. She knew, as her heart filled with joy and excitement, that the baby had come and it wasn't blue, she didn't think blue babies cried. She was excited and happy to have a new baby brother or sister, but as she listened, she realised that it had all gone very quiet, apart from the little noises the new baby was making.

Still she listened, and then Mither Morrison came out. At fifty-three, she was the oldest mother in their camp, and the 'Mither' in any camp was always shown the utmost respect and always had the best of things, partly because some of the residents would be her grown children, and partly because everyone in any camp made sure that the Mither had everything that she needed. She had been quite a character in her day, and even yet, as old as she was, for in those days being in your fifties was a good age, she still managed to bring a spark of light during heavy or hard times. She could make everyone laugh with the old stories she told, and when the occasion warranted it, she could dance a jig with the best of them, though her arthritic bones meant that her jig didn't last very long. With a word or a look, the Mither could make a man feel ten feet tall or chastise him and reduce him to feeling that he was ten years old. She was held in such esteem that she seldom had to chastise, and was more likely to nod and say, "Well done lad, aye well done," and the lad in question, though twenty-four or forty would puff up his chest proudly.

Mither Morrison's hair, once red, was now as white as snow. She wore it partly covered by a colourful thick woollen chequered scarf that she had wrapped around the length of her hair at the back of her neck, and twisted and tied to one side. Her hair had receded back from her forehead a little, exposing a deep brow over watery eyes once as blue as the sky on a summers day. Though her skin was pale, her cheeks were rosy red from daily exposure to the fresh air and the elements. A thick brown woollen dress came down to her ankles, and over it was a sleeveless v-neck jumper hand knitted using many different colours of wool. Over one shoulder was a woollen blanket of reds, yellows, and blues, and the toes of chunky black boots peeped out from her ensemble. She wore heavy gold hoops in her ears and fine gold bangles dangled on her thin wrists as she moved. Her jewellery, and the bright colours that she wore, always drew attention wherever she went.

She was proud of her family too, her son George was married to Mary Ellen's sister Isabella, and they had given her three fine granddaughters. The last one, a late baby, was little Daisy, not yet weaned onto solids, Nellie was five and Jennie was ten. Isabella had miscarried more than once, so she cherished her girls and she was a good mother.

Chapter 2

Coralina looked up as Mither Morrison came through the thick dividing curtain. She realised that the Mither was carrying the tiny baby wrapped in the new white shawl that her mother had knitted. The Mither handed the baby to Coralina.

"Here, watch whit yer daein', an' take the bairn tae yer Auntie Isabella, she'll see tae her. It's a wee lassie."

Coralina looked at the Mither and wondered why she had tears on her face. This was a happy time she thought, as she tenderly and carefully took the new baby in her arms. This tiny baby was her little sister and she was overjoyed. She looked back at the Mither and then suddenly felt confused. She wondered why she had to take the bairn to her Auntie Isabella. Coralina had a worried expression, her eyes were wide and her mouth gaped in surprise, but the Mither only said, "Tell yer Da tae come in on yer way oot."

Coralina stepped into the doorway pausing above the wooden steps, and then made her way slowly down with the baby in her arms. All the men stood suddenly and stared at her. They looked at her anxiously first, and then, as one, they looked at her father as he yelled, "Mary Ellen, nooooo, nooooo!" He screamed for his wife. He groaned as though in agony, as he realised that this could only mean one thing. Coralina, frightened by this sudden change, watched as the men grabbed her father, and held him as he cried. She skirted around them and ran over to her Auntie Isabella's.

Isabella, as well as everyone else in the camp, had been waiting and watching from her wagon as her sister struggled in the throes of childbirth.

"Come in hinny, I'll take the bairn. Go and sit down." Isabella did her best to hide her grief as she took the baby in her arms. Coralina climbed the steps and followed her aunt into her wagon, sat on the bench and watched as Isabella opened her top and fastened her little sister to her ample breast.

"She needs feedin," she said by way of an explanation.

"How come you're feedin her?"

"I'm sorry lass, ye'll have tae wait till the Mither speaks tae ye."

Coralina stood up to go back to her wagon. She was confused and frightened, and wanted to know why her aunt was feeding her baby sister and not her mother. She wanted to know what was wrong with her father.

"Sit doon' lass, stay where ye are, Mither will come for ye when its time."

Coralina was staring at her aunt and she could see that she was upset. Tears began to run down Coralina's face. She didn't know what or why but she knew that something was wrong. She watched her little sister suckle, and she watched as Isabella moved her from one breast to the other. When she was finished feeding, and the baby was content and sleeping, Isabella reached over and placed the baby in Coralina's arms.

"She'll be yours to look after noo Coralina."

Not quite understanding the full implication of the words that her aunt had spoken, Coralina held the baby close, inhaling that new baby smell, and gazed into the child's sleeping face. She was overwhelmed with a love that she hadn't known existed.

"I'm yer big sister," she whispered, and she kissed the baby on her soft cheek.

"Ah'll aye look after ye'," she said, as she rocked back and forward lulling the new baby.

A short while later, Mither Morrison came into Isabella's wagon, and the two women, the younger and the older, looked solemnly at each other as the Mither sat beside Coralina.

"Whit age are ye now hinny?" she asked, although she knew the answer to that question.

"Ah'm seven Mither, Ah'm nearly eight, Ah won't drop her or onythin', Ah'll be careful Mither."

"I, Ah ken ye will lass, Ah ken ye will, yer young yet but yer gonnae have to be strong for Ah have summat tae tell ye."

"Is it ma Da?"

"No hinny its no' yer Da, it's yer Mam. She didnae make it. She gave her last breath tae yer wee sister."

"Whit dae ye mean Mither."

"She's gone lass, she's gone tae heaven tae be wi' the angels, an' ye'll have tae look after wee Mary here. She's your responsibility noo. Gie her tae me an' away ye go across an' say yer farewell tae yer Mam."

Coralina's eyes were wide with terror as she thought about what the Mither was saying. She let her take baby Mary in her arms and in a flash, she was out of the wagon, jumping down the steps, and there, amidst the wagons, was a trestle surrounded by other members of the camp, some were family, and some were friends. As she approached, they parted and she could see her mother lying on the trestle. Thick green glass jars containing lit candles were set around the trestle, but there was space enough for her to approach closely.

"Mam, Mam," she cried as she ran over.

She knew the custom for laying out the dead; she had seen it before and she realised that her mother was gone. She reached over and stroked her mother's cold face, the face that she loved so much, and then she touched her mother's hands, folded over her chest. She stroked her mother's raven hair and she tried to reach up to kiss her, but she was too small. She suddenly felt strong hands lift her up, she knew those hands; they were her father's hands.

"Be strong lass," he whispered to her as he her high enough to reach her mother's lips.

As he put her down, she turned, leapt into his arms once more, and sobbed into his strong chest. Tears coursed down John Kelly's face as he held his sobbing daughter in his arms. He could hear the quiet sobs of those who grieved with him.

The days following her mother's funeral were a blur to Coralina. Her grief was such that she gave all her attention to her baby sister, and the only time that she was parted from her was when her aunt put Mary to her breast.

"Does that make ye Mary's Mam now that yer feedin' her?" she asked one day.

Her aunt looked up and smiled kindly, for she was glad that Coralina had spoken at all.

"No lass, Ah'll no' be her Mam, but Ah'll aye love her as though she was ma ain. She's takin' ma milk so there will aye be a part o' me in her."

"Ah love ye tae Auntie Isabella, and Ah'm glad ye had spare milk."

Isabella smiled, "A mithers' body's a miracle for it gives as much milk as is needed, even if Ah had two suckling bairns Ah could still feed a third. Ah'm still makin' milk for yer wee cousin Daisy, an' ma body'll make as much as Ah need."

Coralina gazed at her aunt with admiration and love in her young eyes. She thought that she was beautiful with her smooth skin and her long straight brown hair cascading over one shoulder. Isabella looked down into Mary's contented face as she fed her. Coralina thought that she looked like an angel, though she had never seen an angel, she was sure that if she had it would look just like her aunt. Thinking of angels made Coralina think of her Mam, and suddenly, the tears began to fall, and they wouldn't stop. Soon she was sobbing; she cried and sobbed, and cried and sobbed some more. She wasn't aware of Mither Morrison coming in, nor was she aware of her father picking her up. He carried her across to the Mithers wagon where they were staying temporarily, put her down on her bed, and covered her with a thick blanket. He sat with her stroking her hair, and he cried silent tears as he wished that things could have been different for his two girls. He knew the road ahead would be a hard one, but he promised himself that he would do his very best by his daughters. Finally, when Coralina was in a deep sleep he rose and left her to rest.

Much later, Coralina woke up her father sat on the edge of her bed.

"Sit up an' take some soup hinny."

She didn't know why but for some reason she felt much lighter. She sat up and her father spoon-fed her from the thick earthenware bowl. Each time he put the spoon to her mouth she would raise her eyes, and look into his strong handsome face. He looked older and sad, and she wondered if she was sick and maybe she was going to go to heaven to be with the angels too.

"Ah'm Ah sick Da?" she asked between spoonfuls.

"No lass, yer no' sick, yer just sad, dae ye feel sick?"

"No Da, Ah feel good."

"Here, take the bowl an' finish yer soup, and then go ower an' help yer Auntie Isabella wi' yer wee sister." He handed her the bowl and stood up to leave the wagon and then he turned and looked down at her, "Yer a good lass hinny, and yer Mam would be proud o' ye. Ah'll be away for a few days hinny so ye'll bide here wi' Mither Morrison until Ah come back."

Chapter 3

John and other members of the camp had held a wake for Mary Ellen until it was time for her burial at Janefield Cemetery. Now that the funeral was over, as was the custom, John and some of the other men in the camp would take the wagon away and burn it. It was thought to be bad luck to live in a wagon in which someone had died. Those who could not afford to replace their home would sell it to a dealer and a new one purchased. The wagon with all the deceased person's possessions was burnt, but there was one thing that John wouldn't burn. Mary Ellen had often spoken to him about the pretty dress she had worn when they had married. She had wrapped it carefully in brown paper and put it away for safekeeping. Each year she took it out, aired it, and treasured the memories it evoked. She always said that one day a daughter might wear the dress on her wedding day.

John took the brown paper parcel across to Isabella's wagon, "Ah've a favour tae ask ye? Ah've Mary Ellen's weddin' dress here. She aye said that someday her lassie might wear it an' Ah cannae bear to burn it. Whit dae ye think. Dae ye think Ah should keep it?"

"Aye John, Ah think ye should 'cause it was her wish, gie it here an' Ah'll take care o' it."

Wagon's were always eye catching and beautifully decorated with the woodwork intricately carved, decorated with fancy scrollwork, and painted in bright colours. More often than not, they would be in a bow-topped style with a heavy canvas cover. John rode to a dealer in the Borders and he had found a wagon, built entirely of wood. It had a narrow floor with the sides sloping out and upwards towards a curved wooden roof. The trimmings were carved in fancy patterns and painted red and gold. Two small spoke wheels to the front and two large spoke wheels to the back attached to the undercarriage giving the frame a good strong foundation. The inside contained everything needed for a family. There was a narrow bed suspended from the roof, which gave access below it to the front of the wagon where Coralina could climb through the stable style doorway to sit by him as he led his horses during their travels. A wood burning

'Queenie' stove fitted against one side would keep them warm during the cold winters, and the flat plate on top of the stove would keep water hot in a small kettle. A bench seat fixed to the opposite wall gave them a place to sit, watch the flames, and chat about their day. There was a plump cushion covered in a fancy tapestry on the bench which when lifted out, revealed a hinged strip of wood that could be unfolded creating a bed, which was perfect for Coralina, and as Mary grew both girls would be able to share it. Tucked away to one side there was a folding table, with two stools in front of it. There was plenty of storage room below the wagon, and between the wheels, and John knew that he could store his small cart, and many other possessions there. Gypsies always enjoyed cooking their food outside on an open fire so there was no need for anything else in the wagon and he was sure that Coralina would be pleased and surprised with their new home.

John was away for more than a week and during that time Coralina watched for her father's return. Isabella and Mither Morrison gave her lots of attention and love but she was understandably very sad.

Grief takes its time to pass and everyone grieves in their own way. Some find solace in tears and solitude, others find it in anger or in work, but Coralina found her solace in looking after little Mary. Sometimes when she looked at Mary, she could see a likeness to her mother and that too gave her comfort. She talked to Mary all the time, and Mary's gaze seldom left Coralina's face. Gradually, day by day, Coralina recovered from the trauma and sadness of losing the mother that she had loved so much.

Coralina heard the commotion before she saw what it was about and when she went to investigate, she saw a beautiful red and gold wagon approaching. Her father was at the reins leading two horses, which he had purchased with the wagon, and his own horse tethered on a rope behind the wagon. Everyone had come out to see and admire John's purchase. Coralina had missed her father; she was excited by his return, but even more excited by the new wagon. Before long the horses were unhitched and led off to graze in a space adjacent to John's other horses giving them time to get to know each other before they would graze together.

Coralina climbed into their new home and sat on the bench opposite the stove. Her eyes were wide as she drew her hands over the tapestry seating and surveyed her new surroundings. One by one, other's came to call and give their best wishes for luck in their new home and each of them brought something useful for them to use. Linens for their beds, Tilly lamps to light their home on dark nights, pots pans or dishes and John was grateful for the support that he had received.

The weather was improving, summer was coming, and Coralina spent her days tidying the wagon, though there wasn't much to tidy, and learning from her aunt how to look after baby Mary. Mentoring Coralina helped Isabella to take her mind off losing her sister. She was a patient teacher, and delighted in showing Coralina how to break Mary's wind after her feed and how to change her. She taught Coralina how to clean the soiled nappies and care for Mary's clothes. Coralina already knew how to care for things around the wagon because she had often helped her mother. Many of the things that she had helped with had become her responsibility now, but she didn't disappoint anyone, and merely took these things in her stride.

When Mary wasn't being fed, Coralina would hold her to her chest and then wrap a big shawl around her shoulders. She then wrapped the ends of the shawl around her tiny waist, crossing them over each other and tying them at the front underneath Mary to support her. For the first three months of Mary's life, Coralina carried her like that everywhere she went. Mary grew fast with the love and care provided for her. As she grew heavier, Coralina began to carry her, still wrapped in the big shawl, but piggyback fashion, and baby Mary's big brown eyes took in every detail over Coralina's shoulders wherever Coralina went.

Chapter 4

George Morrison, Isabella's husband, had inherited his smithing skills from his late father, but smithing wasn't his only skill and he enjoyed working with scraps of wood that he came across. He often saw Coralina struggling with Mary on her back, and with that in mind, he began to put together a cart out of an old wooden box. Gypsies wouldn't discard anything that could be used again, and often found uses for things that home dwellers discarded. He added four small wheels to the box, fashioned a wooden handle, and then lined the box with a pillow stuffed with old clean rags that Isabella had washed and dried for him. He presented the cart to Coralina one day when Mary was about three months old. Coralina saw her Uncle George approaching with the cart. He had to stoop to push it because he had designed it so that it would fit Coralina's height. She watched him and wondered.

"Whit's that ye have there Uncle George?"

"Ye've been carryin' Mary aboot a while hinny, she must be getting heavy. Ah've made this so that ye can shove her instead."

"Uncle George! Ye didnae, did ye, is it really for wee Mary?"

There were tears in his eyes as he looked at Coralina's excited face. He smiled proudly at her.

"Here, gie me the bairn, let's see if she likes it."

Carefully he took Mary from her arms and placed her in the little cart. "She likes it," laughed Coralina as she looked at Mary who was kicking her heels on the soft pillow below her.

"Aye hinny, Ah think she does."

"Whit's that ye have there George?" laughed one of the women, "Ah could be daein' wi' wan o' them."

Coralina could prop Mary up or lay her down, and for a while, she amused herself and Mary by just practising these things, and by pushing her around the camp to show the aunties' Mary's new cart. On fine days, she would leave Mary sitting in the cart in the fresh summer air outside the wagon. At night, when chores were done and Mary was settled, Coralina would climb into her bed in the wagon and watch over Mary in her crib before she herself would drift into sleep, listening to the quiet chatter of the adults who were sitting around the campfire. Many of the adults preferred to sleep outside, especially those with bigger families. In fine weather, they would sleep under the stars but in foul weather, they would erect a bender, then dismantle it and stow it away in the morning. The bender was easily constructed using cut saplings that they carried with them stored under the wagon, or replaced fresh if required, and these were stuck into the ground and covered with a canvas

Each morning after changing Mary's dirty nappy, Coralina would carry her to her aunt to be fed, and then she would run back to her wagon collecting hot water from the kettle to wipe surfaces and wash cups and plates. When all her tasks were done, Coralina would take Mary's dirty nappies and drop the soils in into the dunny before leaving them to soak in a tin pail. Later Isabella would boil them in the large tinny set aside for the wives to boil their whites. Travelling women always wanted to have the whitest wash, and Heaven help those who hung out a white wash with stains showing; they were a very particular lot.

Coralina's mother had taught her to wash her hands and face every morning, and once a week, her father would be bring out the big tin bath from under the wagon, and fill it with warm water to bathe in. Coralina loved sitting in the bath and now that she had Mary to look after, her father would hand the baby into the tinny, and Coralina would bathe and play with Mary while her father would look on proudly as his children laughed.

"Come on now," he would say, "gie me the bairn and get yer self scrubbed, dried, and dressed."

While John dried and dressed Mary, he would think sadly about Mary Ellen. Each time he looked at his children, he saw their resemblance to their mother.

When she was finished, Coralina would reach for the towel and climb out of the bath.

"That's it, into bed and face the wall," he would say, before stripping down and climbing into the tinny for an all over scrub.

Every day when chores were done, the girls in the camp would go and sit with Mither Morrison to listen to her stories. She taught the girls how to sew, knit, and crochet. She taught them how to unpick a knitted jumper and to rewind the wool so that it could be used several times. Arthritis prevented the Mither from doing many of these things with her own hands but it did not stop her from teaching the youngsters. Whilst the younger ones practiced their skills, the old Mither would talk to them, teach them about their history, and sing songs of old.

Coralina loved taking Mary across the camp to sit with the Mither. In the spring, summer, and autumn, the girls would walk in the woods and fields with her gathering wild herbs and flowers, and as they walked, she spoke to them, telling them the best way to dry herbs for use in the winter when the land rested and when things were scarce. She spoke to them about the medicinal uses of different leaves or roots that would make a tea or a poultice to treat wounds, boils, or stomach pains. Those who heard her words did not realise that they were learning valuable survival skills, but these words were remembered, and passed on. Often while the women went about their business, the children's voices were heard through the trees as they learned the words of their songs. The Mither would recite the words and the children would repeat them, sometimes laughing as they did so.

Nettle stings when ye gang past

But grab it noo an' grab it fast

Boil the water un' make' a tea

It builds guid bones n' cleans yer pee.

Docken bides tae ease the sting

fae nettles prickly mood

and if ye faw n' cut yirsel

wi' docken bind the wound.

Borage pretty as it is

hides it's face fae ye n' me

but soak it well an' make' a tea

yer skin will clear for aw' tae see.

Chamomile to ease yer tears

An' wash awa' yer night-time fears

Lavender tae clean yer cuts

An' burns fae that camp fire's spits

Mint will calm the worried heart

An' ease yer stomach's wind.

Sage abides tae clear yer mind

An' make' yer thinkin' smart

An' Thyme's the wan ye need tae use

tae fight the germs that kill

an' a' these herbs are guid for ye

so use them as ye will.

Chapter 5

Gypsy families had camped near Glasgow Green for as far back as anyone could remember. Being central, they could go from there to the Borders for tin; to Lanark for gathering and picking fruit or vegetables, to the Ayrshire coast for whelks that they picked from the shores. On their travels, they would buy flour and oats from the mills. Farm work was a good source of income for them too and the farmers appreciated the seasonal labour for root vegetables. The farmers that hired them during the seasons provided fresh fruit and vegetables and they could earn up to eight shillings a week. Money they earned would help them buy food if they ran out of supplies. Life was hard in those days and they spent every daylight hour working and taking advantage of the seasons, but at least travelling families had fresh air and fresh food. They feasted on fish caught in the streams, whelks picked off the shore between September and April, game between October and February and Hares caught for the pot in August after the breeding and nursing cycle was over. They purchased oats, grains, and flour from the mills; kept their own hens for a regular supply of eggs, and milk or cheese came from the nearest dairy farm.

Seasonal farm work was by far the hardest and the happiest of times for the travelling families, whether they were picking turnips, potatoes, or soft fruits. For children this meant meeting up with friends and families and helping their parents. During the picking season it was not uncommon for the families to work from six o'clock in the mornings until late in the evenings, but this was something that everyone looked forward to, adults and children alike, for they were well looked after and well paid by the farmers. If the farms were close by, travelling families would return to their own wagons at night, but if the farms were further afield, whole camps would just gather up their belongings and move to where the work was. Night times were the best of times, for the fine weather meant singing songs round the campfires and sleeping under the stars. There was always a bender to shelter under if the weather was foul. Sometimes a farmhand would arrive at a camp as early as five o'clock in the morning, and everyone would pile into the farmer's cart happy and laughing, ready to go to work. The farmer's wife would have prepared an urn full of tea, and piles of sandwiches, which they would enjoy before they began their shift. There was always enough to feed everyone. At weekends, a big breakfast of home cured bacon, fresh laid eggs, and homemade tattie scones was served. Bread would be thick, crusty, and still warm from the oven, and butter churned fresh would be as yellow as the summer sun. In those days, many farmers made the travellers part of the family, and it was a natural thing for Gypsy children to become friends with farmer's children.

The beginning of June signalled the start of harvesting and everyone would pile into the fields and begin the days' work. Farmers sold the crops they gathered at markets and fairs or to locals who would go direct to them for their produce. Everyone worked side by side with the exception of the teenagers, who liked to work in their own little group, but they worked hard while they talked and giggled. At night, everyone sat around and talked about the days' work before retiring for a good sleep.

The women's role was primarily to mind the home and the children, but they also earned a living by making lace doilies, bunches of Lucky White Heather, Mistletoe and Holly garlands, and Lavender posies. They sold handcrafted items from door to door in nearby towns or villages. Most of them followed the old religion and if they had the gift of second sight, they told housewives their fortunes. Isabella and George's oldest daughters Jennie and Nellie had learned how to crochet little cotton circles for covering jam and honey pots and larger mats for women to set on their sideboards. They often sat of an evening doing this so that they could sell them when they went around doors with their mother.

During winter, the men would gather mistletoe to sell and while they were climbing trees to collect it, the women would be gathering sprigs, ripe with red berries, from the holly trees to make the Christmas decorations. Spring, summer, autumn, or winter, there was always something to do and no hands were ever idle. The young lads would go with their fathers, learning from an early age how to earn a living. Each family had a separate skill set that they were able to earn from, and they would chip in and share whatever they could if another family ran short. After the harsh realities of winter, they always looked forward to attending fairs in Scotland and England and this was a regular feature of life for them. They looked forward to buying goods, selling their crafts, trading horses, dogs, and ferrets, and meeting up with friends or family members who had moved with husbands or wives to live in other camps.

Sickness was rife for home dwellers especially those with children at school, as head lice, scabies, and ringworm, were common. Worse still were mumps, measles, tuberculosis, scarlet fever, whooping cough, and the many other, often fatal, illnesses that plagued them. Children and the elderly were most at risk, the life expectancy for that time was between forty-five and fifty for the poor and manual workers, and the infant mortality rate was very high. Understandably, travelling families tried to stay away from those who were sick, but their life style had penalties too, and they were often harassed for poaching, vagrancy, or trespassing; and if they were caught, harsh prison sentences were imposed on them. One travelling family that fell foul of the authorities was harassed to the point that they were warned that if they didn't move into a permanent home they would have their children taken from them, and they would be put into the 'poor house'. These words were spoken easily from the mouths of those who did not know what struggle was. Those who were in positions of power or authority did not care that finding a home was next to impossible, and for a travelling family, living in one would be like a prison to them.

Chapter 6

Time passed and both girls were beautiful to look at with long jet-black curly hair and deep dark brown eyes. By the time Mary was four, Coralina, then almost twelve, noticed that Mary had something different about her. Sometimes Mary would stop in the middle of things and just stare off into the distance.

"C'mon Mary," Coralina would urge her, "stop yer day dreamin', help me wi' things."

Then Mary would look at Coralina as though she knew something that her big sister didn't. Sometimes Mary would make an announcement like, "Tom's got a sore leg."

Much later, Tom would be seen limping. Coralina had heard the aunties talking about 'The Sight', and she had a vague idea what it meant, but she had never seen it happening before and it had never happened to her. She was a little afraid of it and a little worried.

This went on for some time before Coralina plucked up the courage to speak to Auntie Isabella.

"Dae ye know whit 'The Sight' is Auntie Isabella?"

"Aye, why dae ye ask hinny?"

"Is it bad for ye, can it hurt ye?"

"Why are ye askin' me that hinny?"

"Whit does it mean Auntie Isabella?"

"Is there somethin' ye should be telling me?" Isabella was looking at Coralina who was twisting her hands in agitation.

"Dae ye think ye have seen summat?"

"It's no' me Auntie Isabella, it's our Mary."

"Whit makes ye think she has the sight?"

"She says things."

"Whit kind o' things?"

"Jist stuff, and then it happens. Sometimes she goes quiet and looks,… Ah dinnae know, jist different."

"It's a rare and precious gift, the gift o' the sight Coralina, yer mother had it. She knew all sorts of things, an' sometimes Ah think she knew way too much."

"But whit does it mean Auntie Isabella?"

"Some people pretend tae have it tae earn a sixpence, some pretend tae have it tae show off an' feel important, but there are some that can see whit's gone afore an' whit's still tae come an' often those that have it can make things happen."

"Whit dae ye mean, like seein' pictures in yer heed?"

"Summat like that, everybody can imagine pictures, but folk that have the sight dinnae imagine them, the pictures just come, an' then the pictures come true."

"Ah don't ken whit tae dae, Ah'm supposed tae look oot for her."

"Ye canny dae onythin' hinny, but Ah'll have a wee word wi' Mither an' we'll see whit she says, dinnae worry yer self Coralina."

The next day Isabella was chatting to her cousin Lizzie, who was married to Arthur Donnelly; he bought and sold pots, pans, stainless steel baths, wash basins, and jugs. They were standing by a fire where a galvi basin full of water was propped over the flames to boil their whites.

"Whit's up wi' ye the day Isabella, ye've a worried look aboot ye," said the Mither as she approached them.

"Ah was jist telling Lizzie aboot a chat Ah had wi' Coralina. She thinks oor Mary has the sight and she's fair feart for her."

"Aye, she has that. She has a power aboot her that Ah huvnae seen the like o' for a while."

"Whit are wi' tae dae Mither?"

"Nuthin' ye can dae, 'cept teach her right from wrang and how tae mind her ain business."

"Coralina says Mary sees things and tells her aboot them afore they happen," said Isabella.

"Ah never mentioned afore," said Lizzie, "but Ah've heard her an' it's a wee bit scary, she gets a look aboot her before she says summat, an' Ah'm aye feart o' whit she's gonnae tell us."

"Aye, it can be a curse or a blessin'," said the Mither, "Ah'll keep an eye on her."

Mary's nature was changing; where Coralina was a sensible, obliging, child who always had a ready smile, Mary often displayed a mean side when she didn't get her own way. Coralina did all that was expected of her, but often when she asked for help, Mary would just give her a look and walk away. Coralina lavished love and attention on Mary, as did everyone else, but gradually Mary was gaining a reputation of being selfish and spoiled. Mary was not slow about lifting her hand and striking another child, and no matter what Coralina said or did, Mary was a law unto herself. Coralina didn't want to tell her father but as time passed Mary's behaviour and attitude grew worse. Eventually Coralina spoke to her father.

"She cannae be trusted Da, if ye tell her tae dae summat she only does it if it suits her, and she's got a vicious streak. She punched wee Daisy an' bled her lip, an' Auntie Isabella was ragin'. She tells lies an' a' when she gets caught daein' summat she blames wan o' the cousins."

John sighed sadly, he too had noticed the changes in Mary, and he blamed himself for being too soft on her. He missed Mary Ellen more than ever and silently sent up a prayer to his wife for guidance.

"Dinnae worry Coralina, Ah'll have a word wi' her an' see if she can mend her ways. We've an early start in the morn to head for the Dalgarven Mill. Ah'll speak tae her t'morra'. Ah've some horses tae shift an' we'll bring some flour an' oats back."

Coralina felt the better for having shared her worries about Mary with her father, and she went to sleep that night with hope in her heart, and a sense of excitement too, for she liked going to Dalgarven Mill better than anywhere. They had been going there regularly for as long as she could remember. For summer trips, they left the wagon at the camp and took a big cart and if it was a long trip, they camped beside it in benders. In colder months, they took the wagon and carried a small flat bed trailer, which was stowed under the wagon. They would re-assemble it, fill it with provisions, and tow it behind them as needed. Coralina loved sitting up in the front of the cart with the sun shining on them as they travelled. She would sing old songs and Mary would join in singing and laughing,

"Be baw babbity, babbity, babbity, be baw babbity, kiss the bonnie wee lassie."

They stopped at various farms along the way and while her father attended to the business of selling and buying horses, they would be playing in the sun and singing their favourite songs. For Coralina, every trip to Ayrshire started with an eager anticipation because she had made friends with the miller's son Robert, and she was always happy to see him when they reached Dalgarven Mill. Robert was a little bit taller than she was and had thick fair hair and blue eyes. She smiled to herself as she thought about the way his hair stuck up at the crown of his head, and how he always tried to flatten it. She liked the way it stuck up, but she knew that when she saw him coming towards the wagon the first thing he would do was put his hand up and flatten the unruly tuft. Sometimes Robert and she would wander down by the banks of the River Garnock and play for a while on the sandbank and then it would be back to the mill for a bite to eat before they began their journey home.

Chapter 7

John Kelly always maintained about ten to twelve horses at a time. He had four for pulling the cart or the wagon. Just two horses pulled the cart on short journeys, but on longer trips, John would have two horses leading and two spare horses on guide ropes. From time to time on long journeys, he would swop the horses over to give them a rest from pulling a heavy load. He kept his other horses for breeding, trading at the horse fairs, or selling to farmers. John had a reputation for knowing all there was to know about breeding the best working horses, known as Vanners. Some would say he had an instinct for looking at a foal and knowing that she would be a great brood mare, or a colt, and knowing that he would sire the best horses for pulling wagons. This trip to Ayrshire was an important one because he already had orders for a few of his horses and he planned to keep his eyes open just in case he came across a fine filly or two to breed. He could make a pairing of filly and foal that would later produce a Vanner that was not only a good worker or breeder, but was also a thing of beauty to be admired and shown off at the horse fairs.

Gypsy Vanners were beautiful horses to look at with their long feathered manes that came almost half way down their bodies. They were a joy to observe when they were trotting or cantering, amusing themselves in the fields, or when they were being ridden fast by the young lads showing off at the various fairs. Thick tails, strong fetlocks, and beautifully coloured coats set them apart from other plainer breeds. Little did anyone know that much, much later, when the war would break out, that these colourful flashy horses would be spared being taken to the front line because of their bright colours.

One of his prime concerns was temperament, and he specialised in rearing horses that were not only powerful, but gentle natured. Even the smallest children were safe on a Vanner. Each day he would take the horses one by one, and exercise and groom them. He would brush their long manes and tails and generally handle them so that they were comfortable around people. He would whisper quietly to them and give them an occasional treat of a piece of carrot or turnip, and they loved him in return. They could sense when he was approaching, picking up their ears and then pointing them forward to welcome his approach. When he handed over his treat, a soft nicker would reward him. One by one, he would go round each horse in turn, running his hands down their legs, and feeling their muscles and tendons. Any sign of heat or swelling would mean that there was a strain or injury and that would need tending to immediately by applying a wrap of cabbage leaves or a mash of Chamomile to ease and reduce any inflammation.

John's cousin and best friend Willie McGuigan had four sons. Three of them were always to be found by their fathers side no matter what he was doing, but his youngest son Johnny, who was two years older than Mary, loved being around the horses, and he was always hanging about his Uncle John. Whenever John went to feed and care for the horses young Johnny wasn't far behind him with his father Willie's words ringing in his ears.

"Don't get under yer Uncle John's feet mind."

"Ah won't Da," would reply the youngster.

Since John had no sons, young Johnny's presence was a delight to him, and he enjoyed explaining what he was doing with the horses, and teaching him how to look after and care for them.

Although she had no need to be jealous, Mary hated the attention that her father gave to young Johnny, and she was often spiteful towards him. Johnny was better natured though, he seldom let Mary's nasty side bother him, and soon, when she realised that Johnny didn't react to her jibes, she stopped bothering him. Before long, young Johnny became an extension to the family and, as on this occasion, John would have a word with Willie.

"Ah'm off in the morning to Ayrshire wi' some horses and bringin' back some provisions. Ah'll take young Johnny if ye dinnae need him for onythin'?"

Willie laughed in response, "He'll moan a' day if Ah say he cannae go. Johnny loves bein' wi' his Uncle John an' the horses."

The next day, at the break of dawn, they were all up dressed, and making their way through Glasgow towards Ayrshire. They would travel about fifty or so miles on this journey, managing fifteen miles each day, with just a few short breaks to feed and rest the horses, and to have something to eat. They would be going to some Ayrshire farms to deliver horses ending up at Dalgarven Mill. Each night they would stop at a suitable place and while John unhitched and saw to the horses, Coralina would unload the tarpaulin and hazel poles so that her father could set up the bender where they would sleep. They always camped in the same places, near streams for fresh water for the horses and for cooking and washing.

John would loosely tether the horses allowing them to graze then he would begin putting the bender together. While he was busy with that, Mary and young Johnny fetched twigs to start the fire and Coralina would set some stones in a circle to contain it and then fetch the kettle to hang over the chitty prop. With the fire lit, and a good flame going, John would hang the kettle over so that they could brew some tea.

This became the pattern with John, Coralina, Mary, and young Johnny travelling around Ayrshire together. John was happy having young Johnny around because he seemed to have a calming influence on Mary. Over time, Mary stopped needling Johnny and then just watched him wherever he went. Her eyes followed him, and occasionally he would look up and smile at her, and she would just draw him a look and turn her back, but before long, she would be watching him again. Mary even began to chat to Johnny. At first it was just questions, 'Why are you doing this or that or where are you going?' Johnny was always polite and even-tempered, and soon Mary realised that she got more attention, nicer attention, when she was polite, than the attention she got, or lack of it, when she was being mean. The mean streak was still there but it did not show itself as much.

Often while Coralina and her father were sitting up at the front of the cart, she would glance across to him, and he would glance back at her and smile, as both knowingly acknowledged that Mary and Johnny were chatting in the back. It was nice to hear them talking, nicer still that Mary was being friendly rather than sullen. The motion of the wagon as it rolled over the uneven roads often lulled the youngsters to sleep but Coralina was too excited to sleep. She had other things on her mind. Coralina was twelve now nearly thirteen and she was beginning to feel quite grown up. Since she did everything that a grown woman did, this was really no surprise, but there was still innocence to her and that in itself was appealing to those who knew her.

Coralina began to think of the Millers of Dalgarven Mill, they were a lovely family and they always had a bite to eat ready for them whenever they arrived. They always made sure that they had something to eat before they left, often giving them a loaf of crusty bread and some cheese or scones to take away with them. Elsie and Mathew were their names, and typical of country folk, they rose early in the day and worked until late in the evening. Running a mill was hard responsible work, as they provided for the needs of everyone in the local area, nevertheless they made time for their visitors. Coralina began to think about Robert and she found herself wondering if he would kiss her, and then she was horrified at the thought. Her cheeks flushed with embarrassment as she realised what she was thinking.

"Are ye a'right lass? … Coralina! Ah'm speakin' tae ye, are ye feelin a'right?"

Coralina jumped guiltily as she realised that her father was speaking to her. "Aye Da, Ah'm fine."

"Ye look a bit flushed hinny, are ye sure yer ok?"

"Ah'm fine Da, honest."

She knew her father would be furious if he thought she was thinking about things like that. She wondered where the thought had come from because she had never thought of anything like that before, but the more she tried to put it out of her mind the more it popped back in again.

These were happy days for all concerned but no one could possibly anticipate what was to come, except Mary that is. She was already seeing pictures in her mind and although she couldn't fully understand them, she didn't like them. She didn't like them one little bit, and this of course altered her mood and her behaviour.

Chapter 8

Often, when they arrived at the mill, Mathew would appear, his hair dusted grey with a fine layer of flour, and a happy grin on his face as he welcomed them, his floury hand outstretched to shake John's. He would have a smile and a word for the girls and young Johnny. Elsie was always busy doing something, feeding chickens, seeing to the few cows that they kept for milking, and sometimes she would greet them, her face red from the heat of the bread oven. She would usher them into the cosy kitchen to sit at a table laden with homemade bread, freshly churned butter, fresh jam, and scones straight from the oven in the big black range.

While John and Mathew looked at the horses and talked business, young Johnny was hanging on every word, taking on board everything that he heard, and learning from his mentor. Mary on the other hand was sitting under a tree in a sulk because no one was paying her any heed, and Coralina had gone down to the side of the mill where she could sit by the stream in the afternoon sun and watch the mill wheel turning as it was pushed by the strong flow of water. Mary could see Coralina from where she was sitting and she saw Robert going over to sit beside her. The pair of them chatted for a while and then Robert, leaning towards Coralina, reached his hand over, touched her hair, said something to her, and Coralina smiled at him with her cheeks turning pink. Mary watched the interaction between the two, and was overwhelmed with a feeling that she couldn't explain. Coralina was hers. She didn't want Robert or anyone else being her friend. She closed her eyes tight, her anger building up inside and her thoughts racing, *"Ah hate him, he shouldnae be touchin' ma sister."* Suddenly she heard a yell, and looked over to see Robert sitting on the ground, holding his wrist and Coralina fussing over him. He had slipped off the wall and landed badly on his hand. Coralina looked over, sensing Mary watching, and she saw her smile at what had happened.

"Away in tae the kitchen an' let yer Mam have a look at that, it might need a poultice Robert."

Coralina hurried over to Mary, "Ah saw ye smirking Mary, and Ah think yer badness is wrang. Ah think ye make things happen wi' yer badness, Ah dinnae ken how, but Ah'm sure its summat ye did."

Mary kept her eyes down but inside she was sad, she didn't want Coralina to be angry with her. She loved Coralina, but she didn't know what to say to her to make things right. Coralina sat under the tree beside her and put her arm around Mary's shoulder. "Talk tae me Mary. Whatever is up wi' ye? Ah know ye can dae things, an' Ah know ye can see things, but ye cannae hurt people."

Mary began to cry, she was confused and frightened and sorry that the thing had happened. She leaned in to Coralina and hid her face in Coralina's chest.

"Can ye talk tae me aboot it Mary?"

"Ah don't know, it jist happens sometimes, if Ah get angry."

"Whit happens Mary?"

"Ah don't know; Ah don't know whit it is."

"Look, here comes Robert, dinnae say anythin' tae him, I like him Mary, he's ma friend."

Mary reached up and hugged Coralina as Robert approached.

"Is yer hand ok Robert?"

"Aye its fine, Coralina, it was jist a bit sore when it happened. Yer Da says tae tell ye that he's waiting for ye."

"Thanks Robert," said Coralina.

"Ah'll see ye the next time then?"

"Aye Robert, we'll be back soon enough."

The sacks of flour and oats were stowed in the wagon, and John was shaking Mathews hand as the girls approached. Elsie came out drying her hands on a tea towel.

"...hanks very much Missus Miller," said Coralina, and she gave Mary a small ...ge.

"Thanks Missus Miller, it was nice to be here," said Mary.

Young Johnny piped in with, "Ah might see ye again Missus."

"Ah'm sure ye will Johnny, Ah'm sure ye will," laughed Mrs Miller.

They climbed up on to the cart piled high with sacks of oats and wheat and waved to the Millers as they set off to their camp for the night. It would be an early rise for them to head back home, and it would be late when they got there. The journey home was uneventful, apart from the fact that Coralina was preoccupied with worrying thoughts of Mary and what she might be capable of. She didn't really understand, and although she wanted to ask Mither Morrison, she was a bit afraid of doing so, because she didn't know what the Mither would say or do about it. She wondered if it was just a coincidence that Robert fell off the small wall and hurt himself, and then again maybe it wasn't.

The rolling of the wagon had lulled Johnny and Mary off to sleep.

"Yer quiet hinny," her Da said, "is there summat troubling ye?"

"Well…"

"Speak up lass."

"It's just, ye know Ah'm the nearest thing tae a Mam that oor Mary has."

"Aye."

"Well its jist that a want tae dae the right thing by her."

"Ah ken she can be a bit o' a handful, but ye dae a guid job wi' her Coralina, an' yer Mam would be so proud o' ye, but if yer worried ye know ye can aye ask me or Auntie Isabella or the Mither. Is there summat ye want tae tell me?"

"Naw Da, Ah think Ah'll speak tae Auntie Isabella."

John was quiet for the rest of the journey, as was Coralina, both engrossed in their thoughts. John wondering if there was something he should know or something he could do better, and Coralina was wondering if she would be doing the right thing by expressing her fears to her aunt or the Mither.

They made good time on the journey home, stopping only once on the road, and they were all ready for something to eat before they got settled down for the night and feasted on tea and the scones Elsie had given them before they left. The next day would be a busy one for John, as he would share out the provisions that he had purchased for the rest of the camp. The horses would be rubbed down, watered, and fed, then allowed to rest after their journey. Before long it would be time to go back on the road again. For Coralina it was a different story; she had made up her mind to speak to her aunt again and that was the first thing on her mind when she woke up.

In those days, marrying outside the Gypsy culture was frowned upon, more so even than in present times. Travelling families were expected to marry within their own culture. It was common for them to marry as young as fourteen or fifteen and to marry first or second cousins. Since they lived in small tight knit groups, keeping themselves to themselves, marrying outside their own community was rare. Families could be torn apart by such an event and those that considered this option would bring shame and disgrace on their family. Gypsy men were aggressively protective of their women and they would go to almost any lengths to prevent such a thing from happening, it just wasn't tolerated.

"Mornin' lass, did ye have a good trip tae Dalgarven?"

"Aye Auntie Isabella, ma Da sold the horses we took wi' us and wi' finished up at the mill. Missus Miller fed us well, an' Ah saw Robert."

The moment Roberts name was out of her mouth she blushed. Isabella, canny as ever, knew there was more to come, but waited to see if Coralina would be forthcoming, or if she would need prompted. There was silence as Coralina stood looking uncomfortable, and Isabella carried on with her chores until after a bit she said, "Let's go sit by the fire an' have a drink o' tea." Isabella lifted the heavy kettle from its hook as Coralina put the teapot on a wooden box by the fire. Isabella water into the teapot and added a small handful of leaves. They both for a few moments, Isabella waiting, and Coralina trying to find the words to begin.

'Roberts nice."

"Aye, Ah've heard yer Da sayin' that they're a nice family."

"He stroked ma hair."

"Did he now?" Isabella said, raising her eyebrows.

Coralina continued in a rush, "The thing is Auntie Isabella, Mary was watchin' from under the trees an' Robert fell off the wall, it was jist a wee wall, an' he jist slipped right aff it, an' Ah think it was oor Mary made him fa'."

For a moment Isabella almost laughed, and then she remembered the conversation she had with the Mither about the sight sometimes being a gift or a curse. She pressed her lips together waiting to see if there was more.

"She's jealous Auntie Isabella, she disnae like me bein' too friendly wi' anybody. Ah tried tae talk tae her, an' she feels guilty, so it must ha' been her."

"Was he bad hurt?"

"Naw no' really, jist a sprain in his wrist, he's a' right but Ah'm worried aboot Mary."

"Drink yer tea Coralina an' dinnae worry yer self, Ah'll have a word wi' the Mither."

"Thanks Auntie Isabella."

"So tell me about Robert?"

"Aw he's nice Auntie Isabella, I like him."

Isabella didn't say anything; she would talk to the Mither, about this as well as what to do about young Mary.

Chapter 9

Later that day the Mither and Isabella sat discussing what Coralina had revealed.

"Whit did ye say tae her Isabella?"

"Ah jist told her that Ah'd have a word wi' ye."

"Aye, its wan tae think aboot," the Mither said, shaking her head worriedly. "The problem wi' Mary is wan thing, but Coralina needs tae mind that she cannae be too close tae Gorja's. She has tae stick tae her ain kind. Ah'll have a think aboot this an' Ah might need tae have a word wi' John tae. He'll no' be happy if he has tae hear this."

A few days later the Mither called young Mary to her side, "C'mon take a walk wi' me Mary." She took Mary's hand in hers and began to lead her away from the camp,

"Whur are wi' goin' Mither."

"Jist a walk hinny, an' maybe a wee seat by the Clyde."

It was nice day, the early morning sun was shining, and the birds were singing in the trees above them. As they reached the old log that was a favourite seat for everyone, the Mither leaned on Mary's shoulder as she eased herself down.

"Sit aside me lass," she said patting the log for Mary to join her.

Mary was worried, she sensed that something was coming but she wasn't sure what it would be.

"Aye we've had many a chat on oor walks hinny."

Mary was silent.

"Whit dae ye see aboot ye Mary?"

"Whit dae ye mean Mither?"

"Ah mean whit Ah say, whit dae ye think Ah mean?"

"Ah don't ken Mither."

"Jist look aboot ye an' tell me whit ye see."

Mary took a breath and looked around, "Ah see the river Mither, an' the grass an' the trees, is that whit ye mean?"

"Aye Ah mean that, an' whit can ye tell me about a' that hinny?"

"It's aye here?" she questioned.

"Aye its aye here an' that's 'cause it lives Mary. It lives 'cause wi' dinnae damage it."

"Ah dinnae ken whit ye mean Mither."

"Everythin' ye see aboot ye has life in it Mary, it's like the music, ye kin hear it but ye cannae see it."

Mary sat and thought for a few moments, and the Mither waited and watched the child thinking and then Mary said, "So when ma Mam died did her music stop?"

"Naw hinny it didnae stop, it jist played somewhere else. The music was inside her an' when her body died the music left its shell an' floated free."

"Is it still floatin'?"

"Aye, an' that's why sometimes ye can see stuff, yer like yer mother."

Mary turned suddenly with her mouth open in surprise and looked at the Mither. There they sat the wise old woman and the innocent child meeting a moment of awareness.

"Ah didnae ken ye knew Ah could see stuff Mither."

"Aye Ah kent, yer Mam could see stuff an' a'."

"She could see the music?"

"Ye could say that."

This was a lot to think about for Mary, part of her was excited that she was the same as her mother, while another part was a little wary that the Mither knew. She had so many questions but didn't know where to start.

"Ye see Mary, sometimes people that can see the music can dae harm as well as guid' if they're no' careful an' they dinnae know what they're daein'. Ah think maybe you might be a wee bit like that."

"Ah dinnae ken whit ye mean Mither."

"Ye've heard yer Uncle Willie playin' the fiddle?"

Mary was confused, "Aye."

"An' it makes a grand sound?" said the Mither.

"Aye."

"Whit would happen if a string broke Mary?"

Mary almost fell backwards laughing at just such a memory, "Aw it sounds jist terrible, Ah remember when that happened before an' Uncle Willie was ragin."

"That's whit Ah mean Mary, when ye damage summat ye break the music."

Mary sat and looked up at the Mither as realisation came to her, and then the tears began to fall. "Ah think Ah broke Robert's music."

The Mither put her arm over Mary's shoulder and Mary leaned in accepting the comfort, but still she cried. "Ye damaged his music Mary. He's a'right noo, but it's worse than that, ye see whit goes aroon comes aroon, so ye need tae remember that, an' if ye stop an' think aboot it ye damaged Coralina's music tae 'cause everythin's connected."

"Whit dae ye mean Mither?"

"It's like throwin' a wee stone in the river, get a wee stone an' throw it in an' tell me whit ye see."

Mary looked about for a bit and then picked up a stone and threw it in the water. She and the Mither watched as the stone landed with a loud plop. Then Mary looked at the Mither.

"Dae ye see the ripples Mary?"

"Aye Ah see them."

"Well the stone landed in the middle o' the water but the ripples keep comin', dae ye see them comin' right back tae the edge here?"

"Aye Ah see them, Ah never noticed that before."

"When ye dae summat bad, the ripples keep movin' until they come back tae ye. Ye can dae guid wi' yer gift, but ye can dae harm tae. Dae guid an' guid things will aye come tae ye, but be sure o' this Mary, if ye dae summat bad it's the hardest thing tae take back, and bad will come right back at ye when ye least expect it."

"Ah'm feart Mither."

Once more, the Mither gave Mary a comforting squeeze, "An' so ye should be hinny, so ye should be. Aye be good an' good will come tae ye."

"Is summat bad gonnae happen tae me Mither?"

"Only if yer no' careful aboot whit ye dae. Ye see yer gift is like the music, if you play a nice tune, ye make people happy an' that makes ye happy. Ye have strong music Mary. Put yer hand out."

Mary put out her hand and the Mither placed her hand above it. "Can ye feel that Mary," she asked.

"Ah feel heat Mither, is that whit ye mean?"

"That's yer music Mary, an' yer music is strong enough tae heal Mary. Yer body is jist a shell tae haud the music, it's the music that gives ye life, it's yer energy."

Mary eyes were wide with amazement, "Ye mean Ah can make a body well when they're sick?"

"Sometimes Mary, but no' a' the time. Sometimes people are meant tae pass on, jist like yer Mam did when she went tae be wi' the angels, but if yer a guid lass an' yer careful whit ye dae ye might be able tae help people instead o' troublin' them."

"Ah think Johnny has good music Mither."

"Aye, yer right, Johnny has got good music an' ye should be nice tae him."

"Ah will Mither, thanks for helpin me."

"Help me up an' we'll go back tae the camp."

Mary was like a different person as they approached the camp; she was smiling and running ahead of the Mither and then running back to have a quick word, only to repeat the process over and over again. Isabella, watching for them coming, breathed a sigh of relief. She could see the Mither laughing at Mary's antics and Mary seemed so happy. It was obvious that the talk had gone well.

Chapter 10

The kettle had come to the boil, and Isabella made a fresh pot of tea for her and the Mither.

"Sit yer self doon Mither an' have some tea."

"Thanks Isabella, that was nae bad, Ah think she understands but time'll tell. Ah didnae have tae let on that Ah kent aboot the wee accident wi' Robert, for she brought his name up hersel'."

"Whit aboot Coralina and Robert, will ye say summat tae Coralina or will ye say summit tae oor John?"

"Does Coralina ken aboot her body changing?"

"Ah dinnae think so,"

"Will ye have a word wi' her Isabella?"

"Me! No' me, Ah'm embarris'd tae mention that," said Isabella her face turning red at the thought. "Ah'll tell oor Jennie tae speak tae her aboot it."

"It's up tae ye Isabella, but after me yer the oldest an' ye'll be the Mither when Ah'm no' here an' ye'll need tae take responsibility then."

"Wheesht, Ah'll no' hear oh that."

"When it's ma' time, its ma' time, nuthin' onybody kin dae aboot that."

Just at that moment, Coralina came over to the fire. Always polite and respectful she said, "Mither, Auntie Isabella, can Ah come an' sit by yo." "Aye, oit Coralina, have ye summat on yer mind?"

"Ah jist wanted tae tell ye that Mary seems awfy happy. Ah'm guessin' ye had a word wi' her Mither."

"Ah did that, an Ah think she understood."

"Ah'm ever so grateful Mither, Ah'm sure she will be a'right noo, thanks."

Later that day Jennie came over to seek her out.

"What are ye up tae Coralina?"

"Nuthin' much how?"

"Jist wanted a word."

"Aye, whit?"

"Aw well, ye see ma Mam wanted me tae speak tae ye about changin'."

"Changin' whit?"

"Ye ken?"

"Ah don't ken whit yer talkin' aboot."

"Ah'm talkin' aboot changin' fae a lassie tae a wummin."

"Dae ye mean like the animals when the bitches are ready an' they go into the heat an' the blood comes?"

"Are ye takin' a rise? Ye should ha' said ye kent."

"Well, Ah jist know aboot the animal's fae whit Ah've seen."

"Aye, it's the same as that, an' ye cannae let a fella' near ye, it'll shame ye an' shame yer family, an' ye have tae keep yer self clean an' stay away fae Gorjas."

"Some Gorjas are a'right."

"Naw Coralina, stay away fae them 'cause ye might get tempted tae be wi' wan, and that would be the end, so jist take a tellin'." With that, not prepared to discuss the matter any further, Jennie turned and walked away leaving Coralina to her thoughts about becoming a woman.

Mary was a different girl after the chat with the Mither. Her behaviour changed considerably, but she still had moments when she lost her way and forgot the lesson the Mither had taught her, but as soon as she remembered, for fear of something bad happening to her, she would try to make amends to anyone that she had scorned. She helped Coralina without too much persuasion, and even young Johnny felt the benefit of this new Mary. Coralina was happier that she had ever been, and that summer was one of the best that she remembered.

Autumn and winter came and went, and soon the daffodils were blooming and everyone was looking forward to getting out on the road and visiting old friends and families once more. Unbeknown to Coralina, who had celebrated her thirteenth birthday, the Mither had had a word with John about Coralina's friendship with Robert, the Miller's son, and at the end of the discussion, they agreed to put some distance between Coralina and Robert.

The first Coralina knew about it was when her father was getting ready to make the first of his trips to Ayrshire and the Dalgarven Mill.

"Ah'm jist takin young Johnny, you'll bide here wi' yer sister and mind the Mither for she's getting on in years."

Never one to answer back Coralina shocked John when she retorted "But Da!"

John turned his head quickly and glowered at Coralina, and she hung her head, but she wasn't happy and she wasn't finished.

"Ah've worked haid a' winter Da, Ah was really lookin' furrat tae goin tae Ayrshire wi' ye."

"Ye'll bide here Coralina, an' Ah'll brook nae argument on the matter."

Coralina ran outside and across the camp towards the river, and when she got there she sat on the log, put her face in her hands, and cried. She started when someone placed a hand on her shoulder.

"Whit's up wi' ye Coralina, why are ye greetin'?" Mary sat beside her sister and she had a fretful expression on her young face; she had never seen her cry like that.

"It's ma Da, he says Ah cannae go tae Ayrshire wi' him."

"Am Ah goin'?"

"Yer no' goin' either."

"Whit aboot Johnny, is he goin'?"

"Aye he's goin', but we have tae stay and mind the Mither. Ah think that's jist an excuse, but Ah dinnae ken why he would dae that."

Mary sat quiet but she wasn't happy either. Over time, she and Johnny had become good friends, and she hadn't once felt that burning jealousy when her father paid Johnny attention, but she felt it now and it troubled her. She jumped up and ran away back to the camp. She saw Johnny making his way towards the horse's field.

"Johnny, Johnny," she called.

Hearing her call, Johnny turned with a smile on his face, but it quickly vanished when he saw her agitation and he hurried towards her.

"Whit's up Mary?"

"Are ye gone tae Ayrshire wi' ma Da?"

"Aye!" he answered in surprise, and without a thought, Mary kicked him on the shin and stomped off. She was quickly yanked back when Johnny grabbed her by the shoulder. Mary was shocked, and so was Johnny, though he didn't show it, for he had always been taught to be gentle with girls.

"Whit did ye dae that for Mary, Ah thought ye were past that stuff, look at ma leg Mary, look at whit ye have done. Ye've skint ma shin," he said as he rolled up his trousers and viewed the graze.

Mary's eyes were full of tears as she looked down at Johnny's leg, but her tears were there for selfish reasons. She was thinking about the consequences of her actions. She had lost her temper again, and done something to hurt someone.

"Ah'm sorry Johnny, Ah didnae mean it."

"Whit dae ye mean ye didnae mean it, did your foot jist connect wi' ma leg?"

Mary laughed, "Yer so funny Johnny."

However, Johnny didn't laugh, and Mary's laugh was quickly smothered as she clamped her lips tightly together, her eyes suddenly filled with tears.

"Aye, Ah might be, but you're no' funny Mary, you're no' funny at a'."

Johnny turned his back on Mary and walked away from her.

"Johnny Ah'm sorry, honest," said Mary as she ran after him, but Johnny was having none of it.

Disgusted with herself, Mary went back to where she had left Coralina and sat beside her. She slipped her hand into her big sister's and the two of them sat there absorbed in their own misery.

Chapter 11

Later Coralina went to see her aunt, "Whit's up wi' ye the day Coralina, it's no' like ye tae be doon in the dumps."

"Mam, Da says Ah cannae go tae Ayrshire wi' him, that me an' Mary have tae bide here."

Isabella knew the reason behind this but wasn't prepared to share it with Coralina.

"He says Ah've tae look after the Mither."

"She's no' so able these days Coralina, Ah'm sure ye don't mind really."

"Ah'm disappointed."

"Ah'm sure ye are hinny, but maybe ye'll get tae go another day."

Coralina thought about Robert. He had been in her mind a lot recently and she was looking forward to seeing him, then she wondered if he was looking forward to seeing her. There was nothing else for it but to get on with things, so she accepted the inevitable and said no more about it, but inside, she felt miserable and unhappy.

Her Da and young Johnny left for Ayrshire early the next day. Coralina and Mary watched them ride off on the wagon until they couldn't see them anymore. Mary had hoped for a wave from Johnny, but he was still annoyed with her and didn't turn his head.

For the next few days Isabella kept a watch over both girls and Coralina did as her father had bid her, and went over to the Mithers a few times each day to see if she needed anything and to take her cups of tea and some dinner.

"How are ye feeling Mither?"

"Ah'm a bit sore an' stiff Coralina, but there's nowt' a buddy kin dae aboot that. Ah've a cabbage poultice on ma knees that could be warmed up if ye have a mind tae take it across tae the fire?"

Coralina waited while the Mither hitched up her woollen skirt and rolled down her thick stockings, and then she helped her to unwrap the poultice.

"Ah'll make ye a new wan Mither."

"Yer a guid lass Coralina, ye remind me a lot of yer Mam, and yer jist as lovely as she was."

It was while her father and Johnny were away on their Ayrshire trip that Coralina's body started the change. She woke in the night with bad pains in her stomach and she felt as though her back was breaking. She curled herself up into a tight ball, clutching her belly and the warmth of her hands started to ease her pain. Finally, she fell into a deep sleep, but when she woke early in the morning, she knew something was wrong. As soon as she saw the blood she had a moments panic, and then she realised what was happening to her. She pulled the bed sheet off the bed and rolled it into a ball to hide the bloodstains, before hurrying across to her aunt's wagon.

"Auntie Isabella?"

"Come away in hinny," said Isabella, and then as she saw Coralina's bundle she realised her predicament.

"Ah've started Auntie Isabella, an' Ah'm no' sure whit tae dae."

Isabella overcame her embarrassment and took charge.

"Come wi' me lass," she said as she rummaged in a drawer for some clean rags.

Coralina, meek, uncomfortable, and self-conscious, followed Isabella across the camp towards the river. Isabella led her downstream to a secluded part of the river and began to show her how to take care of herself.

"If ye get any blood on yer sheet rinse it aff doon stream like this."

Isabella shook out the sheet, placed a corner of it on a flat rock, and secured it in place with another on top of it. She loosened out the folds so that the water would run through the marks removing the bulk of the stains.

"Now stand in the shallows here, crouch doon and wipe yer self clean, then dry yer' self wi' this cloth, an' when yer done put wan o' these rags in yer knickers. Ah'll leave ye until yer done, then come back tae mine. Wring oot yer sheet an' bring it wi' ye an' we'll get it in tae the boil."

Isabella left her, and when Coralina was finished, she took her sheet, wrung out as best she could, back to her aunt's wagon.

"Jist leave it under the step the noo an' come in, Ah'll boil it later."

"Thanks for helpin me Auntie Isabella."

"Jennie tells me ye know whit's happenin', but did she tell ye that yer a wummin once that happens? Dae ye ken that ye kin make bairns noo?"

"Well, Ah dinnae have a husband so Ah cannae make bairns."

"Naw, naw, Coralina, ye dinnae need a husband tae make a bairn. Ye have tae be awfy careful noo that ye have changed. Ye cannae let a fella near ye. Oor kind will have respect for ye, but others, they'll no' care an' would take advantage."

Coralina sat and thought about what her aunt was telling her. "Ah think Ah'm feart Auntie Isabella, whit happens if a fella touches me, will Ah have a bairn?"

"If a fella tries tae kiss ye, and puts his airms aboot ye…then that could be the start o' trouble, so dinnae let it happen, an' keep away fae Gorjas."

While Isabella rummaged in a trunk, Coralina thought about what she had said about Gorjas. She thought about Robert, because he was a Gorjas not a Gypsy. She wondered if her Da hadn't taken her because he thought she liked Robert, and was worried that Robert would touch her. '*Naw, Robert was a nice lad an' her Da liked him*,' she thought to herself.

Isabella had pulled an old sheet from the trunk, "Here, take that across tae yer wagon and tear it intae squares. Hide them somewhere an' change every time ye go for a pee. Fold one up, stick it in yer knickers, an' wash the rag that ye've used. Wash them how a showed ye an' dinnae let anybody see them dryin', its private."

"Thanks Auntie Isabella."

"Jist as well ye never went tae Ayrshire wi' yer Da or ye would ha' been caught oot."

Coralina's face went bright red as she thought that maybe her Da knew that she was going to change and that was why he didn't take her. The next few days were difficult for Coralina as she was plagued with stomach cramps and on one of the days, Mary went to look for her and was startled to find her lying on the bed in the wagon.

"Whit are ye dayin' lyin' doon, are ye sick Coralina?" asked a worried Mary.

"Ah'm fine Mary, Ah've jist got a sore stomach."

""Whit gave ye a sore stomach, did ye eat summat bad?"

Coralina had to think for a few moments of how to respond, she wondered if she should just avoid the question or if she should just tell Mary what was what. She decided on the latter and if Mary asked questions, she would tell her the truth. "Ah didnae eat summat bad Mary, Ah'm changing from a lassie tae a wummin."

"How long does that take?" asked Mary innocently.

In spite of the cramps Coralina laughed. "It's happened already Mary. Jist like the animals, Ah'm bleedin' and Ah'll bleed every month."

"Oh," replied Mary, and then after a little while, standing looking at her sister she said "An' ye get a sore stomach wi' it?"

"Aye."

"Ah' dinnae think Ah would like that Coralina."

"Ye've no' got any choice, it happens tae a' lassies."

"Can Ah try summat Ah've been practisin'?"

"Whit is it ye want tae try?"

"Ah want tae try tae take away yer pain."

Coralina looked at her and then she said "Whit makes ye think ye can dae that."

"The Mither said Ah had good strong music an' if Ah use it right Ah could help people, let me try."

"Ah dinnae ken whit yer talkin' aboot."

"It disnae matter, jist let me try."

"Hurry up then whatever it is yer gonnae dae, get on wi' it."

Mary knelt beside her sister and placed her hands on her stomach and the two girls just stayed like that for several minutes. Mary was aware of the heat building in her hands and she was sure that there was a tingling feeling. Coralina moaned once or twice but Mary stayed as she was, and soon, Coralina began to drift into a contented sleep. When Mary was sure that her sister was sound, she quietly stood, leaned over her, and kissed her cheek. She went outside, sat on the wagon steps, and thought about what had just happened. In her heart, she felt that she had somehow made a difference and she liked that feeling. She promised herself that she would try to help anyone who was sick or sad. It was a much better feeling than the one that consumed her when she was angry or spiteful.

Chapter 12

Young Robert Miller saw John's wagon approaching and ran into the farmhouse to let his mother know, and then he went over to the mill to give his father a shout. He tried hard to contain his excitement and it was only when he walked out with his father that the smile dropped from his face as he realised that neither Coralina nor Mary were on the wagon.

Robert was fifteen now and he had been thinking a lot about Coralina. There were local girls who lived in the village and they were nice lassies, but none could compare with Coralina. He had been looking forward to seeing her and chatting to her, though he would never have admitted that he had a crush on her. Mary was another matter though; she could be a bit of a pest but he would happily put up with Mary for the pleasure of seeing Coralina. His father shed light on their absence.

"Ye didnae bring the lassies wi' ye John?"

"Plenty for them tae dae back yonder Mathew."

"The Missus will miss them; she likes chattin' tae them."

Robert didn't want to show his disappointment, in fact, he didn't want to show his interest in case anyone chided him, so he kept quiet, but he thought about Coralina all day long. It was as though the fact that she wasn't there made his need to see her even stronger, but there was nothing that he could do about that.

Elsie Miller was as hospitable as usual, and after John and Johnny had eaten, they went over to the mill to load up the wagon with flour and oatmeal. Johnny and Robert helped the men and listened while they chatted.

"Where are ye off tae next John?"

"Ah'm gonnae look at some mares just up by Stewarton and Dunlop. Ah'm hopin' tae pick up some good breedin' stock. Ah'll wait an' see whit they're like but if they're good Ah'll take them. A short visit this time an' we'll be headin' aff as soon as we're loaded."

When Mathew went into the kitchen Elsie asked, "They didnae wait long Mathew was there summat up?"

"He jist said they were away tae see some horses."

Mathew and Elsie felt that there was something not quite right, but they would never have guessed that John was trying to keep a distance between Robert and Coralina.

On John's return to the camp Coralina did not mention the trip to Dalgarven nor did she mention Robert. Mary on the other hand had question after question.

"Who did you see? Where did you go? Did you bring back a sweetie?"

On and on the questions went to John and young Johnny until they were both tired of listening to her. She followed them around ending up at the horse field, and then much to her shock John hoisted Mary up and plunked her down on the back of Mizzie, one of the brood mares.

"Da, Da, whit ye daein' Da?"

"Jist hang on tae its mane and sit tight on her back, she'll no' hurt ye."

Mary's face was a picture and John stole a glance at young Johnny who lowered his head to hide his grin. Although many of the girls could ride, it was the lads who usually worked and exercised them, but Mary was driving her father crazy, and he thought she would have enough to think about holding on to Mizzie. All the horses were safe around the children and Mizzie was the gentlest of them all. She had an instinct that made John feel as though she was reading his mind.

Mizzie's feathered mane was thick and long and reached the bottom of her stomach. She was mostly black with large white patches scattered over her hindquarters and shoulders. Looking at her serious face one would realise that she had two different coloured eyes, one brown and one blue. Her feathered fetlocks were thick and white in contrast to her black legs and her thick tail was white like her mane. Whenever she galloped across the field, she was a beautiful sight and John would often stand and watch her.

Mizzie's ears flickered back a little and then forward as Mary settled on to her broad back and then she slowly walked forward. Mary opened her mouth wide in a silent scream, and then suddenly she looked at her Da and started to laugh.

"Oh Da, look, Ah'm ridin' Mizzie!"

John and Johnny exchanged glances again but this time they were both surprised. They both expected Mary to be quiet, and want nothing more than to be lifted down from the horse so that she could scamper back to the camp. How wrong they were, for that was the start of Mary's passion for horses, in particular for Mizzie, and the bond was a mutual one because for some unknown reason Mizzie took a special liking to Mary too.

Mizzie was one of John's finest brood mares; she was seven years old and every second year she gave him a fine foal or filly. John remembered the day she was born and he had loved her since. She could have foaled every year, but John was happier to let her have a year to nurse her young before allowing her to mate again, in the belief that she could foal for longer rather than breeding from her every year and wearing her out.

Mary took every opportunity to run to the horse field and as soon as Mizzie saw her, she would trot to meet her with her tail held high behind her as though she was showing off. Some days if Mary was slow to arrive Mizzie would be waiting for her at the edge of the roped off field, stamping on the ground, quietly snorting her impatience. Sometimes Mary would tease Mizzie and run away from her and Mizzie would run alongside her. Mary's laughter and Mizzie's whinnying could be heard in the camp, and any that watched were sure that Mizzie was enjoying the game as much as Mary was.

One day, John watched the interaction between his youngest daughter and the horse. The top of Mary's head only came up to the middle of Mizzie's stomach, and John laughed at their antics, the pair of them running at full belt. As he watched he saw Mary adjust her pace to mimic Mizzie's canter, skipping as though she herself was a horse, when suddenly Mary reached up and grabbed Mizzie's mane. In the next moment, she was hoisting herself, half hanging upside down, before she managed to wriggle her legs and body onto Mizzie's back. Neither Mizzie nor Mary broke stride and all John could do was stand there and watch in amazement as the two behaved as one, Mizzie's long mane flying as she galloped around the field, and Mary's hair blowing back behind her. His heart almost stopped, and then, as if that wasn't bad enough, he watched Mizzie with Mary on her back leap over the rope that enclosed the horses.

"Holy Mither!" he said, as he started to run, but what he was hoping to do he did not know, and then just as quickly Mary turned Mizzie and rode back to meet her father.

"Did ye see me? Did ye see me, Da?"

Only then did John realise that young Johnny was beside him, both of them looking at Mary with a mixture of concern and amazement.

"Get aff."

One look at her father's face told Mary that he wasn't happy; in fact, he was mad at her. She swung her leg round and slipped to the ground with a sheepish look on her face.

"Whit were ye thinkin' Mary?"

"It jist happened Da."

"Yer aye the same Mary, ye jist dae things with oot a thought, ye gave me a fricht an' ye could ha' killed yer self or hurt Mizzie."

Johnny stood quietly beside them, but he was impressed, and thought that Mary was the wildest, bravest, most beautiful lassie that he had ever seen. Johnny was only eight, coming on nine, but in that moment, he knew that one day he would marry Mary Kelly.

"Away an' help yer sister, Ah dinnae ken how she puts up wi' ye."

Mary didn't argue, she just turned her head and kissed Mizzie's soft nose and then went back to the camp. The camp, of course, was buzzing with Mary's escapade, as a few of the women had seen Mary's leap over the rope and out of the field. Most kept their heads down to avoid eye contact with her as she walked back, but Mary being Mary, held her head high and didn't care what anyone thought.

Coralina was oblivious to Mary's escapade, she was busy fussing with things in the wagon, but although she loved her sister, she was despairing of having to do almost everything herself. Thoughts of Robert occupied her young mind, and she often romanticised about him as she carried out her daily tasks.

Chapter 13

The Appleby Horse fair was held every year in the first week in June. Although there were many fairs throughout the country, this one was the most popular in the travelling community. Almost the whole camp would pack up and travel to Appleby where they would buy, sell and trade and meet up with their own kind. The journey would take at least a week and at the end of the day's journey, those that were camping out would set up their benders and a campfire would be lit in the middle of the camp. Often this was a good excuse to sit around the fire, play a fiddle or accordion, sing songs, and tell stories of previous fairs. Eventually everyone would settle down to rest before another early rise the next morning.

This was something that everyone prepared for in advance; horses and dogs would be paraded around a roped off auction ring while others were negotiated for in private sales where they would barter with each other arguing over prices. Some Gypsies would have purchased rugs from Arab traders to sell on at the fair, while others would be selling galvi basins, pails, and jugs. Cartloads of goods were transported to sell at the fair. Most Gypsy women were good with their hands and they would bring their arts and crafts to sell and exchange with other women, and much showing off, socialising, and celebrating would be done.

The young lads would show off their riding skills by trotting and galloping bareback through the town then they would gather at the River Eden to cool off and wash their horses, but uppermost in their minds would be impressing their peers, and the young lassies. Many a match would be made through meetings at the Appleby Horse fair.

John and his family and almost all of the camp set off for Appleby at dawn one fine morning in the last week in May. The sun had just risen and was warming the early morning dew on the grass, and there was an air of eager anticipation among the travellers. It would be seven or eight days before they would reach their destination nevertheless everyone looked forward to the excursion. Because this was such an important event in their calendar, wagons had been repainted, brasses polished until they were gleaming, and horses groomed to perfection. Of course, the journey being so long, meant that everything had to be refreshed each day before the next part of their travels, but no one minded the task and it was all part of the excitement.

Their personal appearance was important too; for the men, boots would be polished to a fine shine, though that wouldn't last once they started tramping through the field where the fair was held. The wives and mothers would steam jackets and trousers over a pan of boiling water to freshen them up and they would make sure that they had something bright and new to wear too. They preferred to use colourful fabrics bought or traded to make skirts, shawls, and scarves to wrap their hair in; everything had to be perfect.

Coralina had spent weeks making skirts for her and Mary, Coralina's was scarlet and full skirted so that it would look beautiful when she danced, and she had made a white petticoat to wear under it. When it was finished, she tried it on and did a few twirls in front of her aunt showing off her handiwork. She made the same outfit for Mary, but Mary's fabric was multi coloured in shades of blues and yellows. During daytime, they would wear their everyday clothes, but at night when the day's trading was over everyone would dress in their best, and gather together to sit and socialise, pass on messages or the latest news, tell stories, play music, or sing and dance. The lassies would be trying to impress the lads and the lads would be posturing and showing off.

As they got closer to their destination, other wagons would join the procession and locals would gather to watch the arrivals. Some would come to admire, some to stare in fascination, and others to complain, but the travelling families took it all in their stride. They knew that oftentimes those that stared or scorned would actually be the ones who would purchase their wares and services. Mary could hardly contain herself such was her excitement. Coralina was more dignified about the whole thing, nevertheless her grin made her cheeks ache. Young Johnny was travelling in his family's wagon so he was spared Mary's chatter and jostling about.

"For Heaven's sake, Mary have ye worms can ye no' sit still?"

"Da, Ah'm fair excited."

"Jist calm doon, and sit quiet like yer sister."

"Can Ah ride Mizzie along the street wi' the lads."

At that comment, Coralina turned and stared at Mary's audacity, and John did the same. Coralina dropped her eyes quickly, but John stared at Mary, and she knew by the look he gave her that this question should not have been asked. She so wanted to ride out with the lads, and she was too young to realise that this was inappropriate.

"Ye'll sit in the wee cart wi' me an' yer sister, an' that's as near as ye'll get to ridin' wi' the lads."

Mary turned and pulled a face at Coralina but Coralina just ignored her. When they had set up in the field, that would be their base for the duration of the fair, they would assemble little carts from parts that were stored under the wagons. There were large carts used for transporting things that would be needed by the travellers, and those that didn't have enough room to store their small carts could borrow a space in another's cart.

John had plenty of room under his wagon to carry his own cart and he was busy assembling it with Mary looking on watching his every move. Some of her attention was given in the hope that she could get back into her father's good books, but being the tomboy that she was, she was watching, because in her mind, one day, she would be building her own cart to ride through the streets with the lads. She wouldn't be doing that anytime soon, but she was about to do something that would draw everyone's attention, and that people would talk about for years to come.

While John was assembling his cart Coralina was grooming the horse that would pull it along, making it look smart, and it was as though this horse, King, knew that within a few moments he would be clipping along showing off as did everyone else during this parade through the town. Coralina had brushed his mane and tail and had fastened bells to the halter and reins. As soon as the cart was ready and John had hitched up King, he and the girls climbed on to the wooden frame that supported a narrow bench for them to sit on. It was all about showing off how you could handle a horse and cart and not so much about the cart.

"Noo' mind keep yer skirts tucked in and yer feet away fae the sides."

Coralina demurely settled herself, but Mary as always had an answer, "Aye Da, Ah hear ye, Ah'm bein' careful."

The sound of the horses' hooves could be heard clip clopping through the town as Gypsy travellers and locals alike watched. The atmosphere was electric, and everyone was happy and smiling as the riders in the parade made their way to the river Eden. The lads were out, as usual, riding bareback through the streets, some of them taking chances with their antics, and many a gasp could be heard as they passed within inches of carts or spectators. When they reached the river, those on horseback would ride right into the water to cool their horses, and of course, to show off their horsemanship. Some of the cart riders would unhitch their horses and walk down to the river to cool their beasts and let them drink after the thirsty ride; others would stand around chatting, catching up on the latest news or gossip.

Chapter 14

Mary stood and stared in fascination at some Shire Horses that were in the roped off area with Vanners and other workhorses. The Shires towered above the others and Mary watched as some horses were led around the ring and others stood quietly by their owners. Buyers wandered freely among them, looking, nodding to the owners, sometimes drawing a hand down a horse leg, or across their back. Some examined a horse's teeth and this was a sure sign that they were interested in buying. Mary began to make her way around the ring so that she could get a closer look at them.

"Mister, can Ah stroke yer horse?" said Mary. The man she spoke to looked down at her, hardly interested, but nodding his approval. Mary went under the rope and up to the giant of a horse and reached up to stroke its belly. The owner of the horse was chatting to another man and they both glanced at Mary and laughed at her.

"Whit's his name?"

The owner looked down at Mary once more, "Sam," he said indifferently. Mary wandered round Sam stroking the parts that she could reach, her neck straining as she looked up admiring the horse and talking to him.

"Aye yer a grand lad Sam; yer a giant, big strong legs, aye yer beautiful." Sam was listening to Mary but not reacting very much to her compliments. The two men had another quick glance at Mary and laughed at her while carrying on with their conversation.

"Can Ah ride him?" Mary asked,

Both men bellowed with laughter, more intent on doing a bit of business than tolerating a silly wee lassie. "Aye, if ye can get yer self up ye can ride him," he replied laughing with the other man.

Mary turned and walked away, and as far as the two men were concerned that was the end of the matter, but it wasn't the end of the matter to Mary. She made her way around the stallholders and noticed that one woman had a display of early carrots, "Missus, can Ah get a carrot?"

"Away ya' cheeky lass."

"Ah have a coin."

"Ah'll take' yer coin then," the woman said, and handed Mary a couple of carrots.

Mary grabbed the carrots, and ran off back to the horse ring, ducking and diving around people as she made her way back to the Shire horse. The two men were still chatting as Mary approached the Shire. She walked around and stood in front of the huge horse that paid her no mind. Mary took a carrot from her pocket, and letting the horse see it, she bit off a piece, and made exaggerated noises of pleasure as she crunched it. Sam's ears flicked forward in interest and looking down at Mary, he sniffed and snorted at her hair. Mary bit another piece of carrot and palm opened she offered it to Sam. It was gone in a second leaving a large area of moisture on Mary's hand; the Shire was more interested now. Mary giggled as she took a step back and Sam took a step forward. Another piece of carrot was bitten off, offered, and accepted.

The owner and his colleague were half watching and half ignoring Mary, assuming that all she was doing was giving titbits to the Shire. They were only remotely interested in her presence and continued chatting. Mary offered Sam another small piece of carrot, which was eagerly received. She bit another piece of carrot and placed it on the ground between her and Sam. The Shire lowered his head to the ground and snaffled up the carrot. Mary took another step back and once more placed a piece of carrot on the ground between herself and the horse. This time, when the horse stretched down to get the carrot Mary ruffled his mane. She took another step back, broke off another piece, placed it on the ground, and stepped to the side. As she expected the big Shire lowered its head to the ground and without another thought, Mary leaned in, grabbed a handful of mane with both hands, and held on for dear life as the Shire lifted its head and Mary with it. In the next moment, Mary was sitting on the horse's neck, giggling and clinging on for dear life, and then she just wiggled down his neck, onto his back, leaning forward rubbing his face, and telling him how clever he was. Then she sat there proudly looking down at the owner and his companion, who were both standing with their mouths hanging open at her antics, her audacity, and her ingenuity.

"What the devil?" said the owner.

"Did ye see that wee lassie, did ye see whit she jist did?"

"Ah'm fair flummert," was the reply.

"Whose lassie is that?"

"Ah dinnae ken, she's wan o' oors, but Ah've nae idea whit family."

"Ye said if Ah could get up, Ah could ride him, Ah'm up," said Mary confidently, and as the men, and others who had seen Mary's bold move watched; Sam showing off, proudly walked forward and began to circle the horse ring.

Across the field, Coralina was standing by her Da and young Johnny as they chatted with other travellers. There was much for her to see and take in but she became aware of a hubbub of conversation as though something different was happening, and as she diverted her gaze to the source, her mouth fell open. "Da! Da! It's Mary." Her father turned and anxiously looked at Coralina, because he could tell by her voice that there was something not quite right. He started to scan the crowds around him leaning to the left and the right to see if he could see Mary between the folk that were milling about.

"Da! Da! Look!" she said, and pointed to the other side of the ring; and there was his Mary, visible above the crowds, sitting on top of the big Shire horse grinning from ear to ear.

"Holy Mither, that lassie'll be the death o' me." He ran towards the ring, stooped under the rope, and ran between other horses and up to where Mary was. Coralina and Johnny were at his heels when he reached her.

"Get aff!"

"But Da!"

He reached up, grabbed Mary from the horse, and glowered at the owner. "Did you put ma lass up there?" he asked angrily, standing, fists clenched, and ready for a fight.

"Here noo, haud yer horses, yer lassie did it hersel'."

"Dinnae be ridiculous man, she can barely reach its belly."

"Aye, an' that's whit Ah thought when Ah told her she could ride it if she could get on him hersel'. She's a wide wan that yin. Next thing she's conned the big fella tae put his heed doon an' she climbs up his neck. Ah've never seen onythin' like it! Ah recognise ye. You'll be John Kelly then, Ah've seen ye aboot. Ah was awfy sorry tae hear aboot ye losin' yer wife." He stuck out his hand to shake John's.

"Aye, that's me and this vixen is Mary, and she'll feel ma anger on her backside."

"Aye well, she's your lass, but that was a clever thing she did, she has a knack wi' the horses. Whit age is she?"

"She's nearly eight goin' on eighty an' Ah cannae keep up wi' her."

The owner of the Shire and his friend regaled John about Mary's antics and her determination to ride the big horse. While they were speaking, someone sounded a bell announcing the auction was about to start so John shook hands with the two men and holding on to Mary he made his way around to watch the bidding.

The auction was a favourite with all the fair goers as this was where you could see the antics of the bidders; some would merely raise an eyebrow to indicate a bid while others, remaining perfectly still, would simply move their index finger and the eagle eyed auctioneer would spot that and up the price would go. Others yet would wink or nod but the auctioneer didn't miss a trick. When a horse was sold the seller and the buyer would meet outside the ring behind the auctioneer and exchange pleasantries and as the custom would have it, the seller would give a penny to the buyer 'for luck'. It was the height of bad manners not to offer that lucky penny and some would say that if you didn't then you might never sell another thing.

Later in the evening, when they were sitting around the fires it became apparent that the entire fair knew about Mary's antics, and Mary, well she was delighted to be the centre of attention, but John wasn't happy, and Coralina was disgusted with her sister.

Chapter 15

As Mary became more outgoing, Coralina became more reserved and quiet. She continued to love and care for her little sister, she took care of the wagon, and looked after her father's needs, but she was withdrawn and often looked sad. The Mither and Isabella noticed this too, and often asked Coralina what was wrong with her, but she just stated that she was fine and that there was nothing wrong. Mary was so wrapped up in herself that initially she didn't notice the changes in her big sister, but as the winter came, she realised that her sister was ailing for something. Her instincts had been dormant largely because she was more interested in what she wanted rather than what was going on around her.

She began to watch Coralina, and as she watched, she became filled with a sense of sadness so deep that it was painful. Coralina's sadness was hidden so well that Mary found it hard to read the reason for it, and suddenly, looking at her sister that she loved so dearly, silent tears began to roll down her cheeks. Coralina was engrossed in what she was doing, but when she glanced at her sister and saw her tears, she jumped up and went to her side. Putting her arm around Mary's shoulder she asked, "Mary! Whit's up wi' ye?"

"Ah'm sad for ye Coralina. Ah can feel yer hurtin' an' Ah dinnae ken whit tae dae or why yer hurtin so bad."

"Ah'm jist sad Mary, an' Ah dinnae ken why, but dinnae say onythin' tae ma Da or Auntie Isabella or the Mither. Ah'm jist sad that's a'." As the words were coming out of her mouth Coralina had the merest thought of Robert, and at the same time Mary sensed the thought and she gasped.

"Yer thinkin' o' Robert Miller!"

Coralina's face reddened, "Naw, wheesht, yer' wrang."

"Ah'm no' wrang, Ah know yer thinkin' o' him."

"Please Mary, ye'll get me in tae trouble fae Da an' Auntie Isabella, she tell't me tae stay away fae Gorja's an' Ah huvnae seen him, but Ah think o' him a' the time." Coralina was crying now and Mary put her arms around her.

"Ah'm a big lassie noo an Ah ken whit it feels like tae love a lad, Ah love Johnny an' Ah would be fair upset if Ah couldnae see him. Ah'll no' say a word Coralina."

Coralina laughed at her sister through her tears, and then the two girls embraced and cried quietly together, but from that day Mary paid more attention to her sister and tried to be more helpful. As Mary tuned in to her sister she was also tuning into other energies around her, and she began to develop an understanding of her gift. She realised that just by watching someone, just by being in the moment, she could read a person's emotions, and more often than not, she could predict things about them.

That was a long cold winter for everyone, and temperatures were below freezing so keeping warm was a priority for the travellers. John was thankful that he had chosen the wooden wagon with the wood burning stove, which kept the girls warm and cosy. Fetching water from the river meant breaking the ice to access the freezing cold water below. The full pail was carried back to the campfire and decanted into the big galvi milk churns that were used to store the water. These sat near the fire to prevent the water from freezing.

Their over winter supplies were running low, and poaching was the only way to put food on the table. Those who didn't have a stove that they could light or share would huddle in their wagons, their shoulders draped in blankets with only the heat from Tilly lamps to keep them warm, but in such small spaces the heat soon built up and kept them cosy. That was the year that the old Mither died. She just passed away in her sleep. Mary sensed it first, and ran to her aunt's wagon. "Auntie Isabella Ah think summat's wrang wi' the Mither."

Isabella ran across to her mother-in-law's wagon, but Mary hung back afraid to go any further. At first, Isabella thought she was only in a deep sleep, but as she approached, she became more concerned. She looked at the Mither and she could see that her skin was smooth and free of the lines that normally creased her face.

She reached out and touched the Mither's face and it was ice cold. She drew back suddenly as she realised that her mother-in-law was gone. She stood there with her hands covering her mouth as grief poured through her and she thought of her husband George. She tried to think of how she would tell him that his mother had passed over. She didn't know that young Mary had gone to fetch him, and just as she was fretting over how to break the news, George appeared in the wagon behind her. No words were necessary, they just stared in shock at each other, and then Isabella moved to one side to allow George space to approach his mother. He knelt by her narrow bed and took one of her cold hands in his. He whispered silently, "Aw Mam, Mam, whit are wi' tae dae with oot ye?" Isabella watched sadly, as tears wet her husband's face, mirroring her own.

After some time, he stood and turned towards Isabella, took both her hands in his, lowered his head and put his lips to her hands.

"Mither," he said, and Isabella gasped as she realised that she was now the oldest in the camp, and the responsibility of advising, and overseeing discipline, praise and decision making was now hers. This was a daunting thought, and she didn't feel as though she had the knowledge, skills, or experience to fill this role as the Mither of the camp. She was wrong; every day in the presence of the Mither had been a lesson for her, and the Mither had taught her well, nevertheless, she was afraid of what might lie ahead for her.

Isabella and George spent some time quietly grieving and saying silent prayers. By the time they were ready to leave the wagon, everyone in the camp had gathered outside in the cold chill air. George emerged first, and as he appeared on the steps, he stood for a moment and surveyed his fellow travellers, his family, and his friends. All of them, affected by the same sadness, gazed upon him, and as he made his way down the wooden steps from the wagon, each in turn shook his hand, embraced him, and offered words of support.

Isabella had known this would happen, and allowed a little time for these sympathies to be offered before she too left the wagon. Her heart was pounding in her chest as she stood at the threshold of the wagon. One by one, each of the gathering approached her, took her hand, and said, "Mither," to show their respect to her.

They gathered around the fire, sitting up through the following nights, talking about Mither Morrison, sharing memories of things that she had said or done, speaking of how she had praised, chastised, or helped them. They all had memories to share and held several wakes, until it was time for her to be laid to rest at Janefield Cemetery.

The day after the funeral, a sad procession took her wagon, with all her possessions intact, away from the camp to a secluded area, and set fire to it. As they watched the wagon and its contents burn, they grieved for a life lived, and a loved one gone.

Chapter 16

The first signs of spring were beginning to show and that cold, cold, feeling was disappearing. With each passing day, the nights grew shorter and the days grew longer. Snowdrops peeping through the still hard ground delighted everyone who saw them, and spirits began to rise. Now that spring was on the way, they could begin to focus on their plans and tasks to earn a living for the year ahead.

Isabella had been keeping a close eye on Coralina, aware that she had become withdrawn and unhappy, though true to her nature, she never complained. George was preparing to go on the road with his tools, for his skills shoeing horses and sharpening tools would be in great demand around the local farms. John would be making his trip around the Ayrshire farms, where he would negotiate the purchase or sale of horses, and on his journey, he would replenish the stocks of flour, oats, and pulses for himself and the rest of the camp, finishing up as usual at Dalgarven Mill.

Isabella had fretted over Coralina, and she came to the realisation that it was her place to do something about her. She knew John would be at the horse field so she made her way over to find him.

"A word in yer ear John."

"Aye, whit's up Isabella?" he said to his sister in law, straightening up from cleaning the hoof of one of the horses.

"Ah'm fair worried aboot Coralina."

John sighed and shook his head, "Aye, me an' a' she's been awfy quiet, an' even if Ah ask her whit's up, she tells me nowt."

"Well John, she's no' been away fae the camp for a good long while, maybe ye should think aboot takin' her wi' ye this time."

"Whit aboot Robert Miller?"

"She's a sensible lass, an' fae whit ye say about the Millers they're a guid family, jist keep yer eye on her."

"Ah'll see, Ah'll think aboot it, away wi' ye Mither, Ah have a lot tae dae for the morrow," he said, laughing at giving her a formal title. Isabella smiled to herself as she made her way back to her wagon and she felt as though she had achieved something, little as it was.

When John was finished all he had to do to prepare for his trip, he made his way back to his wagon to find Coralina sitting crocheting small cotton doilies that she would trim with fancy coloured beads or shells to sell around the villages in the summer time.

"Whit ye daein' lass?"

"Makin' doilies Da."

"Ye must have a fair few noo Coralina."

"Aye Da, Ah've aboot twenty."

"Ah'm thinkin, if ye could tear yer self away fae yer crochetin', maybe ye would like tae come on the road wi' me the morrow, might happen that ye could sell some doilies tae?"

Coralina sat quietly, for a few moments; she didn't lift her head, afraid to show her excitement, and then, "Aye Da, that would be nice."

John had expected more of a reaction, but he was pleased that Coralina didn't seem overly bothered. "Aye well, get any stuff ye need ready for yer self an' yer sister, an' we'll be off early mornin'."

Mary was in the horse field with Mizzie, and although Coralina was desperate to share the news, she decided to wait until Mary came back to the wagon. She didn't have long to wait, for a short while later Mary came running in bursting full of excitement, having just been told by her Da that they were both going on the trip.

"Coralina, have ye heard? Did Da tell ye he's lettin' us go wi' him an' Johnny the morrow? Ye'll be able tae see Robert."

"Mary wheesht, dinnae mention his name, ma Da'll no' let us go if he hears ye. Get yer stuff ready."

"Are ye no' pleased Coralina?"

"Aye, Ah'm pleased, Ah jist didnae want to be too keen. Away, get yer stuff ready."

Coralina checked on the things that they would need to take with them for the trip, and Mary, while chatting ten to the dozen, busied herself hindering rather than helping. Coralina wasn't listening to any of Mary's chatter. Her mind was on the trip to Dalgarven and seeing Robert again. As with any budding romance, she was filled with fears and her thoughts were racing.

'Did he like her as much as she liked him? What if he had a lassie? Maybe it would be better if she didn't go with her Da. She wanted to see him so badly that she was willing to take the chance.

The Sun had just risen when they set off from Glasgow Green that Monday morning; the March air was clear, but although it was still cold there were signs of spring everywhere. They would travel towards Shawlands passing the grand Pollok Estate, on towards Barrhead, and then by the Crofthead Mill in Neilston. Occasionally they could pick up threads and fabric samples from the mill that the women would use for making new clothes, or repairing old ones. They would save scraps of cloth and remnants for crafts, and then sell these crafts around the villages or at the fairs. After their visit to the mill, they would head along Lochlibo Road, on through Shillford ending that part of the journey at Lugton, a small hamlet in East Renfrewshire, where they would set up camp by Lugton water.

Once the family and the horses were tended to and settled, John would saddle up one of the horses and ride up to West Halket Farm taking a couple of young horses he had brought with him. He had promised them to the farmer, one for him, and another for his neighbour. Later, when the business was done John would walk from the campsite to the Lugton Inn and have a welcome pint of beer, knowing that Coralina would be mindful of Mary and Johnny, and the horses tethered nearby. The landlord at the Inn was always pleased to see him and often gave him a loaf of fresh bread to take away with him.

The next day after an early start they would head for a dairy farm in Dunlop where they would pick up cheeses for the camp. By lunchtime, the party would be feasting on lovely chunks of fresh bought cheese and the crusty bread from the Inn. Everyone was enjoying the trip but none more so than Coralina. With each part of the journey, her excitement grew, although she did her best not to appear too eager, for fear of her father realising that Robert Miller was the source of her enthusiasm.

The last horse was to be delivered to Auchintiber, and after the business was done there it was on through Kilwinning, and finally to Dalgarven. Coralina's stomach was in knots by the time they reached the outskirts of Kilwinning because before long they were turning into the mill yard.

Chapter 17

Robert heard their wagon before he saw it; it could have been anyone coming for flour, but the hitch in his stomach was the sign that he was hoping that it would be John Kelly, and that he would have brought Coralina with him. As the wagon came into view, he was torn between running to it, or standing his ground. He was going on eighteen now, and in Coralina's absence he had filled out considerably. His boyish good looks had developed, and anyone could see that he would soon be a strong handsome man.

Coralina was blushing as she looked at him and smiled coyly. Mary was grinning like a Cheshire cat, and she sneaked a look at her sister who glowered back at her. Young Johnny was the first to jump from the cart,

"Are ye a' right Robert," he said, and Robert acknowledged with a grin and a nod.

"Guid tae see ye Mister Kelly, have ye had a guid journey?"

"Aye Robert, Ah have that, how's the family?"

"They're both good, Ma's in the kitchen an' Da's in the mill. Ah'll tell them yer here," and with a quick glance at Coralina, he turned and walked off to let his parents know that the John Kelly had arrived.

Robert could hardly see in front of him, all he could see was Coralina's face. "*My Lord! She's mair lovely than Ah remembered, Ah'll be heartbroken if she has a fella,*" he thought. He stuck his head around the back door of the farmhouse, "Mam, the Kelly's are here, Ah'm jist away tae shout ma Da." He knew that they were climbing down from the wagon but he didn't dare turn and look, so he carried on to the mill and called his father. "That's the Kelly's here Da." He tried to remain calm and casual as he walked back round to where they were waiting.

"Hello Robert," said Mary, skipping up towards him.

He ruffled her hair, "My, ye've grown a fair bit Mary," and to Johnny he said, "Is this lassie still givin' ye grief?" He was still laughing as he glanced over to Coralina, "Coralina," he nodded at her, "are ye well?"

"Ah am Robert, yer self?"

"Aye, ye'll be ready for a cuppa."

Just at that moment, Elsie and Mathew arrived at the wagon and shook hands with John before leading them all into the kitchen.

"Yer in luck the day John, Ah've jist taken some soda scones aff the griddle; come away in an' sit at the table."

After they had eaten and enthused over Elsie's home baking, John, Elsie, and Mathew sat and chatted while the others went off outside, and while Mary and Johnny amused themselves exploring, Robert and Coralina found time to chat. They walked over to the mill and sat on the mill wall above the stream.

"Ah've' missed ye Coralina."

"Aye, Ah've missed ye tae Robert, though Ah was worried ye widnae' remember me, it's been a fair while, an' Ah thought ye would have plenty tae think aboot."

"Never a day passed when Ah didnae think of ye Coralina."

"Ah'm glad tae hear that Robert, Ah thought aboot ye a' the time. Ah thought ye might have taken a wife?"

"There's only wan lass for me Coralina, an' here she is afore me."

"Oh Robert, ye cannae talk like that! Ma Da would have the skin aff yer back if he thought ye were sayin' such things."

"Yer Da likes me."

"Aye, an' he likes yer family tae, but Ah have tae marry fae ma ane kind, it's expected, an' if Ah dinnae marry a Gypsy lad it would bring shame on me an' ma family."

"Dae ye love me Coralina? That's a' that matters, dae ye love me?"

Coralina had been going to Dalgarven since she was a toddler and she and Robert had played together and run about the fields since they were small. She knew in her heart that there would be no other for her.

"Aye Robert, Ah think Ah have aye loved ye."

"Well Ah'll speak tae yer Da."

"Ye cannae Robert, if ye speak tae ma Da ye'll never see me again, 'cause he'll no' allow it. He'll no' let me come wi' him ever again."

Coralina was silent, crying now, and Robert felt sick to his stomach.

"Dinnae worry then lass, Ah'll no' say a word but Ah'll make a plan. Will ye come away wi' me?"

"They'll come after us; the whole camp will come lookin."

"Ah'll take care o' ye Coralina, they'll no' find us. Just keep things as they are an' dinnae say a word, jist give me yer promise that ye will be ma wife."

"Ah will Robert, Ah promise."

"Ma Da has been guid tae me an' gave me a wage every week for helpin him, so Ah've money put by, enough tae gie us a guid start; we'll jist run aff and get wed, an' that will be that. Dae ye think yer Da will be at the fair in Neilston in July?"

"Aye, 'cause he'll be looking tae show some horses an' pick up some new stock."

"Ah'll make a plan, if he brings ye tae any o' the fairs be ready tae go an' that will be that. If he disnae, well jist be ready whenever he brings you, whether it be here or a fair, an' Ah'll be waitin' an' ready tae go."

"Ah'll be ready Robert, Ah love ye Robert, but Ah better get back; Ah'll see ye in a bit."

Robert went for a walk by the river Garnock. He sat on the sand bed at the edge of the river and stared out in front of him. He had thought that he would spend his whole life here and take over the tenancy of the mill from his father. His mind drifted…Dalgarven was his home, and it had everything that a man could want to set up a home and a family. The mill was at the centre of the community, no doubt, it was hard work providing flour and oatmeal for the village and the surrounding areas, but he loved it. It was a bustling village, where everyone knew everyone else, and they did not have to travel elsewhere for tradesmen, as they were all there within this small community of around thirty or so houses; slaters, saddlers, carpenters or joiners lived and worked within a short distance. The local sawmill supplied wood for building, and the women could find cloth for their clothing or other needs.

He thought back to when he was just three years old; there was shouting and screaming in the early hours of the morning, his father grabbing him from his sleep and running into the yard with his mother. It was absolute pandemonium; the mill was on fire, and the fire had already spread to some of the surrounding buildings. His father thrust him into his mother's arms; she was crying and screaming, and holding him so close that he could hardly turn his head to see what was happening. The barns and byres had caught alight, and his father was in the middle of the melee of villagers trying to save livestock and their homes. He would never forget that day, or the days, weeks and months that followed, when everyone worked together and rebuilt all that was damaged, or destroyed by the fire.

As a small child, he was unable to do much to help, but he watched and learned from his father and others. As he grew, he developed a keen interest in fixing and building things. Now as an adult he could turn his hand to anything; he understood the engineering mechanisms of the mill machinery and could carry out repairs if necessary, he could work with wood, patching or building as required, and he was confident around livestock.

'*Surely,*' he thought, '*Ah kin find any kind o' work; Ah kin turn ma hand tae anything*'.

He sighed a deep heart-wrenching sigh; he loved his village, his home, but he would overcome any obstacle or face any challenge if it meant Coralina would be his wife.

Chapter 18

Coralina and her family left early the next morning to begin the long journey home, and it was with a heavy heart that Robert watched the love of his life leaving in the cart laden with flour and other supplies.

"He has feelin's for that lass," said Elsie Miller to her husband.

"Aye, Ah think yer right, but he keeps them under wraps."

"It's jist as well, for nothin' can come of it."

"Dinnae worry, he'll find a lass soon enough, and then ye'll be nursin' gran' weans," laughed Mathew as he put his arm over her shoulder and led her back to the kitchen.

Robert stood there, watching until the cart was out of sight, and then he took himself into the mill back to work while he thought and planned. The Neilston Fair occurred in the first week of July, he counted out the time in his mind; he had about four months to get ready, but he still had to think about how they would manage this daring escape and where they could go so that no one would find them.

Robert had his own horse and cart that he used to deliver supplies from the mill to anyone that couldn't manage to come for them. His father had helped him to build it the year before and Robert had taken his time about planning the size and style, it was six feet long at the back with deep sides and a storage box under the seat. The box was big enough to carry tools to fix a wheel or help another out while making deliveries. When it was time to leave' he would stow some blankets in the box, along with the canopy that covered the cart when the weather was bad.

He would carry a small amount of feed for the horses; mostly they would be able to graze when they stopped for a rest. As far as their needs went, he had enough money to buy their provisions. There was no knowing how long it would be until they found somewhere safe to settle, so he would be careful with what money he had.

Where to go was the biggest problem that he had to solve. *'Perhaps it should be somewhere fairly remote, but somewhere that Ah could find work, but maybe a town would be better.'* He pondered on this for a while thinking that the first place the Gypsies would look for them would be the mills scattered around the country, but he would do anything, any job, as long as they could be together.

Coralina was just as quiet on the journey home as she had been before they set off, and John began to think it was just because she was growing up and changing. She and her sister were pretty girls, but now Coralina was becoming a beautiful young woman. Her skin was fresh with a golden glow, and her long, wavy black hair framed her face as it tumbled down over her shoulders. John was sure that once she had found someone to love, that would love her equally in return, she would be happy. He began to think of the lads that he knew that were around her age, and he decided that he would do something about finding her a match at the Appleby Fair.

Coralina would have been horrified if she could have read her father's mind, but her mind was racing with other possibilities. She had taken all the lace doilies that she had made, and each time they stopped, she offered them for sale to whoever was around. She sold them all; she had been doing this for several years and her father always made her keep her pennies.

'For yer bottom drawer Coralina,' he would say to her when she offered him her earnings as she always did.

Occasionally she would sort her farthings, ha'pennies, and pennies, and her Da would change her coppers for a bright silver shilling. In those days, a shilling was a lot of money, the average weekly wage being around ten shillings. Coralina had already amassed a small fortune of five pounds and four shillings and this was safely stowed away in her bottom drawer. She decided there and then, that on her return to the camp, she would set aside the four shillings plus the odd coppers that she had earned on the journey. She would give this money to her sister to give her a start with her dowry. Mary would soon have to start thinking about making things to sell so that she too could save for her wedding day. So far, Mary had shown no interest in making things with her hands, preferring to be in the horse field, riding Mizzie, and helping with the other horses. Small though she was, she would carry water, feed, or straw and take on any task that Johnny did, almost as though she was out to keep up with him at least, or at best, better him. Coralina knew that when she left Mary would have little time for indulging in her preferences.

When they finally arrived back at the camp, everyone came out to collect the provisions that John had brought back with him. Money changed hands, and as was the tradition, there was always an extra penny given *'for luck'*. The horses were unhitched and led to the field to graze and then the cart was cleaned, the wheels were oiled and it was stowed away for future use. When everything was back in order, John went across to have a cup of tea and a chat with Isabella. "Well Isabella, Ah dinnae think the trip did much for Coralina's mood. She still seems ower quiet tae me. Ah'm thinking that it's high time she was wed, an' Ah'm thinking Ah should have a chat wi' ma cousins at Appleby Fair'; whit dae ye think o' that?" he said, nursing his cup.

They were outdoors sitting on wooden boxes set by the fire.

"Aye ye might be right John, have ye anybody in mind?"

"Aye, there's wan or two come tae mind but she's never shown any interest in them."

"She's been too busy mindin' Mary, John, that's half the problem."

"Aye, ye could be right. It's by time Ah had another word wi' Mary, she needs tae gie' her sister a break an' help her."

John and Isabella sat there, sipping their tea and musing over Coralina's future and a potential match for her.

"Have ye said onythin' tae Coralina aboot this John?"

"Nah', no' yet."

Neither of them had noticed Mary, who had been sitting quietly on the grass nearby, nor did they realise that she had heard them. Mary slipped away, her mind racing. She couldn't wait to tell Coralina what she had heard.

Chapter 19

Coralina was kneeling on the floor of the wagon going through her things; in her mind, she was planning what she could to take with her, and how she could hide things from her father. Her dowry money was the first thing she looked at, and then she looked for a box that she could use to put the spare shillings and change into for Mary's start. She was doing that when Mary appeared.

"Come wi' me Coralina?"

"Whit for?"

"Jist come wi' me."

"Ah'm busy Mary, Ah've things tae dae."

"Jist listen tae me, ye need tae come wi' me the noo. Ah need tae tell ye summat."

Coralina stood up and followed Mary, "Whit is it?"

"Wheesht, jist come wi' me."

Coralina followed Mary out of the camp until they were well away from anyone that could overhear them.

"Ah have summat tae tell ye."

"Spit it oot then."

"Ma Da is plannin' tae merry ye aff at the Appleby Fair!"

"Whit dae ye mean?"

"Ah heard him talkin' tae Mither Isabella, an' he was sayin' that come the fair at Appleby he was gonnae talk tae the cousins for a fella for ye tae wed!"

"Never! Ye must be mistaken'."

"Ah'm tellin ye, it's because ye have been quiet, they think ye need tae be wed an' startin' a family."

Coralina put her head in her hands and the tears began to flow. "He cannae dae that, he cannae dae that!"

"Ye'll no' have ony choice Coralina, if ma Da says yer getting merried then yer getting merried an' that will be a' there is tae it."

Coralina knew for sure now that she had to make every effort to get away before the Appleby Fair, and she prayed that her Da would take them to the Neilston fair. She couldn't think what she would do if he decided not to take her.

"Whit are ye gonnae dae Coralina? Ah think Robert loves ye."

Filled with the romance of the idea, Mary surprised Coralina by announcing, "Could ye no' run away an' merry Robert?"

"Mary wheesht! Ye'll get us in trouble if ye say that."

"Heavens above," Coralina thought to herself, *"does she ken everythin'?"*

Mary jumped back, realisation dawning on her, "Yer' gonnae run away wi' Robert!"

Coralina leapt at Mary, and grabbed her by her shoulders and shook her hard. Mary was shocked, Coralina had never shown her any anger, and had never laid a hand on her.

"Ah'm warnin' ye Mary, dinnae ever talk like that again."

Both girls were crying now, Mary because Coralina was so scared and angry, and Coralina because she was afraid that Mary might slip up and the secret would be out.

"Ah promise ye Coralina, Ah'll never say a word, Ah promise. Will ye tell me afore ye go?"

Both girls had tears streaming down their faces. Coralina held her little sister in a tight embrace, "Ah'm no' goin' onywhere the noo Mary, an' if Ah am ye'll be the first tae know."

The girls washed their faces in the river, and for a while, they walked quietly, each with their own thoughts occupying their minds. Mary began to think about what her life would be like without her big sister. She began to realise that what, for a moment, had seemed like an exciting thought, would mean that she might never see her big sister again. Coralina already understood that eventuality, and the thought of leaving her family was breaking her heart, but she knew that it was the only way.

Over the next few weeks, both girls busied themselves. Coralina tried to act as normal, but every waking thought was focused on preparing for her departure and thinking about the Neilston Fair and what she would have to take with her. Subtly, she tried to point out to her sister the things that she did on a daily basis. Neither acknowledged the reasoning behind this, but Mary understood, and played her part in listening and not saying a word about the imminent event.

"Whit's wrang wi' these lassies Isabella?" John asked.

"They're jist settlin' doon John, they're growin', ye should be proud o' them."

"Aye', Ah' am, but they're awfy quiet an' they're aye whisperin' tae each other."

Isabella laughed, "Ye should be glad aboot that John, Mary's getting a big lassie an' she's takin' her share. Coralina has been a guid mither tae her."

"Aye, happens ye might be right."

"Ye'll see a change in them when it's time tae go tae the fair they'll start tae get excited then an' ye'll no' get a minute's peace."

However, that wouldn't be the case, because when it came time to go to the fair, both girls would be aware that this could be the last days that they would see each other. John was preoccupied preparing the horses so he didn't pay much attention to the girls, and just let them get on with what they were doing. From time to time Mary helped her father and Johnny with the grooming, and Johnny noticed how quiet she was. He was reluctant to say anything, but he watched her, and he watched the subtleties between her and Coralina. He wondered to himself what was different, or more to the point, what had happened to make things different between them. Coralina had always been the more serious of the two, and Mary was always 'happy go lucky', but she had become more like her sister over the past few weeks. He often saw the girls deep in conversation and wondered about them.

All too soon, it was time to go to the Neilston Fair. Coralina was sick to her stomach and Mary was much the same. The girls climbed into the cart with Johnny at the front in charge of the reins, while John rode behind leading his horses. The sisters sat in the back of the cart whispering to each other, "Whit's gonnae happen Coralina?"

"Ah dinnae ken, Ah'll jist watch for Robert an' see whit happens."

"Are ye scared?"

"Aye."

"Ah'm scared tae."

"Ah've left summat under ma blanket for ye, for yer bottom drawer tae gie ye a start. Ye need tae think aboot makin' some money."

"Dinnae worry aboot that, Ah'll tell fortunes an' get a sixpence for that, but no' the noo, Ah'm too wee, next year maybe, an' Johnny'll look after me."

Coralina nodded, she knew Mary would be able to do that, and she would probably make good money.

Chapter 20

Before long they had reached Neilston and made their way along the road, busy with carts and wagons, carriages and pedestrians, and folks leading or riding horses. Coralina was agitated and Mary was clutching her hand, thankfully, John who was riding King, was too busy leading his sale horses, and nodding to familiar faces to notice how the girls were. Johnny, leading the cart, turned into the fairground, and began to head for the spot that they usually camped in when Mary whispered, "Ah can see him Coralina, OUCH!" she shouted as Coralina gripped her hand tightly.

"Aye, so can Ah."

Once Johnny had halted the cart, John led the horses to the roped off area where he would tie them loosely and let them settle down.

Robert approached the cart, "Hello there Johnny, Ah thought Ah might see ye here the day, are ye well?"

"Aye Robert, are the family wi' ye?"

"Nah, it's jist me the day." As Johnny jumped down from the cart and tended to the lead horse Robert went to the back of the cart and whispered to Coralina, "Ah'll be waitin' at the gate wi' ma cart, come as soon as ye can an' be ready to go." In a louder voice, "Hello there Mary."

With her eyes wide with apprehension, dreading what was about to happen, Mary looked at him and nodded, "Robert."

Robert made his way towards his cart, hitched near the gate and jumped onto it. He waited until there was a space between those coming in then he directed his horse out onto the street to wait for Coralina.

"Johnny, tell ma Da that Coralina an' me are jist away for a look an' we'll be back in a wee while," said Mary, and then she held out her hand to Coralina and said, "Are ye comin' then." Without a word, Coralina took the bag that she had stowed in the cart earlier. Hand in hand, they made their way through the crowds.

Coralina had tears running down her face and when she looked at Mary, she saw that her eyes had filled too. It seemed as though Mary was taking charge, and Coralina knew in her heart that Mary would be fine without her, but the more she thought about leaving her little sister the more the ache in her heart grew.

"Hurry up Coralina," said Mary, as she tugged, almost dragged, her sister between the crowds that were building up. Then suddenly, before Coralina had any more time to think about what she was doing, they reached the gate, and there was Robert, waiting outside the field, anxiously watching for them.

"Go! Go quick! Afore anyone notices, Ah'll aye love ye an' Ah'll think o' ye every day. Send word if ye can; go now hurry."

Coralina couldn't speak for the lump in her throat. Robert jumped down from his cart. "Come tae the back o' the cart, pretend yer reachin' for summat, an' when Ah think it safe Ah'll gie ye a shove, an' ye can climb in an' pull the hap ower ye."

Coralina did as she was bid, and within moments, the cart was trundling away and Mary ran back to where their cart was parked. Coralina's heart was thumping in her chest; she was terrified that at any moment she would hear her father's voice yelling for them to stop. Tears coursed down her face and she sobbed, her heart breaking at the thought of never seeing her sister again. Robert had led the horses down the hill from Neilston into Barrhead and was heading down through Crookston before he felt it was safe enough to stop for a moment to make sure that Coralina was all right, hidden under the hap as she was. He swung round on the bench and lifted a corner of the cover, "Are ye a'right Coralina?" He was shocked when her face appeared, her eyes red, tear streaked and swollen from crying. "Oh ma darlin' Ah canny bide here, but in a wee while it will be safe for us tae stop for a minute. Take a drink o' water from the flask, it'll be a'right." Now he was overwhelmed with guilt and fear wondering if he had done the right thing, beginning to question his choice and fearing for Coralina wondering if she would ever get over her grief. He had decided that they would camp out for the night near Erskine, and then the next day they would take the ferry across the Clyde and travel on towards Loch Lomond. He knew they would need to travel far to be safe from Coralina's Gypsy family and if necessary they would go as far as Fort William and beyond. He would do whatever it took to make a happy and safe life for himself and Coralina.

From Crookston he followed the road to Renfrew and beyond until he found a suitable place to stop. He was keen to share this with Coralina. He settled his two horses, tethering them loosely to allow them to graze and went back to the cart. Coralina was sound asleep under the hap; he lifted a corner and as he gazed at her, he was overwhelmed with his love for her.

"Coralina, wake up sweetheart," he touched her shoulder gently "It's jist me, we're safe' dinnae be scared, sit up, come an' see."

Coralina rubbed her eyes, sat up and looked out over the edge of the cart. "Oh my, that's jist lovely, where are wi'?"

"Erskine, and that's Dumbarton Castle yonder. Come on, ye should stretch yer legs, let's take a walk an' then Ah'll make a fire an' wi' can have some tea an' a bit tae eat."

They walked hand in hand with the sun shining on them, admiring the view and as Robert placed his arm around Coralina's shoulders, she felt a sense of security. He kissed her there for the first time, standing on the hill above the Clyde and she knew that she loved him with all her heart and she knew that he would always take care of her.

Chapter 21

It was almost noon before John realised that something was amiss. He kept questioning Mary, and although she was resilient, before long she was in tears. He was frantic with worry, "Ye know summat, Ah'm sure ye know summat Mary, an' if ye dinnae tell me Ah'll whip yer hide."

"Ah dinnae ken Da, Ah was watchin' the fair, Ah didnae see whur she went."

"If yer hidin' summat fae me, Ah'll never forgive ye Mary, ye'll pay for this Mary, one way or t'other ye'll pay for this."

All Mary could do was stand and cry. She cried for her sister knowing that she would probably never see her again, and she cried for her father, for his anger and contempt of her. John went around the fairground several times. He asked people he knew, and he asked strangers if they had seen his lass. Other Gypsies began to congregate around him offering to set up a search party. Some made their way down to Barrhead and Darnley others went on to Uplawmoor, but no one had seen anything.

Two weeks had passed since that day at the Neilston Fair. Each day her father rode off searching for Coralina. Each night he came back more dejected than before. All thoughts of attending fairs or going for supplies were pushed to one side. After another long day searching John rode into camp, young Johnny took his horse and led it away to attend to it, and John went over to sit by the fire that was set in the middle of the camp. He took a bottle from his jacket pocket and drank from it. The whisky burned as it went down but he felt nothing but the pain in his heart.

The atmosphere in the camp was subdued, and day by day the number of folk who had been searching had whittled away. Those who lived on the camp were reluctant to ask John if there was any news, there was no need really as they could see by his face that he had discovered nothing.

Mary was isolated in her despair, it was as though the life had gone out of her and it felt as though everyone blamed her. John knew that some of Coralina's belongings were gone, so he knew too that she hadn't been taken. Wherever she was she had planned to go, John was certain that Mary must know something about it, but Mary had given her word, and she refused to admit that she knew anything, not even to young Johnny.

Isabella was making a pot of tea one morning and seeing John coming out of his wagon, ready to begin another days searching, she called to him.

"Have some tea afore ye go John."

John walked over and sat beside her at the fire. Trying to get John back to normal life, she asked if he would be going for supplies soon and the effect was startling. John stared at her for a moment, but that moment seemed like an eternity.

"That's it!" he said, as he jumped up, spilling his tea as the cup was thrown to the ground, "That's whur she is!"

Isabella was startled and she jumped up too, "Whur dae ye think she is John?"

"Away wi' Robert Miller!" he said, as he ran off to fetch his horse.

Isabella was left standing open mouthed as she watched John race off. He was saddled up within a few minutes and riding out of the camp at speed. All she could do now was wait and wonder. Mary, seeing the exchange and her father riding off at speed ran towards Isabella, "Whit's up wi' ma Da?"

"Yer Da thinks Coralina's wi' the Miller's!"

Mary stood there, fear written over her face.

"Dae ye ken summat Mary? If ye dae ye better tell me."

"Ah dinnae ken onythin'."

"Well if ye ken summat' ye better tell me afore yer Da comes back."

Mary turned and walked away, leaving Isabella standing by the fire wondering if Coralina was away with Robert Miller, and if she was she thought it was her fault because she encouraged John to take her with him to Dalgarven. She thought that John would be furious with her.

The trauma that Mary had endured over the past few weeks was plain to see. Her puppy fat had disappeared largely due to the fact that she had lost her appetite and wasn't sleeping. She kept worrying about how her sister was, and she feared that her father would never speak to her again. It wasn't her fault, but she felt as though everyone was shunning her as though it was. She didn't understand why she was being blamed; she was still there, it was Coralina who had run away, but that's the way it is with people when they are hurt, angry or afraid, they take their angst out on those who are closest to them regardless of whether they are responsible or not.

Confused and upset, she left the camp and made her way to the horse field and called Mizzie, who was at the other end of the field grazing. Mizzie was sulking, and not prepared to jump to Mary's call, after all she had been neglecting her recently. She called again and Mizzie, lifted her head, gave her a look, and then carried on grazing.

It was just too much to bear. Mary dropped to her knees on the grass, and with her head in her hands she cried her heart out. A few moments later she felt a warm moist tickle on the back of her neck, and startled, she looked up as Mizzie nuzzled her once more. That only made her cry some more, she thought her heart would break. Mizzie nudged her, and Mary stood up and rested her face against Mizzie's neck. The horse snorted and huffed at her, and Mary hauled herself onto her back and rode to the edge of the roped off area. She dismounted, and untying the rope she led Mizzie out of the field, jumped on once more, and rode off across the fields. Johnny had been watching from a distance, and as soon as he realised that she was taking Mizzie out he ran to the field and followed her on one of the other horses.

She cried as she rode, and her mind was preoccupied with thoughts of Coralina and of her Da. She had no thought or idea of where she was going, and she wouldn't have cared anyway. She felt lost, lonely, and alone, and things would never be as they were before. She followed the river, passing the log that she had sat on with her sister on many occasions, but she didn't stop there. She continued to follow the river for another two miles from the camp. Finally, exhaustion set in and Mary slowed Mizzie down to a walk, and led her to a small clearing beside a large oak tree. She dismounted and walked Mizzie to the water's edge to drink.

Johnny followed at a distance; he knew she was hurting but he didn't know how to fix that, all he could do was follow in case she needed him, or in case she hurt herself. When he saw her by the river, he dismounted and walked over to stand beside her. She saw Johnny approaching but she didn't speak, nor did he. When Mizzie had taken what she needed Johnny took her by her head collar, and led her and his own horse to a nearby tree, tying them so that they could graze but wouldn't wander off. He turned to see Mary, sitting there on the grass under the oak tree, knees bent, her arms resting on her knees and her head resting on her arms. Her long dark hair hid her face, but he knew that she was crying. He went over and sat beside her, and there they sat quietly together, neither saying anything to the other. Finally, Johnny spoke, "Dae ye want tae tell me onythin'."

Mary shook her head.

"Talk tae me Mary, dae ye ken whur yer sister is?"

Mary didn't answer, but Johnny asked again, "Dae ye ken whur yer sister is Mary?"

She looked him straight in the eye and truthfully told him that she didn't, she wasn't lying, she didn't know where Coralina was. Johnny shook his head sadly. "Mary Ah've known ye all ma life an' Ah've seen the best o' ye an' the worst o' ye. There is nothin' that ye can say tae me that will shock me, an' if yer worried that Ah'll tell yer Da then you dinnae gie me credit. Talk tae me Mary, tell me whit's in yer mind."

Mary started to sob once more, "Ma sisters away an' ma' Da's no' speaking tae me, an' Ah canny bear it."

Johnny wrapped his arm around her shoulder and pulled her towards him, and slowly they sank backwards to lie on the grass together. Johnny held her in an embrace and whispered into her hair, "Ah love ye Mary Kelly, ye have nothin' tae fear 'cause Ah'll watch oot for ye."

They lay on the grass for a while until Mary's sobbing had subsided, but although she trusted Johnny with her life, she held on to her secret for a while yet. The time would come when she would share, but not yet.

Chapter 22

Robert had left a short note for Elsie and Mathew to find after he had left. It just said, *'Ma an' Da Ah'm sorry tae tell ye that Ah've had tae go away. Don't worry aboot me. Ah'll be in touch as soon as Ah'm settled. Love Robert.'*

They were worried sick, and couldn't understand why he had left, and his note gave no explanation. They had always done their best by him, and he had always been a good son; they were mystified as to why he would leave. As is usual when people do not know the true facts, their minds go into overdrive and begin to imagine all manner of problems. For two weeks they fretted and argued about the reasons why he might have gone, and then out of the blue, when they least expected, a letter arrived. Elsie was in her kitchen kneading dough for bread when the postman stuck his head round her door, "A letter for ye Elsie."

"Eh? Whit's that? Jist put it on the table," she said, holding up her hands covered in dough to demonstrate why she couldn't take it. As soon as he was gone, she grabbed a cloth and started to wipe the dough from her hands. Thinking that it might be word about Robert, she looked at it as though it would burst into flames, and then ran to fetch Mathew from the mill.

"Mathew! Mathew! Come quick."

On hearing her urgent call, Mathew rushed from the mill, "Whit's up wi' ye wummin'?"

"A letter!" she said, hurrying him back to the kitchen. At first they stood and looked at it, till Mathew picked it up and began to read it to Elsie, who was wringing her hands in distress.

'Dear Ma an' Da, Ah'm sorry aboot the way Ah had tae leave, an' Ah wish things could'ha' been different. Ah aye thought Ah would spend ma life at the mill. Ah thought Ah would bring ma wife tae the mill and start a family there, but ye see that was nae tae be. Ye see there is nae other lass for me but Coralina Kelly, an' wi' widnae get her Da's permission tae wed, so wi' have left tae make oor ane life an' maybe wan day wi'll see ye again. Ah huvnae dishonoured Coralina so ye dinnae need tae be ashamed o' me. Wi'll be merried soon. Ye'll aye be in ma thoughts an' prayers. Ah'll be in touch soon

Yer ever lovin' son, Robert.'

Elsie sat down, slumped at the table. Mathew stood by her side, both of them in shock.

"Ah dinnae ken if that's a blessin' or a curse," said Mathew.

"its no' a curse, how could it be a curse."

"Because John Kelly will go crazy when he finds oot."

"It's been two weeks Mathew, he must surely ken."

"Aye, he'll ken she's away, but he might no' ken that she's away wi' oor Robert, and when he does ken…"

Mathew shook his head in despair.

"Whit dae ye think he'll dae?" asked Elsie.

"Who can say, he might try tae find them, an' if he does they could gang up on oor Robert. It's been hard wi' Robert away, it could be harder still if the Gypsies stop buying fae us."

"Dae ye think wi' should try tae get in touch wi' him?"

"Tae tell him his lassie has ran away wi' oor Robert!" asked Mathew in disbelief.

"Ah widnae like tae think he would dae onythin' bad, but Ah widnae like tae think he is worryin' himsel' sick aboot where she might be."

The words were no sooner out of their mouths than they heard him coming, the horse's hoofs clattering on the yard as he rode in.

"Leave this tae me Elsie," said Mathew, as he went to the door.

John was dismounting, and seeing Mathew, he turned and asked accusingly, "Where are they? Ah'm tellin ye man, Ah dinnae want tae hurt ye, but ye better tell me where ma lass is."

Ever the diplomat Mathew replied, "Come away in John."

John was in no mood for niceties but, had little option if he wanted to find out where his daughter was.

"Make some tea Elsie, sit yer self doon John."

"Ah'll stand," it was apparent by his face that he would not take kindly to platitudes and they could smell the stale whisky on him.

"She's no' here John, this letter jist came. Wi' were jist havin' a look at it as ye arrived." He slid the letter across the table to John. For a moment John looked at the letter, and then he looked across the table to Mathew, "That's nae use tae me, for Ah cannae read."

Mathew took the letter back and John slumped in the chair as Mathew read it to him.

"She has shamed me an' the rest o' the family."

"Ye heard it yirsel John, in ma son's words, he didnae dishonour her."

"That's as may be, but she's dishonoured her family, for she's meant tae merry her ain kind."

"It's no' that bad man, can ye no' jist accept it, after a' we're be gonnae be family, an' there'll be bairns in the future."

The words were hardly uttered from Mathew's mouth when John stood up, knocking over the chair that he had been sitting in. He yelled at Mathew, "Family! Family! Ye'll never be part o' ma family! Nor will ma lass! Never! Never again! As far as Ah'm concerned, she's dead tae me an' mine." He scrunched the letter in his hand and threw it to the floor, before making his way to the door, and at the last second he turned and said, "Ye'll no' see oor kind again either, we'll be getting oor needs elsewhere."

Mathew picked up the letter and smoothed it out, and then walked over to comfort Elsie who was standing by the kitchen sink quietly crying. They listened to the sound of John riding away, both of them afraid of what the future would bring. Reading between the lines, if John considered that Coralina was dead to him, then perhaps he would be less likely to try to find them, but still there was a chance that he might go looking with the rest of his camp and the outcome of that would be dire. They also knew that at their time of life they would be unable to continue to carry the heavy burden of running the mill for much longer without Roberts' support.

"Ah've never known him tae smell of the drink Elsie, have you?"

"Naw, no' in a' the time he has been comin' here. Ah think he might be hittin' the bottle hard."

On John's return to the camp he was met by Isabella. She could see he was enraged, and knew that things had not gone well, she was cautious about speaking to him, but knew that she must say something.

"Are' ye gonnae tell me whit's whit'?"

"Wan thing," he said, turning on her and pointing his finger at her, "Never mention her name tae me again." And with that he turned and walked away, leaving Isabella to wonder what he had found out.

It was Isabella's responsibility now to make sure that everyone knew not to mention Coralina, and of course everyone wanted to know what he had found out, but no one dared to ask John, and Isabella was unable to make them any the wiser. It was only later, drunk on the whisky and rambling like a man possessed, that others found out that Coralina had run away with the miller's son.

Chapter 23 Before the Rose, Mary's Story

Everything changed after Coralina ran away. John seldom spoke to anyone except young Johnny. He hardly looked at Mary and only spoke to her if he had to; he no longer trusted her, and he blamed her. Initially Mary was badly affected by her father's reaction, but she was made of stronger stuff, nevertheless the experience changed her. Before, Mary was confident, outgoing, determined, and capable of doing whatever she wanted, and although inwardly she still retained these strengths they were tempered with a seriousness, a quietness, that was difficult for anyone around her to penetrate. She seldom conversed with anyone any more, except for Johnny, and she spent most of her time doing only what she had to do. Mary was always found around the horses when her tasks were done, but she and her father avoided each other, and the general atmosphere around them was uncomfortable.

John, like many others on the camp, had always enjoyed a bottle of beer or an occasional nip or two of whisky, but since Coralina's departure, John had taken to 'the hard stuff' and was often the worse for wear. His cousin Willie, Johnny's father and his brother-in-law George did their best to talk to him about his drinking but eventually they considered him a lost cause and they watched as he neglected his responsibilities, and left young Johnny to pick up the slack. In some ways, this was a blessing for Mary because it was easier for her to be involved in helping with the horses when it was just her and Johnny. Soon even the responsibility of selling the horses and fetching the provisions fell on Johnny's shoulders, while John slouched somewhere in a drunken stupor.

Hard work had toughened young Johnny; he had filled out and matured beyond his years. Anyone seeing the seventeen-year-old would have assumed that he was in his early twenties. In looks, he was handsome, lean though muscular and tall. He still had some growing to do, but he was already taller than his peers were. He had dark hair typical in his family but his eyes were a piercing blue and they often conveyed more than his words did. When Johnny wasn't focused on his work load, his attention was always on Mary and he looked for her if she wasn't close by.

Each day Mary seemed to grow more striking. At fifteen she had lost her childlike looks and was blossoming into a beautiful young woman. She carried herself with grace and dignity as though she was better than everyone else, but really her appearance and attitude belied her inner grief, and all she was doing was protecting herself from the opinions that others may have had of her. She was every bit a typical Gypsy lass with cascading dark hair and the darkest eyes. Mary preferred her own company when she wasn't around Johnny and of late, she had taken to solitary night time walks in the moonlight. Spending time alone sharpened her gift of the sight and with each passing day she was becoming more gifted, though she had learned from experience to keep her impressions to herself.

The Moon fascinated her and she was sure that it wasn't a man in the moon that she could see; she was certain it was a woman; she called her 'The Lady'. Sometimes in the night under the full of the moon she would stand there with her arms spread wide and implore The Lady of the Moon to guide her, to help her to understand her life. She would ask for help to stop her father drinking so much and she would ask that her sister would always be safe and happy. No one told her what to do when she was on her moonlight walks and no one had told her how to chant in rhyme but natural instincts took over and became habit. Perhaps it was hidden in the words of the old Mither and how she made them repeat rhymes about plants and their uses. Mary now had rhymes for every occasion and was quick to create new rhymes whenever she required them.

For wisdom and understanding she would chant,

'Borage with your heed cast doon

Take away ma worried froon

An' sage ye guide, tell me whit's right

Tae still ma worries on this night.'

Sometimes she would seek out dried petals from flowers and plants that she had gathered and occasionally if she didn't have what she needed she would ask Mither Isabella if she had any to spare. Off she would go and sit by the river and grind her petals or seed mixture until it was little more than a fine dust and then she would chant her rhyme and set a light to the dust.

Her thoughts often drifted back to that day that she had spent with the old Mither when she first found out that the old Mither knew that she knew things and could see things. She worried about what bad things would come back to her because she had helped Coralina to run away. She did not think that helping Coralina was a bad thing, but her father blamed her, and she thought everyone else did too. She was more mindful of her reactions to anything that displeased her, afraid of what the consequences might be, but now and again her temper would rise. Others in the camp would approach her if they were feeling poorly as they knew she had a healing gift, but wherever there is a positive, there is always a negative to bring balance.

On one occasion Daisy, Isabella's youngest daughter, taunted Mary as she was walking by.

"Ah dinnae ken why that Johnny bothers wi' ye Mary Kelly wi' yer nose stuck in the air, he'd be better aff wi' wan o' us," she called out after her.

Mary turned, glared at her and pointed her finger in Daisy's direction and then just as suddenly, she dropped her hand, turned and hurried away.

Later Daisy related the event to her sisters and anyone else who would listen. "Ah'm tellin' ye, she pointed at ma stomach an' Ah got such a pain an' Ah had the skitters a' day. It was her, Ah'm tellin' ye. Ah was trippen' ower ma'sel goin' back an' furrat tae the dunny!"

Eventually the gossip got back to Johnny.

"Ah thought ye were by that stuff Mary? Dae ye ken whit Daisy's sayin'?"

"Aye Ah've heard, an' she's talkin' rubbish, Ah didnae dae anythin, Ah nearly did but Ah stopped ma self. It's no' that when they have summat wrang or they want a potion, they come tae me for healin', or when they're hopin tae charm a fella."

When the other girls and women were going around the doors selling doilies and sprigs of flowers to make some money, Mary was telling fortunes, and word travels fast when you are good at something like that. Often when the others would have a door slammed in their face, Mary would have housewives eagerly waiting to hear what she had to tell them. The other girls were jealous of Mary. Apart from her demeanour, she always made more money than they did. Having more money meant that she could buy cloth for dresses or skirts and since Coralina had gone away Mary had started to make her own clothes, with difficulty at first but then with experience she became quite adept at her new skill.

Chapter 24

Mary missed Coralina desperately, and had eventually confided in Johnny that she had known about her father's plans to marry Coralina off and how upset Coralina was at the thought. She had asked Johnny how he would have felt if she had to marry someone else. Johnny stood there looking down at her for she was shorter than he was, and said with finality, "It would never happen."

After Mary's explanation of her reasons for helping her sister, Johnny began to call in at Dalgarven, to speak to the Millers, enquiring if there was any word from Coralina and Robert, although he knew that it was forbidden. Initially, the Millers were understandably cautious, but over time they began to realise that Johnny meant no ill will, instead he was anxious to carry word of Coralina's wellbeing back to Mary. He never ever mentioned to John, or anyone other than Mary, anything that the Millers told him. Soon it became apparent that this was a good way for Mary and Coralina to keep in touch, albeit sporadically. Mathew was able to tell Johnny that Robert and Coralina had a little girl named Emily. Johnny was certain that the Millers knew where Robert and Coralina were, and was just as certain that they had visited them wherever they were, but the Millers gave nothing more away.

On one of his visits Mathew told Johnny that Coralina had been asking if he and Mary were wed yet. This had been on Johnny's mind for some time, but John was in such a permanent state of drunkenness, that Johnny had been putting off the idea of setting a date. It was a foregone conclusion that he and Mary would wed, it was just a matter of time, but Mary held out hope that her father would sober up. That wasn't to be, his health just worsened with the effects of alcohol poisoning. Mary cared for her father; she washed his soiled clothes, she fed him soup when he was too drunk to care about eating, and she covered him to keep him warm when he fell over too drunk to even know where he was.

She found him late one February night lying out in the open. It was so cold that the grass was stiff and his clothes were almost frozen onto him. She ran for Johnny who helped her to get him up and back to the wagon. Together they stripped him out of his sodden clothes and put him to bed after bathing him down with cloths soaked in warm water, but the damage was already done. Eventually he was so ill that he couldn't get out of his bed, but even that wasn't too much for Mary. She cleaned his mess and washed him, tried to coax him to eat, and prepared syrups to ease his rasping cough. Every time she attended to him her heart broke a little bit more, remembering the man he had been, until finally he was breathing his last.

Johnny was in the wagon with Mary, and he watched as the love of his life grieved for the father she had lost years before. He grieved with her, remembering all the good times that they had shared and travelled together. Everything he knew, he knew because this man had taught him. Mary sat cradling her father in her arms holding him up to try to ease his breathing when suddenly his breathing became quick and shallow and he gasped for air.

"Da! Da!" Mary screamed, "Oh Da! Dinnae leave me; take ma breath, Da take ma breath." And her father opened his eyes; he looked tenderly into Mary's eyes, clutched her hand, and drew it to his lips. He kissed her hand and closed his eyes never to open them again. Mary crumpled over her father sobbing uncontrollably and all Johnny could do was sit and watch as he too wept for what was lost. Eventually her tears spent she stood and made to leave the wagon.

"Where are ye goin' Mary?" he asked catching her arm. She turned and looked him in the eyes then looked down at his hand on her arm holding her back.

"Let me be Johnny," she said and as he released his grip, she turned and left the wagon. She ran across the field and through the trees until she reached the river. She found her way by instinct rather than sight because it was a black night in the dark of the moon. She knelt by the river filled with a rage that was so powerful that she felt her heart would burst. Without intention, her mouth opened and she released a guttural scream as she looked up at the dark sky looking for the Moon. Then she yelled,

"Aye hide yer face pretend ye cannae see

But take this, it's the last ye'll hear fae me

Ye took ma sister an' then ye took ma Da

The next time Ah see ye Ah'll hide ma face an' a'."

She cried until she was empty.

Johnny's father Willie came into the wagon to comfort his son for he knew that he had been a great influence in Johnny's life and of course, he grieved too, for he was losing a dearly loved cousin. Willie stayed in the wagon until Johnny went looking for Mary. He knew where she would be and was not surprised to find her on the ground, shivering with the cold, staring blindly ahead of her. No words passed between them as he gently coaxed her to her feet and took her to Isabella's.

Father and son were stoic in their grief over the next few days, as they prepared John for his final resting place at Janefield Cemetery.

"Will ye keep her wi' ye Isabella for wi' have tae burn that wagon?"

"Dinnae worry yer self aboot that Johnny, Ah'll see tae her."

"Ah have a wagon comin' for us when wi' get merried but Ah don't think wi' should dae it till some time has passed and she has been able tae deal wi' her grief."

"Aye lets jist get this ower wi' first."

The following days were a blur to Mary, she couldn't think, she couldn't eat and she couldn't sleep. She wandered, like a zombie, back and forward between the horses and the river that she loved to sit by, her eyes staring straight ahead avoiding any eye contact with anyone. When the first sliver of the Moon appeared, she felt a deep guilt and wandered back to the river.

"Silver Lady in the sky

Ah've come tae tell ye ma tears are dry

Ah'm sorry Ah was awfy bad

Ah didnae mean it, grief made me mad.

Ah'll Aye come back tae talk tae ye

Please Lady dinnae look away."

Just as she was saying those last words, a cloud passed over the moon and hid it from her sight and her heart filled with sadness and dread.

After John's funeral Mary moved into Isabella and George's wagon, much to the displeasure of Daisy. Nellie had only recently married Willie's nephew, Edward McGuigan, who was a skilled carpenter, and Jennie had gone with her husband to live at another camp after their wedding, so it was just Daisy still in the wagon with her parents. In spite of them both sharing the same breast milk when they were babies, the two girls did not have a good word for each other. Daisy felt sorry for Mary's loss, but that didn't mean that she had to like sharing her home with her. She had nothing to worry about because Mary was too grief stricken to care or think about Daisy or anyone else for that matter.

Their wagon was gone now, it had been taken away and burned with everything in it, and she hadn't even a keepsake to hold, to remind her of happier times. Johnny had hardly any time for her because he was tending to her father's responsibilities, seeing to the horses and now that the worst of the winter had passed, travelling here and there fetching provisions for the camp. He had found the time to call into Dalgarven to ask the Millers if they would pass word to Coralina about her father's passing.

"Ah'm right sorry tae hear that," said Mathew.

"Aye, it's been hard on Mary an' she's no' taken it well. Ah expect that Coralina will be saddened tae."

"He jist never got over Coralina runnin' away."

"Naw, it fair broke his heart."

Johnny was leaving when the Millers surprised him with another piece of news.

"Afore ye go Johnny, Ah jist wanted tae tell ye if ye come tae see us again, come tae that last cottage on the Beith Road for me an' Elsie are givin' up the mill an' another family will be runnin it. It's too hard with oot Robert and we're retiring fae it."

Robert leaving with Coralina had wide reaching effects, and Johnny couldn't help but wonder how things would have turned out if there had been another way. A big part of him thought that what they had done was selfish considering the consequences, but at the same time he wondered how he and Mary would have acted under the same circumstances. He knew that he would give up everything for his Mary and he couldn't imagine his life without her in it.

Chapter 25

As the days passed, Mary found comfort in going over to Nellie's wagon keeping her company and enjoying baby Eddie. More often than not, she just sat quietly cradling Eddie in her arms, but she didn't shy away from carrying soiled nappies to the dunny or rinsing them off in the river before they would be boiled. Nellie had the same temperament as her mother and never ever pushed Mary to talk unless Mary started a conversation. The silence and the time spent with little Eddie were healing for Mary. Gradually, day by day, her appetite picked up and she began to feel like her old self. She began once more to enjoy Johnny's company and spending time around the horses, particularly Mizzie.

No one was more surprised than Johnny when a few weeks later, Mary suddenly announced to him, "It's time we were wed Johnny and Ah dinnae want any fuss, jist here, in the camp, but Ah want tae be wed on the first o' May. Dae whit ye have tae dae tae make it happen," and with that parting comment she turned and walked away. Johnny stood looking after her, shaking his head but with a wide grin on his face, then he ran after her and grabbing her by the arm, he spun her around and kissed her passionately on the lips. He took Mary's breath away and some of the children nearby started hooping and cheering and laughing. Mary, being Mary just gave him a look and walked off again but her heart was pounding in her chest and for the first time in months, she felt whole and happy in herself.

"Ah'm gettin' wed!" she thought excitedly to herself *"Ah wish ma sister was here."* For a moment, she felt her emotions overwhelming her and she wanted so desperately to cry but she had cried enough over the last few years and she didn't give in to her feelings. Later that night under a full moon, Mary went out as usual and sitting by the river, she made her wish.

"Bairns Ah want for Johnny an' me

Not one but two maybe even three

Tae be a guid mither is ma intent

An' wi' this dust ma wish is sent

A lassie or two tae bide by me

A laddie for Johnny would make the three

Ah'll teach the lassies whit they need tae know

The laddie wi' Johnny will aye go

Ah ask this on a moonlit night

Under the stars that shine sae bright

A guid wife an' mither is ma intent

An wi' this dust ma wish is sent"

At times like these, Mary felt whole and content and when she returned to the wagon, she did so with a soft smile on her lips. The next day she made her way to Nellie's wagon and went in to give her the news.

"Ah'm right happy for ye Mary, ye'll have tae start thinkin aboot whit tae wear. First o' May, there'll be flowers oot that ye can put in yer hair an' ye'll look bonny."

"Ah have a nice bit o' cloth tae make a dress for ma weddin'."

A bale of red cotton at one of the fairs had captivated Mary and she had bought herself enough to make a dress. She hadn't yet done anything with it, but she decided there and then that this was what she would use to make her new dress.

Nellie was looking at her as though she had something to say, "Whit's up Nellie?"

"Nothin', Ah wis jist thinkin' that would be nice."

Mary was puzzled by the look, but too excited with her own thoughts to pay much heed. After Mary left, Nellie went across to see her mother.

"Mam Ah think we have a wee problem."

"Whit's up Nellie?"

"Did ye no' tell me that after Auntie Mary Ellen died, Uncle John gave ye her weddin dress for safe keepin'?"

"Aye Ah did, that was a long time ago, Ah'm surprised ye remember that. Ah'm gonnae get it looked oot an' freshen it up for Mary. She'll be ever so pleased when Ah show it tae her."

"Mary's got some red cloth an' is talkin' about makin' her dress herself."

Isabella stood looking at her; that was a problem, she didn't want to take away Mary's hope of making her own dress, but she didn't want to hide that she had her mother's wedding dress for safekeeping.

"Oh whit tae dae, whit tae dae," said Isabella.

They both sat quietly pondering the problem, trying to think of a suitable solution and then Isabella said, "Don't say a word tae her, jist let her make her dress an when the time is right Ah'll offer her Ma's dress.

In the following days and weeks, when the weather permitted, if Mary wasn't helping Johnny or Nellie with little Eddie, she would gather her fabric, needles threads and scissors and take herself of to sit by the river and put together the dress for her wedding.

No one threw anything away in those days, buttons or fasteners were unpicked from clothes that were beyond repair, patches were cut out and saved, for they were always handy, and trimmings were saved like treasures. Everyone would have a tin full of buttons and fasteners, and a bag full of bits of trimmings and beads. Some were happy to share while others would guard their treasures, unwilling to share them in case they would need them for their own repairs or projects later.

Mary had Coralina's sewing things, and in amongst her treasures she found a bag of beads. She opened the bag and to her delight discovered a broken hematite necklace that she supposed Coralina had found discarded somewhere. As she sat there by the river, she examined the dark grey stones with a silvery sheen and was thrilled to see the way they caught the light. She decided that she would use these beads on the neckline of her dress. Each day when she was finished her task she would fold up her precious workings and wrap them in brown paper then carry them back to the wagon. She was tired of sharing a space, though she was grateful to her aunt and uncle for welcoming her and looking after her. *'One day soon, Ah'll have ma ain wagon an' it'll jist be me an' Johnny,'* she thought to herself as she hid her bundle under the thin mattress on the bed she shared with Daisy, before going over to spend a while with Nellie.

"How are ye getting' on wi' makin' yer dress Mary?"

"Ah'm happy wi' it Nellie Ah think Johnny will like it tae."

"Will ye tell me whit it's like Mary?"

"Ah cannae dae that Nellie, Ah dinnae want onybody to know whit it's like or tae see it afore ma weddin' day."

Nellie laughed, she didn't think that Mary would tell her anything anyway.

Chapter 26

Mary was heading back to the wagon and there was Daisy, sitting on the wooden steps and blocking her way. She had a smug look on her face and Mary felt like slapping her, but she resisted the temptation and said, "Mind yer self, let me by Daisy."

"Whit, are ye too fat tae squeeze by? Naw it cannae be that yer like a stick. That Johnny'll no' have onythin' tae haud on tae come May.

Mary felt her rage rising as she tried to squeeze by Daisy without touching her but Daisy was determined to annoy her.

"Ah suppose ye think that ye'll look good on yer weddin' day in a red dress?"

Mary stopped dead in her tracks half in and half out of the wagon. A raging mist descended on her as she stood there, and that moment seemed like an eternity as she stared at the bed where she had stored her parcel. She rushed to lift the mattress, the brown paper parcel was still there, but she knew that Daisy had tampered with. She let out such a scream of rage that Daisy, who had been so bold previously, leapt from the step, and as she landed on the grass, she turned to face Mary who was now in the doorway of the wagon. Before Daisy could think or speak, Mary launched herself on her screaming like a banshee.

"Ya' jealous bitch Ah'll scratch yer eyes oot," she screamed as she landed on her cousin knocking her to the ground. Daisy tried to scramble away on her hands and knees, but Mary was on her again ripping at her hair and trying to draw her nails on any part of Daisy's skin that she could reach.

Hearing the commotion, everyone hurried over to watch the spectacle. Daisy managed to get to her feet and began to run, but nothing was going to hold Mary back not even those who tried to make a grab for her, and she took off after Daisy, who ran like a hare in fear of what Mary might do next. Through the trees she ran, with Mary in hot pursuit. Mary caught up with her as she reached the river; she grabbed her by the hair, spun her around, and threw her with all her might. Daisy spun, tripping over her own feet and tumbled head first in to the river. Mary, not quite finished, ran in after her. Who knows what would have happened next if some of the men hadn't arrived, and what at first seemed amusing, now looked as though it was really getting out of hand as the two girls wrestled with each other, both of them soaked to the skin.

George dragged his daughter away and over to where Isabella stood open mouthed in amazement, "Ye deserve everything ye got Daisy 'cause ye have needled that lassie forever, noo get back tae the wagon an' Ah'll see tae ye later."

Johnny had taken hold of Mary; she looked like a wild woman, her eyes wide with anger, and her hair all over the place. He took her further upstream as everyone else dispersed to sit round the fire and chatter about what they had just witnessed.

"It had tae happen," said one.

"That Daisy's been askin for that for a while an' she should ha' known better than tae take Mary on."

Johnny sat by the river with Mary "Dae ye want tae tell me whit happened?"

Mary was crying her face red from the exertion and the rage that was only now beginning to subside. "She was in at ma weddin' dress Johnny, an' threw it in ma face making feel... Ah don't know whit she made me feel. Ah'm sorry Johnny, Ah'm sorry that yer angry wi' me."

"Ah'm no' angry wi' ye Mary, Ah'm jist worried aboot ye. Wash yer face Mary an' take a drink o' water."

It was days before the atmosphere of the episode with Mary and Daisy settled. Mary set a bender up near the wagon and planned to sleep there until her wedding. She kept herself busy preparing her dress, helping Johnny, or chatting with Nellie. Daisy avoided her if she could and tried to keep a low profile, averting her eyes any time Mary was nearby. Night times, sitting around the campfire, were probably the worst because neither wanted to see or look at the other, but living in such close proximity made that difficult. Eventually something had to give and Mary made the first move. There was bated breath as she walked over to where Daisy was sitting. Daisy saw her coming and her stomach clenched as she wondered what was going to happen. Mary stood and looked down at her cousin "Can Ah sit by ye Daisy?" Daisy's eyes were wide with disbelief. She shuffled along the bench she was sitting on and made room for Mary who without another word on the matter sat down. For a moment, conversation in the group hushed, and everyone was looking around at each other. Eventually Mary said to Daisy "Ah'm goin' for tea will Ah bring you some?"

"Aye!" said Daisy in surprise," and watched, confused, while Mary went to the big teakettle and began to pour two cups of tea.

"Ah hope she disnae pour it on her heid," laughed one.

"Ah hope they put this nonsense behind them," said another.

When Mary took the tea back and handed the cup to Daisy, she sat down beside her. They were silent for a while as the murmuring and chatter resumed around them, but although everyone pretended that they weren't watching, all eyes were on them. Then Daisy said, "Ah'm right sorry for goin' in tae yer parcel an' lookin' at yer dress Mary, an' Ah'm sorry for makin' a fool o' it." Mary turned and looked her in the eye,

"Why did ye?"

"Ah don't know, Ah think Ah was jist jealous," said Daisy, and hung her head sadly.

"Jealous? Ye were jealous o' me. Whit is there tae be jealous o'."

Mary knew that feeling; she could remember the trouble that it caused. She slipped her hand over Daisy's and in hushed tones; she told her about the day that she spent years ago with the old Mither. Daisy was as bewildered as Mary had been so she explained to Daisy. "It's like the music, when the string on the fiddle breaks the music is still there but it sounds bad. When you get angry or jealous the music that's in the air gets sour an' bad things happen."

Daisy absorbed this new information and as she was mulling it over Mary said "Ah've nae Mam, ma sister ran away wi' her fella, Ah've buried ma Da, how can ye be jealous. We should be like sisters you and me; your Mam fed me her milk, sometimes you on wan titty an' me on the other Ah've heard them say." Mary was smiling as she said this and looking at Daisy she was happy when she saw a giggle escape from her. The two girls sat there holding hands, closer than they had ever been.

"Will ye stand wi' me as ma maid Daisy?" Daisy looked into Mary's eyes and both girls had tears forming. "Aye Mary, Ah will, thanks for askin' me." At that, both girls threw their arms around each other and everyone present raised their eyebrows in surprise and breathed a sigh of relief. Johnny was so proud of his bride to be and his heart swelled with love for her as he watched the exchange. From that day, the girls never fought again and were as close as sisters should be. They both learned valuable lessons but Mary would pay later for things that had happened, and those things that were yet to materialise.

Chapter 27

All too soon, the wedding day arrived. Isabella, Daisy, and her sister Nellie were fussing over preparations. A circle of stones decorated with wild flowers was set at Mary's favourite spot by the river. Daisy had gathered Bog Myrtle, with its aromatic and aphrodisiac scent for fertility, and Meadowsweet with its profusion of tiny white flowers for love and happiness. These she tied together to make a pretty bouquet, saving some that she fashioned into a garland for Mary's hair. Other women on the camp busied themselves preparing soups and stews for the party and the men busied themselves laying out boards so that the revellers could dance the night away.

Johnny had gone to fetch the new wagon that he would present to Mary during the festivities. In those days, it was legal for a blacksmith to marry couples, so George Morrison would perform the ceremony, he was sitting quietly in Nellie and Edward's wagon going over in his mind the things that he would say to help the happy couple exchange their promises to each other. Isabella, her tasks done went back to her wagon to help Mary get ready. She had just stepped out of the galvi bath and was drying herself off.

"Leave that be, Ah'll empty the bath Mary, jist you get dried for Ah have somethin' tae show ye."

She was standing in the wagon with a loose wrap over her underwear when Isabella came back in; she was carrying a paper parcel. "Sit doon lass. Ah know that ye have been busy makin' yer dress this past wee while an' it's taken yer mind aff things that might have upset ye."

Mary had no idea what was coming and she was beginning to get a little bit worried.

"Whit's up has summat happened tae ma dress?"

"Naw Mary, nothin' like that. Ah jist want tae tell ye summat, but jist remember ye don't need tae feel guilty no matter whit yer choice is."

"Tell me quick Auntie for Ah'm feart noo."

"A long time ago when your Ma died, yer Da came tae me wi' summat tae keep for his lassies. Ah've had it a' this time, an' Ah know Ah could have told ye before ye made yer dress, but it wis makin ye happy an' takin yer mind aff other things so Ah have kept it till noo."

She handed the parcel to Mary but Mary was almost afraid to open it. "Whit is it?"

"It's the dress yer Mam wore on her weddin day."

Mary burst into tears as she opened the paper parcel. She opened the precious contents and could hardly see for the tears streaming down her face. This was the first and only thing that she had ever touched that had been her mothers and her emotions were just brimming over.

She stroked the fine pale blue cotton lawn fabric with tiny sprigs of white daisies all over it. A blue ribbon threaded through the scooped neckline creating a gathered effect and handmade lace edged around the cuffs of the sleeves.

She was crying so much she could hardly speak but through her tears she said, "It's the loveliest thing Ah have ever seen," and looking at her aunt she asked, "Can Ah wear it the day?"

Isabella was crying now and she could remember the day that Mary Ellen had worn it. "Aye, of course ye can wear it, yer no' angry then. Whit aboot yer red dress?"

"Ma red dress, Ah can wear that onytime; Ah can only wear this once an' Ah want tae wear it the day. Thanks Auntie Isabella. Ah dinnae know how tae thank ye for a' ye've done for me these past months."

"Nae need tae thank me Mary, yer jist like wan o' ma ain." Mary stepped forward and gave Isabella a warm hug, "Ah needed tae say thanks, it's meant a lot tae me, an' this is jist so special."

Isabella helped Mary into her mother's dress just as Daisy arrived, garland and bouquet in hand, "Ah made these for ye Mary."

"Oh Daisy that's lovely Ah'm ever so grateful."

"Aw' Mary, ye look fair bonnie in yer Mam's dress. Whit will ye dae wi' yer red dress?"

"Ah'll put it on later for the dancin'," she replied laughing.

Mary's red dress, covered with a cloth to keep dust off it, was hanging on a hook.

"Ye jist look lovely Mary," said Daisy.

Mary was glowing with joy but her stomach was churning with nerves. Isabella reached over and kissed her, as did Nellie, all of them ready to make their way to where the wedding was to take place. It was an emotional time and everyone had tears in their eyes as Mary finished getting ready. "Jist wait a few minutes Mary and then come wi' Daisy."

"Where am Ah goin'?"

"Daisy knows, she'll bring ye," said Isabella as she and Nellie left the wagon. Mary and Daisy stood and looked at each other.

"Ah feel as though Ah've waited for this moment a' ma life Daisy."

"Well it's here noo," said Daisy, "are ye ready to go?"

"Aye, Ah'm ready."

They made their way through the camp towards the trees. "Where are wi' goin' Daisy?"

"Ye'll see in a minute."

"Ah thought wi' would be set up in the middle o' the camp?"

Daisy just looked at her grinning, took her by the hand, and hurried her along. Just as they came to the end of the trees at the edge of the river, Mary caught sight of all her friends and family. Everyone from the camp had gathered and formed two lines for Mary and Daisy to walk through. Mary was blushing and smiling and that was the first sight that Johnny caught of his bride as she walked through the aisle of well-wishers.

Mary realised that she was getting married at her favourite spot by the river and she saw the circle of stones decorated with flowers. Mary and Johnny caught sight of each other at the same time. Johnny thought his heart would burst with pride as he looked at his beautiful bride. Mary's eyes sparkled with love when she saw Johnny in his dark suit, waistcoat, white shirt, and red patterned scarf at his neck. A gold hoop dangled from his ear and his dark curly hair came down over his collar.

Daisy took her straight to Johnny, and he held out his hand for her and together they turned to face their Uncle George who was standing in the middle of the circle. They walked forward together and stood in front of George.

"It's ma duty the day tae witness the joinin' of Johnny Stewart, horse breeder, and Mary Kelly, maiden. Johnny Stewart, dae ye take this lassie, Mary Kelly, as yer wedded wife?"

"Aye, Ah dae, that Ah dae."

"An' you Mary Kelly, dae you take Johnny Stewart, as yer wedded husband?"

"Aye, Ah dae."

"Dae ye have a ring Johnny?" Johnny took a gold band from his pocket.

"Well, put it on her finger and repeat after me, *I Johnny Stewart, do take thee Mary Kelly tae be ma wedded wife, to have and to hold, to honour and care for, tae love and cherish, through sickness an' health till death dae us part.*"

Johnny gazed into Mary's eyes and repeated his vows solemnly.

"An' you Mary repeat after me, *I Mary Kelly do take thee Johnny Stewart, tae be ma wedded husband, to have and to hold, to honour an' obey…*" As George said the words 'honour and obey', there were a few laughs from the gathered crowd, as everyone knew that Mary would find obeying difficult to do. Johnny and Mary laughed too and then Mary without prompting from George continued her vows with, "Aye, Ah'll obey ye, an' care for ye, Ah'll love and cherish ye through sickness and health till ma last breath."

"Have you got the cord Daisy?" Daisy stepped forward and handed her father a length of white cord, which he proceeded to wrap around Johnny and Mary's joined hands. "With this cord ye are bound together in wedlock, let no man put asunder whit has been joined here the day." There was a long pause as everyone waited; Mary and Johnny were oblivious to everyone but each other.

"Ah now pronounce ye husband an' wife."

There was silence as Mary and Johnny stood gazing into each other's eyes.

"Well man, are ye gonnae kiss her or are ye jist gonnae stand there looking glaikit?" said George and at that Johnny leant down, embraced Mary and kissed her passionately on the lips to the raucous cheering of the gathered crowd.

Then the shouting began, Nellie had placed a broom decorated with flowers and ribbons at the edge of the circle of stones, and everyone was shouting, "Jump the broom, jump the broom, jump the broom." And hands still tied together that's exactly what they did, they jumped the broomstick and took off running through the trees, running and laughing whilst everyone else, laughing hilariously took turns at jumping over the broomstick.

Chapter 28

They could hear everyone laughing and shouting as they ran through the trees. Finally, they found a secluded spot and Johnny held Mary close to him and gazed into her eyes. She could feel his heart pounding in time with hers as he lifted her chin and kissed her on her lips.

"It's jist us noo Mary, you an' me an' Ah'll gie ye a good life, Ah promise ye."

"Aye, Ah know ye will Johnny, yer a guid man an' Ah'll be a guid wife tae ye."

Together they lay in the long grass by the banks of the River Clyde and under the warm afternoon sun Johnny made Mary his wife. Later as they made their way back to join the festivities, they could hear the fiddles and accordions and the sounds of the dancer's feet on the boards. The crowd cheered as they came into the camp and of course there were ribald comments that made Mary blush, but they took it all in good sport and laughed with everyone else.

Johnny pulled his scarf from his pocket and tied it over Mary's eyes to blindfold her.

"Whit ye daein' Johnny?"

"Come wi' me Mary," he said as he led her past the dancers, and everyone stopped what they were doing and followed on. Willie had fetched the new wagon and everyone had, at one time or another, unbeknown to Mary, filled it with everything that she would need to give her a good start. Johnny stopped Mary in front of her new home and removed her blindfold to reveal the dark green bow topped wagon. All the woodwork was highly varnished and decorated with hand carved scroll. Two brass Tilly lamps hung either side at the front and there were steps at the back for access. Struts fixed under the wagon would allow them to carry or store whatever they needed and various pots jugs and even a galvi bath hung on the sides.

Mary put her hands over her face and cried. This was beyond her expectations and everyone had been so good to her. She was overwhelmed and she felt guilty because she could have been nicer to many of those who had given her these gifts.

"It's too much, Ah didnae expect a' this, Ah don't know how tae thank everybody."

Everyone was touched and pleased to see Mary showing her emotions and most felt that this could be a turning point in her life, and it was, for a while anyway.

Mary and Johnny ran back to Isabella's and untied their cords, quickly retying them as soon as she changed into her red dress. It had a wide skirt, nipped in at the waist, and trimmed with the hematite beads that she had sewn around the edge of the neckline. She had added an extra tier of material to the bottom making the skirt full, so that it would spin out for dancing. The skirts flounced as she walked showing the black lace that she had attached just under the hem, and the effect was stunning. She had new black shoes with a small block heel perfect for dancing, and she had added red ribbon to lace them up.

Everyone was in the middle of the camp, when Mary and Johnny joined them to a rousing cheer. The fiddles and accordions resumed and everyone toasted the happy couple's health. Someone called out to Johnny "Sing us a song Johnny," others joined in, "Aye Johnny, sing us a song."

Johnny sat where he was on a wooden box, his father Willie sat by him with his fiddle tucked under his chin, Johnny took a breath and began to sing in a beautiful baritone…

'Johnny was born in a mansion doon in the county o' Clare

Rosie was born by a roadside somewhere in County Kildare

Destiny brought them together on the road to Killorglan

One day in her bright tasty shawl, she was singing

And she stole his young heart away

for she sang...

Meet me tonight by the campfire

Come with me over the hill.

Let us be married tomorrow

Please let me whisper 'I will'

What if the neighbours are talkin'

Who cares if your friends stop and stare

You'll be proud to be married to Rosie,

Who was reared on the roads of Kildare.

Think of the parents who reared ye

Think of the family name

How can you marry a Gypsy?

Oh whit a terrible shame

Parents and friends stop your pleading

Don't worry about my affair

For I've fallen in love with a Gypsy

Who was reared on the roads of Kildare

Johnny went down from his mansion

Just as the sun had gone down

Turning his back on his kinfolk

Likewise, his dear native town

Facing the roads of old Ireland

With a Gypsy he loved so sincere

When he came to the light of the campfire

These are the words he did hear

Meet me tonight by the campfire

Come with me over the hill.

Let us be married tomorrow

Please let me whisper 'I will'

What if the neighbours are talkin?

Who cares if yer friends stop and stare?

You'll be proud to be married to Rosie,

Who wus reared on the roads of Kildare.

Mary listened to the words that she had heard many times before, but on this occasion, these words struck a chord and reminded her that her sister had run away. She sat where she was but her eyes filled with tears; she knew that neither Johnny nor Willie meant any offence but it was a sad reminder that her sister wasn't present. When the song ended, everyone clapped and cheered and then Willie stood, walked over to where Mary was sitting and began to play a rousing tune on his fiddle, all the while teasing Mary and giving her the nod that he wanted her to dance. Mary giggled and at first resisted, but Johnny gave her a gentle push and she rose to the occasion. She assumed a taunting pose, with her hands by her sides clutching the skirts of her dress, hitching the sides up a little and looking at Willie. At first, she danced around him, her feet echoing in time to the fiddle. Willie moved to one side and those who had the traditional Celtic drum the bodhran, began to beat out the rhythm, while others joined them tapping the rhythm on the boxes they were sitting on.

Holding her skirts high at the sides now, Mary had the floor and she spun and tapped and taunted and teased, dancing sensuously towards Johnny offering her hand and as he reached out she would spin away laughing at him, looking over her shoulder to tease him and the look she gave him offered more. Those who watched appreciated her dancing skills, and were as amused as she was. Johnny was overwhelmed with love and passion for his sensual bride. Eventually he could stand the taunting no more, and he leapt to his feet and joined her in the dance. Everyone jumped to their feet, cheered and stamped at this exhibition of passion and love between the two.

Chapter 29

Mary was happier than she had ever imagined that she could be. She had a lovely wagon and all the things that she needed. She and Johnny soon fell into a rhythm of working together. Mary would start her day by cleaning the wagon and preparing the food that she would cook later. Johnny would go to the horse field where Mary would join him when she was finished whatever she happened to be doing on that day. When Johnny travelled, Mary was by his side. They were as inseparable as they always had been and there were no teething problems settling in together. All they needed and wanted more than anything was their own baby to love and cherish and make their family complete. Mary often went across to sit with Nellie to chat, and when she did young Eddie would climb up on to her knees.

"Aye, he loves his Auntie Mary," Nellie would often say and Mary would have her face buried in Eddie's neck blowing little kisses on him while he giggled with delight.

"It's been three months, should Ah no" be pregnant already?"

"It disnae aye happen like that Mary, it'll happen when God's willin'," but every month, like clockwork, Mary bled and every time she bled, she cried. Her dearest wish was for a child of her own, a daughter, but Eddie filled this gap in her life.

She was with Johnny tending to the horses when a terrible pain gripped her in her stomach. She doubled over clutching herself and the colour drained from her face.

"Whit's up Mary!" cried Johnny in alarm.

"Ah'm fine, it's jist a pain," and then she collapsed in a heap at his feet.

"Dear God Mary, speak tae me Mary, for God's sake Mary." He gathered her up in his arms and ran as if the devil himself was after him calling all the while

"Mither, Mither!" He ran towards his wagon and Isabella appeared and followed him. He laid Mary down on their bed. "Whit's up wi' her, whit's happenin'?"

Isabella ushered him out of the wagon telling him to fetch Nellie. Mary's skirt was wet with blood and Isabella feared the worst was happening.

"Fetch a basin o' hot water an' bring it quick," she called to him.

"Oh my God, whit's happenin," said Nellie as she rushed to her mother's bidding. Hearing the commotion, Daisy arrived and seeing Johnny in a state of distress outside and thinking that one of the horses had kicked Mary asked him, "Whit's up Johnny, has she been kicked?"

"Naw, she jist got a pain and collapsed, Ah'm worried sick."

Some of the others came around too and sat with Johnny and Daisy while Isabella and Nellie tended to Mary. They stripped off her clothes and washed her down but the blood still came.

"Tell Johnny tae fetch the doctor Nellie."

Nellie stuck her head out of the wagon. "Go for the doctor Johnny." Johnny stood there with his mouth open in shock. One of the other lads called, "Stay here Johnny, Ah'll go, whit will Ah say is wrang?"

"Tell him she's bleeding bad."

Johnny was in a state of shock and didn't know what to do. Someone stuck a glass of whisky in his hand and made him drink it. When the glass was drained, he put his head in his hands and moaned, "Dear God, dinnae let me lose her, dinnae let me lose her. Ah could stand jist aboot onythin' but Ah couldnae stand that."

It was an hour or more before the doctor arrived and Isabella stayed in the wagon with him while he examined Mary.

"Ah'm sorry to tell you that you have lost your baby Mary."

"That cannae be, Ah' didnae know Ah' was pregnant, Ah never missed."

"Sometimes that happens Mary, never mind, there will be other chances."

Mary began to cry and her mind raced. *'Ah was pregnant an' Ah didnae know, maybe Ah did summat Ah shouldnae have done."* She was inconsolable.

"She needs to rest her body now and take things easy for a few weeks and then she can try again," the doctor said to Isabella before he left. He nodded to Johnny who was standing at the bottom of the steps waiting. "Whit's wrang wi' her Doctor?"

"I'm afraid that she has lost her baby but she will be fine now, plenty of rest for a few weeks and then she can try again."

"A baby?"

"A very early pregnancy, now if you'll excuse me," he said and hurried off leaving Johnny dismayed.

Isabella came down the steps, "Ye can go in an' see her now, but she's upset."

He went into the wagon, knelt beside the bed, and put his arms around Mary who was crying quietly. Seeing Johnny set her off again and she wept loudly "Oh Johnny wi' made a baby an' now it's gone Ah'm so sorry."

"Ma darlin', hush now, hush, don't upset yer self," but Johnny cried with her as he thought of the baby that might have been.

Isabella went to her wagon, and searched until she found what she was looking for, a paper bag containing red raspberry leaves. She took them across to Mary and Johnny. "Every morning make a pot of tea wi' a spoonful o' these leaves Johnny and gie it tae Mary tae sup. Two or three times a day ye need tae drink this Mary an' it'll help ye get back tae normal. Mind Johnny, a fresh pot every day an' make sure she drinks it." Then to Mary she said as she was leaving, "Ye'll be fine lass, ye'll have bairns."

Mary struggled to come to terms with her grief and this slowed the healing process. She was prone to bouts of weeping without knowing that she was even going to cry. It was as though she had no control of her emotions. Everyone did their best to spend time with her, trying to console her but losing her father and then her sister and now a baby was just too much for her to bear. Gradually, with everyone's love and support, she began to recover and soon it became just another hurt buried deep in her heart. As much as she wanted to be around Johnny, helping with the horses, he was afraid to let her lift or carry anything in case she damaged herself so she gave up trying. Instead, she spent her time with Nellie, and young Eddie, who was growing fast, would climb on to her knee and take her mind off her worries.

"For a lassie that didnae have any wee brothers or sisters yer good wi' the wean."

"Och Nellie, he's a wee soul an easy tae mind."

"Dinnae you worry Mary, ye'll have yer ane afore long."

Winter came and went and, soon enough, spring was beginning to show signs of arriving. Mary finally appeared to be back to her normal self and Johnny felt relieved and happy, but no sooner were they getting used to things being normal when it happened again and it was the same as before. No hint of morning sickness, no hint of missed cycles, nothing. Nothing at all told her that she was once more with child until the pain doubled her in two, and the blood that poured from her stained her clothes.

She was with Isabella when it happened. "Dear God! No' again!" said Isabella when she saw the blood. Isabella sent for Johnny and together they helped Mary to their wagon. Once more, the doctor came and when he had seen to Mary, he took Johnny aside.

"Bring her into the hospital tomorrow morning; she will need a small operation. It's nothing to worry about."

"Whit kind o' operation Doctor?"

"We need to make sure that everything is cleared away and we can have a better look at what has caused her to miss-carry again. You will be able to wait and bring her home but she must have bed rest for at least a week and wait six weeks before you, well before you and she, you know…"

Johnny was worried sick, but he did his best to play down his concerns as he told Mary where she was going. He expected a reaction but Mary just lay there quietly and didn't say a word. The next day Johnny helped Mary into the cart for the journey to the Glasgow Royal Infirmary.

Chapter 30

Mary was like a shadow of her former self in those first few weeks after losing her second baby. She had lost weight and her skin was too pale with dark circles under her eyes. She didn't speak to anyone unless she was spoken to and she avoided others wherever and whenever she could. She would peek out of her wagon and wait until no one was around before venturing out. Both Nellie and Daisy tried to comfort her but she refused to say a word. Johnny was at a loss and didn't know what to do for the best. Everyone was worried about her.

About seven weeks after her hospital visit Mary finally broke; in the middle of the night while everyone slept, Mary slipped out of bed and left Johnny asleep in their wagon. She had no real plan in mind, she didn't know where she was going or why, she just wandered away from the camp. The full moon meant that she could see clearly ahead of her as she began to walk through the trees towards the River Clyde, not stopping until she reached her favourite spot. In her mind, she cursed; she cursed her life, she cursed the Lady in the Moon, she cursed her body, and finally she dropped to the ground, a silent scream escaping her lips. The pain in her spirit was as real as any pain she had physically so far suffered. She pounded the ground in a rage at her loss and cried herself into an exhausted sleep.

Johnny awoke early just as the sun was breaking and realised that Mary wasn't beside him. He quickly pulled on his shirt and trousers and left the wagon. He went over to the dunny first hoping that she would be there but there was no sign of her. All the wagons were set in a semi circle so it was easy for him to see, but there was no sign of her around any of the wagons either. He went to the horse field thinking that she must be there, she wasn't. He took off through the trees, running now, afraid of what he might find, or worse not find.

Mary was lying in the grass, her clothes wet with morning dew, her hair wild from running her hands through it, and her skin pale and almost transparent. At first, he thought she was dead but she stirred as he ran to her and gathered her in his arms.

"Ah' jist want tae die Johnny, Ah've failed ye an' Ah've failed ma bairns. Ah couldnae haud on tae them."

Johnny tried to console her, "It's a' ma fault, it's 'cause Ah've been bad."

"Whit dae ye mean, how can ye say that?"

"The old Mither told me long ago that if Ah did bad things then bad would come back tae me."

Nerves made Johnny want to laugh almost with relief at the absurd claim but he knew better. "Whit bad things dae ye think ye've done?"

"Ah've been angry an' hurt people's feelin's, Ah helped ma sister tae run away wi' Robert an' it finished ma Da. Ah killed ma Da tae!"

"Mary, Mary, ye didnae kill yer Da, he drank himself tae death an' ye didnae make yer sister run away, she did that herself an' its' no' yer fault. Yer jist sufferin' 'cause ye have lost yer bairns but the doctor said ye can have others." He held her for a while then took his hankie from his trouser pocket and soaked it in the river. He gently wiped her face with the cool wet cloth. "Come on Mary, let's get ye back tae the wagon." He helped her up and together they went back to the camp. Johnny made her some tea and settled her into bed. "Sleep now lass, ye need rest tae get ye better." He sat with her for a while until she slept and then he went across to Isabella.

"She's grievin' bad Mither an' Ah dinnae ken whit tae dae."

Isabella reached across and placed a comforting hand over his. "There's nothin' ye can dae Johnny, it's jist time she needs tae heal. Lovin' her an' takin' care o' her the way ye dae is a' she needs an' before ye know it she'll be back on her feet."

"She has it in her mind that she is bein' punished for bein' bad."

"Whit!"

"The old Mither told her if she did owt bad it would come back tae her."

"Oh Johnny Ah remember that from when she was a wee lassie wi' an awfy temper but Ah dinnae think that has owt tae dae wi' whit's happenin'." "She thinks it's her fault that Coralina ran away or at least it's her fault for helpin' her and she's blamin' hersel' for her Da dyin'. She thinks that's why the bairns came away."

"Mither of God!"

"Ah ken, how dae Ah deal wi' that?"

"Whit did ye say tae her?"

"Ah told her it's no' her fault, but Ah dinnae think it made a difference, She's sleepin' noo, I expect she'll sleep for a while."

"Well wi' jist need tae keep an eye on her an' dae the best wi' can."

Over the next few months everyone looked out for Mary, they kept her company and made sure that she didn't spend too much time on her own. The arrival of summer helped and as her body recovered so too did her spirit. Young Eddie was a blessing because he was the first one to make Mary laugh and the sound was so unusual that those who heard her turned and looked at her with such feelings of gladness that for some it brought tears to their eyes.

No one asked her how she was feeling because that would just remind her of the babies that she had lost. It didn't stop her thinking of them though; they were always in her mind. Johnny began to recover too for he had been in such an anxious state, every bit as sad about his lost children, but more concerned about Mary, and worried about how this would affect them in the future.

By the end of the summer, Mary was almost back to normal. Her colour had returned and she had gained the weight that she had lost following the miscarriage but her monthly cycle had ceased to be regular sometimes bleeding twice in the month and sometimes missing a month altogether. At first, she was concerned, but after talking to the other women, she was reassured that this sometimes happened.

Chapter 31

It had been a good summer and now that October had arrived, folks in the camp were checking their provisions and making ready for the winter months. Mary had gone on a few trips with Johnny and they had visited the Millers in their new rented cottage. They were happy to hear that Robert and Coralina were doing well, but they didn't mention anything about their loss to the Millers. After they returned from one such visit, Mary complained of feeling sick in her stomach.

"Ah must have ate summat bad," she said after returning from one of many trips to the dunny.

"Ye should lie down Mary," said Johnny, concerned.

"Naw, Ah feel fine, it was jist a wee turn for the worst."

Over the next few weeks, Mary continued to be sick and sometimes her complexion took on an almost grey hue. If she had had eyes on the back of her head, she would have seen the other women watching her and giving each other knowing looks, but when she felt sick, she felt so bad that she couldn't begin to notice what anyone else was doing. She began to lose her appetite and then just as suddenly she would be hungry but each time she put food to her lips she had to run away to be sick again. It got to the stage that she could even keep water down and at that time, Isabella took charge.

"Right Johnny, get the cart. That lassie needs tae go tae the hospital." Johnny was shocked but at the same time almost relieved, that someone was making a decision because he was at his wits end and didn't know what to do. Mary was too sick to her stomach to care so she climbed onto the cart without an objection.

They waited for what seemed like ages in the cold tiled corridor and watched porters, nurses, and auxiliaries hurrying about their business until finally a nurse approached them.

"You can go up and see her now; she is in the maternity ward upstairs on the first floor."

Isabella just nodded, but as she looked at Johnny, she almost laughed, as there was a look of shock on his face. "Does that mean she's pregnant?" he asked in amazement.

"Aye, Ah had a feelin' she was."

Johnny ran ahead, taking the stairs two at a time while Isabella made her way up at a slower pace. He reached the ward and scanned the rows of beds until he saw his Mary. Hurrying to her, he folded her in his arms. She was grinning from ear to ear. "Ah'm gonnae have a bairn and the doctor said Ah'm a'right. He said Ah' have a greedy baby an' that's why they have me on this drip."

"Does it hurt ye Mary?"

"Naw, Ah canny feel it. He said Ah have tae bide here till the morra'."

Isabella came into the ward and over to Mary's bedside, she gave her a hug, "Yer' gonnae have a bairn then?"

"Aye, Ah'm really happy, but Ah'm scared as well, but the doctor said that everythin' should be fine this time. That's why Ah' have been so sick."

They stayed a while with Mary until the nurse came and hurried them away.

"It's good timin' Johnny."

"How dae ye mean?"

"Well she can rest up ower the winter an' the bairn will come in the summer an' that will gie it a guid start tae build some strength afore next winter comes."

"Dae ye think it will be… Ah mean dae ye think she will be able tae carry it?"

"Aye, Ah have a guid feelin aboot this wan Johnny, it's been different, she was never sick afore. Ah' think she's carryin' this wan right."

Isabella was right, Johnny brought Mary home from the hospital and from that day, she bloomed as her stomach swelled. Every day she wore a happy smile on her face and she did as she was told, she took things easy spending her time between Nellie's, playing with little Eddie, and Isabella's. She was playing with Eddie when her own baby kicked for the first time. She stopped suddenly and looked at Eddie who looked back at her and then she looked at Nellie who was aware of the sudden change.

"Whit's up Mary?"

"Ah felt it, it kicked me, an' Ah think it kicked Eddie tae," she laughed, "Look at his wee face. Did ye feel the wee baby?" Eddie was just two years old, too young to understand but it was as though he did when he placed his little hand on Mary's bump.

"The wee soul, Ah think he kens," laughed Mary.

The winter came and it was cold and miserable but with every day that passed Mary grew more content and happy. Both she and Johnny were thrilled at the prospect of having their own child. By the time spring came Mary was heavy with child and waddled rather than walked. The baby was due to arrive in May, until then, she passed her time visiting, chatting, and sometimes going to stand by the horses' field to stroke Mizzie and give her a treat. When Johnny went to fetch provisions or sell horses Mary stayed at home. When the moon was full, she would walk through the trees and standing by her favourite spot, she would give thanks to the Lady in the Moon for her blessings and pray for a safe delivery of her baby. When any of the others went off to visit fairs, she and Johnny stayed behind. He didn't want to take her in case anything went wrong but he didn't want to go and leave her behind.

One night she woke, feeling uncomfortable because of pains in her back and Johnny heard the creak of the steps as she left the wagon.

"Mary! Whit's up?"

"Nuthin' Johnny, ma backs jist a wee bit sore an' Ah canny get comfortable."

He pulled on his trousers and went out to join her. "Ah'll make ye a cup o' tea."

"Aye, that would be nice Johnny." Johnny was stoking the fire under the big kettle when Mary got up from the box that she was sitting on.

"Whit ye daein'."

"Ah think Ah need tae pee, Ah'm goin' tae the dunny, oops, too late Johnny, Ah' think Ah've wet ma self'." When Johnny looked over at her, she was bent over; laughing at herself, but Johnny knew what was happening. He dropped the cup he was holding, turned, and ran to Isabella's wagon. George was the first to rouse.

"Whit's up, whit's the ruckus?"

"Wake Isabella, Ah think Mary's started." He ran back across the short distance to find Mary leaning over against the side of their wagon, both her hands braced on the wooden rim. When she turned to look at him he knew that she was in labour, her face pinched with pain. "Dae ye think its ma time Johnny?"

"Aye, let's get ye up the steps an' on the bed."

By the time Isabella had thrown on her clothes, Nellie and Daisy were up too, as well as some of the other women. Everyone was hurrying about filling the big kettle, tearing up cloths, and generally making things ready for the arrival of the new baby. Johnny sat outside the wagon with the men and some of the women. By morning, there was still no sign of the baby. Nellie and Daisy were whispering to each other praying that everything would be all right. "Ah think it's takin' too long Daisy." Just as they were speaking, Isabella came out of the wagon and summoned George, "Away for the doctor George, jist tae be safe."

Johnny jumped to his feet "Whit's up? Has summat' happened?"

"Naw Johnny, she's jist worn oot an' the bairn is takin' its time, better tae be safe than sorry."

"Can Ah be wi' her?"

"No' the noo Johnny jist bide where ye are." It was some time before the doctor arrived and he went straight into the wagon. Another hour passed and eventually they all heard loud lusty cries of the newborn baby.

Impatient, Johnny said, "For God's sake whit's keeping them?" No one said anything in return, they all waited silently now for someone to appear and reassure them that all was well; and Isabella did.

"It's a lovely wee lassie, well she's no' so wee, she's an eight pounder."

"Whit aboot Mary?" asked Johnny.

"Aye Mary's fine, she's worn out an' she's lost a lot o' blood but she'll be fine."

Someone produced a bottle of whisky, and everyone toasted Mary, Johnny, and the new arrival. After what seemed like a long time, the doctor came out and took Johnny to one side. "Mary and your wee girl will be fine but she will need a good few weeks to recover from this birth. There has been a bit of damage, she's lost a lot of blood, and I'm sorry to say that it's unlikely that there will be any more babies."

Johnny thanked the doctor and tentatively went into the wagon. His heart was overwhelmed with love and joy, with tears streaming down his face as he looked at his Mary and his tiny daughter cradled in her arms. He knelt beside the bed and he kissed Mary on her lips and then gently kissed his little girl.

"She's bonny Mary an' she's got rosy cheeks," he said as he gently drew a finger over the sleeping babies cheek, "an' look at her wee lips, she's like a wee rose bud. Whit are we gonnae call her?"

Mary was smiling as she answered, "Rosa, oor wee rose bud."

"Can Ah pick her up?"

Mary handed Rosa to her father, he held her close gazing into her eyes and gently stroked her tiny hand, and then the magic happened, as it always does when a grown man finds that moment of pure love that he feels for his newborn child, and Rosa clutched his finger. Eddie looked at Mary, his eyes wide with wonder, "She's holdin' ma finger Mary, look," and they both cried tears of joy.

Chapter 32

That was a beautiful summer; Mary took her time resting, nursing Rosa, and building up her strength, while Nellie and Daisy took on some of her chores. Most days she sat in the sun enjoying her baby and being amused by little Eddie's reactions to Rose. The first time he saw Rosa, his little eyes lit up with amazement, he stretched over and kissed her on the lips. Mary and Daisy laughed as Nellie said, "Aye there's a match made in heaven." From that day, Eddie was never very far from Mary. Rosa fascinated him, and he watched over her even while she slept. Johnny was so proud of his little family and he was happy that Mary was recovering well enough to venture out on the cart for short trips. He liked showing off his family and was keen to do so as often as possible. Mary had taken to motherhood easily, enjoying every moment that she spent with Rosa, and Rosa was a good baby even when she began teething. She seldom cried and she slept through the night.

"Aye, ye've got it easy wi' that bairn Mary, Ah dinnae think Ah've heard her cryin', she's a wee gem, so even tempered," said Nellie.

"She takes after her Da, Ah don't think she has ma nature."

"Well Ah didnae want tae say that ma self but Ah think ye might be right," replied Nellie laughing.

Mary didn't take any offence at the reference to her younger days.

"Ah wanted tae ask ye summat?"

"Whit?"

"Dae ye still see stuff?"

"Aye, but Ah've learned tae keep ma mouth shut."

"Does it jist happen or can ye make it happen?"

"Sometimes it jist happens an' sometimes Ah can make it happen, why dae ye ask?"

"Well Ah ken ye tell fortunes when ye go aroon the doors, but is that for real or dae ye jist make it up?"

"Ah dinnae make it up!" exclaimed Mary. "An' Ah wonder why yer askin me?"

"It's oor Daisy, she's fair love sick, she likes a fella that she sees at the fairs. Could ye see summat for her?"

Mary laughed, "Aye, Ah could, tell her tae come an' have a drink o' tea an' Ah'll read her. Wait till Rosa's settled for the night."

"Thanks Mary, she'll be glad o' that, she's been on at me tae ask ye."

Nellie was quiet for a bit, obviously mulling over something else that she wanted to say.

"Mary, can Ah ask ye how ye dae that, Ah mean how dae ye see things, Ah mean whit's it like?"

"It jist comes, ye ken, like it's happenin' an' Ah can see it clear, other times its jist a feelin'."

"Di's it happen aw' the time?"

"Naw, that would drive ye crazy," said Mary laughing.

"Can ye dae it whenever ye want?"

"Ah suppose Ah can."

"Can ye see onythin' aboot me?"

"Have ye got a sixpence?" said Mary laughing at her own joke. "Ah'm only kiddin', Ah didnae need yer sixpence."

"Well whit dae ye see?"

"Ye've nuthin' tae worry aboot, but Ah'll miss ye when ye go."

Nellie startled, jumped in her seat, "Whit dae ye mean? Am Ah' gonnae die?"

"Don't be stupid, Ah didnae mean that yer gonnae die Ah meant when ye go somewhere else."

"Where am Ah goin'?"

"Ah'll tell ye after Ah read Daisy's tea leaves."

"So Ah'm a'right then?"

"Aye, yer fine," laughed Mary.

"Dae ye ever see owt bad?"

"Aye, sometimes, but Ah dinnae aye ken whit it means 'cause sometimes its jist a really bad feelin' and Ah dinnae ken whit's gonnae happen'."

"Ah widnae like that."

"Sometimes Ah dinnae like it either."

Later that evening Daisy and Nellie joined Mary and the three of them sat on boxes outside Mary's wagon, each with a cup of hot tea. They were chatting normally, but there was an undercurrent of anticipation, especially from Daisy. Although they had settled their differences just before Mary's wedding, Mary was still closer to Nellie, and Daisy still hadn't achieved the familiarity with Mary that Nellie had with her.

"Are ye done huggin' that cup Daisy?"

"Aye, here."

"That's nae use, ye still have a drop o' tea in the bottom, sup it till its dry." Daisy pursed her lips together to prevent the tealeaves from getting into her mouth and then she gave the cup back to Mary. They sat quietly for a few moments while Mary studied the leaves.

"Whit can ye see?" asked Daisy.

"Wheesht, Ah'm readin' it." After a few moments more, Mary began to speak. "Right the first thing is somebody is gonnae bring ye some news, an' there's a big crowd. There's a lot o' flowers in yer cup tae and that's compliments an' nice things happenin'…"

"Dae ye mean it's ma weddin'?"

"Naw, it's no', there's a journey either side o' it so it looks as though ye go somewhere an' there's a lot of people and then ye come back. Then there's another journey further on. That journey will come after yer ain weddin. Ye'll no' stay here an' ye'll take Nellie wi' ye…"

"Whit dae ye mean, she'll take me wi' her?"

"Two lassies, two men an' young Eddie as well."

"Ah'm no' gone anywhere."

"The leaves say different."

"Where am Ah goin, an' when?" exclaimed Nellie.

"Ah told ye, sometime after her weddin'."

"Who am Ah getting' wed tae?" interrupted Daisy.

"Ah cannae tell ye that, but he has ginger hair."

Daisy gasped, "It's him, it must be him, he's got ginger hair."

"Who has?" asked Mary.

"The fella she's sweet on, Bruce, he's no' fae aboot here, he's fae Carlisle," said Nellie. "He's a Donnelly; ye see him at Appleby an' the like."

Mary's prediction came true later that summer, when they all went to Appleby fair, and Bruce asked George if he could have Daisy's hand in marriage. She was beside herself with excitement and couldn't wait to share her news with Mary.

"Ah'm getting' wed Mary! Ye were right, Bruce asked ma Da for ma hand an' he said aye. Ah'm so happy."

Mary hugged Daisy, "Ah'm right pleased for ye Daisy, when is it tae happen?"

"At the end o' the summer, when the harvest is in. Ah want tae get wed in the camp wi' ma Da daein' ma vows."

"He's right clever, he makes an' fixes wheels for carts, an' he's got plans for the future."

Mary knew this to be true and she knew that this would bring about the next part of her prediction, the part that she was less pleased about because that would take Nellie, Edward and young Eddie away to live somewhere else and she knew that she would miss them very much.

It was a lovely sunny October day when Daisy and Bruce got married and the celebrations went on long into the night. Mary and Johnny were back in their wagon when Johnny asked Mary why she looked so sad.

"Ah'm gonnae miss seein' Nellie an' wee Eddie when they go."

"Dae ye no' mean Daisy?"

"Aye, she's goin' as well, but Nellie an' Eddie will go tae?"

"Who told ye that?"

Mary just raised her eyes and looked at Johnny for a minute and then she said, "Ah've seen it, and they'll be away afore the snow comes."

"Och maybe yer mistaken,"

"Ah'm never mistaken Johnny, an' am surprised that ye would say that."

"Perhaps yer right then." Johnny knew that if Mary had seen it then there was a good chance that it would happen, but he would miss Edward if he left.

Isabella was heartbroken when Daisy and Bruce left to settle in a camp in Carlisle where the Donnelly's lived. George had a tear in his eye as his youngest daughter left with her new husband, but there were more tears to follow only they did not know that yet.

Chapter 33

Isabella and George were sitting in their wagon one evening not long after Daisy and Bruce had left to begin their new life in Carlisle when Edward and Nellie came across to visit with little Eddie. They sat chatting for a while but Isabella had the feeling that something was coming, but she wasn't sure what. Eventually Edward broached the subject that had been hanging in the air. "Bruce has got a guid thing goin' in Carlisle."

George and Isabella both looked over at him waiting for more and Isabella glanced at Nellie who was biting her bottom lip, a sure sign that she was worried about what was to come next.

"Whit's that?" answered George.

"Well ye ken he's a wheelwright."

"Aye."

"Well wi' were talkin' an' he has plans tae build wagon's an' he asked me if Ah wanted tae go in wi' him. He would dae the wheels an' frames for the wagons an' Ah could dae the insides. Ah could make a guid job o' that."

"Aye, Ah'm sure you could," replied George cautiously, knowing there was more to come.

"Thing is, it would mean me an' Nellie an' wee Eddie movin' tae Carlisle."

Isabella put her hands to her mouth and her eyes began to fill with tears.

Nellie rushed over to kneel in front of her mother, "Oh' Mam, dinnae greet, it's no' that far away an' wi'll see ye from time tae time."

"So how come ye cannae dae this here? Bruce could come here," replied George.

"Aye he could but he's established in Carlisle and that's where o' the business is these days. He's getting a lot o' work fae the borders an' the North o' England."

George sat quietly for a few minutes and then he replied, "Aye, Ah suppose yer right it does make sense, but Ah'll be sorry tae see ye go. When are ye thinkin' o' leavin'?"

Isabella gasped as Edward replied, "This week."

Nellie was still kneeling in front of her mother, but now she was crying silent tears. "Oh' Mam Ah'll miss ye tae."

Everything appeared to have changed and the change had crept quietly up on everyone. The last part of Mary's prediction had come true. Daisy and Bruce along with Nellie, Edward and young Eddie had gone to Carlisle. Johnny missed Edward's company and Mary particularly missed Nellie, but she had Rosa to take her attention and she spent much of her spare time keeping Isabella company because she was sad not having her daughters nearby.

All too soon, summer ended and by the end of October, the winter had come in with a bang, one storm after another, and rain for days on end. Johnny was patiently waiting for a break in the weather so that he could make the last trip for their winter supplies. He had put off going until after Daisy and Bruce's wedding, and then he put it off again to wish Nellie and Edward well when they were leaving for Carlisle. When the rain finally stopped, Johnny was reluctant to leave, because Rosa, who was now five months old, had developed a bad cold but Mary thought that it would pass in a few days. She had a bad feeling about it but convinced herself that it was just because she was a mother now, and a mother always worries. Johnny kissed them both before leaving and promised to be back the next day but he had no sooner gone than it started to snow.

Isabella had gone over to Mary's wagon to see how the little one was. Rosa's face was flushed red, her nose was blocked, and she had started to cough. Mary had done everything that she could think of. Isabella suggested trying steam to ease her breathing so she fetched a pot of hot water and placed it on the table. Mary sat beside the table with Rosa in her arms and Isabella placed a sheet over them both so that the steam from the pot would stay under the sheet. This didn't appear to make much difference and Mary could stand it no longer, she was afraid for her daughter.

"Ah'm gonnae take her tae the Royal."

"Ye cannae dae that yer self, a' the men are away, whit ye gonnae dae, walk!"

"Ah'm gonnae run," said Mary and she quickly grabbed a big woollen blanket and wrapped her and Rosa up in it.

"Ye cannae go yer self whit if ye fa' wi' the wean? It's slippy oot there. Ah'll come wi' ye."

"Ye'll need tae keep up wi' me Isabella for Ah huvnae any time tae wait for ye."

At that, Isabella ran to her wagon, and quickly grabbed her warm shawl and head scarf then ran as best she could to catch up with Mary. It had only been seconds since she left Mary but the snow was falling so fast now that she could hardly see her ahead. "Ah'm comin, Mary," she called. Mary was just a dark silhouette on that path. They cut through Glasgow Green making their way to the Royal Infirmary. The going was treacherous and they could hardly see in front of them.

"Wi'll cut up to London Road," said Mary. Isabella was too busy trying to keep upright to answer and she was worried about Rosa. On and on they tramped, through the thick snow finally reaching London Road. They were exhausted but didn't care. All they could think of was getting Rosa to the hospital. Suddenly they heard the sound of horses pulling a carriage. The snow was a little clearer but still falling thick. They stopped for a moment thinking that they could get help and as the carriage neared them the coachman reined in the horses, startled by the sudden appearance of the two women, neighed their displeasure and stamped the ground.

"Help me tae get tae the hospital!" cried Mary.

At that, a wealthy looking man pulled down the window at the side of the carriage and looked down at Mary and Isabella. He stared at them.

"Mister, can ye help me tae get tae the hospital?"

Mary could see a gold ring on his finger. "Can ye help me wi' ma wean mister?" The Coachman was leaning over the side watching for his response. The passenger stuck his finger in the air and made a circular gesture, there was a pause for a moment as the coachman looked at the passenger and the passenger said in a loud voice "Drive on." The coachman paused and tried to explain but the man yelled at him in an American accent. "You have been told coachman, drive on."

The coachman looked down at Mary, shook his head sadly, and then did as he was bid. Mary screamed at the American "Naw, naw ye cannae dae that, ma bairns sick!" but she was speaking to the back of the carriage as it pulled away. Rage enveloped her as she ran after the wagon screaming at the top of her voice.

"Ye saw me runnin' in the dark

An' didnae stop an' didnae park

She was sick ma precious bairn

Ah widnae dae ye any hairm.

Ye think ye are an important maister

Yer nothin but a selfish baistard

Tae you an' yours a send Ah curse

Let bad things happen and then the wurst.

Son or daughter from this day on

They'll suffer for yer deeds e'en when yer gone

Ah send this curse just wait an' see

For ye widnae stop an' help ma wane an' me."

The last of her words were called into the snow for she could not see the carriage any more, but she could hear it and with every ounce of her being, she wished ill on the man in the carriage. Mary's words shocked Isabella, cold as she was these words chilled her in a different way, and they would be remembered for a long, long, time. The visit to the hospital was a short one; Rosa was immediately put on oxygen and kept in overnight while Mary and Isabella waited in the cold hospital corridor. By morning, Rosa was much better and although the hospital wanted Isabella and Mary to leave, they wouldn't go without Rosa. After some insistence, they allowed them to take Rosa home. The sky was bright blue, the sun was shining, and there was not a cloud in sight when the little group left the Royal Infirmary that morning. Mary stopped at the doorway and looked up for a few minutes and then she turned to Isabella and said, "Let's get hame Isabella, it'll be a'right noo."

Chapter 34

Johnny was shocked to hear how sick Rosa had been and dismayed to hear that Mary and Isabella had made their way through the blizzard to the hospital. Mary told Johnny about the wealthy American.

"The coachman wanted tae help but the Yankee widnae let him. Ah was ragin', but he'll get whit's coming tae him for no' stoppin' 'cause Ah cursed him wi' a' ma might."

"Mary, Ah've seen ye cryin' yer eyes oot for daein stuff like that. Ah thought ye had learned yer lesson fae old Mither Morrison. Ye told me yer self whit goes aroon' comes aroon', Ah wish ye didnae dae that."

"Well it's done noo an' he deserves whit's comin', Ah cannae take it back." Johnny shook his head sadly because he was worried about what might come back. He didn't want something bad to happen to either of them or especially to Rosa who he loved more than he could have imagined.

News of Mary and Isabella' late night dash to the hospital travelled around the camp and at the same time so did the story of the curse that she yelled to the wealthy American. Reading newspapers was not common among the Gypsies for at that time, most of them couldn't read, but that did not stop news travelling. There were always travellers coming and going, some would come from other camps and they would just be passing on their way to another town or village. Often they would take the opportunity to stop for a night or two, and share news and titbits from their own camp or whatever they heard on the way. Likewise, they would carry stories back when they returned home, so it wasn't long before Mary's curse became common knowledge. Some just laughed when they heard of it but others would shiver and shake their head.

The following year the story of the curse raised it head again when Edward, Nellie, and young Eddie came to visit Isabella. They had already spent the day going round the camp, saying hello to old friends and family. Nellie took Eddie across to see Mary and was delighted that Rosa was now toddling about, confident on her feet. Rosa stood and stared at Eddie who was nearly five years old now and then she grinned and put out her arms and in her baby voice, she said, "Up." Everyone laughed including Eddie as he struggled to lift her.

"Ah think she remembers him, Ah told ye that was a match made in Heaven," said Nellie. They went outside with the children so that they could play in the summer sunshine and for a while, they watched fascinated as Eddie and Rosa sat in the sun enjoying each other's company. Eddie took Rosa's hand and wandered round the camp with her grinning from ear to ear. "He loves that wean," said Nellie.

"Ah think yer right."

Nellie didn't share the story, she had been keeping it from Mary, but she was anxious to share it with her mother. Much later when the opportunity arose and she was sitting chatting with Isabella she asked, "Dae ye remember when Mary cursed the Yankee Mam?"

"Aye, whit of it? Ah dinnae like tae remember that."

"Edward came hame wi' a story about a Yankee politician that had spent time in Scotland and there was news that he lost his wean, a wee lad."

"Never!"

"Aye, for sure. There was some talk that a Gypsy had cursed him an' noo he's lost his son. They say it was in the newspapers."

"Oh that's terrible, it cannae be true."

"That's whit Ah'm hearin' Mam."

"Have ye told Mary?"

"Naw, are ye jokin' Ah couldnae tell her that. Ah'm sure she meant it at the time, but Ah think she would be fair heartbroken tae think a wee laddie had died because of it."

"Well maybe he was sick, maybe it wisnae the curse."

"Well that's whit they're sayin' in the camps an' on the road."

"Ah dinnae think ye should mention it tae her."

"Naw Mam, no' me Ah'm no' tellin' her o' it."

"Naw Ah dinnae think ye should for it would only worry her an' their life is sweet. Ah wouldnae like tae see summat bad comin' back tae hurt her, an' Ah widnae like tae see her worryin' that it could."

In spite of Nellie and Isabella trying to keep this gossip from Mary, Edward mentioned it to Johnny.

"Heavens above, dae ye think it's true?"

"Well who can say if it's true or no', but Ah thought it would be better if ye knew aboot it."

"Aye yer probably right Edward, Ah have tae think aboot this, Ah dinnae ken if Ah should tell Mary."

Johnny worried about the story he had heard and Mary sensed that something was troubling him. One evening a few days after Nellie and Edward had left, they were sitting in their wagon. All was quiet, and Rosa was fast asleep.

"Are ye a' right Johnny?"

"Aye, why dae ye ask?"

"It seems tae me that there's summat troublin' ye the past few days."

Johnny made no response and this just confirmed Mary's fears.

"Can ye tell me whit's troublin' ye Johnny?"

"Ah didnae want tae worry ye, but Ah think that there is summat ye should know." Mary was more worried now.

"Tell me Johnny, for ma worry will be greater if ye dinnae say whit it is."

"Ah'll tell ye this Mary, but Ah'm only tellin' ye so that ye can dae summat if it's possible."

Mary sat with bated breath waiting to hear what he had to say. "Dae ye remember the night ye had tae rush tae the hospital wi' Rosa?"

"Aye Ah remember it, Ah'll never forget it as long as Ah live."

"Dae ye remember the Yank that widnae help ye an' ye cursed him?"

"Ah dae."

"They say he's a Yankee Politician."

"Whit of it?"

"They say he had a wee lad an' he has died. They're sayin it was a curse on him by a Gypsy."

"Och that's jist rubbish! How could onybody know that?"

"Ye know how stories get passed Mary. The coachman tells the stable lad, the stable lad tells the housemaids, before ye know it everybody knows. Noo they're saying it was in the papers that he thinks the Gypsy's curse was tae blame for his bairn's death."

Mary was quiet, thinking about that night, trying to understand her feelings. She questioned herself, deep in her heart she could not forgive the Yankee, but at the same time she realised that what she had done, the power of the words that she had uttered could have been the cause of the death of a child. She was horrified.

"Dae ye hate me for what Ah said Johnny?"

"Ah could never hate ye Mary but sometimes Ah question yer thinkin'."

All was quiet in the wagon as both of them sat and thought about that night. Johnny wished that he had never made the decision to leave that day. If he had waited another day or two, he could have taken Mary and Rosa to the hospital in the cart and they would never have met the Yankee. Mary's thoughts were on her terror at the thought of losing Rosa and then suddenly, in her mind, she heard old Mither Morrison's voice,

"When ye dae summat bad, the ripples keep movin' until they come back tae ye. Ye ' can dae guid wi' yer gift, but ye can dae harm tae. Dae guid an' guid things will aye come tae ye, but be sure o' this Mary, if ye dae summat bad it's the hardest thing tae take back, and bad will come right back at ye when ye least expect it."

Mary sat there, Mither Morrison's words ringing in her ears and fear of the consequences churning in her stomach. She tried to put a brave face on and pretend that she wasn't bothered, but she was deeply troubled and she realised that she felt guilty that a child had suffered.

Chapter 35

Mary felt sick to her stomach, she tossed and turned unable to sleep, and every time she closed her eyes, she could hear the words of her curse ringing in her ears. Johnny, lying awake beside her, but pretending he was asleep, felt every twist and turn. He was unable to offer any solace to his troubled wife. He was aware of her slipping out of their bed and quietly leaving the wagon. He felt sure that he knew where she was going, her favourite spot by the river. He also knew that on this occasion he should let her be alone. He didn't know what she was going to do, however, he was sure that she would be trying to repair any damage her curse had done.

The moon was waning and instinctively Mary knew that this was a perfect time to ask for something to be sent away. She made her way through the trees and when she reached her favourite spot, she knelt down on the cold damp grass.

"Whit have Ah done, whit have Ah done?" She looked up at the sliver of the Moon and implored,

"Lady of the silver Moon

Help me noo Ah spoke too soon

Ah shed a curse, Ah was feart that night

But noo Ah know Ah wisnae right

Break this curse and make it well

Ah'm awfy sorry, ye can surely tell

Take ma fears an' make things right

Ah beg ye this wi' a' ma might

Ah'm sorry for the curse a made

A curse Ah know Ah shouldnae have said

Take them back Ah beg ye please

Ah'm praying on ma bended knees

Let me an mine aye be well

An listen please tae ma wee spell

Hear me Lady hear me pray

For ne're again a curse Ah'll say."

Mary stayed there for a long time thinking and worrying about what she may have been the cause of, fearing what may happen in the future and then she realised that there was a way she might be able to see ahead. Dawn was breaking as she made her way back through the trees to her wagon. Johnny had the fire going already and water boiled for tea. He saw her approaching, her appearance dishevelled, her dark hair unkempt, her face streaked from crying and her eyes swollen. She walked straight to him and he embraced her and held her in his arms. She was exhausted but sleep was a long way off.

"Dae ye remember that old broken clock ye found Johnny, dae ye know where it is?"

"Here drink this tea, let me have a think, aye, it's in a box under the wagon. Whit dae ye need it for?"

"Jist summat Ah want tae try."

"Ah'll get it for ye."

"Thanks Johnny."

He sat looking at her and was unable to think of what to say to her that would make her feel any better.

"Ah have nae idea how tae help ye Mary."

"There's nothin' ye can say or dae that will make me feel better. Ah've done whit Ah can. Whit Ah did was wrang an' Ah have tae make up for it for the rest o' ma life."

Johnny got up and kissed the top of her head. "Ah'll see if Ah kind find that clock."

Mary heard Rosa stirring as Johnny began to search through boxes that were stored under the wagon. She went in and picked her up smothering her sweet face with kisses. She cried a little too, "Ah'll never let ye oot ma sight ma darlin'."

Rosa, oblivious to her mother's pain, nuzzled into her neck enjoying those first morning moments in her mother's arms.

"Ah've found it Mary."

"Jist leave it there for me Johnny, Ah'll get tae it later."

"Right then Ah'll see ye a bit later, Ah'm away tae see tae the horses."

Mary spent the better part of the morning tending to Rosa's needs and tidying the wagon, later she popped over to see her aunt.

"Yer quiet the day Mary?"

"Aye, Ah've had a rough night."

"Wi' the bairn?"

"Naw Mither, jist summat that's came back tae haunt me."

"Dae ye want tae speak ot it?"

"Dae ye remember the night wi' ran tae the hospital wi' Rosa?"

Isabella's breath noticeably hitched and Mary looked at her questioningly.

"Ye've heard the rumours then?"

"Aye Mary, Ah have, but Ah dinnae think ye needed that worry."

"Well it's better that Ah know of it. Maybe Ah can change things."

"Dae ye think ye can?"

"Well Ah've been up a' night tryin' so Ah jist have tae wait an' see."

"Ah'll keep an eye on Rosa if ye want tae go an' have a sleep Mary."

"Thanks Mither but even if Ah lay doon Ah dinnae think Ah could shut ma eyes an' no' see that damage Ah've done. Ah'll be fine, but Ah appreciate the offer."

Later that night Mary took the old clock apart. She had no need of the workings; it was the bevelled glass that she wanted. She searched in her box of trimmings looking for a square of black velvet that she knew she had and then she laid the curved glass on top of it. It was exactly the right size, but she wanted a box to finish her creation. She began to search in the cupboards and cabinets in the wagon and finally she found a wooden box full of buttons and fasteners. She emptied it out putting all the contents to one side; she would find something to keep these treasures in later, but for now the focus of her attention was the box, the black velvet and the curved glass from the old clock.

Later that evening after they had eaten, and Rosa was settled for the night, Mary spoke to Johnny.

"Ah'm away tae the river Johnny, Ah'll leave ye tae mind Rosa for a wee while."

"Aye lass, she'll be fine wi' me." He stood and kissed her before she left the wagon. "Ah take it ye have a plan?"

"Ah'm gonnae see if Ah can take a look into the future for us."

There was not much that Johnny could say about that because he had no concept of the gifts that Mary had, he just nodded his support.

Mary was careful about gathering all the things that she would need for her task. First into her basket was the box that she had prepared by lining it with the piece of black velvet cloth with the curved glass over it. Next, from her supply of herbs, she added a sprig of Bog Myrtle, a sprig of Rosemary and then from her cupboard she added an earthenware dish, a candle, and finally she placed a cloth to sit on at the top of her basket. On the way to the river, she nipped several leaves from one of the lower branches of an Ash tree. When she arrived at her favourite space, she spread the cloth on the ground and unpacked her basket. She used a stone from the riverbank to grind the Bog Myrtle, the Rosemary and the leaves from the Ash tree earthenware dish. She sat for a few moments to focus her mind on her intention. When she felt that she was ready, she lit her candle and then set the flame to the crushed herbs. Leaning over the smoke from the herbs, she inhaled deeply and used her hand to waft the smoke onto her face. At first, she could feel the smoke making her lightheaded and then the properties began to induce a trance like feeling. She took the wooden box and placed it on her lap so that the light of the moon reflected on it, and then she began to scry in the glass.

At first, she could see nothing but the Moon's reflection but as the effect of the burning herbs began to take effect, pictures began to form. Initially it was almost as though she was seeing through a fine mist but as she concentrated, the pictures became clearer. She wasn't sure of the correct way to do what she was doing but she persevered. She saw Johnny in her vision and he was laughing; she concentrated harder and then she saw Rosa running, laughing with her arms outstretched, and then she saw that Rosa was running to young Eddie. He was laughing too, and he picked her up, swinging her around then put her down and mussed her hair. She saw the whole family at different fairs and Rosa was older and so pretty. She kept looking willing her intention to go as far into the future as she could but the last thing that she saw before she passed out was Eddie handing Rosa a small wooden token carved in the shape of a Rose. She knew in the moment that Rosa and Eddie would marry and she felt a deep sense of contentment.

Chapter 36

Johnny paced about, unable to settle, he was not sure what Mary was actually doing and was feeling useless. Rosa continued to sleep soundly and finally Mary arrived back. Johnny breathed a sigh of relief and clasped her to him.

"Are you a'right Mary?"

"Ah have a really sore head, it's a bad one."

"Ah'll make ye some tea an' then Ah think ye should go tae bed."

Mary drank her tea but she was half asleep before the tea was finished and Johnny took her cup, picked her up in his arms and laid her down to sleep. She slept through the night and late into the morning. When she awoke, Johnny was already away to tend to the horses and Isabella was minding Rosa. "Mither, whit ye daein here, where's Johnny? Is everythin' a'right?"

"It's nearly noon Mary, ye've been asleep for a long while an' Ah've been enjoyin' this wee treasure, here go tae yer Mam," Isabella said, handing Rosa to Mary.

"Ah cannae believe Ah've slept a' that time."

"Johnny was fair worried for ye so Ah came across tae mind the wee one an' let ye sleep."

"Thanks Mither, that was kind o' ye."

"Tis nothin'."

Isabella lifted the teapot that was sitting on top of the Queenie stove, poured a cup of tea, and handed it to Mary. "Drink this lass, an' there's a pancake under the napkin, made fresh this morning. Ye'll feel better wi' summat in yer stomach."

Mary sat with Rosa on her lap, in between bites she gave Rosa little bits of pancake, laughing with Isabella at the happy faces Rosa was making as she enjoyed the treats.

"Johnny said that ye were oot most o' the night trying tae see whit's comin', did ye have any luck?"

"Ah saw a lot o' things Mither, but Ah didnae see owt bad. Ah saw ma bairn growin' aw she was jist beautiful, Ah saw her playin' an' laughin' an' Ah saw her wi' Eddie. Ah think they will wed. He'll make her a fine husband, but after that, it jist got darker an' darker an' Ah couldnae see owt. Ah think maybe Ah fainted, Ah don't think Ah fell asleep an' Ah am no' sure for how long. Ah don't even rightly remember comin back here."

Isabella just nodded. She wasn't sure if this was good or bad, but only time would tell. As it happens, it was just as well that Mary did not see what was coming as the foresight might have killed her. No one could cope with the knowledge of what would happen in times to come, but she didn't see and from that day on life returned to normal for her, Johnny and Rosa.

The whole world was changing around them, not least was the fact that Mary began to call her husband John rather than the Johnny that she had always called him before. By the time Rosa was five years old the first cars were appearing and new opportunities were opening up. People were able to travel farther in a shorter time and there was even some talk of wagons being motorised. Some laughed when they heard and some scorned or scoffed the idea of it. For this camp, everything remained as it had been. Johnny still traded horses and looked after fetching provisions. Mary went along with him and there were often wives waiting to have their fortunes told. They still enjoyed the experience of travelling to fairs and meeting up with their kinfolks and friends and they always looked forward to visits from Nellie and Edward. Eddie was growing fast and he was such a handsome lad and clever too. From an early age, he showed his skills with wood. As soon as Nellie and Eddie would let him handle a sharp knife, he was whittling little bits of wood. Before long, he was making clothes pegs. When he announced that he would sell them round the doors whenever he had made enough of them. Edward and Nellie laughed at his claims, but Eddie was diligent, and before long, his claims became a reality. They didn't laugh when he sold his first batch; in fact, they were very proud of him.

Life goes on as it must do and as time passed Johnny and Mary continued doing what they had always done, breeding, selling, and showing horses. Mary taught Rosa everything that she knew, well almost everything. She taught her how to cook and clean from an early age, and she taught her how to sew on a button or mend a hem, she taught her the benefits of healing herbs, and how to make potions, but she didn't speak to her about spell crafting. When they went to fairs, they met up with Nellie, Edward, and young Eddie and Eddie was always the first to run to them. He missed his Auntie Mary but he missed Rosa more. As soon as they saw each other, they would skip off together holding hands and laughing. From time to time, Nellie, Edward, and young Eddie along with Daisy and Bruce would come back to the camp at Glasgow Green to visit their parents. Those days created special memories for everyone and as always Eddie and Rosa were inseparable.

Rosa had inherited her fathers' temperament and her mother's beauty. From an early age, Eddie's good looks were often the topic of conversation among the young girls wherever he went, but he only had eyes for Rosa. By the time he was twelve years old he was making and selling clothes pegs around the doors and saving for his future. Later he began to construct three legged stools with beautifully turned legs and he sold these as fast as he could make them. Before long, he was carving patterns into the seats and soon he was taking orders, but there was more to Eddie's talent than clothes pegs and stools no matter how pretty the stools were. Often when he was travelling on the cart with his father he would shout to him, "Haud up there Da!" then he would jump down from the cart and run to the edge of the trees where he had spotted a dried up root or a fallen trunk. He could see things in a piece of wood that no one else could, and he could take that wood and spend hours carving out shapes, creating beautiful fruit bowls or plates. He had carved shapes and patterns into the woodwork on his parent's wagon and Nellie delighted in showing off her son's skills.

Eddie was about fourteen years old when, one day, he had just finished carving a bowl when he spotted a small burr of elm that had landed at his feet. Anyone else might have discarded this but Eddie saw something in it immediately. He picked it up and turned it over in his hands, looking at it from all angles and then he sat down and began to carve out the shape that he could see in his mind's eye. First, he smoothed off the edges and when he was satisfied, he began to cut into the surface. He patiently shaped and carved it until it was flat on one side and about two inches across. On the surface, he began to carve the shape that was in his mind. He was engrossed in his project and he had one person in mind during the creation of it, Rosa. When he had finished he once more turned it over and looked at it from all angles and knew, small though it was, it was the finest work he had created. This he created with love in his heart. He carried it in his pocket knowing that the next time he saw Rosa he would give it to her.

Rosa was always excited when they were getting ready to go to any of the fairs, but this wasn't like going to a local fair in Barrhead or Neilston, for they were going to Musselburgh by Edinburgh and they might even get to Portobello beach. She knew that they would meet up with family and friends they hadn't seen but she was more excited at the thought that she would see Eddie again; everyone would be there, especially Eddie.

When they finally arrived at the fair Eddie was watching for them and went to meet their wagon, "Uncle John, Auntie Mary," addressing them as was the custom. He nodded to them but his eyes were for Rosa.

"Can Ah go Da?"

"Ye might ask yer Mam if she needs ye."

"Mam?"

"Away wi' ye Rosa," and then she looked at Johnny and smiled, but he just shook his head. Rosa jumped down from the wagon and ran off with Eddie, both of them laughing and happy to be with each other.

"Ah have summat for ye."

"For me Eddie?"

They were running hand in hand, as they spoke, "Aye."

"Whit is it Eddie?"

"Ye'll see in a minute."

He led her to the edge of the field that the fair was being held in and they both sat on the grass. "Ah've missed ye Rosa, but Ah thought o' ye every day."

Rosa smiled at him still in that early age of awareness but still shy, being with the one she loved, but not truly knowing what that meant yet.

"Gie me yer hand."

Rosa held out her hand and Eddie placed the wooden rose in it. "Ah made this for ye Rosa an' Ah've carried it every day an' Ah would like ye tae keep it tae remind ye o' how Ah feel when we're apart."

Tears filled Rosa's eyes as she looked at it. "It's a rose!"

"Aye, it's a rose for Rosa."

"It's lovely Eddie, Ah will treasure it, an' Ah'll carry it always."

They stayed at the fairground for two days and Rosa and Eddie were together as much as possible, but all too soon, it was time to part.

"Ah don't ken when Ah will see ye next but keep that rose on ye an' think o' me often an' Ah'll be thinkin' o' ye."

Chapter 37

They had managed to get together at several fairs but each time their parting was harder. She would take the wooden rose out of her pocket often, and look at it, treasuring the memories that it evoked and thinking of Eddie. Among her precious things was a box that Eddie had made and given to her at the last fair. It was about eight inches long, four inches wide, and four inches deep. She kept little things in it to remind her of Eddie; inside was a pressed flower, a button from his jacket, and a ribbon that he had bought for her hair. Little things, but looking at them reminded her of him.

Rosa kept her promise and carried the wooden rose in her pocket all the time. The first time Mary saw her looking at her it, she knew exactly where it had come from, but she allowed Rosa her secret and didn't say a word about it. Mary mentioned to John that Eddie had made Rosa a wooden token, "Ah think it's a rose."

"That would be fitting an' Ah'm sure he made a guid job o' it."

She smiled at him as she remembered those first flushes of love.

"Ah will be surprised if they didnae wed each other, they've been stuck like glue since the day she was born."

"Time enough for that Mary. She's only a lassie."

"She's sixteen John, a year or two an' she could be promised tae him an' married no' long after that."

John didn't want to hear that, acting as most fathers do when they think that their daughter might soon be dependent on someone other than them. "Enough," he said and took himself off to the horses. Mary muttered to herself, "Aye he's got a short memory," shaking her head she continued, "he forgets whit we were like an' Coralina was away wi' Robert by the time she was sixteen." She sighed at the random thought of Coralina and wished her well wherever she was.

It was a fine day and she was intent on washing down all the woodwork on the outside of the wagon. She filled a pail with warm water and then rubbed a cloth in the water with carbolic soap. Her mind drifted back; back to when they were younger, and all the changes that they had experienced since those days. She laughed to herself as she thought of the fight that she had with Daisy just before her wedding, and then she blushed as she remembered her father dragging her from the river like a wild woman. She shook her head trying to rid herself of the embarrassing thought. She thought about Coralina and Robert and wondered how different her life would be if Coralina had loved a Gypsy lad and still lived on the camp. Daisy and Bruce were still in Carlisle with Nellie and Edward; she missed them and was always glad to reunite with them and their children at fairs. Isabella was gone now and so was George and she remembered that they had passed within weeks of each other. It was a shock to everyone, and it still brought a tear to her eye, but it brought Jennie back to the camp with her husband Henry, and their three children, Ellen, Sadie, and Lizzie, it was good to see them back where they belonged.

Before too long she had finished cleaning the wagon, and with everything spick and span she went off to join John at the horse field. Mizzie was gone now too; the bond she had with Mizzie was special and no other horse had touched her heart the way Mizzie had, but she liked them all well enough, and she still had a way with them. They were going to Musselburgh within the next few days and John was making sure that all the horses that he was taking looked their best. Rosa could hardly contain herself because she knew that she would see Eddie and she couldn't think about anything else.

"Are yi takin' some doilies tae sell Rosa?"

"Aye Mam; an' Ah have some wi' nice beads an' shells that Ah think will sell easy."

They had done everything that they needed to do to prepare for the trip and now it was time to leave but Rosa was dithering about, her excitement at seeing Eddie was just too much and she could hardly think straight.

"Hurry Rosa yer Da wants tae leave in ten minutes."

"Ah'm hurryin' Ma, Ah'm goin' as fast as Ah can," said Rosa. She hopped about pulling on her black boots and fastening the laces. The last time they had met was at Musselburgh Fair and she couldn't wait to see him again. She was sixteen now, her raven black hair curled and waved over her shoulders and down her back and her green eyes sparkled with excitement.

She turned the wooden rose over and over in her pocket feeling the grooves and shapes that formed the rose. She knew every part of it.

"Hurry up lass," her father called as he hitched the lead horses to the front of the wagon.

"Stop yer day dreamin' and get up on the wagon."

Rosa was sitting up on the front of the wagon with her mother and her father was riding behind them leading the horses that he was taking to sell. The early morning sun was shining and the birds were singing as they travelled along. Four other families were travelling behind them and they all made a pretty parade, each wagon gleaming clean and painted in bright colours.

"Are ye gonnae be telling fortunes Mam?"

"If Ah'm asked."

"Can ye tell mine?"

Mary laughed, "Ah dinnae need tae be a fortune teller tae see what's comin' for ye, it's a' Eddie, Eddie, Eddie."

"But will we have bairns Ma?"

"Aye, lass ye'll have bairns, of course ye'll have bairns."

"Have ye looked then?"

"Naw, Ah've no' looked an' Ah'm no' gonnae look."

"Why no' Ma?"

"It'll be a nice surprise when it comes."

That answer pleased Rosa, but the truth of the matter was that Mary was afraid to look. One of the curses of being able to see the future is that sometimes you see things that you cannot change and after seeing these things, you know that you can do nothing but worry about them.

Musselburgh was seven miles from Edinburgh, and they would water and exercise their horses at the banks of the River Esk. They were all looking forward to getting to the fair for they knew that the showmen would be there with their galloping horses' carousel, which had only been around for a few years. It was such a novelty that it attracted hundreds of fairgoers and they would be camped quite near the fairground. Even knowing that it would be busy at Musselburgh, it didn't take away from their surprise and delight at the crowds that were milling about as they drove over the cobbled stones of the High Street and past Merkat Cross.

There were other families behind and ahead of them and their procession drew gasps from pedestrians going about their business. Finally, they arrived and queued to enter the field where they would camp for the next few days. Other travellers were already setting up stalls to display and sell their wares. Some would come and lend a hand with unpacking, and to share the latest news. The Wilson's, the Boswell's, and the Stewarts called hello and gave a cheery wave.

Chapter 38

The energy around the field was electric and Rosa was bouncing with excitement. Mary tried to calm her but it was hopeless.

"Mind yer ane business Rosa and dinnae let yer Da catch you lookin' at the lads," her mother whispered.

"I'm no' lookin at the lads Mam, Ah was jist lookin' for…" her face burning with embarrassment.

"I know who yer lookin for, it's that Eddie McGuigan. A guid boy mind ye, but dinnae show yer keen."

"I like him Ma, he asked me to remember him last year."

"Wheesht, here's yer Da!"

Suddenly she caught sight of him and her heart skipped a beat as her cheeks began to glow bright red.

"Ma," she whispered.

"I see him."

Rosa kept her eyes downcast as Eddie approached, and not once did Eddie look in her direction.

"Excuse me, Aunty Mary," he said, as was the custom in his culture, "Could Ah speak tae Uncle John?"

"Ye've never had a problem speakin' tae him before Eddie, dae ye think ye might have wan the noo."

Mary laughed to herself as she watched this boy, now a young man, she had loved since he was a baby. Eddie was mortified but he knew that his Auntie Mary was teasing him.

John's heart almost stopped as he came around the wagon and saw Eddie there because he had a notion that he knew what was coming and he would never be ready for this. He glowered at him, "Eddie."

"Uncle John, a word."

"Well, spit it out and Ah'm warnin' ye, Ah'm nae in the best o moods."

Eddie was not happy at John's sharp tone and was equally sharp with his reply. "Ah could come back an' see ye."

"Jist git on wi' it lad. Ah've things tae dae."

Eddie was a confident lad, but what he was about to say meant so much to him that he wanted to create the best impression, nevertheless he was not prepared to be intimidated. He took a deep breath, straightened his shoulders, looked his uncle in the eye, and said, "It's an important thing Ah wish tae speak tae ye about, but if ye huvnae time tae be civil Ah'll come back."

Realising that he had been a bit harsh with Eddie, John tried to start again.

"Jist haud yer horses' lad, ye got me on the wrong foot. Ah feel Ah know whit ye want to speak tae me about an it's churnin' in ma' stomach. Say yer piece."

As John stepped closer he moved to put his arm over Eddies shoulder and realised with some shock that the lad was no longer a lad in fact he was taller and broader than John. He shrugged, embarrassed by the realisation, and stuck his hands in his pocket.

"Let's take a walk Eddie."

Eddie was the next to speak, he stopped mid stride and turned to look John in the eye. He took a deep breath, and said, "Ah've loved yer lass since Ah was wee, an' she was just a babe. Ah've watched her grow and become the beautiful lass like the flower ye named her for. The past four years Ah've worked and saved and every penny is for Rosa's future."

John knew it was coming but now that it had, his heart was pounding in his chest as he looked at the man who would take his daughter away from him. He couldn't find the breath to speak, and he and Eddie stared at each other for what felt to both of them like an eternity.

"Ah'm askin' ye for her hand man," he almost shouted.

Finally, John spoke "Same time, same place, next year, if ye still feel the same ye can ask her yirsel, an' if she agrees ye can marry on the first day of May at the Tinkers Heart."

Eddie did a dance right there in front of John.

"She'll say aye, I know it."

As John walked back to his wagon he could see Rosa helping her mother and his heart swelled with pride and some sadness because he knew that in the not too distant future she would be away with Eddie looking after her on family.

"Ah've jist seen that young Eddie," he said to no one in particular, but really so that Rosa could hear. "Turned into a fine man," he said, as he climbed into his wagon. He poured himself a whisky and sat there and that's where Mary found him, sitting staring straight ahead, his face wet with tears. She sat beside him, placed her hand in his, and gave it a comforting squeeze. She felt as he did, proud and happy for her daughter, but desperately sad at the thought of her leaving them.

Rosa had finished helping her mother and she changed from her travelling clothes to her new dress that she and her mother had patiently sewn together. The skirt was bright red with gold and green abstract patterns and the bodice had a red trimmed white insert with black lacing down the centre. She wandered across to the river and sat quietly by herself admiring the activity around her and looking at her skirt from time to time delighted with the bright blues and reds of the fabric. She was waiting for Eddie and she knew that he would find her. She wondered what he had said to her father, and more she wondered what he had said to him. She had butterflies in her stomach as she thought of the conversation that they might have had. She kept glancing up to see if she could see him, but she remembered what her mother had said about not looking as though she was too eager. How could she not be too eager, she loved him with all her being, he was the other part of her, and then he was there, right beside her.

"Oh Eddie, "Ah'm pleased tae see ye."

As he sat on the grass beside her he gave her a red rose and said, "Ah'm fair pleased tae see ye tae. Ah spoke tae yer Da," he said, grinning from ear to ear, holding her hand and looking into her eyes. "Whit did he say Eddie?"

"He said Aye, no' like that though, his exact words were 'Same time same place next year an' if ye feel the same ye can merry on the first o' May at the Tinkers Heart. Whit dae ye make o' that Rosa?"

Rosa's hands flew to her mouth, "Are ye kiddin' me? Did he really say that? We can be wed at The Tinkers Heart! Oh, my, that'll be grand. Ah'm fair excited Eddie."

"Jist a year and a bit, on the first of May we'll marry above Loch Fyne at the Tinkers Heart, and Ah promise Ah'll love ye forever Rosa if ye'll have me."

He took a beautiful gold ring from his waistcoat pocket and placed it on her finger. She gazed at the tiny diamonds in the shape of a flower and said, "Aye Eddie, Ah will marry ye," as he kissed the happy tears on her face.

They spent a while sitting there on the grass expressing their love for each other in words to each other and in their eyes. They had no thought of anyone else but themselves. Eventually they had to make their way back to Rosa's wagon where Mary and John were waiting for their return. All eyes were on them as they made their way across the field for news travels like wild fire and everyone knew now that Rosa and Eddie were betrothed. Mary and John were sitting outside their wagon as they approached and Rosa ran to her mother holding out her left hand to show off her ring. "Look Mam, look at what Eddie has given me! It's beautiful."

Mary and John stood and each in turn they embraced both Eddie and Rosa.

"It's lovely Rosa, Ah'm happy for ye."

That night everyone gathered to share in the good news; they sang and danced, they played fiddles and accordions, and they generally overindulged until the early hours of the morning. There was another surprise that night and that was the arrival of Eddie's cousin Tam, who was in his early thirties. He had been off travelling; some said he was hoping to find a wife, others laughed and said he was trying to avoid getting married, but Tam had no such thoughts, he was a wanderer but he had reached the point where he was ready to go back to his roots. Tams arrival made it a double celebration.

"Where have ye been Tam," John asked.

"Och man, Ah've been all over Scotland, away as far as Inverness an' beyond." Someone laughed and joked, "Aye yer feet must be loupin' Tam. Everyone laughed at the joke and then he was asked "Whit have ye done?"

"Ah've done a bit o' everythin', worked wi' sheep for a while, worked wi' some Highland Cattle tae, an' horses, but the best was when Ah was workin' wi' a builder, makin doors an' the like."

Eddie came over, offered him a bottle of beer, and sat down beside him. "Ah'm right glad yer back Tam. Will ye bide a while?"

"Aye that's me, Ah'm ready tae settle."

"Can Ah ask ye a favour then?"

Tam turned and looked at him, "Aye Eddie, whit's up?"

"Will ye stand wi' me at ma weddin Tam?" Tam stood up and as he did so did Eddie. Eddie wondered what Tam was thinking because he just stood there looking at him, and then he said, "That's no' a favour Eddie, that's an honour, It would be my pleasure tae stand wi' ye," and he threw his arms around Eddie and gave his younger cousin a crushing hug. The two men stood laughing at each other. "Ye nearly broke ma ribs Tam," said Eddie

"Ye fair took ma breath away," replied Tam both of them laughing at their own enthusiasm. It was a night to remember and everyone enjoyed the festivities.

Chapter 39

The following day everyone had their stalls or tables set up and the crowds were pouring in. Some folk were there to ride on the carousel horses or visit the side stalls where they could throw hoops at pegs pinned to a wall, or throw wooden balls at rows of coconuts balanced precariously on posts. Some would be lucky enough to win a balloon or better still a goldfish. Mary had a fancy tent, made of four tall poles stuck into the ground covered on three sides with fancy purple fabric. Another length of ornate red and gold silk cloth draped across the front to allow eager customers a hint of privacy. A board with a hand painted image of a large crystal ball stood outside the tent. Mary wore a colourful silk wrap over her normal clothes and fashioned a red silk scarf over her hair. Large gold hoops in her ears and several thin gold bangles on her wrists created the image she was trying to portray. This made no difference to what she would say, but it was expected. Inside the tent were two chairs with a table set between them. The table was covered with a purple silk cloth and on the table was an elaborate candleholder with a thick white candle burning brightly, Mary's scrying glass, and a deck of ordinary playing cards. Mary only used the playing cards occasionally for they were only useful to her for looking at what was happening, but she could never see in them why these things would occur.

Within the hour, there were queues of women eagerly waiting to hear what Mary had to say. When a customer come in Mary would tell them to sit in the chair opposite her and place their hands on the table with their palms upwards. First, she would sit quietly looking at their hands as though she was palm reading; in truth that was not Mary's skill, but it gave the customer a moment to settle and then Mary would place her hands on top of the customers. After a few moments, Mary would close her eyes and allow sensations and vibrations the freedom to flow from the customers psyche to hers. This was how Mary could predict things with such accuracy. When she was ready, Mary would open her eyes and look directly into her customers eyes. Some found this captivating, others disconcerting, but Mary, always accurate, would begin to tell them things about themselves. Sometimes she was so accurate in describing events that had already happened that she scared her customer. Other customers wanted to know more, and Mary would tell them to choose some cards. If they were willing to pay extra,

Mary would uncover her scrying glass and begin to gaze into it until images appeared.

She had been working steadily for a few hours when a woman came in and sat down as she was bid, but as soon as she was seated, she said, "I don't want my fortune told."

"Why have ye come then?"

"I have something that I hope you will take from me, because I don't know what else to do." The woman opened her bag and drew out a small package wrapped in black satin and passed it across the table to Mary.

"Whit's in it?"

"Tarot cards," replied the woman.

Goosebumps stood on Mary's back and neck. She had heard of Tarot cards, but had never yet seen them. She looked at the package eager to open it and at the same time fearful. She drew them towards her and carefully opened the package. Inside was a cardboard box, worn at the edges with a well-used look about them Mary asked, "Where did ye get these?"

"We just moved into a new house and I found them when I was cleaning out old boxes that were left in the loft. I opened them and had a look."

"Why are ye givin' them tae me?"

"I thought you would know what to do with them."

"Why are ye no' keepin' them for yer self."

The woman began to cry, "They frightened me, and I am too scared to throw them away in case I get bad luck."

"Dinnae be daft. Ah'll take them an Ah'll tell ye yer future for free."

"No! No, thank you very much, I don't want a reading, I just want to be rid of them," and at that she jumped up and left the tent.

Mary shrugged and thought to herself that if the woman didn't want them, she was glad to have them. She was too busy to do anything more than put them in her bag as there was a queue of people waiting to see her. Word of Mary's accuracy at the fair soon spread and for the next few days, she hardly had time to lift her head. By nine o'clock each evening, Mary was more than ready to close her curtain over and bring in her board. She would go into her wagon and lie down, exhausted from seeing so many people.

Rosa looked after her mother during the day making sure that she stopped for a drink of tea or something to eat. On the last day, when everyone was finished, all the Gypsies would dismantle rides, pack away their stalls, and then gather in the middle of the field and have a farewell party. The next morning, they would be up and away at the break of dawn and by the time local people were moving about, going to work or going shopping, there would be no sign of them. The journey home was a quiet one, as most of them were too tired to think never mind chatter, but overall the fair had been a great success. John's thoughts were on horses, for he had sold everything that he had taken with him and he knew that he would have to build his sale stock up for other fairs. Mary's mind was on Rosa, and that this was probably be one of the last fairs that they would go to together, and Rosa, all she could think of was Eddie. She kept glancing to the ring on her finger, admiring it, smiling to herself and thinking of Eddie.

Chapter 40

In the days, weeks, and months that followed all Rosa could talk about or think about was her wedding. She was impatient and wished that it could be this coming May that they would be married, but she would abide by her father's wishes and wait until after the next fair at Musselburgh. Often she would sit and talk with her cousin Lizzie whom she had asked to be her maid of honour and they would giggle as they chatted. Mary would see them and her heart would swell with pride as she watched her beautiful daughter.

They went to local fairs until the end of the summer and then they occupied their time with preparing things to sell around doors for Christmas time. The women and girls were always making something that they could later sell. Rosa spent much of her time gathering and making things for her bottom drawer. From the time they were little, girls got into the habit of putting things into a trunk that they would keep until they got married themselves. This was common practise in Scotland and everyone did it, not just Gypsies. On cold winter nights, Rosa and her mother would often open the trunk and look through her things. She had white linen pillowcases and sheets that she had patiently sat pulling ten weft threads an inch below the hems, and then gathering the warp threads together using coloured embroidery silks, making patterns of little crosses. There would be gifts given to her on her wedding day from guests who would travel from everywhere to witness her marriage to Eddie. Eddie was busy too, he was building a fine wagon for them to start their married life, and Rosa would not know anything about it until she was his wife.

There was nothing else for it except to endure the long cold winter and look forward to the summer months when they could once more meet again at Musselburgh or other fairs that they both might be attending. Everyone kept busy but being apart was difficult for the young lovers.

At the first sign of spring, Mary began to look out boxes of things that she had stored away that she would need for the coming fairs. She sat outside her wagon and pulled out her fancy fabrics that she used to create her fortune-telling tent. She shook them out and draped them over the wheels of the wagon to air. When she looked in the bag where her candleholder and accoutrements were stored, she came across the black satin wrap. At first, she couldn't think what it was and then suddenly she remembered the woman who had given it to her at the Musselburgh Fair. She took the wrap into the wagon, sat at her table, and carefully opened the satin parcel. Inside was the cardboard box of Tarot cards. The edges of the dark blue box were scuffed and worn and she tentatively opened the flap at one end and drew out the cards. The first card that she saw had a picture of a vagabond wearing a colourful tunic and carrying his possessions wrapped in cloth, tied to a stick, and jauntily balanced over his shoulder. The sun was shining above his head and he was standing at what looked like the edge of a cliff. In the background, she could see the sea. She did her best to try to read the words written below his feet. Strictly speaking, many Gypsies couldn't read or write, but they often had a little knowledge that would enable them to figure out what was written. She knew the first word was 'The' and then she laughed to herself as she realised that the second was 'Fool', she felt like a fool as she laughed.

Her heart was pounding in her chest as she spread the cards out in front of her and then she realised that this was going to be very difficult for her to understand. She counted them first, there were seventy-eight cards in all, and they all had pictures. She sat and thought for a bit and then she began to put similar cards together. There were ten cards with Cups, ten with Branches, which in fact we know as Wands, ten with Coins, we know as Pentacles, and ten with Swords. She couldn't understand the roman numerals, but by counting the Cups, Branches, Coins, and Swords, she was able to discern that they related to each number. Mary placed each individual pile in a row and then began to look at the remaining cards. There were four Kings, four Queens, four pages and four Knights, each of them had Cups, Branches, Coins, and Swords, so she added these to the appropriate piles. She counted the remaining cards, there were twenty-two. She put them to one side and looked at the ones she had put into order.

She sat there looking and thinking trying to figure out what she was missing because she was sure that she was missing something obvious. She went to the chitty prop and poured herself a cup of tea.

"Dae ye need me Mam?" questioned Rosa who was sitting chatting at the fire.

"Naw Hinny, jist bide where ye are."

She went back into her wagon and sat once more at the table looking at the piles of cards and then she jumped up, fetched her bag, and took out the playing cards. She separated them into their suits; there were thirteen cards in all, King, Queen, Jack, in the hearts, diamonds, clubs, and spades. She was tingling now. She counted the playing cards, there were fifty-two. She compared them, the two lots of cards and then she laid each of them in a row. The top row had all the Branches then the Cups, then the Coins and finally the Swords. On the next row below the Cups, she placed the hearts, and then below the diamonds she placed the Coins. That left two suits to figure out. She now had Branches and Swords to place, *"That must mean that spades or clubs are branches or swords."* She decided that clubs should be with Swords and spades should be with Branches. She counted each pile again only to find after several counts that the Tarot cards had an extra card in each suit and then the penny dropped and she knew what was different. She took out the four knights from each of the Tarot cards and counted again and this time they matched. She muttered to herself trying to understand the puzzle,

"So the plain cards have fifty two. The Tarot cards have fifty two, plus four knights, plus twenty two others?"

This was an awakening for Mary and she almost didn't know what to do with herself as she realised that ordinary playing cards actually came from Tarot cards. She had so much to think about, she gathered all the playing cards together and put them away. Then she gathered the Tarot cards that she had been working with and put them in a pile to one side. It was time to apply herself to the mystery of the twenty-two remaining cards, but the effort had left her feeling spent and she decided that she would study the remaining cards in a day or two.

For the next few days, Mary went about her normal routine, however, her mind was busy trying to work out what she had discovered about the Tarot cards, and she was eager to find a minute so that she could sit quietly and study the twenty-two cards that were still a mystery to her.

Chapter 41

For the next few months, life continued as normal but at every opportunity, Mary took herself off to sit quietly and study her Tarot cards. She had managed to decipher the Roman Numerals on the major cards by comparing the numbers on the suit cards, that helped her to put the major cards into their sequence, and each day she laid the majors out in a row and tried to understand them. Finally, it all clicked into place for her, and she realised that the major cards were the cause of changes and the minor cards were predictable reactions, good, or otherwise. The Cups were all brightly coloured and told her about love. In contrast, the Swords were darker in colour and appeared to show problems. It was as she was looking at these things, that she realised the significance of them all. Wands were for springtime, ideas thoughts, and growth. Cups were summer cards and told her about love and romance. The Coins made her think about earning money and she concluded that this must mean harvest and autumn. If that was the case then the Swords were winter. Swords were weapons, but they could also be tools, consequently, they were about action. Each suit had its fair share of good and bad cards that would help her in her predictions.

John made her a new board showing images of the tarot cards to display outside her tent at the Musselburgh fair. It was only later, when she was using the tarot cards for customer readings that she realised that every time she shuffled the cards, if one fell out, it was conveying a message for the person that she was reading for, because the same card would appear during the reading. She was never tempted to read them for herself, in fact she was a little afraid of them, but she would never have admitted that to anyone. She also realised that the images depicted in the cards were personifications of the customer and how that customer felt or would feel.

Mary became so adept at reading the Tarot cards that she could now tell people what things would happen, why these things would happen and how best to act or react. If someone had a problem, Mary could tell that person how to avoid it. If avoiding it was not possible, Mary could at least tell them how long it would be before the issue was resolved and what would happen next. When there were opportunities, Mary could tell her customers about them so that they were able to take full advantage of them. She could predict the timing of things with an accuracy that sometimes even surprised her.

It was common for there to be more than one fortuneteller at fairs, but they only read ordinary playing cards which Mary now knew only told part of the story. Mary now understood the difference, and because of this insight, her reputation grew even more and she always had the biggest queue. As customers came and went from Mary's tent, Rosa stood nearby in case Mary needed anything. At the end of the day, when Mary spoke to her mother, she was laughing.

"Ma, ye should hear whit folk are saying when they come oot yer tent."

"Whit did ye hear?"

"Well there was a woman in the queue waiting for her mither who was in wi' ye an' when the mither came oot she slapped her daughter an' said *'Ye should a' told me ye were havin' a bairn instead o' lettin' me hear it fae a fortune teller.'* Rosa and her mother laughed at this, and Mary was delighted that the cards were proving to be so accurate.

Later that evening, Rosa and Eddie sat with the others enjoying the time that they had together. Eddie, handsome as ever, was wearing his red neckerchief and he had given a matching one to Rosa that she was wearing in her hair. This was a sign to anyone who didn't know them that they were betrothed to each other. They talked about their forthcoming wedding at The Tinkers Heart.

"Whit happens after the weddin' Eddie?"

"Ah'll kiss ye till ye think ye cannae breathe," he replied laughing.

Rosa thumped him playfully on his shoulder, "Ah dinnae mean that, Ah mean where will we go? Where will we live?"

"Well Ah' would like tae bide at the Green, but Ah'd like tae go other places tae."

"Wi' can dae a' that Rosa, wi' can spend a couple o' months jist here and there, visitin' friends an' kin an' then come back an' settle on the Green if ye like."

"Aye Ah'd like that fine."

"Will wi' have bairns Eddie?"

"As many as ye like."

They made a pretty picture, both of them sitting holding hands and with eye for no one but each other. Rosa was crying when it was time to leave and Eddie had to be strong for both of them.

"It'll no' be that long Rosa, ye'll see, the winter will fly past an' afore ye ken ye'll be climbin' the hill tae the Tinkers Heart an Ah'll be there afore ye."

He took her by the hand and walked her back to her wagon where her mother and father were packing up. Mary had dismantled her tent and put her candleholder and scrying glass into her bag. She wrapped the Tarot cards in the original piece of satin and put them in the bag too. She wouldn't need any of these things until the next fair. They all said their farewells and Eddie stood and watched as Rosa, John, and Mary left the fair. He was as sad as Rosa was, but he knew that the next time he would see her he would never have to leave her again. For the next few months, he would concentrate on getting the new wagon ready for her, and he would put all his energy and love into that. Now that Tam was back, he would enjoy sharing the work with him.

Rosa climbed into the back of the wagon, lay down on the bench, and cried. John and Mary knew that she was crying and John whispered to Mary, "Are ye gonnae go back an' see tae her?"

Mary looked at John and said, "Dae ye think that Ah can say onythin' that will ease her hurt John?"

"Naw, Ah suppose yer right enough, better tae let her cry."

The wagon trundled along and eventually Rosa fell into a sleep. When they arrived back at the camp, they began to store away things that they only used for fairs. While they carried out their task, Rosa spoke quietly to her mother.

"Ah had a funny dream when Ah was sleepin' on the way back Ma."

Mary looked at her, "Whit aboot?"

"Me an' Eddie an' a bairn."

"Was that no' a guid dream?"

"Ah'm no' sure Ma, ye see Ah was standin' at the edge o' a field, an' Eddie was at the other end o' it. Ah could see him clear enough, but he had the bairn in his arms an' he was walking away an' wavin' tae me."

The hackles stood on Mary's back and she felt as though the colour was draining from her face. She turned her head so that Rosa wouldn't see her reaction while she pretended that it was of no importance. "Och it's probably jist yer mind playing tricks on ye. Sure ye had jist said cheerio tae Eddie an' yer thinking aboot yer weddin an' startin' a family, dinnae worry yer self. It was jist a dream."

Mary was worried; no Mary was more than worried, she was sick to her stomach and had to take herself off to the dunny so that she could cover her face with her hands and weep. She was not sure what the dream meant, but she was afraid of the worst thing that could happen and she didn't want her fears to be seen by anyone, especially not John or Rosa.

Chapter 42

Mary watched Rosa carefully over the coming months, making sure that she didn't do anything that would bring harm to her, but as time passed, she began to relax and believe what she had told Rosa at the time, *"It was jist a bad dream."* Gradually the memory of the dream began to disappear, and all they thought, and talked about was the coming wedding, but Mary had a niggling feeling that she couldn't quite understand.

"Look Mam, look whit Ah've got in ma trunk," called Rosa

Mary sat beside her and together they looked at all the fine things that Rosa and some of the families had made for her. Mary asked her, "Are ye worried aboot onythin' Rosa?"

"Naw Ma, should Ah be?"

Mary laughed, "Naw Rosa, but have ye spoke aboot where ye will go after yer wed?"

"Oh that, aye, wi' will go travellin' for a bit, see some different places and visit folks we've no' seen for a while. There are some o' Eddie's family that Ah don't ken yet. Ah think he wants tae show me aff," she replied laughing, "but dinnae worry we're comin' back here tae settle on the Green." Then she said, "Ah'm wonderin' whit dress tae wear though."

Mary smiled and went to another trunk that was for her special things. She unpacked it carefully and then produced a brown cardboard box tied with string from the bottom of the trunk. "See whit ye think o' this then," she said as she handed it to Rosa. Rosa took the parcel and reverently untied the piece of string and opened the box. There were two brown paper packages inside; she lifted out the first one and carefully unfolded the paper and she caught a glimpse of pale blue cloth, with tiny sprigs of white daisies all over it. She lifted it out and realised that it was a dress made of fine cotton lawn. She held it up in front of her and looked down at it. A faded blue ribbon inserted through the scooped neckline, trimmed with handmade lace in the same fashion as the long sleeves. There was a white lace pinafore, which came to a point at the front. Mary had tears in her eyes as she helped Rosa to put the dress on.

"Ah wore this when Ah wed yer Da an' ma' Mam wore it when she got wed tae. Dae ye like it Rosa?"

"Oh Ma, Ah love it, can Ah really wear it?"

"Aye hinny it would make me proud tae see ye in it."

"Whit's in the other parcel?"

Mary opened the second parcel, and took out a long net veil, trimmed all around in the same lace as the dress. She placed the veil on Rosa's head and then lifted a circlet of tiny handmade flowers and placed that on top to hold the veil in place.

"Ye look bonny Rosa, quick now tak it aff afore yer Da comes back, and Ah'll get it a' ready for yur big day."

The worst of the winter was past and everyone was looking forward to Rosa's wedding. There were daffodils everywhere and it was almost as though Mother Nature was celebrating too. All Mary could think about was Rosa leaving with Eddie. She was going to miss her terribly and although she tried to be brave, she was anxious about how long she would be away travelling. The wedding date was fast approaching when Rosa asked Mary if she had ever been to The Tinkers Heart.

"Aye Ah have, its lovely there."

"How far is it Mam?"

"Ah think aboot four days travel?"

"That sounds a long way Ma, Ah don't ken where that is."

"Well when wi' leave here wi'll head for Old Kilpatrick and camp up there for the night and then the next day wi' head for Helensburgh, ye'll like it there. From Helensburgh wi' go tae Arrochar. That's the last stop afore wi' head ower Hells Glen tae the Tinkers Heart. Wait till ye see it, fae the top o' the hill ye can see across the water tae the castle on the other side o' the loch. It's a big occasion, folks will come fae everywhere tae go tae a weddin' at The Tinkers Heart. There'll even be folk there that wi' dinnae ken."

"Why is it called the Tinkers Heart?"

"Some say it was a place tae honour Gypsy lads that died in a war, a rebellion a long time ago, an' then oor kind, knowin' it was a special place sometimes got wed there, some blessed their new bairns there, and some went there tae pay their respects tae their loved ones that had passed. Its aye extra special when a couple weds at The Tinkers Heart.

"Ah didnae ken it was so special Mam."

"Well yer Da thinks ye are special an' he aye wants nothin' but the best for his Rosa. It' just a wee heart shape lined wi' quartz stones that sparkle in the sunlight, but it's got a special feelin' tae it."

Later, when her father arrived back, Rosa ran to him and threw her arms around his neck.

"Whit's up wi' ye lass?"

"Nothin Da, Ah jist want ye tae know that Ah love ye and Ah'm gonnae miss ye when Ah'm away."

When Rosa let go and ran off to join her cousin, no doubt to talk of what she had learned, John stood there with tears in his eyes and his heart full of love. When he saw Mary, he asked her, "Whit was that a' aboot, did ye see her. She nearly knocked me on ma backside when she jumped into ma arms, did ye see her?"

Mary was laughing when she replied, "Aye a' saw her, she was askin' aboot The Tinkers Heart. She's excited John."

Chapter 43

Mary was crying, she could see Rosa lying flat out and there was something wrong with Rosa. Her lips were moving, but Mary couldn't hear what she was saying. Over and over, she shouted, "Whit's wrang Rosa, Ah cannae hear ye, whit's wrang?" Eddie was there too, and he looked petrified. Rosa reached out for Eddie but she was getting further away from them and Mary began to scream, but no noise came out of her mouth. She could hear her own heart beating in her chest and she could feel someone grabbing her by the shoulders, trying to pull her away, but she just wanted to get to Rosa so she fought with all her might.

"Mary! Mary!" John was shaking her and eventually she came out of her nightmare, but she still felt as though she was in it. John was alarmed and Rosa, wakened by her mother's distress, was frantically asking, "Ma, Ma whits the matter?"

"Go an' see if the water is still hot in the big kettle an' make yer Ma some tea, if no' jist bring her water." Rosa hurried off to the chitty prop and John turned to Mary.

"Whit's up Mary, whit's up?"

"Ah had a really bad dream John."

"Dae ye want tae tell me whit it wis?"

"Ah cannae remember." Mary was lying and John knew that she didn't want to talk about it so he didn't push her. He took the cup from Rosa and gave it to Mary to drink. "Dae ye think ye can sleep or dae ye want tae take a walk?" Mary was surprised that John would ask her this, she guessed that he knew she wouldn't speak of it and perhaps he thought she would speak of it outside.

"Try an' get some sleep Rosa, Ah'll just take a walk wi' yer Ma."

Rosa got back under her blankets and John and Mary threw a blanket over their shoulders and left the wagon. They walked across the field and through the trees. All was still, but for a few snorts from the horses, wondering what was going on. When they reached the river, they sat down.

"Dae ye want tae tell me whit was in yer dream?"

Mary was quiet and John was patient.

"Tell me Mary."

"Ah cannae put it into words in case Ah make it happen."

"Wis it aboot Rosa?"

Mary nodded and began to cry again.

"Ye ken Mary, ye have been anxious aboot Rosa leavin' would that no' make ye have bad dreams?"

Still crying silently, Mary nodded once more. John sat there with his arms about her; he didn't know what else to do. After a while, the both went back to the wagon and crept in quietly to avoid disturbing Rosa, but she was still awake, worried about her mother.

"Are ye better Mam?"

"Aye go back tae sleep hinny it was just a bad dream, Ah cannae even remember whit it wis aboot noo."

Relieved, Rosa settled down and was soon asleep again.

It was the dream that prompted Mary to do something that she promised herself that she wouldn't. She decided to look at the Tarot cards, but she didn't want anyone to see her. She was rummaging about in one of her boxes under the wagon when John asked her what she was looking for.

"Ah'm jist looking for ma stuff for the next fair," she said.

"Dae ye need a hand?"

"Naw John, Ah've found ma stuff. She made as if she was just airing her cloths but what she really wanted was her little bag that had her fortune telling things. She opened it up at took out the black satin wrapped Tarot cards and then she wrapped her fancy silk cloth around them and called, "Ah'm just away tae the river tae gie this silk a rinse in fresh water John."

She headed off through the trees to the river and sat on the grass. She sat there for a while with the wrapped cards between her hands, pondering on questions that she could ask, but in the end she decided that she would just let the cards speak to her. She closed her eyes, steadied her breathing, and opened the satin wrap. She took out the cardboard box, flipped open the end and took out the cards. She shuffled them in her hands mixing them thoroughly trying to keep her mind free from any thoughts, and then she fanned the cards face down in front of her. For the first time since she had been given the cards, she wished that she knew someone whom she could talk to about Tarot cards because now that she was doing it for herself, she was afraid of doing something wrong and misreading them. She passed her right hand over the cards, about two inches above them, trying to sense which one she should choose first. She drew one card towards her and apprehensively turned it over. It was the High Priestess. That was one card that she didn't fully understand and couldn't interpret its meaning. She wasn't aware that the High Priestess represented hidden information, things that she was not yet meant to know about. Because she didn't understand its meaning, seeing this card did not worry her. She had no concept that this card could bring good or bad so she had no reason to fear it. The next card that she drew was the one with two Cups and she smiled happily when she saw this because it was two young lovers exchanging promises. It was plainly depicting Rosa and Eddie's wedding day. The third that she drew was a major card, the one with the wheel on it. This card made her feel content because the illustration was a large wagon wheel. *'That'll be the journey goin' tae or leavin' the weddin'.'* She drew a third card toward herself and turned it over to reveal the card with ten Coins. The illustration was of lots of people, children and adults, *'That must be the weddin' party,'* she thought to herself, and gathering the cards together, wrapped them in the satin and gave her silk cloth a quick rinse in the river, just in case John noticed. When she went back, she draped her silk cloth over the wheel to let it dry. She was much happier now and content to believe that she had only had the dream because she was worrying about missing Rosa.

Chapter 44

Over the next few weeks, leading up to the wedding, Mary was more content and happy, and they were all looking forward to travelling to The Tinkers Heart. The whole camp could talk of nothing else, but Rosa and Eddie's forthcoming wedding. Those women that could sew were making pretty skirts, tops, or dresses, or cutting cloth into squares to fasten their hair. Those who couldn't sew well were bothering others to help them. The men as usual took all this frantic activity in their stride and left the women to steam their better clothes over boiling kettles. They would wear a waistcoat with a white shirt and colourful neckerchief, but it was women's work to organise that. They paid heed to the horses and the wagons making sure that the wheels were in good condition to make the journey without mishap. Two men would stay behind and miss the wedding celebrations. They would look after the horses or anything else during the time everyone was away. Some made plans to collect provisions or things that they could re-sell at fairs on the return journey. All was well, for a little while anyway, and then just days before they were about to leave, Mary had the dream again. This time John was quick to react and woke Mary before Rosa was disturbed.

"Will ye tell me the dream Mary?"

Mary didn't want to share the dream with John because it would worry him sick. There was no point in them both being worried, and she didn't want to put it into words.

"Ah cannae remember it John."

John knew he was wasting his time trying to force Mary to share the dream if she didn't want to, so he just sat comforting her. It was the best that he could do. The following days were difficult for Mary. She was unsettled and afraid to close her eyes at night in case the dream returned. She was pale and had dark circles round her eyes. She had lost her appetite and even Rosa was beginning to notice that all was not well with her mother.

"Ah'm worried aboot ma Mam," she said to her father.

"Dinnae be, she's fine, she's jist no' sleepin' well, she'll miss ye when yer away, but it'll no' be that long till yer back again and a' this grief will jist be a memory. Ye'll see, after the weddin she'll be fine, jist let her be."

Finally, the day arrived when they were ready to set off. As always, they started their journey at first light. Mary was anxious but she was excited too and she was hopeful that now the journey was beginning she would be too tired to dream. They stopped as planned at some spare ground in Old Kilpatrick and camped there for the night. There was a good campfire burning brightly, boxes out to sit around it, and that was all the reason they needed to sing songs and drink a few beers. The next day, another early rise, and they were on their way. Their journey took them along the River Clyde past Dumbarton Castle, through Cardross and then to Helensburgh. They were beginning to see other travellers in the distance and Rosa wondered if Eddie was among them. That night they camped and partied and everyone was enjoying the excursion.

By the time they reached Arrochar the following day, Rosa's excitement was bubbling over. Mary however was still a bit unsettled. Rosa was sitting up in front with her father and Mary was sitting inside, the rolling of the wagon making her sleepy. Before she lay down, she took the opportunity to draw one Tarot card. It was the one with six Cups. She sat quietly looking at the illustration. There were two people in it; one looked older, possibly a child, the other could be an older child or an adult because the second was stooped over presenting the smaller one with flowers. She realised that it looked like a reunion. She felt relieved that it was a good card for she knew that going to a wedding she was bound to meet people from her past. She was glad that the card did not show something that she should worry about.

Finally, they arrived amid the great gathering of Gypsies camping at the bottom of the hill, and more arriving all the time, but there was a surprise in store for Mary, one that she hadn't seen coming. All her instincts were on Rosa's wedding and the dreams that she had been having, but this surprise would bring her great joy. People were moving about saying hello to folks they hadn't seen for a while, others were sitting around the fire and at the edge of the crowd Mary saw a woman staring at her and smiling. At first, all she saw was a familiar face, and she smiled nodded then looked away trying to place who she was, and then in a moment of realisation, her heart almost stopped when she recognised the face. "Johnny! Johnny!" she called using his name as she had when they were young. She was crying tears of joy as she started to run, she could hardly get the words out, "Its ma sister, its ma sister."

Coralina and Mary ran to each other both crying, both hugging, and then drawing back to look into each other's faces. It was a touching sight to see. John was grinning from ear to ear, and had to wait his turn to embrace his sister-in-law. It was a few moments before Mary and John realised that there were others standing close by. Robert stood off to one side waiting and then it was just a melee as Coralina introduced her family; her grown up daughter Emily, with her husband Edward and their young son Paul.

"Oh! ma sisters a granny!" laughed Mary as she swept young Paul into her arms smothering him with kisses. John and Robert shook hands and embraced warmly.

"How are ye Johnny?"

"Aye it's a while since Ah was called Johnny, she only says Johnny when she's emotional," he laughed, nodding at Mary.

Mary embraced her niece Emily, and introduced Rosa to her Aunt Coralina, her Uncle Robert, and her little cousin Paul. For the next few hours, they shared what each had been doing.

"Ah never thought this day would come Coralina, ma heart is jist burstin' wi' happiness. How far have ye come, how did ye ken?"

"We've had the rent o' a farm near Oban for the last ten years. Paul's family are mindin' it for us while we're here. This was too guid a chance tae miss." The two sisters, grown women now, sat together holding hands, and reminiscing "Robert was worried that he wouldnae be welcome, but Ah told him time heals. Ah hope Rosa and her fella come by the farm when they are on their travels for they will be welcome an' we're anxious tae get tae know them better."

Her Aunt Coralina fascinated Rosa, and she thought about the stories she had heard of her running away with the miller's son. She didn't have to think long about whether or not she would have done the same for Eddie because she knew that if they were separated she would run to him in a heartbeat. She found the opportunity to talk to her cousin Emily about it later. "Aye, Ah know the story well, Ma an' Da have talked about it afore. It's really romantic, but it must have been hard for them tae, leaving family an' the like. Whit aboot yer fella, Ah hear his name's Eddie?"

"Aye, an' Ah cannae wait tae see him, but it's no' lucky afore the weddin'."

The two families enjoyed sharing stories and renewing their relationship and Mary was happy that others from the various camps had accepted and welcomed their arrival. Mary felt a deep sense of contentment, which was something that she had not anticipated.

"Are ye still tellin fortunes Mary?" asked Coralina.

"Aye, an' Ah saw this in the Tarot cards but Ah didnae realise it was you comin' back. Ye could have knocked me o'er wi' a feather, it was such a shock tae see yer face in the crowd." They both laughed and shared their memories of that first moment.

Chapter 45

Mary felt sure that tonight, the night before her beloved Rosa's wedding, she would sleep well, and it would be a deep contented sleep, but that was not to be. The temptation to look at the Tarot was just too great. John was sound asleep, the effect of too many beers; Rosa was exhausted from all the excitement and travel, and she was sleeping soundly too. Mary slipped out of her bed and rummaged in her bag for her Tarot Cards. She threw a shawl over her shoulders, picked up a blanket to sit on, and slipped out of the wagon. She looked around to see if anyone was about, but all was quiet.

She slipped away from all the other wagons and sat quietly under a tree. She settled herself on the grass sitting on the blanket that she had taken with her. It was a cool still night and the moon was full as she opened the satin cloth and placed it on the blanket in front of her. She held her Tarot cards in her hands and thought of the wedding. She fanned the cards in a semi circle, face down on the satin cloth, paused, and then choose one, the six Cups, she smiled knowing exactly what that meant. She sat for a little while thinking about the meeting with her sister and her family and then she choose another card. This time it was the two Cups and once again, she smiled because this was Rosa and Eddie making their promise to each other.

She wondered why she was torturing herself because each time she drew a card her stomach churned with fear, the fear that she might see something that would frighten or worry her. She just wanted to know that everything would be all right in Rosa's future, but Tarot never speaks to please, Tarot shows everything that can happen, good or bad, and it's up to the individual to make the best of changing circumstances and events. Tarot can tell you that something is wrong, but it seldom actually tells you exactly how this will occur, and often, there is nothing that you can do to change things.

She turned another card and it was The Wheel again. She was drawing the same cards, but that was no surprise either because she understood that her situation was the same as it had been the last time she looked, but she wanted to know more, to go further. Bracing herself she took another and this time it was the Eight Branches. She raised her eyebrows and muttered to herself, "That's different, Ah ken whit that is, that's Rosa and Eddie travellin here an' there."

She felt more confident now and took another card, and this time she was thrilled because the card she turned over was the Empress, the young pregnant woman. "A bairn!" she exclaimed to herself as she placed her hands over her heart, this was her dearest wish for Rosa because she knew that Rosa wanted to be a mother. There was no stopping her now, and she took another card and this time she wasn't so pleased. She had drawn the Nine Swords and she knew that this was not a good card, but as is the way when faced with a card that you don't like you are almost compelled to draw another, she did. It was the Ten Swords and her heart was racing.

Her heart was conflicting with her common sense and she had to take another. Things did not get any better for the next card that she turned over was the Three Swords a red heart pierced by three Swords. This was bad, and she had to keep going, but when she turned the next card over, she wished that she had stayed in bed, and remained ignorant, for she had drawn The Tower. She was shaking now, and all her worst fears were materialising before her eyes. She had to choose another, hoping that the next card would assure her that all would be well. She had to bite her knuckles to keep from screaming because the card that she drew meant a funeral. She did not know whose funeral it would be, but she was sure that what she had seen would come to pass, and it would affect her family.

She cried for a long time, but eventually she had to go back to her wagon before anyone woke up. She put the cards away and vowed that she would never read for herself again and lay down on the bed beside John. He stirred and whispered, "Where have ye been?"

"The dunny," she lied.

She stayed awake and got up first thing to wake Rosa and to help her to get ready for her special day. She managed to carry herself and hide her fears, but her emotions spilled over and anyone who saw her tears assumed they were just the tears of the mother of the bride, dreading her only child leaving to begin a new life. Rosa was ready and looked beautiful in her dress with the long veil cascading down her back.

"Ah'll see ye at the top o' the hill Rosa, yer Da will bring ye up. There's a fair crowd gathered tae wish ye well hinny." She took Rosa in her arms and held her tight, tears streaming down her face, and then she turned, her heart breaking, and left the wagon.

"Ah'm ready Da," said Rosa. She was glowing as all brides are. John looked at his daughter and said, "Yer as beautiful as yer Ma was on her weddin' day. Ah'm right proud o' ye an' Ah'm happy for ye, but it will break our hearts tae see ye go."

Rosa hugged her father, "Ah love ye Da an' Ah'll miss ye tae, but it'll no' be that long afore we're back at the Green an' then there might be a wee Rosa's tae sit on yer knee."

They both held each other and laughed together at the lovely picture Rosa's words had portrayed, neither of them knowing what would really happen.

Mary and Coralina stood at the top of the Hill on the edge of The Tinkers Heart with her family beside Eddie's parent's Nellie and Edward. Eddie and Tam were waiting for the bride to appear and the sound of cheering told them that she had started to make her way up the hill.

Mary stood and watched with a deep fear in her heart, pretending that all was well but she knew it wasn't. Someone she loved would die and she knew that this death would be untimely but, she could not tell who it would be, or when it would happen. The crowds parted and she saw John bringing Rosa to the Tinkers Heart, leading her to her destiny, and she cried for what was to come.

The End

The Wooden Rose, 1889
Chapter 1
A Travellers' Camp near Glasgow Green

"Hurry Rosa yer Da wants tae leave in ten minutes."

"Ah'm hurryin Ma, Ah'm goin' as fast as Ah can," said Rosa. She could hardly think straight as she hopped about pulling on her black boots and fastening the laces. She was excited at the thought of seeing Eddie again, tall handsome Eddie with his dark curly hair. She couldn't remember the first time that she saw him, but she had known all her life that he was hers. The last time they had met was at Musselburgh Fair when all the travellers got together to reunite, share good times, meet up with family and friends, and trade with each other.

She was sixteen now, her raven black hair came half way down her back and her green eyes shone under long dark eyelashes. Soon she would marry, and the only boy she would marry was Eddie. Her young heart fluttered when she thought of him. Eddie was so clever with his hands. He was an artist with wood, he didn't just make things, he made beautiful things. He made shelves for his Mam's precious ornaments, and he had carved the shapes himself and painted flowers and ivy down the sides. He made clothes pegs to sell round the doors too, but that was different.

Rosa carried a wooden token in her pocket. When no one was watching, she would take the token out of her pocket, look at it, and think of Eddie. Her Eddie had made it for her when he was fourteen and she was only ten. He had carved a lovely rose on the surface of it, and each time she looked at it or held it in her pocket, she thought of her Eddie. It was just a simple piece of wood, flat, about two inches across and half an inch thick, but she could feel the love in it. She was never without it and had never shown it to anyone. It was something special to her and Eddie.

"Hurry up lass," her father called as he hitched the horses to the front of the wagon.

"Stop yer day dreamin' and get up on the wagon."

She loved her Father; he was a big strong man with black curly hair, arms like tree trunks and hands like shovels. They were taking horses he had bred and trained to trade at the fair.

They were leaving Glasgow today, and it would be two or three days before they would reach Musselburgh. Soon they would meet up with friends and family. There would be horseracing and reunions. The young girls would be posing and showing off new dresses that their mothers or grannies had sewn for them, and young men, boys really, would be strutting and acting manly. Everything had to be perfect in this very proud culture and each family would vie to be and have the best; everyone went to Musselburgh Fair, it was traditional.

Mary's Mother had taught her how to scrub, clean, stack, and stow everything that they needed in, on, and around the big wagon. Pots and pans hung from the sides of the wagon and sang a merry note as they travelled. Everything was spic and span, for they were fussy about cleanliness.

Each night after a long day in the wagon, John would stop in the same place that his family had done for generations before him. There were trees to shelter the tent that they would put down to sleep in, because the wagon would be full of things that they needed when they were travelling and things that they could sell or swop. There was lush grass for the horses to graze on, and a running stream nearby for fresh water.

As soon as the wagon stopped, Mary and Rosa would jump down and begin to unpack the things they would need. They always carried wood to start the fire and Rosa would set that out. Mary would gather the slats from where they were stored under the wagon and she would use these to build a floor for their tent. They often erected their big tent if they were staying somewhere for a week or more, but when they were travelling, the smaller tent was fine for their needs.

With the fire started, Rosa helped her mother while John roped off an area and untied the trading horses from the wagon before turning them loose in the secured space. The lead horses were unhitched and turned loose with the others.

Their two terriers ran around excited to be free, but their big lurcher Suzie was tethered safely, with just enough rope to wander a short distance, otherwise she would have been off exploring and hunting for game. Mary set up the chitty prop, a three legged cast iron pyramid shape with a large hook for holding a pot over a fire, as Rosa fetched the water. Fire lit, kettle on to boil water for tea, and animals tended to, they could now sit and rest a while under the stars.

This is how they travelled; always following familiar routes and stopping at familiar places, each place would hold memories of previous times and previous journeys. Each morning they would rise early, feed the animals and stow all their belongings back in and around the wagon and continue on their journey.

As they neared Musselburgh, they would catch sight of others travelling to the fair and there was a stir of excitement in the air. Finally, they arrived and lined up in a queue to enter the grassy field. They waved and called to other families arriving or queuing. They could see the Morrison's, the Wilson's, and the Boswell's and there were others approaching that they would know, and some of their own family, their second cousins, the Stewarts, would be there too.

Rosa could hardly contain herself.

"Mind yer ane business Rosa and dinnae let yer Da catch you ey'in up these boys," her mother whispered.

Rosa was horrified and embarrassed "I'm no ey'in up boys, Ah was jist lookin' for…"

"I know who yer lookin for," replied her mother. "It's that Eddie McGuigan. A guid boy mind ye, but dinnae show yer keen."

Rosa blushed and her ears were burning with embarrassment.

"I like him Ma, he asked me to remember him last year."

"Wheesht, here's yer Da!"

Chapter 2

It was a hard life being a traveller, but it was a good life and a life that they loved. Mary, Rosa's mother, was a good-looking woman of average height and build, but it was her dark hair and eyes and her self-confidence that made her stand out. She always knew what to do and got on with doing it. There was nothing shy or retiring about Mary, and that was what her husband Johnny loved most about her.

Mary always got what she wanted, and in her younger days, she had had a nasty mean streak about her, but that was before she and John got together. She was more understanding and tolerant as an adult than she had ever been. He was known everywhere for his knowledge and skill with the horses, and it was probably that same skill that he used on Mary, settling her when she was about to fly off in a tantrum, or calming her when she was agitated.

Mary had two loves in her life; Rosa, her darling daughter and John, her big strong husband who in spite of his outward stern appearance, had a soft kindly heart and would do anything to help another. John didn't take any nonsense from anyone though, and could drive a hard bargain making sure that he got the best of any deal.

The sun was shining as John was unhitching his horses from the wagon while Mary and Rosa began to fetch the makings for their tent. They unloaded slats of wood from underneath the wagon for the big tent and with the help of nearby children; they began to put it together.

The wooden shapes for the floor went down first to establish the hexagon shape, leaving an uncovered space in the centre for the stove that they carried with them. Other children would dash in to help, and each would hold a length of wood while Mary and Rosa secured poles to the tops, holding the frame together and maintaining the shape.

There was lots of laughing and teasing as the children supported the frame, then Rosa and Mary, standing on either side of the frame began to throw and catch a big tarpaulin cover up and over. The tarpaulin had cords attached at various points to make the job of pulling the cover over easier.

Often they collapsed on the ground laughing and rubbing their aching arms from the effort of the task. Coloured cloths were fetched from the wagon and draped on the inside walls, and rugs were laid on the boards.

Finally, the stove was set up in the middle of the floor, and a long pipe attached to fit directly under the smoke hole at the top of the tent. The stove would keep them warm at night and with a kettle at the ready, there was always a cuppa for anyone who called in.

Outside, Mary set up the chitty prop, and young Rosa fetched the wood to start the fire. Before long, a large cast iron pot of soup or stew would be hanging from the chitty prop. Food was always cooked outside, keeping the tent free from smells and spills. There was always plenty to share among friends and family members.

The muscles in Eddie's arms bulged below the rolled up sleeves of his red and black checked shirt as he set up at the fair though he was oblivious to the admiring glances from some of the young girls. Thick dark hair framed his handsome face tanned with the summer sun. All he could think about was seeing his Rosa.

Eddie was a hard worker and talented too, he just put his head down and got on with things, and when he was working with wood, his mind would drift off into his plans for the future, the future he saw with Rosa. He knew that he was going to marry Rosa and that they would make a family together.

He could see it in his mind's eye as though it had already happened. A big family, boys and girls; the girls would help their Mam and marry well and the boys, well they would work with him. He would teach them how to look at a windfall tree trunk that others would pass by, and he would show them how to read the wood and see what things they could make from it. He would teach his sons how to create beautiful pieces of work that the wealthy would have on show in their fancy homes.

He was twenty now and had been learning to hone his gift for carpentry since he was a child, starting off just whittling bits of wood into little ornaments, making clothes pegs and selling them door to door. Eddie progressed to making three-legged stools and by the time he was in his teens, he was making special pieces; wooden spoons for stirring the pot, bowls, beautifully turned, carved and polished, containers with lids for sugar and tea, children's pull along toys, garden furniture, and wooden ornaments that the wealthy were happy to purchase. He had made good money and saved every penny he could. He was going to speak to Rosa's Father when he saw him next. He knew he could give her a good life with the money he had put by and his plans for the future.

Rosa was helping her mother to set up their camp when out of the corner of her eye she saw Eddie approaching. She glanced quickly at her mother as her cheeks began to glow bright red.

"Ma," she whispered.

"I see him."

Rosa kept her eyes downcast as Eddie approached, and not once did Eddie look in her direction.

"Excuse me, Aunty Mary," he said, as was the custom in his culture, "Could Ah speak tae Uncle John?"

"Ye've never had a problem speakin' tae him before Eddie, dae ye think ye might have wan the noo."

Eddie shuffled his feet showing his discomfort, but he could see that Mary was teasing him. Just at that moment, Uncle John appeared back from chatting to other family members who had just arrived.

"Eddie," he said, looking at Eddie sternly under heavy dark bushy eyebrows. Eddie's stomach might have been churning, but that was no comparison to what John was feeling. He knew in his soul what was coming, but he wasn't ready to let the apple of his eye, his little Rosa, go that easily.

"Uncle John, a word."

"Well, spit it out and Ah'm warnin' ye, Ah'm nae in the best o moods,"

Eddie bristled at John's sharp tone. "Ah could come back an' see ye."

"Jist git on wi' it lad, Ah've things tae dae."

Eddie drew himself up to his full height, stuck out his chin and his chest, looked his uncle in the eye, and said, "It's an important thing Ah wish tae speak tae ye about, but if ye huvnae time tae be civil Ah'll come back."

"Jist haud yer horses' lad, ye got me on the wrong foot. Ah feel Ah know whit ye want to speak tae me about an it's churnin' in ma' stomach. Say yer piece."

John stepped closer to Eddie to put his arm over his shoulder. Surprised by the fact that Eddie was taller than he thought, he wondered why he hadn't noticed, he was dealing with a full-grown man now, but in his mind and heart, to John, Eddie was still a lad. He did what any other proud man would do to avoid his embarrassment, and stuck his hands in his pockets.

"Let's take a walk," he said to the young man.

They walked in silence away from the hustle and bustle of everyone chatting and setting up for the fair. Both men were a generation apart, but both with the same person in mind. Finally, Eddie stopped, looked his uncle in the eye as he looked back at him, took a deep breath, and said, "Ah've loved yer lass since Ah was wee, an' she was just a babe. Ah've watched her grow and become the beautiful lass like the flower ye named her for. The past four years Ah've worked and saved and every penny is for Rosa's future."

His uncle fixed his gaze on him, just stared at him silently saying nothing while his mind went into overdrive.

The words poured out of Eddie like a desperate plea. "Ah'm askin' ye for her hand man," he almost shouted.

John stared at him, the fear becoming a reality, the pain of that reality written on his face.

"Same time, same place, next year, if ye still feel the same ye can ask her yirsel, an' if she agrees ye can marry on the first day of May at the Tinkers Heart."

Eddie's face lit up, he punched the air and did a dance right there in front of John.

"She'll say aye, I know it."

Eddie ran off back to his pitch and as John walked back to his wagon he watched Rosa helping her mother.

"Ah've jist seen that young Eddie," he said to no one in particular, but really so that Rosa could hear. "Turned into a fine man," he said, and climbed into his wagon where he poured himself a whisky, sat down and stared at the wall in front of him, seeing nothing but the memories of his daughter's birth and early years. Thinking of her blossoming into a beautiful woman, he wondered how he would feel to let her go, to start her own life. When Mary came in his face was wet with tears, she sat beside him and reached over, placed her hand in his and gave it a comforting squeeze. No words were necessary between them for she understood how he felt.

Chapter 3

The atmosphere at the Musselburgh Fair was electric and exciting. Friends and families merged and mingled, lurchers and terriers barked, children played, and the men did what men do. They traded horses, ponies, and dogs, showed their Persian rugs, tin pots and other crafts and looked on proudly at their sons and daughters. They exchanged wares and ideas on how to make a living, places to go to sell their wares, and places to avoid.

The men were a sight to see, all wearing jackets, flat caps, and often waistcoats below. Shirts tucked into dark trousers were clean and white with no collars, but a colourful patterned scarf at the neck. They all stood in a group making loud exchanges as they performed the almost religious ceremony of trading and bargaining. With each offer or counter offer, the men would slap hands, but even that had a specific format. A spit on the palm and a full-handed slap was a deal, but if only fingertips slapped then the bargaining would continue. The seller held his hand out asking, and the buyer would state his offer and slap. The men had idiosyncrasies that would give each other clues to what they were thinking. Some would touch their caps between slaps. Some would turn and pretend to be walking away. Others would complain loudly and throw accusations, but there was always a bargain sealed.

A horse buyer would gradually make his way around so that he could stand directly in front of the horse seller and pretend to be mildly interested. He might stroke the horse, have a look at its teeth, pick up a leg, and feel its joints. The seller would know by this that a sale was imminent and the bargaining would begin.

"Guid enough horse." (Slap)

"What'll ye offer?" (Slap)

"Forty an' not a penny more." (Slap)

"Ah yer jokin' man; Sixty an' not a penny less." (Slap)

"Sixty? Yer a robber Ah'll give forty-five." (Slap)

"Fifty an' ye have a deal."

A spit on the palm and a hand held out, a spit on the palm and a full-handed slap and the deal done.

"Now gimmie a penny back for luck," the buyer would say, and as was the custom, the seller would give the buyer a coin or two and the bargain was sealed.

Young men would stand by and watch the exchanges learning the craft, and then they would discuss among themselves the skills or failings that they had witnessed.

"Aye, he couldha got cheaper," or "He couldha got more if he hung oot a bit."

They in their way would take on board lessons that they had learned, that they would use themselves when their time came. Overloaded with testosterone, they rode their horses bareback, raced each other, and performed tricks to impress the girls. The girls giggled and looked coy and pretended to be unimpressed by the boys.

In the middle of all this, the women gossiped and bragged about their children while they skinned hares for the pot. Some chopped vegetables and fetched split peas and lentils that had been soaked overnight. Dumplings and potatoes added to the stew ensured that there was plenty of filling food all.

Everyone gathered around the campfires and shared the food that had been prepared earlier in the day, and then out would come the pipes and the tobacco for a relaxing smoke. Some of the old grannies would smoke a clay pipe and ponder while they remembered and shared stories about their own younger days.

Those that could play a tune would fetch a musical instrument, fiddles would be fine-tuned, flutes prepared, and box accordions stretched and squeezed. Some would have the traditional Celtic drum the bodhran, and others would be happy with a tambourine or a set of spoons. Others still, with no instrument, would sit open legged on a wooden box and tap a rhythm on the box to accompany the music.

The women and girls would dance and twirl on boards laid out for the purpose; boxes were set out around the space for others to sit on and participate, playing an instrument, or singing, or just enjoying the spectacle. The atmosphere was warm, friendly and exciting, the smell of wood smoke from the fire scented the air, and the night was clear and bright under the full of the moon.

Eddie and Rosa sat side by side quietly chatting. She felt pretty in her new dress, with its full drindle skirt that she had helped her mother to sew. With her head down, she studied the bright blues and reds of the fabric as she wondered what to say to Eddie. They both felt different now that Eddie had declared his intentions. He told Rosa what her father had said. For now, they could sit together or hold hands, perhaps even sneak a kiss if no one was watching, but all eyes would be on them now for it's the traveller's way to be chaste before marriage.

After the fair, the only way that they could communicate would be by messages passed by word of mouth, or for those that could read and write, and at that time, there were only a few with this skill, a note. It would be twenty years before a public telephone appeared, but there were so many of their kind that it was always possible to pass a message from one to another by those who were moving from place to place.

"Ah'm sixteen now, next August when we come to the fair next year Ah'll be seventeen. If ma Da says we can marry on the first of May Ah'll be nearly eighteen an' you'll be nearly twenty-two. It all seems so far away," she said as she looked into his dark brown eyes. His dark curly hair fell over his brow and curled over his collar at the back. They were so entranced with each other that at first they were unaware of the chant.

"Rosa, Rosa, Rosa, give us a dance."

She giggled and got up and moved to the centre of the circle and gave an exaggerated bow. Everyone knew Rosa loved to dance, and had she not been so engrossed in conversation with Eddie, she would have been the first to start the dancing.

The fiddle stuck up, the flutes joined, and the circle of folk began to clap in time to the music. The bodhran beat out its rhythm and Rosa threw her head back with a laugh. She began to dance a jig, her feet matching the rhythm on the boards. She held her skirts up a tiny bit and her black laced boots were visible below them. Round and round the circle she danced, skipping and twirling, the sound of her heels joining the beat of the music, her dark hair flying behind her and then she began to pull other girls into the circle where they joined in the fun of the dance. She was so happy that she wished she was married to Eddie now, and that this could be the beginning of their life together.

As the night ended, a singing voice filled the air and Rosa knew that it was her Father. He was singing the song that his Father used to sing to his Mother.

Johnny was born in a mansion doon in the county o' Clare

Rosie was born by a roadside somewhere in County Kildare

Destiny brought them together on the road to Killorglan

One day in her bright tasty shawl, she was singing

And she stole his young heart away

For she sang...

Meet me tonight by the campfire

Come with me over the hill.

Let us be married tomorrow

Please let me whisper 'I will'

What if the neighbours are talkin'

Who cares if yer friends stop and stare

Ye'll be proud to be married to Rosie,

Who was reared on the roads of Kildare.

Think of the parents who reared ye

Think of the family name

How can ye marry a gypsy?

Oh whit a terrible shame

Parents and friends stop yer pleading

Don't worry aboot my affair

For Ah've fallen in love wi' a gypsy

Who was reared on the roads of Kildare?

Johnny went down from his mansion

Just as the sun had gone doon

Turning his back on his kinfolk

Likewise, his dear native toon

Facing the roads of old Ireland

Wi' a gypsy he loved so sincere

When he came to the light of the campfire

These are the words he did hear

Meet me tonight by the campfire

Come wi' me over the hill.

Let us be married tomorrow

Please let me whisper 'I will'

What if the neighbours are talkin?

Who cares if yer friends stop and stare

Ye'll be proud to be married to Rosie,

Who was reared on the roads of Kildare.

Chapter 4

Travelling families rarely built their own wagons, but Eddie's skills with wood enabled him to do just that, and he wanted Rosa to have the best that he could make. A farmer on the outskirts of Glasgow sold him a small piece of land; Eddie fenced it and built a shed. Whenever he passed a wood yard or sawmill on his travels, he would call in to see what they had. From time to time, he purchased timbers to lay aside so that he could build a wagon for Rosa that he would present to her on their wedding day.

Most of the wagons that he was familiar with had a narrow floors and sides that sloped outwards, but he had seen some showmen at one of the fairs. Their wagons had a wider floor, were taller with a slightly pitched roof, and windows on both sides. He was going to build that style of wagon for himself and Rosa to begin their new life. He had been gathering oak, ash, walnut, and pine and he would use all of it to make the finest wagon that anyone had ever seen. In his mind's eye, he could see the travelling home he would build. It might take a year or more, but he would work night and day if he had to.

Eddie shared his parent's wagon, and he was proud of the work that he had done on it, taking it from a standard style to something that turned heads wherever they went. Their wagon had a narrow floor encased between tall wheels making it safer for travelling over streams and rough ground.

The original body of the wagon had curved support struts covered in a thick canvas. Eddie had remodelled the original interior making cabinets for storage from the floor to waist height. In the centre of the cabinets, he fitted a small pot-bellied stove with a chimney flue running up to the top emerging from one side to allow smoke from the stove to escape.

Eddie fashioned the canvas cover, cutting it into sections that overlapped for protection from the weather and on fine days, sections could be tied back to let in light and air. At the front and back, he added porches with carved side brackets and then painted fancy scroll patterns along the brackets. He cut the door in two halves, allowing the top half of the door to be open while the bottom remained closed, and the addition of strong ropes to the steps allowed the family to raise or lower them at will. Pots, pans, and other necessities hung from racks he fitted along the outsides. The intricately carved wood was brightly painted and polished until it shone like glass. Gold leaf added the final additions to his work of art.

Eddie's parents, Edward and Nellie, were very proud of their only child. Eddie travelled with his parents, but he had his own horse and cart that he used to carry his wares. He spent his days going from door to door selling what he had and when they weren't travelling to fairs he would ride over to his shed and work until late, building the wagon for his Rosa.

Eddie and Rosa managed to see each other now and then when they were attending the same fairs, but Rosa was sad every time they had to part. By the following August when they returned to Musselburgh Fair Eddie had finished building the wagon, and he would spend the next months after the fair painting and decorating the outside, so that it would be completed in time for their wedding in May.

Rosa was watching for him coming, her stomach churning with eager anticipation. She caught sight of him as he jumped down from his cart and they ran to each other. He picked her up in his arms and swung her around in a circle before setting her down and looking into her eyes.

"Aye lass, yer as beautiful as I remember, have ye missed me?"

"Oh Eddie, Ah thought of ye every day."

The thought of parting even for a moment was unbearable for both of them.

Later that day, when everyone had seen to their horses and set up their tents, Eddie took Rosa for a walk along the River Esk. They sat on a log by a tree on the banks of the river, and Eddie took Rosa's hands in his and looked into her eyes.

"On the first of May next year we'll marry above Loch Fyne at the Tinkers Heart, and Ah promise Ah'll love ye forever Rosa if ye'll have me."

He reached into his pocket, took out a beautiful gold ring with tiny diamonds in the shape of a flower, and placed the ring on her finger.

"Aye Eddie, Ah will marry ye," Rosa said, and he kissed the happy tears on her face.

The festive air was richer that night by the announcement that Rosa Stewart was to marry Eddie McGuigan, and people came up to offer their best wishes to the happy couple. Many promised that they would make the long journey to The Tinkers Heart at Loch Fyne to share and witness the marriage between the two families. When the fair was over the loving couple had to part and go their separate ways, and it was likely that the next time that they would see each other would be at the Tinkers Heart on their wedding day

Rosa spent the following months gathering and making things for her bottom drawer. Every girl had to have a bottom drawer, more often it was a trunk, and she would keep things in it for her own travelling home when she married.

She would often open it and look through her things, handling them with love and care and thinking of what it would be like to be Eddie's wife. Inside her trunk were white linen pillowcases and sheets, hand laced by pulling the ten weft threads an inch below the hems, and then gathering the warp threads together using embroidery silks creating patterns of little crosses around each edge.

She knew how to do that too now that her Mother had taught her. Another set of linen trimmed with lace lay in the trunk, and she knew that when she married there would be more gifts from travelling families everywhere. There was a lovely china tea set handed down to use for very special occasions, and some small ornaments that she had collected over the years.

Pride of place among her things was a box that Eddie had made and given to her when they parted on the last day of the Musselburgh Fair. It was about eight inches long, four inches wide, and four inches deep. Eddie had carved the top of the box with fancy scrollwork, and anyone seeing it would recognise Eddie's work immediately. It was a beautiful keepsake and looking at it reminded Rosa how much they loved each other.

As Rosa thought of Eddie, his mind would drift to her while he concentrated on painting the new wagon. Inside he had built storage cupboards in every conceivable space.

His cousin Tam had given him a hand to position the cast iron stove that he built against a wall, which he had faced with tiles to prevent the wood from overheating. The flue ran up the wall and out at the top of the side and a tiled slab beneath the stove protected the floor. The top of the stove had a flat surface so that Rosa could boil a pot of soup or a kettle for tea on the colder days, for in the summer time a campfire outside and the chitty pot was preferred.

Eddie had thought everything through before he started his build and he was not disappointed with the result. It was just one large room, but Eddie had created pull out panels so that the room would divide into sections. There was plenty of room for two comfortable chairs and a table. He could see himself and Rosa sitting there enjoying a chat or a cuppa after a days' work.

He carved and painted the facings on the shelves and cupboards with several coats of paint, and the outside of the wagon was similarly carved, decorated, and finished with gold leaf. Boxes and racks fitted to the sides meant they could carry or store their wares, their cooking utensils, and anything else that they would need while they were on the road.

Eddie had cleverly created an overhang at the front of the wagon so that whoever was leading the horses wouldn't get wet on rainy days, and another at the back so that anyone sitting at the back would benefit from the shelter. He would hitch a trailer behind the wagon filled with the tools of his trade, horse feed, and their tent.

He was very proud of his achievement, and planned to present it to Rosa during the festivities after the wedding ceremony. He tried to picture her reaction to seeing it for the first time. On the journey to Loch Fyne, the new wagon would be concealed under a heavy tarpaulin so that Rosa would be the first to see it.

Chapter 5

Four weeks before the wedding Mary brought out a box and opened it to reveal the dress that she had worn on her wedding day. The fine cotton lawn fabric was a very pale blue colour, with tiny sprigs of white daisies all over it. The scooped neckline had a delicate blue ribbon drawstring, finished with a trim of hand-made lace and this matched the cuffs of the long sleeves. Rosa tried it on and looked down at herself. The hem of the dress came to just above her ankles and over the dress was a white lace pinafore, which came to a point at the front just above the hem.

Smiling and with tears in her eyes Mary unwrapped a brown paper parcel, to reveal a long net veil which was trimmed from top to bottom in the same lace which matched the dress. A circlet of tiny handmade flowers held the veil in place. Mary held a looking glass in front of Rosa and she gazed at her reflection.

"Oh Ma, Ah look, Ah look beautiful." She said this as though she had no idea how lovely she was.

"Ye are that Rosa, yer the most bonny bride Ah have ever seen. Quick now tak it aff afore yer Da comes back, and Ah'll get it a' ready for yur big day."

There was no need for wedding invitations in the travelling community; by now, everyone would know that they were to be married at the Tinkers Heart, and as was the custom, hundreds of travellers began to make the journey during the last week in April. Some would make their way over the 'Rest and be Thankful' turning into Gleann Mor and over Hells Glen to reach the Tinkers Heart, and those that came from the direction of Inveraray would come by Cairndow and the shores of Loch Fyne.

When the camp was set up everyone prepared for the feasting and celebration. They had all brought gifts for Rosa and Eddie; some brought linen, rugs, pots and pans or dishes, others would give the couple an envelope filled with cash to give them a good start in life.

On the first morning of May, Eddie leading the way, they all climbed to the top of the hill, and up to the Tinkers Heart, which had quartz crystals laid out on the ground to form the heart shape. There was an air of celebration and laughter and some sang as they climbed.

There were herrin' heeds an' bits o' breed,

Herrin' heeds an' haddies O,

Herrin' heeds an' bits o' breed,

To carry on the weddin O

Voices rang out the chorus line

Drum-mer a-doo a-doo a-day,

Drum-mer a-doo a dad-din O

Drum-mer a-doo a-doo a-day,

Hurrah for the Tinker's weddin O

It was a fine day, the sun was shining as Rosa and her Father followed the party climbing through the gorse and the heather. The scent of bog myrtle filled the air as their clothes brushed past the wild shrubs. John held Rosa's hand in his firm grip as they climbed the hill. Lizzie, Rosa's cousin and bridesmaid, walked behind holding up Rosa's delicate veil to protect it from the wild gorse or brambles that grew on the hillside.

"Ah'm so proud oh ye lass, ye look mer beautiful the day than a have ever seen ye. Ah cannae tell ye how much yer Ma an me are gonnae miss ye lass, but Eddie's a guid lad an it's aye been you an' him. He'll look after ye of that Ah'm sure."

"Ah know Da, Ah know, Ah'll miss you an' Ma tae. Ah've aye known we'd be wed Da"

From the top of the hill, they looked across at the opposite shore where they could see Dunderave Castle and over to the west lay Inveraray. Cairndow was at the bottom of the hill where the vicar had come from to perform the ceremony.

As they walked between fellow travellers, friends and families Rosa caught sight of Eddie for the first time and her heart skipped a beat. So handsome he was standing there, his piercing brown eyes filled with love as he stared at her. He looked fine in a new brown suit, and his dark hair curled over the collar of his white shirt. Her Father led her towards Eddie who was standing at the quartz heart, he placed her hand in Eddie's, and with a lump in his throat and a tear in his eye, he stepped back to join Mary. Tam, Eddie's cousin, stood by his side performing the duty of best man, and he carried the gold ring that Eddie would place on her finger never to be taken off.

After the ceremony, they all gathered back at the camp in the field by the loch and the celebrations began. There was feasting on jugged hare stew, roasted suckling pig, fresh caught wild salmon, and brown trout. After the feasting, out came the flutes, fiddles and squeezeboxes and the dancing and singing began in earnest.

I ken ye dinnae like it lass, the winter here in toon

For the scaldies a miscaw us, and they try tae bring us doon

And it's hard tae raise three bairns, in a single flae box room

But all tak ye on the road again, when the yella's on the broom

When the yella's on the broom, when the yella's on the broom

I'll tak ye on the road again, when the yella's on the broom

The scaldies ca us tinker dirt, and they spurn oor bairn's in school

But fa cares fit the scaldies think, for the scaldies, but a fool

They never hear the yarlin's song, nor see the flaxen bloom

For they're cooped up in hooses when the yella's on the bloom

Nae sale for pegs or baskets noo that used to bide our lives

But I seem to work at scaldies jobs, from nine o' clock till five

But we ca' nae man oor maister, when we own the warld roon

And I'll bid fareweel tae Breechin, when the yella's on the broom

I'm weary for the springtime, when we tak the road aince mair

Tae the plantin and the fermin, and the berry fields O Blair

When we meet up wi' oor kin-folk, frae a' the country roon

And we yarn aboot wha'll tak the road when the yella's on the broom

Unbeknown to Rosa, as planned, Eddie's cousin Tam had driven the new wagon, concealed under a tarpaulin, all the way to Loch Fyne. Eddie asked Rosa to wait where she was as he had something to do. Rosa was puzzled, but she agreed and sat with her family and friends while Eddie went off to fetch the wagon.

A short while later, when she heard the commotion, she turned and there was Eddie driving the covered wagon led by two fine horses. He jumped down from the wagon and as everyone watched, Tam and Eddie drew back the tarpaulin amid admiring gasps and cheers from the partygoers.

"This is for ye ma darling, a weddin present tae start oor life the gether, this is yer new home."

She thought it was the biggest wagon she had ever seen, and the wooden trims were intricately carved, and painted in bright colours. A proud Eddie helped Rosa up onto the wagon while everybody was cheering, banging posts and shouting good wishes to the happy couple. There were murmurs of appreciation as everyone crowded around to admire Eddie's handiwork and later several of the guests spoke to Eddie, asking if he could build similar wagons for them. Eddie could see that this would be a good way to make a living; doing something, he loved doing with Rosa by his side. Much later, Eddie and Rosa, proudly seated at the front of the wagon, left the wedding amid cheers, well wishes, and laughter, to camp further down the on the loch side.

Mary and John had given Eddie Rosa's trunk, and he had set it to one side in the wagon for her to find. When they arrived at the loch side, while Eddie unhitched the horses and set out food and water for them, Rosa went into the wagon.

The first thing she saw was her precious trunk. She knelt on the floor and opened it. Looking at her things made her think of her Mother and her Father, and although she was blissfully happy, she was also a little sad knowing that she was leaving her childhood behind and becoming a wife.

Chapter 6

By the time Eddie came back in from seeing to the horses, Rosa had set a small fire in the stove with the kettle on the hot plate. There was a slight chill to the night air, but the wagon was nice and warm.

"Would ye like some tea Eddie?"

"Aye lass that Ah would."

Both Rosa and Eddie were nervous, but the simple act of having a cup of tea settled them. For a short while, they chatted about how much everyone had enjoyed and participated in the wedding and their lovely gifts.

Before too long, Rosa was in Eddies embrace, he was gentle and caring as he drew her into his arms and kissed her tenderly. Such was their passion that night that his seed took hold and within a few weeks, Rosa began to notice the changes in her body. She knew immediately that a new life was growing inside her. Eddie was overjoyed when she told him, and he picked her up, swung her around, and kissed her face over and over again.

"Oh ma love, ma lass. Ye have made me the happiest man alive."

Soon they were into their own routine travelling from place to place, where Eddie sold his woodcraft and took orders from customers, and Rosa spent her time organising and cleaning her new home and cooking a meal for Eddies return. There was always time to spare, and Rosa used that time to make small posies of dried flowers and lace doilies to sell round doors in villages they came across.

They planned to spend their first year travelling from place to place, setting up camp, selling their wares, and meeting friends and families far afield that had not been able to travel to their wedding. They would return to camp near Glasgow Green at the end of October, so that they could be close to Mary and John before the baby was due.

Rosa did not have an easy time in her pregnancy; in the beginning it was just morning sickness, and usually Eddie was gone before it took hold of her, but as the weeks passed she wondered how other woman coped as those that she knew seemed to take it in their stride

By the time Rosa was five months pregnant, she was plagued with headaches, and sometimes, dizzy spells overwhelmed her, and she would have to lie down until the feeling passed. Her face, hands, feet, and legs were very swollen and she was always tired. Eddie was worried about her and did his best to look after her, but she never admitted to him how badly she felt.

This was her first child and she did not realise that these things were not normal. She stoically carried on with her daily chores of cleaning and cooking, but as each day passed she found it harder and harder to get out of bed. She was embarrassed and didn't want to admit that she wasn't coping. She was afraid that others would think she was just complaining for the sake of it.

"Women have babies all the time," she thought.

When they arrived back at the camp in Glasgow at the end of October she was seven months pregnant. Mary took one look at her and cried in dismay.

"Oh my God Rosa, look at you. Yer so swollen, that's no normal. Quick John, get Eddie get this wean tae the hospital."

Eddie came running in. "Whit's wrang?"

"She's sick son, Ah think she's got the toxins. We need to get her tae the hospital at Castle Street."

Eddie and John hitched a small cart and made it ready to carry Rosa and Mary to the hospital, but by the time they reached it Rosa was as white as a sheet, and barely conscious.

"Whit's wrong wi' her Ma, will she be awright?" Eddie asked.

"Rosa darlin, speak to me, why did ye no tell me ye wernae well."

She reached out and held his hand as tears ran down her face.

"Save ma baby!" she said, "Save ma baby an' call her Rosie."

"No Rosa, no, wur nearly there yer gonnae be awright."

Tears ran down Eddie's face as he held Rosa in his arms. John ran into the hospital and came back seconds later with nurses and a trolley. They helped to lift Rosa on to the trolley and whisked her away from them. Mary, John, and Eddie, followed the trolley as far as the labour ward, and sat in the cold corridor clutching hands and crying together, praying that Rosa and the baby would be all right. Doctors and nurses hurried in and out of the door that they had taken Rosa through, and all they could do was sit and pray in silence. A nurse took them into a side room and brought them hot sweet tea.

An hour passed before they heard the faintest whimper, the first cry of baby Rosie. They rushed into the corridor with a sigh of relief until they saw the doctor coming towards them, his green scrubs covered in blood and a grim expression on his face. This was not the face of someone bearing good news. Something was wrong. He started the conversation with,

"I am very, very, sorry."

At that, two grown men fell to their knees.

Mary screamed at the top of her voice "Nooooo" she screamed "Nooooo," and she fell to the floor at the doctor's feet in a dead faint.

Little did they know that later, they would all feel that pain again… much, much, later…

Baby Rosie was very premature, and at first, they did not think that she would survive, but she rallied quickly and the doctors agreed to release her to the care of her granny. Night and day, hardly sleeping, she sat with her, caring for her and loving her, pouring the same love that she had had for Rosa into the tiny baby. Friends and neighbours from the community gathered, as is their way, to look after things while Mary cared for her grandchild.

The dreadful day arrived when Rosa was to be put into the ground. The family gathered, with Eddie leading the procession with his cousin Tam supporting him as he carried his tiny baby in his arms. Mary and John with Eddie's parents came next, and all the members of their immediate community followed in two's, three's, and fours.

Along the way, travellers joined them, word of mouth having told them of the tragedy. Hundreds followed the sombre group as they made their way on this sad journey. A specially constructed cart, drawn by four white horses, carried Rosa's flower covered coffin to Janefield Cemetery in the Gallowgate.

Hundreds of travellers all wearing black, their heads bowed in sorrow were already gathered to meet the procession that walked behind the hearse. The Glasgow streets were crowded with people who lived nearby, and they stood along the pavements watching and whispering quietly.

Rosa's casket was lowered into the ground, and the mourners filed past dropping tokens into the grave onto Rosa's casket. Some dropped ivy leaves, others a piece of lace made into a flower shape. Others dropped small posies or a handful of soil.

At the end of the ceremony, Rosa's grave was completely dressed in wreaths and flower garlands, and the mourners stood in silence remembering beautiful Rosa, dancing at the Musselburgh Fairs and on her wedding day at the Tinkers Heart.

Sadder still was the sight of Eddie holding the tiny baby, wrapped warmly in a white hand crocheted woollen shawl, and wearing a warm hat and mittens. He looked a broken man, tears coursing down his face, supported as he was by John, Mary, and his own parents.

"It was the toxins that got her," people were saying.

Some would later know it as pre-eclampsia.

"She might have lived had she known it wisnae normal."

"Aye it's too late noo."

"When its yer time its yer time."

"Look at that poor lad, it's a shame, it saddens yer heart it does."

"How will he manage that bairn?"

"Mary will mind the bairn; Eddie's Ma's no fit. Mary an' John will see them awright."

"Eddies a canny lad, he's got a bit put by."

Eddie had asked Mary and John if they would move into his wagon to help care for baby Rosie. Since his wagon was big enough for the four of them, and they were spending most of their time there anyway, the decision was an easy one. Mary and John traded their wagon to another family, and from then on they all travelled together.

Chapter 7

Time passes as time does, and day by day the pain that Eddie and the family felt began to become bearable. Eddie worked hard giving all his time to building wagons for those that could afford his prices. The money he made was for Rosie's future, but he seldom said a word to anyone, least of all his daughter, but he looked at her. He watched her as she grew and played with other children; every time he looked at her, he could see Rosa in her and the pain was hard to bear. He found himself choked with grief any time he tried to talk to her. It was easier to walk away.

Granny Mary and Pa John on the other hand lavished the child with love and attention. She was often with one or the other and anything she wanted she got, though she seldom asked for anything other than to be around them all the time chatting and fussing and asking questions. She seldom went near her Father, her young mind sensing something and assuming that he had no time for her.

Eddie often spoke with his Rosa in his heart and sometimes he was sure he could hear her voice. She would talk to him about the child and chide him for his tears.

"Let me go Eddie," he would hear her say.

"Mind the bairn Eddie."

"Find another wife Eddie."

"Never," he would say aloud and end his secret conversation.

In 1914, when war was declared, Eddie was among the first of his family and community to volunteer. This was a sad and worrying time for everyone, not just for the travelling community. Those within the community that were too old or unfit took their women and children further into the country for safety's sake.

Many of the travelling women joined the land girls working on farms, ploughing fields using horse drawn ploughs, tending to animals, getting up at five in the morning for milking, and mucking out cowsheds.

Those travelling men that did return came back changed men forever. Some of these lads received medals for their services to King and country, but all of them had scars that would never heal, some in mind and some in body. It was a frightening time for everyone.

Mary was heartbroken that her John never made it home, but Eddie came back wounded in the leg, he was alive and home and that was the main thing. He never spoke of the things he had seen, or the friends and family members that had been lost, but he carried the sadness on his face as most folk did.

Tam came back; he had been one of the lucky ones, if anyone could be considered lucky. During a battle, his officer's horse panicked and threw the officer to the ground almost trampling him. Tam jumped forward, grabbed the frightened horse, and calmed it. He then assisted his officer to his feet and made sure that he was uninjured.

The officer was shaken, but unhurt, and he asked Tam where he got his horse skills. Tam explained his background and experience breeding and training horses, and within weeks, he was shipped back to England to train horses for the war effort. His time overseas had affected him badly though, and working with the horses he loved helped him to recover from the trauma he had experienced.

When the war was over and it was safe to go back to their normal camp by Gretna Green, so many things had changed. Builders were building new homes, and engineers were planning new roads to accommodate the cars that were now becoming more common. The old was beginning to merge with the new, and soon enough everyone began to settle into this new lifestyle.

Some travellers wanted to settle in houses when they returned, but most still loved the life of freedom and fresh air, living on and from the land. Eddie picked up his business where he left off, and once more those that could would go from door to door, selling their wares, sharpening knives, and odd jobbing wherever they could.

One day, when Rosie was about fourteen, she asked her Granny about a box that was on one of the high shelves. She had noticed it before, but had never thought to ask about it.

"Whit's in that box Granny?"

There was a silence.

"Granny, whit's in that box?"

Mary knew the day would come and here it was.

"It's some things belongin' tae yer mother."

"Whit things, are they mine, can Ah see? Please Granny let me see the box."

Mary reached up and handed the box to Rosie, who took it reverently, placed it on the table, and sat down staring at it. She stroked her hands across the top of the box, and then she looked up at her granny.

"Did ma Da make it?"

"Aye, he did."

"Did he make it for ma Ma?"

"Aye."

She stroked the wooden box again, passing her hands over the delicately carved roses and the etched pattern that ran all around the outside edges.

"Whit's in it Granny?"

"Precious things hinny."

"Can Ah open it?"

"Aye."

Rosie slowly opened it. Inside was a piece of lace from Rosa's wedding dress, all that was left of it, for she had been dressed in it for her burial. Her wedding ring had remained on her finger, but her engagement ring was in the box, along with a small circle of wood with a rose carved in the centre. Rosie picked up the ring and tried it on each of her fingers.

"One day when Ah'm bigger this might fit me; Ah'll be able tae wear it."

Mary glanced at her fondly.

"Aye ye will."

She put the ring back in the box and picked up the wooden carving. She pensively stroked a finger over the rose.

"He's clever ma Da tae make this."

"He made it when he was just a lad, and gave it tae yer Ma when she was jist a lass. She carried it awe the time an' thought nae body knew she had it but yer Pa an' me, we knew."

Rosie held it tightly in her hand and thought about the mother that she had never known. She loved her Granny, but she missed her Ma with a soreness that she couldn't put into words.

"Was she pretty Granny?"

"She was right bonnie an' she could sing an' dance better than the rest."

"Dae Ah look like her Granny?"

Mary's eyes were full of tears when she answered.

"Aye lass, yer her double. See for yir self there's a wee picture there."

Rosie picked up the small square photograph and there was her Father, younger and happier than she had ever seen him looking down at her Mother.

"She's beautiful granny."

She studied the images before her and thought of the mother she had never known. The sadness and emptiness inside her made her quiet for a while with her thoughts. She put the picture back in the box and picked up the wooden rose once more. She looked at her granny.

"Can a have it Granny?"

"I don't know lass ye'll have tae ask yer Da."

"He's outside. Will Ah ask him the noo?"

Mary looked outside to see Eddie feeding the horses.

"Go on then if ye like."

Rosie ran outside, "Da! Da! Can Ah speak tae ye?"

Eddie turned and looked down at her as she held up the carved wooden rose. She watched the colour drain from his face and then watched it come back until he was bright red with anger.

"Where did ye git that? Never mind!" he said, and stormed off away from the camp.

Rosie felt the tears welling in her throat. The pain in her heart was unbearable. She thought her father hated her so much that he couldn't bear to talk to her, but she needed him. She needed to talk to him, and she was going to, if he liked it or not. She gathered her courage and followed the path that her father had taken and caught sight of him sitting on a log by a stream. She approached softly and stood just behind him.

"Ah'm sorry a killed ma Ma. Ah'm sorry that ye hate me Da, an' Ah'm sorry that ye canny love me."

He turned sharply, and she was shocked to see tears coursing down his face. He stood and placed his hands on her shoulders and looking into her eyes he said, "Whit dae ye mean, ye killed yer Ma. Ye never killed yer Ma."

"But she died havin me," Rosie was crying too.

"No lass," he said, as he drew her towards him and held her in his arms for the first time since she was a baby.

"Yer Ma was dyin when we got to the hospital, an' there was nuthin wi' could dae, but the last thing she said tae me was 'Save ma baby, call her Rosie', she wanted you tae live."

He choked on his words; swallowing his tears, he said,

"An' Rosie Ah dae love ye, Ah love ye wi' aw' ma heart, it's jist every time Ah see ye Ah blame ma self for no understandin that yer Ma was awffy sick. If Ah had known maybe she couldha been saved."

They held each other tight, both cried cathartic tears, and then they talked as they had never talked before.

Rosie knew that she loved her father, but knowing that he loved her and that her mother's death wasn't her fault filled her with a new deeper love for her him and a happiness that she could not put into words. She looked at his handsome tanned face lined with worry as he spoke to her and for the first time he told her stories about himself and her mother.

He told her about the little wooden rose, remembering when he had carved it and remembering the day that he had given it to her.

"Ah'm glad yer Granny kept some stuff for ye, an" Ah'm heart sorry that Ah could nae tell ye aboot hur afore the noo."

Together they looked at the token that Rosie held in her hand.

"Can Ah carry it in ma pocket Da. Ah'll be careful wi it Ah promise?"

"Aye, of course ye can, yer Ma wid be happy aboot that."

As they walked back towards the wagon, Mary looked out of her window and cried "Oh!" as the tears poured from her eyes. There was Eddie, hand in hand with Rosie, she looking up at him and him looking down at her, and both of them happy and smiling at each other.

"Well Ah never, an' not afore time," Mary thought.

She moved away from the window and sitting at the table, opened the box, took out the picture of Rosa and Eddie on their wedding day, put it in a frame, and hung it on one of the shelves.

Chapter 8

Rosie carried the small wooden rose in her pocket and was never without it. Whenever she thought of her mother, she would put her hand in her pocket and touch the token of love. Whenever she felt anxious or tired, the token gave her comfort and strength.

Following that day when she found her father's love for her, she spent many happy days and evenings in his company. Sometimes Rosie walked out with her Pa learning new routes and places to go to sell sprigs of heather and pieces of lace. He always taught her to be careful about where she went and to trust her instinct. They still went to fairs, but times were changing and more and more travellers were beginning to settle or stay in places for longer periods. Some were getting rid of their wagons and buying motorised vans.

Travelling women tended to sell pegs, china pottery, handmade flowers, and lace for trimming clothes or tableware. Some, gifted with the sight, would tell a fortune for a piece of silver. She knew her Granny Mary had the gift of the sight, for she had heard the other women whispering about it, but she didn't think that she had it.

She once heard them whisper about a time when she was just a baby. They said something about her being sick and Granny Mary was running in the rain to get help when an American gentleman riding by in a fancy carriage refused to stop.

She didn't know any more about it, but she did hear one of the women saying something about never crossing the Mither and she knew they were talking about her granny.

Her granny always told her to trust her instincts. She said if she felt that something was good then it was, but if she felt that something was bad then she should run as fast as her legs would carry her. Her granny was funny with her sayings.

The men folk worked the fields gathering tatties, pulling turnips, or picking fruits. Others would have grinding carts, and they would go around houses and farms sharpening tools. Smithing, breeding, training, and trading horses, lurchers and terriers and sometimes ferrets for hunting was a popular way to earn money.

Eddie's business, building quality wagons for newlyweds and for travellers who were doing well, was growing. His reputation as an artisan brought him many orders, enough that he could enlist the help of men within his own group. He used the shed that he had built on the land purchased from the farmer several years before, and before long he was able to buy more land from the same farmer.

Occasionally he would meet up with Arab traders who brought Persian rugs to the UK hoping to make their fortune. Eddie would buy a cartload and then pass them on to others in his community for a small profit, and they then sold the rugs from door to door. He made time to travel to the fairs at Musselburgh, St James fair in Kelso, and Appleby Horse Fair often taking Mary and young Rosie with him.

Rosie was growing more beautiful by the day and more like her mother in many ways. Even her voice reminded him of Rosa, sometimes he would hear Rosie chatting or singing, and it was as though Rosa was by his side. Rosie's responsibility was to help her granny keep the home clean and cook the food.

There might be fish or meat caught using nets, ferrets, catapults, or dogs and sometimes they would cook squirrels, hedgehogs, hares, and pheasant. When they needed to, they could buy or trade meat from a local butcher, or sell him any excess that they caught. They made flavoured drinks and jams, from fruits that they had gathered, or they would preserve them for future use. They made natural remedies from herbs and stored some in jars or brown paper bags to flavour their food.

When there was time to spare, they would go from door to door selling fancy lace for collars, or trims and wooden clothes pegs. Some homes treated them kindly, but others treated them with scorn and disrespect, throwing things at them and calling them names.

"Why do they call us Tinkers Granny?"

"Its jist their ignorance lass. They think they're insultin' us, but 'tinker' comes from the tinkling' noise that's made from the pots an' pans we sell hangin from the carts."

Over time, Rosie knew where to avoid and where she would be able to earn a penny or two.

As time passed, with the onset of arthritis, Mary was finding it harder to go from door to door selling their wares so, Rosie went on her own. Rosie kept to areas close to where they were camped, so that she could help her granny by fetching and carrying water for cleaning or cooking, and wood for their fire.

Life was beginning to return to normal, but it would never be the same as it had been before the war. There were houses, where before the war there were fields, and factories had sprouted up. By 1923 motorised buses were becoming more common and there were many more cars on the roads and further afield. Everything seemed to be noisier, dirtier and rushed, although for Rosie and the rest of her community, they tried to maintain the old ways.

Mary at fifty-one looked much older than her years. The loss of Rosa and John had added lines to her face. Arthritis troubled her daily and made getting about a painful trial. Her long white hair dressed in a middle parting with pleats on either side was partially concealed under a black crocheted shawl. In her younger days, bright colours were her choice, but since the death of Rosa she had always worn black.

Her skin was weather beaten and lined with wrinkles, but in Rosie's eyes, it was the loveliest of faces.

"Have ye everything ye need Granny?"

"Aye lass Ah'm fine, why dae ye ask?"

"Ah'm gonnae head o'er the Glasgow Bridge this morning. See if Ah can sell some heather an' lace tae folk goin' tae work. Maybe go as far as Kinning Park. Ma baskets fu' o stuff Ah've been makin'."

"Aye, folk might be thinkin' o things tae buy. Ye could take some jams if there's spare."

"Next time granny, ma baskets full tae burstin."

"You mind yir self lass and don't trust a face cause it's smiling at ye."

Rosie was smiling as she leant over and kissed granny on the forehead and went out the door. Her granny had lots of saying like that…

"Keep yer hon on yer ha'penny an' don't gie it away for a penny"

"Ne're shed a cloot tae May is oot."

"Gang wi' the craws git shot doon wi' the craws."

Rosie amused herself laughing and thinking of her granny's sayings as she walked from Fleshers Haugh at Glasgow Green along the banks of the River Clyde.

"Whit's for ye'll no go by ye!"

"Lang may yer lum reek."

"Dinnae teach yer Granny tae suck eggs."

Her basket was packed with small sprigs of heather tied with string into little bunches and pieces of lace were rolled into yard long lengths. Her basket was full, but light enough that she had one hand free to hold out a piece of lace or a bunch of heather to people she passed along the way.

When she wasn't offering something, she would put her hand in her pocket, and finger the little wooden rose token and make a wish for the next person to buy from her. She made her way towards the Glasgow Bridge, and was glad to see that it was teeming with people crossing the bridge to the city and going the other way to the docks and warehouses that ran along the Clyde.

"Lucky white heather a penny a bunch."

"Lucky white heather."

"A bit o' lace for yer missus?"

Not many on the bridge took her up on her offer.

"*In too much of a hurry.*" she thought as she gazed over the parapet and watched people boarding the King Edward steamer. In those days, the Clyde was a hive of activity with steamers, puffers, and small cargo ships from the recently formed Burns and Laird line.

Chapter 9

She didn't have much luck on the bridge as people jostled each other hurrying to wherever they were going. Tramcars and horse drawn dray wagons from the bonded warehouses at Port Dundas, all fought for room to move back and forth. Over the bridge, she headed towards Paisley Road to the tenements in Kinning Park. The tenements were grimy, and some of the children made a fool of her and called her names, but she always managed to sell a thing or two there.

She went from door to door; always staying on the ground floor level of the tenements, and eventually she came to St James Street. She hated the dark dingy closes and the smell that hung in the air. She could never understand why people would want to walk through filth to get to their own door. If she and her granny lived there, they would clean every day and the close would smell fresh and sweet.

There was a man who lived in one of the ground floor flats who always bought a bit of lace for his wife, and he always gave her an extra penny or two for her trouble. Sometimes he offered her a drink of lemonade or a sweetie. She thought he was a bit "away in the heed," because he always laughed when he opened the door to her and announced,

"Have ye come to see Mr James of St James Street?"

She always played the game and said,

"Aye, Ah've come to sell Mr James of St James Street a bit o' lace for yer missus,"

"Will ye come in lass n have a sip o' lemonade?" he said.

Her Granny Mary always told her,

"Never cross the front door when sellin yer wares as ye cannae trust a buddy 'specially if they're nae yer ane kind".

She had never gone in before, but she was tired from her long trek and her throat was dry from speaking to people. Her granny's words forgotten, Rosie stepped over the threshold of Mr James of St James Street's house.

The room was dark, dingy, and dirty, it didn't look as though as though a woman lived there and Rosie wondered why he had been buying the lace. She glanced round the room, the curtains on the window were closed tight, and there was a stale smell filling her nose. Two armchairs sat either side of a dirty fireplace and she noticed a fat man sitting on one of them. He staring at her with a look on his face that made her stomach turn.

By the window stood a wooden trunk with handles on either side and leather straps that wrapped around it fastened with buckles. She felt afraid and didn't know what to say or do.

"Where's yer missus?" she asked, panic beginning to burn in her chest.

Both men laughed at her. She felt Mr James put his hands on her shoulders, and she turned with a start and backed away from him, but the table in the middle of the room stopped her.

"Dinnae dae that Mr James."

"Awe come lass, Ah'm sure ye know whit's whit." he said menacingly, moving closer to her.

She tried to slip past him, but he was between her and the door.

"Come on ye can have a bit o' fun now a bonnie lass like you, Ah've waited a long time for ye."

She screamed as he lunged for her forcing his mouth on hers and splitting her lip. She saw the fat man coming towards them and for a minute, she thought he was going to help her.

"Ah'll hawd her doon." She heard him say.

She tried to scream again as she fought them off like wildcat. She kicked out and bit as Mr James held his big thick hands over her mouth and nose to stifle her screams, but he was choking the life from her. She fought, kicked, and struggled, and felt something hard and heavy hit her on her head. Bit by bit, her strength disappeared, and the last coherent thought she had was

"Granny"

"Ya' crazy bastart' whit have ye done she's deed!" Mr James said to the fat man standing over Rosie's body.

"She shouldha' kept quiet then."

"Whit are wi' gonnae dae?"

"Get her clathes aff and empty her poackets an' that basket. Burn awe that in the fire. Its nearly teatime, the factories are emptyin' and it'll be gettin' dark. We'll stick her in the trunk and dump her in the Clyde."

"Are ye effin' crazy man, how are we supposed to get her tae the Clyde in that trunk wi'oot onybody seein' us."

"They'll think wur sailors gone back tae the boat. They'll no mind us among the melee comin' an' goin' fae their work. They might see us, but they widnae' think we were putting a body in the Clyde. Hurry up gie me a hawn." He laughed

The fat man began to burn the lace and heather in the fireplace, and at the bottom of Rosie's basket, he found the money from her sales and counted it out. "Three shillin's, that'll be ma pay for the dirty work ye huv me daein'," he said, as he put the handfuls of pennies and halfpennies in his pocket.

Mr James was stripping Rosie's clothes off.

"Awe whit a shame she's deed, we couldha had a nice bit o' fun wi' that yin."

The fat man took Rosie's clothes and went through her pockets and found the little wooden rose, "Whit aboot this, dae ye want it?" he asked.

"Naa, Burn it wi' the rest."

The fat man looked at the carving of the rose on the face of the wooden token and slipped it into his pocket. Together they picked Rosie's lifeless body and put her into the trunk then fastened down the straps.

"Whit are wi' gonnae say if anybody asks us whit where dayin."

W'ull just say Ah'm ge'in ye a hawn back tae yer ship." Then he laughed again and said,

"We'll ask them tae gie us a hawn and then they'll no be very long in mindin' their ane business."

They carried the trunk between them along St James Street. They were only a few minutes walk from the Clyde, it was already growing dark, and the rain had started to fall. People were hurrying towards their homes, but no one bothered them. They crossed some spare ground to reach the spot that they wanted to dump the trunk and Rosie's remains.

"Ye ken this is tidal," said the fat man.

"Dae a look' stupit."

"Ah never said that, Ah'm jist remindin' ye."

"Well hurry up, get some o' these big stones an' we'll make sure it goes deep an' disnae move. As soon as it lands it'll sink in the silt."

Hurriedly they gathered boulders and put them in the trunk, and then they closed the lid on Rosie and fastened the straps again. They dragged the trunk to the edge of the Clyde, made sure there was no one around and together they heaved and pushed until the trunk slipped into its resting place. As they walked the fat man pulled his hankie from his pocket, and as he did so the little wooden token spilled out of his pocket and rolled away. Neither of the men even noticed it.

"Where did ye put that money ye found?"

"In ma poakit."

"Aye, well yer buyin, let's go for a pint."

And with that, they sauntered off to the nearest pub.

Chapter 10

Granny Mary had a bad feeling in her stomach and pains in her chest. She didn't know that she was suffering from angina. She looked at the old clock on the wall and then she rose to look out of the window of the wagon. It was raining hard, she knew a storm was brewing and she felt sick. She began to pace and tried to still her mind, but the feeling of dread grew in her.

She had avoided her gift of the sight for a long time and although it was still there it was weaker through lack of use, nevertheless her instincts were screaming at her that something bad was happening, and her worst fear was that Rosie was in trouble, serious trouble.

Suddenly there was a crash and the photograph of Rosa and Eddie fell off the shelf. She put her hand to her mouth and stood there staring as the tears began to course down her face. Slowly she moved to the photograph lying face down by the hearth. With difficulty, holding her shawl over her shoulders, she stooped to pick it up. Rosa's face on her wedding day looked back at her. The picture was undamaged, but the frame had broken beyond repair.

The pain in her heart worsened as the panic grew. She tried to still her fears, but deep down she knew there was something terribly wrong. She opened the door of her wagon and called to a neighbouring wagon.

"Bella, Bella come quick."

Bella came over, "Whit's up Mither?" she said using the term Mither as a sign of respect.

"Have ye taken bad?"

"Its Rosie, summat terrible has happened," she said clutching Bella's hand.

"Send somebody tae fetch oor Eddie an' the lads."

"But whit's happened, whit's happened?"

"Ah dinnae ken, but Ah know it's bad, fetch the men an' be quick. She shouldha been hame afore noo."

Eddie and the other men from the camp had gathered within the hour, and still there was no sign of Rosie.

"Where'd she go the day Granny?"

"Doon by the docks, maybe Clyde Street an' across the water."

The men huddled in a group and discussed the plan to search various areas. Some had bicycles, others horses, and they went off in different directions. Knocking on doors as they came to them or stopping folk in the street. The question was the same from all of them.

"Have ye seen oor lass, she goes by the name Rosie. Sellin' lace she was, maybe pegs. She's a pretty lass wi' long dark curly hair."

Some remembered seeing her in the past, some knew her by name, and some just shook their head and walked on disinterested. There were not so many people on the streets because of the weather, but they continued to search for hours. There were no phones to communicate with each other so at various points along the distance, between the camp and the search area, one of the men would wait so that a signal could be given if anyone found any sign of Rosie, or if she returned home.

All the women gathered together in and outside Eddie's wagon to give and seek comfort. She was one of their own and they would search until they found her. They searched all night, and finally in the early hours of the morning, Eddie and his cousin Tam went into the new Orkney Street Police Station. The duty constable looked up from his desk and eyed the men up and down contemptuously without saying a word.

"Ma lass is missin'," he said.

"What makes ye think she's missing."

"She never came home last night."

"And what age would this lass be," the constable said.

"She's jist turned sixteen," replied Eddie.

He saw the smirk on the constable's face.

"And is there a boyfriend missing as well?"

Tam quickly grabbed Eddie and held him back for he was about to punch the constable on the nose.

"She's a guid lass, there's nae boyfriend. Ah'm tellin' ye she's missin', she never came hame last night an' we've searched awe night for her."

"Wait a minute," the constable said, and left the desk and went through a door behind him into an office.

They could see him through the frosted glass as though he was talking to someone in the office, but when he came back, they could see through the door that the office was empty.

"The gaffer said leave it till tomorrow and if she's still not back come and see us."

They stared at each other for a few moments. Eddie and his cousin knew that the constable was lying, and the constable knew that they knew it, but it didn't matter a jot to him. In his mind, the missing tinker lassie had run off with a sweetheart.

"Come on Eddie," said Tam "We'll git nae help here."

He took Eddie by the arm. He could feel Eddie shaking with rage and frustration in his bones as he all, but dragged him out of the station. In those days when a person was missing, it was unlikely that there would be any action taken until twenty-four to forty-eight hours had passed unless they were vulnerable.

At that time a sixteen-year-old gypsy girl was not considered vulnerable.

They walked up Broomloan Road and onto Paisley Road West stopping people as they went, asking them if they had seen Rosie. They continued on making their way towards the bridge over the River Clyde heading back to where they were camped.

Eddie's head was down, his shoulders slumped in despair, and Tam didn't know what to say to him. What can you say to someone when you yourself think the worst has happened? Just at the corner of St James Street Eddie's shoe made contact with something on the pavement and it rolled to the gutter, he walked on for a moment, and then he stopped dead in his tracks.

"Whit is it man?" Tam said.

"Whit was that, where did it go?" he said as he turned sharply and started searching and there it was, the wooden rose that he had carved for his Rosa and passed to his daughter Rosie when she was barely fourteen. She had carried it ever since.

"Aw' naw!" he cried as he knelt by the kerb, "Naw, naw, naw, she's somewhere here," he said, clutching the wooden rose as though it were a lifeline. It was early morning, and while some would be getting ready to go to work others were still asleep, but that didn't matter to Tam and Eddie. They turned into St James Street and started banging on doors and shouting to people.

"Away wi' ye afore we call the polis, tinkers, bloody cheek," some said.

They went to every door on every floor in each tenement and finally arrived at Mr James's door.

"Aye, Ah've seen her before, but no for a while," he said "But Ah'll watch for her an' tell her yer lookin'."

Finally, they made their way back to the camp to find that about a hundred of their community had arrived to help with the search and were waiting for their return. Such is the nature of the travelling community that yes, they celebrated together, but they also gathered to help each other when one of their own was in trouble or needed support.

Tam shook his head discretely to the gathered men, warning them to give him a bit of time before they spoke to him. They separated as he walked between their ranks, some reaching out to touch his shoulder or arm as he passed with his head down and his face drawn in anguish. The women stood and made way as he approached his wagon.

He stepped into the wagon and looked at Granny Mary. He couldn't speak and nor could she as he held out his hand to show her what he had found. Outside where the travellers had gathered, men women and children shivered as the keening grew louder and louder as Granny Mary wailed in her grief.

Some of the older women came in to comfort her, and Eddie went out to join the men who waited by the campfire. Someone put a bowl of soup in his hand and another set a whisky down beside him. He told them as best he could where they had looked and what they had found at St James Street. They decided that the men would gather at St James Street to begin the search again, and Eddie would go back to Orkney Street Police Station.

The following morning, while Eddie went back to Orkney Street Police Station almost one hundred travellers gathered around St James Street and began banging on doors. This caused some alarm, such an unusual event, that runners were sent to Orkney Street to fetch the police.

The runners arrived at the police station while Eddie was trying to get them to look for Rosie. The sergeant was more sympathetic than the constable had been the day before and he reprimanded him out of earshot of the people who had now gathered in the station.

Communications were poor then, but the sergeant listened to Eddie's report of where he thought Rosie had been and where they had since searched. He told the sergeant where he had found Rosie's token and the significance of it.

The sergeant explained to Eddie that he would notify other stations at the start of the next shift so that constables could search various locations.

There were no mobiles in those days or biro pens. Constables would make notes in their notebooks with a pencil and the radios that they did have merely clicked rather than allowing the opportunity for speech. The sergeant organised a search and instructed officers to go from door to door and leave no stone unturned. The search went on for several days but it was fruitless. The constable who had been on duty on that first day had wasted valuable time, and any trail had since gone cold.

Chapter 11

People that had come to help stayed at the camp for more than a week, but they had to return to their families and their daily life. Day after day, week after week, Eddie searched for Rosie. He searched from Glasgow Green, through the city and over the Clyde. He searched in Kinning Park and as far as Govan, but never found a trace. Some days he walked the banks of the Clyde. He was sure that Rosie would never have ventured onto the docks, but he even searched there. Some days Tam would go with him, but on other days, he insisted on being by himself. He was a constant visitor pestering the life of the sergeant at Orkney Street, but nothing changed.

Each evening he would return to the camp worn out and heart weary. At first folk would look at him as he arrived back and ask

"Any news Eddie?" and he would just shake his head sadly.

He would climb the steps to the wagon only to find Granny Mary sitting staring off into space in silent agony.

Most nights he would lie awake and on the nights that he slept, he would find himself tortured by nightmares. Often he would rise in the middle of the night and he would hear Granny Mary whimpering in a fretful sleep.

Granny Mary was failing fast; her legs wouldn't hold her, and her grief was more than she could bear. She had lost the will to live and was fading away before everyone's eyes.

Bella and some of the other mothers took turns every day looking after Mary, but no amount of encouragement would make her eat a proper meal or leave the wagon. Bella pleaded with her to let her send for the doctor, but Mary demanded that she be left alone. By November, Mary's condition had deteriorated and one morning Bella went looking for Eddie.

"Ye better come Eddie, Ah'm that feart aboot the Mither. The pains in her chest are bad an' she'll no let me call a doctor."

Eddie stopped grooming his horses, not that he was even aware of what he was doing, because his mind was on his daughter. He went into the wagon and there was Granny Mary, white as a sheet, lying on the couch against the wall, her face drawn with pain.

"Ah have seen her ye know, an' whit Ah have seen is terrible, Ah'll never rest until she's found. A lass'll fin' her ye know, but no for a while yet, no for a long while."

The tears coursed down her wrinkled skin. Eddie sat on the couch at her side and held her bony hand. Grief touched him again and stuck a knife in his heart.

"Ah'm gonnae send for the doctor Granny."

"Nah, nah dae nothin' oh the kind. Let me go, let me be wi' ma Johnny, Rosa, an' Rosie. Ah cannae bear this pain o livin'. Let me go laddie, let me go. Take me outside, Ah want to look at the sky wan last time afore Ah go."

Travelling folk preferred to die outside, and those that had gathered to wait in respect had had prepared a bed supported on a trestle. Eddie went to the door of the wagon and looked at Tam who was nearest to him. Tam nodded and a few of the men came into the wagon to support Eddie as he carefully and lovingly lifted Mary and took her outside. Together they laid her down on the bed and covered her with a clean white blanket.

The November air was still as Eddie stayed by her side holding her hand and remembering happier times. Remembering how she had looked as a younger woman when he was courting Rosa. How could so much pain come to someone who had been so kind and loving to him? Friends at the camp gathered sensing that her time was near and none had a dry face. All had memories of Mary and things she had done to help them; she made them laugh when they were down in the dumps, and made them potions from herbs that made them well when they were sick. Aye, everyone loved Mary. Few remembered her darker side, for mostly that side of her character had calmed after she and Johnny had started courting.

As they gathered there, standing guard in her final minutes a robin landed nearby. All heads turned for all had seen it, and as they watched Mary gave one last sigh, one last breath, and the essence of her was gone. She passed quietly away and as she did, the robin took flight singing its mournful, warbling, song. Eddie kissed her forehead and said

"Away then Mither and find yer Johnny, and then the pair o' ye find my Rosa an' ma Rosie. Tell them Ah'll be joinin' them soon enough."

The women lit candles, put them into glass jars, and placed them around the trestle to light Mary's way to the afterlife. Someone went for the undertaker and before long Mary was taken away to be looked after and prepared for her final resting place. She was to be dressed in her best clothes and jewellery, for there was no daughter or granddaughter to inherit. They would bury Mary beside Rosa at Janefield Cemetery in the Gallowgate, until then, the men would stand vigil at the funeral parlour.

Everything and everyone drew to a standstill as four hundred mourners turned up to pay their respects. The solemn procession walked behind the horse drawn hearse, and the four white horse's bridles and headbands were dressed with fancy plumage and brass hangings. The air was still and quiet in spite of the number of people and all that could be heard was the clip clop of the horse's hooves.

After the funeral, the women of the camp provided food for everyone, and they held a grand wake to share stories and memories of loved ones who had passed. Some of the old mither's from other families whispered about Mary's curse, and said that the American's family was already suffering and none could stop the curse now that Mary was gone.

It was several days before people went back to their own camps or homes, and when they were gone Eddie spoke to Tam. In his heart, Eddie knew that his lovely Rosie was gone from him forever and the only consolation that he had was that she was with her Ma, her Granny, and her Papa and that neither of them would be as lonely as he was.

Tam had hardly left Eddie's side since Rosie disappeared. Anyone who saw them would think that they were brothers instead of cousins because they looked so like each other. The main difference was that Tam had red hair where Eddie's hair was jet black.

"Ah'm goin' on the road for a bit Tam, look after things, ye know where everything is."

"Ah'll come wi' ye man."

Eddie put his hand on Tams shoulder and looked into his tear-filled eyes.

"Ah'll be better ma self. You bide here an' look after the wagons, some need finishin', an' the horses. It's aw yours' man."

Tam was choked with grief and could do nothing to help Eddie other than what he asked.

"It'll be here when ye come back."

Eddie patted Tam on the back and said, "Aye man, Ah know."

He started to walk away from Tam, but Tam grabbed him and put his arms around him holding his cousin and best friend for a moment and then the two men parted. Eddie walked away without looking back. He drove his wagon away from the camp towing a trailer behind him. When others asked him where he was going he replied that he was going on a journey and told no one of his destination.

He drove the wagon along the shores of Loch Lomond and onwards to begin the climb over the 'Rest and be Thankful' following the routes that he had taken to his wedding to Rosa sixteen years ago. He turned into Gleann Mor and when he found a suitable derelict spot, he unhitched the horses and the trailer. He dragged the trailer away to one side, took the horses, and hitched them to the trailer. He went back to the wagon, stood for a moment looking inside the home he had created for Rosa then he took some paper, lit it, and threw it inside before turning his back and walking away from the burning wagon.

He continued on his journey with little more than the clothes he stood in, the bedding and the pot or two that he had in the trailer.

He climbed the hill to the Tinkers Heart and there he stood gazing around him, looking at the loch below and the hills and mountains beyond. His thoughts travelled back to the journey that his life had been on, and he thought back to the day he had watched his Rosa, climbing the hill towards him with her Father on their wedding day.

He put his hand in his pocket and drew out the little wooden rose that he had carved twenty-four years before. He held it in his hand as he lay down in the Tinkers Heart, and there he stayed in the middle of the heart and wept until he had no tears left, until he was empty. Eddie was never seen again, but he was remembered for a long, long, time.

Chapter 12 Present Day

Alina Jones listened to her mother's voice as the answering machine recorded the message.

"Dad and I are going to take a drive down the coast and wondered if you would like to come with us. If we don't hear back from you within the hour, we will just go ourselves. I hope you can come."

Alina's face was blotchy and her eyes were red from crying after having an argument with her husband James. She wanted to go with her Mum and Dad, just to be with them and enjoy their company, but she knew that they would immediately know that something was wrong, and she just didn't want to talk about it.

She thought about calling them back and making excuses, but her parents knew her too well, and the minute her Mum heard her voice she would know something was wrong. She hated that she was having problems, and hated her parents knowing about them more.

She knew her Mum would ask her what was wrong and she didn't want to go through an explanation of the argument that she had with James. Two or three times she reached for the phone and changed her mind. What had she become she wondered, who was this dominated woman inside her skin?

James had gone off to his work in the city, he had a career in savings and investments, and they had a nice three bedroom detached home, garden, and a double garage for his and her cars. There was money in the bank that they could afford to spend on holidays, nice clothes, and small luxuries, but things were not as good as they could be.

More often than not, he came home late, missed planned dinners or birthday celebrations, and sometimes even cancelled things at the last minute because of business meetings. This had led to Alina feeling left out and lonely, and although she could have invited friends over to keep her company, James disliked her friends. It was easier to comply with James than argue over it and gradually she lost touch with them. She went upstairs to her bedroom, to lie on her bed and let her mind drift back over their life together.

Alina had worked full time in banking and she remembered the day that tall, dark, handsome James Jones had come to the branch to meet with a customer. He was wearing a navy pin stripe suit, a white shirt, and a navy and white diagonal striped silk tie. All the female tellers glanced at each other, making subtle eye movements to indicate their attraction to the handsome newcomer.

She was giving him a second look as he was giving her one, their eyes met and for her that was it. Cupid's arrow had struck her, and she did not refuse when later, after he had left the branch, someone called her to the telephone.

"Alina Webster," she said, assuming it was a customer. "How can I help you?"

"I wondered if you would like to join me for dinner?" a male voice said.

"Excuse me!" she replied, puzzled. "Who is this?"

"It's James Jones, just call me JJ."

"How do you know my name?"

"It's on the badge pinned to your blouse. I noticed your long dark hair and pretty blue eyes too," he laughed.

"I don't even know you," she replied.

She was smiling when she recognised who was calling her and she knew that she would go for dinner with him; however, she didn't want to appear to be too keen. She whispered to her colleagues and told them about the call from the handsome stranger. She remembered how her work mates had laughed and teased her.

That was the beginning of a wonderful romance with JJ; he took her for dinner to fancy restaurants, bought her flowers, and surprised her with weekends away and gifts. She was twenty-two and being swept off her feet, but in spite of that, neither her parents nor her friends liked him. Her mother said he was smarmy, whatever that meant. Alina could not see any fault in him whatsoever, and six months after they first met, on her twenty-third birthday, he proposed to her by taking her to a house in Bearsden with an 'Under Offer' sign outside. He had suggested that he was 'giving it the once over' for a friend.

"What do you think?" he asked as they walked around the outside.

"It's lovely," she said.

"Come on inside," he said taking her hand and leading her up the three steps to the front door. He took her into the front room and there in the middle was a small circular table with two chairs either side; on the table were roses, a bottle of champagne, and two glasses.

"Oh my goodness," she said mystified. "That's' an unusual way to dress a house for viewing."

Alina's face was a picture to behold as she looked at the table and its bounty. JJ laughed and said, "Sometimes you are so innocent Alina; I put these things together for you."

As she turned to look at him in surprise, JJ promptly knelt in front of her and said, "Marry me Alina, and this will be our home. All I have to do is sign the missives."

In his hand, he was holding a red velvet ring box with a beautiful solitaire diamond ring inside.

There was one small niggle in the back of her mind. As they entered the house, she noticed that the number was sixteen and for Alina, that was not a good number. She had studied Tarot cards and numerology and occasionally read for her friends. The sixteenth card in the Major Arcana of Tarot cards is the Tower. Alina knew that 'The Tower' represented disaster, loss of control and grief. She shrugged off her feelings and allowed the thrill of the moment to over ride her doubt. She should have known better.

The next couple of months were a whirlwind of planning for her wedding, but JJ had no family and a quiet wedding, was what JJ wanted. Now that she reminisced, she realised that JJ always got what he wanted. Her parents were disappointed, especially her mother who, like every mother thought about a daughter's wedding day.

Her parents had no living relatives so it wasn't as though they were offending anyone; at least, that was JJ's argument. In the end they had a quiet wedding at Gretna Green with only her parents, JJ's friend Bob, acting as best man, and Alina's best friend Sheila acting as maid of honour. She knew her parents were disappointed, but in spite of their disappointment, they did their best to support her wishes.

She realised that everything in the past three years of married life had been what JJ wanted, and that she had become complacent and agreeable, even resigning from her job so that she would be at his 'beck and call'.

Chapter 13

Alina was in a deep exhausted sleep dreaming that she was trapped somewhere, and a loud noise was alerting her to danger, but she couldn't escape. Clarity interrupted her nightmare, and she realised her mobile phone was ringing. She looked at the display as she answered.

"Mum," she said, and a man's voice answered her.

"Hello, who is this?" she said, "And why are you using my mother's phone?"

"Is this Alina, your name is the last number called on this phone, I take it that this is your mothers phone?" he questioned.

"Yes, did you find it?"

"Well no, not exactly. I'm Constable Riley, you see your parents have been in an accident. I take it your mother was travelling with your father."

"Yes, yes, oh God what's happened to them, are they alright?"

"I have been given this number to contact next of kin and let you know that they have been taken to The Vale of Leven Hospital. Do you know where that is?"

"Are they alright?" she almost screamed at him.

"I don't have any other information other than where they are. I am sorry," he said.

She grabbed her bag and her car keys, threw the phone into her bag, and raced out of the house. Her MG sports car was in the garage and she fumbled, dropping her keys as she tried to open the 'up and over' garage door. She did not even stop to close it before she reversed out of her driveway. She took the Duntocher Road then picked up the A82 to Alexandria. Thirty minutes later, she was at the main reception desk of The Vale of Leven Hospital.

"My parents are here, I had a call from the police to say they had been involved in an accident, Mr and Mrs Webster, can I see them please, tell me where they are please?" the words rushed out of her mouth.

"Oh, one moment please," the receptionist said.

She left Alina waiting there as she went through an internal door. Alina waited anxiously. A few moments later, the receptionist came back.

"Someone will come for you in a moment if you would like to just wait here."

"Are you Miss Webster?" the receptionist asked her.

"No, Mrs James."

A nurse appeared through the internal door and the receptionist turned and said to her.

"This is Mr and Mrs Webster's daughter Mrs James"

The nurse came around from the reception area and smiled kindly at Alina.

"Is someone with you?" the nurse asked taking Alina by the arm and leading her away from the main area and along a corridor.

Alina turned and looked at the nurse, and said firmly, "Look I don't need anyone with me; I just want to see my parents please."

"Just in here," the nurse said, and led her into a small room and closed the door.

The hair stood up on the back of Alina's neck.

"What's going on, I want to see my Mum and Dad."

"I understand," the nurse said, "please sit down a minute."

"I don't want to sit down thank you, you are not listening to me, I just want to see my Mum and Dad, and I want to see them right now."

"I am so very sorry to tell you …"

Before the nurse could say another word Alina heard a keening sound, getting louder and louder, then she realised that the sound was coming from her. In her heart, she had known this was serious by the way the receptionist looked at her, and by how the nurse behaved, but she did not want to accept the fact that her parents were dead. She doubled over with her face in her hands.

"Oh God I should have been with them. I wish I had been with them. I didn't pick up the phone. I will never forgive myself."

Her tears flowed endlessly and the pain in her heart was unbearable.

The nurse held her in her arms as she sobbed.

"Is there someone you can call?"

"Yes, I will call my husband."

"Let me get you a cup of tea, I will be back in a minute."

She dialled JJ's number and it cut off immediately. She tried again, same thing. She called his office and his assistant answered.

"Can I speak to JJ please? Tell him it's his wife."

"I am very sorry Mrs James, he isn't in the office at the moment," she replied.

"Do you know where he is or when he will be back?"

"I'm sorry no, I don't know when he will be back, he just said that he had a meeting, have you tried his mobile?"

"I have to speak to him urgently. Just ask him to call me as soon as you hear from him."

"I will," said the assistant.

The nurse came in with a cup of tea, some milk, and some sugar.

"Is your husband coming Mrs James?"

"No, at least I don't know, I couldn't get a hold of him, I left a message."

"What happened to my parents?"

"There is a policeman waiting outside to see you. Do you want me to give you a few more minutes?"

"No, I want to know what happened and I want to see my parents."

The nurse went out of the room and came back a few moments later accompanied by a police officer.

"What happened to my parents?" she asked.

"It looks as though your father had a heart attack, and the car veered off the road and down an embankment. Your mother died on impact. No one else was involved."

He paused between each statement trying to break the news gently.

"I'm sorry for your loss Mrs James."

Alina broke down again and covered her face with her hands.

"I don't know what I am supposed to do now," she cried.

The nurse stepped forward, crouched in front of Alina, and took Alina's hands in hers. "We have someone here who can help you, try to drink some more of your tea."

The police officer gave Alina a card with his name and contact details before he left, and Alina tried to call JJ once more, but his mobile was still off.

"Would you like me to take you to the hospital chapel?" the nurse asked.

"I would really just like to see my parents," Alina replied.

"Let's go along to the chapel first; I will take you to see your parents as soon as they are prepared for you."

"I don't understand?"

"They will be taken to a special viewing room."

"Are they badly injured, I mean are they marked?"

"No, they will look just as you remember them."

"No they won't, they are dead. How can that be just as I remembered them?"

The nurse accompanied Alina to the hospital chapel and left her there, telling her that she would come back in ten minutes or so. Alina sat it the little chapel her face wet with tears.

"Please forgive me Mum, I didn't speak to you on the phone because I knew that you would know that I was upset, and I didn't want to talk about it or worry you and spoil your day. Maybe you would still be here if I had answered the phone."

She thought about her Dad, at sixty-five he was seven years older than her Mum was. He had looked older since he had suffered a minor heart attack a couple of years before. When he walked, his steps were shallow, not dragging his feet exactly, but not as sprightly as they had been. He was more stooped than usual and as deaf as a post.

She thought back to times before she was married and remembered the way he would look at her with a twinkle in his eye and a half smile on his face. She would smile back at him and it was as though they shared a secret or a joke that no one else knew about, and then they would laugh at nothing and go off together to the local pub for a game of pool.

Her Mum would look on fondly at the pair of them. She had kept her slim figure and always took care of her appearance. She aged gracefully, not showing her grey hair so much because of her natural blonde colouring. She wasn't vain, she just liked to look nice so she visited her hairdresser every six weeks or so and liked to wear nice clothes. Ronnie, her Dad, loved her dearly.

When they were going out together, more often than not, her father would be waiting for her mother to get ready, and as she appeared, he would say, "Ah there she is, my glamorous Beverly." Of course, at all other times he and her friends just called her Bev. Alina loved her Mum deeply, but she was a 'Daddy's Girl' at heart.

"Oh Daddy what am I going to do without you and Mum?"

Part of her realised that though the loss for her was terrible and almost impossible to bear, her parents would not have to suffer the loss of one before the other.

Alina had been interested in the pagan path before her marriage, but JJ was scornful whenever she brought the subject of faith up and gradually her interest waned, but in her heart, she believed that there was a God and a Goddess.

She respected other faiths, but her own faith gave her the comfort of knowing that her parents would be reborn in another life, and that they would probably be soul mates forever until the end of time.

She knelt in front of the altar, and prayed. She asked for help to bear this terrible ordeal. She asked that her parent's spirits, wherever they were, would find safe passage to wherever the afterlife was. She rose and went to a three-tiered stand that had receptacles for T light candles.

She wondered if the lit candles that were already there represented loved ones who had died at the hospital today. She took two new candles and touched the wick to the flame of a lit candle. She lit one for her mother and another for her father, and wished that their memory would always burn brightly in her heart.

When the nurse came back, Alina followed her through a maze of corridors, the sound of their footsteps echoing in the cold silence. Eventually they came to the viewing rooms. As they entered, the nurse paused and asked Alina if she was ready. Alina nodded and the nurse took her through the next door, and there were her parents, lying side by side on two trolleys. A white sheet covered them both to the neck.

"They look as though they are sleeping."

Silent tears fell as she looked at them. The nurse left her to say her goodbyes, and Alina slowly walked forward to stand between her parents.

"This is where I spent most of my life, between Mum and Dad, holding their hands, going places together," she thought to herself. "I have no one now."

She reached over and kissed her mother's cold lips and her tears dripped onto her mother's cheeks.

"Don't cry my baby girl, don't cry." She heard her mother's words in her mind and in her heart.

She reached over to her father and rested her head on his chest and her arm over his head and she stroked his hair. "Oh Daddy, don't leave me." She cried Memories of happy times came flooding back and she knew then that these precious memories would be all she had to hold onto.

The nurse had told her to take as much time as she needed and she told her to press a buzzer, indicating where it was, when she was ready. When Alina had said her goodbyes, she buzzed the nurse, who returned and took her back to the family room where she was introduced to Mrs Evans from family support.

Mrs Evans held Alina's hand in hers as she said

"I am so terribly sorry for your loss. I'm here to help you with some of the things that you will need to do over the next five days."

"Thank you," said Alina numbly.

"Come and sit by me," said Mrs Evans as she drew Alina towards a table and chairs that were set off to one side of the room. She had a folder full of paperwork on the table, and as she was about to open it Alina stopped her.

"I know you mean well and are just doing your job, but I'm afraid I can't do this right now. I just want to go home. Can't I take it with me and work through it on my own?"

"Yes of course you can, actually I have your parent's belongings here too," she said as she handed Alina the folder. There were two large carrier bags, she carried one, and Mrs Evans carried the other as she led Alina to the main exit of the hospital. Alina opened the boot of her car and placed the bags inside. Mrs Evans took Alina's hand and held it for a moment between her hands.

"This has been a terrible blow for you Mrs James. You may want to see your doctor if you feel as though you are not coping."

"Thank you, you have been very kind," Alina replied, as she stepped into her car and placed the folder on the passenger seat.

Chapter 14

It was almost four in the afternoon before Alina arrived back from the hospital. She unlocked her front door, went into the lounge, lay down on the sofa, and cried herself to sleep with the hospital folder lying on the floor by the sofa where she had dropped it. She had not had a return call from JJ, but she was so numb with grief that she did not even realise that he had not called her back.

It was nearer seven pm when his key in the door woke her from her exhausted sleep. She heard the thump of his briefcase as he dropped it in the hall, and then the tinkle of his keys landing on a glass bowl by the hallstand. She sat up trying to focus, wondering if she was still in an awful nightmare as the memory of what she had been doing earlier came back to her. Her long dark hair tumbled over her face and her eyes were puffy from crying all day.

"Look at the state of you." JJ said as he walked into the lounge undoing his tie and kicking off his shoes.

"Where have you been?"

"Where do you think I have been? I have been working. Have you been lying there all day?" He said.

"Why didn't you call me back?"

"I was busy and now I'm not, what did you want anyway."

"My parents were killed in a traffic accident on the Loch Lomond Road."

"Oh! Well that's not so good," he said as he made his way out of the room.

"I'm going for a shower; it's been a long day. Would you like me to pour you a brandy or something?"

She looked at him, and for the first time she really saw that there was no substance to him whatsoever. Was that his support? *'Well that's not so good'* did he really just say that? She questioned herself as she went up to their bedroom and put her pyjamas and a change of clothes into a bag. She went to the shower, reached in, and turned off the water.

"What the hell are you doing?" he shouted angrily "I'm getting ready to go out."

"And I am going to spend the night at my parent's house. I have too many things to do and it would be easier from there. I will be back sometime tomorrow or maybe the next day."

"Fine, whatever, I can fend for myself for a couple of days. Make sure that you take your mobile in case I need to speak to you," he said indifferently, as he put the water on and turned his back to her. She looked at him in disgust.

"Selfish B," she thought to herself. She would take her mobile, but she wouldn't answer if he called her. She was not spiteful by nature, but this was an entirely different scenario.

Her parents house was in nearby Milngavie, a mere ten minutes away, and she could easily have done what was necessary on a daily basis, but her need to be close to her parents in some way was great, and the lack of support from JJ just confirmed her desire to spend a night or two at her parent's house.

Unbeknown to Alina, JJ was rather pleased with her decision.

She had never noticed before, but the minute that she stepped through her parent's front door, she realised that she could smell them. She opened the hall cupboard and took out her Dad's scarf and the jacket her Mum used when she was pottering around the garden and she carried them upstairs to her parents' bedroom. She clutched them tightly to her chest as she lay down on their bed and breathed in their scent.

She tossed and turned unable to stop crying and around four am she got up and went downstairs to the kitchen to make herself a cup of tea and some toast. She took her snack back up to the bedroom and climbed into her parents' bed. The sick feeling in her stomach began to ease as she half-heartedly ate her toast and drank her tea. She lay back down and tried to think about what she had to do in the morning and she remembered the folder that Mrs Evans had given her; it was still in the car, but exhaustion overcame her and she drifted off into a deep sleep.

When she woke up, she looked around the room, puzzled for a moment. The reality of yesterday's events came flooding back. She dragged herself out of bed and went downstairs and into the kitchen. She put the kettle on to make coffee and then went out to her car to collect the folder, the bags from the hospital and her overnight bag. She made her coffee, took it through to the sitting room, and glanced at the wall clock; it showed seven am.

Everything she looked at evoked a memory. She had bought that clock for her father on one of his birthdays and she remembered him saying that every time he looked at it he would think of her. The tables had turned now and every time she would look at it; she would think of her Dad.

She curled up on the sofa, picked up the folder and took out the papers. Right at the very top of the papers was the death certificate signed by a doctor at the hospital. She was not aware of the tears until she realised she could not see through them to read. She noticed the date first. Her parents had died on the twenty second. The significance of the number twenty-two did not escape her attention. Twenty-two is the number that represents crossing a bridge to a new beginning. She wondered what this would mean for her and for her parents too.

She believed in an afterlife and imagined them in a beautiful garden, her father sitting on a comfortable deck chair reading a newspaper or simply watching and smiling at her mother as she pottered among the flowers. Wiping her eyes, she began to read the next lot of papers. The first page revealed the title,

"What to do after someone dies"

Get a medical certificate from a GP or hospital doctor to register the death.

Register the death within five days and request documents required for the funeral.

Arrange the funeral by yourself or employ a funeral director to arrange it you.

The next title was

"Gather the following documents and information."

National Insurance number

National Health Service number

Date and place of birth

Date of marriage or civil partnership (if appropriate)

Child Benefit number (if appropriate)

Tax reference number

Notify the family doctor

Contact the deceased person's solicitor and obtain a copy of the will or if there is no solicitor search the deceased papers to locate a will.

Begin funeral arrangements - you will need to check the will for any special request

If relevant, a completed form should be sent to the local Social Security or Jobs & Benefits office regarding the deceased's benefits (if appropriate)

The next title suggested

"Who else to contact"

Insurance Companies to notify them of the bereavement and cease any policy

Banks or building societies (and accountant if appropriate) to close any accounts

Mortgage provider to freeze payments and consider future options

Hire purchase or loan companies to advise them of the death

Credit card providers'/store cards to cancel cards and close accounts

Utilities and household contacts to advise them of the death and arrange for final readings

Landlord or local authority if they rented a property

Royal Mail, to re-direct mail

TV or internet companies to cancel contracts

Telephone and mobile phone companies to cancel contracts

Local councils

The employer (if appropriate)

The school, college, or university (if appropriate)

The relevant Tax Office

National Insurance Contributions Office (if appropriate

Child Benefit Office (if appropriate)

UK Identity and Passport Service, to return and cancel a passport

DVLA, to return any driving licence, cancel car tax, or return car registration documents

Alina looked at the documents in dismay and wondered how she would be able to cope with everything that she had to do.

Chapter 15

Alina sat staring off into space numb with grief; she couldn't think straight and didn't know where to start and she didn't know how she was going to cope. Her Mum was a well-organised person and she knew that she kept paperwork in an antique bureau in the study. She decided that the bureau would probably be the best place to start.

Just as she was about to begin her search the telephone rang. Alina turned and looked at it and dreaded picking it up. For a moment, she wondered if it was JJ, and then realised that he would most likely call her mobile. She picked up the phone.

"Morning Bev, I saw your light on, fancy a quick breakfast coffee?" said her mother's best friend and next-door neighbour Nancy.

"Nancy it's not Mum, it's me Alina." The lump in her throat almost choked her.

"Sorry Alina, are you ok?"

Alina found it hard to talk, "Can you come round?" she asked,

"I'll be there in one minute"

Nancy called upstairs to her husband Davy.

"I think something's wrong next door Davy, I've just spoken to Alina, and she sounds upset. I'll give you a shout in a bit."

Alina went to open the back door; she knew her mother and her neighbour's habits and knew that Nancy would come to that door.

"Oh my God you look awful Alina, what's happened pet, where's your Mum, has something happened to your Dad?"

Alina could not speak, she turned and put the kettle on and began to make Nancy a coffee.

"Speak to me pet, what's happened?" She said as she took Alina by the arm and turned her around to face her. She saw the tears coursing down Alina's face and wrapped her arms around her.

"There, there now, come on pet, tell me what's wrong" They both went through to the sitting room and Nancy sat Alina down then sat beside her.

"Oh Nancy they are both gone."

"Gone what do you mean gone?"

"They were killed yesterday on the Lomond Road, they said that Dad had a heart attack and lost control of the car and Mum died by his side."

"Dear God." Nancy slumped back into the chair, the colour had drained from her face, and she held her hands to her mouth as though she was trying to hold back her grief at the loss of her dear friends.

"I spoke to them yesterday, they told Davy and I that they were going for a run in the car. Oh, my God I cannot believe they are gone. Davy will be shattered, let me call him round."

Nancy went to the back door, called to her husband to come round, and waited there to close the door behind him.

He knew by the look on her face that something was wrong.

"What's up?"

"It's terrible news Davy, Ronnie and Bev were killed in a car accident on the Lomond Road yesterday."

"Never!"

"Come through to the sitting room, Alina is in a state, she looks like she has not slept for a week."

As he entered the sitting room, Alina stood up and went to him. She had known them most of her life and it was easy for her to lay her head on Davy's shoulder as she sobbed.

"There there, pet, just you have a good cry." He fondly patted her back looking over her shoulder at his wife while trying to console Alina. Nancy stood with tears falling from her eyes.

"I don't know how I'm going to cope without them."

He shook his head sadly his eyes full of tears.

"Well, we'll help you all we can to get through these difficult days. Have you contacted anyone yet?"

"No, not yet."

"Right, it's early yet for contacting people so let's get some food into you before we start and Nancy and I will help you. When did you last eat girl, you look as though you are ready to drop and you cannot function on an empty stomach. Here sit on the sofa and put your feet up. Nancy make us some breakfast love and I will call the surgery. Dr Naven should be informed. I'll leave a message for the receptionist to phone here urgently."

He came back into the sitting room and spoke to Alina.

"Just you rest a bit and I'll give Nancy a hand in the kitchen."

Alina did as was suggested; she put her head back on the corner cushion, and closed her eyes as she listened to Davy speaking to Nancy about the call to the surgery. Dr Naven was Davy and Nancy's doctor as well as hers and her parents. She knew he would be shocked too.

Nancy was putting together scrambled eggs and toast. She was as familiar in Bev's kitchen as she was in her own, but moving around her friend's domain, touching things that she knew Bev and Ronnie would never touch again made her very sad and she cried while she went about her task.

Davy patted her shoulder and asked her, "What can I do to help love?"

"Just set a tray for Alina while I plate these eggs."

They took the food through to the sitting room; Alina sat up and Nancy put the tray on her lap and encouraged her to eat. After they had finished eating, Nancy asked Alina if the hospital had given her a death certificate.

"They gave me a whole pile of stuff; it's all here in this folder."

Nancy opened the folder and spread the contents on the coffee table.

"We should contact the undertaker and then insurance company."

"Davy, I remember Bev saying something about it all being arranged. I know she has papers somewhere."

"Mum would have kept anything like that in the bureau."

Nancy began to search through the bureau and found what she was looking for in the bottom drawer. It was no surprise to Nancy that Bev had left everything neat and tidy in a folder.

She had included both her and Ronnie's wills, contact details for their lawyer, the insurance company, and the funeral director.

"She has everything organised here Alina, Davy and I will start making phone calls. The next of kin has to hand the death certificate into the registry office so Davy will take you there this afternoon. I just need your Mum's mobile to get the numbers of people that we should call."

"The hospital gave me those two carrier bags with their clothes and things; it might be in one of them."

"Shall I take a look?"

"Please, I can't bear to open them."

"I'll take them through to the kitchen."

Nancy picked up the bags and carried them through. One bag had Ronnie's clothes and shoes in it. The other had Bev's clothes, shoes and her handbag. Inside the handbag was her mobile phone, her purse and Ronnie's wallet. There was a cellophane pouch, and in it were Ronnie's watch, and Bev's necklace and earrings. Nancy's heart flipped a beat because she had bought them for Bev last Christmas.

She gathered the clothes, shoes, and jewellery, took them upstairs and put them in the bottom of the wardrobe in their bedroom. She set Bev's jewellery and Ronnie's watch on the dressing table.

She thought of Alina's husband. He should have been by her side at this difficult time, but she expected that his appearance would be limited for, as she had agreed with Bev, he was a selfish man and thought of no one but himself. She and Davy would help Alina, through this; it was the least they could do.

Chapter 16

She looked around at the sea of faces, all gathered to bid farewell to her Mum and Dad. There were so many people there that she didn't recognise, but everyone came to her and offered their sympathies and condolences.

The funeral was over and she was numb and bereft. JJ had put in a late appearance and tried to pretend that he was being supportive, but she could see that he was only doing so for the sake of appearances. He had no sooner arrived than he was gone again, 'pressure of work' being his excuse. That fact embarrassed her more than anything did. He had done nothing to help or support her, and it was Nancy and Davy who had helped her to organise everything even though they were grieving too.

She had spoken to her parent's solicitor and her parents had left everything to her including the house, which was mortgage free. In the weeks following the funeral, with Nancy's help, she emptied cupboards, wardrobes, and drawers giving things to charities. She kept some of her mother's favourite pieces of furniture, like the antique bureau and a small gate leg table with matching chairs upholstered in deep red velvet.

She told Davy to help himself to anything that he wanted from her Dad's shed and garage, and she gave Nancy her Mum's collection of books. Davy helped her to arrange self-storage for the things that she wanted to keep.

She had hardly seen anything of JJ during that period and had to avoid Nancy's questions about where he was and why he was not helping her. She made excuse after excuse often, lying to hide the humiliation that she felt about his lack of support.

Finalising her parent's estate and dealing with all the legalities that this involved took up most of her time. More often than not by the time she got home, he had already been home and had gone out again only to come back late at night. She often pretended that she was asleep rather than have an argument about nothing if he thought she was awake. She often found her face was wet with tears even though she had not realised that she was crying.

The days flowed into weeks, her parent's car had been a right off and the insurance company offered her a cash settlement; the house had sold very quickly and there was nothing left to do except one thing. She went to see Nancy and Davy.

"Come in Alina, I'm just putting the kettle on,"

"Is Davy in?"

"Yes did you want him, he's in the sitting room, go on in and I will bring the tea through."

"I wanted to see both of you actually,"

"Go on through, I'll be there in a minute."

Davy stood up and gave Alina a hug.

"Come and sit here pet, how are you today?"

"I'm OK. I wanted to see you and Nancy together to thank you for everything that you have done for me these past weeks."

"There's no need to thank us," said Nancy catching the conversation as she came through carrying the tea tray.

They sat for a little while drinking their tea and not really saying very much at all.

"Nancy, Davy, there are no words to express my gratitude to you and I will never forget what you have done for me."

"Stop it now," said Davy.

"No please let me say what I have to say. This has been a terrible time for all of us I know, but especially so for me and I know that you are aware that JJ has not been around much to help. Anyway what I am trying to say is there are some things that belonged to Mum and Dad that I want you to have, and I'm sure that they would want that too."

"You've given us enough lass, we don't need anything more." said Davy.

Alina took two boxes out of her bag and gave one to each of them. Davy opened his box and in it was Ronnie's gold watch.

"He wore it all the time Davy. I would like you to have it as a keepsake."

Nancy was opening the box that Alina had given her and when Alina turned to speak to her, Nancy had tears streaming down her face.

"These were so special to Bev, I remember when Ronnie gave them to her, it was their twenty fifth wedding anniversary. She always loved opals, but was really surprised when your father gave her them."

They both looked at the matching necklace, earrings and bracelet.

"Memories" Nancy said, "That's all we have of them now and they're precious. I will treasure these Alina."

"I'm really touched Alina." Davy said, "I miss him more than I can say and I will treasure this and accept it with a humbled heart."

When Alina left their home, she knew that she probably would not see so much of them. Every visit would be a reminder that her parents were no longer next door. There was a feeling of finality to their goodbyes that day. She would come back, but she didn't know when.

She had been operating on autopilot and now there was nothing to occupy her days or sleepless nights. She caught sight of herself in a shop window a few months after the funeral and was shocked to see her reflection. There were dark shadows under her eyes, her face looked gaunt, and her hair looked limp and lifeless. On impulse, she went into a nearby salon and asked to have her hair cropped short. The receptionist told her that she had had a cancellation and advised her that if she could wait ten minutes someone would be available.

An hour later, she came out of the salon; her long dark hair was now just a memory. The stylist wanted to shampoo, condition and style it, but she told her to crop it as short as it would go. The stylist tried to dissuade her, but Alina was determined and after an argument, she got her own way. Cutting her hair did not make her feel any better.

She was still grieving the loss of her parents, JJ was indifferent to her loss, her grief, and as the relationship between them worsened, she blamed herself. He arrived home later that night and Alina was sitting waiting for him.

"Look at the state of you, what have you done to your hair? It's a mess."

Alina looked at him her eyes filled with tears; she shook her head.

"Look there is no point in dragging this out much longer, I have met someone else. You don't take care of yourself and I haven't been able to entertain colleagues for months. I don't know what's become of you and I wonder why I married you in the first place."

Alina's mouth was open in disbelief. He was right, she hadn't been taking care of herself and she was struggling with her loss, but if he had given her some support, things may have been different. She had lost weight, wasn't sleeping well, and had been torturing herself to distraction trying to make things right, and failing at every turn. He did not want her; he was in love with another woman.

Suddenly her hurt turned to rage.

"You are a selfish B. Not once have you offered me any support, sympathy, or tenderness. If it had not been for Davy and Nancy helping me I would never have been able to cope. You have always had somewhere else to be, something more important to attend to and I have let you treat me with indifference for months. Do you remember what you said to me when I told you that my parents had died?"

"What the fuck has that got to do with anything?"

"Don't you dare use that language. You said, 'Oh that's not so good' and then you went for a damn shower."

Back and forward the argument went. Even though he tried to turn her words and blame her, her rage made her stronger. She was standing up to him in a way that she had never done before. For the next hour, they raged at each other. She followed him upstairs and still they raged at each other. She began to feel afraid of him as he realised that he was losing the argument and his attitude became vicious.

He pushed her over and she landed on the bed; while she was down, he grabbed her by the throat choking her with his eyes blazing. She drew up her leg, kneed him as hard as she could between his legs, and as he doubled over in pain, she wriggled free, and ran to the other side of the room.

She grabbed her mobile and said, "Touch me again and your precious career will be over."

He looked at her with such loathing and contempt that she wasn't sure that he was even the same man that she had married. He turned and left the room; she listened as he went downstairs, and then she heard the front door slam shut and his footsteps on the gravel as he made his way to the garage. She looked out of the window as he accelerated out of the driveway.

Chapter 17

She could not bear to stay in the house another moment and she began to regret that her parent's house was already sold. Without thinking of what she was doing, she began to pack an overnight bag. She did not know where she was going, but she certain that she wasn't spending another night in what had been her home.

As she was going through the wardrobe, something made her stop what she was doing. Her instincts were buzzing. She began to go through some of JJ's pockets and found credit card receipts for meals at the same fancy restaurants that he had taken her to when they were dating. There were receipts for flowers, chocolates, and jewellery and none of them had been for her. Now she was frantic, and started pulling open drawers, tossing the contents out onto the floor and searching for clues to his adultery. She gathered all the receipts that she could find and sitting on their bed, she began sorting them into purchase dates. Some of them were more than eight months old. He had been lying all along, blaming her grief as the reason for everything.

She left all the receipts on the bed, and the drawers that she had searched lying open. Before she left the room, she glanced back at the mess she had made and almost grinned; it looked as though there had been a burglary.

She left it as it was and he would know that she had found him out and knew of his lies. With her bag over her shoulder, she left the home where she thought she would raise a family.

She threw her bag in her silver MG sports car and with no real idea of where she was going she drove along Duntocher Road towards Great Western Road and continued through Old Kilpatrick and Bowling. She remembered that the Dumbuck House Hotel was not too far away from where she was. She picked up the Glasgow Road in Dumbarton. As she approached the hotel, she hoped that they would have a vacancy and if they didn't she would just keep driving until she found somewhere to stay.

The hotel was a pretty white two story building that was around two hundred years old, but it was well maintained and had been modernised in keeping with its old world charm. She parked her car in the car park, threw her bag over her shoulder, and tried to look confident in spite of how she felt. The receptionist was polite and friendly and confirmed that they did have a vacancy. As she completed the registration form, she noticed that her room number was eleven; eleven, the number for justice and balance. She took some comfort in that.

The room that she had been given was a large room facing outwards over the front of the hotel. There was a king size bed dressed with white linen sheets, duvet, and pillows, accessorised with a turquoise silk throw and cushions. A matching headboard and curtains gave the room an elegant yet restful appearance.

She unpacked her bag, and began to hang up the few things that she had brought with her. She took her toilet and make up bag through to the bathroom and as she was putting her overnight bag away she realised that she had brought her trinket box.

She opened the small wooden trinket box and scattered the contents on the bed, then sat down to go through the treasures that were there. There was a shell from the beach, which was a reminder of the first picnic that she and JJ had shared. She threw it in the waste paper bin. She picked up the odd pearl earring that had been her mothers and she could remember, as a child, asking her mother if she could keep it. There was a tiny witch on a broomstick that had come from a Christmas cracker, and various ticket stubs from places that she had gone to with JJ. The ticket stubs joined the seashell in the bin. She tenderly handled an old tiepin that had been her fathers and held it sadly in her hand. So many memories, some good, and some not so good flashed back.

Among all the trinkets was a round wooden carving measuring almost two inches across. It looked very old and was worn smooth around the edges and on one side, but beautifully carved on the face of it was a rose. She looked closely at it and admired the details. She thought back and remembered that she had bought it on one of the last shopping trips with her mother. They had gone into several antique and charity shops and she remembered that she had looked at it for a few moments, decided against it and then went back to the counter and bought. She remembered laughing with her mother over the purchase and her Mum saying that it must have called to her.

She threw away everything that reminded her of JJ and sat on the bed holding the little wooden rose, turning it over in her hand and thinking about her future. Her stomach churned with anxiety as she worried about her next step. She went to the side dresser and picked up the kettle to take it to the bathroom to rinse it out. She filled the kettle from a bottle of fresh water that was on the courtesy tray and set the kettle to boil. When the kettle boiled Alina went through the motions of making coffee then kicked off her shoes and sat back on the bed with the little rose just laying there beside her. She picked up the complementary newspaper from the bedside table. She was not really reading it, just turning pages numbly while her head was somewhere else and occasionally staring at the opposite wall. Collecting herself again, she turned another page and a box advert drew her attention.

PSYCHIC ROAD SHOWS

Britain's top Psychics

No appointment necessary

Her heart flipped, the hotel that she was staying in was holding the event the next day.

Alina had her own deck of Tarot cards and had read for friends, but had always kept them out of JJ's sight. He was against 'things like that' and his ridicule of her interests had made her put them away, but she wondered now if by putting them away she was also putting her own essence away too.

When did she stop being herself she wondered? She realized that day by day and bit by bit he had been reshaping her ideas and moulding her into being someone that she was not. She realized that she had no one to blame, but herself because she had allowed this to go on.

Her parents were never sure of her choice of life partner and neither were her friends, but she was caught up in the romance and charm of him and could only see what he wanted her to see. One by one, she had lost touch with friends. He always dissuaded her from them, casting his negative thoughts and feelings on her about her friends until it was easier to live by his opinions.

The next morning, she showered, did the best she could with her cropped hair, and resented the fact that in her angst she had cut it so short. Alina looked through her makeup bag and found some lipstick, blusher, eye shadow, and mascara. Feeling a little more confident, she was about to go downstairs to check out the psychic fare when she glanced at the bedside table and saw the wooden rose. She went over, picked it up, stroked it with her thumb, and put it in her pocket. Before JJ, she had always worn a pouch on cord around her neck and in it she carried little things that held some significance to her. She resolved to start carrying a pouch of special things again. Life was better when she had done that.

Chapter 18

There were several people moving around the reception area as she approached the room where she assumed the psychics were and spoke to a woman who looked as though she was the organiser.

"Excuse me."

"Where have you been, you are late?" the woman said taking her by the arm and leading her into the room. "We have people waiting."

"I am sorry, there has been a misunderstanding," she replied as the woman talked over her.

"I don't need to hear your excuse just now we don't have time, where are your things?"

"I am trying to tell you; I came to make an appointment."

The woman drew back and looked at her deeply. She felt as though she was looking into her soul.

"Let's start again," the woman said, "My name is Madame Cassandra, I apologise for my mistake, but I want to ask you a question and I am sure the answer is going to be yes. Do you read the cards?"

"Well yes, but not for a long time I just came to…"

"I knew it," the woman interrupted "I know a psychic when I see one, even if you do not know it yourself. Help me out dear, a new reader should have arrived last night. You can take her place, sit here and I will make sure that you get plenty of business today."

She gave Alina that piercing look again as she guided her to a table and chair.

"Consider it destiny guiding you," Cassandra said.

"I don't have anything to work with," said Alina in dismay.

"That will not be a problem; I will be back in a minute, now just you compose yourself."

Alina looked around at the other psychics, seated at tables around the edge of the large conference room. A few looked back and nodded or smiled, but Alina was so bewildered by this strange turn of events that she didn't know how to react other than to nod back. A few minutes later Cassandra arrived back with a decorative cloth for the table and a box about the same size as a shoebox.

"I can give you ten minutes to set up and then I will open the doors and let everyone in. We have quite a queue outside now and some have people have appointments so you will be busy."

"Wait," Alina said "I'm supposed to check out; my bags are still in my room."

"Give me your name and room number and I will tell the hotel that you are staying another night," and with that Cassandra just walked away leaving Alina to get on with setting up her table.

She spread the cloth and opened the box to find a pack of Rider Waite Tarot cards, some crystals, a desktop tape recorder, a dozen blank tapes and a notepad and pen. She wondered if this was serendipity or if she was opening Pandora's Box. She wondered too if the little wooden rose was somehow a catalyst steering her in a new direction.

She felt as though the little rose token was calling to her so she put it on her table for luck and as a reminder of the shopping trip with her mother. Within a few minutes, she had her first client, and although she was nervous, it did not show and the client left happy. By the end of the day, she had seen ten clients and had made two hundred and fifty pounds. Cassandra's table fee was fifty pounds from each reader and she covered the cost of advertising and room hire.

Cassandra came over to collect her table fee and have a chat with Alina.

"Well, how was that for you today?"

Alina smiled for the first time in what felt like a while. "Actually once I got started it was ok. I have never read for so many people in one day, it was always a bit of a secret before, I just read for myself or a few friends in time of need."

"Yes, but this is your time of need Alina," Cassandra replied knowingly. "You can join the road show and start a new life or you can go back to misery and confusion, it's up to you, but don't think for too long."

"What would be required if I join?"

"Day after tomorrow we are off to Carlisle, we will spend two days there and then go on to Manchester for two days. After this tour, we take a five-day break and start again. We cover the whole of the UK. The next trip is for twenty-one days and we are off to Ireland."

Alina only took a moment to think, she could go home, pack what she needed including her cards.

"I'm in," she said and felt excitement build in her stomach.

The panic began to build in her chest as she drove back to her house. She made up her mind that if JJ's car was there she wouldn't go in, because she had seen a nasty steak during their argument and she was afraid of him. Her heart was thumping as she drove into her street. Thoughts ran through her mind,

'his car might be in the garage, he might be home and have the lights out.'

Clutching her house keys in her hand Alina unlocked the front door of their home. There was no sign of JJ's car in the driveway and she peeped in the garage window. There was no sign of the car there either and that that reassured her, but she was still afraid that he would return while she was in the house.

She wanted to pack as much as she could and did not want to forget anything or explain what she was about to do. She wanted to be in and out of the house as quickly as possible. She had completely lost her faith and trust in the man that she had loved and believed had loved her.

Before leaving the hotel, Alina had made a list of things that she did not want to leave behind. Going upstairs, she checked her list while her heart fluttered and beads of perspiration began to trickle down her face. She hated to admit to herself that she was afraid of him now, and she was panicking that he would arrive and try to prevent her from going or create a confrontation. She did not want him to make a fool of her and what she was about to do.

She had brought her empty overnight bag with her and she threw it on the bed with two large suitcases from the top of the fitted wardrobes. She noticed that he had picked up all the clothes and things that she had thrown about during her search the night before. She was worried and afraid of how he might react if he came home while she was packing.

She threw as much as she could into the cases, emptied her cosmetics from the bathroom into a vanity case, rammed her hairdryer on the top, and grabbed her laptop in its carry case. She ran into the little study and began to rummage through the desk picking up documents that she thought she should take with her, trying to think of things that she might need, things that he might withhold as a grudge, birth certificate, bank statements, passport, and driving license.

She struggled downstairs with her luggage, in a panic to escape from what had been her home. There were things that she would have to leave behind, but perhaps she could collect them later. Her mind was racing, as she put her cases into the trunk of her car. She ran back into the house for her overnight bag and her laptop. "Oh God," she thought, "My Tarot Cards."

Her mind whirling, she tried to remember where she had last seen them. She would need a cloth for her table. "No," she thought, she could buy one, there would be time to do that when she reached Carlisle.

"Just get the cards," she thought, as she ran into the house and across to the welsh dresser in the dining room. She lifted down a workbox from the top opened it and to her relief, there they were along with Rune cards and a beautiful crystal pendulum.

Back in the car she started the engine, "No!" she yelled to herself, "Leave a note, oh God, paper pen, where?" She couldn't do it; she couldn't go back into the house. He would know that she was gone when he saw the cases and her clothes were missing. Her hands were shaking as she put the key in the ignition of her car and drove away into the night and back to the hotel. She parked her car and the concierge saw her struggling with her luggage and came out to help her.

"Let me help you, madam,"

"Thank you,"

"I thought you were only staying one more night," he said as he smiled at her and competently gathered her cases and put them on a luggage trolley.

"Yes, I am, but I'm going on somewhere else," she replied.

Alina approached the reception as Madam Cassandra appeared from the hotel lounge.

"Back already," she said,

"Yes," Alina replied, "Why do you ask?"

Madam Cassandra laughed,

"You have only been gone about an hour or so, and it looks as though you managed to squeeze a lot into that short time. You look stressed, go up to your room and take a few minutes to freshen up, then meet me in the lounge and we can go over some details."

"I just want to see if I can stay another night and leave for Carlisle from here."

"Leave it to me," Madam Cassandra said, "Off you go and freshen up, and I will see you in ten minutes."

When Alina went back down to the hotel lounge, some of the other readers were sitting with Madam Cassandra. She beckoned Alina over and passed a brandy to her.

"You look as though you need this," she said.

One of the girls smiled at her and patted the seat beside her to welcome her and Alina sat beside her and accepted the drink.

"Sally," the girl whispered, introducing herself.
Alina smiled at Sally and then addressed Madame Cassandra. "Thank you Madame Cassandra."

"Just call me Cassandra; you are one of us now."

She breathed a deep sigh as she relaxed into her chair and then she felt the panic begin to rise in her chest as her mind began to race through irrational scenarios.

"What if he happens to come in and sees me here? What if he approaches and starts a scene?"

She could feel her colour rising in her face.

"Could we maybe chat about the details over breakfast?" she asked Cassandra, as she stood up ready to leave the table.

"I would really prefer to go upstairs and sort my things out if you don't mind."

She looked at the other psychics sitting at the table and wondered if they could see everything that she was feeling and all that was happening in her life.

Cassandra smiled, "Off you go, seven am in the breakfast room, I will see you there."

Back in her room Alina sorted through her luggage and checked all her documents to be sure that she had not left anything important behind. She had nothing to worry about as far as financial matters were concerned. The money from the sale of her parent's home, and the insurance settlements were in a savings account in her name only. She was financially secure, but she had only two hundred pounds in her personal account. She had available credit on her personal credit card, but she would not touch the joint savings or current accounts. Then she remembered that she was actually earning money reading tarot cards and smiled to herself.

She did not want anything from JJ, but when they had married, three years previously, her parents had given her ten thousand pounds as a wedding gift. It had added to their joint savings account which had a healthy balance and she knew that she was entitled to her share.

Recognising that JJ had a mean streak gave her cause to think that he would not stop short in making her life miserable even though he was involved with someone else. Although she did not want any part of him, she had taken the most recent bank statements as she felt as though she might need them for any final settlement. She would see a lawyer when she came back from this tour. She hung her clothes, sorted her makeup, and then took a long hot relaxing bath before climbing into bed exhausted.

Chapter 19

The dream woke her; she could hear footsteps walking up and down the corridor outside her room. They got quieter as they receded and then they would grow louder as they returned. She was terrified that JJ had somehow seen her car and was trying to find her. It was several frightening moments before she realized that the footsteps were in fact her heart beating so loudly that it sounded like a person marching up and down the corridor. She could not remember what the dream was about just that there was an old woman in it.

The woman had white wispy hair drawn back tightly away from her face, lined and wrinkled with age. A black crocheted shawl partly covered the old woman's head and shoulders. Below the shawl, the woman wore a thick dark woollen skirt and old black leather boots peeped out from under the hem of the skirt. The hands that clutched the shawl under the old woman's chin looked thin and gnarled with arthritis. Her face looked contorted with grief and she had a pleading look in her eyes. That was all Alina could remember and although the old woman was not threatening, the dream had scared her.

She got up and opened the little fridge in her room, took a miniature brandy bottle out and put the kettle on to boil. She put the brandy in a cup; added a spoonful of sugar, topped it up with hot water from the kettle and climbed back into bed. "I'm just scared," she said to herself, "It's just the unknown." When she had finished her nightcap, she put her cup on the nightstand and got back out of bed to fetch her own Tarot cards.

She was afraid to read her cards for herself, afraid of what she might see. She carefully un-wrapped her cards form the silk cloth; held them reverently in between the palms of her hands and with her heart pounding and her head aching she tried to still her mind and settle her thoughts. She closed her eyes and said a prayer to herself.

Please show me what I need to know when I need to know it.

Help me to listen to my heart with understanding and to speak with wisdom.

Please show me what I need to know now.

She shuffled her cards taking her time to think about recent events and what the future may hold for her, and then she made a decision and said aloud "I am only going to turn one card, please show me what lies ahead?"

She spread the cards in a circle on the bed and carefully selected the one card. For a moment, she held it in her hands, almost afraid to turn it over. Steeling her resolve to what she might see she turned the card over and burst into tears.

As the tears ran down her face, she began to smile and laugh because instead of her worst nightmare she was looking at the best possible outcome, the ten of cups.

"Everything will be alright; in fact, everything will be better than alright."

She closed the cards, folded them in the silk cloth and still holding them she lay down. As soon as her head touched the pillow, she fell fast asleep.

She woke the next morning a six am, put the room kettle on to boil for that first coffee hit and went to the bathroom to take a shower. Fluffy white towels and a basket of delights made her sigh with relief. Shampoo, conditioner, shower gel, and moisturiser, at least she could go through the motions of pampering and lulling herself into believing that all was well.

When she had showered, she came out of the bathroom and caught a glimpse of herself in the full-length mirror that was on the wall. She actually gasped when she saw herself, really saw herself for the first time in, she didn't actually know how long.

Naked, she could see her hipbones sticking out and her stomach looked hollow. She peered up close to the mirror and studied her eyes. Bright blue, they were her best feature underneath her dark hair, but it was not long anymore; it looked as though it had been hacked with a razor. It was too short and there were shadows under her eyes. "Get a grip," she told herself. She had always been proud of her figure and had, by her mother's example, always taken care of her appearance.

Looking at herself now, she realised that since her parents had passed she had forgotten about herself and her self-esteem. For a second, only a second, she thought that it was no wonder that JJ had found someone else and then she remembered his affair had started long before her parent's accident.

"Had it only been the night before last that she had walked out? Blind idiot," she thought of herself.

She felt ashamed when she thought of her parents; she could see her mother's face when she told her that JJ had asked her to marry him. Her mother had put her arms round her and told her that she was happy for her if she was sure that she was making the right decision. In her heart she believed that she was, but she also knew that her mother did not like or trust him. Alina's father never said much about the relationship, but he had a way of observing that said a thousand words.

Alina believed that once they knew him, really knew him, they would come to love him too. JJ had no living family and Alina felt that that was partly the reason that he made excuses not to visit her parents. She felt that he did not know how to interact in family situations. She knew different now, it was just his way of keeping her apart from them and making it uncomfortable for Alina when she went to visit without him.

Looking at her reflection in the mirror, she knew that she had to take better care of herself. She had not worked since her marriage as JJ preferred her to stay at home and since he had a well-paid career in investments, she did not really need to work. She realised this was just another aspect of control, of manipulating her life.

They had entertained his friends and colleagues, but not hers, as he did not really want them to be invited. Dinner parties always had the excuse of networking and her friends were not suitable for that. Before long, she and her friends had drifted apart and she felt guilty that she had neglected them.

"I'm stupid, skinny, and bordering on ugly," she thought "but no more."

She made her coffee and while she was having it, she picked up her mobile phone and switched it on.

It had been off since she checked into the hotel. It was no sooner on than the message beeps began to flood in. Twenty text messages came in, all from JJ, getting progressively more irritated and angry at her "Irresponsible behaviour." "Where are you? How dare you? Get back here right now." Blah-blah-blah, on and on he went, venting his anger.

He did not love her, but he was furious that she would leave. He had lost control of her and was finding that difficult if not impossible to deal with. She sent one text.

"We are finished and you will hear from my lawyer soon."

She would speak to the lawyer who had handled her parent's estate and if he didn't handle divorce cases, she was sure that he would be able to recommend someone who did. From now on she was on her own; she knew in her heart that everything would work out, her cards had confirmed that last night and she would hold on to that thought. Once more, she looked at her five-foot six-inch frame in the mirror. It all begins now she thought to herself.

She took her makeup bag and applied a little makeup to her face trying to disguise the dark circles under her eyes. The hair was another problem, perhaps a spiky do, but she had no mouse or gel. "Improvise... ok," she took some soap that was still a little wet and rubbed it on her hands then used it on her hair as though it was a gel. The effect was excellent.

She rummaged through her clothes and found a simple ankle length black dress with long sleeves and a plain round neck. She picked up a colourful red and black pashmina that had long black fringes around the hem. She had thought would be useful to cover her table. Instead, she draped it over her shoulders and fastened it with a pin. She looked good, shadows under the eyes disguised, a little eye shadow to compliment her eye colour and a vivid red to her lips matching the colour of the pashmina.

On a whim, she unfastened the pashmina and crossing it over and around her waist and fastened so that the long fringes draped down the side. "Hmmm, I look like a gypsy girl," she thought; and that's how she wore it as she went downstairs to meet Cassandra in the breakfast room.

"Good Morning Alina, you look like a different person today, much brighter," Cassandra said.

"Thank you, I feel much brighter."

"I wanted to apologise for the mix-up when you arrived yesterday morning. A new psychic was joining the group and I assumed it was you. I am glad that she did not come now. Destiny intervened."

"I believe you are right," Alina replied.

Over breakfast, Cassandra discussed the schedule for the road show and explained and how it operated. Alina admired Cassandra while she explained things. She looked like a slightly plump, Spanish mama, with sallow skin, a round face, dark eyes and eyebrows, and her jet-black hair drawn tightly into a bun at the back of her head. Alina felt that she could share her fears and worries with Cassandra.

In spite of her gentle appearance, Cassandra was an efficient business woman and her psychic road show was a well organised and successful operation. Cassandra handled all the advertising and advance bookings for the venues and booked the hotel accommodation for the psychics that would attend. There was apparently a bank of about twelve psychics, but they did not all travel with the group at the same time.

Cassandra gave Alina a schedule of the events and the locations. Together they went over the list so that Alina could decide on which events she would attend. "Mark me down for all of them," Alina said.

"Are you sure?" Cassandra replied, "April through to November?"

"Yes mark me down for all of them, there are days in between when we won't be travelling and I can use my mobile phone and email for anything else that I need."

Cassandra reached over the table and placed her hand over Alina's hand. Alina almost drew back, but let her hand remain where it was. Cassandra looked into her eyes. "You don't need to tell me what you have been through, I can read it in your entire being, but you need some stability too and that means you will need an address so that you can have your mail redirected to somewhere to pick up between shows."

Alina bowed her head, the reality of her situation hitting home.

"Look," Cassandra said, "You can use my address for the next few weeks, but then I expect you to get something more permanent sorted out."

"Thank you Cassandra," Alina said. "That's really kind of you, but I think I may be able to use a friend's address."

After breakfast, Alina made a call to Nancy and Davy to explain her situation. They agreed that she could have her mail sent to them and although they were sorry for what she had been through, they were glad that Alina had finally seen JJ for what he was and was beginning a new life.

"Keep in touch pet, we will see you when we see you, and we will call you if anything comes in that looks as though it's important.

Chapter 20

The trip to Ireland had been a success, and she had enjoyed visiting different towns every day even though she didn't manage to do any sightseeing. On her return from Ireland, she checked into the Travel Lodge at Paisley Road Toll. Nancy and Davy wanted her to stay with them, but she needed to stand on her own feet, find herself, and make her own way in life.

She knew she would have to find a furnished flat with immediate entry. Her internet search had shown that there were many flats available, but more often than not, the date of entry would occur when she would already be away on her next trip. She was not yet ready to think about buying a house of her own, and was not even sure where she would settle or when she would want to make that commitment.

Finally, she found one that she thought would be ideal. It was just off Hillington Road South in a quiet cul de sac. It had private parking and a security entrance, two bedrooms with a master en-suite, a lounge, kitchen, & main bathroom. Gas central heating and double-glazing was a plus. It was close to the M8 motorway, which meant that she did not have far to travel to pick up the motorway for her next and subsequent tours with the psychic fair. The best thing about the advert was the words "Available for immediate entry."

She called the agent, a Miss McNeil, and made an appointment to meet her at the property that afternoon. She began to think of what she would need to take with her, "Driving license, passport, and a bank statement should be enough," she thought. How wrong she was. Miss McNeil was very nice and very efficient and the flat was just what she needed. After viewing the flat, Miss McNeil produced an application form and gave it to Alina for completion. She took it with her back to the Travel Lodge and sat down with a cup of coffee to complete it. By the time she had scanned through it, she was disheartened and dismayed. They wanted so much information and confirmation about details in her life and some of them she knew would fail. Apart from that, she did not want any correspondence getting into JJ's hands even in error.

Apart from wanting her contact details they wanted information on where she worked; how long she had been there *'if less than three years, previous information.* her address, and *'if less than three years, previous information.'*

They wanted to know her marital status, if she was an owner, council tenant, private tenant, or living with parents or friends.

"If I was in any of these situations I wouldn't be looking for a furnished apartment," she thought. If all of that wasn't enough the form asked for her credit history, details of her employer and whether she was employed, self employed, on contract, retired or an unemployed student.

She threw the application form to one side, lay back on her bed exasperated and deflated. Lying there quietly she looked around the room. The room was nicely furnished, and it was a good size giving her plenty of room to move around and had everything in it that she needed. There was an en suite bathroom with a bath, and a shower. The double bed was comfortable, and she could relax and watch the wall mounted television set from the armchair that was set off to one side. Ample storage space for her luggage and clothes meant that she would not be tripping over her things and a desk along one wall with an upholstered chair would provide a good workspace. Wi-Fi was free so browsing the internet and emailing would not pose any problems.

She began to calculate her options; staying in a furnished flat would cost her approximately five hundred pounds a month, plus council tax, electricity and gas whether she was in the flat or on tour. If she stayed in the Travel Lodge after every tour, it would cost her forty-nine pounds a night and that meant that five nights would only cost two hundred and forty-five pounds with no additions for electricity, gas or telephone lines for broadband access. Admittedly, that was for a week, but she would be away most of the time and when she was back, it would mostly be for two or three nights. Chances were that her outlay would be less than one hundred and fifty pounds for each period that she was off.

She jumped off the bed and went to the reception area. "Could you tell me if you have any preferential rates for frequent visitors?"

"Yes we have," answered the receptionist, "but only with advance bookings."

"What would that rate be?" Alina asked

"It depends on the amount of visits and how far in advance you book, but if you were coming back four times for example I could reduce the rate to thirty-nine pounds."

"Let me get my tablet, I have all the dates I need in it"

By the time Alina had booked her return dates, she managed to get the rate down to twenty-nine pounds a night and she was delighted.

Alina sorted through her luggage and organised it so that things she would need were in one case and things that she didn't need could be stored in the other case and left in the boot of her car for the time being. She managed to organise her work clothing so that she would just carry one suitcase, her workbox containing her cards, tablecloth and accessories, and her vanity case. Her tablet would give her access to the internet and she could store names and addresses of clients on it. Her laptop would remain in the car with her excess luggage and she could use it if she needed to.

Alina had earned more than she thought was possible during her trip to Ireland. She had taken names and contact details from everyone that had come to her for a reading and planned to contact them in advance of any return trip to ensure a full diary of appointments. She had enjoyed travelling from place to place, meeting lots of different people, and the busy life style.

She began to realise that with each day that passed, she was becoming her old self, and the more she thought about it, she realised that she was more than she had been before. Her previous business mind that was so active during her banking career was now helping her to be the best that she could be following her new esoteric path. She felt as though she could accomplish anything now.

Chapter 21

Alina and Sally, the first girl that she had met when she joined the group, had become good friends and spent a lot of time together. The friendship she had with Sally had helped Alina to find herself again, and although Alina was friendly the other girls that she worked with, Sally was the one that she was closest to.

Sally was the opposite of Alina; she was shorter and very blonde, rather than dark like Alina. She had a serious considerate side to her nature, but more often than not, she was making Alina laugh. Often, at the end of their working day Sally and Alina would get together to have dinner or just chat and enjoy each other's company.

Sally was knowledgeable about many of the esoteric disciplines and had told Alina that she was a white witch. Although Alina followed the pagan path she felt that she didn't know enough to comment.

Sally was nice and to Alina that was the only thing that mattered. She did wonder though if being a white witch gave Sally her calm understanding nature. No matter what happened on any given day, Sally would remain positive and suggest that the Goddess knew what she was doing and that everything happened for the right reasons.

Sally even managed to make sense of the loss of Alina's parents and the breakup of her marriage. She suggested several scenarios that could have happened to her parents, and she explained that witches believe that they come back and experience life and love again. Sally said that when you have a soul mate, you could have that soul mate for eternity not just for that specific life.

Later when Alina thought these things through, she found comfort in realising that her parents would always be together no matter what journey they were making.

As far as the breakup of her marriage with JJ, Sally explained to Alina that she was on the wrong path.

"It's like this," said Sally "imagine that you are walking along a road and it splits in two or three directions. You choose one road and then suddenly come to a brick wall and can't go any further. What do you do?"

"Go back," said Alina.

"Before you go back what do you do?"

"I don't know. You can't do anything else because the wall has stopped you."

"Exactly," said Sally "when you choose the wrong path you are stopped in your tracks and can't move forward."

"Meaning?" questioned Alina.

"OK when you were with JJ who were you and what direction were you moving in?"

Alina sat quietly thinking and then said, "You are right you know, I had stopped being myself and I had become his trophy. I was stopped in my tracks. Even the things that I believed in were pushed to one side, but thinking of it now, I don't know where my tracks are leading me."

"We don't always know where our path leads us Alina, but we should always pay attention to our inner feelings. We should always listen to that inner voice that tries to guide us and tells us when something is not right. When you don't trust your instincts things go wrong, and then things get worse until you stop and change direction."

Sally's words made a lot of sense to Alina and she vowed to pay attention to her instinct in the future. Sally introduced Alina to psychometry; reading an object that belonged to someone by holding it and sensing the vibrations stored in the object. The reader could then accurately tell the owner of the object things that had happened in their life.

They had several amusing evenings practising this discipline and on more than one occasion, they would be falling about on the bed laughing like teenagers.

Alina soon fell into a pattern of travelling with the psychic fair and staying at the Travel Lodge between tours. As always, she carried the little wooden rose with her.

She had started to put little things into the velvet pouch that she wore on a long cord around her neck, and that is where she carried the wooden rose. From time to time, when she wasn't busy, she would open the pouch, take out the rose, and remember the last excursion to the antique shops with her mother.

Nancy and Davy had allowed her to use their address for any official correspondence, and she visited them often between tours and sent them postcards when she was away. They were always happy to see her when she visited during her days off, and she was getting used to the fact that other people now lived in her parent's home. Her life was running smoothly and she was happier than she had been for some time.

The only 'fly in the ointment' was the recurring nightmare of the old woman. She began to keep a notepad by her bed, but as always, when she woke up all she could remember was what the old woman looked like. One night she woke up after having a dream of the old woman, she decided to consult her Tarot cards to try to understand what her dream could be telling her.

She sat up in bed, un-wrapped the cards from their silk cloth, and held them in her hands for a few moments while she pictured the old woman in her mind's eye.

She drew one card, 'The Hermit.'

"Something from the past, a light at the end of the tunnel," she wondered aloud. Perhaps 'the light at the end of the tunnel' was referring to her personal journey. She drew another card and recoiled, anxious; 'The Tower' trauma, disaster, not a nice card to have in a reading and it made her feel concerned. She drew one more card, 'The High Priestess'. Secrets, hidden information. She drew one more, 'The High Priest', information will be revealed - uniforms. She puzzled over these cards not really understanding their significance. All too soon, these things would become clear to Alina and take her on a journey down yet another path.

Anxious about what she had seen and what it may have meant to her life, she shuffled her cards thoroughly and asked into herself what was in store for her, and then she drew one card, 'The Nine of Cups' wishes granted, she thought to herself, closed her cards, and lay down to sleep reassured once more.

Chapter 22

Often during fairs, Cassandra would nominate a psychic to do a demonstration for people waiting to have their cards read, and each psychic had to take their turn. Some readers were accurate in their predictions, but Alina was sure that some just made things up. She disapproved of this and kept well away from those that aroused her suspicions, and Cassandra was no fool either; she soon got rid of anyone that she felt did not come up to her stringent standards.

Alina had performed demonstrations using her Tarot cards, but on this day, Cassandra mistakenly announced that Alina would be demonstrating psychometry. *Was it a mistake or was it by design?* Alina moved to the centre of the floor and stood in front of the eager audience. She asked if anyone would like to give her an object to read. Several people raised their hands, but one young woman was drawing more attention to herself.

"Me, me, me." She was calling and waving her arms to Alina.

Alina pointed to her and the woman, laughing, came forward and handed her a ring before returning to her seat. Alina held the ring in her hands, placed it on the tip of her finger and turned it several times. She closed her hand over the ring and then closed her eyes. There was silence in the room and everyone waited quietly to see what Alina would say. The young woman was looking from side to side grinning.

Alina opened her eyes suddenly and looked straight at the young woman and to others it looked as though she was gazing into the woman's soul. Alina's expression was serious and annoyed.

"You tried to trick me, but you haven't. This does not belong to you."

There were gasps from the audience and the young woman's face was bright red with embarrassment.

Alina walked to the other side of the room where other women sat. She reached over to one of them and handed her the ring.

"I believe this belongs to you."

The woman took the ring sheepishly and apologised.

"I'm really sorry, sometimes my friend is a bit over enthusiastic, but I don't believe she meant any harm."

Alina leaned over and whispered in her ear, "You will have a baby before a year has passed."

At that, the woman burst into tears and her friends huddled round her.

"What did she say?" What did she tell you?" they asked.

What Alina didn't know was that the woman had unsuccessfully undergone fertility treatment.

Alina ignored the disruption, chose someone else to continue her demonstration, and finished to rousing applause from the group.

Later the two women came over to Alina's table; the first apologised for trying to trick her and the second told her about the unsuccessful treatment that she had endured.

"You have given me hope. Thank you very much." She leaned over and hugged Alina.

Later Sally and Alina talked about the experience.

"I knew you could do it, but even I am surprised. How did you know?"

"I don't know, it was just a feeling and at first I was annoyed and then I remembered what you said about everything happening for a reason, so I went with the flow."

Her reputation was growing and more often than not Alina was fully booked before arriving at venues. Sometimes there would be a freelance reporter and photographer waiting to interview her, and she was always a little uncomfortable about that, but Cassandra insisted that it was good for the fair.

One day a young girl about eighteen years old came over and asked if she could have a reading. She was smiling and appeared to be a bright bubbly person. She was wearing a dark coat and her hair was windblown as though she had been waiting outside for a while.

"Of course," Alina replied. She smiled at the girl and gestured to her to sit down. The girl sat down and Alina took her name and asked her for her contact details.

"I'd rather not say, what do you need them for?" said the girl whose name was Alison.

"I drop an email or a card to clients when I am coming back to the area, but it's ok if you don't want to be contacted."

Alina smiled at her and began to prepare the cards for her reading. She shuffled them thoroughly and then handed the deck to Alison.

"Close both your hands and think carefully of your questions, but don't tell me what they are. When you are ready place the cards here on the centre of the mat."

Alison held the cards and thought seriously about her question and after a few minutes, she placed the cards on the mat.

"Cut the deck into three even piles using your left hand."

The girl took her time and made the cuts. Alina lifted a crystal dowser and began to dowse over the first cut, then the second and then the third. In her mind, she was asking the dowser to show her which deck held the answers to Alison's questions. There was no reaction from the first two, but the crystal began to spin over the third cut. Alina picked up the first two and put them to one side before laying the cards from the third cut in a circle for an astrological spread.

She put the cards out by laying the first card face down in the centre of the circle. Moving to the nine o'clock position, she began to lay the cards out, face up, in an anti-clockwise direction. She looked up at Alison who was staring at her intently. Her expression had become worried; her lips pursed together tensely, her brow frowning.

Alina reached over and placed her hand over one of Alison's and said, "You hide your grief very well." and she watched as the tears began to run down the girl's cheeks. Alina had a lump in her throat, almost reduced to tears too.

"Have you ever had your cards read before?" Alison shook her head.

"Do you know anything about Tarot?" Alison shook her head again. She looked terrified. Still holding Alison's hand, Alina said.

"I'm going to tell you a little about myself and I'm going to give you a lesson in Tarot, and when I am finished you will know that everything I have told you is true."

"Some time ago I lost my parents in a tragic car crash, and it was bad enough that I had lost them, but worse was the feeling of terrible guilt that I had let the answering machine take my mother's last call to me rather than picking up the phone and speaking to her. I had been arguing with my husband and didn't want her to hear it in my voice. You know what mothers are like, they always know. Anyway shortly after that my husband left me for someone else."

Alina was watching Alison as she told her story.

"I thought my life was over, and sometimes I even thought of ending it and then something thing happened. I picked up my Tarot cards and I asked one question, I asked the cards to show me what lay ahead and then I drew one card. The card I drew made me cry with relief because it was the best card in the deck. You have that card here." Alina pointed to the ten cups.

Alison's shoulders jerked up and down as she sobbed silently and Alina was not aware that tears were running down her face too. She handed Alison a tissue.

"It gets even better than that Alison, if it had been nine cups I would be telling you that your wishes would be granted, but the ten cups can only be better, beyond your wishes, beyond your expectation."

Alison put both her hands over her face and rubbed at her eyes she was still crying, but now she was laughing too. Alina laughed with her.

Chapter 23

Alina began to explain the Tarot reading to Alison

"Now let's sort out this mess that has been around you. All these dark cards, the swords, these are your problem cards. Each position tells me the area of your life affected by the card whether it's good or bad. I would describe the Tower as your worst nightmare; it's all about loss of control in your life. The Five Pentacles relates to financial matters, look at the picture. That's you in the picture, feeling lost and alone, cold and hungry, feeling as though no one cares.

When I am looking at this second card in the 'house of finances', I look too at the card relating to your career and health because these positions are related. Look at the card what do you see?"

Alison began to describe the card.

"I see a woman behind swords and she is wearing a blindfold and her hands are tied."

"That's you Alison, that's how you feel right now, but remember you have the ten cups and we know that no matter what has gone before everything is going to be better than you can imagine. Look at the number on the card Alison and tell me what it is."

"It's eight." She said.

"The suits only go as far as ten so this means that you have two things to do and only you can know what these two things are. Two responsibilities, two tasks perhaps, but as soon as you have done these two things, the suits have to begin again.

"What number do you think they will begin with?"

"One?"

"Absolutely," said Alina, pointing to the Ace swords in the twelfth house. This is where your anxieties lie and the power of this card will allow you to cut through your anxieties and find a new beginning."

Alison was now beginning to scan the pictures on the cards and beginning to look more enthusiastic.

"Do you see your third house, relating to family and news? Nine Swords, we are getting closer to achieving the ten that we need for the new beginning. You have something to do concerning a member of your family before you can reach that level. The fourth house is showing me your home life, and the Moon tells me about your depression and anxiety."

Alina continued with the interpretation of the cards making sure that Alison understood everything that she was telling her.

"This fifth house tells me about romantic matters and you have an awful card here. The Knight Wands is all about abuse Alison, it can be any kind of abuse, emotional, physical, verbal, financial, spiritual or sexual, but no matter which way it's looked at it is abuse, and you have to get away from it because it or the person who is causing it will not change."

"Your seventh house, which tells me about partnerships and relationships, confirms how this is affecting you. Look at the card and tell me what you see."

"A red heart with three swords piercing it."

"What do you think that means Alison?"

"Heartbreak."

"Yes."

Alina and Alison looked at each other across the table. Alison could hardly believe that Alina, without knowing anything about her, could tell her so much about her life and the things that she was going through.

Alina, of course did not know the specifics, but she could understand the associated events and emotions that the cards were showing her.

"That is the worst of the cards Alison, now let's look to the future for the best is yet to come. This next house deals with endings and new beginnings. Look at the card, look carefully on the Magician's table and tell me what you see."

Alison took the card in her hand and looked closely at it.

"There's a sword there!"

"Yes, there is what else?"

"A branch, a cup, and a coin."

"That's right Alison, although in Tarot we would say a wand for the branch and when there is only one it becomes the Ace of Wands.

On the Magician's table there are four aces, the ace swords, the ace wands, the ace cups, and the ace pentacles, but in your cards there is only one ace missing and that is the ace wands. That ace will bring you new ideas, motivation, excitement and enthusiasm, and it will come within the next six weeks.

In the house of travel and education, you have the ace pentacles, which is fantastic; new doors opening, your chance to learn some new skill perhaps go to college or university. The tenth house is for your hopes and dreams, and you have the ace cups. This will bring you love, joy, and contentment, but you have one problem in the house that deals with your friends and colleagues, and this card 'the devil' tells me that there is a bad influence here and that perhaps it's time to stop listening to someone that is leading you in the wrong direction. It can also mean that you are afraid of someone in that circle. You can cut through your anxieties with the ace swords, which will empower you, and finally the best of all in the middle of your reading the ten cups. It does not matter what has gone before all you need to focus on is your future."

Alison was smiling when Alina looked across at her.

"Thank you so much, I don't know how you did that, but you have made all the difference to me."

"You are very welcome Alison. Are you confident about your future now and what you should be doing?"

Alina stood up and moved around her table and Alison threw her arms around her and hugged her warmly before she left.

Alina took a break before seeing her next client and after having a cup of coffee, she went back to her table to begin again. About an hour and a half later, after she finished reading for another client, Cassandra came over to her table carrying a bouquet of flowers.

"Oh they are lovely, have you got an admirer?" Alina said.

"They're not for me, they're for you."

"What, who from?"

"A girl called Alison, she had two bunches of flowers, one for you and one for her mother. She told me to tell you that she was going home to her mother, and that before she had come to see you her plan was to take her own life."

Alina's eyes were wide and her mouth gaped open at Cassandra's words. She knew that reading cards for people was a massive responsibility and that readers had to know what they were doing, but Alison's message really brought that fact home.

Cassandra put her arms around Alina and held her for a few moments.

"You gave her hope Alina; she only had despair in her life before you read for her."

Chapter 24

Time passed as time does and soon Alina was becoming dissatisfied staying in travel lodges between trips. She had kept some things in storage from her parent's home, and after the divorce, some things from her own home, nevertheless, not having a permanent place of her own to return to meant that she was reluctant to buy things that she saw and admired on her travels. She began to itch for her own place, a place that she could call home. She didn't want to admit that she was also becoming tired of the constant travelling, staying in top hotels while on tour, and eating fancy foods. Sometimes she just fantasised for a plate of homemade mince and tatties or a bowl of chicken soup like her mother used to make for her.

Thinking of that made her think of the last time that she had spent the day shopping with her mother. She fingered the pouch hanging from the cord around her neck. In it was the wooden rose from the antique shop, the odd pearl earring, the mate of the one that her mother had lost years before, her father's tiepin and the little witch on a broomstick. Yet though the memories that these things evoked saddened her, they also brought her some comfort.

She shared her feelings with Sally.

"What do you want to do?" Sally asked.

"I want a home; I want to stop travelling about."

"Are you going to stop seeing clients?"

"No definitely not, I love what I do and I love feeling as though I have helped people to make choices. No I don't what to stop, but I want to be in the one place where people can come and see me in my own place."

"So where do you want to live?"

"Definitely Glasgow, somewhere central, easy access for clients. An extra room to see clients in and it must be somewhere safe just in case JJ gets any stupid ideas."

JJ had continued to harass her even after their divorce, paying her more attention than he had when they were together. She had changed her mobile number, but if she was going to work from home she would have to advertise her services, and if he was still of a mind to bother her, it would only be a matter of time before he found out where she was. Perhaps she was being paranoid, but the content of some of his texts during the initial breakup had scared her.

"Do you want me to do a spell for you?" asked Sally smiling at her.

"No thank you, you and your rituals. I have watched you so often I could do it myself if I wanted to and I've read all your books too." Alina laughed at her.

"Are you going to tell me that you are not just a tiny bit interested?"

Alina looked at Sally and smiled.

"It's not that I am not interested, I'm just not ready; maybe once I get my own place I will feel more like taking it a bit further. I have certainly seen some positive results from watching you, and many of the things that you have explained resonate with my own feelings."

"Have you read your cards on it?"

"Nope."

"Are you going to?"

"I don't know, maybe."

"You will keep in touch won't you." said Sally, her eyes tearing up. "I don't want to lose your friendship."

Alina jumped up from her chair and went across to hug Sally.

"Numpty, you're my best friend, of course we will keep in touch. Remember I have lost friends through neglect before and I don't plan to repeat that mistake.

When I get this house you will be helping with the move and the decorating." Both girls hugged and laughed.

Occasionally, Alina would browse the internet or she would pick up a property newssheet, but as always, the next trip got in the way. One day as destiny intended, she was waiting for her next appointment to arrive when she noticed a newspaper left behind by an earlier client. Alina picked it up to browse while she was waiting and she caught sight of an advert that drew her attention.

Property for Sale

4 Riverview Drive, The Waterfront, Glasgow

This is an extremely spacious three bedroom, (1 en-suite), top floor apartment with lounge, dining room, kitchen, and guest bathroom. Attractive views of the River Clyde and residents' parking.

A reception hallway, bright spacious lounge with fireplace, patio doors, and balcony that overlooks the River Clyde. A modern fully fitted kitchen complete with wall and base units, and appliances. Two of the three large bedrooms have fitted wardrobes, and feature shallow balconies. The property has double-glazing, central heating, and is accessed via secure entry. There is ample residential parking on this development on the southerly banks of the River Clyde and there are excellent transport links with nearby access onto the M8 motorway. Offers around £158,000 are invited.

Throughout the day, in between clients, she looked at the advert again. Her instincts told her that this could be the one.

The last three years had been traumatic to begin with and then transitional as she began to rediscover herself and who she really was and wanted to be. At twenty-nine, she felt that she should be in control of her life's path. She was stronger and more confident in herself and she realized that this was the time to make some serious decisions.

She was still sitting at her table with her cards in front of her while she thought about the property at Riverview Drive. She reached out, placed her left hand over her Tarot deck, and then fanned them out in a semi circle. She closed her eyes, touched one card, opened her eyes, and turned the card over.

The card she had was 'The Hanged Man'. This was a good sign indicating life-changing events. The number associated with it was twelve, adding the one and two together would achieve three. Three in numerology meant growth, expansion, and fruitfulness.

She spoke to Sally over dinner that night.

"I read my cards, well one card."

"What! When?" exclaimed Sally

"Today, in between clients, I pulled a card."

"Whatever for?"

"I saw a house advertised that might be the one."

"And you never told me"

"I'm telling you now." Alina laughed.

"Where is it, what's it like, tell me all about it?"

Alina had cut the advert out and had put it in her handbag. She drew it out and handed it over to Sally.

"Wow Alina, this looks great. I love it. What are you planning to do about it?"

This was the last day of what had been a fourteen-day tour and they were at the Concert Hall in Glasgow. She would have five days off and that was plenty of time to arrange a viewing, and if all went well, to see her lawyer before the next tour was due to start.

"Well if you don't have any plans for tomorrow I thought that I would call the agent to arrange a viewing, and I thought my best friend would come with me."

"You just try and hold me back. Oh I'm so excited now."

They chatted over their meal and Alina said she would call Sally to let her know what time to meet her at the flat. Sally left to go to her home in Largs and Alina went back to her usual Travel Lodge. She called the estate agent in the morning and the appointment was set for noon that day. She could feel things falling into place.

Chapter 25

The Country Wide estate agent was waiting for them when they arrived and very professionally showed them around the flat. Alina could see that Sally could hardly contain her excitement. She kept glancing over at Alina behind the agents back and mouthing "Wow." Alina loved the apartment; she stood at the little balcony and looked across the Clyde. She could see the 'Squiggly Bridge', and from the apartment, she could walk over the bridge into the city centre to browse the shops, visit chic bars or restaurants, or she could just walk along to the left from the apartment and she would be at The Quay. There was a cinema and several restaurants there too.

"Maybe I could get a little dog." She wondered.

"Are dogs, pets allowed in these apartments?" she asked the agent.

"Yes absolutely, the walkway outside is ideal for walking a dog and your next door neighbour has a little 'Scotty' dog. She is very friendly."

"The woman or the 'Scotty' dog?" Alina heard Sally saying as she laughed at her own joke.

"Sally!" Alina reprimanded her, but could hardly contain her own laughter.

The estate agent laughed too. "Actually they are both very friendly, Mrs Brodie is my aunt, and Jock's the dog. I'm a dog lover so it would be hard for me not to like Jock."

Sally was still making faces and she raised her eyebrows at Alina as she walked out of the agent's line of sight. She nodded at the estate agent behind his back and mouthed "Nice butt", making a grabbing gesture with both hands as she did so. Alina turned quickly away from Sally. She could not look at her without laughing; she could feel her face blushing.

He did have a nice butt, he was about six foot and lean, but not skinny. He had a look about him that said he enjoyed a game of football or tennis. He looked fit in more ways than one. His dark hair was nicely styled, but had an almost unruly look to it. The agent interrupted her thoughts and she was almost embarrassed as though he knew that she had been thinking of him.

"I will leave you ladies here for a bit to browse around the apartment on your own. Just close the door behind you and I will meet you in the car park."

He offered his hand and as Alina placed her hand in his she said, "Thanks, Mr Buchanan, we won't take too long."

"Please, call me Ronnie," he said, still holding her hand.

"Oh!"

"Something wrong?" he questioned at her exclamation. They were still holding hands and making direct eye contact and as far as Sally was concerned for far too long.

"No, no nothing, that was my father's name, you just surprised me that's all. It's not a name I hear often these days."

Sally was almost dancing behind him mouthing, "It's a sign it's a sign."

Alina ignored her, and smiled at Ronnie releasing her hand from his.

"We will be down stairs shortly."

As he left the apartment, Sally and Alina giggled at each other.

"You are such a bad influence Sally."

"That's why you love me. I make you laugh and I can remember a time when we first met that I wondered if you knew how to laugh." Changing the subject quickly, she added "But he is nice and the apartment is fabulous. What are you going to do?"

"I'm going to make an offer; I want this house, I want it to be my home, it feels right."

"Wait, don't you think you should see if you can get a mortgage first?"

"Actually I don't need a mortgage, I have enough in the bank to just buy it."

"Excuse me, do you mean we have been friends all this time and you never let on that you are loaded? Well I know who is buying lunch," said Sally as she hooked her arm through Alina's arm. "Let's go and have that lunch now."

They went downstairs and met Ronnie in the car park. He handed her the home report.

"I've downloaded it already so I don't really need it thank you. You will hear from my lawyer today so you might want to give your clients a 'heads up', I will be putting in an offer, but they will only have until noon tomorrow to accept or decline, and if they accept it will be a cash purchase so there will be no waiting for mortgage approvals."

Ronnie raised his eyebrows, looked at Alina and said, "That was a quick decision; I must admit I didn't expect that to happen so fast. I will speak to my clients and let them know to expect your offer."

They shook hands with each other and then Ronnie nodded to Sally as he got into his car. Before Alina and Sally reached theirs, he was on his phone calling his client.

Alina sat in her car and called her lawyer. "Offer them the asking price with a close of noon tomorrow. Can you have that couriered over to their lawyer?" Alina gave her lawyer the property details and the contact numbers for the estate agents.

"What now?" asked Sally

"Lunch, I'm buying," laughed Alina, "and then we wait."

At ten o'clock the next morning Alina's mobile phone rang and she jumped up to answer it, wondering if it was the estate agent calling, but when she looked at the display it was Sally.

"Have you heard anything?"

"No it's only ten o'clock; get off the phone, they could be calling right now."

"I can't stand the wait; I have been awake half the night, I'm coming over, I'll be there in less than an hour. If the news is good we'll celebrate and if not, well I'll be your shoulder to cry on."

Sally arrived at the travellers lodge an hour later and Alina already had her jacket on to go out.

"Let's go for brunch, we'll go in your car since it's still warm."

They went to one of the cafe bars in the city and ordered breakfast and coffee. "Make sure you can get a signal in here," said Sally.

"What for?"

"In case the agent or your lawyer calls of course," replied Sally,

"Oh I don't need to bother about that."

"Why! Have you gone off the idea?" said Sally dismayed at Alina and surprised that she had changed her mind.

"No I haven't changed my mind," she said calmly stirring her coffee. She looked up at Sally and grinned. "It's mine, it's mine, my lawyer called right after you, and my offer has been accepted."

"OH MY GOD oh my God, oh my God," said Sally bouncing up and down in her seat. "How could you hold that in?"

Alina laughed, "So that I could see this reaction."

Both girls had tears in their eyes and both were happy with the result.

"You've bought a house; I can't believe it, that was so fast."

"Well the offer has been accepted, but it will be about six weeks before all the paperwork, searches and stuff has been completed, but my lawyer will get the missives signed as soon as possible and my accountant will arrange for the funds to be released."

"What are you going to say to Cassandra? She'll be upset when you tell her you're leaving."

"I'll be upset too and I am dreading her disappointment. She has been so good to me, and if it wasn't for Cassandra, who knows what I would be doing or where I would be right now. She changed my life, and both of you helped me to find myself."

Chapter 26

When Sally dropped Alina back at the Travellers Lodge, Alina called Nancy and Davy.

"Can I pop up this evening?"

"Of course, you don't even need to ask, you know you are always welcome here," said Nancy.

"Yes I know that, but I wanted to be sure that you were both at home, I have some news for you."

"Have you met a nice man?" questioned Nancy smiling and hopeful.

"I'm always meeting nice men, but it got nothing to do with that. It's something special and I'm giving nothing away until I see you. Is seven o'clock ok?"

"No, make it earlier; if you come now you can help me make dinner, it's your favourite, 'Haddock Mornay Pancakes'. I can't wait to see you; we have both missed you very much."

"I've missed you both too."

Later they all sat down to a dinner of smoked haddock. The fish was cooked in a little milk and butter, broken into bite size chunks then covered in a cheese sauce. Alina had helped Nancy to make the pancakes flavoured with a touch of herbs, and then Nancy put a large pancake on each plate, heaped a generous serving of cheesy haddock in the middle, and then folded the pancake over the top. Alina garnished the pancake with grated carrot and added the side salad.

"So what's this news you have Alina?" asked Davy.

Alina reached down into her bag that she had brought to the table and handed the schedule to Davy.

"I thought maybe you and Nancy could come and visit me sometimes and maybe I could make you dinner."

Davy looked at the picture on the front of the schedule and then he handed it to Nancy.

"You've bought this, well I'm proud of you pet well done, this calls for a celebration. Let me open a bottle of wine."

Davy left the table to fetch the wine and Nancy came round the table to hug Alina.

"I'm so happy for you Alina and I'm proud of the way you have handled things these past few years. It looks lovely and I can't wait to see it."

They talked about the house during the meal and then went through to the sitting room to relax with their coffees. Nancy and Davy offered Alina the spare room so that they could relax and enjoy the rest of the evening.

During previous visits, Alina had mentioned to Nancy that she had been having strange dreams, but she had never gone into detail about them. Davy had elected to wash the dishes and while he was in the kitchen, Nancy spoke to Alina.

"Are you sleeping better or are you still having the dreams?"

"No I still have them, it's the same dream all the time, and I have been having it more often recently."

"What is it you are dreaming about, you never said before and I didn't like to ask?"

"I see an old lady, white hair drawn back in a middle shed pleated at either side. She looks very sad and it's as though she's imploring me, but I don't know what she wants. She wears a black shawl and a thick skirt that comes down to her ankles."

"Maybe it connects to your gypsy blood."

"WHAT!"

"I said maybe it connects to your gypsy blood."

"Nancy I don't know what you are talking about. I don't know anything about having gypsy blood."

"I'm sorry pet maybe I shouldn't have said, but your Mum told me that one of her ancestors was a gypsy girl who ran off and married a miller's son and caused such a ruckus in the family at that time. Both sets of parents disowned them. I wonder why she never said. It was all very romantic when she told me. That's probably where you get your gift."

Alina's mouth was hanging open when Davy came through from the kitchen and started topping up their glasses.

"Did you know about Bev's gypsy heritage Davy?"

"Married a miller?" Davy replied.

"Aye that's right, did you know about her family?"

Davy thought for a moment, standing with the wine in his hand. "Aye it comes back to me now, I think, no, am sure she was a gypsy girl and the two families banished them."

"Did your Mum never mention it to you Alina?" asked Nancy.

"You know, when I was little my Mum used to tell me a bedtime story about a gypsy princess who gave up her kingdom and ran off to marry a miller's son. That must have been what she was talking about, but I never thought it was real."

Nancy and Davy were quiet as they watched Alina processing this information.

"That's it, that's why I keep having the dream. Amazing, wow, I'm a gypsy, how exciting is that?" She laughed then held up her glass.

"Cheers," she said still laughing. "How would I find out? There must be travellers somewhere that are relatives of mine. Wow, I don't know what to think or where to start, but I am thrilled to bits. I might have family still alive. Maybe the old woman is a relative? Wow, I hope I dream of her again soon, maybe I can find out what she wants me to do."

Alina didn't dream that night and if she did, she didn't remember. She slept soundly in Nancy and Davy's spare room and the next morning after breakfast, she called Sally to tell her what she had found out.

"What are you going to do about it?" asked Sally.

"Nothing just now, I have too much to think about re the new house and organising things that are in storage, but once I am settled I am going to find out everything that I can. I know my Mum had a load of old papers and documents that I have never looked at, but they are in a case in Nancy's loft for safekeeping. When I'm settled you can help me to go through them if you want."

"You bet," said Sally.

Chapter 27

Eight weeks later Alina stood outside her new home waiting for Sally and the removal vans to arrive. She was a different person now, confident in her five foot six slender frame, her dark hair now healthy and long and a sparkle in her blue eyes. She stood beside her car and looked over the River Clyde and back at her apartment on the top floor. Daffodils bloomed on the well-kept grass verges, which edged the residents parking zone, shrubs and trees provided an area for the birds. She watched a robin pecking around and there was a sense of calmness in the fresh morning air. The robin came really close to her feet and she had an overwhelming urge to speak to it.

"Hello Robin, what do you want little bird, have you come to welcome me to my new home, or are you letting me know that this is your patch?"

Sally drove up and laughed as she said, "Do my eyes deceive me or did I just see you speaking to a bird?"

"Yes you did."

"By the way, Cassandra sends her love," Sally said as they hugged each other.

Alina knew that she would miss working with Cassandra and it had been hard saying goodbye, but that part of her life was over now and this was her new beginning. She was confident that she had chosen well and the fact that her house number was four added to that feeling of confidence as the number four indicated stability and security, exactly what she needed and wanted in her life, stability and security.

Before too long the removal van had arrived bringing her belongings from storage, and she spent the next few hours directing the removal men and telling them where to put her things. Davy and Nancy had come along to help and with Sally there too, the task was so much easier. She had ordered a new three-piece suite and bedroom furniture for her bedroom and the guest room. The spare bedroom would have a small two-seater settee, which she found in an antique shop. She had it professionally re-upholstered in rich red velvet to match her mother's mahogany antique chairs and gate leg table that had been in storage.

Nancy unpacked bed linen and made up beds while Davy worked with a hammer and picture hooks taking instruction from Alina about where to hang her paintings. Sally and Alina hung sheer muslin drapes on the brass curtain rails that were already in place over the patio doors, which opened on to the shallow balconies in the lounge and the master bedroom.

After Nancy and Davy went home about four o'clock, Alina and Sally, who was staying over for a few days, took a walk through each room with an objective eye. They started at the front door as though they were entering the house for the first time. The walls were soft shades of cream or oyster making it easier for Alina to place her things without worrying about clashing colours.

With their backs to the main door, they were looking at a wide hallway that now had a small antique mahogany reception table with bowed legs and a lower shelf. Two soft bucket chairs sat either side, which would allow the next client to sit and wait, and Alina would add fresh flowers to the Chinese vase on the top of the table, and some magazines to the lower shelf. Davy had hung three 'old masters' which continued the antique theme.

A door to the right of the wider part of the hallway opened onto a bedroom, which had a front facing balcony overlooking the Clyde. Alina had decided to use this room for private consultations. She had placed the red velvet covered two-seater settee against the far wall, her mother's antique bureau in the corner and on the opposite wall, her mother's circular mahogany gate leg table, and matching velvet covered chairs. Her workbox containing her Tarot cards and other accessories was already sitting on the table waiting to be unpacked.

"I love the fancy scroll work on the chair frames," said Sally.

"Hmm, me too, I think it looks nice and restful for clients, don't you?"

More paintings were hung in this room and these were scenes of trees and landscapes in soft watercolours. On the far wall stood a music centre so that Alina could play soft background music; and a built in wardrobe doubled as a discreet mini office, storing her laptop, files, and other paraphernalia.

A door to the left of the main door led to the guest bedroom and Nancy had been busy in there making up the bed. New bedding was dressed in soft lavender shades; later Alina would add drapes over the bed using sheer chiffon matched with a silk overthrow. The bedroom furniture in this room had come from her parent's house, and comprised of two cream and gold ornately designed bedside chests and a matching dressing table and stool, upholstered in cream and gold to match the furniture. The style was 'French Chic'. The three paintings here were all of ballerinas in various positions of the dance, and Alina had bought these when she was married. Patio doors overlooked landscaped gardens to the rear of the property.

As the hall narrowed, it led to an ensuite bedroom on the left, which Alina would use, and it too was dressed in soft shades, this time of pearl and cream. The furniture in this room was all built-in and comprised of wall-to-wall wardrobes with sliding mirrored doors, which opened to reveal an abundance of hanging and shelving space with room in the middle, which housed a vanity unit, complete with stool and recessed lighting. Alina planned to accessorise the walls with large prints of red poppies and peony roses.

At the end of the hall to the right was the dining room and here she used her parents antique dining room suite. The table was in a six-seat position, but a recessed pullout allowed it to extend to eight seats. There were two carver chairs and four dining chairs with a matching sideboard, all in rosewood.

Alina had hung small prints of posters depicting 'French Cafes' and had placed two large silver candelabras on the sideboard adding a nice touch.

The Kitchen was a dream of modern technology with stainless steel fittings, cooker, oven, and grill. Concealed white goods and a multitude of storage and work surfaces completed the picture.

The dining room led through to the lounge and in the corner was Alina's favourite purchase, a wraparound Persian blue corner suite with deep soft cushions. A Japanese style coffee table sat in front of the suite and two deep matching armchairs sat opposite. Two tall freestanding shelves echoed the Japanese style that Alina favoured, and she knew that there were several ornaments still packed in boxes that would look perfect on these shelves. Muslin drapes dressed the main widows and moved softly from the air coming from the open patio doors.

Chapter 28

The house was in order and all the boxes that could be unpacked were flattened and ready to go to recycling. There were still some boxes stacked to one side in the lounge.

"What's in these boxes?" asked Sally.

"Books, I am going to need book cases for before I can unpack these, but right now I think I need food more. Are you hungry?"

"Starving," said Sally.

"We could order in, what do you fancy?"

"Chinese would be good, Lemon chicken and fried rice."

Alina switched on her laptop and searched for the nearest takeaway Chinese Restaurant and once she had the number, she called the restaurant and placed the order. About fifteen minutes later her doorbell rang.

"That was quick," said Sally.

"It can't be the delivery; how would they get in through the controlled entry? They have to buzz the house number for access."

Alina went to the main door and looked through the spy hole to see an elderly woman with white hair on the other side of the door. For a moment, the white hair gave her a jolt, but she opened the door.

"Hello dear, you're in then, I'm just back myself I've been away at my friends. I'm Mrs Brodie and this is Jock," she said indicating the Scotty dog at her feet. Jock was looking up at her expectantly.

"I've brought you some shortbread and a wee half bottle of whisky. My nephew Ronnie told me you might be moving in today."

Alina laughed and welcomed her and Jock in and then introduced her to Sally.

She looked around the sitting room.

"Oh my, it looks as though you've been here for months, everything in its place, its lovely dear and I hope you'll be very happy."

"Thank you, would you like to see the rest of the house?"

"No my dear, I just wanted to welcome you. If you need anything you only have to ask."

Shortly after Mrs Brodie and Jock left, the buzzer at the main door sounded the arrival of their meal. Alina pressed the entry button on the control panel and when the delivery driver arrived at the door, she swopped money for the carry out bag of food.

While they were eating, Sally asked Alina about the 'gypsy blood story'.

"I was amazed and delighted when Nancy told me about that. I must have family somewhere and I would love to make contact. I wonder if the old woman I dream about is an ancestor."

"Did Nancy bring the box of documents? We could start there if you like."

Alina went to the built in wardrobe in what was now her designated consultation room cum office and fetched the box of paperwork. She was anxious about opening it fearing that the sight of her parent's death certificate would upset her, but she took comfort from the fact that Sally was there with her, and she always knew how to lighten a mood.

Alina and Sally moved to the dining room and sat side by side at the table. Alina opened the box and right at the top was her parent's death certificate. Below the death certificate was a manila folder and Alina opened it to view the contents. The first thing she saw was her parent's marriage certificate.

"Look there's lots of information on here."

"Sally, I can't do this. I don't even know if I want to do this, not just now anyway."

"Do you trust me?"

"Of course I do."

"Ok, if you are happy to let me copy all the relevant documents, I will take the copies on tour with me and I will research them in the evenings."

"Are you sure?"

"I could really get my teeth into this Alina, of course I am sure, and if I find anything I will let you know."

"Thanks Sally, sometimes I wonder what I would do if I didn't have you for a friend."

Alina and Sally took the papers through to the office and copied the documents and then Alina put the file away on the top shelf.

They spent the rest of the evening chatting and before going to bed having decided to rise early and go shopping for more bookcases or shelving.

After a breakfast of coffee and pancakes drizzled with Maple Syrup Sally said, "Right, let's go shopping for some book cases and maybe new shoes."

They took Sally's Nissan, which had more room than Alina's MG to carry bookcases in, and they spent the rest of the day shopping for bookcases, buying new shoes, and having a pub lunch.

On their return home, the girls built the bookcase and set them out in the hall, master bedroom, and lounge.

All too soon, it was time for Sally to head home to Largs to prepare for the next psychic fair. They said their tearful goodbyes and although Alina was sorry to see her go, at the same time she was glad to have her home to herself.

Over the next few days, more boxes of ornaments and oddments arrived from storage and Alina unpacked them and set things out on shelves and in cupboards. It was quite hard for Alina emotionally because she had not seen many of the things that were unwrapped since she had cleared her parent's home.

Exhausted from unpacking, Alina decided on a long hot bath and then early to bed. She filled the bath with water and some relaxing Himalayan Bath Salts, put some ambient music on to play on her stereo, stepped into her bath, lay back and closed her eyes.

"Coralina! Coralina!" the voice called to her, "Coralina!" Alina looked up as a mist surrounded her, but vaguely, through the mist, she could see the old woman, her hands stretched out in front of her.

"What are you asking me for, what are you trying to tell me?"

"Find her, you're the one."

"Find who?"

Suddenly, Alina woke up, still in the bath, music still playing in the background. She had only been dreaming, but the woman had spoken to her and that had never happened before. Alina felt troubled. She thought that she was probably over tired from moving in and sorting through all the boxes. Memories had been stirred with each opened box making unpacking an emotional journey. She tidied the bathroom, threw her towels in the washing machine, and climbed into bed.

The next morning, she awoke feeling refreshed and well slept, and went through to the kitchen to make her first cup of coffee. She took her coffee through to the sitting room, went over to the patio doors, and opened them.

Nancy had brought her several patio plants in large ceramic pots as a housewarming gift and as she opened the sliding doors, there was the robin hopping about among the leaves of the Acer and the fern. She wondered if it was the same robin that she saw when she was waiting for the removal men arriving.

She got bread from the kitchen and crumbled some to drop around the plant pots and she felt happy about the visit from the robin. Sipping her coffee, she watched as the robin hopped about pecking at her offering and thought about what she would or should be doing next.

After having a shower and pulling on her leggings and a sweater, she went through to her office. She searched the demographics of several newspapers then analysed the advertising costs. Once she had done that, she began to think about and plan her own advertising campaign.

There were brochures and business cards to think about, and she wanted to take plenty of time to avoid making mistakes or missing out relevant information.

She had choices to make, she could take her requirements to a professional printer, or she could do it herself. She decided that she would do it herself; she had all the tools that she required, laptop, printer, scanner, and assorted software. All she really needed was good quality brochure paper and card for the business cards, and she could take her time about picking up these things from a stationery supplier.

It did not take Alina very long to settle into a new routine of seeing clients and studying her subject. She developed a new habit of casting a circle each morning to meditate quietly on her new life, and those things that she hoped to achieve. Sally came to stay overnight between tours, and they would see a movie or go out for dinner, but Alina didn't mention that she been casting circles.

She loved her new home and life was good.

Chapter 29

The old woman continued to appear in her dreams, but since that first time, in March, just after moving in to Riverview Drive, she never spoke to Alina again. Mrs Brodie had become a regular visitor, often bringing homemade scones or a pot of soup and Alina appreciated her kindness. She often mentioned that her nephew Ronnie, the agent who had shown Alina the flat, had asked after her and asked if she was settling in.

It was May now and the days were brighter, warmer, and showing signs of the summer to come. Alina had taken a computer course, learning how to build a website, and she was busy in her office modifying it when she heard her door. She knew that it would be Mrs Brodie because the bell for the main door had not rung. She rose and went to open the door and was surprised to see Ronnie standing there.

"Oh! Sorry, you surprised me for a moment. I thought it was Mrs Brodie, you're Ronnie aren't you?"

He was smiling at her, but it was a shy smile rather than an overconfident one, and for a moment, she heard her mother's voice in her head saying, "Not like that smarmy JJ." The thought surprised her.

He had a covered plate in his hand and Alina guessed that it was something from Mrs Brodie.

"Would you like to come in a moment?"

"Aunt Nessie asked me to bring you some scones."

"I am due to stop for a cuppa, would you like to share a scone and a cuppa?"

"Only if I'm not keeping you back, Aunt Nessie said that you work from home."

"I do, come in?"

She held the door further open and closed the door behind him.

"Shall I put these in the kitchen?"

"Yes," she laughed, "you know the way."

He stopped as he entered the sitting room and Alina almost bumped into him.

"This is lovely; I really like what you have done here."

"Thanks, it's very much to my own taste and style rather than following trends. I'm quite esoteric in my taste."

"I can see that," he said. He walked over to Alina's shelves and began to look at her books and her Japanese and Egyptian style ornaments.

Alina went into the kitchen, switched on the kettle, got out two cups and plates for the scones, and began to fill the coffee machine with water for a fresh pot of coffee.

He came into the kitchen and set the plate on the tray that Alina was preparing.

"Tea or coffee?"

"Coffee would be great thanks."

When Alina had seen Ronnie before he was dressed smartly for business, wearing a shirt and tie, but today he was more casually dressed in denims, tan boots with brown leather cuffs and a chunky brown sweater. Very dark eyes, dark hair, and showing a hint of fashionable stubble, made him very nice to look at, but Alina was not interested in romance; definitely not, but if she was he would be worth a second look.

"Here, let me take that," said Ronnie picking up the tray when Alina had finished making the coffee.

"Take it through to the sitting room please."

They sat on the rich blue sofa with the tray on the coffee table in front of them. Ronnie poured the coffee and Alina watched him. He looked up and smiled at her and she almost blushed.

"What?" he said smiling at her.

"Nothing."

She wondered what was wrong with her. She felt tongue tied; didn't know what to say or what to do with herself.

"You said your Dad's name was Ronnie, what does he think of your new home?"

Alina took a breath, "I lost both my parents a few years ago. My Dad had a heart attack when they went out for the day, and my Mum was killed when their car crashed."

He reached over, covered her hand with his, and looked into her eyes.

"I am so very sorry Alina; I know that pain. A drunk driver killed my parents when I was just fourteen. My mother died immediately, but my father was in a coma for a long time before his body finally gave up the struggle. I went off the rails a bit, got into the wrong company, and missed a lot of school, but Auntie Nessie took charge and I wouldn't be who I am today if it hadn't been for her love and support."

It was an awkward moment, but Auntie Nessie at the door distracted them, and in she came with Jock, who bounced all over Alina and Ronnie.

"Jock, behave yourself, he has no manners at all," she said, but she was proud of the little dog and she knew that neither Alina nor Ronnie was bothered in the slightest.

"I'm off to the shops now Ronnie, but you've got your key to get in haven't you. Why don't you two young things go out on a nice day like this?"

Alina wondered if she was trying to set them up, and she could see by the look that Ronnie was giving his aunt that he had noticed that too, but Nessie just smiled knowingly and off she went.

"I'm sorry about that Alina."

"Don't worry Ronnie, she means well, but just to be clear, and please don't take this the wrong way, I am happy to have you as a friend, but I don't want anything else."

"Don't worry about that Alina, but we may have to pretend to keep Nessie off our backs," he laughed.

They were still laughing when he left, the awkward moment forgotten and a new friendship beginning. He promised to pop in again and Alina agreed that she would look forward to that.

Alina was settling into a comfortable routine. She kept in touch with Cassandra from time to time, and had dinner with Nancy and Davy at their house or hers. Sally was still touring, occasionally visiting on her five-day breaks, and giving her little bits of information about the family tree that she was researching for Alina.

Clients came to see her often and she read for oversees clients on the telephone. She still wore the velvet pouch on a long cord around her neck and often when she was working, without even being aware of it, she would stop to think of what she was going to type on her keyboard, or say to her client, and she would hold the pouch with her right hand identifying each object by feel.

Ronnie came to visit now and again, and they fell into the habit of taking Jock for a walk by the river. Auntie Nessie had instigated this initially and often watched them from her window. In the beginning, they walked side by side, but apart, however before long, they were walking closer, and more recently they would walk arm in arm. Auntie Nessie was a wise woman in her own way.

"That's nice, that's nice, things are moving along nicely," she would say to herself, smiling.

Suddenly Alina realised that Ronnie was an important person in her life. "*How did that happen?*" she thought to herself, then she began to argue with herself about her feelings and even tried to convince herself that it was her imagination. She didn't open the door when Ronnie came across the landing. He thought that perhaps she was in the bath or seeing a client. He went downstairs with Jock and there was a heavy feeling in his chest, but he wasn't sure why.

Alina sent Sally a text.

"Where are you?"

"On tour."

"Yes, but where?"

"Aberdeen."

"In a twin or double?"

"They only had twin why?"

"How long will you be there?"

"Why all the questions? Two more days."

"Still using the Palm Court?"

"Yes."

"Coming across. Will see you later, ok to share?"

"Yes what's wrong?"

"Nothing. C U in a bit."

Then she jumped up, threw some stuff in her overnighter, and went downstairs and into her car. She was already gone when Ronnie came back from his walk with Jock.

Chapter 30

During the long drive to Aberdeen, Alina thought about Ronnie, and in her mind, she went over everything that she knew about him. She knew that he was close to his aunt and visited her often. That showed a caring side to his nature, and although they had spent time chatting while they walked Jock she didn't really know much more about him than that. She knew he was an estate agent and that he lived in a flat in Pollokshaws. She knew the kinds of films and music that he liked, and they had talked about books that they read, but she didn't know anything else about him. He had never talked about anything personal or serious, but then, thinking about it, neither had she.

By two thirty in the afternoon Alina was in the Palm Court Hotel having a late lunch while she waited for Sally. She had already spoken to the receptionist to let her know that she would be sharing the room. Between clients, Sally came out and gave Alina the room key.

"What's wrong?"

"Nothing, does there have to be something wrong?"

"Yeh, there does. Why else would you drop everything and suddenly appear?"

Just at that, Cassandra came over and gave Alina a big welcome hug.

"Oh oh, man trouble," said Cassandra.

Sally turned and looked at Alina.

"Is it?"

"Nooo, I just wanted to do something different."

She gave Sally a look that said drop it. Sally just shrugged and went back to her table and left Cassandra to chat for a few moments with Alina. When they had finished chatting, as Cassandra was moving off, she turned and said, "You know where I am if you need me Alina." She had that knowing expression on her face that Alina had come to love.

Alina went up to Sally's room and lay on the bed to wait until she had seen all her clients. Later they ordered room service and over dinner, Sally risked broaching the subject again.

"Do you want to talk about it?"

"Not really, but it's hardly fair to suddenly land on you and not tell you why, and I don't believe I will get a minute's peace until I do tell you."

"Is it Ronnie?"

"Yes."

"What's wrong?"

"I think I like him?"

Sally began to laugh and Alina was furious.

"I don't know why you're laughing."

"You've always liked him."

"I mean different 'like'."

Sally was still laughing and teasing her now.

"How many kinds of like are there?"

Alina drew herself up and glared at Sally.

"Alright, alright, I promise I won't tease you anymore. Tell me what's wrong."

"I have started getting butterflies in my stomach when I know he is coming or when he arrives unexpectedly."

"Aw' that's lovely."

"No, it's not lovely. I don't want to have these feelings. It will never work, his house my house. I don't want things to change. I'm happy with things as they are or as they were before the butterflies started. I don't want to lose his friendship."

"Did he ask you if he could move in?"

"Don't be ridiculous?"

"Did he ask to marry you?"

"Of course not?"

"What's all the fuss about then?"

"I told you I like him, well more than like him."

"And what is the problem here?"

By this time Alina, her dinner only half eaten, was out of her chair and pacing as well as she could in the small room. Sally was watching bemused and continued to eat.

"I have only known him for six months and look what happened before."

With that, Alina sat on one of the beds and put her head in her hands. Sally sat beside her, drew her hands down from Alina's face and held on to them.

"Alina look at me," Alina looked at her dear friend.

"Ronnie isn't JJ, and you are not the young girl who was infatuated by his empty promises."

Sally put her arms around Alina and told her that the best relationships come from strong friendships. Friends become friends because they like each other and have things in common. Relationships break down because passion rules the attraction, and when the initial passion has burnt out there is only emptiness left.

"Get into to bed Alina, sleep on it and you will see that I am right."

Alina took Sally's advice and slept soundly.

The next morning bright and early, Alina woke up and had a shower before Sally stirred. Alina was filling the kettle for coffee when Sally got out of bed. It was Alina's turn to laugh, Sally's long blonde hair was all over her face, and there were sleep creases where she had been lying on the bracelet that she had forgotten to take off.

"What time do you want to go down for breakfast?" said Alina, still laughing at Sally.

"I ordered room service last night while you were sleeping; two full breakfasts, so that we could chat about the family trees. I want to tell you what I have found so far."

After Sally had showered and dressed, they sat down to breakfast and Sally updated Alina on the results of her search.

"From what Nancy and Davy remember the gypsy line came from your mother's side of the family, so here is what I have found, some of it you might already know, but bear with me. Your line goes back to a Robert Miller.

He was the miller's son that ran away with your great, great, great, great, grandmother. He was definitely sixteen because his birth is registered in 1866 so we can only guess that she was around that age. Oh by the way, you'll never believe what her name was."

"Don't keep me in suspense, tell me."

"Her name was Coralina; I bet that's where your name comes from."

"Never, you are joking, I heard the old woman calling that name."

"You heard her calling Coralina?"

"Yes in a sort of dream or meditation, I'm not quite sure which."

"The more we find out the more amazing this gets."

"You have done some great work Sally."

"I have only just started, there's more. They married in 1882 and had several children, who all died in infancy except their first-born child Emily."

Emily would be your great-great- great, grandmother, and she married Edward Devlin in 1903. They had two children; Paul Devlin was born in 1905 and Cora Devlin was born in 1907. Your great grandmother Cora Devlin married George Alexander in 1930 and had a daughter who would be your grandmother Sarah Alexander. She was born in 1933, and she married Charles McGregor in 1952. Your mother Beverly was born 1954.

Now if we go back to Paul Devlin; he was your great-great uncle, he married a Patricia Cairns in 1933 and then they emigrated to America in 1937, but I haven't caught up with them yet, and really at this time I have no idea where they are, but I will keep searching."

Sally handed the sheet of paper that she had printed the information on to Alina.

"I can't believe that you have found so much information. Thank you Sally. This means that I might find that I have family. Even if they were in America, it would be nice to know that I wasn't the only one.

"Right, I better get downstairs and back to work, I'll see you later then."

"No Sally, I was being stupid yesterday, but as usual you have set me straight. I'm going to head home now."

"Are you sure? You could stay another day."

"Thanks, I'll see Cassandra downstairs and let her know that I am leaving."

Alina was about to speak to Cassandra, but she could see that she was busy chatting to new clients, so they waved and blew kisses to each other.

Chapter 31

Alina had stopped off at the nearest supermarket to get some shopping on her way home, and as she gathered her shopping bags from the boot of her car, Ronnie drove in to the car park and parked beside her.

"Need a hand?"

"Hi Ronnie, yeh, that would be good, thanks?"

"Are you expecting a siege?" he laughed.

"No nothing so dramatic, the freezer is empty, and the cupboards are bare."

Inside she was thinking that she should act normal, but her heart was racing and there were butterflies in her stomach. Why hadn't she noticed how handsome he was, she thought he was attractive, but now he looked as though he had just stepped out of a fashion magazine. He was wearing a chunky dark blue cowl neck sweater over a light blue t-shirt and loose fitting jeans. His face was melting her heart. When he wasn't seeing clients the clean cut look was replaced by a dishevelled casual appearance. She wanted to move nearer him to get closer to that glorious smell of after shave and feel that stubble on her... she stopped where she was; her mouth hanging open, staring at his back as he climbed the stairs ahead of her.

"Oh my God, what am I thinking?" For a moment, she imagined his face against hers and she was embarrassed at herself.

He must have felt that she had stopped and he turned to look down at her.

"Alina are you alright?"

"Yes, I just thought of something."

They reached her door and she put the key in, turned the handle, and went straight through to the kitchen. Ronnie followed in behind her and put her bags on the units.

"I'll leave you to it. I'll be next door if you need me." He leaned over and kissed her on her cheek and left.

She stood there stunned; she wondered why he had done that, he never had before. She could hear him whistling as he left and shut the door behind him. She wondered if he was a mind reader, and then she began to think that she had made it happen because she had pictured it too clearly in her mind.

"I have spent too much time with Sally in her circles," she muttered to herself.

"I'm not a witch. I don't think I am. I just do witchy stuff, hmm… maybe I am a witch."

When she shared a room with Sally during tours, she was happy to sit in when Sally cast her circles. She didn't think that made her a witch, but she did have the same beliefs. Sally created magick, Alina only watched. She did believe that God was both male and female, but that didn't make her a witch. She did understand the power of air, fire, water, and earth, but that didn't make her a witch either. She was happy studying her Tarot cards, Rune Stones, Numerology, and Astrology. She was fantasising about Ronnie, but that didn't mean that she was falling in love with him.

"Oh my God, not falling in love with him. Where did that idea come from?"

She realized that she was slamming cupboard doors as she put her shopping away. She dumped things in the freezer without thinking about any kind of order. She began to pace around her apartment. Her energy was throbbing and she did the only thing she knew to settle down.

She had freestanding candleholders in each corner of her sitting room and each held a chunky pillar candle. She looked around her room to make sure that nothing was out of place, and then taking a lighter with her she walked over to the east corner and lit the first candle. Walking around her room clockwise, she lit the east candle, the south candle, the west candle, and then the north candle. She picked up an incense stick and walked around the room fanning the incense into the air.

As she passed her stereo, she pressed the play button to listen to Oliver Shanti, nice relaxing music. She stood in the middle of the room, raised her arms high above her head, and felt energy pouring into her body. Lowering her arms, she sat down on her sofa, leaned back, and relaxed. The music comforted her, and soon her heart was beating normally and her mind had settled.

She closed her eyes and listened to the soft sounds playing in the background. She allowed her mind to wander on a journey of meditation and in the distance, she could see a field, and feel a fresh breeze on her face and in her hair. As she got closer to the field, she could see a small copse of trees. Birds were singing and the sunlight dappled through the leaves and cast shadows ahead of her.

She began to realize that there was an old gypsy wagon hidden in the trees. It had four big wheels and a bow shaped top covered in a dark green canvas. The trim on the wagon looked like oak; the beautifully carved wood was dark with age and the paint had worn through with the weathering, but there were traces of gilt among the patterns. Two long wooden arms stretched out to the front for hitching horses to, to pull the wagon. These long arms too were beautifully carved and painted.

She realised that someone was there. She had never seen anyone in a meditation when she had meditated with Sally, she had seen majestic scenery, wolves, eagles, even dolphins and whales, but this was different. She didn't feel uncomfortable or afraid as she looked closely at the trees where she was sure someone was standing.

The old gypsy woman stepped forward, smiled at her, and handed her a red rose. Close up, she could see the beauty that had been in her face when she was a younger woman, and her hair wasn't white it was silver. Alina smiled in return and accepted the rose. The old woman turned and walked away and Alina watched until she could no longer see her. Then she too turned and walked in the opposite direction through the trees back across the field.

Alina drifted from meditation to sleep and when she woke an hour or so later, she puzzled over the meditation. Rising slowly, she stretched and went through to the kitchen where she had left her mobile, switched it on, and sent a text to Sally.

"Call me when you're clear, xxx."

When her phone rang, she knew it would be Sally.

"Hey what's up?"

"I cast a circle and did a meditation."

"You what?"

"You heard me."

"Well done you, I'm surprised."

"Actually, I have been casting circles and meditating since I first moved in, I just didn't what to make a big deal of it."

"And you never mentioned. Why?"

"I didn't want you to think I was trying to be a witch."

Sally laughed and through her laughter she said, "You don't try to be a witch, you are a witch, or you are not a witch. Being a witch isn't about casting circles. Being a witch is a way of life, being a witch is believing, and behaving in a certain way. Casting circles just helps you to focus on what you believe you can do. I have known you for nearly four years now and in that time we have had many conversations about Mother Earth and the power of the four elements air, fire, water, and earth. I have always believed that you are a witch, but you just didn't know you were, and now you do. What happened anyway?"

"What makes you think something happened?"

"Alina, you didn't call me just to tell me that you had cast a circle, what happened?"

Alina told her about the meditation and the old woman giving her the rose, and asked Sally what she thought that meant.

"She has been appearing in your dreams for how long?"

"Since my parents died, four and a half years now."

"Every time she appeared before she was imploring you, she looked as though she was pleading with you wasn't she?"

"Yeah that's right, always."

"And now she gives you a rose."

"Yes, but what does that mean?"

"Well you must be getting closer to whatever she wants you to do or to find. What's different, has something happened or something changed?"

Alina was silent.

"Something has changed, tell me Alina."

"Ronnie kissed me."

Sally let out a yell and Alina could hear her dancing and laughing over the phone.

"Was it a passionate snog?"

"Stop it! Sally get your head out of the gutter. It was tender; it wasn't even on my lips, it was just different, as though he cared."

"Well I have no doubt that he cares, but in view of our recent conversation regarding your feelings perhaps his are changing too."

"Yes, but did I do that?"

"What do you mean?"

"Did I make that happen, I'm really worried?"

"Did you do a spell?"

"No."

"Well how could you possibly make that happen?"

"I'm too embarrassed to say."

"Alina, tell me."

"When I came home, I met him in the car park and he carried my shopping upstairs. I could smell his after shave and he looked, oh I don't know, he just looked…"

"Gorgeous," laughed Sally, as Alina was tormenting herself.

"Well yes, but I got this overwhelming picture in my head of his face close to mine and his stubble on my skin."

Sally was laughing so hard the tears were running down her face and she was holding her side, which was aching with the strain of her laughter.

"Oh Alina, sometimes you are so innocent, that's not a spell, that's lust. You're lusting after a very handsome man that's been a good friend for the past few months. Relax, you haven't put a spell on him, but cupid's arrow may have struck."

"Do you think that's why my old lady came to me in my meditation and gave me the rose?"

"Could be, or it could be that you are getting closer to something. I don't know, we'll have to wait and see."

"I don't know what to do."

"About what?"

"I don't know what to do about Ronnie and my feelings."

"Alina, do nothing except what comes naturally, and follow the path that destiny lays out ahead of you and you will be fine."

"Why don't you read your cards Alina?"

"You know that terrifies me, I might see something that I don't want to see."

"Then don't look, are you ok now?"

"Yes I am, thanks Sally. I feel really stupid now."

They said their bye's and ended the call.

Chapter 32

Alina went to her office and opened the workbox that she kept her reading accessories in; she drew out the wooden box of Rune Cards and her reading mat and placed them on her reading table. She sat down, unfolded the mat, and opened the box containing the Rune Cards. She sat quietly holding the cards between her hands, she took a deep breath and into herself she asked, "Please show me what I need to know."

She placed the deck on the right side of the mat and deftly using her right hand swept the cards into a circle from right to left. She paused, thought of her life as it was, and then she drew one random card. As always, Alina was afraid to turn the card over, but steeling herself, she turned it over and looked at it.

The symbol was 'Mann'; written it looked like a sharp 'P' with another 'P' in reverse and both letters touching each other. For Alina this was a positive sign, and her experience with this rune indicated that there was someone around her that she could depend on and trust. She wondered was the symbol showing her Sally or Mrs. Brodie or even Nancy and Davy who were still an important part in her life.

As she was thinking about these things, she heard a knock at her door. Thinking it would be Mrs. Brodie, she went to the door and opened it to find Ronnie standing there. His black hair looked dishevelled as though he had been running his hands through it, and he looked stressed when only a little while ago he was whistling as he left after carrying her shopping.

"Ronnie, come in, are you alright?"

"I came to see if you were alright Alina. I was worried that something was wrong."

"Oh Ronnie, I'm sorry if I worried you, it's just, well its just things I can't explain. Come on in and have some coffee. Put the kettle on." She told him.

The Rune Card was referring to Ronnie; he was the person she could trust, why had she doubted that, she already knew she trusted him. It was her feelings that she was unsure of, her own insecurity was suffocating her and preventing her from experiencing her true feelings. She was afraid that if he really knew her and her beliefs, the fact that she enjoyed casting a circle, that she was psychic - if he knew these things, he may just turn his back on her, or worse try to change her, and the thought of that hurt her deeply. She had only just found herself, could she give that up for a man who may not even feel as she did. It would be like JJ all over again, becoming someone she wasn't to please another person.

She was standing in her office staring at the cards on her reading table when Ronnie came through to tell her the coffee was ready. She turned sharply, surprised that he had followed her into her sanctuary and anxious to hide the spread of cards.

"What's wrong Alina, please tell me. I can't sleep for thinking about you since the other day. I know something's wrong and I can't understand why you don't trust me."

"Oh Ronnie," she said as tears filled her eyes, "I'm so afraid that I will lose your friendship."

He drew her towards him, wrapped his strong arms around her, and held her close. He lowered his head and kissed the top of her head buried in his deep chest. The swell of love for her in his heart was unbearable. He just couldn't keep it in.

"You'll never lose me Alina, I'm so in love with you that all I want to do is be with you for the rest of my life. Please don't cry."

She raised her head, her eyes and face wet with tears as she gazed into his deep brown eyes. "You're in love with me?" she said incredulously.

"I'm in love with you." He smiled down at her.

"That's what has been wrong with me; my feelings for you have been changing and we have spent time together, but you don't really know me, not the real me. There are things that you don't know that you may not like, and I don't really know you either. I'm afraid"

"What's to know that I don't already know? Do you think that I don't know that you are a very gifted psychic, that you see things, that you have your own ghost, that you're probably a witch?"

Alina looked at him, astonished by how much he knew.

"Alina, I have been in and out of your house for more than six months now; I've seen your candles, smelt your incense, looked at your books on the shelves, and heard your music playing. Everything about you says witch to me."

"I don't even know if I'm a witch! And what do you know about a ghost?"

"The old woman with the silver hair who hangs about. I've seen her lots of times."

"You have! Why have you never mentioned her to me and why have you never said anything about the rest of it?"

"Alina I was happy to be in your company, having coffee, taking Jock for a walk, the rest was personal; and I felt if you wanted to share anything with me you would and you didn't, so I respected your privacy."

They were still standing together, Alina had her arms around Ronnie's waist and he had his arms over her shoulders. They had never been this close before.

"Come on let's go and have some coffee."

"Do you want to know what I was doing when you came to the door?"

He glanced over her shoulder and looked at the cards fanned out on the table. "Reading your Runes, Mann, that's a good one to have."

Alina's face was a picture of confusion and surprise

"You know the Runes?"

"And a lot more besides. Let's go and have that coffee and a long chat and I'll tell you the things about me that you didn't know."

Chapter 33

Alina washed her face before rejoining Ronnie. He had made the coffee and set it on the coffee table in the sitting room. They sat side by side facing each other, occasionally sipping from their cups of coffee, and Ronnie told her his story. He reminded her of a conversation that they had had about his parents dying when he was fourteen. He told her that his life had crumbled before him.

Auntie Nessie had temporarily moved into his family's home to look after him, and night after night he suffered from terrible nightmares. He stopped going to school, got into fights, and then one day he was caught shoplifting. He told her how pathetic it was, because he felt stupid being caught and going through all that for stealing a stupid magazine.

Auntie Nessie spoke to the police and the newsagent and somehow made it all go away. He remembered how ashamed he was and how upset his aunt had been, but she held him close and told him that she loved him, and that she too missed her sister and brother in law, his parents.

He confided in his aunt that his parents often appeared to him and he was afraid of the future. If he had to go and live with his auntie, he might not see his parents again. She promised that she would stay in his home until he was mature enough to decide what he wanted to do.

She told him that if he had no guardian, he would go into foster care, because he was too young to live on his own, but the condition was that he would attend school regularly, get good grades, and stop fighting otherwise he would be on his own.

About nine months after his parents died, he told his aunt that they had stopped coming. She explained to him that they had come because they were worried about him, but now that he had settled down and was attending school, they knew that they didn't have to worry anymore and were able to continue on their journey to the afterlife.

He explained to Alina that this experience raised more questions, and from that point onward, he had read everything that he could lay his hands on about spirits and guardian angels, about religion and beliefs, and that these things had led him to reading about Tarot and methods of prediction.

"We have more in common than you thought Alina; I don't want to change you or anything about you. You are perfect just the way you are. Do you want to tell me about your old lady? I would like to know everything about you."

Alina not only told him about the old woman. She went back to the beginning and told him about her life growing up; about meeting and marrying JJ and how he changed after they were married. She told him that she had changed too, and that she blamed herself for allowing him to manipulate her. She talked about the tragic way she lost her parents and how unsupportive JJ had been. She mentioned Nancy and Davy that he had already met in passing, and how they had been her rock through it all.

They laughed together about how she had joined the psychic fair and how Cassandra had mistaken her for someone else. She remembered the shopping trip that she had with her mother only days before the accident, and while she was talking about the visiting the antique shop, she opened her pouch and took out the wooden rose to let him see it.

"Can I hold it?" he asked.

"Of course."

He held the wooden disc and looked at the delicately carved rose.

"It's a little work of art," he said as he closed his hand over the disc, "It carries some powerful energy, love and joy, sadness and fear, terrible fear and something else that I can't quite put my finger on."

"Yes, I feel that too, I think it goes back to my parent's accident."

"Anguish, that's the feeling that I get, but I think it goes much further back than your parent's accident. Perhaps that's what the old woman is connected to."

"Oh my God, you could be right; and there's more, I think I have gypsy blood. Nancy told me that my Mum had mentioned having gypsy blood, and I then remembered what I thought was a fairy story that she used to tell me at bedtime about a princess who ran off to marry a miller's son."

"You should try to find out about that, my gypsy girl." He laughed.

"Sally has been researching that for me, and she has managed to trace my family to Paul and Patricia Devlin who emigrated to America in 1937. She is going to try to find out more about them."

They talked until the early hours of the morning, and Alina asked Ronnie if he still lived in his parent's house.

"No, when I was about sixteen I began to realise how difficult it was for Aunt Nessie to keep two houses going, so we sold it and I moved in with her. It was selling that house that got me interested in becoming an estate agent, and soon after I started working for the agency, I got the chance to buy a flat. I stayed with Auntie Nessie and decorated it in my spare time and when it was done; I sold it for a profit and bought two more. I live in one flat, but I sold the other and I have been buying and selling houses ever since."

"I have six rented properties just now, but hope to have more in the not too distant future."

They talked and talked until they were both exhausted by the day's developments. Ronnie stood up when he was ready to leave and Alina walked him to the door. He wrapped his arms around her and kissed her tenderly on her lips; her heart flipped a beat and the butterflies in her stomach began a crescendo that rose up to meet her heart. The scent of his after-shave was a pleasure to inhale and his smell, his essence, was all man.

Ronnie savoured her lips, enjoying her taste, he didn't want this moment to end, but he knew that this was not the time to take things any further. Alina had a vulnerability about her and he would not take advantage of her.

As she closed the door behind him, she turned and leant her back against it, her heart pounding, but a smile on her face.

"I'm in love with a wonderful man and he is in love with me."

She heard the engine of his car start and she blessed him with a wish for a safe journey. Auntie Nessie, never a good sleeper, listened to the car driving away and smiled to herself.

"A good match made," she thought to herself, "all that from sending him across to Alina's door with a plate of scones," and smiling, she settled down under the covers to sleep contentedly.

Chapter 34

Alina slept soundly without dreaming and woke up feeling content and refreshed. She cast a circle, and did a morning ritual. When she was finished, she made herself a cup of coffee and settled down on her sofa to compose a text to Sally.

"Ronnie and I talked. Speak later," and pressed send.

Seconds later, her phone beeped for in incoming text from Sally "Good?"

She replied "Great!" and received

"Can't wait, xxx."

Sally called during her next break and Alina told her everything that had happened, especially that Ronnie had said that he loved her. Sally was delighted with this development, as she knew more than most how Alina had avoided any kind of relationship with the opposite sex since her marriage to JJ had ended.

She knew that Alina had a mature, capable nature in most areas of her life, but where men were concerned she was a vulnerable individual. Sally had met Ronnie briefly several times and as well as being very handsome, he appeared to be a genuine person. They made plans for Sally's next visit on her five days off, and they talked briefly about the search for family in America.

Alina went through to her office to check her appointments and to mark Sally's visit on her desktop calendar. She checked and answered emails and from time to time her thoughts returned to the evening before and Ronnie and each time they did, she smiled to herself and enjoyed a feeling of contentment and anticipation.

Still thinking of Ronnie, she began to doodle on her notepad working out the significance of the numbers in his name. She didn't need a graph to work with numerology, but if she had done, she would have written down the numbers one to nine across a page and then the alphabet below those numbers. The letter A would be under the number one and the letter I would be under the number nine, the letter J would begin at one, and so on.

She calculated Ronnie's first name to begin with and discovered that the total was thirty-nine. Adding the three and the nine together gave her twelve and adding the one and the two gave her three. She was happy with that number as it showed a kind caring person confirming what she already thought. Her name number was one and these two numbers added together became four. That was a good combination because the number four gave stability.

Curiosity stimulated she began to work on the vowels, because the vowels gave insight to the inner personality. His inner personality number was twenty, which then became two. Twenty showed her that he considered things deeply before acting, that he was a dark horse and never gave much away. She knew that too, but it was reassuring to have these things confirmed.

It had been some time since she had looked at her own numbers so she thought for a moment and calculated the vowels in her name Alina. With her eyebrows rising in surprise, she realised that the vowels in her name added up to eleven, representing justice, and then two, the same as Ronnie's vowel numbers. More significant was the fact that adding Ronnie's inner personality number with hers gave the number four again.

She was smiling to herself when her phone beeped to alert her to an incoming text. She looked at the display, pleased to see that it was from Ronnie, and read the message.

"Good morning gypsy girl, are you free at any time today? x"

"Clear all day today booked solid Tuesday and Wednesday. Sally coming for a few days Thursday and Friday. Thought the three of us could go and visit Nancy and Davy?"

"Sounds good, I have some news. Good News, C U later. x"

Alina phoned Nancy, and she suggested that Alina join her for lunch.

"I can't come for lunch because I want to be at home this afternoon, but I can drive over now if you are not too busy."

"That would be lovely pet, just you come when you are ready."

Nancy put the kettle on when she saw Alina's car arriving, and they hugged warmly when she went into the house.

"I feel as though I haven't seen you for ages, and I have so much to tell you. How have you been, and where's Davy?"

"He just popped out to get a Danish pastry; he knows how much you enjoy them. We're fine. Take your coat off then come and sit down and tell me your news."

"I'll wait for Davy because he will want to hear this too, but between you and me, there has been another little development."

Nancy was smiling at her and she reached over to place her hand over Alina's hand.

"Oh Nancy, you know you have been like a mother to me since Mum died and sometimes I forget how important you are."

She reached over and kissed Nancy on the cheek.

"You'll have me tearing up girl. We love you too, you're like the child we never had, and we couldn't be any prouder of you if you were our own. So what's the secret you have? Tell me before Davy comes back."

"It's not so much a secret,"

"You've met someone nice?"

"Not met."

"Its Ronnie then, I'm so glad, he is such a lovely chap, always polite."

Alina laughed, "How did you know it was Ronnie?"

"Women's intuition," laughed Nancy, "and I have had a couple of chats with his Auntie Nessie too."

Alina told Nancy about the past couple of days and was just finishing her story when Davy arrived back, armed with a bag of Danish Pastries. He immediately came over and wrapped Alina in his arms, as Nancy went through to the kitchen to bring through the tea tray.

They sat down, and Alina reminded them of the day that they had mentioned to her about the gypsy girl who ran away to marry the millers' son.

She then went on to tell them about Sally's search of her mother's lineage and what she and found so far. Davy and Nancy were surprised and delighted with these new developments.

Before Alina left, she mentioned that Sally was coming for a few days and that they were going to come and visit one evening.

"That will be wonderful Alina. Come for dinner and why don't you bring Ronnie and his Auntie Nessie too if they can make it."

Davy looked at Nancy with a puzzled look on his face, wondering what she was up to and behind Alina's back Nancy winked at Davy, and he just shook his head and muttered under his breath "Women, always up to something."

After Alina left, Nancy told Davy the good news and he was every bit as pleased that Ronnie and Alina were now in a relationship.

"It's about time that she had someone to look out for her." Davy said,

"And he is such a personable young man."

"Better than that…"

"Now, now, Davy, don't speak ill of anyone it's not like you."

"I know, I know, but when I think back to Bev and Ronnie having that accident and everything she went through, and he didn't lift a hand to help or support her."

"It's in the past and best left there," replied Nancy firmly, and Davy went back to his newspaper, the conversation over.

Chapter 35

When Alina arrived home, after her visit to Nancy and Davy's, she changed into smart trousers and a colourful slashed neck top and then added some fresh lipstick. She checked her appearance in the mirror. Like her mother, she always tried to look her best, but she was getting ready for Ronnie to arrive and that made her nervous.

She fussed with her hair, and turned this way and that to see herself from different angles. She grabbed a handful of hair and held it up in a bunch behind her head, she tried it swept to one side, and then she just brushed it down again and left it as it had been. She added a quick spray of La Perla, her favourite perfume, blotted her lipstick. Her stomach was churning in anticipation.

She went over to her candles and lit them one by one, east to north. She lit some incense and pressed play on her CD player. The soundtrack from August Rush was playing and she always found that uplifting and inspiring.

Ronnie kissed her on the lips and held her close when he arrived.

"Hello Gypsy Girl."

"Hello Dark Horse."

"Dark Horse?"

"Yes, I did some numerology on your name today and your inner personality numbers tell me that you are a dark horse." She laughed.

"Did you do your own?"

"I did, I'm a dark horse too."

"You're more of a filly Alina, a gypsy filly."

They were laughing as they walked through to the kitchen and Alina started making coffee as Ronnie got out the cups and went to the fridge for milk. Anyone looking at their ease with each other would have thought that they had been together for a long time.

"What's your news?" she asked as they sat down.

"I've handed in my resignation?"

"Oh I don't know what to say, is that a good thing?"

"I have the rented properties to look after and I have another two that need quite a bit of work. I don't have enough time to work at the agency and look after my properties and fortunately, I have enough in the bank now that I don't need to worry. I prefer working for myself anyway."

"That's great then, I'm happy for you. When do you finish up?"

"Friday will be my last working day; I have annual leave that's been carried over which means my actual leave date is three weeks from now, but Saturday will be the start of the new me."

"What are you doing on Thursday evening?"

"Spending some time with you I hope?"

"You and Auntie Nessie, Sally, and I have been invited over to Nancy and Davy's for dinner. Can you come?"

"I can and I don't think Auntie Nessie has plans for Thursday, but I'll check."

As it turned out Auntie Nessie was free on Thursday, and was delighted to accept the invitation.

Sally arrived as planned and the two young women got ready for their evening out. Sally was eager to hear all about how Alina and Ronnie's relationship was progressing and Alina was happy to share.

"Is he a good kisser then?"

"Sally, enough," laughed Alina.

"Come on no secrets, oh my God you are blushing."

"Stop it you are putting me off; I am trying to put on my mascara."

"Seriously though Alina, I have never seen you this happy, whatever it is that he has done to you its brought out an inner joy."

"Sometimes, when he isn't around, I have these fears that it's not real; and then he arrives and wraps his arms around me and the whole world just stops, and it's only him and me in that moment."

"Aw... that's so lovely, you are making me cry."

As if on queue, Ronnie arrived and Sally got to see their warm embrace for herself as Alina and Ronnie kissed.

"Get a room you two."

Ronnie and Alina both laughed and separated and Ronnie took Sally in his arms and kissed her on her cheek.

"Did you feel left out Sally?" laughed Ronnie,

"Oooh, my knees have gone all week, be still my beating heart," laughed Sally placing the back of her hand on her forehead and pretending to faint.

Auntie Nessie arrived, and together they made their way in Ronnie's car to Nancy and Davy's. They had a thoroughly enjoyable evening and Sally amused everyone with tales of her adventures during her trips with the psychic fair.

Nancy had cooked a lovely meal of Scottish salmon, dressed with hollandaise sauce, and served with new baby potatoes boiled in their skins and drizzled with butter and fresh mint. Auntie Nessie had made meringues with fresh cream and brought them with her as a contribution to the meal, and everyone had these with berries on the side.

Over coffee, Davy, Nancy and Auntie Nessie had a moan about the price of electricity and gas and then reminisced about days gone by dancing at the 'Savoy', although they were quick to add that it was in the later days before it closed its doors.

Alina and Ronnie sat quietly side by side and enjoyed the banter as it went back and forward. The older generation sneaked glances at them and enjoyed watching their closeness. Nancy refused to let anyone help with the clearing up, but Nessie insisted on giving a hand, and the two women went through to the kitchen for a gossip. Nancy asked, "I know you had a hand in this didn't you?"

"Well maybe a little push and a little wish."

The two ladies laughed together.

"I'm glad," said Nancy.

At the end of the night, Nancy and Davy stood at their door and waved everyone off. Davy had his arm over Nancy's shoulder and he looked down at her fondly.

"That was a lovely evening and a lovely meal sweetheart. It's so good to see Alina happy. She has a good friend in Sally and I have a feeling that Ronnie is the one for Alina."

"I think so too Davy."

"Better than that waste of space…"

"Now Davy, let's not spoil the mood by bringing up his name or his memory. Let's leave that in the past where it belongs."

When they arrived back at Riverview Drive, Ronnie kissed Alina tenderly and said good night before going across to Auntie Nessie's having decided to spend the night there.

Alina and Sally decided to have some hot chocolate and they both curled up on the sofa and chatted before going to bed. Alina told Sally of Ronnie's spiritual journey and the fact the he knew about Tarot and Runes, and that he had seen the old woman several times.

"You are joking," said Sally.

"No seriously, he told me he had seen her, in fact he asked me about her before I even mentioned her."

"He is a better fit for you than I imagined, it's good to have a partner in your life who understands your interests."

"I know; I feel quite blessed."

"Do you understand what I am always talking about now Alina? The Goddess knows what she is doing. She led you to that first psychic fair which led you here to meet Ronnie."

"I do now Sally and finally I can look back and be glad that JJ was such a pig otherwise I might never have met you too."

Chapter 36

On Friday morning the girls went out for breakfast to the west end of Glasgow, and then spent a couple of hours going up and down Byres Road browsing the shops before returning to Alina's home to wait for Ronnie who was coming over later. Sally updated Alina on the search for family and was able to tell her what she had found.

"Ok, bear with me, we last spoke about Paul Devlin he died in 1982 and his wife Patricia Devlin died in 1984. Both died in the US. Their son Thomas Devlin was born in 1940, in 1966 he married Jo Beth Mclean and they gave birth to a daughter Joanne the same year.

In 1986, Joanne marries, strangely enough, a John Miller; I feel as though we are going full circle here. Joanne's father, Thomas died in 2009, her mother died in 2012, and we are still in the US. Now I don't know if Joanne and John were just slow about starting a family or if there was a problem, but finally in 1997 they registered the birth of a daughter named Rosemarie.

That makes her eighteen and Joanne and John Miller will be about in their late forties. From what I can gather, so far, tracing your direct line, you have living relatives. Unfortunately, they left America and for the time being, I don't know where they are, but they did come to the UK. I expect they left America because both her parents were dead now."

Alina was thrilled to find this out.

"My goodness that's fantastic news, they could be here in the UK?"

"Yes, they could, unless they have moved again so leave it with me a while longer and I will see what more I can find out. I might be able to trace them."

When Ronnie arrived, Alina and Sally updated him on the latest news and then they began to discuss the continuing appearance of the old woman. Alina had made a list dating back to the first time that she could remember seeing her in her dreams. The three of them went over the list, and all concluded that although

Alina had connected the wooden rose as a reminder of the loss of her parents, it was more likely that it was a link in some way to the old woman.

"Have you ever done Psychometry over the rose?" asked Sally.

"No, never."

"Perhaps we should."

"I'm not sure about that, on the brief moment that I held it I could feel a powerful energy, not bad, but very powerful," answered Ronnie.

"I think I should, otherwise we may never get to the bottom of why the old woman keeps appearing."

Finally, after discussing it from every angle, Alina made the decision that she was the obvious choice to do psychometry on the rose.

The three of them stood up at the same time, almost in silent agreement and straightened cushions on the sofa and armchairs, tidied magazines on the coffee table, cleared away the coffee cups and generally made sure that there was nothing out of place or creating an air of disarray.

Without ceremony, Alina lit her four pillar candles and an incense stick. Ronnie and Sally made themselves comfortable on the armchairs on either side of the sofa, and Alina settled on the sofa.

Everyone was quiet for a few moments and then Alina opened her pouch and removed the rose from it. She looked at it for a little while and then, closing her eyes and resting her head against the back of the sofa, she took some deep relaxing breaths. She focused her attention on the rose while she fingered it gently in her hand. Sally and Ronnie were watching her closely and as they watched Alina's face, they could see that she was beginning to smile.

"What do you see Alina?"

"A pretty little girl with dark curly hair; she's about four, and its summer time and she is running towards a little boy who's about eight. He's putting his hand out and she takes it. They are both happy."

"Where are they?"

"I don't know, it's countryside. She's skipping and he's looking down on her."

"Are they brother and sister?" asked Ronnie.

"I don't think so, wait, they're turning, someone's calling to them. She has let go of his hand and she is waving to him. Rosa, her name is Rosa."

Alina opened her eyes and looked at Ronnie and Sally. She was amazed at what she had seen and Sally had goose bumps all down her back. Ronnie got up, went to the kitchen, and came back with a glass of water, which he handed to Alina.

"Drink," he said, "you're as white as a sheet."

"I'm ok, really I am; that was such a lovely picture, I can't believe I saw all that and I could feel it too. I felt as though I was there, right there beside them. Her name is definitely Rosa, I heard her mother calling her."

Sally had not said anything at all and when she did, she surprised Alina.

"I'm really impressed Alina, I knew you had the gift, but I didn't realise how strong it was. I couldn't have done that; I would only have received impressions, but you were right there. You described that as though you were watching a film."

"I know." Alina stretched out the 'know' in amazement. "I want to do it again; I want to find out more."

Ronnie was being protective. "I don't think you should, not just now, take a break first," he suggested.

That suggestion was like showing a red rag to a bull; Alina looked at him, and for a moment, JJ flashed into her head. She read Ronnie's suggestion as telling her what to do and didn't realise that he was concerned for her. He saw the moment in her face, a stubborn set of her lips and eyes that surprised him, but at the same time, he realised what had sparked the reaction.

"I'm not telling you what to do Alina, I'm just a bit worried that too soon might be too much."

She felt like a fool misreading his intention.

"I know Ronnie, I reacted wrongly, I'm sorry I misunderstood, but I think I would like to do it again."

"It's up to you."

Sally observed the interchange between the two of them, at first embarrassed by the static and then uplifted by the love that they showed for each other.

They all took up their original positions and Alina began to concentrate on the rose again.

Once more, she began to smile, "There is a big crowd, and everyone is happy. They are all on the top of a hill and there is a loch below them. Everyone is looking down the hill; it's a wedding, I can see the bride with her father coming up the hill, it's not a bridal dress, but she looks like a bride and she's wearing a veil. The bride is standing at the edge of a heart shape made out of white rocks, they look like crystals." Alina was quiet as she watched and then…

"Wait, it's changing, it's a different time and its cold outside."

"Who do you see?" asked Sally.

"I don't know; it's as though I am looking through someone's eyes, as though I am looking, as though I am that person."

Ronnie was on the edge of his seat; Sally was beginning to feel uncomfortable.

"I'm in an old close and its smelly, really old and dark, I don't like it. I'm knocking on a big dark wood door. Oh, it's ok a man's opening it and I know him, he's laughing. He steps back and invites me in. I feel uncomfortable, I'm in the house it's dirty, there's someone else there, now I'm afraid."

Suddenly, Alina dropped the rose and grabbed her throat. She went rigid; she was choking and struggling on the sofa. Ronnie and Sally both jumped over towards her at the same time. Ronnie was pulling her hands from her throat and shouting.

"Alina, Alina, you're ok, you're safe, I've got, you come back, come back to me. Dear God what's happening to you?"

Sally in a panic ran to the kitchen and ran water over a cloth, then she ran back with it and began to wipe Alina's face with the cold cloth. Ronnie was cradling her in his arms and Alina was sobbing.

"He killed me, he killed me."

"No he didn't you're home, you're safe, you're with me, I've got you babe, I've got you."

Sally went through to the bedroom, grabbed a cover from the bed, and took it back to the sitting room. She wrapped it over Alina who was still cradled in Ronnie's arms. She went over to the stereo, checked what CD was in the stereo, and then pressed play. As ambient music began to play in the background, Alina drifted into a deep sleep in Ronnie's arms. He was almost afraid to let her go, but he gently eased her back on to the sofa, put her feet up, and took off her shoes. He covered her tenderly with the throw from the bed and stood up.

Breathing a deep sigh, he turned to Sally and said.

"What the hell happened there?"

"I don't know Ronnie, I've never seen anything like that, and I had no idea how sensitive she was. For goodness sake, I only taught her to do psychometry. Most people just get an impression, but that was although she was there, in the past, in whatever was going on."

Ronnie was sitting at the table on one of the dining chairs opposite Sally. He was running his hands through his hair as he looked at Sally, his face full of the anguish that he felt.

"I thought she was going to die. I couldn't bear that."

"Don't be silly. She wouldn't have died," said Sally, and she got up and went to the bathroom. She stood with her back against the door and as she slid to the floor, she covered her face with her hands and cried her heart out. At first, Ronnie had thought that Sally was being flippant until he heard her crying, and he realised that she had been as frightened as he was. He let her be for a few minutes and then he heard the water running.

He went to the kitchen and made a pot of tea and as she came out of the bathroom, he called quietly to her.

"In the kitchen Sally."

She came into the kitchen and he walked over to her and put his arms around her.

"I thought we had lost her; I feel so responsible." Sally began to cry again.

"Neither of us could have anticipated that happening."

Chapter 37

Alina was asleep on the sofa when Ronnie and Sally took their tea into the dining room where they could watch her and chat quietly without disturbing her. They were shaken by the effect of the experience on Alina and they were concerned for her. Alina stirred as they talked and they both went quickly to her side. Ronnie knelt down and stroked her forehead.

"Are you feeling alright?"

She stretched and smiled, "Actually I feel good." Then as the visions came back to her, she sat up quickly.

"Oh that was terrible!"

"Don't talk about it just now, you gave us quite a scare, are you certain that you are ok? I'll make you some tea. Ronnie, another cup?"

"Yes please Sally, a splash of whisky in it maybe?"

"In tea?"

"I believe it's good for shock." Sally laughed at him.

When she came back with the tea Alina was sitting up and she had colour back in her face. Sally poured tea for the three of them and then Alina talked over everything that she saw. She closed her eyes and tried to recall every detail.

"I could see a crowd of people, men, women, and children at the top of hill and below I could see a loch. They were all in a happy mood, eager, and looking down a path. Yes, they were standing on either side of a path, and then I could see below them a bride coming up the hill.

I don't know when it was, but it looked like a long time ago. The men were smart, but they looked hardy, as though they worked on the land, and the women were all wearing long skirts and dresses of the period, whenever that was. The bride wasn't wearing a wedding dress as we know them; she was wearing what looked like a cotton dress, it was soft and moving in the breeze and it had tiny flowers all over it. She was wearing a long veil, longer than her dress, that came right down to the ground. I could see wild flowers in the posy that she carried. There were Bluebells and Red Campion and sprigs of Heather with blue ribbons trailing from the posy.

Her father was looking at her, I think she was maybe about five foot four and he looked about six feet tall. He was big in stature, he looked important and he was clearly very proud. She was smiling and nodding to the people who were watching and I could see her glancing up trying to catch sight of the groom, but I didn't see him at all."

She took a deep breath and opened her eyes.

"It was such a lovely scene to see, it was as though I was there."

"Do you think it was Rosa who was getting married?" asked Sally.

"I don't know, it could have been, she looked similar, but older obviously. She did have dark curly hair though."

"What else can you remember?" Sally asked.

Ronnie was quiet, just observing until Sally asked that question. He turned his head and glanced at her. Clearly, he was not sure that he wanted Alina to recall that part of the experience yet.

"Everything changed then and instead of watching a scene unfolding I was part of the scene. I was walking into a dark dingy close. I could smell stale urine and there was dirt on the floor. Rubbish had gathered around the edges against the walls. I felt as though I was carrying something, but I'm not sure what it was.

I was standing in front of a black door and the paint was cracked and peeling. I don't think it was paint, I think it was old varnish. Anyway, a man opened the door, I knew him, but I didn't like him, I don't know why I was there. He was big man he had a rough face and a rough look about him, but he was laughing and joking. He was wearing a striped shirt with no collar and it was creased and stained down the front.

He invited me in, and I don't know why I went in, and I could hear a voice in my head saying, let me get this right, no I can't remember, but it was something about crossing a door. When I went in there was a big fat man sitting by the fire, and the way he looked at me was disgusting, and then I felt the first man's hands on me. They jumped me, I was screaming, but the first man was holding his big fat hands over my mouth and my nose and the other one was groping me."

By this time, Alina was sobbing and Ronnie had moved to the sofa beside her and put his arms around her shoulders to comfort her.

"I couldn't breathe, I was suffocating."

"Shh now shh..." Ronnie reassured her.

Sally asked, "Were you Rosa, was it Rosa being attacked?"

"I don't think so; no I'm sure it wasn't Rosa."

"I don't think we should do any more on this Alina, Sally do you agree?"

"I do. I think we should leave this alone for a bit to give Alina a break from it. This appears to have been building up for some time, since the wooden rose in fact, and there is probably more to find out before we know the underlying cause of this mystery. I have to leave first thing in the morning, Ronnie are you staying here tonight?"

"Sally!" exclaimed Alina.

"Well I will be leaving early and I am not leaving you alone."

Ronnie put his arm around Alina.

"Don't worry babe I won't take advantage of you, not while you are vulnerable, I can sleep on the couch."

"Don't be ridiculous Ronnie. I will be in the spare room; you can be with Alina."

Alina was mortified. It was so typical of Sally to organise her.

"He doesn't have any pyjamas here!" exclaimed Alina and then felt incredibly childish.

Sally gave her an exasperated look that said 'grow up' and Ronnie just grinned.

"I guess that's that settled then," laughed Ronnie as Sally kissed them both on their cheeks and then went off to the bathroom to get ready for bed.

"Would you like some more tea before you go to bed?"

"Yes I would love some."

Ronnie went to the kitchen to make the tea, and when he returned with the two cups of tea they relaxed and chatted about what they would do the next day now that Ronnie was finished with the estate agents. When the tea was finished and Alina could no longer delay the inevitable, she got up to go to the bedroom.

"I will be through shortly Alina."

Later, Ronnie went through to the bedroom. Alina was fast asleep; he sat on the edge of the bed and looked at her sleeping. He loved her so much and he wondered how and when that had happened. He slipped quietly and carefully into bed beside her to avoid disturbing her, and he fell asleep holding her close. Early in the morning, Sally, leaving quietly, woke him up and he was amused to find that Alina's leg was almost pinning him to the bed and her arm was over his body. Rather than react to his natural urge he eased himself out of bed and went through to the guest bathroom for a shower.

Chapter 38

Ronnie was in the kitchen grilling bacon and whisking eggs. He looked as though he was in command of the task of making breakfast. His hair was still damp from his shower and he was just wearing jeans slung low on his hips. Alina looked him up and down from his damp hair to his bare feet and her mouth watered. He was simply delicious to look at. Sensing her presence, he turned and smiled at her.

"Coffee's ready, breakfast will be ready in a minute."

She blushed as he looked at her, she had cleaned her teeth, washed her face, and brushed her hair, but she felt silly standing there in her pyjamas while he cooked breakfast in her kitchen.

"Thanks for staying last night. Where did you sleep?"

"Beside you, you were out like a light when I came through, but you had me trapped under you when I woke up this morning. I saved your modesty and slipped out of bed." He grinned at her and she blushed again.

"Do you want to take the toast through to the dining room?"

She gathered herself and picked up the toast and the coffee pot, and he followed with breakfast on a serving plate and then returned to the kitchen for plates and cutlery.

Over breakfast, he asked her what she would like to do.

"I think I would like to walk on a beach. We could get Jock and go somewhere if you like."

"I'll go next door and get a change of clothes from Auntie Nessie's and I'll pick up Jock too."

"I'm embarrassed; she will think we slept together."

"We did, we slept together all night," he laughed.

"You know what I mean."

"Auntie Nessie is a woman of the world and thinking that we made mad passionate love all night will delight her, so stop worrying your modest head."

When they were both ready they put Jock in the car and drove to Largs. They spent the day there enjoying their time together, chatting, walking Jock along the beach and throwing sticks for him. The streets were bustling with shoppers and day-trippers. About thirty motor bikes were in the car park and the bikers were chatting and admiring each other's bikes. They had lunch at Nardini's then had another walk along the beach with Jock. By the time they returned to Alina's, Jock was tired out, but Alina and Ronnie felt thoroughly refreshed.

"Would you like to go to the Uplawmoor Hotel for dinner tonight?"

"I would love that," she said surprised by the sudden invitation and then she laughed.

"Is this our first date then?"

"Yes I suppose it is."

"Well yes, I would love to go on a date with you." He kissed her on the lips.

"I am going to head back to my flat and change my clothes; I'll pick you up at seven. I'll drop Jock off before I go."

She felt as though she missed him before he was even out of the door.

Sally called during a break to ask how she was feeling after the events the day before. Alina told her that she was none the worse, that Ronnie had made breakfast, and that they had been to the beach with Jock.

"He is taking me to the Uplawmoor Hotel for dinner tonight. I can't believe how nervous I am."

"What's to be nervous about?"

"After dinner."

"Dessert?" laughed Sally.

"Don't be funny."

"Alina, stop over analysing things, what will be will be, and what will happen will happen."

"That's easy for you to say, but I haven't been with anyone since JJ."

"Oh, well then, I think Ronnie has more to worry about than you have."

"Now you're being silly and I'm trying to talk seriously with you."

"Just go out tonight and enjoy it. Ronnie is a decent guy; he is hardly going to force you into doing something that you are not ready for."

"Yes, you're right, I was over analysing. I better go and look out what I'm going to wear."

"Don't forget, matching underwear, preferably sexy," laughed Sally as she was hanging up.

Alina browsed through the hanging rail in her wardrobe; there were a couple of dresses that she had never worn yet, and as she looked through them she decided on a short navy blue fit and flair dress with a slashed cowl neckline. The fitted bodice pinched in at the waist with two deep pleats then flared out over her hips.

She applied a little shadow, some mascara, finished with a quick sweep of blusher to her cheeks, and then went to look in her jewellery box for earrings and a pendant, choosing a delicate chain with a sapphire pendant and matching earrings. A spray of her favourite perfume, La Perla, a touch of lipstick and she was ready. The pouch containing the wooden rose was already in her tan silk clutch bag, which matched the colour of her high heels.

Ronnie arrived on time and when she opened the door, she was thrilled by how handsome he looked.

"You look lovely Alina and smell delicious too." He stooped to kiss her on her lips.

"We're dressed to match," she smiled as she admired him in his Navy silk mohair suit. His navy and white checked shirt was open at the collar, but he had a tie in his pocket just in case.

"I thought we would go for dinner first and then to a late showing of Interstellar with Anne Hathaway and Matthew McConaughey."

"I'd love that; I've seen it advertised."

The drive to the hotel in the village of Uplawmoor took about thirty minutes and they chatted nonstop on the journey. Alina had never been there before, and was delighted to see the small two-storey white and black trimmed hotel as they drove into the almost full car park. As Ronnie negotiated parking his BMW, Alina noticed the Three Gold Star and AA Rosette plaques.

The inside was a delight, with a cocktail bar to the left and a huge brass canopied fireplace in the centre of the lounge. Comfortable sofas and chairs were scattered around the space, and the staff were welcoming and courteous as they showed them to a sofa and offered them drinks.

The head waiter approached and presented them with a menu each, and while they perused a mouth-watering selection of starters, main courses and desserts, their drinks arrived. Ronnie had ordered Alina a glass of Châteauneuf-du-Pape and still water for himself. They both chose the chef's Chicken Liver Parfait with a red onion & orange marmalade for their starters, and while Alina chose the Chicken Lattice stuffed with mushrooms, Ronnie chose a Moroccan Chickpea Tagine.

They talked and laughed while they enjoyed their meals and each other's company. By the time the meal was over neither of them could manage dessert, but they lingered over fresh coffee until it was time for the late showing of Interstellar.

On the drive home, after the film, which they both loved, Alina relaxed listening to Elbow playing on the CD, and she thought over the past months, from meeting Ronnie when he had first shown her the apartment until now. She thought about how they had become good friends and then closer still, and she remembered how he had told her he loved her. They walked upstairs together and Alina unlocked her door and walked into her apartment with Ronnie just behind her. She turned suddenly, stood in front of him, her heart thudding in her chest and said, "This is where I could say, thank you very much, this has been a lovely evening," then she reached up, took hold of his lapels, pulled his face down to hers, kissed him passionately on the lips, and savoured the taste of him. His tongue flicked over hers as he picked her up in his arms and lifted his foot to kick the door shut behind him.

Chapter 39

On Sunday morning, she woke up early feeling content and happy. Ronnie was in a deep sleep as she slipped out of bed and went in to run the shower in the ensuite. She was singing quietly to herself as water ran over her body.

"Meet me tonight by the campfire

Come with me over the hill.

Let us be married tomorrow

Please let me whisper I will."

Ronnie stepped in beside her and squeezing a handful of shampoo on to his hands, he began to lather her long hair,

"What are you singing?"

She luxuriated in the feeling of his hands in her hair,

"I don't know just a tune I can't get out of my head."

"It sounds like the kind of song a gypsy girl or boy would sing."

"Really, so it does, I don't know where that came from."

Later, over breakfast, she could hear the song in her mind. "I'm wondering about that song; do you think it's connected to my old woman?"

"I was already mulling that over."

"What do you think?"

"I think it is,"

"Yes, you are probably right. After breakfast I would like to get out my Runes and maybe ask some questions, see what comes up."

"I think that's a good idea."

Ronnie cleared the table and stacked the dishes in the dishwasher while Alina went to her office to fetch the workbox containing her reading accessories. She set her reading mat on the table and opened the wooden box that contained her Rune cards. She set the Rune box to one side and placed the cards on the reading mat.

"I've seen lots of Rune stones, in fact I have a set of hematite Runes, but I have never seen Rune cards."

"I came across them a few years ago and I find them good to work with when I am seeing clients, I have stones too, but I prefer to use the cards. Do you mind if I light a few candles, set the right energy?"

"I would be surprised if you didn't. Shall I help? You could light east and west and I will light south and north if you like, balance the energy, male and female."

"Perfect, yin and yang."

They stood together side by side and Alina lit the first candle to the east. Together they walked to the south and Ronnie lit the second candle. Alina lit the west candle and Ronnie finished by lighting the north candle. They walked over to the coffee table together and sat side by side on the sofa.

"How are you going to do this?" he asked as he lit an incense stick.

"I think I will just ask to be shown what I need to know regarding the old woman."

She held her cards in her hands, and silently recited her usual prayer finishing with, "*Please show me what I need to know so that I may understand more about the gypsy lady and what she wants from me.*"

She placed the deck of cards on the coffee table to her right and efficiently, using her right hand, she fanned the cards to her left in a semi circle. She closed her eyes, thought for a moment, and then pointed to one. She opened her eyes, drew that card towards herself, and turned it over. She had chosen Eoh.

"This is probably talking about you Ronnie, as this is the card that I often consider to be a helping hand. I have a favourite Rune book on the shelf. We should have a look at what is written for this just in case we miss something."

"Let me get it."

Ronnie came back to the sofa and sat down. Alina fanned through the pages.

"Yes here it is." She handed the book, open at the correct page, to Ronnie as she gathered the cards.

"Traditionally it relates to travel and movement for instance when you are moving home and neighbours or friends gather to give you a helping hand to move to your new home. Since neither of us is moving, it probably relates to you giving me a helping hand."

"When did you last look at this Alina?"

"I don't know, a few years ago, why?"

"There is a sentence here that might be quite relevant," and he read it aloud.

"Theirs were travelling folk, but they had settled at this camp for some time."

"And look at the illustration, it's a gypsy wagon."

"Oh, perhaps it's relating to the old woman's background, her heritage."

"Try another; be more specific with your question."

Alina sat with the cards for a moment and asked into herself

"What am I looking for?"

She fanned the cards as before, paused, then pointed to a card and drew it towards herself before turning it over. She had drawn Thurizas, the Rune of caution.

"Look at the picture Alina, it has a rose in it."

"I remember this one; the story tells us to mind the thorns when picking roses, to handle things with care."

"What do you carry in your pouch Alina?"

"Oh my goodness, I didn't make the connection, it's a rose. That's not making sense, I can't be looking for a rose, and I already have a rose."

"It must be connected to the rose Alina, perhaps the rose belongs to Rosa that appeared when you did psychometry. Ask another question."

"This has to be the last one today. I never like to draw more than three for myself."

She fanned the cards, paused, then pointed to a card and drew it towards herself. This time she turned over Lagu.

"What did you ask, Alina?"

"If I am looking for a person, where is she or he?"

"Lagu is caution again; it deals with the emotions telling us to be patient and to wait for the right time before acting. It's not making sense to me."

Suddenly the hairs stood out on the back of her neck, she looked at Ronnie.

"What is it, what's wrong?"

"Whoever we are looking for is in the water. The illustration shows water. I'm sure that we are looking for someone who is lost or hidden in water."

They both jumped up as the patio doors slammed open, blowing out the candles and for just a second Alina saw the old woman.

They stood looking at each other.

"Did you see her Ronnie?"

"Yes, I did, I think we are getting closer. I think it is a woman who is missing and I think she is in water, and it might be Rosa."

Alina stood up, went over to close the doors and as she reached the patio doors she called to Ronnie, "She's on the sidewalk by the river. Oh my God! Ronnie, I think whoever she is looking for is in the Clyde. Oh dear God, it's too terrible to imagine."

Ronnie put his arms around Alina and comforted her as she sobbed.

"We're getting closer Alina, we'll get to the bottom of this, we'll do everything we can to find her."

Suddenly the scent of roses filled the air, Ronnie and Alina looked at each other and smiled.

"Can you smell them Alina?"

"Yes, it's beautiful. It feels as though she is telling us that she is happy with what we have found so far. How are we ever going to find whoever it is who is missing?"

"I think for the time being we need to take a break from this to gather our thoughts, and then we should do some research on the internet and maybe the Mitchell Library. We should be able to track newspapers that were topical during..., oh we can't search newspapers, and we have no idea what period we are researching."

Ronnie looked despondent as he realised the enormity of the task.

Chapter 40

They pondered over the enormity of their task and then Alina suddenly announced.

"I know a way that we could maybe narrow it down."

"How?"

Alina was grinning as she opened her workbox and drew out a six-inch long crystal dowser, which was about an inch thick. It had a copper band over the top with an eyelet, and a heavy silver chain was threaded though the eyelet. Beaten copper spiralled from the top to the bottom of the crystal, with copper wire following the path of the beaten copper. The wire secured two small magnets attached to either side of the crystal.

From the bottom of the workbox, Alina drew out a notepad and two pens, and began to peel off sheets of paper and tear them into small squares.

"I'm intrigued," said Ronnie as he watched her.

"It's my dowser. So what do we know so far?"

"Well we think we are looking for a girl called Rose who was murdered and she lived in a gypsy caravan."

"But we don't know when."

"No."

"So if we guess at when travellers lived in gypsy caravans, what would be your 'guestimate'?"

"I suppose from the 1900's to maybe the 1970's."

"That's good enough to start with," said Alina, and she began to write the years from 1900 to 1970 on eight squares of paper and then lay them out face down on her reading mat. She spread them about, mixing them up and then asked

Ronnie to place them so that they were not touching each other. When he had done so Alina placed her elbow on the tabletop to keep her arm steady, and then she suspended her dowser holding the chain draped over her index finger and held in place by her thumb.

She held the dowser over the first piece of paper; nothing happened, then the second and the third with the same negative reaction. When the dowser reached the fourth piece of paper, it began to pull to the right.

"Can you see that?" Alina asked.

"What's it doing?"

"I think it's the fifth and coincidentally the number five relates to questions being answered?"

She suspended the dowser over the fifth piece of paper and it spun fast.

Ronnie turned over the piece of paper and read out the year.

"It's the 1920's."

Alina tore ten strips of paper and wrote each year from 1920 to 1929 on each piece. Ronnie scattered them around the table as before and Alina began to douse once more. There was no response from the douser as it passed over the first six pieces of paper and then on the seventh it began to spin.

"I bet its 1923."

"Why do you say that?"

"A hunch."

"Spill, what gives you the hunch?"

"The number twenty-three is often associated with abuse, turn it over."

Ronnie slowly turned over the paper and jumped back laughing, but in awe of what he saw. The year 1923 was on the paper.

"Alina," he laughed, "you are really scary. Did you even have to dowse?"

"Well yes, I would never have taken the chance on something so important, but I had a feeling."

"Ok what now? We have the year, so that leaves three hundred and sixty four days of newspapers to search through."

"Well let's try adding months such as January 1923, then February 1923 and so on."

They shared the task between them and once more, they wrote the year and month on squares of paper and placed them on the reading mat. Alina began to dowse again but this time the year and months were visible. She began with January 1923. When she reached May 1923, the crystal began to rotate.

"That's it then, it looks as though whatever happened occurred in May 1923, only thirty-one days of newspapers to read, fifteen days each if we do it together."

"We'll go to the Mitchell Library tomorrow if you like." said Ronnie.

"Thanks Ronnie, I'm glad that you are helping me with this."

Monday and Tuesday were clear for Alina, as she had no clients expected until Wednesday, giving her spare time to devote to the search, and now that Ronnie was finished at the estate agency, he could spare as much time as necessary. Since the library was twenty minutes away from her apartment, they decided to walk rather than take a car and have to think about parking in the city.

They admired the library as they approached it and looked at the stunning building with its distinctive copper dome, bronze statue and striking classic facade. Inside was every bit as imposing and whilst it was tempting to spend time exploring various exhibits and collections, they made their way to the fifth floor where archives where stored.

The librarian directed them to back issues, suggested the Glasgow Herald as a good place to start their search, and instructed them in the use of the microfilm machines. They settled down to the task and worked until almost one o'clock. Ronnie turned and looked at Alina who was engrossed in her task.

"How does lunch sound?" At first, she was so engrossed in her study of the material that she didn't even hear him and then she stopped and looked at him.

"Did I hear the word lunch?" she grinned, and they both stood at the same time.

"Let's go down to the ground floor, I am sure there is a cafe there."

In contrast to the main building, the cafe was light, modern, and almost full in spite of being a Monday. They managed to find a free table, looked over the menus and then Ronnie joined the queue to order Cajun Chicken Panini's and coffees.

Over lunch, they discussed their searches. Ronnie had started at the end of the year 1923 on the first day of May, whilst Alina had started at the last day and was working backwards.

"How are you getting on Alina?"

"My eyes are melting," she laughed.

"Yeah, mine too. Have you any hunches?"

"Yes, but I'm not telling."

"Come on, share."

"I'll write it down and we'll see if I'm right." She took out her mobile, opened the 'memo' app, and typed in the date she thought would shed a result, saved the note, and closed her phone.

They both laughed as they gathered their plates and piled them on their tray, before going back to the fifth floor to resume their search. The search appeared to be easier in the afternoon, perhaps because they had refuelled, or maybe they were just getting used to searching. At four o'clock Alina made an announcement.

"Found something."

Ronnie went to join her at her station and stooped over her shoulder to read what she had found. There, in black and white at the bottom of the page were the words, *"Police rushed to the area of Kinning Park to break up an unruly crowd of travellers who were causing a nuisance and creating fear and alarm by tramping through closes, banging on doors allegedly in search of a missing girl. No arrests were made and the unruly mob was disbanded."*

"That's it, don't you think?"

"I think so, maybe," replied Alina.

"Scroll up, what is the date?"

She did as he asked and at the top of the page they both read aloud together,

"The Glasgow Herald Saturday May 23rd 1923."

"What did you think it would be?"

She took out her mobile opened the note that she said and handed it to Ronnie so that he could read it for himself. He looked at the text display and there was the date twenty-third of May 1923.

"Alina, that's just not possible, but I am looking at it. I can hardly believe my eyes, how on earth did you know?"

"I told you, twenty-three, it's a funny number, there are hundreds of statistics about the number; on very few occasions, during a reading, I have known it to represent a soul mate, but I would say that ninety percent of the time, for me anyway, it represents abuse of some form or another."

"Let's go home."

They closed things down, thanked the librarian, and began the short walk home. They were both quiet on the journey and Alina was worried that Ronnie was perhaps having second thoughts about being involved with someone like her. She was beginning to wish she had held her gift back, and then she remembered her promise to herself after her relationship with JJ.

This is who she was. Things that she felt, saw, or understood were things that made her who she was and she was not going to change for anyone no matter how painful it would be.

"Are you angry Ronnie?"

"Angry? What about?"

"About things I see and know."

He stopped there in the street, traffic thickly congested only feet from them, and he put his hands on her shoulders and looked into her eyes.

"Nothing you do or see or say makes me angry Alina, confused, yes, I'll admit to that, but angry? Absolutely not. I admire your gift, but it scares me a little, you are so on point. It doesn't scare me that much though that it would change my feelings for you, if that's what you mean."

Alina breathed a sigh of relief as he leaned down and kissed her passionately on the lips to the accompaniment of passing cars honking their horns. They laughed together and continued toward Alina's apartment. Auntie Nessie joined them for dinner that evening and after she left, Ronnie left to spend the night at his own flat.

Chapter 41

Ronnie had business to attend to the following day and wanted an early start; he also wanted to give Alina some time to herself so that she could prepare to see her clients the next day. Sally was due to arrive on Thursday around lunchtime with the latest news on her search of the family tree, so they arranged to meet again on Thursday to discuss what they had found out and decide on the next step.

Ronnie arrived first on the Thursday and Alina was happy to see him, she had missed his company even though it had only been for one day. He wrapped her in his arms and kissed her on her lips.

"Hello my Gypsy Girl, I have missed you."

"Hello my Dark Horse," she laughed.

"What, didn't you miss me?"

"I did, but I didn't want to admit it."

"Is Sally here yet?"

"No, but I expect her anytime now."

Alina had set the table so that they could have lunch; she had prepared some potato salad, cooked ham and chicken, salad greens, tomatoes and fresh crusty bread that she had shopped for in the morning.

Sally arrived a few minutes later and as usual was bursting with energy and enthusiasm. She hugged and kissed both of them and hung her jacket in the hall.

"Ooh lunch, I'm starved and I have a lot to tell you."

Over lunch, Sally started the conversation, giving Alina news of the last trip and passing on regards to Alina from Cassandra and the other psychics.

"Saving the best till last I have found more family connections."

"That's great Sally," said Alina enthusiastically.

"The last time we spoke about this I mentioned that I had got as far as Paul Devlin who married a Patricia Cairns and then moved to the United States in 1937. In this most recent search, I have found their son, Thomas Devlin. He married Jobeth McLean in 1966 and they had a daughter Joanne in 1997."

Sally stopped to chew a mouthful of chicken and crusty bread.

"Sally that's amazing, I can't believe how good you are at this stuff."

"Wait, there's more, we know that in 1882 Coralina ran off and married the miller's son Robert Miller, and then one hundred odd years later in 1986 Joanne married John Miller."

"1986, that's not that long ago Alina, you could still have traceable relatives," Ronnie said.

"I know; I am excited at the thought."

"Ok, so Joanne and John had a daughter Rosemarie in 1997, that means she'll be eighteen now. I honestly don't know what the relationship will be, cousins I suppose three or four times removed, but that doesn't really matter, what matters is, they are family. The thing is I'm still searching The National Archives, and hopefully I will find something. There is also the 'Voters Roll', I'll search there too, but I am sure that they are here and I will find them."

Alina jumped up from the table and went around it to hug Sally who was sitting on the other side.

"Oh my God that's amazing Sally. I don't know what to think. Goodness! I may have passed them in the street and not known."

"See, I knew you would get carried away with it all, they could be in Brighton or Wales or Ireland for all I know, but I will keep trying to find them."

Alina frowned, but only for a moment and then she was excited again.

"I still think the progress you have made is amazing."

When the lunch was finished, Alina and Sally cleared the table and stacked the dishwasher while Ronnie made coffee. They went through to the sitting room to relax and talk over the latest developments in the search for clues about the old woman.

"So tell me what has been happing with you guys?" Sally asked.

"We decided to cast the Runes last Sunday and Ronnie helped me to cast a circle, nothing elaborate, just candles and incense."

"Really! Good for you Ronnie, I didn't realise that the mysteries interested you so much, I'm impressed. That would be a nice balance of male and female."

Alina went on to tell Sally about the three runes that they had chosen and the significance that they held.

"We were checking with the Rune book so that we didn't miss anything. It was Ronnie who noticed the illustration in the first one Eoh; it was a gypsy wagon.

I thought at first that it was referring to Ronnie because he was helping me, but I think the wagon was the connection because Ronnie went on to read the text in the book and it talked about a travelling family.

We could be just connecting dots influenced by the revelation that I have gypsy blood, but I don't think so."

"So the old woman may be from a travelling family Alina, what do you think Ronnie?"

"Yes I agree with that too, and something that hasn't been mentioned," he said cautiously "it may be someone from Alina's distant family."

Both girls exclaimed together, "Oh My God!"

"I didn't make that connection Ronnie."

"Nor did I," said Sally

They pondered on that for a few moments, each with their own thoughts then Ronnie continued.

"The next Rune had a rose in the illustration."

"You're joking, seriously, which one was it?"

Alina replied, "Thurizas, caution! I'm not sure if it is telling us to be cautious or if it was appearing because of the rose in my pouch."

"Oh I have no doubts about that Alina, I'm sure it's about the rose."

"Alina asked a third question to establish if we were looking for a person and where that person would be and she drew Lagu."

"Oh my God, in water, whoever it is may be nearby?"

"That's not all; the patio doors slammed open and when I went to close them the old woman was standing outside on the footpath. Ronnie saw her too."

Then Ronnie said, "Suddenly the room was filled with the scent of roses, and we may be way off base, but putting everything together we think we are looking for a girl, possibly the body of the old woman that appears to us, and we think she might be in the river. Her name might be Rosa."

Ronnie and Alina went on to tell Sally of their search at the Mitchell Library, and how Alina had dowsed over slips of paper to establish a year to search, and then did the same again searching by months.

"Alina had a hunch of the date that we would find something, but she wouldn't share. She put the date in her phone, and then, when we found an article that we thought could be relevant, she let me see the date and she was spot on."

"What did you find?"

"You have the copy of the piece don't you Ronnie."

"I put it in your workbox," he said and got up to fetch the paper that he had copied the text to and gave it to Sally.

Sally took it, studied it for a moment, and then began to read aloud, *'Police rushed to the area of Kinning Park to break up an unruly crowd of travellers who were causing a nuisance and creating fear and alarm by tramping through closes and banging on doors allegedly in search of a missing girl. No arrests were made and the unruly mob was disbanded.'*

'Oh my God! This is Kinning Park, but this new bit is now called the Waterfront, it must be here somewhere. That's quite upsetting; to think that a girl went missing is bad enough, but that perhaps she was never found…"

"Alina was upset too, but I think we have to put that behind us and try to find her if at all possible."

"How did you know the date Alina, I bet you used numerology didn't you? I knew you were good, but sometimes you really surprise me by how accurate you are. What's the next step?"

"I have been thinking about this for a few days, since we found the article really, I think I should go to the police."

"We'll come with you, what do you think Ronnie?"

Before Ronnie could answer, Alina said, "No, that's not a good idea. They will never believe us and will probably think we are time wasters. You have your reputation to think of Sally and you too Ronnie. I will go myself."

"What about your reputation?" they both asked simultaneously.

"Don't misunderstand me, please, I could never have done all this without your help, but I can't allow either of you to risk your livelihood on this."

Ronnie and Sally looked at each other. They both knew and understood Alina and although in some ways, she appeared vulnerable, and sometimes insecure, when she made up her mind about something there was no stopping her.

"Do Nancy and Davy know anything about this?" asked Sally.

"No, I haven't told them all the things that have been happening, they just know that the old woman appears in my dreams."

"Maybe you should talk it over with them," said Sally.

"Why?"

"If your parents were still here would you talk it over with them?"

Alina looked chastised. "Yes I guess I would."

"Well, Nancy and Davy have been like parents to you, and it's only my opinion, but I think you should tell them everything, and Aunt Nessie too, because when and if news of this breaks they will all be involved one way or another."

Alina had tears in her eyes.

"I don't want anyone's life to be disturbed by this, but I feel driven to follow this course. You are right, I know you are."

Ronnie reached over and held Alina's hand. "You do what you have to do Alina and we will be there for you no matter what the consequences are."

Ronnie and Sally hugged Alina comforting her.

"Ok I'll give Nancy and Davy a call and ask if they would like to come for dinner tonight. Do you want to nip across the hall and ask Auntie Nessie, Ronnie?"

Chapter 42

Alina, Sally and Ronnie shared in the making of spaghetti bolognaise; Ronnie chopped onions, garlic, and skinned tomatoes, Sally gathered and chopped oregano and parsley from the herb pots that Alina had started growing on her veranda, while Alina browned the minced beef. Sally went on to preparing garlic bread and then when everything was in the bolognaise pot Alina added tomato puree, grated parmesan and a stick of celery.

"Celery?" said Sally.

"Shh, secret ingredient," laughed Alina and left the pot to simmer. The table was set for six and Ronnie had gone to the off license to pick up a couple of bottles of red wine.

There was almost an air of apprehension as they sat in the sitting room waiting for everyone to arrive. Alina was nervous, but no one was surprised about that, as what she was about to tell Nancy, Davy, and Auntie Nessie, might come as a bit of a shock to them.

Auntie Nessie was watching from her window for Nancy and Davy's car to arrive so that she could go into Alina's at the same time. She gave it the right amount of time and opened her front door, which was opposite Alina's, and they all went in together.

Auntie Nessie was wearing a plain grey skirt with a twin set in her favourite colour of pale pink that suited her grey hair and smooth complexion. She had added a hint of blusher, pink lipstick and had on a matching set of pearl earrings and necklace. She had already met Nancy and Davy a couple of times and they enjoyed catching up and asking after each other.

Nancy was wearing a fine knit dress in bottle green and although her hair was grey now she often used a mid brown rinse. The effect as the rinse washed out and as Nancy's hair grew, gave her bands of silver at each side and tonight she had gathered her hair up from the sides with two attractive slide combs. Davy as a courtesy to the fact that he was out for dinner had changed out of his baggy grey trousers and favourite holey cardigan and T shirt at Nancy's insistence, and was wearing smart jeans and a white polo shirt.

Ronnie entertained the three of them and offered something to drink while Alina and Sally went to the kitchen to put on the spaghetti, warm the garlic bread, and prepare a side salad. The water had been on the boil so there wasn't long to wait before everyone sat at the table with delicious food in front of them.

Sally, Alina, and Ronnie had talked about how and when they should tell the family; and they decided rather than tell all of it before or after dinner, they would try to keep it casual, as casual as it could be anyway, and tell them during dinner. This wasn't going to be an easy task as Nancy, Davy, and Nessie were so busy chatting and laughing, taking turns at exchanging snippets while they ate, that no one could get a word in edgeways.

Sally, Alina, and Ronnie looked at each other grinning and making eyes at their elders. Ronnie held his fork in his hand level with his wine glass, he mouthed and nodded to Alina "Will I?", and he motioned ringing his fork against the glass to attract them.

Alina and Sally both laughed, Alina nodded and Ronnie tinkled his fork against his glass and made a coughing sound "Ahu mmm."

They looked up as one, and everyone laughed together and settled down as they wondered if there was going to be an announcement. Nessie and Nancy gave a quick glance and a secret knowing look to each other, thinking that the announcement was going to be one concerning rings and they were equally happy to think that.

There was an empty silence, and as they waited for news to fill it as Ronnie said encouragingly, "Alina has something to tell everyone, go on Alina."

"Recently memories of little things have been coming to me and there is a reason for that, I'm sure now. I suppose I should start with a fairy story that my mother told me when I was a little girl. Until a few months ago I had forgotten the story, but now I remember all of it."

She told this story...

"Once upon a time, long, long, ago there was a group of gypsies who travelled in tall colourful wagons. Big wheels held the wagons up and long wooden poles attached the horses that pulled them along from place to place. The wooden insides and outsides of the wagons were painted in bright colours with hints of gold here and there.

The big group had smaller groups, and each of the smaller groups had their own place that they returned to when they were not travelling from fair to fair, or farm to farm, but they travelled often and getting back to their own place was like a holiday. There were hundreds of people in the big group, they were all there together;

And then my mother would sing this song"

Alina sang it just as her mother would have.

'The Morrisons', Cunninghams', and the Stewarts', too

The Boswells' and Marshalls', the Deadmans', sure.

Douglas, and Wilson, Donnelly and Kelly

There they all were under the trees.

Not forgetting the family of Lees.

Some families would go this way and some families would go that, but always, always, always, they would come back to that place that was theirs; they called it home.

In every group, every woman was every child's granny, or mother, or auntie, or cousin or sister. In every group, every man was every child's Grandpa, Father, uncle, cousin, or brother. They called it family.

You see, to travelling folk, family is everything. Family is all you need. When you have family, you feel safe and loved, but when you don't have family, you always search and wonder.

In one particular family there were two daughters who were princesses, and both princesses were beautiful, good, clean, and kind.

The little princess loved her older sister and learned how to wash the pots and clear the fire before the wagons moved in the mornings. They travelled all around Scotland, but the princesses liked Ayrshire the best. The older princess she liked it best when they went to Dalgarven Mill in Kilwinning. The miller was a nice man and gave them fresh baked bread and bags of flour in exchange for his horses being shod.

The miller had a son who was about the same age as the older princess and they knew each other from when they were little. They waved eagerly when they saw each other, and if there were a moment or two to chat or play, they would take advantage of it, but as they grew, so did their friendship for each other. Soon they were no longer just friends; they loved each other; they would steal a moment to run in the fields with the sun in their hair and smiles on their young faces.

The princess sang a song when they were together, and the miller's son would say to her, 'Sing me your song Gypsy Girl' and she would sing in her lilting voice."

Alina sang,

"Meet me tonight by the campfire

Come with me over the hill.

Let us be married tomorrow

Please let me whisper 'I will'

What if the neighbours are talking?

Who cares if your friends stop and stare?...

One day the song became true when the miller's son asked the princess to marry him.

'I can't, I can't! She cried.'

'Don't you love me?' he asked.

'With all my heart, but you and me are different and I can only marry from my kind.'

Her heart broke as she realised her family and her group would never agree to the union.

'Run away with me,' he said.

On the night that she ran away, the older princess told the little princess that she was leaving.

"But we're family?" little sister cried.

"I know and I will always love you, but little sister, when you find love that pure and true it does not matter if you are different kinds, if you find love don't let it go."

And with that the older sister slipped out into the night and was gone, but for a long, long, time she missed her family, and she would sing her song,

'Meet me tonight by the campfire

Come with me over the hill.

Let us be married tomorrow

Please let me whisper 'I will'

What if the neighbours are talking?

Who cares if your friends stop and stare..."

There was total silence in the room when Alina finished talking.

Alina continued with her thoughts and feelings.

"I didn't notice until Mum and Dad died, but I think there has always been a feeling of not knowing who I am. It came to a head when they died and more so after I left JJ. At first, I just thought it was the transition, but it all makes sense now and I want to know who I am and where I come from. What makes me who I am? Why do I yearn for family? I think the old woman must be family, I want to find her, to see how I can help her, and I think I know where she is."

Alina excused herself and went to the bathroom to wash her face. Her insides were in turmoil and in her mind, all she could see were the silent looks of concern on the faces of Nancy, Davy, and Nessie.

Chapter 43

For a few moments after Alina had left the room everyone was lost in their own thoughts. Alina had touched their hearts with her words, and then Nancy broke the silence when she turned to Davy and said,

"Poor lass, I never knew she felt like that Davy."

"Nor I, and it saddens me to think that we missed it. She always just gets on with things."

"And all this time she has been hurting inside, Nessie said, and thinking of us before herself,"

Ronnie and Sally began to tell them more about the dreams and the appearances when Alina came back through to the dining room. The conversation continued as Ronnie, Alina, and Sally talked about the various methods that they had used to find information, summing up with the newspaper clipping.

"The thing is," said Davy, "the newspaper clipping says a young girl went missing, but it's an old woman who appears to you. I don't understand that; wouldn't it be the young girl who would appear to you?"

"I don't know either Davy, but it doesn't alter the fact that the woman keeps appearing and it seems to be connected to the young girl. I just know that I have to go to the police and ask them to search in the Clyde. I am sure they will think I am some kind of fool, and I am worried that the newspapers get a hold of this and that's why I wanted to forewarn you. I don't want you to be troubled by this."

Davy stood up and went around to Alina on the other side of the dining table, "Come here lass." He took her hand and she stood up as he wrapped his arms around her. "We may not be your real family, but we love you very much and we will support you no matter what you decide to do."

"Hear, hear," chanted Nancy and Nessie. And everyone gathered around Alina offering their unconditional support.

"Let's go through to the sitting room and I'll pour us all a drink," Ronnie said.

"Not for me thanks, I'm driving."

"Stay the night, Nancy, Davy; you can use my spare room since Sally has Alina's."

Nancy and Davy looked at each other and nodded.

"That's kind of you Nessie I think we will be happy to take you up on your offer." Then to Ronnie he said, "A whisky or a brandy would be great."

Ronnie poured drinks for everyone while the women cleared the table and stacked the dishwasher. The task done, they joined the men in the sitting room.

"So what's the next step Alina?" Davy asked.

"I will go to the police station at Helen Street on Monday, I want to think about what I am going to say over the weekend, and I think I will go out with my dowser tomorrow and walk a few hundred yards around here."

They discussed the recent events over drinks and then Nancy and Davy went next door with Nessie. Sally was leaving to have a couple of days at home in Largs the next morning, so she kissed Ronnie and Alina good night before going to the spare room. Ronnie and Alina relaxed on the sofa and talked about how the news had gone down with their families.

"They just took it in their stride," Alina said.

"Did you expect them to react in a different way?"

"Well I didn't really know what to expect."

"They love you very much Alina and Aunt Nessie already loves you too, so it's understandable that they would want to support you, and I love you too. Come on, it's been a long day and you look worn out, let's go to bed."

The next day after breakfast, Nancy and Davy popped in to say bye to Alina and Ronnie before they left for home.

"Do you want to do anything over the weekend Alina?"

"I think I just want to lie about watching old westerns and be a couch potato; is there something that you want to do?"

He laughed, "Yes be a couch potato, watch old westerns with you, and we could be really lazy and order in later."

"Fantastic."

They took the time to themselves relaxing and trying to avoid the subject of dowsing for a body and seeing the police. Ronnie lounged back on the big sofa and Alina lay on the other end with her feet in Ronnie's lap. When they checked the TV planner, they saw that there was a John Wayne film, 'The Quiet Man', not exactly a western, but definitely worth watching. As they watched the old movie, Ronnie massaged Alina's feet and stroked her legs, such a little thing, but a tenderness that she had never experienced with JJ. She wasn't comparing JJ and Ronnie, but she was comparing the way Ronnie treated her. He treated her with consideration, kindness, and tenderness and when he loved her, he treated her as though she was his Goddess.

He turned, his gaze distracted from the film,

"What?"

"Nothing."

He was grinning at her, "I could feel you staring."

"I was just thinking."

"About what?"

"About you and the way you care, just the things that you do. You make me feel happy inside."

"Alina, I will do everything I can to make you happy and that's a promise; come here."

She swung round on the sofa as he pulled her onto his lap and wrapped his arms around her.

Ronnie made sure that Alina had a restful weekend. He knew the strain that she had been under and he knew that worse was to come on Monday. He wanted to go to the police with her, but he also knew that she had ideas about her independence and that, at this stage in their relationship, she would consider his insistence controlling rather than supportive as intended. He would be close by so that he would be there for her when she would need him most.

Chapter 44

There was quietness between Ronnie and Alina on Monday morning as they showered, dressed, and had breakfast. Alina was nervous, and Ronnie was concerned for her and the reaction that she might get when she went to the police station.

"I have been thinking about this and I have decided that I want to ask a professional dive company for information first, before I go to the police."

"That's probably a really good idea Alina."

"Do you know anyone?"

"No, but I'll Google it."

They went through to the office together and their search revealed several dive companies, however, Clyde Commercial Diving had a local telephone number, and being quite close to where they were it seemed the ideal place to start. The director's name was Jim Patterson. Alina made the call and asked to speak to him, but he was out of the office.

The receptionist said that he was returning from the highlands having been involved in the repair of a Cal Mac ferry, but she took Alina's number and said that she would pass a message to him and he would call her back. An hour later Jim Patterson called, and arranged to meet her the next day at ten am at his office in Loanbank Quadrant, just off Helen Street.

Alina breathed a sigh of relief after the call, not because she was relieved that he had called back, but because she had another day before it would begin.

"Come on Alina, let's go to a property auction."

"What? Are you buying property?"

"Not necessarily, but we should do something completely different today and there is a property auction in Kilmarnock Road."

Alina's mood brightened immediately.

"I've never been to a property auction."

"It's exciting, I'm sure you'll enjoy it and it will be a distraction."

They went in Ronnie's BMW; the Waterfront was a convenient location to access anywhere in Glasgow since it was so close to the access points for all major and minor routes. Ronnie drove his BMW out of the waterfront, turned left towards the junction at Morrison Street, and then they followed the turns to pick up the M77, which led them directly to Kilmarnock Road, only ten minutes from the apartment.

There was an air of anticipation and excitement in the auction hall as people shuffled about whispering to each other, trying to look as though they weren't interested, and waiting for that moment when they would start bidding for the property that they wanted. Some people were there to buy homes for themselves, but many of the buyers were property developers.

Alina found it fascinating to watch, and from time to time Ronnie would draw her attention to someone or other so that she could watch how he or she bid. It was a fascinating process and it served Ronnie's purpose of distracting Alina from her concerns.

After the auction they went for a bar meal at one of the local pubs and then headed back to the apartment. They called in to see Aunt Nessie and took Jock for a walk before spending the evening with Nessie in her apartment.

Alina asked Ronnie to stay the night when they left Nessie's apartment.

"I would like you to go with me to meet Jim Patterson tomorrow."

"Of course I will."

"But I still want to go to the police station myself."

"I understand Alina, stop worrying, we will take things one step at a time and I am going to be here whenever you need me."

The next day they went to meet Jim Patterson at Clyde Commercial Diving as arranged. Jim was actively involved with Strathclyde Police Underwater Search Unit, and his experience included diver training, and operations including recovery of missing persons or articles.

They found that Jim was very helpful in answering Alina's questions, and he explained some of the historical facts about the Underwater Search Unit set up in the 1960's after the Peter Manuel murders. Alina asked about the possibility of finding a body and the condition a body would be in had it been in the Clyde for almost a hundred years, and Jim explained about the previous dredging of the Clyde by the Clyde Navigation Trust, which became the Clyde Port Authority. Jim told her that if a body was there it was likely to be below six feet of silt unless it had been disturbed for some reason, and the likelihood was that only bones would remain.

Jim told her that her first point of contact would be the police and that she should contact them in the first instance, and that they would do a search. He went on to explain that the resources that the police had these days may restrict the amount of time they could search, but assured them that if they were unhappy he would be willing to search on their behalf.

Alina asked Jim how much notice Clyde Port Authority required, thinking that it could take weeks for consent, but Jim explained that it was a safety notification to the CPA so that shipping in the area would know that the divers were in the water. He shook their hands as they left and assured them that he would do what he could if it became necessary, and both Ronnie and Alina thanked him for his input and advice.

"He was so helpful wasn't he Ronnie, and he didn't seem to be put off by the fact that I am a psychic or that we were trying to trace a body that we really didn't know for sure was there."

"Do you feel more confident now?"

"Yes I do; would you take me to the new police station now?"

Ronnie drove his car out of the car park and turned right into Helen Street. It only took them five minutes to get there, and Ronnie dropped Alina off at the main door while he went to wait in the visitor's car park.

Her heart was thumping as she went through the blue swing doors and into the reception area. Several officers were going about their business moving between offices and there were some rough looking individuals sitting in waiting areas.

For two pins, Alina would have turned and run out of the station, but she willed herself to the reception desk and stood in front of it facing a uniformed police officer.

"Miss?"

"Can I speak to someone in the Underwater Search Unit please?"

The officer looked at her as though she had horns.

"Can you tell me what your business with them is and I'll see what I can do?"

"I would really rather just speak to one of them direct thank you."

"There might not be anyone here that can help you, so if you tell me why you need to speak with them I will try to help you."

"Is there somewhere that I can explain privately?"

Alina could see that he was exasperated, but she stood her ground and looked him in the eye.

"Give me a minute?"

He left the desk and a few moments later a door in the reception area opened and the officer called her over and asked her to take a seat.

"Someone will be with you in a minute."

She assumed that he went back to his desk duty so she waited where she was, but began to wonder if she was being ignored because it was about fifteen or twenty minutes before anyone came to see her. A young constable came through the door.

"Can I help you miss?"

"I wanted to see someone from the Underwater Search Unit."

"There is no one here from that unit so if you tell me what it's about I will try to help."

"I wondered if they could do a search for a body in the Clyde."

He raised his eyebrows and drew back at the nature of her request.

"Where is this body?"

"Near the Waterfront development where I live."

His attitude changed and became more professional.

"Let me take some details."

He opened a document on the computer on the desk in front of her and asked her for her name address and occupation. She felt uncomfortable saying professional psychic, as she knew what misconceptions this would lead to, and the minute she gave her occupation his eyebrows rose again, but he made no comment.

"Now tell me about this body, where did you see it?"

"Well that's the problem, you see I haven't actually seen it, but I know it's there."

"Did you overhear someone talking about the body?"

"No, you see, the thing is, I have been having dreams, and all this goes back to the 1920's..."

Before she could say anymore, the constable put his hand up in front of her and stood up.

"Just give me a minute."

He went out of the door that he had come through and she heard him saying, "Is this a windup?"

Then there was muted conversation and she could only hear a few words, dead body, psychic, time waster, and then a lot of laughter. She felt humiliated, a lump formed in her throat, her lips began to tremble, and tears began to run down her face. She stood up and without further ado, she left the office that she was in and hurried past the reception and out of the police station to look for Ronnie who was already watching for her coming out. He drove the car forward meeting her at the entrance to the station. He knew by the tears that it had not been a good experience.

Chapter 45

On the short journey home Alina was quietly sobbing to herself, more from embarrassment and frustration that anything else, and Ronnie let her cry believing that it was better for her than holding it in. When she stopped crying she wiped her eyes and blew her nose trying to compose herself.

"They laughed at me, they made me feel stupid and embarrassed."

She told him everything that had happened and asked him to take her back to Jim Patterson's office.

"Alina I think you have been through enough, why don't you give me his number and I will call him and ask him to organise a search?"

Alina took her phone from her handbag and handed it to Ronnie. He pulled over to the side of the road and made the call.

"Hi there Jim its Ronnie here, I came in earlier with Alina, we would like you to go ahead with a search please."

"I take it that it didn't go well at the police station then?" he asked.

"No; quite the opposite, so we would like to go ahead with the search please."

"Well you followed proper procedure and you can't be faulted for that. I have a space in the diary tomorrow morning around ten o'clock if that's good for you?"

Ronnie agreed to the appointment and gave Jim Alina's address.

"I'm taking you home now and no arguments; you cannot carry this burden on your own. You need a big brandy and some rest."

Alina hadn't the energy to argue so she just lay back in the comfort of the big saloon car and closed her eyes.

When they arrived home, Ronnie ran her a bath, put candles on each corner of the bathtub, and sprinkled some Himalayan Bath Salts and some bubble bath into the water. He went through to the sitting room and pressed play on the stereo. He knew that chances were whatever was first to play would be ambient and it was.

Alina was sitting on the sofa with her eyes closed going over in her mind the frustration and embarrassment that she was feeling. She opened her eyes when Ronnie took her hand and led her into the bathroom.

"Oh Ronnie, that's just so lovely, thank you."

"Get your clothes off and get into the bath and I'll bring you a brandy."

She did as she he told her without another thought. As she sank into the warm water, she felt all her cares leaving her, at least for a while. She lay back in the water and sipped at the brandy; she could feel the warmth of it easing the anguish she felt inside as the water eased the tension in her muscles. She emptied her mind and rested.

The next morning, refreshed after a sound dreamless sleep, Alina was ready when Jim arrived. Ronnie opened the door for him and he gave Jim a brief outline of the events that brought them to where they were. Jim took it all in his stride; clearly, he was a sensitive open-minded man who understood that he was playing an important role in this drama.

Alina and Ronnie went outside with Jim and Alina began to use her dowser. She held it as before in her right hand with the chain suspended over her index finger while her thumb held it in place. She walked from the edge of her entrance to the left towards the Glasgow Quay. She had only gone about ten yards when the dowser began to spin furiously. Ronnie and Jim looked at each other for a moment and then Jim picked up his mobile and began to make a call to his office.

"Christine, prepare a risk assessment, other paperwork and notify Clyde Port Authority of a dive tomorrow morning from ten a.m., and then check with some of the other divers and see who will be available to partner me on the dive. I'll text you the coordinates and expected duration shortly."

Jim took a permanent marker from his pocket and made a mark on the paving where the dowser had indicated and then they went back to the Alina's apartment. There were contracts to be completed and Alina made Jim some coffee while he was preparing them. Once they were completed and signed, they shook hands and Jim left, promising to be back at ten the following morning.

The next morning around nine thirty, two vans arrived and parked near the area that Jim had marked. The two men with Jim began to unload their gear, various tools and prepared their equipment for the dive.

"Do you want to go down and watch Alina?"

"I don't know, I'm not sure, it will be terrible if they find something and terrible if they don't. Yes, I want to be there."

Together they went down to watch. A small crowd began to gather, curious about the goings on. This was Alina's worst fear, knowing that anyone in the crowd could call the newspapers and she didn't want that to happen.

Each diver took turns in the deep murky water, which was so dark that it was impossible to see your hand in front of your face. Powerful flashlights did little to make things any easier for them. Turn after turn they took until about two o'clock in the afternoon Jim, who was currently diving, surfaced, and gave a thumbs up. Alina assumed that they must be giving up for the day at least, as Jim was helped out of the water. He took off his facemask, tanks, and flippers, and barefoot walked over to Alina. He looked at Ronnie, then back at Alina, and said, "Found a human bone."

That was the last thing Alina heard until she came to sitting on the walkway, as she had simply passed out, and both Ronnie and Jim had caught her and lowered her gently to the ground.

"Give me a minute, I have to call the Strathclyde Police Underwater Search Unit. They have to secure the scene until we recover the remains."

The other divers were already pushing people back and creating a barrier around the area.

Ronnie took Alina home and called Nessie to come over. Ronnie was already making Alina drink hot sweet tea when Nessie arrived.

"Sit with her Auntie Nessie I've got to go back down."

Within minutes, the place was swarming with police who were erecting barricades and screens to isolate the scene. The Underwater Search Unit arrived and spoke at length with Jim and then they too began to dive. An officer from the Underwater Search Unit came to the apartment with Ronnie to interview Alina, to ask her how she knew about the body and why she hadn't informed the proper authority.

Alina did her best to explain what had led her to believe that a body was there, and explained that she had been to the police, but they had laughed at her. The officer did not have much to say about Alina's treatment, but he didn't look very pleased.

"It may take some time to recover all the remains, but we will keep you informed," he said before he left. The CID arrived next and began to question, Alina treating her almost as though she had done something wrong, until Auntie Nessie stood up and gave them a piece of her mind. They too left saying that they would be back.

Ronnie sent Sally a quick text.

"We hired divers Remains found in Clyde. When are you free?"

Within minutes, a text arrived from Sally.

"Cancelling my appointments. I will be there first thing in the morning."

Then the telephone started to ring and Nessie answered,

"This is Mrs Brodie; can I take a message for Alina?"

She didn't hear the name of the person calling, but she did hear the word 'newspaper' and promptly put the phone down.

With some considerable coaxing Nessie managed to steer Alina into the bedroom and into bed.

"A good sleep is what you need now. This has all been a bit of a shock for you. I'll stay here, don't you worry about a thing."

Alina was asleep within minutes and thankfully didn't hear the telephone continuing to ring.

"We should unplug that land line Ronnie."

He did just that and then began to pace.

"This is so hard on Alina, I think I will give Nancy and Davy a call," he said, and used his mobile phone.

"Hello?"

"Davy it's started, divers found human remains and the place is swarming with police and newspapers."

"Oh lord, how is Alina taking all this?"

"Nessie has put her to bed and for the moment she is fast asleep, but it was a shock for her. I suppose part of her didn't want to believe that there was a body."

"Nancy and I will be over shortly."

"Why don't you wait till the evening; it may be a bit calmer then?"

"Perhaps you're right, I'll speak with Nancy when she comes back from the shops, see what she thinks."

"I'll call you when Alina wakes up."

Just as he closed the phone, the external door went. He pressed the buzzer to see who was there.

"It's Jim Patterson."

"Come on up Jim, but don't let any reporters try to sneak in."

Ronnie opened the door to let Jim in and shook his hand as he entered the apartment.

"That's us finished now Ronnie, I must admit I don't really know what to say. I was open to the possibility that we might find something, but you know her accuracy with that dowser was astounding. I was speaking to the inspector downstairs at the scene and gave him a little of the background. We both agree she could probably help a lot of people."

"She is sound asleep just now; she will glad that you called and you are probably right, but she is in no fit state to help anyone just now, she needs time to reconcile all this and we still don't know who we have found."

"Well anyway, tell her I called and I would be happy to work with her anytime."

"She'll appreciate that Jim. Can I get you a coffee or something?"

"No, we're packing up and heading back to the office, just give her my regards and tell her to pop in and see me anytime."

Later that night Nancy, Davy, and Sally arrived and Alina had already showered and changed. Nessie had watched over her like a guard dog throughout the day; when she was sure that Alina was all right, she roasted a chicken and cooked a big pot of chicken soup to feed everyone.

Chapter 46

The Underwater Search Unit took several days to recover all the remains and take them to the city morgue for the pathologist to attempt to discern the cause of death, and establish whether a crime had been committed. Newspapers carried various headlines: -

'Human Bones Found in Clyde.'

'Glasgow Psychic Finds Body.'

There was even a mention on the television, but through it all, Alina and the rest of the family refused to be named or interviewed, and neighbours who may have known them kept tight-lipped. Some Glasgow residents came along to the spot that the bones were recovered from and laid flowers at the scene.

A few weeks later, a police inspector came to the apartment; Ronnie had been staying there permanently since the discovery so he pressed the buzzer to release the external door and was waiting to let him in.

"I've just come to let you know that the tests have been completed, and it has been established that the remains were that of a young girl, probably between fifteen and eighteen years old, and that she was murdered. The pathologist believes that the remains have been in the Clyde for around a hundred years."

Ronnie and Alina looked at each other.

"When will the body be released?" asked Alina.

"There are still some formalities to go through, but probably within the next week. I will let you know for sure. I take it you want to claim responsibility for the burial of the remains?"

"Yes, thank you."

"I wonder if I might speak to you on another matter."

"Of course."

"The thing is, we have open unsolved cases of missing persons and I wondered if you would be interested, you and your team, in having a look at them?"

Again, Ronnie and Alina looked at each other. Alina laughed for a moment, "Are you serious? I don't have a team, this has been an experience that we all shared, but we're not a team."

"Perhaps it's something that you would consider; these are my contact details and the numbers listed will take you directly to me, I hope you will think about this as I am sure that you will be able to help us close some cases and put some people's minds to rest."

He stood up and handed Alina his card.

"I won't take up any more of your time; I'll let you know when the remains are ready for collection."

"I'm sorry, forgive me, I didn't mean to sound flippant, you just took me by surprise."

"No offence taken, just get in touch when you have had time to consider my offer and we will talk about the possibilities some more."

After the inspector left, Ronnie said, "I wonder what Sally will make of that offer?"

"I do too, we can ask her, she will be here tomorrow. She sent a text, said she had news. She said not to make any plans."

The next day Sally arrived; she was always excited and upbeat, but there was something about her enthusiasm this time that was different. She could hardly wait to take her jacket off and settle down.

"Sit down, both of you. I want to tell you what happened yesterday. I was in Carlisle and a client came across to me for a reading. I told her to sit down and waited while she got comfortable, and then when I asked for her name and address as per usual, she said, 'Joanne Miller'. I nearly fell off my chair, but I kept it together and began to prepare the cards.

I kept looking at her and I could see that she was a bit uncomfortable to the point where she actually asked me if something was wrong. Anyway, I told her to put her hands over the cards and think of her questions, and then as always I fanned them out and told her to choose the ones that she wanted me to read. She made her selection and I began to place them in the horoscope spread. Alina I saw America! I had to stop reading for her, I knew it was your Joanne, so I just told her everything, and it is her!"

"No Way!"

Alina jumped out of her seat as Sally did the same. Ronnie watched in amazement as the two of them, holding hands, danced on the spot.

"Can you believe it! She came right up to my table. She is so excited."

"I can't wait to talk to her."

"You won't have to; she will be here in about an hour."

Alina was pacing now. She had never felt this excited about anything.

"She's coming here? In an hour?"

"Actually they're coming here, her husband John and their daughter Rosemarie were waiting in the lounge of the hotel, so she went to fetch them and they know everything. The three of them are coming, your family Alina, your family."

Sally started to cry and Alina joined her. The two girls hugged each other and quietly sobbed with the emotion of this new development. Ronnie could only stand by and shake his head, but deep down he felt the power of the emotion as it flooded through him.

"What the hell," he thought to himself and wrapped his arms around both of them.

Alina could hardly contain her excitement, she kept going back and forward to look out of the window.

"Oh my God! I think this is them," she said, as a large white Bentley drove slowly into the Waterfront.

"I have to go down," she said as she rushed to the door.

Alina reached the main door as they pulled in to park. The registration plate read 1986 JM. It had to be them. The woman in the passenger seat caught sight of Alina and waved and the man looked over and grinned.

Joanne got out of the car, ran towards Alina, and threw her arms around her.

"You have the look of family about you," she said, and kissed her. Alina felt as though she was looking at a younger version of her mother, but with dark hair. She was every bit as fashion conscious as her mother too, and she looked smart in a beautiful black knitted dress with diagonal white stripes and chunky jewellery.

"I might be your cousin, or even your aunt several times removed, but who cares, you're family. Meet John and Rosemarie."

John was a bear of a man, dark haired, tall and broad shouldered. He looked as strong as an ox. When he hugged Alina, he hugged her so tight she could hardly breathe. He was in casual wrangler jeans, tan cowboy boots, a white polo shirt and a Giorgio Armani belt, which was a nice salute to style, and then there was young Rosemarie.

Alina felt as though she was meeting a young niece, and she was so pretty. Long brown hair cascaded down her back and blue eyes looked at her coyly as she came towards Alina for an embrace. Her jeans had sparkle down each side seam and the matching denim jacket had more diamante on the shoulders. They all had tears in their eyes as Alina took them inside and upstairs to the apartment.

Ronnie had called Nancy and Davy, they were on their way over, and Nessie was already there. Everyone was talking at the same time and the air of excitement was palpable. Young Rosemarie was watching in almost bewildered amusement and tolerance of her elders then Nancy and Davy arrived, and it all started again.

Chapter 47

When they had all finally settled down, Joanne began to give Alina some information that would make things clear for her regarding her dreams and the appearance of the old woman.

"Our direct lineage goes back to Coralina Kelly who ran away to marry Robert Miller. I know from Sally that you are familiar with this side of the story, but there is more. We travellers are very committed to family and we like to keep ourselves to ourselves. In those days, it was very rare for a gypsy girl to marry a gorger, someone that wasn't a gypsy, and gorgers frowned on any of their kind marrying gypsies.

When Coralina and Robert ran away it broke two families' hearts, and caused a lot of trouble at the time. Soon it was too late to find them and no one who knew would admit to knowing where they were. They went on to have the family that you know of, but later we all began to share stories, and as we know, it Coralina had a sister called Mary.

Mary married John and they had only one child, which was unusual as in those days' big families were common. Rosa their daughter grew up and married Edward. They say he was a fantastic carpenter and that he had carved a little wooden rose when he was only a boy, and he gave it to Rosa when she was about ten or twelve."

Alina by this time had paled, and she was staring open mouthed at Joanne. She looked at Sally, and Sally said, dragging out the syllables, "I knooow!"

Joanne picked up the story again.

"From time to time, Coralina was able to get messages to Mary, but as a child Coralina made Mary swear to keep her secret, and she was afraid to tell anyone that Coralina kept in touch so she shared her secret with no one. Coralina heard about Mary and John's wedding and Rosa's birth, and later all about Rosa and Eddie's wedding on the Tinkers Heart.

Sadly, Rosa died of pre-eclampsia as she was giving birth to her daughter Rosie. There are a lot more stories to tell, but we know that when Rosie was about sixteen she went missing while she was out selling from her basket. The story handed down is that while Eddie was searching he found the wooden rose that he had carved for Rosa at the corner of St James Street and Paisley Road West. St James Street has since been renamed Seaward Street."

"Oh my God! That's just down the road," said Alina, and Joanne nodded as she had already done some research herself. Joanne continued.

"Rosie had been carrying the carved rose for a few years so when Eddie found it he knew that she was around somewhere, but the police never found any sign of her. Sally told me your story and about the dreams that you were having. She told me about the old woman and the remains that have been recovered."

Joanne started to cry and Alina immediately went to kneel beside her chair to comfort her.

"You have been seeing old Mary, Coralina's sister, and the remains that were found are young Rosie."

Everyone in the room had tears in their eyes or was openly weeping; finding someone's remains was one thing, finding out later that those remains belonged to your family was something else entirely, and everyone in the room felt that pain.

"We are all so grateful to you Alina, and to Ronnie and Sally for the part that you played in this experience. The story told over the years is that hundreds searched for Rosie, and many never gave up hope of finding her. Those that remember will always be grateful.

We would like to be involved in the funeral arrangements. Janefield Cemetery is where the rest of the family are and if you have no objection, we would like that to be her final resting place, and please do not take any offence, but you will not have to pay for anything. Everyone will contribute to Rosie's burial."

Although for a short while the mood was subdued, it wasn't very long before things got back to normal. Joanne, John, and Rosemarie agreed to stay for a few days at Nessie's apartment as she had two spare rooms, and then they all went out to dinner at the Hilton in Glasgow.

They devoted the next few days to arranging with the city morgue for the release of Rosie's remains, and with the undertakers to set the date for the funeral. They agreed on the following week. Joanne, John, and Rosemarie were going home to Carlisle for a few days, but before they left, Joanne had something to tell Alina.

"Do you remember how Sally and I met?"

"Yes, you went to get your cards read."

"Yes that's right; John and I were undecided about whether we should stay in the UK and where we should stay, or whether we should return to the States. There have been so many opportunities, but we couldn't make up our minds. Anyway, I just wanted to tell you that we have taken this as a sign and we have made up our minds. We are going to stay and we will be looking at houses and business opportunities here, in Glasgow."

Alina threw her arms around Joanne.

"I'm so glad Joanne; it's going to be wonderful having you all here."

All too soon, the day of the funeral arrived. Joanne had arranged the transport and at ten a.m., a large black stretch limo arrived to pick up Alina, Ronnie, Sally, Nessie, Nancy, and Davy. Everyone was dressed in black as a sign of respect, and everyone wore a red rose on his or her clothing as a token to Rosie.

Joanne and her family followed behind in another black stretch limo, and as the cars turned out of the Waterfront estate, they caught sight of a beautiful white horse drawn carriage. Two police motorcycle riders escorted the two cars and the horse drawn hearse. Alina and the rest of the party looked on at the amazing white carriage with glass sides and gold trim along the edges.

Four white horses pulled the carriage, steered by two coachmen wearing formal black long coats and top hats. Inside the glass carriage was Rosie's white coffin, a wreath of red roses that spelled out 'Rosie McGuigan' resting against the side of it, and white rose petals were scattered all over the top and sides of the coffin.

The four white horses held their heads proudly as though they were aware of the importance of their task. White plumage decorated the tops of their heads and the bridles and harnesses were white leathers with highly polished brasses.

Alina was stunned to see police controlling the traffic and hundreds of cars all parking to attend the funeral. While the carriage waited, they got out of their car at the same time as Joanne and her family, and together they walked silently behind the carriage. As they walked, hundreds of travellers joined the procession all without exception wearing a red rose.

Alina stood with Ronnie, Sally, Nancy, Davy, and Nessie to her right, and Joanne, John and Rosemarie to her left. The minister gave a beautiful talk on loss, hope, and never giving up, and then Alina watched as groups of mourners filed past and threw flowers and tokens as a sign of respect into Rosie's grave. As each family came past, they approached Alina shook her hand and offered her an envelope containing money and stated their family name: -

"The Boswells', for Rosie's headstone."

"The Wilsons', my family searched for a long time, this is for Rosie's headstone."

"The Morrisons', my granny told us Rosie's story, this is for her headstone."

And so it went on, so many names, so many emotions. Joanne had tears in her eyes, but she was smiling proudly. She whispered, "Family, you're one of us now."

Alina had no idea that she was sobbing, and Ronnie had tears streaming down his face. He was overwhelmed with love and pride for Alina.

The procession took an hour to complete and as the last mourner passed, Ronnie and Sally, followed by Joanne, John, and young Rosemarie, stepped forward to pay their last respects and drop their mementoes into the grave. Finally,

Alina stepped forward and removed her pouch from around her neck. She opened it and took out the little wooden rose, then stood for a moment thinking of that day out with her mother when she was inexplicably drawn back into the antique shop to purchase it.

She thought of the journey that she had been on since, from seeing Mary in her dreams to finding Rosie. She felt Ronnie returning to her side and putting his arm around her waist, and then Joanne came and held her hand followed by John and Rosemarie. They all stood together united in their love and grief. Alina took a last look at the wooden rose, kissed it, and then threw it into Rosie's grave. Through her tears, she looked over the heads of the departing mourners, and there, in a sudden mist, was Mary younger, than in Alina's dreams. By her side was her Johnny in his First World War uniform. As the mist began to clear, she saw Rosa and Eddie hand in hand looking towards Rosie, running to towards her parents. Family united in love.

"Can you see that?" she whispered to Joanne.

"Family, Alina, we're always there for each other."

That's what it's all about, family, and that's the traveller's way.

The End

After the Rose, breaking the curse
Chapter 1

The Circle cast, the candles lit, and a sliver of the waning moon shone its light in through her window. Alina wore nothing but a sheer sapphire blue gown, and when she raised her arms in salutation of the Goddess, the moonlight outlined her silhouette. She called the Guardians of the Watchtowers at each of the four quarters, to watch over her while she performed her ritual. She blessed each in turn, using smoke from the incense for the element of air to the East, her altar candle she used to represent fire at the South, water represented the West, and salt at the North represented the earth. She focused on her intention and when her mind was clear of all except her desire, she began to recite her request to 'The Lady'.

"A curse was sent some time ago and many did it harm.

In angry words the curse was made knowing it would return

But, anger blinded common sense and warnings heeded not

For in her rage the Mither's words sadly were forgot.

With all my might and all my will those words I wish to break

And end the pain and suffering that the angry one did make

Time has passed and will again, as new days come and go

Lady hear my plea, break the curse, please make it so.

I make amends for words that should never have been sent

Ever shall I try to help others with good intent

Lady listen, hear my call, hear my honest plea

And grant my wish, please make it so, this curse no longer be."

She stood in quiet supplication with her hands clasped in the prayer position and said,

"And it harm none so mote it be."

She was still for a time, thinking about the past, and thinking about her ancestor Mary. The story handed down spoke of Mary, who on a wild winter day, with the snow thick on the ground, and a gale blowing hard, issued a curse. The story told was that Mary was making her way to hospital with her baby Rosa who was very sick. A fancy carriage, with a passenger who was described as a pompous, wealthy American, slowed down to look and when he saw that she was a Gypsy, he refused to stop and help her. Mary, enraged and distressed, uttered a vile curse, cursing him and his family for generations to come. Some said the curse caused the assassination of one of his descendants in the 1960's. No one ever said that family's name aloud fearing that it would stimulate the curse. Some went as far as saying that the curse touched each generation of Mary's family.

Alina, an only child, who was unaware of any living relatives, only heard these stories when she first discovered her extended family, after her parents had died. She thought of those dark days in the past, when life for her ancestors was much harder. She thought about the tragedies that had befallen Mary after making the curse. Mary's family had suffered too, and she wondered how Mary's life would have been had she not been enraged when the American refused her a lift in his coach. What road would Mary's life have taken? What choices would Mary have made, and how would these choices have affected Alina's life today?

She knew by her pagan faith that whatever you put out returns threefold, do good and good will return, do bad and bad will come back to you. Alina was sure that the curse was still present, and would be, until someone was able to break it. Breaking the curse was her mission and she knew that she would do everything in her power to make amends for Mary's curse. She thought about the unforeseen course of events that had led her from being a recently bereaved daughter and unhappy wife, to being a divorced professional psychic travelling all over the country. She was sad that her parents were no longer with her, but now that she had found her true faith, she had the understanding that they would live again, and this gave her comfort.

A cloud began to pass over the moon and she stirred from her thoughts and moved to the East quarter of her circle. She began, quarter by quarter, to give thanks to the Guardians of the Watchtowers, and to offer back for their use the powers and energies of air, fire, water and earth that had not been used. She snuffed out her candles, and opened her circle. She placed her crystals, wand, athame and chalice on her altar tray, along with her incense holder, and the small bowls for water and salt. She took the tray through to her office and stored them safely in her magickal cupboard, where they would remain until the next time she would use them. She changed into casual fleecy trousers and a knitted jumper, and then wrapped a thick blanket around her shoulders to keep her warm while she sat on her small balcony overlooking the River Clyde. The sky was clear, and bright with stars, and there was a cold December chill to the air. In her mind's eye, she could see past events unfolding before her, and if she was honest with herself, she would admit that sometimes, she found it difficult looking out at the river without remembering.

Mary's daughter Rosa had died during the birth of her first child Rosie, and Mary, heartbroken by the loss of her beautiful girl in childbirth, poured all her love and care into looking after baby Rosie until one day, when Rosie was just a young teenager, she disappeared while out selling trinkets. Travelling families came from everywhere to help with the search but no one ever saw Rosie again and no one knew what had happened to her.

Sometimes it takes harsh experiences to awaken the spirit and such was the case with Alina. First, the tragedy of losing her parents when her Father suffered a heart attack while driving on a day out with her Mother, and then her realisation that her husband JJ was cold, uncaring and unsupportive, leading to her leaving him. Stripped of everything that she knew, a new path opened before her, and her spiritual awareness came to the fore.

So much had happened to her in the last few years; she knew she would never come to terms with losing her parents, but each day that passed helped her to remember them without that deep gut-wrenching ache in her heart. Now she could think of them and think of the happy times that they shared. She glanced over to the ceramic flowerpot sitting in the corner of the balcony. The rosemary bush had flowered profusely during the summer, and that made her smile. She thought back to the simple ceremony that she had performed to remember and honour her Mum and Dad. She had written them a beautiful letter telling them how her unhappy marriage to JJ had ended; she had hidden her unhappiness from them when they were alive, but they knew, even though she never said anything, they knew.

In her letter, she wrote about the day she left JJ, and how, when she was checking into a hotel for a few days, she had accidently bumped into Cassandra, the organiser of a psychic tour. That meeting had set her on a new path. She wrote about her friendship with Sally, and how much they laughed together and how supportive Nancy and Davy, her parent's closest friends, had been. She expressed her love for Ronnie and his Aunt Nessie and even little Jock the West Highland Terrier. The paper was wet with her tears as she poured out her heart and wrote about all the things that they had not been around to see or hear from her lips.

When she had finished writing her letter, she put some fresh soil in a clean pot and then folded her letter several times, until it was a square, small enough to place on top of the soil. She added a little more soil to cover the letter and then fetching the small rosemary plant, for remembrance, she re-potted it on top of the letter. She packed soil around the plant to hold it firmly, watered it, set it in one of her Mother's favourite ceramic plant potholders, and sat it on her windowsill. She lit a T-lite candle in front of it every morning, and this helped her through her grieving process. Each time she re-potted her plant she wrote another letter, once again telling her parents of events that had occurred since the last time. She kept a diary on her pc of everything that had happened since she started touring with Cassandra's Psychic Fair and it was her way to keep copies of the letters that she had written to her parents and planted in her Rosemary pot. She occasionally wondered if maybe one day, her notes would form part of a book. Her plant was much larger now and it was strong enough to sit out on the veranda all year. It gave her comfort every time she looked at it, and she could now think of her parents without shedding tears.

Chapter 2

Alina had loved her flat and she had loved living here especially now that Ronnie was in her life. She enjoyed having Ronnie's Aunt Nessie living next door, and then there was Nancy and Davie, who had been a great support to Alina when her parents died. They often came for dinner and sometimes, her newly found cousin Joanna would join them with her husband John and their daughter Rosemarie. The women would gather in the kitchen, sharing tasks and the latest news, laughing and enjoying each other's company as they prepared food, while the men set the table, opened the wine, and talked about things that men talked about, football, rugby and cricket. Sometimes her friend Sally, who had become like one of the family, would be able to join them and she would entertain them with amusing stories of things that had happened to her since she saw them last.

When Alina had shared her dream about the old gypsy woman, a chance remark from Nancy opened up a completely new world for her. When Alina was a child, her Mother used to tell her a fairy story about a Gypsy princess and how the Gypsy princess had run away to marry the millers son, leaving her little sister behind. Alina had believed that the bedtime story was just that, a bedtime story, but Nancy's remark, *'Maybe it connects to your gypsy blood,'* stunned, and at the same time thrilled Alina. She realised that she might actually have relatives, family that she could call her own. Sally suggested later, when she told her about this new revelation, that she should search through her parents papers and when Alina admitted that she was too raw to do that Sally volunteered. It was thanks to Sally's research that Alina discovered her roots, and now Alina had family that she could see on a regular basis, and she would always be grateful for that. Part of her wished that her Mother and Father were still alive to enjoy these evenings too.

She had to force herself to think of the positives that had come out of this experience, but no matter how hard she tried, there were moments when things would just flash into her mind. She relived the memories of Mary haunting her dreams, and then Mary's spirit appearing in front of her. At the time, she had no idea who Mary was or that Mary was part of her family, or even that she had died many, many, years before. When this began to happen to her, she knew that Mary wanted her to do something, but at first, she didn't understand what that was. The dreams and appearances, the help from Ronnie who was the love of her life, and her good friend Sally helped her to discover the reason for Mary's appearance.

Together they solved the one hundred year old mystery, using Tarot and Runes, then using Psychometry and Dowsing. Following the clues that these disciplines offered, they located the remains of Mary's granddaughter in the River Clyde very close to Alina's apartment. A little carving of a wooden rose had started the chain of events. Unbeknown to Alina, Eddie, one of her ancestors, carved the wooden rose and gave it to Rosa as a gesture of his love for her. After Rosa died the token was hidden away in a box but one day Rosie came across it by chance, and from that day she always carried in her pocket. When Rosie disappeared, Eddie found the carving lying in the street at Kinning Park. Who knows what journey the wooden rose had made, eventually ending up in a charity shop where Alina found it? Alina and her Mother were out shopping, and they had gone into the charity shop to browse. She had picked up the wooden rose and put it back several times, then just as they were leaving the shop, she quickly turned back and purchased it. She and her Mother had laughed about the rose calling to her. That was the last time she saw her Mother alive.

The memories of finding Rosie's remains, so close to where she lived were always present and she shivered as she thought of the headlines in the Newspapers.

"Human Bones Found in Clyde - Glasgow Psychic locates Body."

She flushed with embarrassment every time she thought of those headlines, and the reporters clamouring outside hoping to get an interview. She realised that this was her path, her journey in life, but she knew, with some certainty, that everything happens for a reason. She might never know the reason for all these things, all she knew was that she would trust her instincts, and look for the signs, the events, or the unfolding situations that would take her to the next step, whatever that step would be.

Sometimes these feelings pulled her down but she hid them from Ronnie. Her flat at Riverview Terrace on the River Clyde, was handy for clients to come for consultations, but there was a sadness hanging over her. She didn't know if it was because she had found Rosie's remains so near her home or if it was something else. She knew that she should discuss this with Ronnie, but she wasn't sure how he would feel about moving and she wasn't even sure where she wanted to move to. She decided that she would to talk to Ronnie about this, but not yet.

Alina looked over as Jock jumped off the sofa and started running around and then she heard the car. "Are you a little psychic dog," she said laughing as she picked him up in her arms. She went through to her bedroom and over to the window where she could look down at the car park. If Ronnie and Aunt Nessie had returned the car would be there and sure enough, it was in its usual spot. She opened the apartment door and let Jock have his way, and she laughed as he ran excitedly to welcome them home, slipping and almost running on the spot as his little feet tried to get purchase on the polished hallway. Nessie picked him up, uttering endearments and Jock excitedly licked her face and hair, as she tried to avoid his eager kisses.

Ronnie had taken Aunt Nessie to see Funny Girl at The Menier Chocolate Factory in the West End in London and Alina had stayed at home to look after Jock. Soon they were settled on the sofa with coffee as Nessie shared her excitement of watching Sheridan Smith playing Fanny Brice and singing the songs made famous when Barbara Streisand starred in that role on Broadway.

"It was so exciting, I have never been to a first night performance before, and Ronnie spoiled me the whole time. It was the best birthday present I have ever had."

Nessie chatted nineteen to the dozen, and was more than ready to go next door to her apartment by the time they had finished their coffee. Alina offered to call her when dinner was ready, but Nessie had other ideas. She wanted to unpack her weekend bag, load her washing machine and then have a quick nap before a light dinner. It had been a busy weekend with early starts, long days and late nights and she was tired out but very happy.

Ronnie wrapped his arms around Alina, "I missed you," he told her.

"I missed you too." They stood in front of the veranda doors holding their embrace for a few moments and enjoying the feel of each other's love. "Did you do a circle last night?"

"Yes, I did."

"Have you any plans for later."

"No I thought you would probably be tired after your weekend entertaining Auntie Nessie." They both laughed and then Alina asked, "Do you have something in mind Ronnie?"

"Why?"

"You have a look about you as though you were holding something back."

"Can I not have any secrets from my Gypsy Girl," he asked grinning. Alina laughed at his endearment. She loved hearing him call her his Gypsy Girl. He had given her this pet name since she first discovered her Gypsy roots.

"No, you can't have any secrets," Alina laughed at him. "Well," she said, drawing the word out, "tell me."

"There's nothing to tell really, I just thought we could do something nice."

She was looking at him with a puzzled expression on her face, trying to figure out what he was hiding. "At home or out?"

"What would you like Alina."

"A surprise."

"I can arrange that, a surprise it will be then," he said grinning. "Now I have to go out for a bit, but I will be back shortly."

She laughed to herself as he kissed her, picked up his jacket and left. She hurried through to the bedroom to watch him going to his car. She would never have admitted it to him but she loved watching him, she loved looking at him. His dark hair always had a tousled look about it and at six feet tall with a lean build he was nice to look at. Dark eyebrows over dark brown eyes gave him a serious look, but he had the kindest heart. As if sensing her, he turned and looked up, saw her at the window and blew her a kiss, she laughed and blew one back.

Chapter 3

Alina smiled wondering what Ronnie was up to as she went through to her office to check her emails. There were a few to sort through; some of them were the usual junk, but there were also some messages that needed replies. One was from a repeat client asking for an appointment for a telephone reading, and there were a few from potential clients asking about her services, better still was an email from Sally.

Her mind flashed back to how she had met Sally. She had just made her escape from her husband and had booked into a hotel until she had worked out what she was going to do. She was crossing the foyer when a woman, mistaking her for someone else, ushered her into a conference room. Madame Cassandra was the organiser of a psychic fair at the hotel. She thought that Alina was a new psychic who, as it turned out, hadn't arrived. Cassandra instinctively knew that Alina had the gift and she talked her into taking the place of the psychic who had let her down.

That first evening, after seeing clients all day, Cassandra introduced Alina to the other psychics, and although they were all very nice, she had bonded with Sally, a white witch, and they had been friends since. As her friendship with Sally grew, so did her understanding of those things that she had always believed in. She had never cast a circle, yet she believed in the power of your words, deeds, and actions. She had never knowingly cast a spell, and yet she could remember a time before she married JJ when her spirituality had been important to her.

As she got to know Sally she confided in her more and more, telling her snippets of her life and her experiences. She told Sally about losing her both her parents, and how Nancy and Davy had taken her under their wing, helping to organise their funeral and almost becoming surrogate parents in the process. She entrusted Sally with her Mother's old papers that had been stored away, and Sally spent months researching her family line.

Alina was amazed to learn that she had come from a long line of Gypsy's on her Mother's side and that she had family she had never known about. For Alina this was a blessing, but it posed problems too because once the relationship with her newly found family developed, she learned of Mary's Curse. Alina was afraid of the curse. She often wondered if she had lost her parents because of it. She wanted more than anything to break the power of the curse, but she wasn't even sure that she knew how to do this. She had only recognised and developed her pagan beliefs through her friendship with Sally, although, in Sally's words, Alina was a natural witch, more intuitive, and more powerful. Nevertheless, Alina still felt very much a neophyte.

"Would the curse come back to haunt her?" she wondered.

Every month, during the dark moon, she performed her ritual and recited the verse that she had created to break the curse, but she had no way to know if it would work.

She maximised Sally's email, "Hey girl, save Wednesday for me - passing through - Will be there around four. Cook something nice for me."

She quickly typed a reply "Great. Looking 4ward 2 seeing you. Love as always. A."

Ronnie didn't arrive back until around six thirty, he was grinning from ear to ear, and clutching Chinese take away carrier bags.

"Surprise!" he called. "Get the plates out, I come bearing Chinese and a Sandra Bullock movie."

Alina was delighted, her favourite food and her favourite actress. She quickly set out some tablemats, plates, and cutlery.

"On your knee or at the table?" he asked.

"Spread it out on the table and we can have it on our knees, what do you think?"

"I'm happy with that."

They plated up their food, moved over to the sofa, and settled down to watch Sandra Bullock playing FBI Special Agent Sarah Ashburn with Melissa McCarthy playing her reluctant partner. They laughed at the antics of them as they fought with each other, solved the crime, and eventually became the best of friends. When the film was finished, Alina was stacking the dishes in the dishwasher when Ronnie came into the kitchen carrying Alina's long black coat and holding it out for her to put on.

"Are we going somewhere?" she said as she put her arms through the sleeves, laughing at him at the same time.

"You said you wanted a surprise, well surprise!"

"I thought the Chinese food and the film was my surprise."

"No, that was just the prequel."

He was leading her out of the door as she asked,

"Where are we going Ronnie?"

"It's a surprise," he laughed.

"Ok," she dragged out the syllables, raising her eyebrows wondering what he was up to, but fully prepared to go along with his plan whatever it was. "Will I have to wear a blindfold?" She laughed as they reached his Range Rover.

"Not yet," he said, grinning at her as he was getting into the driver's side of the car.

As Ronnie drove, Alina sat quietly wondering what was coming next. He drove along Paisley Road West and on through Paisley where he turned off following the signs for the Royal Alexandra Hospital. As he drove past the hospital, Alina turned to him laughing and said, "Thank goodness, for a minute there I thought you were taking me to the hospital."

"That would have been a surprise," he laughed, "but no, definitely not the hospital, we're nearly there."

It was a beautiful clear night with no clouds in the sky and as Alina admired the first sliver of the moon, Ronnie drove up hill passing Glennifer Country Park. The car park there was known locally as "The Car Park in the Sky" because of its location and spectacular views over Paisley and Glasgow. He continued to drive and then turned off into a quiet country lane. Parking the car, he turned and said to her. "Promise me that you will sit here for a few minutes without trying to see what I am doing."

"I promise, but I'm curious."

"All will be clear in a moment, I will call you when I am ready," he said as he got out of the car, went around to the back of it, and opened the boot. Alina waited. At first, she could hear him at the boot of the car, and then all was silent. She waited; and while she waited, she watched the moon, thinking how happy they were together.

Taking a shortcut one day, searching for a property, Ronnie had come across this particular spot and immediately knew that it would be a perfect for the surprise that he was planning. It was a small copse of trees but there were four large trees, perfectly positioned in the East, South, West and North, with a clearing in the middle. He had returned to the same spot the previous month to make sure that the moon would be visible from the middle of the clearing. He was excited and at the same time nervous. He loved Alina so much that he wanted this moment to be perfect for her.

Chapter 4

Ronnie made his way to the clearing between the trees carrying the box that he had taken from the boot of the car. Unpacking the box he placed small T-light candles set in glass jars on either side of the path leading to the circle of trees, and lit them. Next, he placed four lanterns at the foot of each of the large trees and lit the T-lites inside each lantern. From East to North he cast the circle around the trees using his Athame to draw the circle line. Returning to the centre of the circle he placed the point of the Athame in the ground, and then to the East, he placed a small pot containing a sage smudge stick to represent the element of air. At the South, he placed a tall candle for the element of fire. At the West, he placed a small bottle of water for the element of water and finally at the North he placed a dish of salt to represent the element of earth.

He returned to the East and began to call the Guardians of the Watchtowers. Taking the bound sage, he lit it and watched as it began to smoke. He swirled the stick, holding it high and said,

"May the guardians of the Watchtower of the East purify and charge this quarter. With the air that I breathe, and the smoke from this sacred herb, I am air."

He moved to the South, picked up the tall candle, set a flame to it and holding the candle aloft he said,

"May the guardians of the Watchtower of the South purify and charge this quarter. With the flame of passion that burns in my soul and the flame of this candle, I am fire."

He moved to the West of the circle and picked up the bottle of water, held the water aloft and then sprinkled some on the ground as he said,

"May the guardians of the Watchtower of the West purify and charge this quarter. With the water that nourishes Mother Earth, that gives us life, and runs in my blood, I am water."

He moved to the North of the circle, picked up the jar of salt, held it aloft for a moment then as he sprinkled salt on the ground he said,

"May the guardians of the Watchtower of the North purify and charge this quarter. With the salt of life and the salt of earth that runs through my fingers, I purify and charge the North. I am earth."

He moved to the centre of the circle, stood facing the moon, spread his arms wide and said,

"With the love that burns in my heart I purify and charge this sacred space that I may love, honour and cherish the Maiden, the Mother, and the Crone and the Goddess in my life, Alina."

He turned and faced the path that he had lined with candles, and taking his Athame from the ground, he pointed at the edge of the circle and created a doorway. He stepped towards the edge of his circle and called Alina.

She heard his call and as she stepped from the car and turned in the direction towards the back of the car, she saw the candles lighting her way and she grinned with delight. She walked the few paces he had lit for her and she reached the edge of his circle where he stood waiting. He put out both hands and she placed her hands in his as he said to her,

"The temple is erected, the circle is cast, let none be here except of their own free will. In which manner do you come here?"

She knew the mantra and she replied,

"I come in perfect love, perfect truth and perfect trust."

He drew her into the circle, into his arms, and kissed her passionately on her mouth. Her heart was beating furiously in her chest. She was amazed that he had done such a lovely thing to surprise her, but the surprise was only just beginning. When the kiss ended, he drew her towards the centre of the circle and guided her to stand where the moonlight would shine on her face. He knelt in front of her, held her hands, looking up at her he gazed into her eyes, and began to speak.

"I kneel on Mother Earth, before the Lady of the Moon, so that my vow be witnessed. Alina, you are the Goddess in my life and I worship and adore you. Forever I will love you and care for you. Forever I will stand by you and keep you safe. I ask in return only one thing. Alina, my Gypsy Girl, my Goddess, my love, say you will be my wife and make my life complete."

Ronnie reached into his pocket, took out a small square of blue silk cloth, and opened it to reveal a beautiful white gold ring, which had a pale white moonstone shimmering with subtle shades of blue set in the centre of the band with two diamonds on each side of the gem. She could hardly speak, the lump in her throat choking her and the tears of joy on her face.

"Yes, Yes," she said as she drew him up to stand in her embrace and together they savoured this precious moment.

Without thinking, without planning, Alina, facing the waxing moon raised her arms high above her head and drew down the energy of the Goddess. Once more Ronnie dropped to his knees and placed the palms of his hands on either side of Alina's shoes, stooped forward and kissed her feet as a sign of his adoration to the Goddess within her. He raised his eyes to gaze on her and was almost awestruck by her beauty as the light of the moon shone on her. He stood once more and they embraced, remaining quiet, both thinking of the wonderful moment that they were sharing.

"Shall we close the circle together?"

Alina took his lead, walked to the East where she stood, raised her arms and said, "Take for your use Eastern Watchtower any powers of air that have not been used." She opened the hanging lantern, and nipped out the candle flame, stooped and snuffed out the smudge stick before returning it and the lantern to the centre of the circle.

Ronnie walked to the South where he stood, spread his arms wide and said, "Take for your use Southern Watchtower any powers of fire that have not been used." He nipped out the flame of the tall candle then opened the lantern, and nipped out the small candle flame then returned them to the centre of the circle.

Alina walked to the West, stood and raising her arms high she said, "Take for your use Western Watchtower any powers of water that have not been used." As before, she nipped out the candle flame in the lantern and poured the remaining water onto the ground.

Ronnie, standing at the North spread his arms and said, "Take for your use Northern Watchtower any powers of earth that have not been used." He nipped out the lantern candle, emptied the remaining salt onto the ground and taking the Athame he pointed it in an anticlockwise direction he said, "With love and gratitude, I thank the Lord and Lady for the blessings they bestow on us. The sacred circle is now closed."

Ronnie gathered all his alter tools and began to pack them in the car. The night air was cold now, and Alina was happy to sit quietly and gaze at the beautiful ring Ronnie had placed on her finger.

Chapter 5

Alina was excited about Sally's visit, and since she had no appointments, she was able to spend time preparing Sally's favourite meal, roast pork with all the trimmings. Ronnie had left early, heading for the Ayrshire Coast to meet clients who were interested in buying a property that he had recently renovated. After he left, Alina set the oven to high before getting the pork shoulder from her fridge and washing it. She peeled some onions, cored and peeled some apples and set them in the bottom of a self-basting roasting tin. She put the pork on top of the onions and apples and then poured a little olive oil over the top before sprinkling a generous amount of sage onto the meat. She turned the oven down to a low heat and put the roasting tin on the bottom shelf where she would let it cook slowly all day.

Alina thought about how she would tell Sally about Ronnie's proposal and, in her mind, she could picture several scenarios and Sally's reactions to each of them. In the end, she decided that she wouldn't mention it at all and wait until Sally noticed her ring. She smiled to herself and thought that Sally would notice it as soon as she arrived. As it turned out, Sally would have other things to catch her attention and this new development would come as a surprise to Alina too. It came in the form of a text from Ronnie about an hour after he had left the house.

"GG just got a text from my old mate Gus. Picking him up at Glasgow Airport, flight from Oz arrives three thirty. He's dying to meet you. Told him he could come for dinner??? Sally will be there too won't she? He'll stay with Aunt Nessie she has a soft spot for him."

Ronnie had spoken of Gus often and she knew that they messaged each other now and again, but she had never met him. This would be an interesting evening and Alina was looking forward to it.

"That's great Ronnie, will be nice to meet him – yes to dinner – yes to Sally – Aunt Nessie will probably come over too. Love you – c u la8er."

"Love u 2."

She read the message again and smiled at the abbreviation of his pet name for her, Gypsy Girl, (GG) l.

Alina busied herself with preparations for the dinner, she cleaned and quartered strawberries put them into a bowl and ground some black pepper over them to bring out the flavour, before putting them in the fridge. Later, she would whip double cream, add crushed meringues that Auntie Nessie had baked, and fold in the strawberries for Eton Mess, everyone's favourite dessert. She prepared potatoes for roasting and cut carrots into julienne strips then soaked them in cold water with star anise. She planned to part boil the carrots then strain them before slow simmering them in butter and a little honey to finish them off. Happy with her preparation she spent an hour in her office before having a shower and fixing her hair before Sally and the others were due to arrive.

With all her tasks done, she made some coffee and while she waited for Sally, she sat thinking about Gus, and wondered how they would all get on together. He had been in working as a motorcycle mechanic in Victoria, New South Wales, Australia. She wondered if he was coming for a holiday or if he was returning permanently.

Sally's arrival interrupted her musings and the girls hugged each other. They were so different in their appearances; Alina was five foot six, with a slender, but shapely frame, dark hair a sparkling blue eyes while Sally was shorter and very blonde with green eyes. Alina had quietness to her nature, while Sally was always so full of life. She always arrived like a whirlwind, with stories to tell, and things to laugh about. She would talk ten to the dozen while Alina listened, smiled and laughed with her. Finally, Sally went to the spare bedroom, to unpack her overnight bag and she continued to call out conversations from the bedroom while Alina went to the kitchen to check on the food. Sally was in full flight verbally

"So Cassandra brings in this new woman, a palm reader, she's late, and clients are already coming in. Cassandra shows her to her table near me, and she starts unpacking a brief case! Next thing she has a customer sitting in front of her, and she presses the customers hand onto one of those old inkpads filled with some kind of black ink or dye and then she presses the woman's hand on a sheet of paper."

"Are you serious?"

"Honest, the woman's face was a picture," Sally was laughing, she was laughing so hard she was bent over holding her stomach. "She handed the woman a cloth to wipe her hands, and then started to follow instructions and read out her interpretation from a book on palm reading. I was mortified, and the customer wasn't happy either. Cassandra stormed over and took the client by the arm to lead her away, and she told the 'palm reader' to pack up and leave."

"How did Cassandra appease the client?"

"She gave her a gift voucher for a reading from any of the other readers and she came to me," said Sally laughing.

"What happened with the palm reader?"

Sally cringed as she told her, "She kicked over the display board on her way out."

"Oh dear!" said Alina laughing, covering her mouth in horror at the thought. Sally just stood her eyes wide with surprise, staring at Alina. "Do I see what I think I see?"

Alina blushed and began to laugh, "What do you think you see?"

Sally grabbed Alina's left hand and gazed at her engagement ring, "Oh, My, Goddess," is that what I think it is. "Oh, My, Goddess, it's so beautiful," and then she started to cry, "Oh I'm so happy for you I could cry."

"You are crying Sally, and now you have made me cry too."

The two friends hugged each other. Emotions overflowing, they made their way to the sitting room and sat on the sofa.

"When did this happen, I want to know all the details."

Alina began to tell Sally of Ronnie's return from Auntie Nessie's birthday trip to London and everything that had happened after.

"What did Nessie say?"

"She is delighted, preening and posturing as though it was her idea. We called Nancy and Davy and I think they had a wee cry too."

"This is such a lovely surprise, I am so happy for both of you."

"There is another one to come."

"You're pregnant!"

"No, silly I'm not."

"What is it then?"

"Ronnie and I would be really happy if you would be Maid of Honour at our hand-fasting."

Sally threw her arms around Alina, both girls cried happy tears together, and then they laughed at each other's show of emotions.

"There's more to come."

"Oh no, I don't think I could handle any more. What is it?"

"You'll see when Ronnie comes home, and speak of the devil that sounds like him now."

Chapter 6

Ronnie unlocked the door, and as he and Gus went into the flat, they were laughing and chatting to each other. Sally hearing their voices looked at Alina puzzled.

"He's got someone with him?"

"Yes."

"Who is it?"

"Best friend just back from Australia, that's the other surprise," and just as she finished speaking Ronnie and Gus came through into the sitting room. Alina walked forward, shook Gus's hand, kissed him on the cheek saying, "It's good to finally meet you Gus," and then turning she said "Sally, this is Gus, Ronnie's friend."

Alina turned to kiss Ronnie and when she looked at Sally, she was surprised to see that her face was bright red and her mouth was hanging open.

"*What's wrong with her,*" Alina wondered. Sally was still standing there and Gus was trying to shake her hand. "You didn't tell me that there would be two beautiful women here to greet me Ronnie," he said as he took Sally's hand in his.

"Oh what a charmer you are Gus, come and sit down. Would you like a bottle of beer or a glass of wine?"

"I'll get it!" said Sally quickly, and she hurried into the kitchen, tripping over her own feet in the process.

"A beer would be great Alina; I'm so glad that journey is over," he said leaning back on the sofa. "I'm glad to meet you at last and I love your home, it has a lovely atmosphere, very relaxing," he said, nodding and looking around the room.

"Thanks Gus, I'm glad you like it, I am looking forward to hearing all about your life in Australia," she said as she went to join Sally in the kitchen.

"I'll have a beer too Alina, do you need a hand?" asked Ronnie.

"Thanks Ronnie; I think Sally's got it covered."

Alina went through to the kitchen to find that Sally was hanging over the sink splashing cold water on her face. "Are you OK Sally?"

"AM I OK, are you kidding me? You might have told me Adonis was coming for dinner. OH… MY… GODDESS… she enunciated, and I tripped over my feet, I'm so embarrassed, be still my beating heart," she whispered vehemently as she held both hands over her chest.

"I have never seen you like this, what's wrong with you," laughed Alina.

"Did you see his eyes, one blue and one green and that blonde hair? I'm not stopping, I'm going home."

"Pull yourself together Sally; you are acting like a fourteen year old. Calm yourself down."

"I can't, I'm telling you my heart is pounding. He shook my hand and it was like an electric charge."

Alina began to realise that in all the time they had known each other, she had never seen Sally in male company or in social situations apart from family gatherings, and she had never seen her smitten with anyone. She was only now discovering that Sally was not as confident when it came to actually meeting and talking to the opposite sex. Alina was quite taken aback to realise this, but it also explained why Sally was still single. Alina actually wondered if Sally was a bit afraid of having a relationship, and she remembered that Sally had often joked about waiting for her wizard to sweep her off her feet.

Sally was looking better than she had ever done. When Alina first met Sally, her blonde hair was straight and hung down over her shoulders and her skin was very pale. Her sparkling green eyes drew your attention though and her smile always lit up any room she entered, but recently she had her hair trimmed and instead of the straight style, she curled it into soft waves, which framed her face beautifully and gave her a much softer look. She had put on a little weight, which accentuated her figure and gave her curves where before she had only had angles.

Ronnie walked into the kitchen. "Is everything OK girls?"

"Yes fine, everything is just fine," said Sally sharply.

Ronnie looked at Alina puzzled, and she just laughed, nodded her head towards the sitting room and imitated Sally's earlier display of tapping her hand over her heart.

"Oh," said Ronnie grinning, as he went to the fridge to take out a couple of bottles of Bud.

"I'll bring the glasses Ronnie," said Alina, nodding her head towards the sitting room giving him a hint that he should leave her to calm Sally.

"Whatever's got into you Sally?"

"I'm embarrassed, I can't think straight. I don't do meeting new people."

"Are you kidding me? You meet new people every day."

"That's different, that's work, this is personal and he's a stranger and he's drop dead gorgeous."

"You're acting as though you have never seen a handsome man before. Come through, or Gus will think there is something wrong."

Alina left Sally in the kitchen and went through to join the men and then she called out to Sally, "Oh Sally, I forgot to pick up the glasses, will you bring them when you come."

"I'll help if that's OK," said Gus standing up and heading for the kitchen.

"Yes, of course, make yourself at home Gus. Grab the bottle of Asti from the fridge too please."

Alina had another look at Gus as he was walking into the kitchen. She could see what Sally was attracted by. He was tall and he looked particularly good in straight leg jeans and a ribbed white jumper that fitted where it touched and outlined the physique of someone who liked to keep fit.

As Gus entered the kitchen, Sally had her back to him and was standing at the sink. He looked at her standing there and admired what he saw. She was wearing a long sleeved black T-shirt with the shoulders cut out and a deep V in the back. Her black skirt, he would remember as a flouncy sort of thing, was full and had tiny sparkles subtly scattered all over the fabric. He watched her leaning over the sink splashing water on her face.

"Are you OK Sally?"

She jumped at the sound of his voice behind her and turned suddenly, surprised by his appearance, and again overcome with embarrassment. *"Oh my Goddess,"* she thought as she looked at him smiling at her. *"That smile could split the clouds and let the sun through."* It had been a very long time since Sally had succumbed to the charms of a good-looking man.

"Yes, yes I'm fine. Do you always sneak up on people?"

"You look flushed. Are you sure that you are feeling well, maybe you have a temperature."

"Oh for goodness sake, I'm fine."

He started to laugh at her… "You're a fiery one, aren't you?"

"I can't see what you're laughing at."

"I'm laughing at you, all angelic and looking as though butter wouldn't melt in your mouth, but breathing fire like there's a dragoness inside you."

"Oh don't be ridiculous!" Sally exclaimed, her own embarrassment making her angry.

Gus laughed again and Sally was tempted to throw something at him, but since this was Alina's kitchen, she thought better of it. Gus stood there with his hands in his pockets, rocking back and forwards from his heels to his toes, amused and stirred by Sally. He watched her getting more flustered and could think of nothing else but kissing her. He paused as the thought occurred to him and his eyebrows rose in surprise at his sudden urge to press his lips against hers. *"Where on earth did that come from?"* he thought to himself.

Sally glared at him. They stood facing each other like two enemies poised, ready for battle. "Ah shit," said Gus as he stepped forward, pulled Sally into his arms and kissed her full on the lips. Sally melted on the spot. Her arms fell limp by her sides, her body tilted backwards as his lips devoured hers. She felt her tongue touch his as though it had a mind of its own and she was shocked. He put his hands on her shoulders, drew back and looked at her. Her face was a picture of amazement. She could not believe that he had the audacity to do such a thing and yet she felt robbed as he took his lips from hers. Without another thought, she promptly stepped back and kicked him on the shin.

"Ouch!" he yelled, hopping about on one foot as he rubbed the assaulted shin, and once more threw his head back and laughed.

"I don't like you," said Sally.

"That's a shame because I might just have to marry you."

"OH PLEASE…" she said dragging out the vowels and as she pushed past him she said contemptuously, "Join the queue."

"Watch this space," he said and still laughing he picked up the glasses and followed her into the lounge.

Alina and Ronnie looked at each other and grinned. He whispered to her, "Did you put a spell on them?"

"It looks that way doesn't it, you know I would never do that, but from here it looks as though Cupid's arrow has struck Sally and gone straight through her heart into his. Where's the bottle of Asti Gus?"

He looked at Sally and grinned before glancing at Alina and saying "Oops, I'll get it now; I had other things on my mind."

Chapter 7

Alina had lit scented candles around the lounge and soft ambient music was playing in the background. Sally and Gus sat opposite each other and while Gus sat back, with his long denim clad legs stretched out before him, Sally, in contrast, was on the edge of her seat, looking anything but relaxed. She couldn't make eye contact with Alina or Ronnie either and her face was still red, but Gus was cool calm and collected and he looked as though he had been to Alina and Ronnie's home many times before.

Alina asked, "So what are your plans Gus? Is this a short break or are you home for good?"

"Definitely home for good Alina, though I have still to make up my mind where I am going to set my roots down. My parents have been running a guesthouse for years and Dad has been complaining that it was getting to be too much for them. I finally talked them into downsizing so they have sold up and bought a bungalow in Largs and I'm…"

Before he could say anymore, Sally exclaimed "Largs!"

Gus glanced over at her, "Yes," he laughed, "you sound surprised."

Sally shrugged, "My parents have a bungalow in Largs!"

"Really, where?"

"On the Greenock Road, the first row of houses coming from Greenock, just after the 'Welcome to Largs' sign."

Gus threw his head back and laughed aloud. "Do you live with your parents?"

"Yes, when I'm not touring."

"That's exactly where they have bought their bungalow, on the Greenock Road."

"Oh my goodness, I know the house, I saw the for sale sign. Is it the second house, the one with the tall glass apex to the front?"

"I believe so; I haven't seen the outside, just some internal pictures and pictures of the great view from the front of the house. Where is your parent's house?"

"It's about four houses further down towards the town," Sally replied.

"Well if I decide to stay with my parents we will be neighbours."

Sally kept her head down, refusing to comment further. Alina saved the day by asking Sally to give her a hand with dinner by setting the table while Ronnie went next door to fetch Auntie Nessie. When Sally started setting the table, much to her displeasure, Gus began to help her. In the kitchen, Alina smiled to herself as she listened to Gus chatting away and she was sure that Gus would melt Sally's cold front. Over a lovely meal, the conversation flowed and Gus amused everyone with stories of places he had been, and amusing things that had happened during his stay in Australia. Finally, when the dinner was over Ronnie topped everyone's wine glass up and stood to make a toast.

"I have missed you a great deal Gus, occasional emails don't make up for the company of a good friend and your return has come in good time because I have a favour to ask you."

Gus was puzzled by this announcement and couldn't think what this would be about, but Alina was grinning from ear to ear and Auntie Nessie was smiling confidently because she always knew what was going on even before anyone else did.

"I asked Alina if she would be my wife, she has said yes, and I would be honoured if you would stand with me and be my best man."

Gus almost knocked his chair over, standing suddenly and walking around the table to throw his arms around his friend. He had a huge smile on his face as he clasped Ronnie by the shoulders, and with a hint of an Australian accent creeping in to his statement he said, "Oh mate, it would be my honour to stand with you."

He hugged Ronnie tightly and patted his back. Turning to Alina, who was sitting looking up at their display of affection, he stooped and took her hand, and kissed it saying, "You'll make a beautiful bride Alina and it's my honour to be part of your special day."

Alina laughed at him, "Gus you are such a charmer, but there's a catch so you might want to hear about that before you agree so quickly."

"We're not just having a wedding we are having a hand-fasting."

Before she could say any more Gus laughed and said, "Oh I know all about that, does that make me a wizard then?"

Alina slapped his arm fondly, "No it does not."

"Shame, no matter, it will still be my pleasure, though I have always envied Ronnie's ability to make magick happen, but I have a condition."

"What's the condition?" was Alina's amused reply.

"Well I take it the Maid of Honour will be Sally here?"

"Yes, of course."

"Well then I'll be delighted, especially when Sally is there to show me the ropes."

Aunt Nessie, tired out, left them to their celebrations, giving Gus her spare key to use. "Make yourself at home son," she addressed him fondly. "Ronnie will show you where everything is, but I'm off to bed now, I need my beauty sleep," she laughed, and as she reached up to kiss him on his cheek, she gave him a sly look and a hint of a knowing smile. "Something in the wind, and all the way from Australia," she chuckled and Gus, grinning, winked at her as he walked her to her door.

"I think there's a bit of the sorcerer in you Auntie Nessie." Nessie just laughed and knowingly tapped her nose three times, with her index finger.

"So when is the big day then, the first of May?" he said returning to join them in the lounge.

"You seem to be very knowledgeable about the Old Ways Gus or were you just guessing?"

"I did a bit of reading when Ronnie told me about you and some of the amazing experiences that you had all shared and I found the whole thing fascinating."

"Do you mean the experiences or the Wiccan path?"

"Well both really, it must have been an upsetting, but maybe rewarding experience too, I read about the old ways because I have always had questions about life and death issues, and to be honest with you, the more I read the more I understood. What about you Sally, how long have you followed this path, or is that a rude question?"

"It's probably a rude question, but I'll answer anyway. I have been on this path since I woke up and realised that sometimes people wear a fake persona. They pretend to be who you want them to be and then one day the mask slips and their real nature is revealed. When that happens, someone gets badly hurt. Now if you'll excuse me I'm tired and am off to bed."

Alina realised that she was biting her bottom lip, embarrassed by Sally's reply. Ronnie looked puzzled because he hadn't seen this side of Sally either. Sally kissed them both good night, but turned to Gus and said "Good night Gus, sleep well."

"Good night Sally, you sleep well too."

When she left the room, Ronnie asked Alina "What's wrong with Sally, I have never known her to be abrupt like that?"

"Me neither?"

"Someone broke that girl's heart," Gus said, to no one in particular.

"She has never mentioned anything like that to me," answered Alina.

"But you would never ask the questions Alina, you always let people share if they want to, I'm not saying that's a bad thing just that some people find it easy to want to know everything about everyone and you're not like that," said Ronnie.

"I suppose you're right, I don't pry. I'm sorry if she was a bit sharp with you Gus. Honestly she is the nicest person."

"No worries Alina, she will get to know me soon enough.

Chapter 8

She was trapped, surrounded by a thick mist, she couldn't see what was ahead of her or for that matter what lay behind her. Her face was wet with tears but she didn't know why she was crying. She inched forward a little at a time, feeling with the tips of her toes, afraid that the ground might disappear ahead of her. Her heart was pounding in her chest; she didn't know which way to turn. She began to realise that ahead of her the mist was brighter, not clear enough to see through, but definitely brighter. She thought she could hear a voice calling to her, *"I've got you, reach out, take my hand,"* but it was so faint she couldn't be sure. Sliding her right foot forward, maintaining contact with the earth beneath her feet, she moved forward. *"Reach out, take my hand."* She wanted to reach out, but she was afraid. She placed her right foot firmly on the ground and gradually moved her left foot looking for solid earth. *"I've come for you, reach out, I'll catch you if you fall."* She raised her arm, stretching her hand out, reaching into the mist at its clearest point. *"Take my hand,"* the voice said. She stretched a bit further, her fingers groping in the mist, and then she made contact. *"Jump, I'll catch you,"* and with a leap of faith she jumped, and he caught her. She felt his strong arms around her and for the first time in many years, she felt safe. She pressed her face against his broad chest, and breathed a sigh of relief as she opened her eyes to look up into his.

"Oh my Goddess!" she exclaimed aloud as she realised that she had been dreaming. She lay there in Alina's guest bedroom, astonished and wondering what the dream was all about, and then she looked at the clock on the bedside table. *"Oh my Goddess it's past ten."* She was always up early and couldn't understand how she had slept so late. She quickly showered and threw on a pair of black leggings and a baggy cotton top. When she went through to the lounge, Alina, Ronnie, and Gus were already sitting at the dining table having coffee. Everyone, in cheerful moods, bid her a good morning, but although she had slept late the strange dream was troubling her and Alina could see that she was puzzling over something.

"Are you Ok Sally?"

"Funny dream."

"Do you want to share?"

"No not just now, I think I will ponder on it. What I need now is coffee, strong and black."

As she sat down at the table, Gus filled a cup from the coffee pot and pushed it across the table to her. All was quiet as everyone watched her take her first sip and then she looked at them, "What?" they laughed together and Gus said, "We are just waiting for the caffeine to take."

"It's getting there now," Sally smiled. "So what did I interrupt?"

"Wedding talk," said all three together and laughed.

"Oh good, I'm awake now," said Sally enthusiastically, and just as she was finishing her sentence her phone began to ring.

"I'll get that," Ronnie said getting up from the table; he went to the sideboard where the landline unit sat in its charger. Everyone watched while Ronnie listened.

"Yes, of course, yes I remember you now,… Today?... Can you hold for a moment?" he said and covered the phone with his hand. "It's Inspector Collins, he wants to come and chat to us, and he said he could be here in half an hour."

Alina sighed and nodded as Ronnie confirmed over the phone. "I saw this coming," said Alina.

"How?" asked Gus.

"I was putting talcum powder on my Tarot cards yesterday and The High Priest fell out, face up on my mat."

Now Gus was intrigued, "You put talcum powder on your Tarot Cards, is that a magickal thing to do?"

Alina and Sally laughed loudly together, leaning over shoulder to shoulder. Alina could hardly speak for laughing, and tears were running down her face as she and Sally enjoyed Gus's innocent, but funny question.

"Oh Gus, I'm so sorry for laughing at you," and she laughed again. "It's to make the cards easier to handle, easier to shuffle."

"Now I feel like a right idiot."

"Don't, honestly we are sorry for laughing at you," said Sally, but she was still laughing.

"So what does The High Priest card mean?"

"Well among other things, it signifies uniforms, but keys too, and when I thought about it later I figured that perhaps it was because you were talking about your parent's new house, and then Auntie Nessie gave you her key."

"That's amazing Alina, would you read my cards sometime?"

"Yes of course I will."

They all began to clear the breakfast things away and then sat down to wait for the Inspector.

"I'll make myself scarce when he comes," said Gus.

Alina and Ronnie answered together telling him that there was no need, and just as they were discussing that, the intercom buzzer sounded announcing the arrival of the Inspector. Ronnie went to the hall to buzz him in and wait for him coming up to the apartment. He wasn't alone, he had brought a plain clothes officer with him and he said, "I hope you don't mind but I brought Detective Inspector Bob Graham with me."

Introductions made, Alina answered, "No not at all, would you like some tea or coffee."

"That's very kind of you but no thanks; we don't want to take up too much of your time. We wanted to run something past you so I'll hand over to D.I Graham."

Sally was giving them the once over, taking in everything about them. Inspector Collins was probably in his fifties, handsome as he was in his uniform, the lines on his face made him look as though he had seen it all. D.I. Graham was younger, Sally guessed at him being around thirty-five or so. He was good looking, brown hair, sincere brown eyes and very smartly dressed in a well cut dark grey suit, a white shirt and a grey and blue patterned silk tie.

D.I. Graham cleared his throat and began to tell them the reason for their visit. He nodded towards Inspector Collins, "Ian, that is, the Inspector and I have spoken about it several times and, well the thing is, when I was still at school a girl in our year went missing. At that time I only knew her and her friends by sight, but I remember how terrible it was. It may have been that incident that made me join the force, but anyway, a friend of the missing girl continues to call every year, hoping that there is some news. Inspector Collins happened to mention it to me, and I told him that I knew about the incident. The long and short of it is that I have been appointed to give it one last try and I was intrigued by the stories about how you managed to find a missing girl." He paused, hoping that Alina would volunteer her services, but when she didn't say anything he continued, "I wondered if you and your team would be interested in taking it on."

Alina leaned forward with her elbows on her knees and her face in her hands. Everyone was very quiet till finally she exhaled a deep breath and said, "You speak as though we are a team that have done this regularly, but we are just friends who met a situation and dealt with it in our own, albeit unique, way. The situation was a personal one, although we didn't know that at the time."

"I'm sorry, a personal one, I don't understand?" said D.I. Graham.

"The girl we found was one of my ancestors, she was family and it was a painful and difficult experience."

"I can understand that, and I am sorry to ask you to go through a similar experience, but with all due respect did that not also bring closure, bring relief to the family once she had been found and laid to rest?"

"Yes it did, and I reconnected with family members that I hadn't known existed."

Alina looked at Ronnie who shrugged his shoulders indicating that it was up to her. She looked at Sally who was waiting to see what Alina's reaction would be, before showing any of her feelings on the matter. Alina got up from the sofa and went over to the patio doors, opened them and stepped outside to the fresh crisp air. Ronnie followed her and stood behind her with his arms wrapped around her.

"Let me make some coffee for you guys," said Sally, jumping up quickly and going through to the kitchen with Gus following behind her.

"What can I do to help Sally?"

"Get the cups and put them on the tray, and the sugar bowl too, the milk jug is in the fridge."

"Did you see the colour of Alina's face? She went as white as a sheet."

In the lounge the two Inspectors glanced at each other, wondering what the outcome would be to their request.

Alina and Ronnie came back into the lounge and sat down as Sally and Gus brought the coffee tray through from the kitchen.

"I will have to think about this," said Alina, "I'll call you in a few days and let you know what my decision is."

They did their best to make small talk while they drank their coffee, but Alina couldn't wait for them to leave so that she could think about the implications of their request, and discuss the matter with the others. The Inspectors finished their coffee and thanked Alina and Ronnie before leaving.

"Do you think she will help?" asked Bob Graham as they made their way to the police car.

"Now I could answer that if I was the psychic, in fact if I was the psychic we wouldn't need her help," laughed Ian Collins.

Everyone was subdued after the police left and no one knew quite what to say until Sally broke the ice, "What do you think Alina?"

"Honestly? I really don't know what to do. It brought such trauma and publicity the last time and affected the whole family, Nancy and Davy, Auntie Nessie, I don't know if I want to go through that again."

"But it brought rewards too Alina, you found family that you didn't know you had because of it," said Ronnie.

"I know, and the thought of someone suffering, not knowing what had happened to a loved one…, that's unbearable. How do you feel about all this Ronnie?"

"I don't want to influence you either way Alina, but I will support your decision no matter what it is."

"You Sally?"

"I feel the same as Ronnie," she replied.

"Count me in, if I can be of any help," said Gus who had been sitting watching the interactions of the three close friends.

"Ok this is what I think. I believe the Goddess opens doors for us to go through, for whatever reason, and 'She' has opened this door. We should go through it together, all four of us, or the police would have called at another time. I will call the inspector tomorrow and tell him that we are willing to take this to the next stage, whatever that is. Is everyone happy with that?"

They all stood at the same time and gave each other 'high fives'.

While they were still standing Gus asked, "Are you going home to Largs today Sally?"

"Do you want rid of me?"

"On the contrary Sally, I was hoping to enjoy your company. I wondered, if you were going that way anyway maybe you would give me a lift. You said your parents live near mine."

"Oh, sure, I will be leaving in about an hour."

Chapter 9

After Sally and Gus left for Largs, Alina and Ronnie sat chatting about the proposed investigation and the potential impact on their lives.

"We have to have their word that there will be no publicity during or after, no matter what happens."

"Yes I agree Alina. We'll talk to them about that before we begin. We'll have to look at the case notes and try to find a good place to start our search."

"We should get our diaries out and make notes of things that we don't want to disrupt."

"Good idea Ronnie," said Alina, going through to the office to fetch hers and Ronnie's desk diaries while Ronnie went through to the kitchen to make them fresh coffee. They sat at the dining room table, diaries open, steaming coffee cups in front of them.

"First thing in mine, apart from one or two morning appointments, is Yule on the twenty first. It would be nice to do a circle with the four of us to introduce Gus to this aspect of our lives. Let me check the position of the moon first." Alina checked the lunar chart, "Yes, Monday the twenty first the moon is waxing in Taurus. That will be perfect."

"Imbolc is next, on the second of February," Ronnie said, while Alina checked the positions of the moon.

"It will be better to hold our Esbat on the first of February as the Moon is void off course on the second. It's moving between Scorpio and Sagittarius and if we have any spells to do they could go wrong if we work during the V.O.C period."

"Ok, that's it marked in. What about Ostara?"

"The twenty first of March is good, Moon in Virgo and not V.O.C.," said Alina.

"What about Beltane, our wedding day?"

"The Moon is V.O.C until three thirty three in the afternoon and then it is fully in Pisces. We could have the ceremony at three forty five. That would work."

"That's settled; we'll work around these dates and do our best to avoid the investigation disrupting our lives. If you text Sally times and dates I will do the same for Gus, and I will send you and Sally his mobile number too."

"Done, I suppose I should really give the Inspector a call and arrange a meeting." As Alina picked up the card D.I Graham had left, her stomach was churning. She dialled the number and he answered after two rings.

"D.I. Graham."

"Hello, it's Alina Webster here, I am just calling to say that we will try to help you, but we would like to have a chat with you before we begin."

"That's great news. I can pop over around four if you have time?"

"Yes that will be fine, see you then."

The Inspector arrived as expected and they sat down to chat about the case.

"The case intrigued me more so because I was in the same year as Maureen Devlin and Fabiana Sinclair. Maureen went missing when she was just thirteen. Fabiana was the last person to see her; they had gone to Craigton Cemetery. Her parents were very strict and she had been warned not to go there so, when the police asked, in front of her parents, where they had been, she lied. She was afraid that her Father would beat her if she had told the truth, but the next day, on her way to school, she went into the police station and told them. It's very likely that this delay in receiving accurate information prevented the officers in charge of the case from finding Maureen, and I guess that Fabiana has felt guilty about her missing friend ever since. She has never given up, and now that I've managed to wheedle my way into this I want to find out what happened and close the case. Maureen's parents never got over her disappearance; they are both deceased, and her brothers are in America, but each year like clockwork, Fabiana gets in touch to ask if anyone is looking at the case. I haven't been able to discover anything at all, and I'm glad that you are willing to have a look at this."

"Do you know anything about the previous case that we worked on?" asked Alina.

"Inspector Collins was very impressed, although he did say that you had met with some scorn when you first tried to enlist official help."

"Someone leaked the story to the newspapers and we had days of newspaper reporters and TV crews camped outside. We will try to help you on the condition that there is no publicity whatsoever," said Alina.

"Well no one will hear it from my lips, I can promise you that much. I have the files in the car. Shall I bring them up?"

While he went to collect the files, Ronnie asked Alina "What do you think?"

"Honestly, I don't know what to think. I just hope he keeps his word. I would like to meet Fabiana though. We could probably pick up some helpful vibes."

The detective inspector came back in carrying a bundle of manila folders crammed full of papers. "This looks like a lot to go through, but to be honest it's doubtful if you will find anything that has been missed. It's all door to door enquires that led to nothing and statements from pupils at her school."

"We would like to meet Fabiana if that's possible," said Ronnie.

"Absolutely, leave it with me and I will try to arrange it."

"Why don't you just give us her contact number and we will call her direct and arrange for her to come here," answered Ronnie.

"Well, the thing is, she doesn't know that I have approached you so if you don't mind I will contact her first, and once I have spoken to her I will call you with her contact details."

"Why didn't you tell her?" asked Alina.

"I didn't want to get her hopes up. You might have refused to help."

"I understand. Let us know when you have spoken to her and we will take it from there."

"Thanks for agreeing to do this, I am sure that Fabiana will be relieved that there is going to be a fresh attempt at solving this. I'll be in touch." He shook hands with them and left the apartment.

Chapter 10

He dialled Fabiana's number and held the phone to his ear, listening to it ringing.

"Hello."

"Fabiana, it's Bob."

"Hello Bob?"

"Can I come and see you?"

"Yes, of course, have you found out something new?"

"No, but I do have something that I want to run past you."

"Yes ok, when do you want to come?"

"If you are not busy I can be there in twenty minutes."

"Oh, yes, ok. See you then."

She closed the phone and sat down to wait; drumming her fingers on her table as she wondered what Bob would tell her. He arrived twenty minutes later as promised and she let him into her flat. Her face was white as they sat opposite each other. Bob was leaning forward his, legs apart, his elbows balanced on his knees. They were each studying the others body language. Her back was straight, her knees tight together, her hands twisting over and over each other, obviously nervous about what she was going to hear. She could have been beautiful, but anxiety and sadness had caused dark circles under her eyes. Her black hair, drawn back painfully from her forehead and fastened in a tight bun almost displayed how keyed up she felt. Everything about her said tension. She waited…he spoke,

"Some time ago, I heard of a one hundred year old mystery that was solved by a woman who lives in one of the apartments in the Waterfront at the River Clyde. The thing is, I have been to see her, and she is willing to have a look at the case."

"I don't understand, a woman, not a police woman?"

"Well no actually, she's a psychic."

"I really don't care what she is, or who she is for that matter, if she thinks she can help I would want her to get all the information she needs."

"She wants to call you and arrange to meet you."

"Oh!"

"What do you think?"

"I hate meeting people."

"I know that Fabiana, but you said you would be happy if she got all the information that she needed."

"But why does she need to meet me?"

"Let me give her your phone number and you can ask her that when she calls you."

Fabiana fingered a chain and pendant that she was wearing as she sat mulling over her apprehension. Her life had been a troubled one, a difficult childhood filled with unhappy memories and then the disappearance of her one true friend when she was only thirteen. When she was sixteen, against her parent's wishes, she left home to go and work in a hotel in Blackpool. At first, she was employed to work in the bedrooms. She cleaned all the rooms every day and made up the beds, and whenever a guest departed she stripped down each bed and prepared the room ready for the next guest. She was still young, but the years of doing her Mother's bidding gave her a good foundation in housekeeping, and the owners were impressed.

When the season ended, they invited her to stay on permanently and they promised to teach her all about the catering industry. For Fabiana this was the light at the end of the tunnel. She worked hard and she found that not only did she learn about catering, she came to understand what family was about, and how other people lived, by observing the owners and how they lived and responded to their children and family members.

"Give her my number then. I just want to know what happened, and I want her found. I will never be at peace until she is."

Bob thanked her, and as she walked him to the door he turned and looked at her, wondering how she would be if this were finally resolved. He remembered how shy and pretty she was at school, he offered her his hand, she looked down at it and finally placed her cold hand in his.

"I have a good feeling about this Fabiana," he said as he shook her hand, but she just nodded, dispirited.

She closed the door and stood for a moment, wondering if she had done the right thing, before going back into her sitting room to sit on her sofa. She leant back, and fingering the chain and pendant that she wore around her neck, she closed her eyes, trying to think about that last day with Maureen. She knew in her heart that if Maureen were still around they would have been best friends. Her own life might have been so different. Maureen was the only person that she had ever truly trusted. She wondered if she and Maureen would have gone to Blackpool together.

She remembered that first day when she saw the bedroom that was to be hers during the season. She had never had a bedroom all to herself. The owner, Mrs Mitchell, apologised for it being quite small, but Fabiana thought it was wonderful. It was down in the lower ground floor at the end of a long corridor. The window faced a brick wall with railings at the top and a path leading to steps up to the back car park.

Small pink rosebuds decorated the papered walls, while the door, window frame, and skirting boards were all painted white gloss. A single bed sat in the centre of one wall with fresh linen placed at the foot of the bed. Her family still used blankets, so seeing the continental quilt was a delight for her, and she touched each piece of matching pink linen, feeling the clean softness. She had made her bed, unpacked her few possessions delighting in the fact that she had her own chest of three drawers, a wardrobe, and two bedside cabinets either side of her bed. She had tried the switches on both bedside lamps, switching them on and off, and on and off again, smiling to herself. She remembered sitting on the bed looking across the room at the small sink, which had fluffy pink towels hanging on rails at either side of the basin. She remembered flopping back, lying down, laughing loudly with happiness at her good fortune.

Then she thought of Maureen and the tears began to fall again.

Alina was updating the calendar on her PC when her desk phone rang.

"Hello, Alina here."

"Alina, its Bob, D.I. Graham, just a quick call to let you know that I've spoken to Fabiana, she said it would be ok to give you her number. She might be awkward to deal with; she's suffered with anxiety and depression for years, most likely the unfinished business of Maureen's disappearance coupled with some family issues."

"Don't worry about that Detective…"

"Call me Bob please."

"Thanks, as I said, don't worry about that, I'm experienced in dealing with people who are troubled. She'll be fine with me."

Alina made a note of the number and decided to wait until she had conferred with the others before calling to arrange a meeting.

She sent a text to Sally first. 'Have the woman's number, when are you next free?' Her reply came almost immediately.

"Got next Mon Tue Wed off, Thu Fri Sat and Sun working in Edinburgh."

Alina replied, "Will check with Gus. B back to you."

She copied the text to Gus and pressed send on her phone.

"Anytime, no car yet, is Sally around to bring me?"

Alina smiled to herself; she wondered if that was just an excuse to spend time with Sally.

"Here's her number, message her."

"Got it from Ronnie, will she reply?"

Alina was grinning when she sent a bewildered emoji. She knew Ronnie would be flexible so she took a deep breath and dialled Fabiana's number. She waited while it rang, and rang…and rang, finally going to the message centre.

"Hello, this is Alina here, Detective Inspector Bob Graham gave me your number and said that it would be ok to call and arrange a meeting with you. I'll call you back in an hour or so or if you want you can call me."

She left her number along with the message and sat for a few moments at her desk wondering if Fabiana was actually there, just not picking up because she didn't recognise the number. She was right; she had exactly pictured the scene; Fabiana was standing by the phone her hand outstretched, anxious to pick up and at the same time too anxious to do so. She listened while Alina spoke. She liked the sound of her voice, and at the last moment as she reached for the phone Alina finished her message and hung up.

Chapter 11

"What time did you say she was coming Alina?"

"Two o'clock, Bob is bringing her. He's going to drop her off and I suggested that one of us will take her home. Sally and Gus should be here around noon."

"Don't you think it might be a bit intimidating to come in to a room with four strangers, especially when she is anxious?"

"I do Ronnie, but I also think that if we are doing this together, each of us may pick up on different vibrations, so although I agree with you, weighing it up I still think it will be for the best."

"Yeah, you are probably right." He took her in his arms and kissed her fondly, and then they sat down to chat and wait for the others to arrive.

"How do you think Gus and Sally are getting on?"

"I couldn't even begin to guess at that answer Ronnie. She obviously thought he was drop dead gorgeous and then she fell to pieces at the thought of being in his company. I have never seen her like that."

"Have you ever seen her in a relationship?"

"No, come to think of it, I haven't."

"No dates or casual flirtations?"

"No, and we have never seriously discussed that either. I mean she would make occasional jokes or comment on a good looking bloke, but she has never shown any interest other than that."

"Gus made a comment that she had been badly hurt, has she ever mentioned that."

"No she hasn't, the only thing she has ever said is that she was waiting for her wizard to appear, but it was said as though she was joking."

"Maybe Gus is her wizard and that's why she went off on one."

"Hardly."

"Don't you think so?"

"I was going to say that he wasn't her type, but I have no idea what her type is. Maybe you're right," she laughed. "Maybe Gus is her wizard."

The buzzer sounded their arrival and Ronnie went to open the door. They hugged each other warmly and Alina made a pot of tea and some sandwiches.

"Is there a plan, or are we going to wing it?" said Sally between mouthfuls.

"Let's just go with the flow and see if we can get her settled and relaxed first. She should be here in about an hour."

"Are you sure that you want me to be here Alina, I feel out of my depth, what do you want me to do?"

"You are meant to be here Gus. At this moment, I have no idea why, but I trust my instincts. This is just the first visit and there may well be more, so for the moment sit quietly, listen and observe, and pay attention to any nuances. We will go over everything later."

At two o'clock as promised, D.I. Bob Graham arrived with Fabiana and Alina welcomed them in.

"Fabiana Sinclair," Bob said as Alina offered her hand.

"Please, welcome, come in and I will introduce you," said Alina taking control. "This is Fabiana Sinclair everyone," and indicating to each one in turn she introduced them to her. "This is Ronnie my fiancé, and our good friend's Sally and Gus. Please, sit down and be comfortable."

Fabiana shook hands with each of them in turn, albeit reluctantly, before sitting in the armchair that Alina indicated. She was obviously nervous and kept glancing at Bob, who was still standing, as if for reassurance. He nodded to her as if to let her know that she would be fine.

"I will give you a call when my shift is finished Fabiana, but right now I have to get back to work. Have you got a minute Ronnie?"

"Yes sure," he said and he followed Bob to the door.

"Don't let Fabiana see the case files. Not that there is very much in them, but seeing them is not a good idea in case it plants unreliable information in her thought processing."

"I understand, don't worry I will keep them out of sight until she has gone and one of us will see her home safely." He shook Bob's hand before joining everyone in the sitting room.

"Would you prefer to be called Mrs Sinclair?"

"I'm not married, Fabiana's fine."

"Would you like some tea or some coffee?"

"Just water, please."

Sally got up immediately and went through to the kitchen, returning with a jug of water and a glass, which she set down on the small side table beside Fabiana. When Fabiana looked up to thank her, Sally gave her a bright reassuring smile.

Alina was the first to speak, "Did Bob explain to you why he thought we could help?"

"He didn't really explain anything; he just said that you had found someone before, and that you were a psychic, but I don't really know what you do or how you do that."

"Well in one way or another everybody is psychic. As children we are all capable of seeing or hearing things and our instincts are very sharp, but it's often discouraged or not used and without practice our gifts slowly fade into the background. I am sure that you have had experiences in the past when you have thought of someone and then later that person calls you, or you meet them unexpectedly. Sometimes we might feel as though someone is watching us and when we turn around a friend is trying to catch our attention."

Alina and the others noticed, as she mentioned 'feeling as though someone was watching' that Fabiana shivered.

"Have you had that kind of experience Fabiana?"

"No, well maybe, I'm not sure."

"No matter, we use our psychic abilities, and other means, such as Dowsing, Tarot cards and Runes to try to find clues, and then we follow the clues, but I have to emphasise that we have only done this once before and we were only trying to understand a particular situation. We can't make any promises other than we will do everything that we can to try to help you."

Fabiana nodded and said "Thank you. What do I have to do?"

"You can tell us a little about your friend. What was her name?"

"Maureen, she was kind to me and we laughed a lot. I don't remember laughing before I met Maureen."

Tears began to trickle slowly down Fabiana's face as she remembered. "I try hard to see her face but all I can see is her blonde hair. She had beautiful hair. It came down to her shoulders in waves and when the sun shone on it, it glistened like gold, and she laughed a lot. My parents liked her."

"Can you remember the last time that you saw her?"

"No," was the quick reply.

"What is your last memory of her?" Alina asked.

"The ice rink, she took me to the ice rink. I had never been before and it was really exciting."

Alina and Sally glanced at each other; everyone could see that Fabiana was becoming uncomfortable.

"That's great Fabiana. I think we have done enough for this first visit. I would like to take you home now and we can arrange to get together another time, maybe in a few days?"

Before Alina had even finished speaking Fabiana was on her feet, anxious to leave.

"Yes that's fine."

Alina left with Fabiana to take her to her home in Mosspark. All was quiet as Alina drove and eventually she broke the silence.

"Was it as bad as you thought it was going to be?"

"No not really, but in recent years I have found it harder and harder to mix with people and I am overwhelmed with feelings of guilt though I have no idea why. What will happen next?"

"We will try to find out as much as we can and in a few days we will get together and see if we can take this a little further. How do you feel about meditation?"

"I have never been able to do it, but I have tried. My doctor said it might help with my panic attacks."

"What about regression, has anyone ever tried that with you?"

"No," and after a pause she spoke again. "I am frightened of that."

"What is it that frightens you?"

"Remembering."

"Remembering what?"

There was another long pause before Fabiana answered. "Remembering things that I couldn't cope with I suppose."

"Don't you want to get to the bottom of this?"

"Yes, I do, but I don't want it to be my fault."

"But you have all these feelings of guilt now, and perhaps if you remembered, you would realise that what happened in the past was not actually your fault."

"What happens if I remember something and discover it was my fault?"

"Well then you will feel guilty, and since that is how you feel now, then nothing will have changed except you may actually have found out what happened to your friend."

Alina glanced over at her as she spoke and realised that Fabiana had tears on her face.

"I'm sorry if this is too much for you. We don't have to go any further if you don't want to."

"No. I feel as though I must at least try."

Alina was just pulling up to the kerb outside Fabiana's house. "Ok, you have a think about it over the next couple of days, and if you want us to go ahead you must call me and we will set aside some time for the next meeting. Would that be ok with you?"

"Yes, thank you very much for today." Alina got out of the car at the same time and gave Fabiana a warm hug, but Fabiana kept her arms by her sides and didn't respond to the offered show of empathy. Alina stood watching while Fabiana walked up her path, her shoulders hunched over and her head down, deep in her own thoughts. Alina didn't see the curtains twitch in a nearby house. As she drove away she felt a deep sorrow for Fabiana.

Chapter 12

By the time Alina arrived back at the apartment the case files had been spread out on the table, and Sally, Gus, and Ronnie each had a folder in their hands, and were sitting quietly reading them. As each folder was read it was passed to the next in line. They looked up in unison as she came in. "How did you leave things with her?" asked Ronnie.

"I spoke to her a little about meditation and regression. She is definitely frightened to remember, but I think she understands that she might not be any worse off by remembering, she could even feel better in herself. I've suggested that if she really wants to go ahead, she should call me in a few days."

Just as Alina finished speaking, the phone rang…

"Hello, Alina speaking. No, it won't cost anything at all. Don't worry about that." She turned to the others who were watching and waiting. "That was Fabiana, she was worried about how much it would cost. It never occurred to me that she would think we would charge for this."

With a large pot of coffee on the table in front of them, they all settled down to read the case notes. By early evening they had gone through every piece of paper pertaining to the case. Ronnie was the first to break the silence, "I think we could break for something to eat. Shall we order in Pizza?"

"Ham and pineapple for me," said Gus.

"Pepperoni, probably for Sally too," said Alina looking over at Sally who nodded and agreed.

"Absolutely," she replied.

Ronnie got up and made the call to the Pizza Place, and everyone else, stretching their legs, began to organise the table, as though this was a regular occurrence. They passed each other backwards and forwards going in and out of the kitchen fetching plates, napkins, and glasses for Pepsi.

"So what do you think so far?" said Gus as he settled down in front of his pizza.

"I think we should leave it alone, let our thoughts settle, and enjoy our dinner. After dinner, we will talk it all over, and compare our thoughts and impressions," answered Alina.

Everyone thought that was a good idea, and settled down to relax and enjoy the food.

Gus and Ronnie were engaged in conversation talking about motorbikes and cars, and that gave Sally the opportunity to ask Alina about her wedding plans.

"Have you thought about what you are going to wear Alina?"

"Not yet, but I think I will know it when I see it. I don't want all the trimmings of the traditional white wedding, but of course I want it to be special. The only thing that we have formalised is the registrar, time and place to be confirmed."

"Do you know where you want to have the Handfasting yet?"

"Still thinking about it," Alina laughed.

"Listen girls, Gus is just telling me that there is a bike show on all week at the SECC, with stunt riders and stalls. We could all go tomorrow if you fancy it, before we get down to this serious stuff, what do you think?"

"I've never been to a bike show; do you mean bicycles or motorbikes?"

"Motorbikes, Sally, Motorbikes," Gus said with emphasis.

Sally and Alina looked at each other and then they grinned and answered together, "We're in."

They decided that Gus and Sally would stay the night, Gus at Auntie Nessie's and Sally in the spare room as usual rather than them travelling back to Largs, and then back into Glasgow in the morning. When they were finished eating they took plates and cutlery through to the kitchen and Alina stacked the dishwasher while Ronnie made coffee, and Sally and Gus wiped the table and set out the case files so that they could refer to them and compare notes. Back at the table, they all sat to express their opinions and impressions.

"How about we start with you Sally? You had the earliest file didn't you?"

"Maureen was reported missing at ten p.m. when she didn't return home. Her parents stated that when she was with Fabiana, she was always home by seven p.m.; but if she was out with friends close to home, her time to come in was nine thirty. They knew that she had gone to visit Fabiana, and when she didn't arrive home by nine they thought she was playing with friends who lived nearby. The whole family, the parents and two brothers, went out to look for her, but none of her friends had seen her so they called the police at ten. Apparently, the police went to Fabiana's house just before midnight. The house was in darkness and no one answered the door."

"I had the next file," said Gus. "I took the first half, and gave the second half to Ronnie. Mine didn't have much to report, just the same questions and negative answers from the door to door enquiries. Some neighbours saw the girls walking up the road together; some reported seeing Fabiana walking home alone, but no one saw anything suspicious. The police certainly did their job calling into each house, knocking on every door, and making return visits to houses that had no one at home, but they learned nothing. One or two of the neighbours mentioned someone called Sanny Wilson, apparently he was a flasher, in and out of prison, but there was no more than that in the file I had."

Alina continued with, "I can pick up from there Gus. My file had more about Sanny Wilson in it. He was a repeat offender, in and out of prison for exposing himself to the girls in the area. A passerby found him lying bleeding and unconscious on Kingsland Drive, quite close to his home on the other side of the road from the graveyard. The man who found him called an ambulance and stayed with him until it arrived and he was taken to The Southern General. The call was logged at 4.15 p.m. There is a bit about the caller's interview, but he knew nothing about the missing girl, and only happened by chance to come across Sanny Wilson because he had finished his work an hour early that day. That's as much as I had in my file. Over to you Ronnie."

"Thanks Gus. The police interviewed some of Maureen's school friends on Monday morning, but apparently the teachers weren't too happy about it. Later that day they went to Fabiana's home and interviewed her. There are some notes about her behaviour as the interviewing officer felt that she was holding something back, and she appeared to be scared of her parents. There is a note on the file that she went into the police station before school the next morning to admit that they had been playing in the graveyard and got scared. She was asked what scared them, and she said that they thought someone was watching them, so they made a plan to count to three and run their separate ways. She thought that was just after 4 p.m. and she went home. She was very worried about her friend. What do you have Alina?"

"Mine is all about the searches, the areas that were covered, notations of things that were found that might or might not have been connected, and then there are some notes about Sanny Wilson. He was cleared from the inquiry and he couldn't remember very much about what had happened to him. From time to time, over the years, there are additions to the notes especially in more recent times when it's obvious that Fabiana is trying to make them re-open the case, but in short we have nothing except a little bit of information that is not likely to help. I think Fabiana holds the key, and meditation, regression or hypnosis is the answer, and if not the answer, I think at least it will give us somewhere to start."

"Do you think you will be able to get her to agree to any of that?"

"Only time will tell, only time will tell."

Chapter 13

They walked the short distance, crossing the pedestrian Tradeston Bridge over the River Clyde, commonly known as the Squiggly Bridge which took them to the exhibition centre. They were more than happy when they arrived, as the car park was packed full of motorbikes belonging to enthusiasts, who had no doubt travelled great distances to enjoy seeing all the latest bikes that would be on display and of course to enjoy the stunt show.

The hall was packed, mostly with men wearing bike gear and carrying crash helmets, identifying their personal interest, while others were there out of curiosity, or just to watch the show that was due to begin around two o'clock. Loud music boomed, and various stages were set up with skimpily clad models dancing to the beat of the music and vying for the attention of potential buyers. Crowds stood around watching, before moving on to the next display, each retailer trying to outdo the next. They spent the morning wandering around, browsing stalls selling hot dogs, burgers, soft drinks and sandwiches as well as teas and coffees. There were rows and rows of motorbikes proudly displayed by retailers and many of the stallholders were selling motorbike clothing or goods and accessories. Tattoo Artists were doing a brisk trade and people stood and watched as customers had their tattoos applied.

While Ronnie and Gus were drooling over motorbikes, Sally and Alina found a unit selling gothic fashions. There were velvet and lace corsets, skirts and dresses, and as they were browsing, something caught Alina's eye. She was looking up at a rail of dresses, suspended from the top of the stall.

"Excuse me," Alina called to the stallholder.

"Yes can I help you?" the woman replied.

"I can see a hint of blue velvet, I think it's a dress, could I see it please?"

"Yes it is a dress from the 'Dark Angel Collection' I stock these in my shop and thought I would take the chance and bring a few to the show with me. Hold on, I will get it down. It's a twelve, would that be suitable?"

"Perfect," answered Alina while the woman reached up using a long pole to catch the hanger.

"How on earth did you spot that Alina?" asked Sally.

"I have witchy senses," she laughed in reply.

"Oh my Goddess, it's stunning," exclaimed Sally, as the woman brought the dress over. Now that is was in front of them they could see that it was crushed velvet, the colour changing from dark blue to electric blue. The neckline, cut in a deep V, had an overlay of sculptured black lace which continued to just under the bust line. The long sleeves were only attached under the arms leaving the cut away shoulders bare. The hem of the sleeves finished in a point of black lace, which would rest over the back of the hands. The dress flared out to an A line at the hem which had a visible underlay of black net

Alina held the dress in front of her. "What do you think Sally?"

"I love it."

"I'll take it," said Alina.

"Don't you want to try it on?"

"No thank you, I am certain it will be just perfect."

"Is it for something special?"

"It's for my wedding."

"Will you have a handfasting?"

Alina smiled at the woman, "Yes, Merry Meet," she said in the traditional greeting used when witches meet each other.

"Merry Meet to you both," the woman replied and offered her hand to Alina and Sally. "I hope you have a wonderful day filled with blessings."

They returned her offered handshake and began to chat about the old ways. "I had a feeling about you both," she said.

Alina smiled, "I'm Alina and this is Sally who will be my maid of honour."

"Really, have you decided what you are wearing Sally?"

"No, I wanted to wait until Alina had chosen her gown."

"Well I might just have the right one here. I didn't have room on the rail to hang it up. It's in dark green, give me a minute." She went to the back of the stall and disappeared behind a curtain.

"I love green, where has she gone?" whispered Sally.

"They probably have a van full of stock behind the stall."

Just at that moment, the woman returned holding the dark green dress. It too was crushed velvet and the colour changed and shimmered from dark green to light green as the fabric moved.

Sally gave a sharp intake of breath when she caught sight of it and she reached out eagerly to take it and hold it against her. She could see that although the fabric was the same, this dress was form fitting with a high, almost polo neck, but as she turned it on the hanger, she realised that the dress had a keyhole cut out at the back from the shoulders almost to the waist.

"Do you love it Sally?"

"I love it."

"So do I, we'll take them both," said Alina, and as she was delving into her bag for her purse Sally replied,

"No Alina, I'll pay for mine."

"No you won't, this is my treat and remember, karma insists, if you say no then blessings stop coming so what do you say?"

Sally laughed and said, "Thank you Alina and I hope many blessings come your way. Seriously, Alina, I love it and I appreciate your gift of it to me. I'm excited; now that we have the dresses, we can go shoe shopping."

They made their way around the hall looking for the Ronnie and Gus and came across them drooling over sports bikes.

"What have you two been up to?" asked Ronnie as he leaned over and kissed Alina who was grinning happily.

"Oh nothing," she answered in a singsong voice, smiling at Sally.

"Just a little shopping," said Sally holding her bag behind her back.

Soon it was time for the show to begin and they enjoyed the next hour or so watching stunt riders performing amazing tricks, riding up high ramps at speed, and flying right off the end, spinning full somersaults, sometimes letting go of the handlebars and then catching them again before landing perfectly, then skidding to a stop close to the crowd barrier. The noise of engines roaring, and the crowds screaming and cheering with delight was intense. The smell of fuel and burning, the engines revving added another dimension to an already exciting spectacle. By the time they show finished, they were ready to head back to the apartment, and they joined the crowds crossing the Squiggly Bridge. Many visitors, who had driven to the show, had parked their cars on the Tradeston side of the Clyde to avoid the congestion at the exhibition centre. The atmosphere was friendly with folk chatting to each other and happily reliving their recent experience.

Chapter 14

Gus and Ronnie decided to go across to Harry Ramsden's to get fish and chips for their supper on the way back from the Bike Show, and the girls continued on home to put the kettle on and set the table. They sat down to wait for the men to return and Alina took the opportunity to broach a subject that she had been thinking of.

"I wanted to ask you about something?"

Sally, puzzled by this opening, looked at Alina and wondered what she was about to say. "Go on."

"Well first if this is none of my business just say so, I won't be offended."

"What on earth is it?"

"Well, in all the time we have known each other you have never mentioned a boyfriend, you know, the serious kind, and I wondered why."

"What's made you ask now and never before?"

"I don't like to pry Sally, and I would never have asked, but Gus said something."

"Gus! What did Gus say," answered Sally sharply.

"He just said that he thought that someone had hurt you badly, he looked sad when he said it. That made me feel as though I hadn't been a very good friend. I mean maybe I should have asked before."

"Gus said that?"

"Yeah."

"Hmm, I wonder why?"

"Who knows how men think, he just came out with it."

"That was very observant of him."

"Is it true?"

"Yes it is and I don't dwell on it, but you're my best friend and I don't have a problem sharing it with you. I was seventeen when I met him; my friends and I were at a night out and he was there. He was older than I was by a few years, but I was captivated when he started paying attention to me. I fell for him hook line and sinker.

My friends didn't like him, my parents didn't like him, but I couldn't see past his good looks, his charm, and his 'gift of the gab'. Within a few months, he had rented a flat and talked me into moving in with him. I defied my Mum and Dad and moved in. We had eight months together and for the most part, I was happy and felt grown up. I went to work every day, I was working in an office and he was running his own business.

Later it became obvious that he didn't have a business and he didn't work anywhere, but I didn't know that at the time. He took care of everything. He did the shopping, paid the bills and often had dinner ready for me when I came home. He liked things done his way and became moody if I suggested an alternative; mostly I was happy to comply.

Anyway, I came home from work one day, it was the twenty-third of December, and the flat was empty, completely empty. I thought we had been burgled; personal bits and pieces of furniture that I had bought were gone, my jewellery, CD's, stereo, and TV, gone. I couldn't understand what had happened. My mind was racing and I was panicking, wondering if he had confronted burglars, and they had taken him. These were stupid thoughts that I couldn't control. Then I wondered if he was at the police station reporting the theft. I don't know why I looked in the built in wardrobe, but when I did, all my clothes were there, untouched, then I looked in his wardrobe and all his clothes had gone. Letters and papers littered the floor. I just dropped to my knees in shock."

By this time Alina was sitting, leaning forward with her elbows on her knees and her hands covering her mouth, shocked at what she was hearing.

"My grandmother had left me a little money, and when we first began to live together he suggested that we open a joint account. I sat there on the floor and I began to go through the letters, I discovered that the rent was in arrears and the property owner was threatening eviction and court action. There were unpaid bills from companies that I had never heard of, and the bank statements revealed that he had emptied most of the joint account including the money my grandmother had left me. He broke me; he broke my heart and he broke my spirit, I felt defiled."

"Oh my Goddess Sally, what did you do?"

Sally laughed bitterly, "I called my Mum. She and Dad came and collected me. I was so ashamed. It was a terrible thing to happen at Christmas."

They sat quietly for a few moments, Sally reliving the memory and Alina digesting what she had just heard.

"I fell into a deep depression and stupidly tried to take my own life."

"Oh no," exclaimed Alina. "Why?"

"I was broken, ashamed, and every time I looked at my Mum and Dad all I could see was that they were grieving for me. It was stupid and I am glad to say that it was a feeble attempt." She paused and then laughed, "Otherwise I wouldn't be here."

"Oh Sally I am so sorry for what you must have gone through."

"Well it's in the past and it will stay there, but I made myself a promise. I will never let that happen to me again, so casual flirtations are fine, but nothing else."

"You know Sally, not all men are like the one who hurt you."

"Yes I know that, but I am the woman who has been shaped by that experience."

Just at that moment, they both heard the men arriving back and they ended the conversation, but Alina had a heavy heart.

"Sorry that took so long girls, it was mobbed there. I think everyone that was at the show had the same idea, and we are starving," said Ronnie.

"Tea is made and the table is set so let's dish up," said Alina.

They were all ready to sit down, eat, and chat about the next step.

"I've spoken to Cassandra, I have told her I won't be back on tour for a few months. I want to be able to help with this mystery without having the distraction of touring with the Psychic Show," said Sally.

"Are you sure Sally?" Asked Alina, "that's a lot to give up; we are only one week into December?"

"Yes I'm sure; I was going to be off from the 19th December anyway so really I am just taking an extra few weeks or so either side of the dates I had already planned."

"I'm clear too," said Gus "I won't be making any fixed plans until the New Year."

Gus was watching Sally, he was sure that she was worried about something, but hesitant about asking her in case she jumped down his throat again. Sally glanced at him a few times; knowing that he had so easily seen through her defences made her think that there might be more to him than just good looks. Gus just couldn't help himself and he whispered over to her, "You ok Sally?"

Sally smiled at him and his heart just swelled. "Yes Gus, I'm fine. Just a memory."

After they had eaten and cleared away the table, they went through to the sitting room and began to study the case files once more, trying to glean every bit of information and making notes.

The phone ringing interrupted them, putting her file to one side, Alina got up to answer it. It was Joanna, Alina's distant cousin, calling to ask if they had made any plans for Christmas Day and suggesting that everyone came to hers for Christmas dinner.

"We have a big crowd here Joanna, why don't you three come to us?"

"Are you sure?"

"Yes of course, it will be lovely to have you and it will give you a chance to meet Ronnie's friend Gus, he's just come back from Australia."

"That's great, I make a traditional 'Clootie Dumpling', it's an old family recipe and we always have it at Christmas. I'll bring one for us to share."

"That will be lovely Joanna. We'll see you then."

As she returned to sit in her chair, she stopped and stared. Sally and Gus were sitting side by side on the sofa, engrossed in what they were reading, and Gus had his hand over Sally's; she wasn't objecting. As she watched in surprise, Gus lifted his hand and turned a page and the moment was gone. Sally looked up, "What's wrong Alina?"

Alina laughed, "Nothing Sally, nothing at all."

It was one o'clock in the morning before they had finished studying the files and discussing their thoughts and they all agreed that it was time for the next step.

"I will call Fabiana in the morning and arrange to bring her here as soon as she can make it, but now I am more than ready for bed," said Alina.

"Oh me too," said Sally, standing up, stretching her arms and yawning.

"Aunt Nessie will have switched the electric blanket on to full on my bed," laughed Gus, "I will have to switch it off and throw the covers back to let it cool before I can get in to it."

"She loves to spoil us," laughed Ronnie.

"Well goodnight everyone, see you in the morning," said Gus before he left to cross the hall to Aunt Nessie's apartment.

Sally fell into bed exhausted and ready to sleep but as soon as her head touched her pillow, her mind began to race. At first, her thoughts were on Fabiana and then her missing friend Maureen, but before long, her thoughts turned to Gus. She was more settled being around him and was beginning to see past his good looks to the kind person that he was. She made up her mind to try to be nicer to him, and she flushed a little thinking about the times she had been short with him when he probably didn't deserve it.

Chapter 15

Sally drifted off to sleep while visualising a beautiful meadow. She wandered barefoot through the flowers enjoying the feel of the soft grass between her toes. Suddenly she was enveloped in a mist so thick that she couldn't see anything. She became afraid, so afraid that she couldn't move. *'This isn't right,'* she thought, and then she heard the voice calling to her.

"This way Sally, come back to me, reach out, I'll catch you."

Her heart was pounding in her chest as the fear overwhelmed her.

"Give me your hand Sally, I won't let you fall."

Sally wanted to turn and run, but she knew that there was nowhere to go. She moved her foot slowly in front of her, her bare toes feeling the grass.

"Closer Sally, come closer, reach out and I will catch you."

She reached out a little too far and began to fall, tumbling head over heels, and as she opened her mouth to scream, strong arms caught and held her. She pressed her face against a strong chest, but she wanted to know who this was and she began to raise her eyes to see her rescuer. She uttered the words *'Who are you?'* A deep warm laugh rumbled in his chest as he replied, *"I'm your wizard."* As the words penetrated her mind, her eyes opened and she woke up.

She didn't know what this dream was about and she didn't know who this was that was catching her, but she did know that it was beginning to bother her. She wanted to know what the dream was trying to tell her.

Sally was up first; she was in the kitchen making French toast, bacon and scrambled eggs when the others came through. "Ronnie would you go next door and tell Gus that breakfast is ready?" said Sally.

"Yes, sure, right on it," answered Ronnie while giving a quick surprised look to Alina as he passed her in the kitchen. Alina just laughed.

"You ok this morning Sally, did you sleep well?"

"Awful actually, I keep having a strange dream Alina."

"What's it about?" Just as Alina asked the question, they heard Ronnie and Gus returning.

"I'll tell you later."

Sally put the scrambled eggs in a serving bowl, and piled the French toast and crispy bacon on to a platter to carry through to the dining table, Alina carried through the coffee pot.

"Smells good, looks delicious," said Gus. "Auntie Nessie offered me a 'Govan Roll'," he said laughing.

Sally looked mystified and asked, "What's a Govan Roll?"

"I had to ask that question too, apparently there was a baker's shop near the Govan Shipyards where all the workers went to buy food for their tea breaks or lunches. Auntie Nessie said that hundreds of men queued right round the corner to get rolls filled with sausage, bacon, black pudding, egg, 'tattie' scone, and dumpling."

"What! All on one roll?"

"Apparently so, but maybe she was exaggerating."

"Oh my Goddess, breakfast on a roll," said Sally.

Alina poured coffee while they all helped themselves to breakfast.

"So if everyone is in agreement, I think I should call Fabiana to ask her about coming over, today if she can make it. I think the sooner we get started on this the better," said Alina.

Everyone agreed, and as soon as breakfast was finished, Alina made the call. Knowing that Fabiana didn't have a car, she suggested that she would drive over and pick her up within the hour, and Fabiana agreed.

"I'll come with you Alina," said Sally.

"Ok."

They put their coats on and made their way to the car.

"I hope you are going to tell me about your dream Sally."

"Are you reading my mind?" laughed Sally.

During the short journey, Sally relayed the dream to Alina.

"What do you think it means?"

"I wish I knew, it seems strange, what was the last thing on your mind before you went to sleep?"

"I told you, I was visualising a beautiful meadow."

"No, what were you thinking before that Sally?"

"Em, let me think; I was thinking about Fabiana and her friend Maureen. It must have been terrible for her."

"That makes sense of the mist then, the unknown. Perhaps you were imagining her falling and got that mixed up super imposing yourself into the dream, but I'm curious about the wizard. Can you remember anything else that was in your mind?"

Suddenly Sally remembered that she had been thinking about Gus, and as the thought appeared in her mind, her face began to flush. Alina turned and looked at her for a moment.

"What? What have you just thought of, you have gone all pink Sally," laughed Alina. "Come on, spill the beans, and tell me everything."

"No nothing," said Sally clamming up.

"Is it private?"

"No it's not private; it was just a passing thought."

"Well, tell me then."

"Oh for the sake of peace, I just had a passing thought of Gus."

Alina was grinning now, but trying hard not to show it and then, unable to hold it in any longer she began to laugh and sing, mimicking Sandra Bullock in one of her Miss Congeniality movies *"You've got a cru..ush, you're liking Gu..us, you want to ki...ss him."* While she sang her silly song, she rocked her shoulders from side to side as though she was dancing.

Sally made a fist and punched her not too gently on her thigh. "Stop it, I have not, and I do not want to kiss him. It was just a passing thought."

"Well if you did want to kiss him I wouldn't blame you, he is a really nice guy."

"Yes I think I am beginning to see a nicer side of him, but trust me I am not going to kiss him any time soon."

They were both lost in thought for the rest of the journey.

Fabiana had her coat on and was watching for Alina arriving. As soon as she saw the car pulling in at the kerb she hurried to her front door and began to lock it behind her, testing it several times before she was satisfied.

Alina got out of the car to meet her and said "I brought Sally with me."

"Hello Fabiana," said Sally, but Fabiana just nodded and got into the back seat where she sat twisting her hands together nervously. She kept her eyes down and it was apparent that she was not interested in making conversation.

"Don't worry Fabiana, you are in good hands and we won't let any harm come to you. Who knows? We might just be able to solve this puzzle," said Sally.

The journey was a short one, but as Alina drove them back to her home Fabiana's life flashed before her. Some memories were clear, very few were happy. The best memories were those that she shared with Maureen and thinking of them made the tears fall.

No one had noticed the curtains twitching in the house nearby.

Chapter 16 Fabiana

She stood in the kitchen staring dreamlike out of the window above the kitchen sink. Her mind drifting, not thinking of what she was doing, but wishing that she could be doing something else. The skin on her hands had wrinkled from being in water for too long. The expression on her face was one of sad acceptance of the fact that she couldn't go out until the kitchen was immaculate. She wasn't even sure if the girls that she wanted to go and talk to were friends, but she wanted them to be her friends.

Sometimes when she was walking to the local shop to get something for her Mother, she would see the other girls playing outside their houses, and they would stop, and stand and stare at her. Sometimes they would whisper, as though they were talking about her, and then they would laugh, as though they were laughing at her. Sometimes they would run up and fall into step behind her, but she was shy and she didn't really know what she was supposed to do, so she just kept walking. Maybe she was supposed to speak first, but she didn't want to do that in case she was supposed to wait for them to say something to her. She had a friend before when she was in primary school, but her friend had moved away and Fabiana had no one now.

She thought that her parents were too strict, so were other parents, but her parents were bad tempered and strict. Other mothers helped with the housework, but her Mother was bossy and lazy, and wanted her to do it all herself. Her Mother said it was her duty, and she was always shouting at her, and her Father had a temper that frightened her. She was not supposed to talk to anyone from the scheme, but she wanted to be the same as the other girls, not different, and she didn't know why she wasn't supposed to talk to them.

When her Mother said 'do the kitchen', it meant 'do everything'. Her heart fell when she had opened the wooden kitchen door with the brass knob; she knew it was brass because polishing it with 'Brasso' was one of her jobs. When she went in to the kitchen, a nappy pail full of cold water and soiled nappies was in the sink. Her Mother was old fashioned. She often saw disposable nappies for sale in the local shop, but her Mother flatly refused to use them and would only use terry towelling ones. She hated doing the nappies; she knew that the hard bits were already down the toilet because that was another of her jobs. She hated the smell of the water when she tried to empty the pail, the smell of ammonia nipping her eyes and catching her breath. She had let the cold water run into the pail as she tilted her head to one side, leaning away from the smell. She had held her breath, scrunching her face in distaste and concentration. Gradually the pail emptied of dirty water without making any spills. She didn't want spills or splashes because she would get a row for that. She swished the nappies around in cold water until her hands were blue, and then she squeezed the water out of them and stacked them on the draining board. She rinsed the pail, added Fairy soap powder, and then let the hot tap run until the water was hot enough to scald her. One by one she added the wet nappies. The pail was almost too heavy for her to lift, but she was careful, and she managed to get it out of the sink and onto the floor out of her way.

She hoped her Mother would wash the nappies later, but if she didn't it would be another job for her. She cleaned and scrubbed the sink and the draining board thoroughly, having put a little splash of Dettol into the clean water. There were dirty dishes on the kitchen table and she knew that she had to wash them too. She had finished washing the dishes now, but she kept her hands in the warm water while she stared out of the window, looking across to the gardens that backed on to hers.

She stood watching the girls chasing each other and laughing. She wondered if they had to do dishes and stuff. She didn't think so because they always seemed to have plenty of time outside. Her Mother said that at thirteen she was too big to play and that she had responsibilities. Sometimes she just wanted to talk to the other girls about the music that she heard them talking about, people like 'Take That' and 'Wet Wet Wet'. When her Father was home, she wasn't even allowed to watch music programmes on the TV. He watched documentaries, war stories, and news programmes, and when it was just her Mother at home, she only wanted to watch old films.

Sometimes she would hear the girls all singing together as they walked to school, and she wondered how they knew all the words to the songs. They always seemed to be happy, but she never really knew what that felt like. She just wanted to be the same as everyone else. She didn't even look like the other girls.

Her Father was Scottish but her Mother was Italian and had brown skin; her name was Yolanda, she had sort of brown skin too, and had to have an Italian name as well, Fabiana, such a stupid name, and she didn't know anyone else who had such a stupid name. She knew it was a stupid name because the girls said so. Sometimes they called after her in a sing song way, "Fabiana, Fabiana, Fabiana," but when she turned…, they would giggle and run away. They had names like Margaret, Brenda, Linda, and Maureen. Her two baby sisters had stupid names; Perlita and Gabriella, well maybe not stupid, because she liked their names, but they were different, and she just wanted to be the same as everyone else, but she wasn't.

Her hair was short, curly, and black, combed in a side parting, and her eyes were so brown that sometimes they looked as though they were black. She wasn't the only girl in the school that had pierced ears, but she was the only girl who had her ears pierced when she was a tiny baby. For as long as she could remember, she had worn tiny gold stud earrings with a little turquoise stone. Her Mother said that was for protection. She remembered that when she was in primary school one of the teachers called her out and tried to take the earrings out, but she struggled and cried and later, when she told her Mother, she was so angry that she went to the school the next day and complained. The other girls had pale skin, blue eyes, and they had long hair that they could pleat, and the pleat would go half way down their back. Some of the girls would have a ponytail, and some wore bunches held up at each side with ribbons. She couldn't do that and she didn't have ribbons anyway.

When she was finished cleaning the kitchen she went through to the living room to ask her Mum if she could go out. Perlita was about six months old and was stuck to her Mother's breast. Gabriella was a year and a half and she was sitting up in the big pram in the living room quietly playing with her teddy. Fabiana walked over to the big pram and kissed her little sister who giggled with delight.

"Can I Mum, can I go out now?" She was carrying on the conversation that she had had three or four times already, but there was always another job.

"What time is it?

"Three o'clock."

"Half an hour and then come back and peel the potatoes."

It wasn't fair, half an hour; she was just about to go when her Mother called to her, "Take Gabriella with you; put her in the push chair."

"Muu-uum," she said, dragging out the vowels in frustration. "By the time I get her ready and walk round the block it will be time to come back; do I have to?"

"Do as you're told, and don't answer me back or I'll speak to your Father when he comes in."

With a sigh, Fabiana fetched the pushchair and carried it outside to the front door, then she went back into the living room and lifted her little sister Gabriella out of the pram. Gabriella giggled, launched herself into Fabiana's arms, grabbed a handful of hair in each hand, and pulled herself to Fabiana's face, where she promptly smothered her big sister in wet kisses. Fabiana laughed as she tried to put the baby's jacket, hat, and mittens on. She didn't want to take her, but she loved her very much, and Gabriella was such a good-natured baby that she always managed to make her laugh. She carried Gabriella out and put her in the pushchair, then she grabbed her jacket, and off she went out of the gate and up the road.

Being February, it was cold outside, but not raining, apart from the cold it was a nice day. She turned left at the corner of Queensland Drive and Ladykirk and then walked on towards Kingsland Drive. She thought she would see some of the girls because it was a Saturday, but she could neither see nor hear them anywhere. She crossed Ladykirk Drive and turned right into Kingsland, having decided that she would walk up Kingsland, then take the first right and the first right again back into Ladykirk, and then home.

She knew that she would pass Dean's house; she liked Dean, they had never spoken, but he always watched her, and when he saw her at school or on the street, he would lift his hand shyly and wave at her. She thought he was about fourteen because he was a year ahead of her at school. As she passed, she glanced over and saw him at his window. He waved, and she smiled, but didn't wave back. She was so embarrassed that she didn't watch where she was going and tripped over her own feet, and that made her even more embarrassed. She thought about Dean as she walked up Kingsland Drive. She had listened quietly to the girls talking about him in school and they said he was American. She thought all Americans had lots of money and wondered why his family lived in an ordinary council house like hers. She wondered what they were doing here, and she wondered what 'Mormons' were because she heard one of the girls saying that. She would ask her Dad, he knew everything. She would never have done that if she knew what was to follow.

Chapter 17

The thump-thump-thump reverberated through the house and the old woman shook her head sadly. She knew it was her son beating his head on the wall in his bedroom upstairs. At least, when he was doing that she knew where he was. *"Better that than exposing himself to young lassies and scaring the living daylights out of them. I wish they would lock him up for good,"* she thought to herself. Thirty days inside and she would have thirty days of peace, and then he would get out again and be back inside within weeks. It made no difference really, because she was so ashamed of him and the things that he did that she hid from her neighbours. She sat by the coal fire that she had lit herself; she had carried out the ashes, and carried in the coal, and he would never give a thought to her age or the condition of her health. All he thought about was his dirty habit. She couldn't cope with him, and no one seemed able to help her. She sat in her chair and waited for death, and no matter when it came, it wouldn't be soon enough.

She listened to his footsteps running down the stairs, then the sound of the front door opening and slamming shut behind him. She clutched her rosary and began to pray that he wouldn't see any lassies out by themselves. She didn't need to glance at the clock on the tiled fireplace to know that school was getting out, but she did, and the time read three thirty. *"Mother of God, he's away hoping to catch them coming from school."*

It would be dark soon, and it was cold outside, as she sat there listening to the buses driving up and down Kingsland Drive. She could hear the sounds of neighbours passing the time of day, and normal noises made by people going about their business, but things were always quieter when he was around. The neighbours were afraid of him too. She was sure everybody knew their name, and she had heard the whisperings on the few occasions that she had passed a neighbour.

"There's that old Mrs Wilson, you know about her son Sanny?" They would nod together conspiratorially.

"Shame for her," and they would shake their heads and glance at her, but she would keep her head down and her headscarf clutched tightly under her chin.

--00--

The pain in his head was unbearable as he ran to the end of Kingsland Drive, across Berryknowes Road and into Craigton Cemetery. His open coat flew behind him as he ran, and as he ran, the pain in him started to fade as something else grew. The cemetery opened out in front of him, the wide-open drive lined on either side with mature Yew trees, and different paths leading off to plots with headstones that marked the graves. Some of them looked as though they had been there for hundreds of years and other had toppled over and were lying face down in the grass.

He liked the graveyard; he could hide there and watch people. If he went over to the far left hand corner, he could force his way through the rough undergrowth, climb the wall into the railway station, and make his way up onto the platform. From there he could go up the stairs and out of the station at the top of the Berryknowes road and he knew that if he stood there, as though he was waiting for someone coming off a train, he could watch down the hill to either side. If any lassies' were about he would see them coming before they saw him. If lassies' were going down the hill from the station towards Kingsland, he could nip back into the station, down the stairs, onto the platform and over the wall into the graveyard. Then he could run out of there and come up behind them at the gates of the cemetery. It made him laugh thinking of that. If lasses had passed and were going down the hill to the shop in Drumoyne, he could nip across the road and through a gap in the iron railing and into the football playing fields, and then he would run along where they couldn't see him, and come out in front of them. It didn't matter where they were on Berryknowes, he could find a way to get in front of them and show himself, or sneak up behind them and scare them. He was so clever it made him laugh again. He collapsed into a heap in his favourite hiding place, his 'hidey hole' as he thought of it. The ground was cold underneath him, but he didn't feel it, and if he did, he wouldn't care anyway. He was going to sit there until it was dark. He had never touched any of the girls, but he thought about that and while he thought about it, he touched himself.

--oo--

Mrs Wilson dragged herself out of her chair, went into the kitchen, and began to cook a pot of mince and potatoes. Her movements were slow and measured as she browned the mince in the pan. While she watched it she cut up an onion and a carrot, then she peeled the potatoes and put them on to boil. She added the carrot, the onion, and an Oxo cube to the mince, and topped the pot up with water, then set it on the stove to bring it to the boil. When both pots were boiling, she turned the gas down to a tiny peep and let them simmer. She took the kettle that she had boiled and added tealeaves to a little pot and made herself a cup of strong sweet tea. As she took it through to the living room, she thought about Sanny. She didn't know what had happened to turn him into the monster that he was now. He had been such a good little boy and had worked hard at school, but in the last five years he had lost his job and had been in and out of prison for 'minor' sexual offences, though in her mind, no sexual offence was minor. At twenty-eight, he should be married and bringing up his own family.

Sanny heard the girls talking from where he hid; he sneaked out of his hidey-hole and peered through the fence at the side of the graveyard. There were three of them huddled together, walking quickly, going up the hill toward the station, occasionally one or other of them would look back as though they were looking out for him. He laughed at this thought, and turned towards the cemetery wall and quickly climbed over it onto the railway platform. He was running up the stairs, past the ticket office to get outside before the girls reached the top of the hill. As he reached the platform, he heard the sound of a train approaching and that infuriated him, because there would be too many people about, and they would see him. He ran on anyway and when he reached the station door, he peeked out and there were the girls, almost at the top of the hill. He ducked back inside and waited until they passed and then, as passengers began to come up behind him, he ran across to be on the other side of the road where the playing fields were. He could cut through the broken railings, hide in the grounds, and wait for the girls to head back home. They would be going for milk or bread or to the chippy next door to the cafe for fish and chips.

There was no lining in the pockets of his coat because he had cut them out. His hands were in his pockets and he touched himself while he waited for the girls to come back.

Chapter 18

Fabiana's Father got off the train and turned left to walk down Berryknowes Road. At the corner, he turned right into Queensland Drive. He was always smartly dressed and at this time, because of the cold February weather, he was wearing a coat that came almost to his ankles. The coat covered the dark suit that he always wore with a white shirt, tie, and waistcoat. His hat was perched on top of his head tilted very slightly to one side and he smoked a pipe. The sweet scent of St Bruno tobacco followed his steps as he walked. The walk was no more than four minutes, but he was a well-known man in the area, tall and handsome, with a smile or greeting for those he passed, and people would always acknowledge him politely. If someone stopped to chat, his journey would take a minute or two more.

Fabiana was home now, and she and her Mother looked up as they both heard the train at the same time. From the living room window they could look across the spare ground, where the wood from the saw mill was sometimes stored. The railway line ran right past the other side of the spare ground.

"Watch for your Father coming."

Fabiana knew the drill, from the living room window she would look up the road to her right, and she could see iron railings that lined Berryknowes Road. The train would pull into the station and then a few minutes' later she would see passengers spilling out of the station door at the top of the hill. Some would go to the right and walk down the hill towards Drumoyne and others would go left and walk down Berryknowes Road towards her street, Queensland Drive. As soon as she saw her Father, she would go into the kitchen, fill the kettle, and sit it over the flame on the gas cooker. Her Father liked to have a cup of coffee when he came home. She would open the oven knowing that there would be food for her Father that her Mother had made earlier in the day. She would light the oven and turn the heat to gas mark four. After he had his coffee and changed his clothes her Mother would take a plate of dinner to him on a tray, and he would sit in his chair by the window and enjoy his meal.

He was a different man at home from the man that neighbours knew. She loved her Father but he terrified her, because his moods were quick to turn, and she never ever knew what would trigger them next. Her Mother could trigger them just by complaining about her as soon as he came home. Sometimes, her Mother would lie and say something like, "Your daughter didn't do the dishes," when she had done them, or "Your daughter answered me back," when she hadn't. He would just turn and give her that look and pause and stare, almost as though he was daring her to say something, to answer back, but she knew better than to do that. Answering back, denying the lie, or saying anything at all, and she could be flying across the room after a heavy slap around her head or worse. If she kept her mouth shut, the punishment was almost like a reprieve. "Get to your bed," he would say.

Without a word, she would climb the stairs. She knew if she looked at her Mother, she would see a smug expression on her face. She would sit upstairs in the cold bedroom, under the covers with coats piled on the bed to keep her warm, and think about why her Mother did things like that. She thought it was so that her Mother could be important, but even though she thought that, she didn't really understand what that meant. She knew that in a little while her Father would have eaten, and dishes would need done, and Gabriella would need to be changed, bathed, and put to bed, and her Father would call her, and he did.

When he was in a good mood, she liked talking to him, and sometimes he was funny and did funny things, but her Mother would glare at her at times like those, as if she was jealous. Sometimes she would think of things to ask him just to hear him talking nicely to her. Gabriella was in her cot sleeping and she was washing her Father's dishes when he came into the kitchen.

"Daddy."

"What?"

"What's a Mormon?" she could feel the air chill.

"Where did you hear that word?"

"Is it a bad word? I didn't know."

"I asked where did you hear that word?" she could feel him getting angry and she was scared.

"One of the girls in my class said that Dean's a Mormon."

"Who's Dean?"

"He's just one of the boys in school."

The words were no sooner out of her moth when his anger exploded. He swung his arm at her, his fist catching her, a hard blow on the side of her head, the impact knocking her to the floor. He threw his cup of coffee towards the kitchen sink and the china shattered and scattered with the impact. Fabiana tried to stand as her mouth filled with blood. She was on her hands and knees staring up at him in terror, afraid that he might kick her face. He looked down at her on the floor and asked her.

"Have you been talking to him?"

"No Daddy, I don't know him."

"Don't talk to him, ever. Get that mess cleaned up and get to bed."

"Yes Daddy."

She kept her head down as she got on with cleaning coffee from the walls and surfaces and picking up the broken china. Wrapping it in newspaper, she put it in the pail under the sink. She worried for a moment whether she should take it outside and put it in the bin, but she could get a row for going outside. She could always go and ask, but that could get her into trouble too. She could hear them taking in the living room. They spoke Italian when they didn't want her to know what they were talking about, but although she never responded to anything that they said in Italian, she had been listening to it all her life and she understood every word.

She left the broken china in the pail, had a quick look around to make sure that she hadn't left anything that they could complain about, and then gingerly she went to the living room door, tapped on it and said.

"I'm finished Daddy."

"Get to bed," came the reply, and she went upstairs listening with baited breath because she knew that he would go into the kitchen to search for something that she hadn't done, and he did. She lay there listening. Sometimes she stayed awake all night, cold and hungry, huddled under the coats, waiting for the morning to come.

Chapter 19

She was walking to school on Monday morning when she realised that some girls were walking not far behind her. A quick glance and she saw that it was Brenda, Linda, Margaret, and Maureen. Linda and Margaret were the worst of the four. Part of her wanted them to be her friends, but she didn't really want to be friends with them, when sometimes they shouted things like, "Fabiana eats a banana." She hated it when they made fun of her like that. Linda was always untidy. She had long blonde hair that came down over her shoulders but it was straggly, and her shirt was always open at the neck with the knot of her school tie half way down her shirt. She always looked as though she was ready for an argument. Margaret was prettier with long dark wavy hair and she always wore coloured headbands, but she had such an attitude and always acted as though she was better than everyone else was. Brenda and Maureen were nicer than the other two and prettier in a softer way. If she saw them when they were on their own they would smile and say hello to her in a nice way, but they were quiet when the other two were making a fool of her.

She kept her head down as she limped to school. Her feet were hurting because her shoes were too tight and there was no point in complaining because she knew it would make no difference. She got new shoes for the first Sunday in May; she didn't know why it was that day in particular, and she got wellingtons for the winter. Sometimes, a neighbour along the street would hand in a bag of clothes, 'hand-me-downs', that her daughter had grown out of. They lived in a bought house and the daughter went to a posh school, but she didn't know where. She was always excited when the 'hand-me-downs' came as sometimes she got to keep things, but her Mother would keep things that fitted her.

She was engrossed in her thoughts when she felt someone hurrying up beside her, but she kept her eyes down.

"Have you hurt yourself?"

She turned with a surprised expression on her face, and then her surprise turned to embarrassment as she realised it was Dean. Thinking quickly she said,

"I've stubbed my toe." She couldn't admit that her shoes were too tight. She became more embarrassed by the minute and her face was bright red, but he didn't appear to notice, or if he did, he didn't say anything about it. They walked together quietly for a few minutes and then he said, "I have something for you."

"For me?"

"Yes," he replied smiling.

"Why?" she asked in surprise.

"Because it's Valentine's Day tomorrow."

"Oh," she said as he handed her a paper bag, which was folded over, and taped closed. She stopped in her tracks and looked at him.

"Are you going to open it?"

She was in a blind panic now because her Father would go crazy if he knew she was talking to him. She looked about frantically and then she began to unfold the paper. Her mouth opened in amazement as the contents shone; it was just inexpensive costume jewellery, but to Fabiana, it was as precious as gold. She took the necklace out of its wrapping and looked at it and her eyes filled with tears. No one had ever given her anything so beautiful. The bottom half of the chain had six triangular shapes filled with Mother of pearl, and as she looked at them, she could see shades of iridescent pink and white. Dean saw the tears and asked, "Don't you like it?"

"It's beautiful, thank you very much." They began to walk the rest of the way to school and Dean slipped his hand into hers. Fabiana's mind was in turmoil, part of her was happy that Dean was holding her hand, but another part was terrified that someone would see and tell her parents. She glanced over her shoulder and she could see the girls behind her and the surprised look on their faces. They started making kissing shapes with their mouths, and Fabiana was embarrassed. She wanted to keep the necklace but she knew that she couldn't. Her parents checked everything, her schoolbag, her pockets, she even saw her Mother looking inside her shoes, and she wondered what she thought they would find. When they reached the school, Dean turned and said to her, "I'll maybe see you after school?"

"Yes, yes ok, I have to run, thanks for the necklace Dean." She couldn't remember a thing that he had said to her while they were walking together.

She was sitting in her English class as the teacher droned on about punctuation and composition but she wasn't listening. In her mind she was wondering where she could hide the necklace; perhaps she could wrap it carefully and bury it somewhere. She was so busy worrying that she didn't hear the teacher calling her name. "Fabiana! Fabiana!"

"Yes sir?"

"Are you feeling alright Fabiana?"

"No sir, I don't feel well."

"Get your things, and go along to the nurse's room, tell her I sent you, you are very pale."

Fabiana, embarrassed by the attention, knew that everyone was looking at her as she picked up her schoolbag and left the classroom. She made her way down the stairs from the first floor English class and along the corridor towards the nurse's room, which was close to the big double doors of the school entrance. She didn't stop at the nurse's room though, she just kept walking, and then she was running right across the playground, and out of the school gates.

She hurried along Kirriemuir Avenue and then crossed the main Paisley Road West. She walked up Berryknowes Road and as she reached the top of the hill she realised that neighbours going to the shops might see her, and that prompted her to quickly cut through a path that led to the Moss Heights. From there she followed the path to the left and entered the rear of Craigton Cemetery. She was scared of being in the cemetery, but she was more scared of anyone seeing her out of school and telling her parents. She had never done anything like that before, at least never without her Mother insisting that she stay off school for something that she wanted her to do. Sometimes her Mother made her stay off school to go to the rent office to pay the rent, or to watch her little sisters while she went somewhere.

Her hand clutched the necklace in her pocket as she walked, while her mind raced frantically thinking of where she would put it so that no one would find it. She found a place to sit and hide herself, and she put her head in her hands and cried. It was cold sitting in the graveyard, but she couldn't go home before school finished. Suddenly she had a thought. She took off her trench coat and began to examine one of the pockets. The stitching had come loose before so that her pencil or any coins would fall through into the lining at the hem. She had sewn the hole closed some weeks ago and as she examined the repair, she could see that she could carefully pull on the threads and reopen the hole. She took her metal compass out of her pencil case and used the sharp point to unpick the stitching. She sat for a while doing that and then she edged the necklace into the gap and stood to shake the coat so that the necklace would fall down into the hem. She knew that when she got home she would have to re-stitch the hole again, but she was sure that neither her Mother nor Father would find the necklace. With her mind at peace now she decided that she would go home, and just tell her Mother that she had been sent home sick. She knew her Mother would find plenty for her to do.

She hurried down towards the long drive that lead to the main entrance to the cemetery, and she kept looking over her shoulder. She knew about Sanny Wilson and felt scared that he might be about. She felt safe when she was hiding among the shrubs, but now that she was out in the open, anyone would be able to see her, and if he were there, he might come after her. She had the compass in her hand and she thought if he chased her, she could use it to protect herself. The gates were in sight now and she ran towards them, then out and across Berryknowes Road into Queensland Drive. She was nearly home and some of the panic was leaving her. She breathed a sigh of relief as she opened her gate and went up to the front door. Her Mother saw her coming and opened it.

"Why are you home early?"

"I was sick and the nurse sent me home."

Her Mother reached over and felt her forehead. "You don't feel sick you feel cold, where have you been?"

"It's really cold outside Mum."

Her Mother gave her as suspicious look. "Hang your coat up Fabiana, and change your clothes."

Fabiana could feel her face turning red at the mention of her coat, but she kept her eyes down, hung her coat on the hallstand, and loosening the knot of her tie, she went upstairs to take off her school uniform.

Chapter 20

She sensed that something was different when she woke up at eight o'clock the next morning. She went downstairs and looked in the living room, and was surprised to see her Father sitting there with her Mother. She thought her Father was on his early shift, and he would usually be away by now. She looked at her Father and then she looked at her Mother. There was definitely something strange going on. Her Mother had that look about her as though she knew something and her Father… something was brewing.

"Have you got anything to tell me Fabiana?"

"No Daddy."

"I am going to ask you one more time and I want the truth, have you got anything to tell me?"

"No Daddy, honest."

"You're a liar," her Mother exclaimed contemptuously. "You see Tony; I told you she was a liar."

Fabiana was in shock, she couldn't believe what was happening when suddenly her Father held up the necklace that Dean had given her, and dangled it in the air in front of her.

"Oh God what am I going to say?" She thought frantically to herself. She could feel her face burning, she felt sick to the bottom of her stomach, and now she had to lie, so she did.

"Oh I was looking for that, I thought I had lost it, one of the girls asked me to stick it in my pocket. Where was it?" Her heart was pounding as she tried to remain calm.

"Which girl?"

"Brenda."

"Why did Brenda give it to you?"

"I don't know Daddy; maybe she didn't have any pockets."

"Where does Brenda live?" asked her Mother.

"Down by the David Elder Hospital somewhere, I don't know exactly."

"Go and get your breakfast and then get back to bed," her Father said.

"I need to get ready for school Daddy."

"You're not going to school today."

Fabiana could do nothing more than what she was told. She left the living room and went into the kitchen. She could hear her Mother and Father talking in Italian, but she couldn't make out what they were saying. She leaned against the kitchen wall trying to hear, but it was all just a mumble. She poured herself a cup of tea, put some jam on a slice of bread, and then went upstairs to sit in the bedroom. Her mind was racing. She didn't know what would happen next. She lay down on her bed and covered herself with a blanket, the tea going cold and the sandwich untouched.

The house was quiet when she woke up about an hour later. She was already in trouble and it couldn't get much worse so she ventured downstairs. She tapped on the living room door and stuck her head around to peek in. Her Father was sitting in his chair staring straight ahead. "Are you not at work today Daddy?

"Nightshift."

"Oh, I thought you were early shift. Where's Mum?"

"She's gone to ask Brenda's Mother about the necklace," he said without looking at her.

"I don't know where she lives so how will Mum find her house?"

Her Father just turned and looked at her and stared. She knew she was pushing her luck, and she knew that he was probably containing himself until her Mum came back. The big pram was away so that meant that her Mum had taken her little sisters with her and she would be walking rather than taking a bus. It would be ages before she came back.

"I'm going up to bed. Bring me a cup of coffee and a sandwich and then do the dishes. When you are finished get back to your room."

Fabiana went into the kitchen and put the kettle on as she listened to her Father going upstairs. She had to get away, but if she opened the door, her Father would hear her. She looked out of the kitchen window. She could climb onto the sink, out of the window and then across the next-door neighbour's fence, if she went that way he wouldn't hear her, and he wouldn't see her from the bedroom window. She didn't know what she was going to do or where she was going to go, and she didn't have any money.

When the kettle boiled, she made the coffee and took it upstairs to her Father. "I'm just going to do the dishes now Dad."

"Right, and get straight back to bed when you're finished."

She went downstairs and as she passed the hallstand, she lifted her coat and took it into the kitchen. She turned on the tap and filled the basin thinking about how she would manage to climb out of the window. She knew her Father would hear the water running and he would listen for the sound of her washing the dishes. She opened the kitchen window, which she often did so that she could throw scraps of toast out for the birds. She lifted the plates and cups and carefully washed and dried them before drying the basin and setting it to one side. She crept quietly to the bottom of the stairs and listened. All was quiet for a few moments and then she heard the muffled sounds of her Father snoring. She knew that any unusual sounds, like opening the door, would wake him. She tiptoed back into the kitchen and holding her breath she slowly closed the door, put on her coat and hoisted herself onto the draining board. She braced herself and then slowly inched the window up until it was wide enough for her to get through it. With her heart pounding in her ears, she slithered out of the window and on to the garden bench below it. Staying as close as she could to the wall, she climbed over her neighbour's fence; cut across her neighbour's garden, climbed over the next garden fence, and then she ran to the next one and climbed over the third fence.

She stopped to catch her breath, and from where she was she couldn't see her Father's bedroom window, and that meant that he wouldn't be able to see her, but in her panic, she could almost feel him chasing her. She ran up towards the fence that separated the back gardens between Kingsland Drive and Queensland Drive, and climbed the fence into the back garden of a house that was on Kingsland. She knew the couple that lived in that house, but they were always at work and they didn't have any children. She ran along their path and out of their gate where she stopped to gather herself, "Which way, which way?" she thought. She turned right following Kingsland all the way over to Hillington Road South and made her way to Crookston Road. She kept her head down as she walked up past Leverndale Hospital. She stayed on the Pollok side of the road and was glad that the streets were quiet now.

She had been walking for about half an hour when she reached the corner of Kempsthorn Road, and suddenly she was startled to hear someone calling her name. She glanced around quickly, ready to run and was horrified to see one of the girls from the group that made a fool of her. She didn't know what else to do so she waved and tried to keep on walking, but Maureen beckoned to her and started walking towards her.

"You not at school?"

"No."

Maureen kept pace with her as she walked. "What you doing up here?"

Fabiana stopped and faced her. She was so nervous that she was twisting her foot backwards and forwards on the pavement. She put her head down thinking about what she could say, but she couldn't form the words so she said nothing. Maureen could see that she was troubled.

"Are you OK?" she asked putting her hand on Fabiana's arm.

Fabiana's eyes were full of tears when she looked at Maureen, and the lump in her throat was choking her. Maureen took a firm hold of her arm and said, "Come on in to my house and get a cup of tea."

Fabiana tried to pull away from her, "No, I can't, you don't understand, I can't let anyone know where I am," she cried, finding her voice.

"Oh my God, you've ran away haven't you."

"Please don't tell your Mum, I need to get away."

"Don't be daft, she not in, the house is empty, and I'm doggin' school."

In spite of the fact that Fabiana was running away, to hear Maureen admitting that she was skipping school shocked her.

"Come on, honest, nobody's in." Maureen led Fabiana into her house and through to the warm kitchen where she made some tea for them both. Fabiana was shivering in spite of the warmth in the kitchen; the realisation of what she had done was scaring her. She put her hands over her face and began to cry.

"What's happened Fabiana?" Drying her eyes, and holding the cup of hot tea in her hands, she began to tell Maureen about the necklace that Dean had given her, and her parents finding it. She told her about lying to them, and that her Father wouldn't let her go to school while her Mother was away trying to find Brenda's house.

"What did you do, how did you get out?"

"I climbed out the kitchen window and cut across the gardens. I'm so scared I don't know what to do or where to go."

Unexpectedly Maureen reached over and gave her a hug. "Don't worry; you can stay here till three o'clock. That's when my Mother comes home, but I don't know what you can do after that."

While they chatted, Maureen was busy buttering slices of bread and spreading jam on them, and then she wrapped them in a clean cloth and put them into a bag with some biscuits

Maureen asked, "Have you got any money?"

"No, nothing."

"I've got some, here, you can have that."

Fabiana was astounded; the girl who had been making a fool of her since she started high school was offering her pocket money, and giving her shelter.

"Why are you doing this when you have been making a fool of me?"

"Och that's Linda's fault, she's a pig, but if we don't side with her she makes us miserable. Tell you what, I'm going to start calling you Ana for short and she'll probably get fed up annoying you."

Fabiana liked the sound of that, but didn't think her parents would, and then as soon as she thought about her parents, she remembered her predicament. She jumped up, "I have to go; I have to get away as far as possible."

"Here, take this, it's not much, but maybe you can get a train somewhere," said Maureen, thrusting the coins into her hand, "and take this, just in case you get hungry." Maureen handed the bag of sandwiches to Fabiana.

"Thanks Maureen," she said, and hurried from the house.

Chapter 21

Ten minutes after Fabiana had climbed out of the kitchen window, Yolanda came back from shops with her bag of groceries hanging on the handle of the big pram. Perlita was fast asleep inside the pram and Gabriella was sitting up on the toddler seat attachment perched on top of the pram. With Gabriella tucked under her arm she unlocked the front door and took the toddler inside. Dropping the shopping bag in the hall she took Gabriella into the living room and fastened her into her high chair before going back to pick up the shopping, which she carried into the kitchen and put on the kitchen table. She bumped the big pram up the three steps into the house and wheeled it into the living room. She thought that Fabiana would have come to help her, but when she didn't she went upstairs to get her. She went quietly because she knew that Tony would already be asleep. She hated when he was on a week of nightshifts, because everyone had to keep quiet until he was up and getting ready for work.

She was already angry when she opened Fabiana's bedroom door and she was ready to berate her for not coming downstairs to help her, but Fabiana wasn't there. She went back downstairs and into the kitchen, but she wasn't there either. She looked in the living room and the bathroom, and then she went outside to look in the back garden. She began to wonder if the next-door neighbour had called on her for a favour so she went there, but when she knocked on the door there was no reply. She hurried back into the house and went through all the rooms again, this time calling for Fabiana. This woke Tony up, "Where's Fabiana?"

"She should be in bed."

"She's not in the house, I've looked everywhere."

"For God's sake," he said, sitting on the edge of the bed and pulling on his trousers.

"Did you tell her I was looking for Brenda's house?"

"I told her as soon as she came downstairs."

"She not in the house," she said as she followed her husband around.

"Fabiana, Fabiana!" he shouted angrily, and then he too opened the door and went around to the back garden.

"She's not there."

"I told you, she's not next door either." He looked at the hallstand touching each of the coats and jackets and then he opened the hall cupboard and looked at the coats and jackets in there too. He was running his hands through his hair turning this way and that, not quite knowing what to do.

"I'll kill her when she comes in."

"She wouldn't go out without permission."

"Well she's not here."

Before long they were in an intense argument, shouting and screaming at each other until both babies were crying. While Yolanda saw to the children, Tony went upstairs, kicked off his slippers, and put on his shoes and a warm jumper before going back downstairs. He took his coat and hat from the hallstand and as he was putting it on he said, "If she comes back before I do send her straight to her room. She will feel my belt when I come home."

He went up Kingsland Drive and met one of the neighbours going to the local shop. "Do you know a family here that have a son called Dean?"

"Oh yes, the American family, nice people, not that house," she said pointing, "the next one along with the pretty lace curtains."

"Thanks," he said, and without another word walked on. He didn't notice and didn't care about the puzzled look he was getting from the neighbour, who stood for a moment watching him. He banged on the door and an attractive woman of about thirty five opened the door. She smiled at him and said, "Can I help you?"

"Is my daughter here?"

"I think you must have the wrong house."

"Have you got a son called Dean?"

"Yes, he's at school, why?"

"My daughter mentioned his name the other day, and then we found a necklace hidden in the hem of her trench coat."

"Yes Fabiana, I helped Dean to choose it for Valentine's Day."

He looked at her, his expression surprised, "You know my daughter then."

"No I don't, look, why don't you come in and tell me what this is about."

He took off his hat and followed the woman into her living room.

"Sit down please, can I offer you something, tea, coffee?"

"No. My daughter is missing."

"Oh my, that's terrible. Why would you think she was here?"

"She lied about where she got the necklace."

"Look Mr… I'm sorry I don't know your name," she said holding out her hand as though to shake his.

"Tony Sinclair," he said reluctantly offering his hand.

She continued, "My son goes to the same school, he said Fabiana was a nice girl, but I don't think they have said more than a few words to each other. He told me he liked her, and would like to give her something for Valentine's Day, and I thought that was sweet. I had no idea it would cause such a problem. Why would she have to run away?"

The question remained unanswered. "I'm very sorry, but I am sure that Dean has no idea where she is. Have you notified the police?"

"I should contact the school first, I'll go there now."

"You can use my telephone and call the school secretary; I have the number, I'm in the parents association," she explained gesturing to the phone on her hall table.

"If you don't mind, Mrs...."

"It's Amy, Amy Young," she said as she dialled the number and spoke to the secretary." She turned and looked at Fabiana's Father with a worried look on her face. "She's not at school, she's marked absent. Maybe you should call the police now."

He left after making the call to the police station, and Amy thought about him after he left. She thought that he looked and sounded angry rather than worried, and she wondered if that was why Fabiana had to lie about the necklace, and why she felt that she had to run away. She prayed that the girl would be safe and well.

Shortly after he arrived home, a police car pulled up and parked outside. He opened the door and let two police officers in. When he had given all the information that they asked for, he put his coat on and went out to search again. It was after three o'clock so he made his way to the high school and waited at the gates for the pupils to begin coming out. He stopped a few that he recognised and asked them if they had seen Fabiana, but no one had. Dean had finished his class early and when he arrived home, he was shocked to find out that Fabiana had run away because he had given her a necklace.

Chapter 22

Fabiana decided she would keep walking until she was too tired to walk anymore, and then she would get on a bus. She had no idea where she would go, but she knew that many red buses ran along Paisley Road West so she made her way back down Crookston Road and turned right at the bottom onto Paisley Road West, heading in the direction of Paisley. She was now heading into an unfamiliar area and part of her felt a sense of freedom, as long as she didn't think about what she was doing.

By the time she reached the edge of the town she was limping quite badly, her tight shoes causing her toenails to cut into her skin. She wished she had new shoes that fitted; she wished that she had put on her wellington boots, but they would have chaffed her legs. She wished that she had somewhere to go, she almost wished that she hadn't run away, and then she thought about the beating that she would have gotten when her parents found out that Dean had given her the necklace. She was sure that they would find out.

She turned and looked over her shoulder as she approached a bus stop and she saw a red bus coming. It said Johnston Castle on the front, and when the bus stopped she climbed on. There were bench seats facing each other, but beyond them, there were seats that faced forward. She sat in one of them and slipped her feet out of her shoes. Leaning back, she relaxed for the first time that day, and enjoyed looking at the different places that she passed.

Suddenly she was aware of someone shaking her shoulder and she woke up with a start. She hadn't even realised that she had fallen asleep until the bus driver woke her to tell her that they had reached Johnston Castle. She got off the bus and wandered around for a bit, but it was getting dark and she was scared. She realised that she had made a stupid mistake. She didn't know anywhere here. She realised that she should have stayed closer to home where she could hide in the graveyard, and even sleep there, and maybe some of the girls in the street would bring her food.

She made her way back to the bus stop and got on a bus going to Glasgow. She climbed on and paid her fair. This time she stayed awake and when the bus reached Paisley Road West, she stood waiting for it to stop. She was walking down Berryknowes Road, heading for the shortcut through the Moss Heights to the cemetery, having decided to hide there, when she saw the police car coming up the road towards her. Her heart started to hammer in her chest and she tried to hurry to get to the short cut before they would reach her. Just as she was turning into the path, she heard the car stop and a door slam shut. She kept walking, but the police officer ran up behind her, and put his hand on her shoulder. "You'll be Fabiana then." At that, she burst into tears and the floodgates opened. She couldn't stop crying. She heard the police officer speaking into his radio saying, "We've picked her up on Berryknowes Road."

They drove her straight home, and her Father and Mother came out of the house before she was even out of the police car. She kept her head down and as she approached her Father, he smacked her hard on the side of her head. She hated him in that moment and she hated her Mother too. She didn't hear the officer chastising her Father for hitting her. She went straight into the house, upstairs to her bedroom, and lay on the bed sobbing.

She wasn't allowed to go to school for the next few days, and very little was said to her apart from "Here's your dinner," or "Watch your sisters." She was scared to go back to school knowing that everyone would be talking about her and she was embarrassed about that, but when she did go back everyone wanted to talk to her and be her friend. She resented that because they hadn't wanted to be her friend before she ran away. She didn't want their friendship now, except Maureen. Maureen had helped her, and Maureen stayed close by her at school. They were becoming good friends in spite of the other girls, and she liked Maureen. She never saw Dean again, but she thought of him often and remembered his face. He had brown wavy hair that was longer than the other boys wore theirs and he had nice brown eyes. She thought that his parents might have sent him to another school and she blamed herself. She never saw the necklace again either.

Things were terrible for her at home; at every opportunity, her Mother would mutter under her breath "Liar," and each day, before her Father came home, her

Mother sent her to her room, and she had to stay there while he was in the house. She didn't know if that was her Father's rule or if it was just her Mother's way of being spiteful. When she was at school, Maureen was like a breath of fresh air, she made her laugh and she could confide in Maureen, but Maureen was also a bad influence. Sometimes when school finished Maureen would say, "Bring a sandwich tomorrow and we'll dog school."

Fabiana, Ana to Maureen, was terrified about this and always afraid that her parents would find out, but Maureen had an answer for that too. "You get into trouble for nothing, so you might as well get into trouble for something." Maureen was bold, she had brothers, and that made her more daring. Eventually Fabiana started skipping school with her. Sometimes they would go to Bellahouston Park and sometimes they hung around the graveyard, but they always had fun.

Whenever they skipped school, Fabiana would get notes of homework and the previous day's lessons that she had missed, and she worked extra hard to catch up. She would drag her tie off her neck on the way up her garden path and then she would go straight upstairs to take off her blazer and school uniform. Once she had changed out of her school uniform, she would do her Mother's bidding, and with everything done to her Mother's satisfaction, she would go back to her room and study.

When Maureen and Fabiana were skipping school, they would often joke and shout to each other "Quick run, here's Sanny Wilson," and then they would run, screaming and giggling, before collapsing on the ground. There would be no sign of him because yet again, he was in prison, but that wouldn't last for long. He would be released soon, and they would become the centre of his obsession.

Chapter 23

Old Mrs Wilson was pacing up and down, watching from her living room window, and then pacing away only to return and look out again. She was wringing her hands with worry and silently saying her prayers, "Hail Mary full of grace, the Lord is with thee, Blessed art thou among women…" She said her rosary prayer repeatedly; The Lord's Prayer first and then she repeated The Hail Mary ten times, it wouldn't stop the inevitable from happening, but it gave her some comfort.

She looked at the days scratched off on the calendar that was pinned on the wall to one side of the fireplace. He was due out of prison today, he had been away for three months and then it would all start again. From her house at the bottom of Kingsland Drive, all she could see were the cemetery gates, but she was sure that he would go there before he went anywhere else. At least the local girls had had a few months of freedom while he was in prison. She hoped their families would keep them in the house or in their gardens from now on, but people were complacent, and always thought it would never happen to them.

--00--

He had a couple of pounds in his pocket when they released him, and the first thing he did was jump on a train and head into Glasgow Central Station. He wondered around the city for a while enjoying the freedom, but relishing, savouring the anticipation, of getting back on a train to take him to the station at Cardonald. It wasn't home he was keen to see, it was his cemetery. He was a strange character to look at with his sandy coloured hair, cut as though someone had stuck a bowl on his head and cut around the edge of it. The fringe was too short at the front making his forehead look longer, and the neckline at the back was too high. He had small decayed teeth, narrow lips, and puffy bags under his eyes. Most people gave him a wide berth when they saw him, but it wasn't his looks that drew wary glances, it was his demeanour. It was a warm day, yet he was wearing a coat, with his shoulders hunched, and his hands in his pockets. He kept his head down and avoided eye contact with anyone, clutching the coat close to his body. When he did raise his eyes, his glances were furtive.

Finally, he could stand the anticipation no longer and he made his way to platform thirteen to board the next train to Cardonald. His stomach was churning with eagerness. The journey would only take seven minutes, but for him it was a long seven minutes. As the train approached his station he hung back, letting passengers go ahead of him before he got up to leave the train. He didn't want anyone behind him. He didn't want anyone to see him jumping over the wall into the cemetery, instead of going up the stairs and out through the station exit.

One or two women in the same carriage recognised him and he could see them muttering. He didn't care, but he knew that they would be talking and telling folks that he was out. He stood there waiting until he was the last to leave the train. He watched their legs going up the stairs and disappearing out of sight and then quick as a flash, he ran to the wall that separated the platform from the graveyard. Putting one hand on the wall, he vaulted over it into the thick undergrowth and he landed with a sense of pure euphoria. He stood there inhaling the familiar old musty smells. Everything was quiet including the birds, almost as though they sensed that a predator was in their midst. He relieved himself of his pent up feelings and sighed with pleasure.

She saw him coming through the cemetery gates and her heart fell. She turned and ran to unlock the door, because it was easier to do that than have to open the door to him acknowledging his presence. She lost sight of him when he walked behind a bus letting passengers off at the bus stop, but there he was again, and he would be in the house in less than two minutes. It would all begin again, the clump, clump, clump, of his feet going up the stairs and then his footsteps moving about in his room. It would only be quiet when he was sleeping or standing at the window watching and waiting.

She knew he wouldn't come in to say hello to her, and she was glad about that. He would just go back to his usual routine, and sadly so would she, because she didn't know what else to do. She would wash the clothes that he would drop at the kitchen door. She would leave food on a plate sitting under a lid, over a pot of water. If he were hungry, he would light the gas under the pot and when the water was boiling, the food would be warm enough for him to eat. She could see all this in her mind's eye, and she wished she could see him choking on it.

She wished that there was somewhere that she could go, somewhere to get away from this hell on earth, but only death would free her, so she would wait patiently, and in her mind, it wouldn't come soon enough. Then the banging started, thump, thump, thump. She knew he was banging his head off the wall, and she wondered if he did that when he was inside, then she wondered why they didn't do something about it, and why they didn't try to stop him from hurting himself. Prison didn't help him; prison didn't do anything for him at all. She knew that things could only get worse.

All was quiet for a time and then she heard him coming downstairs and going into the kitchen. She heard him looking under the lid that covered the food on the plate. She heard him lighting the gas, and she heard him pulling out the kitchen chair, its feet dragging across the uncovered stone floor. After a time she heard him shout as he scalded his fingers when he lifted the hot plate, and she heard him dropping it onto the kitchen table. She listened to the noises that his cutlery made across his plate as he ate his dinner, and then she heard him putting his plate in the sink. She knew that he wouldn't rinse it and she hated him for that too.

The front door opened and he went out. She got up, went into the kitchen, and washed his plate, she really wanted to put it in the bin, but she was smarter than that. She could control what plate he used by washing it and using the same plate to lay out his next meal, but that was all she could control. Now that he was back, she would stay downstairs and sleep on the couch. He wouldn't come into the living room and she wouldn't go out of her way to communicate with him. That's just the way it was, and she preferred it that way. She couldn't stand to look at him. She didn't know where he went and she didn't care, well she cared, but she couldn't do anything about it.

When she was finished tidying the kitchen, she made herself a cup of tea, and took it through to the living room. She sat quietly drinking her tea and when it was finished, she lay down on the couch with her rosary beads clutched tightly in her right hand, and pulling a cover over her shoulders, she began to say her prayers, "Hail Mary full of Grace," but no amount of praying would change what was to follow.

--00--

He turned right when he left the house and walked quickly down Kingsland Drive. When he reached the bottom, he turned right again and followed Berryknowes Road until he came to the shortcut up to the Moss Heights. Half way up that path, he could turn into the back of the graveyard. He was laughing to himself and he thought that it felt good to be home. It was getting dark and that pleased him. He couldn't wait to know what tomorrow would bring, but for tonight, he was going to wander around all his familiar paths to see if there had been any changes while he had been away. He had several hidey-holes that he used and they looked just the same, if a little overgrown. He wandered all over the graveyard all the way up to Craigton and then turned and made his way back down to Cardonald to his favourite spot. The last train was gone and the railway station closed. He jumped over the wall, onto the platform and nosed about. He sat on one of the benches as though he was waiting for a train, but in his mind, he wasn't thinking about trains, he was thinking about other things.

His Mother was fast asleep in the living room when he crept back into the house; he knew she was asleep because he could hear her quiet snores as he stood outside the door with his ear pressed against it. He moved upstairs silently and went into his room and then suddenly, without warning, he began to laugh, quietly at first, and then it got louder and louder and that is what woke Mrs Wilson up. She covered her ears with her hands, still clutching her rosary beads and she cried and prayed, and cried and prayed some more, but the laughing didn't stop for some time.

Chapter 24

Tony Sinclair didn't trust his daughter, he didn't trust anyone. As a door to door debt collector, he heard lies all day every day; "I'll make it up next week," or "Call back later my Mum's not in." He hated his job and he hated the people he called, they were all liars, and since his daughter had lied about the necklace and then been brazen enough to run away, he hated her too. Yolanda always said she was a liar, but in truth it was Yolanda who was the liar. Tony could hardly believe that Fabiana had the audacity to run away, but he only had himself to blame. She was so afraid of his temper, and what he might do, that for her, running away was the only solution.

Fabiana had always been a good girl, and she had never done anything to justify her parent's treatment of her, but since the running away episode, he detected changes in her. She was more likely to question their demands, whereas before she had blindly obeyed. Her Mother Yolanda saw the changes too and she was unhappy about them, although she couldn't quite put her finger on what the changes were. Fabiana did what she was told, no more and no less. Before, she would have done things automatically, but now she waited until her parents told her to do something, and if the opportunity arose she would try to question them.

For Fabiana, the atmosphere at home was always tense, sometimes unbearable. She dreaded the school holidays, at least going to school got her away from her parent's demands and contempt. She wondered how she would cope without seeing Maureen at school every day, but as usual, Maureen had an answer for that too. They were sitting in the playground one day chatting about Fabiana's parents.

"Invite me to your house," Maureen said.

"I can't do that, my Mum and Dad would be furious."

"I bet they won't."

"Trust me they would, they would probably chase you away."

"What would happen if I just came to your door?"

"I don't know, it's been a long time since anyone has come to the door for me. My Mother would be rude and shut the door in their face, and my Father would swear at them and chase them off."

"Well we'll find out soon."

"What are you going to do?"

"What shift is your Dad on?"

"He's off for the next few days, but on Monday he starts a week of early shift."

"Perfect, just behave as normal and I will see you tomorrow."

The next day, Saturday, Fabiana was up early as usual. She had to put her school clothes into the washing machine and while she was waiting for them to wash she had to clean her room, then clean the living room, then go to the shops for her Mother. She had butterflies in her stomach, dreading what the day might bring when and if Maureen turned up unannounced. Her Father was working in the vegetable garden, her Mother was sitting in a deckchair watching him, and enjoying the sunshine. She could predict exactly what would happen next and because of that, she had a pencil and paper in her pocket when she went outside to hang out the washing.

"You can go to the shops now, get a pencil and paper and I will tell you what to get."

"I've got paper and pencil here." Fabiana sat on the grass and began to write out the shopping list.

"Take the big pram and one of your sisters."

Fabiana didn't speak, she just went for the big pram and stuck one shopping bag on the clip handle, and put two others on the tray that was fastened under the pram, and then she lifted Perlita from her Mother's lap and fastened the clips on her safety harness into the pram.

"Do you want anything Daddy?"

"No," he replied curtly. Fabiana couldn't help glancing at her Mother and wasn't surprised to see her smirk at her Father's sharp retort. She wondered if this torture would ever stop. She waved bye-bye to Gabriella and set off along Queensland Drive heading for the shops on Lamberton Drive. She looked at her list; she would go to McCoy's the greengrocers for all the vegetables, and then after that she would go next door to Galbraith's for sugar, tea leaves, spaghetti, and rice. The next shop was the dairy; she went there for Vienna bread and rolls before going to the butchers for square sausages and mince. She had to wait in a queue in each shop, and although it was nice to hear neighbours chatting and laughing, she was agitated because she knew if she took too long she would get into trouble. She always made sure that the provisions were fresh, because her Mother would check them when she put them in cupboards. Fabiana seldom got to eat any of the things on the shopping list apart from bread, and occasionally jam or a sausage. As soon as the shopping was packed away her Mother locked the food cupboard and tucked the key in her bra.

--00--

If she was honest to herself Maureen would admit that she was a little bit nervous as she walked down Queensland drive to Fabiana's house. She could hear voices coming from the back garden as she walked up the path, so she followed her instincts and just kept walking rather than knocking on the door. As she rounded the corner of the house she saw Mr Sinclair weeding between rows of small plants. He stopped, stood up straight and looked at her.

Maureen walked forward with a bright smile on her face and her hand outstretched offering to shake his hand. "Hello Mr Sinclair, I'm Maureen, is Fabiana in?" Caught off guard, he extended his arm, and as they shook hands, he laughed at the cheek of her, but he was impressed by her manners.

"Oh hello Mrs Sinclair, I didn't see you sitting there," and she hurried over making the same friendly gesture to her. "Is this Gabriella? Can I hold her?"

Before Yolanda could say anything, Maureen had picked up Gabriella and sat on the bench beside her, bouncing Gabriella on her knee to the baby's delight. Tony and Yolanda were both dumbfounded at this forward, but friendly girl, and they didn't quite know what to make of her.

Yolanda studied this girl who was sitting beside her, "You go to the same school as Fabiana?"

"Yes we are in the same year. My Mum and Dad said that I could come down and spend the day with her because they are both working today. Would that be alright?" she said, giving them her most endearing smile.

Tony was trying to figure out this girl, he thought that she was a bit forward, but there was something about her that he admired, perhaps it was her nerve. He didn't answer Maureen, he just carried on doing what he had been doing before she arrived, but that sent a signal to Yolanda that he approved, otherwise he would have chased her and told her not to come back.

Fabiana took the shopping from the pram and piled it at the door, before wheeling it round to the back of the house so that her Mother could look after Perlita while she put the shopping away. She was shocked to find Maureen sitting in the back garden holding Gabriella on her knee and chatting to her Mother. She stood there with her mouth open wide and heard her Father saying pleasantly, "Your friend Maureen's here." She didn't know how to respond to her Father. She looked at her Mother and then at Maureen.

"Put the shopping away, and then you can go out for half an hour," said her Mother. She took the key to the kitchen cupboard from her bra and handed it to Fabiana. It was warm from the heat of her Mother's body and Fabiana hated that feeling.

"Can I help?" asked Maureen. Yolanda didn't answer her, but she reached over and took Gabriella from her arms and that was all the confirmation that Maureen needed.

"Close your mouth, you'll catch flies," whispered Maureen, giggling as she took Fabiana by the arm and walked her round to the front door.

"How did you manage that? I can't believe you are here."

They went into the kitchen and Maureen hitched herself up onto the kitchen table and sat, swinging her legs, watching Fabiana putting the groceries away.

"I think we should take the babies for a walk when you're done."

Fabiana smiled at her friend as she was shaking her head. "That won't happen."

"Wait and see, just wait and see."

While Fabiana was putting the last of the shopping away, Maureen went round to the back garden.

"Mrs Sinclair, can Fabiana and I take the babies for a walk in their prams."

Yolanda looked at her husband; he had stopped what he was doing and looked back at Yolanda. He gave her a slight nod, and she said to Maureen, "Be back in an hour."

Maureen was skipping when she went back to the kitchen. She did a silly dance, hugging Fabiana, and said, "We have to be back in an hour, let's get the babies in the prams. Can I take the big pram?"

Fabiana was laughing, "I don't know how you managed that."

Fabiana took the cupboard key back to her Mother and then the girls got the babies organised for their walk.

"What was all that with the key?"

"She keeps the food locked."

"Why?"

"I don't know; she just does, doesn't your Mother lock the food cupboard?"

Maureen laughed, "Are you kidding, my brothers would riot and probably break the door down. So what happens when you are hungry?"

"She opens the cupboard and leaves bread and jam on the table."

"What about dinners?"

"She cooks for my Dad when I am at school and leaves it in the oven, I expect she eats when it's ready and if there is anything left after my Dad has eaten I might be allowed some."

Maureen had tears in her eyes as she looked at Fabiana and listened to her talking. She felt so sad for her. "You must be hungry sometimes."

"I'm always hungry, except at Christmas."

Maureen laughed, "What do you mean, except at Christmas?"

"Well at Christmas she makes a big fancy spread and it stays on the table all day and I am allowed to eat whatever I want."

"Are you serious?"

Fabiana looked at Maureen's shocked face. "Yes I'm serious, is that not the way it's supposed to be?"

Maureen shook her head sadly, and Fabiana began to feel embarrassed as though she had revealed something that wasn't normal. "No it's not normal, and I hope you don't get angry with me for saying so, but I think that's a disgrace."

From that day, Fabiana and Maureen maintained a strong friendship and Fabiana discovered a little more freedom. The downside was her parents often compared her to Maureen, asking her why she couldn't be more pleasant like her. She couldn't tell them that the reason Maureen was more pleasant was because she had different parents, but that was what she thought. She was so happy that summer, spending time with her friend, and she had no idea that it would all end so suddenly.

Chapter 25

Sometimes his headaches were so bad that he couldn't lie down, lying down always seemed to make them worse. On those days, he paced backwards and forwards. Sometimes he would run from the house along the road and into the graveyard, his Mother would hear the door slam, and watch him from her window. This was a bad day, he felt as though he had a vice clamped tightly round his head as he made his way to his favourite hiding spot. He sat among the undergrowth rocking back and forward with his knees bent, his elbows on his knees, and his hands cupped over his head. The fit didn't last long and he didn't even know that it had happened, but when he came to a short while later his trousers were wet with urine. He had never done that before, and he couldn't understand how or why that had happened. He fumbled in his breast pocket for his packet of aspirin; taking several out of the packet, he swallowed them dry.

The sound of girlish laughter alerted him and he peered through the bushes. He saw two girls running and laughing, he recognised one of them, he had seen her walking to school, she was local and he was sure that she lived on Queensland Drive, but the other he had never seen. He crept out of his hiding place and stalked them. He followed them at a distance, all the way through the graveyard, and watched them exit at the Craigton end of the graveyard on Paisley Road West at the junction of Mosspark. He stayed in the graveyard wondering if they would come back that way or if they would go along the main road. He waited until a team of gardeners arrived and he didn't want them to see him, so he carefully sneaked away, avoiding the main paths, staying close to the undergrowth.

The one with the dark hair intrigued him, it was curly hair and framed her face and he could imagine that her eyes were brown. The other one was pretty too, with long blonde wavy hair, and her skin was rosy pink from the summer sun. He liked the way they giggled with each other; even after they were gone, and he couldn't see them anymore, their voices rang out in his head. He knew he would enjoy watching and waiting for them. That would be his mission from now on, he would watch for them every day, and he would jump out at them when they least expected it. He laughed as he thought of his plan.

Maureen and Fabiana were sitting in the cafe on Paisley Road West, and this was a first for Fabiana. She had never been to a cafe before, and sitting opposite Maureen made her feel quite grown up. Although she liked this experience she didn't know what she was supposed to do, and consequently her face was flushed with embarrassment. Maureen on the other hand was quite comfortable in her surroundings, her confidence shone through as she went up to the counter, ordered, and paid for two bottles of Coca Cola. The woman who served her took two bottles from an old fashioned, glass fronted, cold cabinet. She popped the metal caps off using a bottle opener screwed to the side of the cabinet, and stuck a straw in each bottle. Condensation made the bottles wet, and they were icy cold to touch so Fabiana and Maureen made a show of trying to reach the straws with their lips without their hands touching the cold wet bottles. They giggled a lot as they enjoyed themselves.

"I can't believe that you have never been in a cafe before, are you kidding me?"

"No honestly, I am never allowed to go anywhere unless it's to the shops for my Mother or around the block or school, or some other message to run."

"That's not right, it's not normal."

"It's normal in my home."

Maureen felt sorry for Fabiana and was determined to see that from now on she would be able to do things that girls her age took for granted. "From now on be as nice as you can even though you may not feel like it, I am going to ask your Dad if we can go ice skating."

"Good luck with that, he will say no," said Fabiana sadly.

When they were finished their drinks they made their way back, keeping to the main roads. Maureen waited at the bus stop at the top of Kingsland for the number twenty-three bus, which would take her home to Pollok, and Fabiana ran the rest of the way home. She was happier than she had ever been. She didn't know what it was that her parents liked about Maureen, but she was glad that they did. It was almost as though they trusted Maureen more that they trusted her and if Maureen suggested an outing the answer was always yes, but if Fabiana suggested it first, the answer would always be conditional, 'Take your sister', or it would be 'no', or you have to do this or that first. Her Father was still suspicious of her movements, always questioning, as though he was trying to catch her out, but since there was never anything going on, Fabiana just answered his questions. She often wondered what went on in his life to make him so suspicious about her. Sometimes, she felt as though he was following them, but when she told Maureen that, she had laughed at her.

While she was out, a neighbour had handed in a bag of clothes that her daughter had finished with. Fabiana was keen to see what she had brought, because sometimes she handed in things that Fabiana would get to wear. She rummaged through the bag and pulled out a couple of floppy sun hats. She tried both on, one at a time, and laughed at her reflection in the hall mirror.

"Can I keep these hats Mum, one for me, and one for Maureen?" Her Mother turned and looked at her and then looked at the hat's thinking for a moment that she might want them, but for once she wasn't mean and she said. "I don't want them."

Alina happily clutched the hats close to her and continued to rummage in the bag, spotting something that was bright red and it drew her interest immediately. She held it up and looked at it. It was an angora bolero with short sleeves. Her Mother had already taken what she wanted to keep for herself, and Fabiana was surprised that this beautiful bolero was still there, but then she realised that it was too small for her Mother. She tried it on and looking at her Mother she asked, "Do I get to keep this too?" Her Mother didn't even look around, instead she just replied, "If you want it."

Alina was sure that her Mother had made a mistake, but she wasn't about to question her. She put it on and ran to look in the mirror again. She decided that she would wear it one day when she was going out with Maureen and she would take the sunhats with her too, she knew they could have fun with them. The school holidays were almost over; they only had Friday, Saturday, and Sunday left, and then it would be back to school on Monday. Her school uniform, washed and pressed, was hanging behind the bedroom door, but she knew that she wouldn't be allowed out on Sunday just because there was school the next day.

Chapter 26

He was obsessed with the dark haired one, and he had followed them from a distance, watching them and hoping that he would be able to get in front of them. He raged on the days that he missed them. He thought about the blonde girl too, but the dark haired one, she was special; she was so different from the other girls. He fantasised about her more than he fantasised about the others. He was angry with them too because they never kept to a routine so he could never anticipate where they might be going. Sometimes they had a pram with them; sometimes it was a pushchair, but he wanted to get them when they had neither, because the fun was in the chase, the fun was when he suddenly appeared in front of them, and they showed their fear and ran. Thinking of that made him laugh in spite of his anger.

He had followed them up Berryknowes Road and he had followed them through the graveyard on a couple of occasions, but on one of those occasions he realised that someone else was watching, someone else was following them. The graveyard was his place. He didn't know the other man, and he was scared in case the other man was watching for him, but when he thought more about it, he realised that the man was always watching the girls. It didn't matter who he was watching, he didn't want anyone to see him apart from the girls.

He knew the blonde one lived in Pollok because he had seen them standing at the bus stop, and as he watched he saw the dark haired one crossing the road to go home, so he knew that the blonde was going to get on to the next bus. He was only a few yards from the previous bus stop so he took the chance and jumped on the bus and sat downstairs. When the bus stopped at the next bus stop, he watched the blonde one getting on and going upstairs to sit on the top deck. He found it hard to contain his laughter that day, sitting downstairs on the bus knowing that that the blonde one was upstairs. He kept his head down and grinned to himself as he watched the passengers getting off at each stop until finally he saw her getting off. As soon as the bus started to move away from the stop, he got up and stood at the opening ready to jump off at the next stop, but watching her continually to see where she was going. Before the bus had even reached the next stop, he saw her walking up the path to her house. He laughed when he saw that.

He wondered how she would react if he just waited outside her house and followed her. He pictured the scene in his warped mind; she would come out of her house and walk down her path. He would be hiding out of sight while she walked to the bus stop and when he saw the bus coming, he would run and get on behind her. He wondered if she would see him and be frightened; he wondered what she would do if he sat right next to her, or if her head would be so full of going to meet the dark haired one that she wouldn't see him at all. That was still to come. He liked to take his time, planning his moves.

The next day he hid in the lane that connected Queensland Drive and Kingsland Drive. He could hear buses each time they passed on Kingsland Drive. He was watching for the fair-haired one. It would only take a minute or two for her to walk from where the bus stopped and then he would see her coming down Queensland Drive. He watched and waited, getting more and more agitated with every minute that passed. From time to time, he had to go and hide in the middle lane whenever he saw someone walking up or down the road. He didn't want anyone to know he was there. Another bus passed and he watched; then another bus and he waited, peeking out from the middle lane. His heart leapt; there she was, walking down the road. He waited and watched to see the house that she would go into, and he tried to gauge which one it was. She disappeared from sight as she turned into the gate. He waited, stepping from foot to foot in an agitated dance; his hands in his pockets, his shoulders hunched, his eyes wide, staring. They were taking too long and he began to think that they might not be coming out. His frustration was too much for him to cope with and his head started to pound. Every sound was agony and he could stand it no more. He left the lane and hurried to the right toward the cemetery. He hurried along, heading for sanctuary to his hiding place in the graveyard.

He sat in his den hidden by the railway wall on one side and by the shrubbery on the other; his hands were on his head now as he rocked back and forwards, back and forwards, overwhelmed by the all consuming blazing red pain in his head. He keeled over to one side with his hands on the ground supporting his body and vomited, and then everything went black as he slumped to the ground.

He came to lying among the bushes, the smell of his own vomit strong around him, but he lay there anyway unbothered by his own smell or by the fact that he had urinated on himself again. Eventually he pulled himself from his confused state and stood up carefully, looking through the bushes to make sure that no one was around before creeping out and making his way back to his Mother's house.

She saw him coming; she always did, living in a state of fear and contempt. He came into the house slamming the door behind him and he stomped up the stairs. She heard drawers being opened and slammed shut as he rummaged for something. She heard the water running in the bathroom, and then she heard his footsteps going back to his bedroom. The springs creaked as he sat on his bed and then she heard his boots dropping one by one on the floor. She listened, trying to fathom out his movements. He came down stairs and went into the kitchen. She heard him filling the kettle and setting it on the stove. She waited. She heard the whistle on the kettle began to boil and when it stopped suddenly, she knew that he had turned the gas off. She listened to him making a cup of tea and then she heard him going back upstairs. She waited. After a while, she heard him snoring so she got up from her seat and went quietly through to the kitchen, and there on the floor were his soiled clothes, left in a heap for her to clean. She hated him. He was her son, but she hated him with a vengeance, and she prayed as she filled the washing machine with hot soapy water.

Chapter 27

Maureen and Fabiana were sitting on the grass in the back garden. They had spread a rug on the ground and they were playing with Gabriella and Perlita. Fabiana's Father was at work and her Mother was indoors watching an old musical on the television. Fabiana and Maureen would not be going anywhere; that was the rule, if her Father was at work, she had to stay at home. Sometimes though, her Mother would send her to the shops, but she always qualified the demand with the words, "Don't tell your Father." She knew that her Mother would call her a liar if she mentioned to her Father that she had been sent to the shops, so it wasn't worth the trauma that telling him would cause.

This being Friday, there was a good chance that she would have to go to the shops, but she was quite happy going to the shops or staying at home because she had Maureen for company. Maureen was quite happy to hang around the garden too, now that Fabiana was coming out of her shell. At first Fabiana had been withdrawn and quiet, but as their friendship grew Maureen discovered that she was fun to be with. She had a good sense of humour and a nice nature too. Maureen really liked being in her company. Neither of them had any idea that while they sat and enjoyed the sunshine, Sanny Wilson was obsessing about them.

When the musical finished Yolanda came out to the back garden and as soon as Maureen saw her she asked, "Mrs Sinclair do you think we could go to the ice rink tomorrow afternoon?"

"What do you mean?"

"The ice rink, in Paisley, I go there every Saturday and it would be great if Fabiana could come too."

Yolanda was quiet, obviously thinking about it, and Fabiana sat with her lips pressed together, waiting to see what would happen. She kept quiet because she knew that if she made a fuss and pleaded to go her Mother would be more likely to say no.

"What do you think Mrs Sinclair, can we go together?"

"If the house is clean; I'll speak to Tony. What time do you go and when do you come back?"

"It starts at two so if we could leave here at half past one and we could be back by half past five."

Yolanda said nothing; she just turned and walked back into the house.

"Blackmail," said Fabiana.

"What do you mean, blackmail?"

"There will be a price to pay; wait and see, she will want something done."

"Why can't she just ask you if she wants something done?"

"I don't know; I just know that if I ask to go out or to do something she will want something in return, and even if I do whatever she wants, she could still change her mind."

"That's terrible."

Fabiana kept her eyes down, sad, embarrassed, and unable to explain. "My Dad thinks that he is the boss in the family, but he's not, she is, she manipulates everything."

A short while later Yolanda called to Fabiana, "Come in and peel the potatoes for dinner."

Maureen accompanied her into the kitchen and the girls exchanged glances with each other but, Fabiana shook her head. They whispered to each other as they stood at the kitchen sink. "That's not it, she will want something else, and I usually peel the potatoes anyway."

Maureen sat at the kitchen table and watched Fabiana getting a pot from the big kitchen larder, putting the freshly peeled potatoes into it and filling it with water. She couldn't understand the dynamics of this family and she wasn't really surprised that Fabiana had run away. It was as though they didn't actually talk to each other; just do this, do that, go here, go there. She never saw them chatting, smiling or being nice to each other.

Yolanda came into the kitchen and put the kettle on to make herself a coffee. Behind her back Fabiana gave Maureen a look as though to say "Wait for it."

"If you take the curtains down and wash the windows first thing in the morning, I will ask your Father if you can go to the ice rink." She picked up her coffee and went back through to the living room.

"That's it; I knew it would be something more than peeling potatoes."

"Why couldn't she just ask you to wash the windows?"

"I don't know Maureen; this is just the way it always is."

"Can we do them now and I will help?"

Fabiana laughed aloud and then whispered, "If we did them now she would think of something else for me to do."

Maureen shook her head sadly, her home wasn't like this. Both her Mother and Father worked and if help was needed, her Mother asked for it. In fact, the more Maureen thought about it, she realised that everyone pitched in anyway. Her family chatted and laughed with each, but she never saw anything like that when she visited Fabiana. Before Maureen left to go home, she told Fabiana that she would come tomorrow anyway, and if she wasn't allowed to go to the ice rink she would just stay with her since it was the last Saturday of the holidays.

While she was in the kitchen washing her Father's dinner dishes, she heard them speaking in Italian and she knew the proposed trip to the ice rink was being discussed, but she was determined that she wouldn't mention it. She made her Father a coffee and took it through to the living room. The babies were settled for the night and her parents were sitting watching the television.

"Your Mother tells me that you are going to the ice rink tomorrow."

Fabiana glanced at her Mother and then her Father and waited to see what was coming next.

"How will you get there?"

"We can get the red bus from Paisley Road West."

"Well if you are going by Berryknowes Road, stay out of the graveyard."

Fabiana's head tilted to one side as she glanced at her Father wondering why he would even mention the graveyard. They didn't need to go through the graveyard. She pictured it in her mind. They would be able to see the gates to the graveyard from the bus stop at Berryknowes Road, but there was no need for them to go into it. She gave it no more thought; she was too excited about going to the ice rink.

Early the next morning, before the babies were awake, she crept out of bed and went downstairs. She made herself tea and a slice of toast and then she fetched the ladder from the hall cupboard to begin her task of taking down the curtains and cleaning the windows in the living room. She had folded the curtains, left them in a pile in the kitchen and had started on the inside of the windows before anyone else surfaced. In her mind, she was planning her day. She wanted to have time to herself, to wash her hair, and look for trousers and a jumper to wear to the ice rink. She knew that she had seen trousers in the bag that the neighbour had handed in and she hoped that they would fit her. Perspiration was running down her face and her back by the time she finished on the last bay window. Her Mother came and inspected her work, standing to one side and then the other, making sure there were no streaks.

"You can do the outside now."

"Mu-uum," she dragged out the word, "I'm scared doing the outside, and the ladder wobbles on the ground."

Yolanda just looked at her, said nothing, but the look said enough. She knew that if she didn't do the outside of the windows she wouldn't get to the ice rink. There was nothing else for it so she heaved the wooden ladder onto her shoulder, and half-dragged, half carried it outside. She opened it wide and placed it where she thought it was least likely to topple over and stood on the first step, bouncing a little to see if it was steady. There was some movement, the edge that was on the gravel was stable, but if she wanted to reach over to the windows, two of the ladders feet had to be on the soft earth. She wandered around the garden looking for a solution and found a piece of wood that would fit over the soil and give the ladder some stability. It worked, and delighted with her own ingenuity, she began the task of cleaning the outside windows.

By the time Maureen arrived Fabiana was exhausted, she had done the windows, run to the shops for her Mother, hung out the washing and she had only just finished getting ready. Maureen was delighted that she was allowed to go with her. This was close to being the last time that the girls would ever see each other, but neither of them knew this, for if they had, things might have ended so differently.

Chapter 28

He was watching for them, hoping that they would come out and he was going to follow them. He had seen the blonde arriving and he had waited patiently, standing at the edge of the lane on Queensland Drive, peeping out occasionally and tucking himself in among the hedges if he saw anyone passing.

He was angry when he did see them, because instead of turning right and coming towards him, they turned left. He turned and ran as fast as he could up the lane, and at the top of the lane he turned right into Kingsland Drive. He knew that if he ran to the top of the hill he would see them coming out at the corner of Kingsland Drive and Ladykirk. As he reached the crest of the hill a bus passed him and he saw the girls reaching the bus stop. The blonde girl had her arm out signalling the bus to stop. "Ahrrgg," he yelled angrily. He hadn't even noticed what number the bus was. He kept running, his face contorted with rage, his lips pressed tightly together, his hands clutched into fists. The bus stopped to let passengers off and when it pulled away there was no sign of the girls. He was enraged, but still he ran, and then the bus turned left into Tweedsmuir Road. He knew then that it was a number twenty-three bus and that it would be going along Paisley Road West towards Pollok. He stopped where he was. He decided that they must be going to the blonde's house.

Agitated he turned to go back, then stopped and turned again; he was frustrated and angry because this spoiled his plan. He decided that he would go to the bus stop, wait for the next bus to Pollok and wait for them coming out of the blonde's house, but of course, the girls were not going to Pollok. For the time being, they were safe. He waited ten minutes for a number twenty-three bus and then when he got off at Pollok he wandered up and down for several hours, never far from Maureen's house, always watching, always waiting, always hoping for a sign of them coming, but it didn't happen.

Eventually, he made his way back down Crookston Road heading for Cardonald. He turned right on to Paisley Road West, and continued along the busy through route until he came to Berryknowes Road. He was tired and still angry, but the all consuming rage had left him, and he once more began to plan his next obsessive move. From Berryknowes, he took the shortcut to the graveyard, and made his way to his hiding place, where he could sit undisturbed, wonder and plan. His head was pounding and he felt sick in his stomach, but nothing would distract him from his mission. He wanted to see the girls; more than that, he wanted them to see him, but only when he was ready.

--00--

Mrs Wilson was in her kitchen making a pot of mince. She always made mince and potatoes on a Saturday. When he was inside the meal would last two days. A half pound of mince, and diced vegetables, a carrot, a small piece of turnip and an onion, all cooked slowly together in water until the liquid had all but disappeared. A pot of Ayrshire potatoes sat on the cooker and she would set the heat under them when the mince was nearly ready. He was out of prison so the meal would only last one day.

There were dirty clothes in the washing machine. She had bought it a long time ago from the Electricity Board Shop, paying a bit extra money every month on her electricity bill. It had a big drum with a wheel set inside to agitate the water and a wringer on the top so that she could feed the clothes between the two rollers that would squeeze the water from her wet wash. In fine weather, she would hobble on arthritic legs out to the back garden, and hang her washing on the line, but if it were raining, she would hang the washing on the old pulley fixed to the kitchen ceiling. It had four wooden bars suspended on two metal hangers and she could lower and raise it at will with the rope that fastened at shoulder height to a hook on the kitchen wall. Letting the empty pulley down was easy, but pulling it up with a full wash on it was hard on her hands and shoulders.

She turned the gas down to a peep under the pot of mince, lit the gas under the potatoes, and taking her time, she went outside with her basket of washing. The sun was shining, but her heart was heavy. She had her back to the house when she heard her gate slam, her heart skipped a beat, and she turned so that she could face the house. Each time she raised her head to fasten something to the clothes line; she glanced at her windows hoping to see where he was. When she was almost done, she saw his bedroom curtain move. He was upstairs in his room now and she silently thanked God. He wouldn't come down until he heard her settle in her front room.

When the potatoes were ready, she mashed them with a splash of milk and a tiny knob of butter. She added them to his plate with some mince, and set the plate on a pot of water with the gas turned on at a peep below it. She got her plate from her cupboard, served herself a small portion, and carried it through to the front room. She ate as she listened for him. All was quiet, for a little while anyway.

He sat on his bed staring at the wall in front of him. His feet were flat on the floor, his shoulders hunched, his arms resting on his knees, his hands clutched into fists. He squeezed his eyes shut tightly as the headache began to form. He could feel his pulse pounding in his ears as the pain grew. He wasn't aware of standing up, nor of walking to the wall. He didn't even know that he was pounding his head against it. Thump, thump, thump, and his mothers heart beat in time as she listened downstairs to his pounding. She was afraid. She was afraid for him, for herself and for the innocents that he would go looking for shortly. She heard him opening his door and running down stairs and out of the front door. "Mother of God, help me," was the silent prayer that she uttered. She picked up her rosary and fingered each bead as she recited her prayers beginning with The Lord's Prayer.

Chapter 29

The journey to the ice rink was a short one and Fabiana remembered with embarrassment some of the journey from the time when she had run away. She thought for a moment that if she hadn't done that then maybe she and Maureen wouldn't be friends, so in a way she was really glad that it had happened.

"The next stop is ours," said Maureen as she stood up.

Fabiana's stomach was churning with excitement, "What happens if I can't skate?"

"Don't be silly, I'll help you, you'll get the hang of it."

They hurried down a side street to the entrance and went through the double doors to a world that Fabiana had never experienced. The noise seemed to echo around her. She could hear loud dance music, and around her other skaters just arriving calling out to each other. Her heart was pounding with anticipation. There was an entirely different smell to the ice rink, different from anything she had ever smelled before. Boys and girls were standing in groups chatting to each other and laughing. Fabiana blushed; she felt so out of place. Some of the girls were wearing tiny short skirts over thick flesh coloured tights and they had on beautifully whitened skating boots. Other girls had on brightly coloured, long baggy jumpers, and some wore knitted hats, but more for style rather than anything else. There was a chill to the air, but she loved the feel of it on her face. They were still in the foyer and hadn't even reached the ice rink.

Fabiana handed her ticket money to Maureen and stood gazing around the foyer while Maureen paid. "Come on, close your mouth, you look like a fish out of water," laughed Maureen.

"Wait, did you get me hire skates?"

Maureen stuck her hand through Fabiana's arm and hurried her along, "Trust me," she said, "I have a surprise for you."

They walked along the hall and Fabiana was aware of the sound of skaters, the blades of their boots making an echoing sound as they walked on the wooden floor to and from the kiosk for drinks. They were confident and poised on their skates as they walked and she wondered if she would ever be able to do that. She could hear the voices and music coming from the rink getting louder as Maureen led her to the right, and up a set of stairs passing some boys, skates on, running down the stairs taking them two at a time.

Fabiana turned and stared, "How can they do that without breaking their neck?"

Maureen just laughed, and then they were at the top of the stairs, and all Fabiana could do was stand, staring at the crowd of people, most around her own age, some a little older, skating around the rink. Maureen grinned at the expression Fabiana had on her face. Row upon row of bench seats surrounded the ice rink, each a row higher than the row below. Various skaters were sitting in random groups or alone, chatting or tying on their skates, standing and stomping their feet to make sure their boots were a good tight fit.

"I usually sit half way up, you get a better view of the rink, but we'll sit here at the bottom so that you don't have to go downstairs until you are used to it."

"But we didn't get boots."

"I told you to trust me," Maureen said as they took their seat. She heaved her bag onto her lap and took out her skates and with a grin on her face, looking at Fabiana, she took out another pair, "These were my Mum's, but she said that you could have them, here, take the blade guards off and try them on, they're your size." Maureen didn't tell Fabiana that she had told her Mother all about her and how her parents treated her.

Fabiana's eyes filled with tears, she didn't know what to say. She didn't know what to be more surprised about, that fact that Maureen's Mum skated or the fact that she had said she could have her boots.

"She whitened them for you last night, just in case you would be allowed to go. Come on; hurry up, put them on."

Fabiana sat for a moment, holding the boots, staring at them and then she looked at Maureen and grinned, "I've got ice skates, I can't believe it."

"Oh! I told her that your parents were a wee bit weird, so she put a note inside them to give to your Dad, so that you won't get into any bother when you go home with them. I hope you don't mind."

Fabiana turned and looked at Maureen and suddenly she reached over and hugged her. "Thanks Maureen, thanks for being my friend and thank your Mum for me too."

Her eyes were full of tears as she undid the laces. "What's this?" she said as she pulled something else out of the first boot.

"Thick socks, forgot to tell you that you would need them. Put them on and get the boots on, come on, I'm nearly done," said Maureen as she pulled at her laces.

Fabiana took off her shoes, pulled on the socks and put her feet into the boots. Maureen knelt down in front of her and pulled tightly on the laces. "They have to be really tight to support your ankles." When she was done, she prompted Fabiana to stand up.

"Stamp your feet and wiggle your toes to make sure that you can move them."

Fabiana did as she was told. "They feel ok, and I can stand ok too."

"Walk up and down for a bit and then we will go onto the ice."

Fabiana's knees were like jelly as Maureen took her hand and led her to the step down onto the ice. "Keep your knees loose and glide as though you were pointing your feet to the left and the right. Stand here and watch me."

She stood holding onto the barrier as Maureen stepped confidently onto the ice, skated around in a small circle, then turned and skated back to the barrier offering her hand. Fabiana took her hand and her first tentative step onto the ice. She was panicking, "Stay close to the barrier please Maureen."

"You'll be fine; you can't go all the way round hugging the barrier, look, some folk hang about the edges chatting."

"I'm scared, I might fall and hurt myself," and then she did. She was on her backside on the ice, and she had no idea how she got there. She looked up at Maureen, bent over laughing. "You made that happen, you said the word fall," and at that Maureen was beside her, sitting on the ice, laughing with her. By the time the session was over, Fabiana's legs were aching, her face was sore from grinning and laughing and she had just had the best day of her life.

On the way home Fabiana told Maureen that she didn't think she would get out the next day, being the day before schools went back, but Maureen said she would come anyway. Maureen got off the bus at the stop nearest to Crookston Road to walk the rest of the way home, and Fabiana stayed on to get off at the stop nearest Tweedsmuir Road just ten minutes from home. She knew that she would remember this day forever. Other reasons would make her remember this day too, but she was yet to know that.

Chapter 30

Fabiana and Maureen ran up the road together, clutching each other's arms and giggling as they ran.

"I don't know what came over them. I was sure that they wouldn't let me go out today. That was painless."

They stumbled over each other being silly and loving every moment. Fabiana was wearing the red bolero and they each wore one of the hats that the neighbour had handed in. They turned right on to Berryknowes Road at the top of Queensland Drive. They were so intent on giggling with each other that they were not paying attention to anything or anyone else around. When they were half way along Berryknowes Road Fabiana asked, "Where will we go?"

"Let's cut up the lane into the graveyard."

Fabiana stared at her for a moment and said, "Why, 'you know who' might be there."

"I've got something to show you and it's a secret."

"What?"

"Wait and see," said Maureen, laughing as she hurried her into the shortcut.

"This bit always scares me," said Fabiana, "Look at that railing up there at the top of the hill, the way the tree behind the railing is shaped always looks as though it's a person hiding, waiting to jump out."

They both giggled again and clutched each other as they made their way into the graveyard. They sat down on the grass, in a small clearing behind buchoo near some gravestones. From where they sat, they couldn't really see very much, and they guessed that no one would see them, but they were being watched.

"What's the secret Maureen?"

Maureen put her hand to her mouth, drummed her fingertips on her lips and said laughing, "Hmmm, let me think, how much is it worth to you? Oh I know, let me wear your bolero."

"Don't be daft, just tell me."

"Nope, let me wear your bolero and your hat too and maybe I'll tell you." She fell over on to her back laughing at her own silliness.

"Let me wear your silver chain then," said Fabiana taking off her bolero.

Maureen sat up and lifted her chain over her head and taking Fabiana's hat off she placed the chain, which held a little heart pendant, over her friends head saying, "My Mum gave me this, she used to wear it when she was a girl, promise me that you will keep it safe."

"I promise Maureen," Fabiana said laughing, and she perched her hat on Maureen's head as Maureen was putting on the red bolero. Maureen took the hat off her head and pulled up her hair, tucking it under the hat before fixing it on again at a jaunty angle.

"Ok, tell me your secret now."

"I have to show you my secret."

"Show me."

Maureen fumbled in her pocket and took out a packet of cigarettes and a box of matches.

"Oh my God, where did you get them?" said Fabiana.

"I pinched them off my big brother; he was annoying me before I came out. He will be wandering around looking for them and it will drive him mad. Serves him right, he was tormenting me. Come on, let's try." She opened the packet and offered it to Fabiana. Both girls took a cigarette each. Fabiana stuck it under her nose and sniffed it.

"It doesn't smell too bad."

Maureen put the filter tip in her mouth and exaggerated inhaling the unlit cigarette.

"You look ridiculous." Fabiana laughed.

"I am a rich movie star, and everyone loves me," Maureen declared in a funny accent, posing, posturing, and adjusting the red bolero, changing the tilt of the hat in various positions, and trying different accents. Fabiana rolled on the grass, laughing until her tears fell. Maureen took a match and said, "Right, we'll do it together." Fabiana took a match and together they struck their matches, placed the flame to the ends of the cigarettes and sucked deeply. They both breathed in, and then promptly gagged and choked falling over each other retching and coughing.

"Oh no that's awful, I don't know why people smoke," said Fabiana. She looked at Maureen whose face was almost green.

"I feel sick and I feel dizzy, but I quite like it," laughed Maureen, "let's try it again."

They put their cigarettes to their mouths, but didn't suck so deeply. Fabiana fell over onto the grass, "I think I'm going to be sick and my head is going round and round." She looked at Maureen, "You've done this before, haven't you Maureen, tell me the truth."

"OK I tried a quick puff once."

"I'm not doing it anymore."

Suddenly Fabiana turned and looked around her and Maureen took notice.

"What is it?"

"Shhh! I heard something."

The two girls sat quietly looking around them as a crow let out a warning caw. The hairs stood on the back of their necks as they sat and listened. All had gone quiet, even the birds were silent. Fabiana looked around and looked up and there was the crow sitting on a nearby tree, alert and watching.

"I'm scared," whispered Maureen.

"So am I, do you think it's him?"

"I don't know. What will we do?"

"We should run."

"Ok. We will count to three and then you run one way and I will run the other and I'll see you at school tomorrow. Just get up slowly as though we are standing talking and then I'll count to three," said Maureen. "One, two, three," and they ran as though the hounds of hell were after them.

There were two watchers that day in the graveyard and one of them was only interested in catching the one wearing the red bolero. He took off after her and as he made his grab for her, she tripped and fell, cracking her skull on a gravestone. The other watcher was on higher ground and he saw what happened. Saw the blood and the limp form of the one in the red bolero. He cried silently and rocked his body back and forward, back and forward and he leaned over and began to bang his head on a gravestone and still he cried. With blood leaking from the wound on his head from the continued bashing, he stumbled from the graveyard and down the path onto Berryknowes Road. He staggered as he ran, and made it to the corner of Kingsland Drive where he collapsed unconscious on the street.

The other watcher, horrified by what had happened, reached down and turned the girl over. In his head he was screaming "NO, NO, NO" but his scream was a silent one. He dropped to his knees and wept. He frantically looked around him and saw a fresh grave with piled high with flowers. He picked the girl up and carried her to some shrubs where he hid her body, and then he gathered some loose dirt and covered the blood so that it couldn't be seen. He made up his mind that he would come back when it was dark and bury her in the fresh grave. No one could ever know what he had done.

Chapter 31

Fabiana ran to the big path where she could see the main gates at the top of Kingsland Drive and she kept running until she was nearly at her gate. She slowed down to walk because she didn't want her Mother asking her if something had happened, she always seemed to know everything. Her Mother had told her to be home by five, and she expected her to ask why she was home early. She needn't have worried though, as soon as she went in to the house her Mother had things that she wanted her to do, and while she carried out the endless list of her Mother's demands, she thought about what had happened. She couldn't shake that feeling of terror. For a moment as she relived the experience she was sure that she had seen someone else, but that couldn't be possible so she quickly closed her mind on that thought. She knew that she would probably laugh about it with Maureen when they went back to school tomorrow.

There was a police car in the schoolyard the next morning, but Fabiana paid it no heed, assuming that it was a talk or a demonstration for the first year pupils. Her first two periods were for art and Maureen didn't take art so she didn't expect to see her, but she was surprised that Maureen wasn't at the English class. She watched for her all day. Later, after school, a police car arrived at their door.

"Get upstairs Fabiana," her Father said.

She made her way upstairs, but she tried to listen over the banister as her Father opened the door. She heard them talking and then she heard her Father bringing them into the house. After a little while, he called her downstairs. Her heart was pounding because she didn't know what this was all about, and she was afraid that she was going to get into trouble for something. She went into the sitting room and stood quietly. There were two police officers standing beside her Father.

"They want to ask you about Maureen," he said.

She looked at them in a panic wondering what Maureen had done.

"You saw Maureen yesterday?" one of them asked.

"Yes."

"Where did you go?"

Because her Father was watching her, she couldn't tell them that she had been in the graveyard. There was panic was written all over her face. She didn't want to get into trouble, but she didn't want to get Maureen into trouble either.

"Where did you go?"

"We just went up Berryknowes Road as far as Paisley Road West."

"Did you talk to anyone?"

Fabiana had no idea where this was going. "No, just each other."

"Did Maureen say that she was unhappy or that she wanted to run away?"

"No!" She wouldn't do that."

"Did you tell her about the time that you ran away?"

"No, well yes, I mean no." She had to think fast, she didn't want Maureen to get into trouble for giving her sandwiches and money when she had run away.

"What do you mean Fabiana? Is it yes, or is it no?"

"We didn't talk about it yesterday; we only talked about it at the time, after I ran away. Maureen wouldn't run away."

"Why do you say that?"

"She was happy, she loved her family."

"Was she frightened about anything?"

It briefly flashed across her mind that Maureen had pinched her brother's cigarettes, but she knew it couldn't be that. She put her hands to her mouth and started to cry.

"Have you remembered something?"

"NO!" She was sobbing now.

"Why are you crying if you haven't remembered something?"

"Because there must be something wrong and I'm worried."

Fabiana's Father stood up, went to her side and put his arm around her.

"I think that will be enough now, she has told you what she knows."

This startled Fabiana, the last thing she would have expected would be support from her Father. She would have expected him to shout and swear at her, but not this. He ruffled her hair and told her to go and wash her face. Fabiana shut herself in the bathroom, sat on the toilet and cried.

"I have to tell them, I have to tell them but he'll kill me for being in the graveyard and smoking," she thought to herself. She heard the front door opening and the police leaving.

The two policemen sat in their car outside for a moment.

"She was hiding something," said the driver.

The other one nodded, "I got that impression too. We should let her sleep on it. We can call in there tomorrow afternoon again and see if she opens up about whatever it is."

Fabiana came out of the bathroom to find her Father waiting for her. He smiled at her and put his hand in his pocket. "Here, take this, go and get yourself a comic or something?" She stood looking at the money in her hand and then looking at her Father. She had to beg to get pocket money, even money for sanitary towels, and he was giving her money without having to ask for it. She was mystified. Fabiana lay awake half the night worrying about Maureen. She didn't know how to help, but she made up her mind that she would go into the police station the following morning. She knew that she had to tell them about being in the graveyard.

She left the house earlier than usual and arrived at the police station before nine. She asked to speak to the police men that had been at her door. A man wearing a suit came out and called her into an office. He told her that they weren't on duty yet, but he said that he knew about Maureen and that he could help her. Fabiana told him that she and Maureen had been in the graveyard.

"Why didn't you tell the police officers yesterday?"

"Because my Dad was listening and he would batter me for being in the graveyard and for smoking. I was frightened."

"So he doesn't know any of this."

"Please don't tell him?"

"No I won't, you had better get off to school now, you're going to be late, and stay away from the graveyard."

Fabiana never saw Maureen again. Every day she watched for her and every day she hoped she would see her running across the playground with a big smile on her face, but it never happened. She continued to wear the silver pendant with the little heart on it, and neither her Mother nor Father asked her about it, not did they even mention her absence, and that was strange too. Her heart was broken; in the days, weeks, and months that followed, Maureen was seldom out of her thoughts. She knew that she would probably never have another friend like her. She kept to herself and seldom smiled and she struggled to forgive herself for not being brave enough to tell the police the truth in front of her Father. She didn't think that feeling of guilt would ever leave her, and there were moments when it would touch her and she would put her head down and experience a deep ache in her heart and a dreadful feeling of guilt. She knew she would never forget Maureen, and she didn't.

She wondered if Sanny Wilson had taken her, but a few days after Maureen disappeared, while she was shopping for her Mother, she heard neighbours talking about him.

"Aye, they say he was found lying unconscious on the street, and was rushed to the Southern."

"Terrible, jist terrible."

"A brain tumour they say."

"Was that why he was always botherin' the lassies dae ye think?"

"Maybe so. His poor Ma! Whit a life she's had."

"They say he'll be normal now."

"Who knows? A terrible thing," the woman said.

Fabiana stood quietly eavesdropping, listening to them talking in hushed tones about him.

"And did you hear about the lassie from Pollok that's disappeared, at first they were saying it could have been him but apparently he's innocent."

"Terrible the things that happen," said the first lady, "Just terrible."

"Nae news on the missin' lassie then?"

"Ah huvnae heard."

Fabiana was on the verge of breaking down and crying by the time it was her turn, but she held on to her crashing emotions and finished her Mother's shopping. When she went home with the shopping she, as usual, put everything into the cupboards, and then went up to her bedroom where she lay on her bed and cried herself to sleep fingering Maureen's little heart pendant, and thinking of her friend.

Chapter 32 Alina

When they arrived at the apartment, Alina led the way with Fabiana following and Sally behind her. Alina could feel the nervousness radiating from Fabiana. As she opened the door she said,

"We'll have some tea to warm us up before we begin Fabiana, how do you like yours?"

"Just black."

"I'll make it Alina," said Sally.

While Sally was in the kitchen making the tea Alina did her best to make Fabiana comfortable.

"Take a seat on the sofa Fabiana; you have met Ronnie and Gus before."

Fabiana nodded and sat down, feet and knees together and hands clasped tightly on her lap. She was so anxious that she appeared rigid by comparison to the others, who were sitting back relaxed and composed.

Ronnie broke the ice. "You look really afraid Fabiana, but just relax and put your faith in Alina, she won't let any harm come to you."

Sally brought the tea through and handed out cups to everyone. Alina sat down beside Fabiana. Turning her body to face her, Alina reached out and held Fabiana's hand and began to explain what was about to happen.

"When you have finished your tea, I am going to light some candles and play some soft music. All you have to do is kick off your shoes, sit back, close your eyes, and relax. I am going to be talking to you, taking you on a nice safe journey. You will be able to talk to me if you want to, and we can stop any time you like. All you have to do is say stop. Is that ok?"

Fabiana nodded and, finished with her tea, handed her empty cup to Sally who was standing nearby. Alina put a footstool under Fabiana's feet and tucked a soft chenille rug around her making sure that she was warm and comfortable, while Sally took the cups through to the kitchen. Ronnie lit the candles and Alina went over to the stereo and pressed play to activate the CD that was already in place. It was one of Alina's favourites, Tai Chi by Oliver Shanti. Everyone except Alina settled down as the first track, Huanquitan Garden, began to play softly in the background and Alina began to speak slowly and quietly.

"Close your eyes and take deep relaxing breaths. Breathe in through your nose, hold it for one moment, and then let it out through your mouth. Imagine or visualise that each breath you take is filling your entire being with positive light energy. Every out breath rids you of any negative energy."

Alina watched Fabiana as she spoke and she could see that she was following her instructions.

"Just listen to the quiet sounds of the music and allow your mind to drift."

After a few moments, Alina resumed, speaking slowly and softly. "Imagine or visualise that each positive breath you take is sweeping right down through your body as far as your toes. This breath travels around your body searching for any negative energy so that you can rid yourself of it as you breathe out." Alina paused again giving Fabiana time to process the exercise.

All was quiet as everyone listened to the sound of the harp strings playing. Birds chirping in the background of the track almost made the listener feel as though they were there in the beautiful garden.

"Listen to the music as you breathe slowly and deeply. Imagine that you are in a beautiful Japanese garden. Everything is peaceful and calm, the sun is shining brightly as you take your first step to explore your surroundings."

Alina watched Fabiana as she spoke and she could see her beginning to relax. The stress lines were beginning to disappear from her face, and her shoulders began to lower as the tension that she held began to ease. Alina realised that with the stress removed, Fabiana was quite beautiful. She could imagine what she would look like if she loosened the tight bun from her hair. She needed fresh air too, and that would add some colour to her very sallow complexion. For a moment, she wondered what she would look like happy and smiling.

"Continue to take long deep breaths as you begin to walk through the garden admiring the beautiful flowers that are growing there. As you wander, you will begin to hear the sound of water flowing. You follow that sound and come to a pond with a fountain in the centre of it. At the edge of the pond there is a low seat and you make your way towards it. The water looks cool and inviting. Your instincts tell you that these are healing waters. You know that if you sit by the pond, and immerse your feet in the water, you will begin to feel the healing energy flowing into your body. You can see yourself sitting on the seat, and you place your feet in the cool healing water. You smile and wiggle your toes as the cool water washes over your feet."

Alina was watching Fabiana carefully, and she was happy to see that there was a hint of a smile forming on her face. She noticed that she was wiggling her toes. This was a good sign, and Alina knew from these signs that all was well with Fabiana, and that she was following her guided journey. The track ended and a new one began; oriental voices singing in a language, not understood, nevertheless enjoyed for its beauty and melodious sound.

"Keep taking slow deep breaths as you relax and enjoy the feeling of healing energy, and allowing it to rise up through your body. You feel calm and at peace with the world."

Alina allowed Fabiana to drift into the space that the guided meditation and the music were taking her for a few moments.

"I am going to bring you back to the beginning now Fabiana. I want you to get up from the side of the pool and make your way back through the garden." Alina waited and then instructed her further.

"I want you to stretch your legs out in front of you and then relax them."

Alina watched and waited but Fabiana didn't respond because she was deep in her meditation.

Fabiana, it's time to come back now so listen to me; scrunch up your face muscles as tight as you can and then relax them."

Fabiana was slow to respond, but after a few moments, she scrunched her face tightly and relaxed.

"That's good, now stretch your legs out in front of you and then relax them."

This time Fabiana responded at once.

"Take a deep breath in through your nose, blow it out through your mouth, open your eyes and stretch your body and relax."

Everyone watched as Fabiana took a deep breath, stretched, opened her eyes and looked into Alina's eyes and smiled, but remained quiet, and then, almost as though she just began to realise where she was, she sat up quickly. Alina reached out and placed her hand on Fabiana's shoulder. "You are ok, just relax."

Fabiana relaxed, leaning once more into the back of the sofa. For a moment, everyone was quiet and then Alina asked, "How do you feel?"

At first Fabiana didn't speak and then, with tears in her eyes, she said, "That was a wonderful experience; I didn't want to come back, though I heard you, I didn't want to come back." A tear trickled down her face and Alina, touched by the emotion of the moment, reached out sympathetically and held her hand.

"I saw everything; I was wearing a Japanese costume and my hair was piled up high on my head. I felt like a geisha girl. I am quite taken aback and I don't know when I last felt so … actually, I felt a lot of things. I felt well, I felt safe and warm and comfortable. Thank you so much."

"Good, that's good," said Alina and she glanced over to the others. Sally got up and filled a glass from a water jug which was on the table, and she brought it over and offered it to Fabiana, who drank thirstily.

"Thanks Sally," said Alina, and then speaking to Fabiana she said, "I would like to have a chat with you about your life and your family."

"Do you still have your parents?"

"Just a Father; I haven't seen or spoken to him since I was a teenager. My Mother's dead."

"Oh, I'm sorry."

"Don't be, I envy people who grieve having lost a Mother. It means that their Mother loved them; I never had that so I don't grieve for the loss of a Mother. I grieve for never having known a Mother's love." She laughed ironically as she saw the shock in Alina's face, and then she explained further, "My Mother was cruel and manipulative. She was fifty percent of the reason I left home in the first place and I hadn't seen her for years. When you grieve the loss of a Mother you should remember how lucky you were in the first place to have had a Mother's love."

"What about sisters or brothers?"

"I have two younger sisters who left home, as I did, as soon as possible. They are in the States and I only hear from them at Christmas time."

Everyone was taken aback by Fabiana's story, short as it was, and there was nothing that they could say so everyone remained silent until Alina spoke.

"I don't want to do any more with this today Fabiana, I would like to try again tomorrow, but when you go home I would like you to practice this exercise tonight. If it's ok with you, Ronnie and Gus will run you home now and one of us will pick you up at eleven a.m. tomorrow."

Fabiana looked first at Ronnie and then Gus. She looked as though she was deciding if she could trust them, and then she gave a small, embarrassed smile, and said, "Yes, that will be fine."

Alina ejected the CD and gave it to Fabiana so that she could listen to it, and telling her to remember to bring it with her the next day. After they all left Sally said, "Wow, it must be terrible to feel that way, that you have had a Mother, but a Mother that you couldn't even grieve for."

"I know, nevertheless, that went much better than I expected. Let's have some coffee," said Alina sadly.

Chapter 33

"So what's the plan?" asked Sally.

"Light the candles cast the circle, and leave an opening at the door to let them come in. We'll close the portal and start immediately after they arrive."

"Music?"

"No, everything should be quiet for the regression. We don't want her mind to wander and she may be influenced by any music that we play. I will get her to sit on the sofa as before, but I would like you to sit beside her Sally and hold her hand, just in case she begins to get agitated or afraid. I am certain that there are things that she doesn't want to remember. Her mind has shut them out to protect her."

"I'm ok with that."

Sally could see stress lines furrowing Alina's brow as she watched her setting up. "Are you worried?"

"Well I am concerned, we are plainly going back to somewhere that she has been avoiding for a large part of her life and she is vulnerable, but I think her desire for closure outweighs her fear of remembering."

Gus and Ronnie had picked Fabiana up and when they arrived back the room was already set up. Alina made Fabiana comfortable and Sally sat down beside her while the men sat in the armchairs on either side of the sofa. Alina, taking the crystal wand that she had used to draw the line of the circle, moved to the door that they had come through and finished closing the circle.

"I'll hold your hand if you don't mind," said Sally reaching out to Fabiana.

Fabiana held on tightly and Sally whispered to her "Don't be afraid. We are all here for you Fabiana."

"Just relax, close your eyes and breathe deeply and slowly," said Alina. Both Sally and Fabiana settled into a comfortable position and as Alina watched, Fabiana and Sally closed their eyes.

"Breathe positive light energy in through your nose and feel it flowing into your body. Allow this light energy, carried by your breath, to travel down to your feet, and as it returns exhale through your mouth blowing away any negative energy. Breathe slowly and deeply and relax. Feel all the tension disappearing from your body and your mind."

As she spoke, Alina paced quietly around the room watching each of the others in turn. Ronnie and Gus looked very relaxed and comfortable sitting in their chairs with the legs uncrossed and their feet flat on the floor, but Sally and Fabiana were slipping into a deep meditative state.

"Breathe deeply and relax."

Alina paused and watched.

"Keep your eyes closed and your breathing slow and steady. Fabiana I want you to think back to a happy memory. Think of that happy time, and see yourself in that time and place, remembering and feeling the joy that you felt." Alina watched Fabiana's face and she could see her eyes flickering under her closed eyelids. Fabiana was smiling.

"What are you doing Fabiana?"

Fabiana was slow to answer but when she did answer, she answered with a smile, "I'm working."

"Where are you Fabiana?"

"I'm in the hotel."

"Where is the hotel?"

"It's in Blackpool."

Alina, not knowing anything about Fabiana's life, was puzzled.

"And you're happy?"

"Yes, I'm happy."

"What age are you Fabiana?"

"I'm seventeen."

"Let's move further back to another time."

Fabiana shifted her position and Sally, feeling her movement, squeezed her hand gently to reassure her. Alina waited until she looked settled before she spoke again.

"What are you remembering now Fabiana?"

"The first time I went to the ice rink."

"Can you tell me about it?"

"It's cold and noisy, there are lots of people talking to each other, and there are queues of people waiting to hire ice skates."

"What noises can you hear Fabiana?"

"Pop songs, people talking, laughing, and calling to each other, and I feel excited. I can hear the noise that their skates make as they walk backwards and forwards on the wooden floors."

Fabiana was smiling broadly now. "People are wearing long woollen jumpers all different colours and some are wearing hats, the girls have pompoms on theirs and some boys are teasing the girls and stealing their hats, but the girls are laughing at them. I don't know how they can run, balanced right up on the points of their skating boots."

Suddenly Sally said, "I'm getting pictures, I'm there too."

Alina didn't expect this development and she decided to let it run its course. Fabiana interrupted her train of thought.

"I can see the ice now, it's a big circle and people are all skating around. Maureen is giving me a pair of skating boots. It's a present from her Mother and I think I might get into trouble, but there is a note from her for my parents. I'm excited and happy, and the boots are beautiful."

Alina was processing her thoughts as Fabiana was speaking and had an idea that she thought might work. She had decided that if she could get Fabiana to talk about the ice rink and that happy time, when they resumed the regressive meditation, Fabiana might be more open about the things that until now, she was unable to remember.

"Ok, now I want you to come back to today. Think about where you are now, sitting on the sofa, relaxed and happy. Stretch your legs out in front of you, and relax. Scrunch up your face and relax. Take a big deep breath in, blow it out and open your eyes."

Fabiana opened her eyes and looked at Alina, waiting, Sally did too.

"That was great Fabiana. Can you tell me more about that day at the ice rink?"

Fabiana smiled, "I remember how embarrassed and nervous I was and I remember the smell. I don't know if it was because it was an old building or if it was the smell of the wood and maybe the ice, but it was a special smell and I have never smelled it anywhere else. I liked it."

"What did you wear?"

"I don't remember what I wore at the beginning, but later I wore a big red and white striped fluffy jumper. I have no idea where I got it."

"Did you have boyfriends at the ice rink?"

"No, never," she replied adamantly. "I was far too shy and nervous for that, but sometimes you would see girls that had boyfriends, skating around with them.

The girls would skate forward and their boyfriend would be skating right in front of them but backwards, holding their hands. I always thought that it was really romantic."

"Did you go anywhere else with Maureen?"

"Sometimes we went to…. No I don't remember."

"Where were you going to say that you went?"

"I don't remember."

"Ok Fabiana, that's fine for now. Would you like to go for a walk with Sally, maybe get some fresh air and clear your head before we try again?"

Fabiana nodded and Sally got up, and discretely picking up Alina's crystal wand, she opened the portal to go and fetch coats.

After they had left Ronnie said, "You have a plan?"

"Yes, I thought if I could get her to open up and be specific I could take her to her last memory."

"That might work."

"I hope so."

A little while later, Sally and Fabiana returned and once more Alina closed the circle and settled everyone down.

"Are you comfortable Fabiana?"

"Yes."

"Good, let's begin by breathing slowly and deeply. Breathe in positive light energy and blow out any negative energy or any fear that may be lying below the surface. That's good, breathe in slowly and blow away any worries or fears."

Both Sally and Fabiana were deeply relaxed, warm, and comfortable, as Alina guided Fabiana into the next part of the regression.

"Let me take you back to the time that you spent with Maureen."

"I'm getting pictures," said Sally, and Alina leaned over and patted Sally's hand to acknowledge her. "Can you tell me where you are Fabiana?"

Fabiana didn't answer and Alina waited before speaking again.

"Visualise you and Maureen in that happy place and time where you are laughing and happy."

All was quiet for a few moments but Alina could see by their rapid eye movements that both Sally and Fabiana were participating and seeing something, and then Sally said, "We're in a cemetery sitting on the grass near an old gravestone and we're laughing."

Alina said, "Go on."

"I've got cigarettes, I've lit one and Fabiana is shocked. We're fooling around and laughing and I'm pretending I am a film star. We're swopping hats and giggling."

"What else can you see?"

"We're serious now and I'm taking off my necklace and giving it to Fabiana. She is taking off her cardigan, it's a bolero, and I'm putting it on. She's letting me wear it, and I'm letting her wear my necklace."

Alina was listening and watching when suddenly Fabiana sat bolt upright crying. Sally had tears running down her face too. Alina went quickly to Fabiana's side and sat next to her. "You're ok Fabiana, you're ok, just breathe deeply and relax." Gus had gone immediately to Sally's side and he was holding her in his arms as she came alert. Ronnie was standing looking on anxiously holding out a box of tissues.

"We need another break. Let's have some tea and then we will decide if we will continue today, or try again soon."

"How do you feel now Fabiana?" Alina asked after they had finished their teas and coffees.

"I would like to go home now."

"That's ok Fabiana, Ronnie and Gus will drop you off. Would you like to try again, maybe the day after tomorrow?"

Fabiana paused for a moment, as though she was considering what to do, and then she answered positively, "Yes, I definitely want to try again, I'm scared, but I want this to end and I am ready to do whatever it takes to get to the bottom of this."

"Good," answered Alina, and Fabiana stood up and suddenly hugged her saying, "Thank you for doing this for me," and then she reached over and hugged Sally who was feeling emotional and had tears in her eyes at Fabiana's display of trust and gratitude.

After Gus and Ronnie left with Fabiana, Sally asked Alina, "What do you think?"

"I think we are making progress, but not in the way I expected."

"I knooow!" exclaimed Sally then continued, "Remember when you channelled Rosie, though that was terrible and with me it wasn't like that, but I could see everything clearly, more than that really, I could see and feel it as though I was participating."

Alina was sombre for a moment and then looking at Sally she said "When I channelled Rosie, I wasn't watching a murder, I was being murdered and it was horrible. Think about this Sally, what if the same kind of thing happens to you?"

"Well if the same thing happens, you are all there to do the right thing and bring me back. We have to try it; we have to do what we can to help Fabiana. If we were not meant to do it this way, the Goddess would not have given us this task and the ability to handle it."

"Ok, we will try the same thing tomorrow."

Chapter 34

Later that evening, after they had cleared away their dinner dishes, Alina covered the table in a soft black leather cover, which she had made several years ago, especially for spreading out her cards. She brought her workbox from the office, but no one would ever guess the contents because it was a small black polypropylene tool case. She set it on the table, while Sally went around the room, from left to right, with a smoking incense stick. Ronnie had already cast a circle line. He then he followed behind Sally, and one by one, lit the four pillar candles that Alina always had set in the four corners of the lounge. They both intoned quietly to themselves, calling the quarters, while Gus sat quietly watching. He spoke quietly to Alina, "Should I be doing something?"

"Just wait."

Sally went to the occasional table in the centre of the room that had been set up earlier as an altar, and placed the still smoking incense and holder on it. She picked up a dish of consecrated water and approached Gus with her hand outstretch toward his. He looked up at her, reached out his strong hand and took hers as he stood to join her.

"We would be honoured if you would assist us. Take this consecrated water, which of course represents the element of water."

Gus, touched by the sincerity of the gesture from Sally, felt moved in a way that he had never felt before.

"Of course, if you will help me," he said.

Sally led him to the East corner of the room and said, "Repeat this after me, with air, fire, water, and earth, I purify and charge the East. I am air." Gus repeated the words solemnly, and as they moved to the next corner, Sally instructed him to sprinkle some of the water from the dish, around the edge of the room, from the East to the South.

"Now say; with fire, water, earth, and air I purify and charge the South. I am fire."

Gus repeated the words and they continued to walk around the room, then Sally said, "With water, earth, air, and fire, I purify and charge the West. I am water."

Alina and Ronnie watched Gus and Sally working amicably together and listened to Gus repeating the correct words. When they moved on to the North corner of the room Gus turned to Sally and whispered,

"Wait." Then he continued, "With earth, air, fire, and water, I purify and charge the North. I am North."

As he finished speaking, he turned, looked into Sally's eyes, said "Thank you," and leaning forward, he kissed her gently on her lips.

They returned to join Ronnie sitting at the table while Alina stood preparing herself. Gus, sitting next to Sally leaned over and whispered to her, "Are we about to do a ritual?"

"No, but we are doing something a little bit different. Casting the circle and working within it, concentrates our energies."

The three of them sat, silent and unmoving in their chairs, as though they were watching a master at work, and indeed, they were, though in this case it was a mistress, 'A Mistress of the Tarot.' Alina looked up from what she was doing and looked at each in turn, then, injecting her sense of humour said, "What?" and laughing at them continued with, "Do you think I am Paul Daniels, about to perform a trick."

They all laughed and the mood lightened at once, for the Goddess appreciates humour too, then Sally said, "Do you know that you look quite different whenever you begin to work with your cards?"

"What do you mean different?"

"I'm not sure if I can explain it."

"Try."

"Well, it's almost as though you have become a Goddess."

"Oh that's a bit extreme," laughed Alina.

"Seriously, you change, in a beautiful way."

Ronnie suddenly spoke, "Sally's right Alina, I have seen that in you every time, but I thought it was just because I love and admire you so much. You almost become ethereal in my eyes."

Gus and Sally laughed at Ronnie's declaration.

"Oh stop it the pair of you, you are embarrassing me. Enough of this nonsense," she said, taking her box containing Rune Stones and Rune Cards. Of all the discipline that Alina had studied, Runes where by far her favourite. With Tarot there were choices; decisions could be made or avoided that would change a predicted outcome, however, with Runes there were no choices. If the Runes predicted an outcome, whatever that prediction was, that would be the outcome.

Alina sat down at the East position of the round dining table; Ronnie was next representing fire, then Sally representing water, and lastly Gus who represented earth. Alina placed the prepared Rune cards on the centre of the mat in the middle of the table. She treasured her Rune Stones, but she was always aware that overuse could chip them, so she preferred to use her Rune Cards. Sometimes on a morning when she had no plans, Alina would close her eyes and select a random Rune Stone to ask what to expect during the day and the stones were never wrong, but for readings, she always used her Rune cards.

Since Gus was new to this experience, Alina said, "We are going to ask the Runes for guidance in our search. Gus, would you begin by placing your left hand over the cards. Take a moment to think of a question and when you are ready, move your hand away. Don't say what the question is until I have read the card and given the answer."

Gus reached out and covered the Rune Cards with his left hand, and sat quietly until he had formed his question in his mind, and then he moved his hand away. Alina fanned the cards in a semi circle and said, "Point to one card Gus." Gus pointed to a card and Alina drew it towards her and turned it over to see the symbol and interpret the meaning. When Alina turned the card over Gus was surprised to see that the card he had drawn was blank

"It's blank?"

"That's a card with a very profound meaning Gus; it means the answer to your question is inevitable, in other words it can't be avoided, what you thought about will happen. What was your question?"

"I asked if Maureen would be found." The atmosphere in the room was quiet and tense.

Alina had a notepad beside her so that she could take a note of Gus's choice. She gathered the cards together, shuffled them, placed them on the mat as before "You next please Sally," said Alina.

Sally placed her left hand over the deck of Rune cards, concentrated on her question and removed her hand. Alina fanned them and Sally pointed to her choice. She had drawn Sigel, the symbol for success or victory.

"What was your question Sally," Alina asked, her hand was poised over the notepad ready to note down the question and the symbol.

"I asked if our efforts would be the reason that Maureen would be found. Sigel suggests that would be the case. That's a good sign, I'm happy about that."

"I am too Sally, I am too."

Alina gathered the cards again, shuffled them, and placed them on the centre of the table so that Ronnie could place his hand on the cards next. When he had formed his question in his mind, Ronnie lifted his hand, Alina fanned the cards once more, and Ronnie pointed to the card of his choice. Alina turned the card over to reveal Eolh, the Rune of protection.

"Protection, that's a good card considering my question."

Alina asked, "What was your question Ronnie?"

"I asked if what we are doing would harm Fabiana in any way, so I am pleased to see the Guardian Angels of the Runes."

Everyone breathed a sigh of relief knowing that no harm would come to Fabiana because of anything that they were doing. Regression, going back to traumatic circumstances was risky, but Ronnie's question, answered with Eolh gave them confidence that they could proceed without undue risk.

Alina gathered and shuffled the cards, placed the deck in the middle of the mat, and quietly formed her own question in her mind. When she was ready, she fanned the cards and chose one at random; her card was Yr.

Sally said, "I'm not sure of that one, it's about going back is it not? What was your question Alina?"

"I asked where we would find Maureen."

They gathered round to study the card and talk about their understanding of it.

"It links to the past, repeating things that you have done before, overcoming obstacles and trying again," said Alina.

"I'm not sure if I can make sense of that," said Sally.

"Let's look at some of the other interpretations," said Ronnie, getting up from the table and going to one of the bookcases. He came back with The Secret of the Runes by Horik Svensson, and began to flick through the pages looking for Yr.

"Here it is, page forty, a few sort phrases, listen to this.

"Yew is outwardly a smooth tree, hard and fast in the earth. The shepherd of fire, twisted beneath the roots, a pleasure on the land!"

Flicking through the pages, he found another reference on page fifty-eight.

"In brief it is associated with graveyards and is associated with death and resurrection. The last few lines say that there is a way out of any difficulty as long as the situation is approached in the correct manner."

"Oh Blessed Mother!" exclaimed Sally, "Look at the illustration in your card Alina," and together they studied it.

The hair stood up on the back of Gus's neck and he said, "I am not easily scared but that's a graveyard. This is spooky."

"She must be in a graveyard? There was mention of the graveyard in the files," said Sally.

"The police searched the graveyard, as well as nearby gardens, it was in the files, and I have another question," said Ronnie.

Alina prepared and set the cards on the table so that Ronnie could cover them with his hand while he thought of his question. When he had done so Alina fanned the cards in a semi circle and Ronnie touched a card. Alina drew it towards her and turned it over. The card was Ansur.

Alina asked, "What was your question Ronnie?"

"I asked if any of our group would come to any harm during this search."

"What does Ansur mean?" asked Gus.

Sally answered, "It's all about communication, listening and speaking, anything to do with communication."

Sally asked if she could try another question. "Ok, but this should be the last one. I don't like to overdo the questions," said Alina as she prepared the cards again. Sally covered the cards with her left hand and when she lifted her hand, Alina fanned the cards and indicated that Sally should choose the card which contained her answer. Sally pointed to the card that she wanted Alina to turn over and this time the card was Peorth.

"What does that mean?" asked Gus.

"It' a secret," answered Ronnie.

"Oh sorry!"

"No," said Ronnie laughing. "It's not a secret from you. The card speaks of hidden or secret information. It means the future will reveal the answer to your question. It can be a good or not so good answer. If someone is keeping a secret from you, it is likely that you will find out what it is; on the other hand, if you are keeping a secret, well, it won't be a secret for very long. What was your question Sally?"

"I asked how we would be harmed by communication. I suppose it was probably a wasted question."

Chapter 35

The next morning, Alina was, as usual, the first one up. She liked to rise early and perform a morning ritual to begin her day. Her candles were lit in the four corners as she stood in front of her patio doors and raised her arms high above her head, allowing the morning energy to flow through her. She clasped her hands in the prayer position and drew them down in while saying,

"You who are the source of all power and light please show me what I need to know when I need to know it. Help me to listen with understanding and speak with wisdom. Grant me the serenity to accept the things I cannot change and the wisdom to change the things I can change. Show me what I need to know so that I may understand."

She spread her arms open and continued, "The world is an abundant place, I am grateful for those gifts which I have already received and I am open to those gifts which are waiting to come to me. I thank the Lord and Lady for my blessings on this beautiful day."

Ronnie came up behind her just as she finished her ritual and put his arms around her waist. He kissed the back of her neck and she leaned in to him.

"Good morning Gypsy Girl, I miss you."

"What do you mean, you miss me. I haven't been away."

"Yes I know, but you haven't really been here either. You need a break, just the two of us."

Alina turned, still in his arms, and they kissed passionately.

"Is that coffee I smell? Oh! Get a room you two," said Sally, who was only half-awake.

"We are running away today Sally," said Ronnie smiling at her.

"I'm taking my coffee and going back to bed then." Then picking up her freshly poured cup she headed back to the guest bedroom.

"Let's have at least the morning just to ourselves."

"I like the sound of that. Where are we going?"

"Let's go somewhere for breakfast first and then we will take it from there."

Gus arrived as they were getting ready to leave and Ronnie whispered to him, "I am taking my lady out for the morning, make yourself at home. Sally went back to bed with her coffee and is probably fast asleep now."

Just as they as they were going out the door, Alina added, "Help yourself to anything, there is plenty of food in the fridge, and the coffee machine is on. We'll see you in the afternoon."

"Do you mind if I have a look at the Rune books Alina?"

"Not at all Gus, they are on the bookshelf."

Gus poured himself some fresh coffee, and settled down with several Rune books on the sofa beside him and began to read. He had been fascinated by the way the runes appeared to link directly to the questions that had been asked. He spent the next hour reading and digesting the information and began to form an understanding of how they worked. His stomach rumbling reminded him that he hadn't had any breakfast so he put the books to one side and wandered into the kitchen to look for food. He stood and browsed the open fridge, found eggs and bacon and put them on the kitchen unit. A short search later and he had a bowl to whisk the eggs in and a non-stick pan to use to scramble them. He worked out the mathematics of turning on the grill and covering the grill tray with foil he laid out strips of bacon.

It was the smell that woke Sally and she wandered through to the kitchen, in her dark blue cotton pyjamas covered with little white stars, to see Gus standing there looking completely silly, wearing Alina's apron, in front of the cooker.

He looked up a smiled at her, and her heart skipped a beat. She resisted the temptation to smile back and just looked at him. "You look ridiculous," she said.

"Hmm, you're not a morning person then, give me your cup and I will pour you a fresh coffee."

"I can do it myself."

He raised his eyebrows but didn't say anything in reply. Sally moved closer so that she could see what he was making and her stomach rumbled in appreciation. Gus had halved the tomatoes and laid them out beside the bacon. He had found a jar of dried mint and he added a knob of butter and a pinch of mint to each tomato. Butter was sizzling in a pan on top of the cooker and he added sliced mushrooms and a clove of garlic to the pot. The butter was melting in the non-stick pan ready to add the beaten eggs.

Gus turned to her, "Are you hungry?" He stirred the eggs into the pot and continued, "I have made enough for both of us."

"Thanks."

"It's almost ready; do you want to plate up?"

Sally put her cup down and Gus took two plates from the warming drawer and handed them to her. She put bacon and tomatoes on each plate and left the grill tray to one side, then took the offered pan of mushrooms and added them to the two plates. Gus added the eggs and they carried their plates through to the dining table. Gus went back to the kitchen for the coffee pot and the toast rack.

"I can feel you watching me," he laughed.

"I'm not watching you, I'm just looking."

"Same thing."

"No, it's not. Just looking means I am curious, watching means I'm interested and I'm not."

Gus put his cutlery down and looked straight at Sally. For a moment, he just looked without saying anything and then he said, "You know Sally, with a little effort you and I could have a conversation, a normal conversation, without you feeling as though you have to defend yourself. I am never going to do you any harm and I like you well enough that I would be pleased if we could just be civil with each other, but you confuse me. You run hot and cold. One minute you are polite and the next…"

As he was looking at Sally, he realised that her eyes had filled with tears.

"Oh my God Sally, what's wrong, please don't cry."

"I'm not crying I'm embarrassed. You are right and I can't help it. I just don't know how to behave around you."

Gus reached out across the table and placed his hand on top of Sally's, "It was the kiss wasn't it. I should never have responded to my instincts like that; I just found you irresistible."

Sally's face turned crimson and a giggle escaped from her. She wiped her eyes with her napkin and said, "I've never been called irresistible before."

"Just be yourself Sally."

"I'm sorry Gus."

"No need, but you will be sorry if your breakfast gets cold, c'mon, eat."

With that, the awkward situation was gone, and Sally realised that she was being silly and possibly childish too. Gus was a nice guy and didn't deserve her sharp treatment. She made up her mind that she would stop putting up barriers and be nicer to him.

After they had finished eating Sally went for a shower and Gus cleared away the dishes and tidied the kitchen. Much later in the afternoon, when Ronnie and Alina returned, Gus and Sally were sitting at the dining table with rune books spread around them. They were engrossed in discussing the various interpretations and they both looked up and smiled as their hosts arrived back. Gus said "Coffee?" The answer was a resounding yes, and he was laughing as he went to the kitchen to make a fresh pot.

Sally asked, "Where did you lovebirds get to then?" as everyone sat down. "We went for a run down the coast and stopped at Troon. We had breakfast there and then went for a lovely bracing walk along the shore. I found a Mermaids Purse," said Alina as she took it out of her pocket.

"What's a Mermaids Purse, can I see it?" Alina handed it to Gus.

"Is that real, it looks like plastic," Gus asked as he turned the purse over in his hand and inspected it. It was about two inches long, one end blunt and the other end had curly fronds.

"It's empty now; I found it on the tide line. It's the egg sac from skate or dog fish."

"What do you do with them Alina?"

"I keep them with odds and ends that I might need for rituals or casting spells. What kind of spell do you think it would be useful for?"

Everyone looked at Gus while he thought about the answer to Alina's question and then he exclaimed happily, "I've got it. Fertility."

Everyone laughed at his eureka moment and then Alina asked, "Good, what else Gus?"

Gus turned it over in his hand looking at it from various angles and then he said, almost reluctantly, "Protection."

Everyone looked at each other, impressed by his insight. Alina laughed and Gus responded, "Am I wrong, of course I'm wrong, that was probably a stupid answer."

"No Gus you're not wrong, you're exactly right, but none of us expected you to say that, well done. Can you tell me why you said that though?" he shrugged his shoulders and then he said, "It protects the eggs; it's all symbolic isn't it."

"Absolutely Gus and that was a good observation. Many people when they start out try to complicate things, but it's all very simple if you keep it that way. I'm impressed; we'll make a wizard of you yet." As she said this she glanced at Sally who blushed and cast her eyes down to avoid eye contact with Alina.

They spent the rest of the evening quietly relaxing. They knew tomorrow was going to be a big day.

Chapter 36

The room was prepared, the circle cast, the candles lit and Fabiana, who had arrived earlier, was sitting on the sofa beside Sally who was holding her hand. Ronnie and Gus were sitting in the occasional chairs and Alina was standing in the middle of the room.

"Are you comfortable Fabiana?"

"Yes, I'm nervous, but I'm comfortable."

"This time Sally is going to attempt to channel whatever you remember so it will be a little bit different. This time, you don't have to tell us where you are or what you see. If we are successful, Sally will channel your thoughts, images and memories and she will tell us what she sees. If you feel afraid or anxious, all you have to do is say stop."

"Ok."

Prior to Fabiana arriving Sally and Alina had discussed the procedure and agreed that as soon as Sally began to see images, she would raise her hand briefly to sign to Alina.

Everyone was quiet as Alina began to speak in a soft clear voice, "Breathe slowly and deeply taking positive light energy down to your toes, hold it for one moment, and as you breathe out, visualise that you are ridding your body of any negative energy."

She waited a few moments, watching Fabiana and Sally drift into a deep relaxed state and then she began to speak again.

"Breathe slowly and deeply and see sparkling energy filling your entire body and soul." Alina paused again allowing time for her words to take effect. "You are comfortable, safe, and warm, and your mind is drifting back in time to a happy memory."

Sally raised her hand a little and Alina knew that pictures were beginning to form.

"What can you see Sally?"

"We are grinning at each other and running."

Alina waited to see if there was more but Sally remained quiet.

"Where are you running to?"

"I don't know, I think we are just running, and we are happy as though we have done something that we are happy about or are going to do something, but I don't know what."

"Let's go back in time, to the ice rink."

Alina waited and watched and then Sally began to speak.

"I'm there; I'm on the ice, we are skating round the rink and the air is cold on my face. We are looking at each other and we are happy."

"Let's go back to the last time that you were both together."

Alina watched as Fabiana shifted slightly in her position, but she also saw the subtle movement of Sally squeezing her hand in a reassuring way."

"Take your time; just remember that last day that you spent together."

Sally spoke, "We are in the cemetery, we are laughing and I want to wear Fabiana's red bolero, but she says no. I am bribing her with my heart pendant. We have swopped hats too, and we are laughing so hard our stomachs ache. We are leaning into each other, holding each other up we are laughing so much. I'm wearing her bolero now and she is wearing my necklace."

Sally became very quiet and her expression changed from one of joy to one of concern.

"Go on," Alina said.

"I think someone is there, watching us, and I'm scared, but Fabiana thinks I am pretending. The birds have gone quiet now, and Fabiana is scared too. We're making a plan; count to three and we will run in separate directions, go home and meet up tomorrow at school. We're whispering," she looked as though she was about to say more, when suddenly she stood up as though to run in a panic, and then she dropped like a stone to the floor in a dead faint.

Everything happened at once; Fabiana sat bolt upright and burst into tears. Gus was the first to reach for Sally, diving out of his chair he swept her into his arms and held her close while Ronnie and Alina tended to Fabiana. She was still upset and crying quietly, but Alina guided her to a chair so that Gus could lay Sally out on the sofa. He held her in his arms, whispering in her ear. "I've got you Sally, I've got, you're safe, I've got you."

Ronnie handed Fabiana a glass of water and a tissue and spent a few moments reassuring her while at the same time he was looking over to see if Sally was responding. Alina fetched a blue grass sage smudge stick, lit it, and using a feather she directed the smoke over Sally. After what seemed like an eternity Sally, still wrapped in Gus's arms, opened her eyes, smiled at him and said "I've been dreaming about you," and then she burst into tears.

They made sure that Fabiana had fully recovered from the experience and Ronnie was given the job of taking her home. Alina made a call to Inspector Collins, knowing that he was friendly with Fabiana. She suggested that it might be prudent for him to call in and see her later if he had the time. He asked about the progress they had been making, but Alina told him that she would update him later; she was more concerned with keeping an eye on Sally.

"I'm really tired," said Sally.

Gus, who had been fussing around Sally since her collapse said, "Come one Sally, you should lie down, get some sleep."

Sally seemed reluctant to leave the room.

"Come on Sally, I'll sit with you." He took her hand, she stood up and Gus led her through to the bedroom, glancing over at Alina for approval. She nodded to him.

Sally lay down and Gus covered her with a chenille rug that was draped over the foot of the bed. He tucked her in, stroked her forehead and said. "Close your eyes Sally; get some sleep. I will be right here," and he sat in the occasional chair to watch over her. Sally drifted over very quickly, but her sleep was a restless one and Gus could see that she was troubled. After watching her torment for a few minutes, he lay down on top of the chenille rug, wrapped his arms around her and held her while she slept. Her agitation stopped almost immediately. Ten minutes later, when Alina looked in to see if Sally was ok, she saw that they were both sound asleep.

Ronnie arrived soon after that, and seeing him driving up, Alina opened the doors for him and signalled for him to come in quietly.

"Is she ok?"

"Sound asleep. Gus is lying down with her."

"You're joking!"

"Seriously, she is wrapped in his arms, and they are both out for the count."

"Well what do you know? We should get some rest too. Let's switch off the phones and lie down."

Chapter 37

Sally was the first to wake and as she came around from a dreamless sleep, she realised that she felt warm, comfortable and safe. At first, she thought that she was dreaming and then she realised that she was in someone's arms. She opened her eyes, looked straight into Gus's eyes and he smiled at her. Her face flushed with embarrassment and she began to sit up to move away from him.

"Be still, you are fine where you are," he said holding on to her.

He held her close, wrapped in his arms and whispered into her hair, "You scared me half to death Sally."

"It wasn't a nice experience," she said and shivered at the thought.

"I can't even begin to imagine what it was like for you. Does that always happen?"

"I suppose it depends on the circumstances, I have only seen something like that once before when Alina was channelling, but I knew what I was letting myself in for."

"What happens now?"

"We will sit around and talk about it."

Just at the moment, Ronnie knocked on the bedroom door and looked in. "We heard you talking, anybody fancy Chinese for dinner? We are just about to order in."

Sally answered first while she glanced at the clock on the bedroom wall, "Dinner? What times is it, Oh my Goddess it's six thirty, have I been asleep that long?"

Ronnie laughed, "Don't feel bad, we have been asleep too. We just woke up half an hour ago and we are so ready for food."

Ronnie left them to organise themselves and while Alina set the dining table with plates, cutlery and napkins, Ronnie telephoned the nearby Panda House and placed an order for delivery. Just as he finished the call, Gus and Sally came through to the lounge. Alina went over to her immediately, embraced her warmly, and kissed her on her cheek. She placed her hands on Sally's shoulders and drew back to look at her face, "You look much better than I expected."

"I feel better but I am so hungry. What did you order Ronnie?"

"A set meal for four; Chicken and Noodle Soup, Spare Ribs, Sweet and Sour Chicken, Beef Curry, Fried Rice, and that comes with Prawn Crackers and a side of mini spring rolls," he said reading off a list that he had jotted down."

Gus was laughing as he said, "And what did you order for everyone else?"

Sooner than expected the food arrived and they all sat down at the table to enjoy the feast, exactly what they needed to refuel for the next part, and although none of them discussed anything relating to the earlier events, they all knew that after the meal was finished they would begin to talk about Sally's experience during the regression.

They settled down in the lounge and Alina asked Sally if she was ready to share what she had experienced.

"There were two men."

"What do you mean, there were two men?"

"It's difficult to explain this, it was as though I was Maureen, and I knew what Fabiana was thinking and she knew what I was thinking. At first we thought it was just one man, Sanny Wilson, but there was another man watching, and there is more. I felt things and I am not sure if Fabiana or Maureen, for that matter, felt these things."

Sally was quiet for a moment, processing what she was trying to say. "We were whispering to each other that we thought someone was behind us over to the right, but without saying the words I knew that there was someone else, but I am not sure if Maureen felt that too or not, or even if Fabiana felt that. I felt more than that though and it scared me more than the thought of them watching."

"What did you feel Sally?" Alina was concerned about what her friend was going through.

"I felt rage, horrible, horrible, rage from the other man. Knowing that Sanny Wilson, if it was Sanny Wilson, was watching us was frightening but not threatening, but the other man…" Sally shivered as she remembered the feeling and the experience. Gus, who was sitting close to her on the sofa, put his arm around her shoulders.

He asked, "What happened next?"

"I think Fabiana did feel something because at first we were, well, just scared that Sanny Wilson might be watching us, but suddenly at the same time, yes I'm sure that at the same time we both felt terrified. It wasn't the man that we thought was Sanny Wilson who killed Maureen, it was the other man, but it wasn't Maureen he felt that rage for. His rage was for Fabiana." Sally was crying by this time, Alina had tears in her eyes and she felt overwhelmed by the intensity of the memory that Sally was sharing.

Sally dried her eyes and continued, "The angry man killed me but, I should say Maureen, but he thought he was chasing Fabiana."

"I don't understand Sally," said Ronnie.

Sally began to sob, "I was wearing Fabiana's, no Maureen was wearing Fabiana's red bolero. He was after Fabiana. I don't think he meant to kill me, but I fell against a grave stone as he made a grab for me."

Alina and Ronnie looked at each other; they were both concerned because Sally kept referring to the experience as though she was Maureen.

"He dragged me into some bushes and left me there. I might not have died if he had gone for help. Bastard!"

Gus wrapped Sally in his arms and comforted her, while Ronnie fetched a bottle of brandy, poured some into a crystal glass and offered it to Sally. "Would anyone one else like a glass?" Everyone nodded their agreement.

"Fabiana has blanked this out; I wonder if she did know that there were two men, and I wonder who the angry man was. Do you think she knew who it was? I have a terrible thought, but for the moment, I will keep it to myself. I think the next step with Fabiana is to see if she will agree to another regression, but this time I will question her about the things that you have seen Sally."

Chapter 38

Mrs Semple was an old woman who had nothing much to do with her time. Most days she sat by her window, twitching her curtains and watching the comings and goings of her neighbours. Various health conditions kept her housebound, but a little bit of gossip added highlights to an otherwise dull and boring life. She lived a couple of doors along from Fabiana and she knew exactly who she was. Before she moved to her present house in the Shaws, she had lived in Cardonald, not far from Fabiana and her family.

She had always been a busybody, delighting in spreading stories, and sometimes she was even responsible for creating them. These days, she didn't sleep well, and would often sit by her window in the dark. Day or night, if a car stopped, she would peer out to see who it was and she would make notes in her little book. She didn't have any friends, and her only family lived in England. The daily visit from her care worker was her only real sounding board for the latest piece of empty gossip. Her care worker, Sheila by name, who was in her thirties, didn't like Mrs Semple, but, dedicated to her profession; she did provide Mrs Semple with good care, not letting her feelings interfere with her job. Mrs Semple often irritated her; she was a very negative woman and never had a good word to say about anyone so most of the time, when Mrs Semple was badmouthing this neighbour or that one, Sheila gave her a deaf ear, in other words ignored her ranting until one day, she tuned in to the end of a conversation.

"I'm sorry Mrs Semple, what was that you were saying?"

"Ah'm talkin' about that lassie next door, fancy airs and graces, Fabiana they call her. Ah'm saying she's getting about mair' than usual. Ah've seen two different cars pickin' her up."

"Did you say something about murder?"

Mrs Semple turned away from the window and stared at Sheila, giving her a hard stony look, "If yi' paid attention tae me when Ah'm talkin' yi' would have heard me the first time."

She muttered under her breath about young folk and ignoramuses while Sheila pursed her lips together to prevent herself from answering. Sheila carried on counting out the day's medication and placing the pills in Mrs Semple's special dish. Mrs Semple liked things done a certain way, her way. Sheila waited; she knew that Mrs Semple would relay the story again, and she did.

"Ah'm saying, Ah lived in Cardonald when she was just a lassie and I remember that she hung aboot wi' a wee blond pal, that was murdered."

"How do you know she was murdered?"

"Well she disappeared and was never seen again. Ah'm tellin' yi' she was murdered. Look, there's wan o' them cars just stoppin'."

Sheila went to the window and saw Alina getting out of her car and approaching Fabiana's path. "She's probably having her cards read."

"Whit' dae yi' mean havin' her cards read."

"That's Alina; she's quite a well known psychic. I've been to her before."

"Here they come, here they come," said Mrs Semple and Sheila went back to the window.

Mrs Semple continued her observations, "She's no havin' her cards read in the car."

Sheila wondered about that for a moment too. Most psychics would have you come to them, or would come to the client and spend an hour or so, but she thought it was unusual for a psychic to arrive several times and pick up a client. Still, it was none of her business and none of Mrs Semple's business either.

At the end of her shift Sheila was glad to get home, she kicked off her shoes as soon as she went through her front door, ran upstairs peeling off her uniform, then went into the bathroom to wash and put on her house jammies. Downstairs, she put the kettle on for a cup of tea and while she waited for it to boil, she took a casserole from the fridge that she had prepared and cooked the night before, and put it in the oven to reheat. She took her tea through to her lounge and sat down to relax before her husband of ten years came home. Derek worked for one of the daily newspapers and more often than not, he was home on time, but there would be an occasional phone call to let her know that he would be late because of some breaking story.

"So how was your day today, was Mrs Semple in fine form as usual?" he said laughing, as they sat having dinner.

Sheila was grinning as she answered, "She drives me nuts, but I have to be sympathetic as it must be awful for her, no nearby family, stuck in her house every day watching other people going about their business."

"What did she have to gossip about today?"

"Today she was ranting about a neighbour and something about a missing girl that she claims was murdered."

His reporters instincts kicked in, "What was she saying?"

"She has seen her getting picked up and dropped off over the past couple of days and it's given her something new to rant about. It was a bit odd though."

"Odd, why?"

"Because she got picked up while I was there by that psychic Alina. I said she was probably getting her cards read."

He puzzled over her reply for a moment and then he asked, "She just picks her up and then later drops her off?"

"Yes."

"She doesn't go in and read her cards?"

"It doesn't look like that."

"So what's the neighbour's name?"

"Let me think, ends in Ana, yes Fabiana."

"Very interesting."

"Oh don't tell me," laughed Sheila, "you smell a story."

"That's just how it happens, Sheila."

After dinner, he helped Sheila carry plates through to the kitchen and while she stacked the dishes in the washer, he went upstairs to his cubbyhole of an office. Sheila was engrossed in a TV programme that she had recorded the night before, but he was searching the internet for any reference to Alina or the name Fabiana.

The hair on the back of his neck stood up and he shifted in his chair as he caught the reference to Alina on the Google search page.

'Psychic locates body in the Clyde. 100 year old mystery solved.'

He knew that name rang a bell and he began to recall the coverage. He scrolled through the pages and clicked on all the relevant links and even some that were irrelevant, and then he sent a text message to his boss.

"Wont b in 2morrow. Following a lead."

He went downstairs to join Sheila on the sofa, but he didn't mention to Sheila what he had discovered or what he was planning to do the next day.

Alina drove to Pollokshaws to pick up Fabiana the following morning. She had spoken to her on the phone, asking her if she was prepared to have one more session, possibly the last one, and Fabiana had agreed. She had no idea that Mrs Semple was watching from her window. She didn't even know of Mrs Semple's existence, but worse, much worse was the fact that Sheila's husband Derek, the newspaper reporter, was parked on the other side of the road, taking photographs of her as she went to meet Fabiana. He took more shots of her opening the car door for Fabiana and then driving away. He followed them talking to himself as he drove.

"Now what's going on here? Whatever it is, I will find out."

They didn't have far to go and Derek realised that she was turning into the apartments at the Waterfront. He knew from the records that he had seen during his Google search, and from research that he, as a reporter had access to, that Alina was taking Fabiana to her home.

"Now let's see what happens next," he muttered as he concealed his car out of sight, close enough to watch.

Chapter 39

Alina took Fabiana's jacket and hung it on the coat stand in the hall beside her own. Ronnie, Gus and Sally were sitting in the lounge waiting. They had lit the candles in the four corners and some incense was smoking on a holder. The atmosphere was quiet, if a little tense.

Fabiana sat on the sofa and Alina asked her, "How do you feel Fabiana?"

"I'm scared."

"Can you tell me why you are scared?"

"I think it's my fault that Maureen is missing, dead." She was crying now and Alina waited to see if she would say anything else. After a while, Fabiana said. "He was after me."

"Who was after you Fabiana?"

"I don't know, I don't know," she sobbed.

"Why do you think this person was after you?"

Alina sat close beside her, leant in towards her and held her hand, "Why do you think it was meant to be you?"

"We had swopped clothes."

Alina waited and Fabiana continued, "He thought Maureen was me, don't you see, he thought Maureen was me."

Everyone could see Fabiana's distress and they all felt her emotional pain as it surfaced.

"Who was it Fabiana?"

"I don't know."

"Ok, let's stop for a bit."

Sally took Fabiana through to the guest bathroom so that she could freshen up. "Just take a few minutes to yourself Fabiana, you are doing really well. We will get to the bottom of this."

Fabiana looked at Sally and said, "There is part of me that doesn't want to get to the bottom of this and I don't know why."

Sally nodded and said, "I'll leave you to it."

When Fabiana returned Alina broached the subject that she knew would probably put Fabiana in a state of alarm.

"Fabiana, would you be prepared to take us to the last place that you were with Maureen."

Fabiana just leaned forward, her elbows on her knees and her hands covering her face. "Oh God, oh God, oh God," she murmured. "Oh please don't ask me to do this?"

"We won't force you to do anything you don't want to do Fabiana, but if you want us to help you we need to go to that place. You will only have to take us there once; the rest will be up to us. You won't have to ever go there again."

"What choice do you have Fabiana? You are, and have been, struggling with this for years and you have the chance now to help us to find out what happened to Maureen. This is a choice that you have to make for your own peace of mind and for Maureen's sake too," said Sally.

Fabiana sat up and looked at Sally, "You're right, I know you're right. I'm just so scared Sally." She looked at Alina and said, "When do you want to go there?"

"Now," said Alina.

"Are we all going?"

"No just you, Ronnie and I."

Fabiana stood up, "Ok, but you have to promise me if I get too scared we will stop right away."

"I promise you Fabiana. If you want to turn back at any time, we will."

Derek was watching from his vantage point and he saw Alina coming out first, followed by Fabiana and then Ronnie. He picked up his camera from the seat beside him and began to take pictures as they all got into Ronnie's Range Rover. Derek was pleased with himself that he had parked where he could see them coming out. He had been expecting Alina's car, and would have missed them if he had been parked somewhere else. They turned out of the estate and headed along Paisley Road West with Derek following them. "Turn to the right here and it's just over the hill," said Fabiana as they reached Berryknowes Road.

She was leaning forward watching the road as they reached the top of a hill and then said, "If you can park near those flats there's a short cut, or at least there used to be. Ronnie turned into a side street and parked. He and Alina turned and looked at Fabiana in the back seat, "Are you ready Fabiana?"

"Yes, it's now or never, but I feel sick to my stomach."

Derek drove past them as they got out their vehicle. He drove to the end of the road, watching them in his rear view mirror and he saw them turning to the left. He pulled a U-turn, tucked his car in behind another parked car and ran after them. As he reached the corner, he saw them on the other side of the street cutting through between a big house and some flats. He waited for a moment, afraid they might see him, and then he too crossed the road and followed, risking another picture as he hurried after them. He saw them turning off the path and into the graveyard.

"Mostly we came in this way so that no one would see us because I wasn't allowed to go into the graveyard," said Fabiana.

The well-worn track was obviously a short cut and was still a favourite place for kids to play games, and perhaps scare each other. Fabiana gripped Alina's hand, and Alina knew that they must have been getting close to where they sat so long ago.

Suddenly they came to the spot and Fabiana exclaimed, "Oh God!" and turning her back to the others, promptly threw up. She was retching and heaving and tears were running down her face, which was as white as chalk. Alina gave her some tissues. Fabiana settled her emotions and said, "This is where we sat, I am sure of it."

"Ok, that's enough for now; we will go back to the car and drop you off at home. I think we can manage the rest ourselves, but if we need you we will call you."

Derek watched the entire episode, taking more pictures. He ran ahead of them and jumped into his car, his adrenalin pumping with excitement. He knew he was onto something. As the small group came down the path Derek was waiting ready to follow. He watched them getting into the Range Rover and, allowing a couple of cars to pass he pulled out and followed them. He recognised the route and assumed that they were taking Fabiana home so he kept his distance and pulled in at the end of the street to watch where they would go next.

He saw them dropping Fabiana off, and as they passed him, he pulled out and followed once more. He felt certain that they would be heading back to the apartments on the waterfront and when they turned off to do so, he continued straight on before turning once more and heading back to his desk at the newspaper office.

Chapter 40

When Ronnie, Alina and Fabiana left to go to the graveyard, Gus and Sally sat in the apartment in silence, each waiting for the other to speak. Gus was developing strong feelings for Sally and he knew that she was warming to him, but he felt as though he had to be very careful in any approach he made to her. While he was thinking of her, she was thinking of him. She realised that she liked him and was afraid that perhaps she more than liked him. She didn't want to go there. Her last relationship broke her in two, and she did not want to experience anything like that ever again. In her mind, it was better to be single. Her train of thought was interrupted when Gus spoke to her, "We should do something."

"Like what?"

"I don't know, just something, instead of sitting in silence. Why don't we go for a walk, its chilly, but nice outside?"

"I'll go next door and ask Nessie if we can take Jock."

"Let's do that then."

Auntie Nessie was pleased to see Gus and Sally and delighted that, on one hand they were going for a walk together, and on the other that they were taking Jock who loved getting out. Gus had spoken to Nessie on one of the nights that he had stayed over at her apartment. She was trying to encourage a match that she had said was, 'a match made in Heaven' but Gus told her that there wasn't much chance of that happening.

As she watched them from her window, she had a smile on her face and she muttered to herself "Aye, they make a lovely couple." Gus picked up a stick for Jock and the little terrier was jumping up and down, excited and anxious to carry it. Both Sally and Gus laughed at Jock's antics as they played with him. Gus looked at Sally, and all he could think was how beautiful she was; he was beguiled by her.

"What?" Sally said.

"Nothing."

"You're staring at me."

"No I'm not, I'm just looking."

"Staring."

"Ok then, staring."

"Well stop it, you are making me nervous."

"You are just so goddamn beautiful Sally, how can you tell me not to stare at you."

"Oh, now you are just being ridiculous Gus, and if you don't stop I am turning back."

Just at that moment, Gus tripped over Jock and trying to avoid hurting the little dog, he overbalanced and landed on the ground with a thump. He sat there looking up at Sally who was bent double laughing. Jock was cavorting around him as he sat on the ground with a look of dismay on his face. Jock was jumping all over him yipping and trying to lick his face, "Aw Heck," he said, and just lay down on the ground and let the little dog have his way. He was laughing too and Sally felt love swell in her heart as she watched him acting the fool, a grown man on the ground just to please a little dog. When Gus looked up Sally had tears rolling down her face, but she wasn't laughing. Gus jumped up, "What's wrong Sally, what's wrong?"

"Nothing."

He wrapped his arms around her, but she kept her elbows tucked in and her arms between them.

"Stop hugging me," she vented.

Gus stepped back shocked and surprised, his hands, palms facing forward in a gesture of surrender, his emotions going from compassion to confusion. He looked at her for a moment and as she returned his gaze, all she could see in his face was sadness and rejection. "I'm sorry Sally," he said and turned to walk back to the apartment.

"No!" she yelled at his retreating back, "Gus," she called after him and ran to him catching him by the arm. He turned and looked at her as she said, "I'm so sorry Gus, really sorry, I keep hurting you and I don't know how to stop. Please don't go."

"You confuse me Sally, you confuse me, you beguile me, and you drive me nuts. You are my first thought in the morning and my last thought at night. I don't know what to do to prove to you that I will not hurt you. I have strong feelings for you Sally, and I don't think that they will ever go away."

"I'm scared Gus, so scared."

"I am not the man who hurt you Sally."

"No Gus, I know that you're not, but I am the woman that the hurt shaped."

"Give me a chance to prove myself to you Sally, that's all I ask for, just give me a chance. Be my girl, let me take you out, let me hold you in my arms and kiss you, love you."

"Ok."

"What! Did you say ok?" Gus yelled laughing, picking her up in his arms and swinging her around in a circle. They were both laughing, though Sally was laughing and crying at the same time. Jock had to get in on the act too and he was dancing around and under them. Aunt Nessie watched for them returning, and wasn't slow to notice that this time they walked hand in hand, and were looking at each other and chatting as young couple do.

By the time Ronnie and Alina returned, Gus and Sally were sitting on the sofa holding hands. Both of them looked happy, and Alina knew in her very bones that they had been kissing. She and Ronnie looked at each other sending an unspoken message to each other, and they both laughed. Gus and Sally were eager to hear about everything and they all settled down and talked about the experience with Fabiana, discussing the next step.

"I'd like to go back there tomorrow, just you and me Sally, see if we can pick up any vibrations, sensations."

"Yeah, ok, I'm up for that."

Ronnie smiled over at Gus, "We have a free day then, I feel left out, what about you Gus."

Gus laughed knowing fine well that Ronnie wasn't feeling that way at all. "I'm sure we'll find something to occupy ourselves with," was his response.

Later, after dinner, they opened a couple of bottles of wine and enjoyed a sociable evening. They decided that they needed to put a little distance between the investigation and themselves, to let their minds settle and their thoughts and instincts to appear. They laughed and joked, shared experiences, and told stories, always staying away from the subject of Fabiana. Ronnie and Alina saw the difference in Sally and Gus and they were both happy about this change for different reasons. Ronnie knew that Gus had feelings for Sally, but really didn't think that he would conquer her resistance, and in fact had told him so. Alina was happy because Sally was happy, and her happiness could be seen in her face. They were all little tipsy when it came to bedtime and Ronnie and Alina headed off to bed leaving Gus and Sally to say their goodnights. Gus kissed Sally passionately as they stood by her bedroom door. She thought her heart would explode and she had butterflies in her stomach. She giggled, "I swear I can see colours when you kiss me like that."

He kissed her once more, "Good night Witch," he said and left to go across to Nessie's. She leaned against her bedroom door and grinned.

Chapter 41

The next morning they all slept later than usual, but the incessant ringing of the telephone woke everyone up. In her sleep, Alina had heard the phone, but in her half awakened mind it became part of her dream. It was only when she felt Ronnie stir that she suddenly came awake.

"Oh what time is it?"

"Its nine thirty," replied Ronnie.

Sally was emerging from her room at the same time as Ronnie and Alina and together they went through to the lounge. Alina looked at her telephone, which had stopped ringing by the time they got there. The message light was flashing, indicating four messages. She pressed the play button and the machine announced the first message.

"Alina its Nancy, call me back as soon as you get this."

Then the second message played out, the automated voice saying, 'Message two.'

There was silence and then whoever the caller was cleared the line.

'Message three.'

"Alina, Bob Graham here, can you pick up," there was a pause as he waited and then his voice on the tape said, "Call me back as soon as you get this message. It's important."

'Message four.'

"Alina its Nancy, call me as soon as you can."

Alina, Ronnie, and Sally looked at each other, alarmed and wondering what was going on. Alina didn't know who to call first, but she was worried that maybe something had happened to Davy. As she reached for the phone to call Nancy, it rang. She picked it up.

"Hello."

"Oh thank God Alina. Have you seen the papers?"

"No, what's happened?"

"Alina, you are all over them, get Ronnie to go out and get them and then call me back please."

"Ok, ok."

Alarm showed in Alina's face and in her voice as she turned to Ronnie, "Apparently I am all over the newspapers; would you go and get them Ronnie."

He was already dashing to the bedroom to change from his pyjamas and was out the door within a few minutes while Alina was answering yet another call.

"Its Bob, I'm coming right over," he said and hung up.

"My Goddess Alina what's happened?"

"I don't know Sally, but my stomach is churning."

They went into the kitchen and were putting the kettle on for coffee when the doorbell rang.

"I'll go," said Sally.

Gus was standing there with a grin on his face, pleased that Sally was the first one he saw, but his smile fell away half way through his greeting, "Good morning Witch. Sally, what's wrong?"

"I don't know yet, we are waiting for Ronnie to come back with newspapers. The phone has been bouncing off the wall and apparently Alina is all over the newspapers."

"Oh my God, is it about Fabiana, is she ok?"

"She's in the kitchen and she is obviously worried."

"Maybe it's something good."

"Well, there has just been a call from Bob Graham and he is coming right over."

"Oh, that doesn't sound good."

They went through to the kitchen and Gus went up to Alina and put his arms around her, "Don't worry until you know what it's all about Alina."

"Ronnie will be back in a minute and then we will know what it is." No sooner had she said the words than Ronnie arrived back with several newspapers under his arms.

"Is it bad?"

"It's worse than bad Alina."

He spread the newspapers on the dining table and the headlines were stark.

PSYCHIC ON THE SEARCH AGAIN

COLD CASE PSYCHIC SEARCHES

WILL PSYCHIC FIND MISSING GIRL

Worse than the headlines were the photographs; Fabiana and Alina getting into Ronnie's Range Rover, Fabiana and Alina standing in the graveyard, a clear shot of Fabiana, obviously distressed, another of Alina comforting Fabiana.

"Oh my Goddess! Who has done this, who took these pictures?" exclaimed Alina, as she paced, agitated, worried, and angry."

The door entry buzzer sounded and Sally ran to the window. "It's Bob, I'll get the door."

Bob was plainly angry when he came in. "Can you explain this?"

"Are you serious? Are you suggesting that I had something to do with this?" Alina responded angrily.

"Now hold on a minute, don't you dare come in here and make accusations. This kind of publicity is the last thing any of us would want, and we made that clear to you from the beginning. Look to your place first, who have you told?" Ronnie said.

"You're right, I apologise. I shouldn't have jumped to conclusions. Fabiana is in a terrible state. Reporters have been calling and arriving at her door. If it's any consolation, she doesn't think that it came from you."

The situation calmed somewhat as they sat down around the table to discuss this new development.

"I should call Fabiana but I don't imagine that she will be picking the phone up," said Alina.

"No, she won't, but she will probably want to hear from you or speak to you. If you have a note pad handy, I will write down her email address. You can email her."

Alina handed Bob her note pad and Bob jotted down the email address. "I've added mine too so that you can keep in touch. Look I'm sorry again for jumping to conclusions, but I will get to the source of this," he said, before leaving to go and see Fabiana.

After he left Alina called Nancy and Davy to explain what it was all about.

"Who do you think leaked the story Alina?"

"I have honestly no idea Nancy."

"Davy and I were so worried when we saw the newspaper, we just couldn't believe it. Having to go through the same publicity again, it's just terrible. We know how much you hate that. What will you do now, will you stop searching."

"No I can't do that, I made a promise to Fabiana and I have other reasons for wanting to continue."

"What other reasons sweetheart?"

"Oh, you will think I am silly."

"I would never think that Alina, never."

"It's the curse Nancy, I don't want Mary's curse to touch my family again, and I have made a promise that I will do whatever I can to help people. I think helping people will help to break the curse."

"Well you go right ahead dear, and do whatever it takes to make you feel safe."

When Alina ended the call to Nancy she returned to sit with the others.

"I'm not up on these things, but do you remember when we did the Runes?"

Everyone turned and looked at Gus.

"Go on," said Alina.

"Ronnie asked if anyone would come to any harm, and the card said communication."

"Yes, that's right, he choose Ansur."

"Well, doesn't it follow that newspapers would come under communication?"

"You're absolutely right Gus, well remembered. The cards also said that we would find her and I want to keep going."

"I'm in," said Gus.

"Me too," said Sally.

"We're all in Alina," said Ronnie.

"Can I ask a personal question Alina?"

"Of course you can Gus."

"Can I ask what you were talking about when you mentioned a curse to Nancy?"

"A long time ago one of my ancestors, that I knew nothing about, put a curse on someone. Rumour, or story handed down says that Mary, my ancestor, put a curse on an American politician who was an ambassador or some such thing to Scotland. They say that every generation has been touched by this curse."

"Why did she curse him?"

"Her baby was very sick and she was trying to get to the hospital, the snow thick on the ground, when this carriage came past. The driver slowed to stop, but the man in the back yelled at him to go on."

"Oh my God," interjected Gus "Is that the…?"

"Don't say the name; whatever you do don't say the name. It's bad luck. The rumour says that if anyone mentions the name, the curse awakens and strikes."

"But how does that affect you Alina?"

"It's the threefold rule Gus, first do no harm."

She recited it to Gus.

"Bide the Wiccan Law you must,

In perfect love and perfect trust

These words the Wiccan Rede fulfil,

If it harms none, do what you will

What you send forth comes back to thee,

Ever mind the law of three

Follow this with mind and heart

Merry meet and merry part."

It has touched every generation of the American's family, but it has touched every generation of Mary's family too, and I am one of Mary's descendants. I have to try to do something to break the curse because I don't want it reflecting on children that Ronnie and I might have, or children that our children have."

The hair was standing up on the back of Gus's neck as he listened to Alina.

"What can you do to break it?"

"To be honest with you, I don't really know, but I have made an oath to the Goddess to do my best to help those in need, and I have asked the Goddess to protect me and mine, and to break the cycle of this curse."

"How did you find out about all that Alina?"

"Oh my Goddess, that's a story for a long evening, but suffice to say that Mary began to appear to me, first in my dreams and then in spirit. We all worked together, Ronnie, Sally, and I, and we managed to find out why she was appearing. We used every means possible to analyse her reasons. She wanted her granddaughter's body found. She had disappeared one hundred years ago; she was in the Clyde, just outside really. I'm surprised that Ronnie hasn't mentioned all this to you."

"Close your mouth Gus, you look like a fish," said Sally laughing, and then she stood up and taking him by the hand she said, "Come on let's go and get Jock, and take him for a walk. Alina needs some time to herself and I will tell you the whole story." She turned to Alina and asked her "Do you want to tell Nessie what's going on, or would you like me to do it while I'm there?"

"I'd appreciate that Sally, but tell her I'll see her later too. If this is anything like the last time the press will be all over the place."

Chapter 42

Sally and Gus were pleased and relieved to see that all was quiet outside when they left the apartments. They had spoken to Nessie, explaining what had been happening, and how these events had come about. Nessie reassured them that she wouldn't be put out, no matter what happened, and she told Sally to let Alina and Ronnie know that they shouldn't worry.

Once more, they were walking hand in hand and when Gus looked at Sally, he saw that she was grinning.

"Share," he said.

"Share what?"

"You are smiling to yourself."

"I'm happy, and this feels so, well so normal. You and I walking along like this, holding each other's hands and a wee dog skipping along beside us."

"It is normal Sally."

"Yes I suppose, but not usually for me."

"I want to spend time with you Sally. I want to share things with you, ordinary things, and the things that you do too. I want to be with you and make you happy."

"I would like that Gus, I really would. It's going to take some getting used to. My parents will be shocked."

"What about; that you have a boyfriend?"

"Exactly, they have never seen me with anyone since, well, since before."

"Will you trust me enough to tell me about it?"

"I will, I promise."

"That's good enough for me."

"What about you Gus, have you left a trail of broken hearts in Australia."

Gus laughed, a deep hearty laugh, "No, I made sure that I didn't get involved with anyone. I worked hard, saved hard and sometimes played hard too, but the women I socialised with were all part of the larger group of expats. Most of them were young married couples trying to make a better life. Admittedly, one or two of them tried to play matchmaker, but I knew that I was coming home and I didn't want the complication of having to choose. I knew that it would have been hard for me, or anyone that I did commit to, to struggle between staying in Australia and moving to Scotland, so I enjoyed myself, but stayed unattached. Now that I have come home and I have found you Sally, I feel as though an empty space in my heart has been filled."

These words, spoken with such sincerity, stopped Sally in her tracks, and she stood staring up at Gus. He was unaware of the effect that his words had on her and she knew in that single moment that she was head over heels in love with him.

"You're staring at me now Sally."

She had a lump in her throat as she tried to reply, and she had to swallow first before she spoke. "I think that must be the loveliest thing that anyone has ever said to me."

"What, what did I say?"

"That an empty space in your heart has been filled."

"That's how I feel Sally, you have filled it. I didn't know it was empty until you filled it. It's how I felt when I came home from Australia and saw my parents. I knew I had missed them, but I had no idea how much until I saw them again. Looking at you Sally is like coming home."

Tears were streaming down Sally's face now as Gus placed his arms around her and held her close, kissing her hair, breathing in the scent of her.

"I love you Sally."

He kissed her lips tenderly, "Make a life with me Sally and I promise I will make you happy."

"It's too quick Gus."

"When you know, you know. Will you give me a chance to prove it too you."

"Yes Gus, I will."

"That's all I need to know Sally. Come on; let's head back, you're shivering."

Sally laughed, "I'm in shock Gus."

"Well don't be, because this is the start of our life together as a couple."

They weren't aware of the traffic passing to and fro or the people who, like themselves, were out enjoying the fresh winter air, but those who saw them could see a couple, very much in love and happy with each other's company, even the little terrier looked happy. It came as a shock to them when they turned towards the apartments to see the press gathered outside.

"What the heck!" Gus exclaimed.

"Oh my Goddess it's the papers, quick, we'll go in the back way," said Sally as she pulled Gus around.

They hurried to the back entrance and Sally took out her phone to text Alina.

'Have you seen the press outside? We are at the back door.'

She sent her message and a second or so later, they heard the beep indicating that the latch was unlocked. Just as they were pushing the door, one of the reporters who had spotted them came running towards them and yelled, "Hey!"

Gus ushered Sally in quickly and closed the door behind them.

"Did he recognise you Sally?"

"No not at all. I don't even know that he would recognise me. He is probably just trying to get in by any means."

As they entered the apartment, they saw that Alina and Ronnie were packing.

"What's happening?" asked Gus.

"I've got a house ready to let, I was hanging on to it to see what you were going to do Gus, just in case you might want to rent it, but by the looks of things we might all be moving in to get away from this nonsense outside."

"Cool, all of us?"

"There's room for the four of us."

"Ok, I'll get my bag ready."

"Me too," said Sally hurrying to her room.

They had the bags ready at the front door when Alina said, "How are we going to get out without them fallowing us?"

"Will they know my car?"

"I don't know Sally," said Alina.

"Why don't Gus and I take the bags down and put them in the car, and if no one pays us any attention we will call you and you can follow. My car is parked at the back door anyway, so they won't see you."

"What happens if they do know your car and crowd around you?"

"We will go for a drive into town, try to lose them and play it by ear. You and Ronnie wait till you hear from us."

"My stomach is churning," said Alina.

"Mine too but the Goddess will be with us," and then she looked at Gus and said, "Ready Gus?"

Alina said, "I will stand at the window for a few moments to draw their attention."

"Good idea," said Gus, "Let's go."

Together they took the four bags down the stairs and out the back door. The reporter was standing nearby, but he didn't associate Sally and Gus with the scoop.

"Uh oh," said Gus.

"I know, I see him, what will we do?"

"Call Alina and tell them to stay put for the moment."

"Then what?"

Gus grinned and sighed, shaking his head, "I have no idea."

They drove a short distance along Paisley Road West and pulled over beside a row of shops.

"We need a diversion," said Gus. As he sat there thinking and gazing ahead he noticed a hairdressing salon. "I've got an idea, it might be stupid but it's the only thing I can come up with."

"What is it then?"

"Where can we get a wig?"

"A wig, do you mean for a disguise? That might work; we could make her look like an old woman."

Sally turned the car around heading for Salon Services, a wholesale hairdressing supplies shop, which she knew was just over the Jamaica Bridge. She pulled into their car park and went inside.

"I'm looking for a wig, for display purposes," she said to the sales assistant.

"Do you have an account with us?"

"No not yet, I am just renovating a new salon and want to put something in the window to advertise when the salon will be opened. I hope to get all my fittings here once all the structural work has been completed."

Recognising the possibility of major sales to come, the assistant began to show the range of wigs, encouraging her to choose modern shades and styles.

"Hmm, I'm aiming at an older market," Sally lied.

"What about this range?"

Sally was delighted and chose a grey wig with tinted blue highlights, an older style with a modern twist. "This one will be perfect," she said, and paid for her purchase.

"I have put a trade account application form in the bag with your receipt, just fill it out and hand it in the next time you are passing. Good luck with your salon."

"Thank you," said Sally hurrying out of the shop.

"Got it," she said as she got into the car grinning. "Now what?"

"Drop me off at a café; I'll wait while you go back for Alina. You can pretend you are helping an old woman to your car and maybe Ronnie could leave first, and then you could pick him up on the way past."

"That's a great idea," Sally said, "I'm sure we passed a café on Paisley Road West, I'll drop you there and pick you up in a bit."

"Sounds good to me."

Sally sent a text to Alina to let her know that she was on the way back so that Alina would be ready to let her in. When she arrived back she explained the plan to Ronnie and Alina.

"I'll leave now, I know where that café is so I'll meet Gus there, but if there are any problems, call me on my mobile and I'll come back immediately." Ronnie kissed Alina tenderly before he left.

"Do you think Nessie has a walking stick?" Sally asked.

"Let's go and ask her."

The girls crossed the hallway to Nessie's home and when she opened the door to Alina wearing the new wig, she laughed aloud.

"My goodness girl, what have you done?"

They explained the plan and Nessie was really enthusiastic about helping.

"Yes, I've got the very stick, and you can wear my old tweed coat, it's too old fashioned for me; I don't know why I bought it, but there you go, it has a good use after all."

Alina put the coat on and Nessie fussed with fastening it and adjusting the wig. "Now let me see you walking."

Alina walked across the room and turned to look at Nessie and Sally.

"That will never do, you walk like a young woman Alina. Bring your shoulders down and your head forward and limp a little." Alina and Sally were laughing as Nessie took the stick from Alina and demonstrated.

Alina tried again.

"That's it, that's much better."

"Oh my Goddess!" Sally exclaimed and then laughing she said, "You look just like an old woman."

Aunt Nessie fussed with the girls hugging them and encouraging them. "Now go and don't look round if you see anyone. Keep your head down and feel the pain, remember you're an old woman."

The girls thanked Nessie and made their way out to the back car park. Alina sent a text to Ronnie to let him know that they were safely in the car and on their way, and when they reached the café the men were waiting outside for them. They laughed as they caught sight of Alina. "Don't say a word," warned Alina who felt ridiculous in her disguise.

"Where to?" Sally asked.

"Go back over the Jamaica Bridge and turn left onto the Broomielaw," said Ronnie while trying to keep a straight face.

In spite of the funny side of things, they were vigilant on the journey, and they were relieved that no one appeared to be following them.

Chapter 43

As they approached the apartments at Lancefield Quay Ronnie said, "Turn left into this car park Sally."

The South facing apartment was on the second floor overlooking the Clyde on the opposite bank from Riverview Drive where Ronnie and Alina lived.

"Oh my Goddess, is this where your flat is Ronnie? I have always admired these from Alina's balcony, I love the way the frontage is shaped. I always think the shape of them looks like a cruise liner, you know the way the windows and balconies are tiered, and I can't wait to get inside."

"If you like the outside you'll love the inside Sally, Alina has not been here yet either. This is one of my favourite letting homes; I have been holding on to it to see what your plans were Gus. If you want a base here, it's yours."

"Appreciate that Ronnie, once we get past all this, you and I can have a chat about some ideas that I have."

Sally drove up to the secure parking entrance and Ronnie keyed the remote control allowing them into the designated space that Ronnie pointed out to her. Both Sally and Alina were excited to see the apartment for the first time, and they made their way upstairs followed by Ronnie and Gus carrying the luggage.

"Oh Ronnie, this is so lovely," said Alina as they entered the reception hall. She leaned over and kissed him on the lips. "I am so proud of you."

Sally was in too much of hurry to stop and offer compliments. She was hurrying through to see the view from the conservatory and the balcony which overlooked the River. "We can see right across to Riverview, Alina look," she said laughing. Dropping the bags in the sitting room, Gus walked out to join Sally. "This is truly wonderful Sally. I can see us sitting here of an evening, looking out over the Clyde and enjoying a glass of wine."

"Us?" Sally responded in surprise.

"Yes us, why not? You heard what Ronnie said, if he is serious about renting this to me I could happily base myself here, but it would be even better if you were here with me too." They were leaning on the balcony rail, the cool breeze on their faces, Sally taking on board the offer that Gus had just made. Suddenly she grinned and the words tumbled out of her mouth before she could even think about refusing, "Yes, I'm in. I would love to stay here with you," then she had a second thought and trying to cover her embarrassment she continued, "Oh sorry do you mean as in a flat mate, I mean using both rooms, oh gosh, I'm mortified."

Gus put his head back and laughed aloud and then he grabbed her in his arms and said, "I don't want a flat mate Sally I want a partner." He took her hand and headed through to the lounge where Alina and Ronnie were standing.

"We'll take it," said Gus.

"We? As in both of you together?"

"Yes, together, as a couple."

Ronnie grinned at his best friend and said "When you make up your mind, you don't waste any time." He stepped towards him; they shook hands and gave each other a typical man hug, shoulder touching shoulder. Alina and Sally gravitated together and gave each other proper hugs, body touching body, arms around each other, and they both had tears in their eyes. "I'm so happy for you Sally," said Alina.

"Me too," giggled Sally wiping a tear from her cheek.

"Come on, let's go and see what the bedrooms look like Sally." Alina held Sally's hand as they went to investigate the two double bedrooms. Both bedrooms had ensuite bathrooms with separate glazed shower cubicles and there was an additional guest washroom.

"This is fantastic Sally, the conservatory and balcony stretches all the way along the front of the house. You can step out first thing in the morning and watch everyone else hurrying to and fro while you relax and enjoy your coffee."

"I love it," said Sally, and then on a more serious note, "I'm nervous."

"You don't need to be nervous Sally, Gus is a lovely man; he won't let you down, I have a good feeling about this. Come on, let's put the kitchen to good use and find a kettle."

Alina wasn't surprised to find that there was a set of matching storage jars with tea, coffee, and sugar on one of the worktops.

"Someone will have to go for milk," Alina called through to the men.

"There are sachets of coffee creamer in the cupboard above the kettle, we can use them till we go shopping," Ronnie said, as he came through to the kitchen and began to open the appropriate cupboards for cups and creamers and the drawers for spoons.

"Oh my Goddess, the fridge is full of stuff. I must phone Nessie and ask her to take the perishables to her house and use them up if she can."

"It's all in hand Alina, no need, I have spoken to her, but give Nancy and Davy a call and let them know that we are here for the time being. When I think of it though, Nessie has probably already done that," he laughed, knowing that his aunt was as sharp as a tack and would already have thought of that.

Alina asked, "What about bed linen?"

"Two starter sets of everything in the hall cupboard," answered Ronnie.

Sally and Alina made eyes at each other, "He's so blinking organised," laughed Alina, "he thinks of everything."

Mischievously, Sally said, "Oh no, I have forgotten shampoo."

"In the bathroom, cupboard under the sink," Ronnie answered. He turned and looked at Sally and Alina as they both burst out laughing.

"What? I hate it when people come to view and open cupboards and there is nothing to see so I put things in them to give them so that they get a lived-in feeling."

He looked at Gus and Gus looked back at him, every bit as mystified at the women laughing. They both shrugged and Ronnie shook his head and said, "Women; come on Gus, let's get out of here. We'll go and get some food and let the women unpack and sort things out."

The beds were dressed with just the ornate day covers, so after the men left, the girls made up the beds before unpacking their bags and toiletries. When they were finished, Alina fetched her workbox and began to set out her candles and incense, pentacle, athame and dishes for salt and water. She always had a little container of salt in her workbox and while she set that out Sally took the small water pitcher through to the kitchen to fill it. When everything was in place they each went to their chosen bedrooms and used the ensuite bathroom to wash their hands and face and mentally prepare to cast their circle when the men returned. Alina took an incense stick, lit it and carried it through the house, entering each room, allowing the smoke to spiral around the doors and windows.

Shortly after finishing her task the men returned; Ronnie smelling the Nag Champa incense turned and looked at Gus and said with a contented sigh, "We're home."

After putting away the shopping they gathered in the lounge.

Gus asked, "What are we doing?"

"We are doing a simple ritual to bless the house and keep us safe, don't worry we will guide you."

Chapter 44

Alina was standing at the coffee table in the centre of the room, which was set up as an altar. She lit the altar candle and then guided Gus to stand at the North quarter representing earth. Sally took up her position at the West representing water, opposite Gus, while Ronnie stood in the South representing fire and Alina moved to her position in the East. They all stood silently for a few minutes and then Alina took up the taper from the altar, lit it, and returned to the East lighting the candle and saying in a clear voice, *"Here do I bring into the East light and air to illuminate this temple and bring it the breath of life."*

She moved to the South and handed the taper to Ronnie who lit the South candle saying, *"Here do I bring into the South light and fire to illuminate this temple and bring it warmth"*

He moved to the West and handed the taper to Sally. Taking the taper, she lit the West candle saying, *"Here do I bring into the West light and water to illuminate this temple and wash it clean."*

Sally continued on to the North and whispering instructions in his ear, offered the taper to Gus who took it, lit the North Candle and said, *"Here do I bring into the North light and earth to illuminate this temple and build it in strength."*

Alina raised her right arm, and focused her energy for a few moments then drew the sign of a pentacle in the air above her head. She pointed her finger to the ground at her feet and began to walk from the East to the West drawing the circle line reciting her opening, *"This circle line I do prepare let no one enter should they dare, and if they dare and if they must, let it be in perfect love and perfect trust."*

Alina returned to the centre of the circle with Ronnie. They raised their arms high in a gesture of salutation and Alina said, *"We call upon the guardians of the watchtowers to watch over us and guide us."*

Ronnie continued with, *"The air that we breathe, the fire that motivates us, the water that nourishes us and gives us life and the earth that supports us in every way."*

Alina responded with, *"May the Lord, the Lady and the Great Spirit guide and protect us."*

Returning to their own places, all four stood with their heads bowed in silent prayer for a few moments and then Alina stepped once more into the centre of the circle and began to recite in verse the words that she had prepared for the occasion.

"Bless this house in which we bide

Keep us safe for we must hide

Let none who sees us give a care

Until we finish what we must share

A refuge for us this home will be

Prying eyes will never see

To help another, this work we do

And we will share it two by two

We ask The Lady high above

To bless our wishes with light and love

Keep us safe and from harms' way

Grant our wishes on this day

We ask this from Goddesses three

And it harm none so mote it be."

Alina beckoned the others to come to the centre of the circle, and lifting the chalice that she had placed on the altar earlier she held it forward for Ronnie to fill it with water from the pitcher. Sally stepped forward and raised her right arm high, concentrating on building the energy and then she placed her index finger in the water and said, *"Salt is life, here is life, blessed be without strife."* She stirred the salted water three times and then she indicated to Gus to do the same. Feeling a bit self conscious, but eager to participate, Gus raised his right arm and closed his eyes to mimic what he had seen Sally doing and he was amazed to feel the energy building and flowing through his veins. For a moment he glanced at Sally and then he put his finger in the water, stirred three times and repeated the invocation, *"Salt is life, here is life, blessed be without strife."* He felt empowered by the experience and glanced at Alina who nodded her approval before performing the same exercise saying once more, *"Salt is life, here is life, blessed be without strife."* Finally, Ronnie placed his finger in the water and he said *"Salt is life, here is life, sacred be without strife."* He placed the chalice on the altar and they each returned to their positions, once more standing in quiet contemplation.

Alina, once more stepped into the circle, joined by Ronnie and they took it in turns to give thanks to the Lord and Lady and the Guardians of the Watchtowers for their blessings saying,

"Take for your use Eastern Watchtower any powers of air that have not been used."

"Take for your use Southern Watchtower any powers of fire that have not been used."

"Take for your use Western Watchtower any powers of water that have not been used."

"Take for your use Northern Watchtower any powers of earth that have not been used."

Alina announced that the circle was now open, but the work would continue. She and Sally took the chalice filled with consecrated water and sprinkled the blend around the perimeter of every room.

When they had cleared everything away they sat down to chat and Gus was eager to talk.

"That was amazing; I really felt the energy flowing though I must admit I did not expect that. It makes me feel as though I have been going around half asleep, unaware of the possibilities if you are open to the energies that are around."

"Welcome to our world Gus," said Alina, while the others laughed at his amazement.

"You will get used to it Gus, but it will never cease to amaze you," said Ronnie.

"I feel energised, raring to go. I feel as though I need to do something, anything," responded Gus.

"Really!" said Sally, "Well you can make the dinner tonight." She was laughing as he replied, "Sure no problem, I'm on it."

As good as his word, Gus prepared them a meal; he and Ronnie shut themselves in the kitchen and shared the task of preparing salads, crushing garlic to make garlic bread and grilling steaks while Alina and Sally chatted over a glass of wine in the conservatory.

It was a beautiful evening and the air was crisp and clear as they sat and watched the city life. Alina was relaxed, but Sally was pretending to be. She was sitting with one leg crossed over the other, but her foot was tapping restlessly.

"Are you anxious about something Sally?" Alina asked.

"I'm worried about tonight, well maybe not so much worried as a bit nervous." For a moment, Alina couldn't think what she was talking about, and then she realised that Sally would be sharing a bed with Gus.

Alina laughed, "When the time comes you won't be, so stop worrying."

"Yeah, I suppose you are right. Anyway what's our next step in the search Alina?"

"Tomorrow you and I to the cemetery I think and take our dowsers with us."

"Surely you are not thinking of dowsing for a body in the graveyard."

"I am, but I have an idea, I'm going to ask Bob if he will ask Fabiana to let us borrow Maureen's pendant. We might be able to pick up some vibrations from it.

I don't think the press are likely to follow him so I will ask him to meet us at the Bellahouston Hotel."

"That's a brilliant idea, Alina."

"Right ladies, dinner is served," announced Gus as he and Ronnie carried the food through to join them in the conservatory.

Just as they finished eating, Alina's mobile phone announced the arrival of a text message. She opened it and began to read and then put her hand to her mouth in a gesture of concern.

"What is it Alina?" Gus asked immediately.

"She handed the phone to him and he read the message aloud, **"Leave well alone or you could end up in the ground too."**

"Oh my Goddess!" exclaimed Sally.

"Where the heck did that come from, who sent that?" asked Gus.

"Unknown caller," said Ronnie shaking his head, "but it could only have come from the person responsible for Maureen's disappearance, the killer, and plainly, he's seen the newspapers headlines."

Alina had visibly paled and Sally tried to comfort her by holding her hand.

"I don't care who it is, I won't be stopped."

"Maybe it's a crank," said Sally hopefully.

"Where did they get your number Alina?"

"I'm a professional Psychic Gus; my numbers are all over the internet." She paused and then said with a sad shrug, "I'm not hard to find, let's just ignore it."

"No I don't think you should ignore it," said Ronnie. He was pacing about the room now, working things out in his mind. He continued "It's not so much where did someone get your number, but who would go to the bother, and how did they know what you were doing? It can only be the killer. Who else would know that Maureen was 'in the ground' if not her killer?"

Alina leaned forward covering her face with her hands while Sally jumped up saying "Oh mercy, what are we going to do?"

Resigned, Alina sat up straight and said, "I have made a promise and I will keep to it. You don't have to come tomorrow Sally, but I'm still going."

"Where are you going tomorrow?" Gus and Ronnie said at the same time.

"The cemetery," answered Sally.

"We're all going then," said Ronnie.

Chapter 45

He skulked about the graveyard looking for Alina, but someone else was watching him, while he watched for her. He tried to pretend he was just reading the gravestones, but the other man recognised him. They were both older now but he knew him and knew why he was there. He knew he was there to stop anyone from finding out what he had done all those years ago. In that small area, there were two men; one who had good intentions, while the other only thought of himself and feared the consequences of his past misdeed. One would go to any lengths necessary to hide the truth, the other was as determined to stop him from harming anyone else.

Sanny Wilson had spent months in hospital recovering from brain surgery, and months more learning to walk and talk. Memories were scarce and in the first few months, he found it hard to differentiate between memories and bad dreams. As time passed, he began to recall some of the things that he had done and he was ashamed. Because of his shame, he put these things to the back of his mind and refused to acknowledge them or dwell on them.

Now after all these years, having seen the newspaper article about Alina and Fabiana, he thought about these things again. The more he thought about them, the more he dreamt. It had only been a few days since he saw the first article. He went back out to the local shop and bought several newspapers, devouring every piece of information and reading up on the story.

His life was so different now, his Mother passed long ago; he was holding down a steady job as a delivery driver, and he had a flat in Pollokshields. He no longer suffered from the agonising headaches and no longer tormented the young girls in Cardonald. He cringed with horror if he allowed that thought to enter his mind. He kept to himself, minding his own business and he had no friends.

He paced up and down in his small flat letting the memories come. *"Could he have done something, should he have done something"* he tortured himself with random accusations and feelings of guilt. He looked at Fabiana's photograph in the newspaper, head down looking sad, forlorn, and troubled. Even though she was older he could see the child in her face. She should have been beautiful; instead she looked withdrawn and older than her years. He thought that he couldn't change the past, but he could maybe do something about the future, and that's when he decided to take some time off and revisit his past.

First, he walked down Kingsland Drive, past his old house. He shed a tear as he thought of his old Mother and how his illness had affected him and the consequences of it had affected her. The hair stood on the back of his neck as he crossed Berryknowes Road and went through the cemetery gates. He felt sick with contempt for his old self as he wandered some of the paths that he used to take. That's when he saw him, the other man, much older now, but he was sure it was him. Then he verbally, mentally, tortured himself again *"What if he was wrong; what if he wasn't recalling actual events, but the makings of a nightmare, but if that was the case, why would he recognise the man now?"*

He watched him for a bit, even passing close by him, and he knew, deep in his heart, he knew. As he continued to walk in the opposite direction, he realised that this was no manifestation of a nightmare; he was looking at the man who killed that wee girl. He vomited where he stood and he wished that things could have been so different.

Enveloped in his own rage, the other man paid him no heed; he was too busy thinking, worrying, and anxiously trying to figure out what to do next. *"That damn psychic and her, Fabiana, she was always trouble. Why couldn't she just have left well alone?"* he thought to himself angrily.

"I'll put a stop to this. If I can just get the chance to get my hands on her…" he muttered.

He thought back to those days when he still had a family but his temper had chased everyone away. *"They deserved everything they got."* He thought to himself *"He was better off on his own "* For a moment, he remembered the times when people smiled when they met him in the street. No one talked to him now and he didn't talk to them either. His temper had etched his face showing him to be a gruff angry old man. He lived in the same house he had lived in all his life, but the neighbours were different now. Young families surrounded him and they had noisy children. He alienated himself by complaining about the children playing. In fact he complained about everything; even though he didn't maintain his garden, he complained about cats peeing in it, he complained about dogs barking, cars parking, all he ever did was complain. Some neighbours were suspicious that he had poisoned their cats, but they couldn't prove anything. When he had words with anyone, or took a dislike, he made his neighbours feel vulnerable. His neighbours watched out for each other, probably because of his behaviour, and they talked about him creeping around gardens, up to no good, when the owners were out. He was a horrible old man, no one had a good word to say about him and he didn't care.

Sanny watched him, the old man; he looked dirty, unkempt, and he looked mean. Sanny felt sick as he worried about what the man would do. He followed him at a distance and saw him leaving through the cemetery gates and crossing the road over to Queensland Drive, and he realised that the man still lived in the same house. For a moment, flashbacks overwhelmed him and he had to stop and steady his breathing. His heart was pounding in his chest and perspiration was running down his back, making his shirt stick to his skin. He continued to follow and as he had thought, he saw the man going into the same house. He looked at the house on his way past. His memory of it was of a clean well-kept garden, and bright clean windows, but now the windows were dirty and the garden overgrown. The well-maintained neighbouring houses accentuated the neglect. He remembered with disgust how, years ago, he had watched this street, to catch sight of Fabiana and Maureen. While he remembered, a lump formed in his throat and almost choked him. He let the tears of shame, humiliation and regret fall, and he made a promise to himself, to Fabiana, and to Maureen, that he would stop this man from doing any further harm. He made his way home and the first thing he did was open his laptop and switch it on. He opened his browser and in the search bar he typed 'Psychic Alina.' There were several listings, but he found the contact details that he was looking for. His next search was for internet cafés and he found a listing for one not too far from his home. He made his way there, and took up a position where he wouldn't be overseen by other users or any cameras. He took a note from his pocket and read Alina's email address, then copied it into the new email before tying his message all in capitals.

"YOU ARE IN GREAT DANGER – BE CAREFUL"

He sat looking at it for a second or two and then he clicked 'High Priority' above the address bar and then 'Send'.

Chapter 46

"I think you should give Bob a ring and let him know about this. Apart from anything else, he should know about this, so that he can keep an eye on Fabiana," said Ronnie.

"Yes, I suppose you are right, I hadn't thought about that side of things, I suppose she could be in danger too," replied Alina.

Ronnie made the call to Bob who told him that he would go and see Fabiana first and then he would call round to Riverview.

"That's the thing Bob, we've moved. We are keeping a low profile, as far as we can, until this is done. I don't want the press following anyone attached to the story being followed here."

"I'm a cop Ronnie, I won't bring my car and I'll make sure that I'm not followed. Give me the address."

Ronnie recited the address to him and Bob told him that he would see them later.

"I'm not happy about this proposed visit to the cemetery tomorrow," Ronnie said to Gus

"I don't blame you; I'm not in favour of it either. What can we do about it though? What about suggesting to Alina to postpone the search till after the wedding?"

"Are you serious? That would be like a red rag to a bull, Alina is not easily moved once she has made her mind up about certain things," replied Ronnie laughing aloud.

"Really, she seems to be very laid back, understanding, and easy to talk to."

"Yes she is, but she is also a product of a previous relationship in which she was bullied and manipulated. Alina is a law unto herself when she has made up her mind, but give credit where credit is due; she is all of those things that you mentioned and much more. She is my better half and she brings out the best in me."

Gus was quiet for a moment, thinking about what Ronnie had said.

"Penny for them," said Ronnie.

"I was just remembering something that Sally had said about being the woman that a past relationship had formed. Its true isn't it; we are our life experiences all rolled into who we are in the current moment."

"That's very deep for you Gus," said Ronnie surprised by Gus's insight.

"Its hanging around with you guys," he laughed and then continued, "it makes you think. I'm in love with Sally."

Ronnie laughed, "Tell me something I don't know."

"I mean really in love, the 'I want to spend the rest of my life with you' kind of love. Last night, holding her loving her, I felt for the first time in my life that I was at one with another human being; it's as though she is in my soul. No she is my soul, she's my Goddess."

Ronnie laughed again and patted his good friend on the back.

"Yep, she's the one, so what are you going to do about it?"

"Marry her," answered Gus.

"Is someone else getting married?" Alina asked as she came through from the kitchen with Sally following behind. Ronnie made big eyes at Alina, letting her know not to say any more, as Sally asked, "Who's getting married?"

"We are," said Alina, catching on immediately.

"I'm just going to check emails, I'll be through in a minute," said Alina. Ronnie had set up a temporary office space in the master bedroom and her PC was already on. She sat down at the little work space and opened Windows Live Mail and then clicked on the send and receive icon. She watched as seven messages came flooding in. Two of them went straight to her delete folder; the other five needed her attention. She responded to them one by one, some were general enquiries about her services, one was a question about numerology and finally she came to the last one, and when she clicked on it her heart began to thump.

"YOU ARE IN GREAT DANGER – BE CAREFUL"

She sat there for a moment looking at, not believing what she was reading. Then she clicked on the word 'From' in the inbox. There was no name, just a series of numbers; then she right clicked on the numbers and a window dropped down. She moved the mouse down to the bottom to properties and clicked on that. A new window opened offering her the choice of 'General' or 'Details' she clicked on details and then 'Message Source'. A new window opened showing all the information about the email. There were numerous numbers and codes followed by the actual message, but she wasn't able to identify very much from her search.

She was sitting there staring at the screen when Ronnie came through smiling, "Your coffee is getting cold." He saw that there was something wrong by the way she was sitting. "Alina, what's wrong," he said with concern as he approached her. "Print that out, we'll show it to Bob when he gets here," he said. He put his hand on her elbow, "Come on." She stood and melted into his arms and cried, and he held her close stroking her hair and wishing that she didn't have to go through this.

"I know you won't stop babe, but if this gets too much for you, no one will blame you or think any less of you if you do."

She went through to the ensuite bathroom and splashed cold water on her face and Ronnie waited by her side, stroking her hair when she had finished. "Come on, we should show this to the others."

They took the printed email through to the conservatory where Sally and Gus were chatting. Ronnie handed the email to Gus and Sally leaned over to read it with him.

"This isn't from the same person, the tone is different. The first one is a direct threat. This one is more like a warning or advice from someone else. In the beginning when all this took place, there were two men. This has got to be the same two men?"

They were studying the email and its message properties when Bob arrived.

"Sorry, it took me a little longer than it should have, but I was being careful. I jumped on the subway for one stop, and then on again before I got off at Saint Enoch's. It's only a twenty-minute walk from here. I cut through a few lanes and I promise, no one followed me," he laughed, and then he looked at the others and continued, "What's the story?"

Ronnie handed him the printed email and he watched Bob as he stood there reading it.

"Can I take this? I'll give it to one of the IT guys and see if they can glean any more info from it and we might be lucky enough to get an ID from security cameras."

"I know who sent the email. It could only have been Sanny Wilson, but if you question him, stop him, then we might never find Maureen's killer or her body. You started this Bob; you brought this to me, you brought Fabiana to me, you wanted me to solve this mystery, and now you are talking about taking this email to the IT people to get an image. All I am asking is that you protect Fabiana while this is going on and leave us to solve the mystery."

Alina's determination surprised Bob; he looked at the others, and it was obvious that they stood with her and had the same opinion.

"Fair enough," he said as he handed the printed email back to Alina.

"Thank you, Bob."

"Well I won't keep you. I am heading over to Fabiana's just to make sure that she knows where we are at."

Chapter 47

After breakfast the following morning, they piled into Sally's car and drove towards the Craigton Cemetery.

"There is another entrance to the cemetery off Paisley Road West at Mosspark, I think we should go in that way and then at least we will be able to see if anyone is around rather, than going in from Berryknowes Road. What do you think?" Alina asked.

"Good idea," said Ronnie.

"Keep me right with directions please Alina," answered Sally.

"Over the bridge and turn right Sally, and then it's a straight road. We go past Riverview and it's not much further on than that. I will let you know when it's time to turn off."

From time to time, they looked over their shoulders, making sure that they weren't being followed, but no one was about that looked suspicious.

"Indicate right Sally and turn in at the next opening. I'm sure there is an entrance down at the bottom of this street."

Sure enough, as they reached the bottom of the drive they could see the rear gates leading through to the graveyard.

"Should I drive in, the gates are open, or should I park?"

"It might be better to park the car Sally, just in case they shut the gates and we can't get out," said Alina, and then she said, "I think we should split up and go in two and two."

"Why?" asked Ronnie.

"I really don't know, I just think we should."

"Ok, you and me together and Gus with Sally. We will head straight for their last meeting place and Gus and Sally, you two should circle around and see if anyone looks out of place. Do you know how to get there from here Sally?"

"Yes I can get us there; at least I think I can."

The two couples split up going right and left but ultimately heading for the other end of the graveyard that was accessible by the shortcut at Berryknowes road. It was very quiet apart from council workers that Gus and Sally could see from the direction that they had taken.

Ronnie and Alina were quite near the area that they were aiming for when they saw and old man wearing an overcoat and hat and carrying a small bunch of flowers. He knelt as they passed as though he was praying at a loved one's grave. Out of respect, they turned their heads away and did not stare at him, but Alina had a bad feeling. She should have trusted her instincts, but she put that feeling down to the fact that they were approaching the last place that Fabiana saw Maureen.

They caught sight of Sally and Gus approaching from the other direction, passing someone wearing dark jeans and a dark fleece jacket. "Did you see him, did you see him?" asked an agitated Sally, carrying flowers, as she and Gus hurried up to them.

"The old man with the coat and hat on," she replied.

"Calm down Sally, he was laying flowers on a grave," Alina answered.

"Yeah, that's what you were meant to think, but after you passed he stood and stared at both of you, and then he threw these flowers to one side, and hurried away when he saw us."

"You stay here with the girls Ronnie, I will take a scout around and have a look for him," said Gus, and with that he took off at a sprint to see where the old man had gone.

They continued on to the place where Fabiana and Maureen played. When they reached the spot Ronnie asked, "What now?"

"This is a really stupid idea, I did think we should dowse, but now that I'm here I realise that even if I get a positive reading, there is no way that the police are going to start digging up in the graveyard without concrete evidence. Let's go home."

Gus met them on the way down. "No sign of him, are we done? Did you find something?"

"Stupid idea!" exclaimed Alina angrily as she stomped ahead. She was shaking her head and muttering as Sally ran to catch up with her. Gus and Ronnie followed behind exchanging glances, the kind they make when they don't know how to handle a woman who is angry with herself.

Sally kept quiet and let Alina rant under her breath when suddenly she stopped, grasped Alina's arm and said "Wait, do you feel that?"

Alina stopped and looked at her, and then she too began to sense a change, stillness, coolness in the air. The men felt it too, stopped behind Alina and Sally, and waited.

"There's a presence," said Sally.

"It's Mary, I know her presence," and just as Alina was saying the words Mary appeared about thirty yards ahead of them. They stood and stared and then as quickly as she had appeared, she was gone again.

"Did you see her?" Sally asked. Ronnie and Alina nodded in agreement, but Gus was bewildered, "What, where, who, what did you see."

Sally moved to him and took his hand and said, "It was Mary."

"What? Do you mean Mary, the ghost?"

"Yes."

"Damn, I wish I had seen that." Sally squeezed his hand affectionately as she stood there watching the spot where Mary had appeared. "Damn," he said in a whisper.

Sally leaned into him and whispered, "You will be able to." He leaned down and kissed the top of her head.

Ronnie took Alina by the hand, "Let's go and put a marker on that spot where Mary stood. You never know, it might be important, we might need it later."

Everyone jumped when Alina's phone beeped a message. She looked at the caller display, with Ronnie looking at it too, and they saw the words, unknown caller.

Alina opened the message and read it aloud, "He is watching you. Be careful."

The hair stood on the back of their necks and goose bumps tingled on their arms as they looked around, the men adopting positions of protection to look after their women.

"Let's get the hell out of here. I don't want anything happening while Alina and Sally are here," said Ronnie.

"I agree," said Gus placing a protective arm around Sally.

"We can't go straight back to Lancefield in case whoever it is has a car and follows us," said Alina.

"Let's go wedding shopping, that will be enough to put anyone off following us. What do you need Alina?" Sally laughed.

Alina smiled, not really feeling it, but not wanting to disappoint Sally she said, "Shoes."

"Yeah, shoe shopping," grinned Sally, doing her very best to lift Alina's mood.

Ronnie and Gus drew eyes at each other and Ronnie said, "Shoe shopping it is then."

They drove into the city, found a place to park the car and set off walking.

Alina found exactly what she wanted in the first shop; a delicate heeled strappy shoe in electric blue. There were only two straps, studded with tiny star shaped diamante, holding the shoe on and these sparkled as she moved her feet while she was trying them on.

"Alina they are perfect," said Sally.

"They are aren't they," smiled Alina while the men just looked puzzled at how happy the women were over a pair of shoes.

"Will you be able to walk in them Alina?" Gus asked.

"I'll carry her if she can't," said Ronnie and they all laughed.

With the serious mood broken, they went for lunch before returning to Lancefield.

Chapter 48

Bob came over in the early evening to discuss the events from earlier that day. After looking at the text, he asked, "What's your thought on this Alina?"

"Taking the reports from the case files and everything else that has been happening I, well we, think that the threatening message came from the killer, though we don't know who that is, but the other messages we think are from Sanny Wilson. They suspected him and cleared him, but he must have been there. He must have seen the killer."

"That was out thoughts too, but he was in hospital for a long time after Maureen went missing and when he was recovering he didn't have any memory of the events of that day. It could be that all this press coverage has rekindled his memories."

"Are you any closer to knowing where Maureen can be found?"

They all looked at each other, wondering what Bob's reaction would be to hearing that a ghost had shown them something.

"Tell him," said Ronnie.

Alina took a deep breath and composed herself. She told him everything that had happened from the time they entered the graveyard, and how just as she was giving up, Mary appeared.

Bob took on board all that Alina was saying and he didn't look too surprised or taken aback by Alina's revelation. He expected strange developments because he had read up on the case notes that Alina had been involved in before when she had located Rosa's remains.

"Did she show you where Maureen is?"

"Well no, not exactly, but I think where she stood is the spot."

"That's good enough for me Alina, thanks, can you show me where it is."

"I will, I don't want Alina or Sally going back there. When do you want to go?" Ronnie said.

"If you think you can find it in the dark, now would be as good a time as any."

Ronnie stood up, "Let's go, we left a marker at the spot," he said.

"What did you leave to mark the spot?"

Ronnie laughed and said, "The flowers he threw away, Sally picked them up."

Bob laughed aloud at his answer and said, "They might come in handy."

"We'll go in off Berryknowes Road Bob, I expect the main gates will be closed and it's nearer Berryknowes Road anyway." He turned and spoke to Gus, "I'm pretty certain that the girls are safe here, but you'll stand guard Gus?"

"Consider me on guard duty Ronnie," Gus laughed.

After Ronnie and Bob left, Gus spoke to Sally, "When we were at the graveyard you said I would be able to see ghosts?"

"Spirit," Sally said.

"Ok, spirit."

"Yes."

"How? When?"

"When we teach you," said Sally grinning.

"Don't torment him Sally, show him," said Alina.

Sally got up from the chair she had been sitting on, and walked over to Gus who was sitting on the sofa. She stood in front of him and spread her arms a little way to each side, took a deep breath and composed herself. She was concentrating on her energy field and building her aura. When she was ready she said to him, "What can you see?"

"You," he said.

"Keep looking at me but try to look beyond me."

"What do you see?"

"You." He shrugged his shoulders, mystified.

Sally walked over to him, put the thumb of her right hand on his forehead between his eyebrows, and chanted a few words under her breath. She raised and lowered her thumb a few times while she chanted and then returned to her position standing once more with her arms spread slightly apart.

"What do you see Gus? Look at me, but beyond and through me. Allow your focus to distort a little."

Sally focused on her energy as Gus tried to understand what she was talking about and then he said suddenly, "Oh my God Sally, you are glowing."

"I'm not glowing; you are just looking at my aura."

"That's amazing. Why don't I know about this? Why doesn't everyone know about this?"

"Because they have lost touch with their spirituality, and are too busy running about trying to earn more money so that they can spend even more money on material things," said Alina.

"Will I see ghosts, I mean spirits now?"

"No, but this is a good start Gus. Practice this often and try to be in the moment instead of letting it pass you by, if you are blessed and if there is a need for spirit to be around you, then you will see spirit," said Alina.

As Ronnie guided Bob to the spot where they saw Mary's ghost, he described the old man they had seen and asked Bob what he intended to do.

"I will talk to the bosses and see if they will sanction a trap. If they agree I will set up a few wireless cameras and a few guys dressed as council workmen. With any luck, we will get him. I'm hopeful that this old man is the killer and that he will tell us where Maureen is."

"What do we need to do Bob?"

"Absolutely nothing, leave the rest to us and who knows this could be over sooner than we think."

They left the flowers where they lay and made their way back to Bob's car on Berryknowes Road. No one was watching them. Bob dropped Ronnie off at Lancefield Quay telling him that he would be in touch soon.

"Wait, wait, stand there a minute," Gus said to Ronnie as he came back in. Ronnie stood looking at Gus and then he asked, "What are you doing?" The girls were falling over themselves laughing as Gus peered, this way and that.

"I'm trying to see your aura."

Ronnie shook his hand, "You've got this bad Gus. Keep working at it."

"Can you do it Ronnie?"

"Yes, but I've had years of practice and you will find that it is easier when you are not trying so hard. The girls are taking the Mickey right now and having a good laugh watching you try."

Gus turned and looked at Sally and Alina who were trying hard to look innocent.

"Did you make all that up?"

"No not at all, but it was fun watching you Gus. Stop trying now, it will happen when you least expect it."

"Whatever you do, don't ask them how to push someone over without touching them."

"Aw you're kidding me now," said Gus.

Ronnie shook his head and Gus looked at the girls, "Really?"

They both nodded at him.

"You do it," Sally said to Alina.

"No you do it, he's your guy."

Sally asked Gus to stand in the middle of the room with his back to her and his eyes closed. She made sure that Ronnie was standing close to him, just in case he fell over. "Ok I am going to pull you forward with nothing more than my energy and your energy."

She had demonstrated this phenomenon at shows on a few occasions, and to avoid the possibility of autosuggestion, if she said she was going to pull, she would always push instead.

"Are you ready Gus?"

"Yes," he said.

Sally stood still, on the opposite side of the room, and consciously raised her energy. When she felt that she was ready, in one swift movement, she raised both her hands and pushed. As soon as she did, Gus began to teeter, and then suddenly he was swinging his arms trying to regain his balance while Ronnie made a quick move to catch him.

He quickly opened his eyes in amazement. "I can't believe that you just did that. I can't believe that you can DO that," he said with emphasis.

Sally was laughing smugly, "You wouldn't like to see what I can do when I'm angry," she joked.

Chapter 49

For the next week or so, Alina and Sally concentrated on their plans for their Yule celebrations. They planned to perform a circle at midnight on Yule Eve and then have a day of festivities with all the family. Everyone would be welcome to arrive from first thing in the morning, and there would be food and drink all day long. Her cousin Joanna would be there with her family; Gus and Sally's parents were coming, Auntie Nessie, Nancy and Davy made up the rest of the group.

They were sitting having breakfast when Alina's mobile rang. The assigned tone let everyone know that it was Bob and they were hopeful that he might have positive news. Alina, nervous about what Bob would have to say, handed her phone to Ronnie.

"Hi Bob, its Ronnie here."

"It's all over. I can be there in half an hour and I will let you know what's happened."

"That's great Bob, we'll see you then."

He handed the phone back to Alina. Everyone was quiet, each with his or her own thoughts. Alina was the first to speak, "Oh my Goddess I wonder what's happened, I wonder if they found Maureen."

"We'll find out soon enough," said Ronnie.

By the time Bob arrived, they had finished their meal and were sitting in the conservatory. Ronnie went to the door to let him in and saw that he had a black eye.

"That looks painful," he said taking Bob's coat and hanging it on the coat stand.

"It looks worse than it is," Bob replied.

They went through to the conservatory where everyone was waiting with baited breath.

"It's done," he said. Everyone was on the edge of their seats as Bob began to tell them what had happened. "We set up the cameras and waited and sure enough, he turned up. We watched him skulking about for a bit and then he went straight up to the grave that where you had left the flowers to mark the right one. We had taken away the flowers prior to that or he might have realised that there was something fishy going on. Anyway, he made a bolt for it and for an old man he put up quite a fight, hence the black eye. He kept screaming about you Alina, and Fabiana, how you should have minded your own business. I don't think that he would have hesitated for one minute to cause you some serious harm. We arrested him for assaulting an officer, namely me, and that gave us grounds to hold him and question him."

"Let me get you some coffee Bob."

"That would be great Alina."

Alina hurried to the kitchen and was back in a few moments with Bob's coffee. She handed it to him and sat down to hear the details.

"At first he wouldn't answer any questions, but eventually he broke down and admitted that it was an accident. His excuse was that he thought she, Maureen, was Fabiana."

"What, I don't understand," said Alina.

"He's Tony Sinclair, Fabiana's Father."

Alina stood up in horror, her hands over her mouth in shock, as she and everyone gasped.

"He had been following them, but he didn't see the girls swapping clothes so when they bolted he went after the one that he thought was his daughter. No doubt, he would have beaten her, but he said Maureen tripped and hit her head on a head stone. When he saw that she was dead, he panicked. He will spend the rest of his life inside."

"What about Maureen, did you find her?" asked Ronnie.

"Yes we did, exactly where your ghost stood. He buried her in a fresh grave on top of someone's coffin. That's not all though; Sanny Wilson turned up while we were struggling with Sinclair and he came forward and made a statement.

"What was Fabiana's reaction to all this?"

"It was dreadful, she broke down completely, but I think, in her heart, that this was something that she suspected, or even knew all along. I think it would be a good idea for you to stay here at Lancefield Quay for a while yet. A statement has been released to the press and it won't be long before they put two and two together and come looking for you."

"What about Fabiana, won't they harass her too?" Sally asked.

"I have taken her to my place," Bob said.

"Oh!" said Sally and she glanced at Alina, raising her eyebrows slightly and then she said, "Are you together? Oh I'm sorry; I shouldn't have asked that, it's none of my business."

Bob laughed and said, "I think I have always loved her and didn't know it. This has brought us together. I'll look after her."

Sally being Sally gushed and said tearfully "Oh that's so lovely, something good coming out of something bad. I'm happy for you both."

"Thanks," said Bob, a little embarrassed and then he continued, "I'll leave you now, but if there is anything you need just give me a call."

Ronnie fetched his coat and as he was putting it on he looked at them all one by one and then he said, "I don't know what to say, thank you just isn't enough, this could never have happened without all your help. Maureen will be laid to rest,

Tony Sinclair will be in jail, Fabiana will get better, and we are together. How does the words 'thank you' cover that?"

Alina and Sally stood up and went to him, they stood at each side of him and hugged and kissed him on his cheeks. He blushed, nodded at everyone and left.

They all stood looking at each other for a moment or two and then Gus said, "It's a bit of an anti-climax isn't it. Makes you feel as though you want to do something."

"Why don't we all go out for a bit?" Sally suggested.

"I have a better idea," answered Ronnie, "Why don't you and Gus go somewhere, because I have plans for my Gipsy Girl," he said hugging Alina and kissing her passionately on the lips.

"Oh, get a room you two," laughed Gus. "That's a damn fine idea. Come on Sally, let's go." Sally didn't need a second bidding; she hurried to the bedroom, ran a brush through her hair, sprayed some perfume on her neck and wrists and applied some lipstick. A quick glance in the mirror and then she grabbed her coat from the wardrobe. "Ready to go," she announced as she met Gus putting on his jacket in the hall. "We're off," he called as he took Sally's hand, gave her a quick kiss, and led her out of the door, both of them laughing.

"What plans do you have for me?" Alina asked Ronnie.

"Come and sit by me," he said, leading her through to the conservatory.

They sat facing each other Ronnie leaning toward Alina, clasping her hands in his, a serious look on his face.

"You are worrying me now Ronnie."

"The thing is, I know you like your independence and you like to make your own decisions, but ever since they recovered Rosa's remains, when you look out over the Clyde, I see sadness in you and it tears me apart. For the last year or so, while I have been looking at property for the business I have been watching for something that I thought you might like, and I have found something that might be perfect. That is if you want to move, but I would like us to have a fresh start when we are married, somewhere that we can bring our children up."

Alina put her face in her hands and began to cry.

"Oh Alina, please, don't cry; we will stay where we are if you don't want to move, I understand."

"No it's not that," she said, throwing her arms around his neck. "I love you so much Ronnie, I do want to move, but I was worried that you were happy where we were and worried too about leaving Nessie. I love my apartment, but honestly, I am sad every time I look out the window. Tell me everything; where is? When can we see it?"

"We can see it today if you like. Dan, a friend of mine owns it; he bought it as an investment and he is ready to sell it. I asked him to hold it until I had a chance to speak to you about it."

"Yes I'd love to see it, where is it?"

"Gateside, near Beith, I'll give him a call now and we can pick up the keys. Damn, the car is at Riverview."

"We can walk across the bridge; the reporters have probably all gone now anyway, at least until the next lot of stories hit the press."

Chapter 50

"Where are we going?" Sally asked as Gus hurried her along the road.

"Everywhere," he said laughing down at her.

They walked into the city and along to Argyle Street and then as they reached the Argyll Arcade he turned her in and said "It's years since I have been here, let's go in. My Mother and I came here before I went to Australia to buy a watch for my Father's birthday."

Sally had never been to the Arcade and the rows and rows of upmarket jewellers' shops and by the high domed glass roof impressed her.

They looked in several shop windows, Sally gasping at some of the stunning jewellery on display. Gus was watching her all the time, observing what drew her interest. Every time she saw a bracelet or pendant inlayed with emeralds she would gasp and say, "Look at that one."

"We'll go in here," he said.

Sally assumed that he was looking for something for his family so she wandered around aimlessly looking at all the different displays while Gus chatted to an assistant.

"Sally," he called to her, hold his hand out, smiling. She went to him and he led her through a doorway. "Sit here."

"What are you buying?"

"You'll see."

The assistant that he had been chatting to came into the small viewing room carrying several trays and began to lay them down in front of Sally. Her eyes were huge and her mouth was hanging open as she gazed at row upon row of emerald rings, diamond and emerald rings, rings that were set in rose gold, yellow gold, and platinum. Then she looked at Gus who was grinning from ear to ear. The assistant was grinning too, but all Sally could do was stare at Gus and then at the rings.

"I thought it was time you had an engagement ring Sally."

There were tears in her eyes and the assistant was shedding a tear too.

"Oh my Goddess," said Sally, "Are you serious?"

"What about this tray, do you see anything you like here?" asked the assistant.

Sally stared in wonder at the dazzling display, afraid to make a choice, not believing that this was really happening. The efficient assistant was watching her and saw that her eyes kept going back to one particular ring. She lifted it from the tray and said, "Try this one on for size," and she slipped it on to Sally's finger saying, "This is a lovely choice, seven graduated emeralds on a straight high mount set in platinum. The straight design allows the wedding band to sit snugly beside it."

It fitted perfectly and all Sally could do was sit and stare at it. Gus interrupted her reverie by asking, "Do you like this one? Would you like to try any other on?"

Sally shook her head indicating no, she couldn't speak for the lump in her throat. Gus laughed, "Does that mean no you don't want to try on any more or does that mean no, this is not the one?"

"This is the one Gus," she said.

"We'll take this one," said Gus to the assistant.

"Would you like to see wedding bands?" the assistant asked.

"Yes why not," answered Gus.

"No! Mercy me," exclaimed Sally.

"Why not?" asked Gus, "We are going to get married aren't we."

"Yes, of course, it's too much."

"Sally, nothing is too much for you." He leaned in and kissed her as the assistant went to fetch more trays. When she returned, she brought rings that would fit both Gus and Sally and they chose matching platinum Celtic design bands.

"I can't wait to get back to Lancefield to show Alina and Ronnie," said Sally.

--00--

Ronnie and Alina had walked over the bridge and retrieved the car without incident; the press were tired of waiting and had no doubt gone off to chase up other scoops. Dan was in his car waiting for them at Riverview. They shook hands as Ronnie made the introductions, "Keep them for a few days Ronnie in case you want to go back for another look. It's been nice to meet you Alina."

As they drove to Gateside, Ronnie told her what he knew of the cottage.

"It was originally two attached farm cottages. Dan bought them both when they came up for sale at the same time and he converted them into one house, but he created an adjoining door between the two, so that one could be used as a granny apartment, or for letting purposes, so there is room for Nessie or anyone else for that matter."

"I can't wait to see it."

They drove through the village and then turned off down a lane, passing low hedges either side of open fields and then she saw the property for the first time. Ronnie parked in the driveway and Alina stood outside the car looking at the cottage. Because it had been two cottages in the past, the gravel driveway had two openings, one on each side of the property, which was about sixty feet long. The white walls were freshly painted and the black painted corner stones, apexes and window frames stood out. Above the door there was a carved and varnished wooden sign with the name Myrtle Cottage etched into the wood. On either side of the main door, Alina could see Wisteria growing on the walls; Clematis grew on the other side and she knew that this would be beautiful to see in the summer. She turned her back to the house to see what view was like from the dormer windows in the roof, delighted that it overlooked fields. She wandered around the side of the house and in that moment, she fell in love with it. A large well-kept lawn spread out before her surrounded by a beech hedge; some trees were scattered here and there on the edge of the lawn and a decked area covered by a Japanese style pergola. There were no houses blocking the view at this side of the cottage either.

Ronnie was standing quietly beside her, watching her, taking in her expressions, waiting for her to give her opinion. She turned to him and moved into his arms, looked into his eyes and said, "I'm home."

Ronnie laughed with relief and disbelief, "You haven't even been inside yet."

"I don't need to be inside to know that I love it here, it's perfect."

They spent the next hour going through the house, looking at the layout of the main part of the cottage first. There were exposed stone walls, oak floors and an open feature fire place in the lounge. Dark wood beams on the ceiling gave the room character, and double windows let in plenty of light. The dining room also had an open fireplace and double windows. The huge kitchen was big enough to hold a kitchen table and it was fitted with modern units, and an Aga cooker. She wandered through the kitchen into the utility room and saw that the back door was a stable door allowing the top half to be open to let air in while the bottom half remained closed. She laughed aloud and spun around. "I love it. I love everything about it. Can we buy it?"

"I will call Dan now and tell him we are going ahead," said Ronnie. After he made the call, Ronnie told her how happy he was that she liked it because he had fallen in love with the house too.

"I can't wait to tell Sally. I am so excited and I feel as though a weight has been lifted off my shoulders."

Chapter 51

Alina and Ronnie were having coffee in the conservatory at Lancefield, making plans and deciding when they would move and what they would do about Alina's apartment at Riverside when Gus and Sally came back from their outing. They were both laughing and chatting as they came in.

"What are you two so excited about?" Alina asked.

Sally could hardly contain her excitement, she looked at Gus grinning and he looked back at her and said, "Show them."

Sally held out her left hand with pride, and Alina jumped out of her chair, taking her hand for a closer look she said, "Oh Bless, that is just perfect, and it's so you." She hugged and kissed her friend and both of them shed a tear or two. Ronnie hugged Gus and said, "This calls for a celebration, we'll have a party."

"Let's wait till everyone is here at Yule and then we'll announce it, but we could open a bottle now," Sally said grinning at Gus who produced a bottle of champagne from a carrier bag and said "Taaa Daaa!"

Ronnie went for glasses while Gus stood and opened the champagne, Sally and Alina were too busy drooling over Sally's ring. They all stood to make a toast and Ronnie, holding up his glass said, to new love, old love and forever love, here's to a long and happy life together, here's to the four of us. They touched glasses together and drank their toast and then they all happily laughed and hugged each other before sitting down to chat about what they had been doing.

Alina and Ronnie looked at each other and smiled.

"What secret have you two got?" Sally asked.

Alina was grinning from ear to ear when she replied, "We've found a house, well no, Ronnie found a house, we've been to see it and I love it."

"Yeah! Double celebration," exclaimed Sally, "Tell us all about it, have you put in an offer, where is it, when do you move?"

"Whoa, one question at a time," laughed Ronnie and then he told her everything that she needed to know.

"It's in Gateside, a little village near Beith; the offer has been made and accepted because I know the guy that is selling it and I got first refusal, and we haven't decided when we will move yet. That about covers it I think."

"Do you have a schedule, can I see what it looks like,"

Alina answered, handing her phone to Sally, "No schedule was needed because it didn't go on to the open market, but I took some pictures."

Sally and Gus looked at the photographs and they enthused over the layout, the size of the cottage and the gardens. They were still chatting about the cottage when Alina's phone started to ring. Sally handed her phone back to her, and Alina answered it with a simple hello, then she closed the phone. No sooner had she closed it than it rang again. She sighed deeply and switched her phone to mute before saying, "Reporters."

"It's started then," said Sally.

"Yes, but I am not going to let anything spoil this lovely happy time for us. I'll screen my calls later and if there are calls from family or clients, I will call them back. The worst of this should be over by the twenty first and we can enjoy Yule back at Riverview."

The girls went through to the kitchen to prepare an evening meal, both of them giggling and a little tipsy from the champagne. Alina took some steaks from the fridge and brushed them with a blend of mustard powder and Worcestershire sauce before placing them under the grill. Sally sliced mushrooms and prepared tomatoes and they chatted while throwing together a salad. Gus and Ronnie were in the conservatory chatting about property.

"I hope you don't mind, but I wanted to ask you if you had ever thought about taking on a partner, or more specifically would you consider taking me on as a partner?"

"Would I mind? I am delighted; I can't think of anyone that I would enjoy working with more than you. I was actually waiting to see what you were thinking about and then I was going to broach the subject. It looks as though we are already on the same page."

"That's great Ronnie, I have savings to invest the property business interests me, and I know we would work well together."

"Yes absolutely," Ronnie said and they shook hands and then hugged each other the way men do, shoulder to shoulder.

"It's just as well I bought a few bottles of champagne isn't it," laughed Gus as he topped up their glasses and called through to the kitchen. "We have something else to celebrate Sally, Alina, bring your glasses for a top up."

They came through asking together, "What is it, what are we celebrating."

Ronnie and Gus touched their glasses together and Ronnie said, "Gus and I are going to be working together in the property business."

"It's the Magician," said Sally.

Gus looked at her puzzled but Ronnie and Alina knew exactly what she was talking about.

"In the Tarot," Sally said, "when the Magician comes around he creates new beginnings. Where are your cards Alina?"

Alina went to her where her workbox was and came back with her tarot cards. She fanned them out on the table and everyone stood waiting,

"Go on, pick one," prompted Sally.

"Who?" Gus asked.

"Anyone, we are all experiencing this together."

Gus reached out and for a moment deliberated over which card to choose and then he pointed to one.

"Look at it then, it won't turn over by itself," laughed Sally.

Gus drew the card forward and cautiously turned it over. "Aw no way, if I didn't see this for myself I wouldn't believe it." He laid the card face up on the table, The Magician.

"See I told you," said Sally, "That's the way the cards work."

"Welcome to life as we know it," laughed Ronnie.

"You have to teach me how to read them Sally," said Gus.

"All in good time, all in good time," replied Sally.

"I'm not in favour of doing a circle when we have all been drinking, but I think it would be nice if we did one in the morning to give thanks for all these lovely things that have been happening to us," said Alina.

"I'm in," said Gus and Sally together.

"We're all in," said Ronnie.

Chapter 52

Everything was back to normal; Ronnie and Alina were home at the Riverview apartment, Gus and Sally had moved in to Lancefield Quay and most importantly, the reporters had found new stories to follow and new people to harass. Gus and Sally had already seen the new house at Gateside and looked forward to sharing odd weekends with them. Nessie had been to look at the new house too and while she loved it, she was not ready to move. She was happy where she was and didn't want to change her routine.

They had had their Yule ritual privately on the eve of Yule and now it was time to gather with their small group of friends and family. In the morning before the celebrations had begun, Alina took a little time to herself to write another letter to her parents. She shed a few tears while writing to them; telling them all about Sally and Gus's engagement, and how Gus and Ronnie were going into business together. She told them about the cottage at Gateside and its beautiful garden. When her letter was finished, she went out on the veranda and carefully removed some of the soil from the rosemary plant then she buried her letter among the roots and carefully replaced the soil.

Ronnie was waiting, knowing what she was doing, when she came back in from the veranda. He wrapped his arms around her and said, "I'm so sorry that they are not here to share this with us Alina, but in my heart I know that they are watching over us, just as my parents are too."

Everyone began to arrive around noon and pictures of the cottage were passed around to those who hadn't seen it yet. Among the guests who had been invited were Bob and Fabiana. Alina and Sally were amazed by the change in Fabiana's appearance. The tightly drawn back hair style was gone, instead her hair hung down over her shoulders in thick dark waves. It was plain to see that there was a bond between Fabiana and Bob and Alina was glad that she had trusted her instincts and invited them. She knew that Fabiana was on her own and from a brief conversation that Ronnie had with Bob, she knew that he had never married. Alina could see by the protective gestures that Bob made, holding her hand and staying close by her, that romance was in the air and in her heart she wished them well.

Nancy and Davy brought Trifle; Nessie brought home-made Chicken Liver pate and Cranberry sauce, and Sally and Gus's parents brought Mince Pies and Mulled Wine and Joanna and family brought Clootie Dumpling mad from her old family recipe. They were all mixing well with each other as Ronnie and Alina chatted about their plans to move in before the handfasting, so that they could have the wedding feast in the back garden of the new cottage. They ate good food, laughed at the lucky tokens they found in Joanna's dumpling, toasted with glasses of mulled wine and chatted nineteen to the dozen. Sally had been struggling to keep news of her engagement to herself and had discreetly hidden her ring in Gus's pocket. They had earlier planned that Ronnie would make the announcement and he winked at Sally as he stood up and clinked a spoon against his glass. Gus slipped the ring onto Sally's finger and everyone was quiet.

"We have had a lot to share and a lot to talk about today, but there is more to celebrate with everyone. Is the champagne ready Gus?" Gus nodded, he was excited and nervous; he had already met Sally's parents, and they loved him, but suddenly, he felt as though he should have spoken to Sally's Father first.

"No wait a minute, not yet," he said suddenly, and then to Sally's Father he said, "Jack, can I have a quick word?"

Sally's Father looked puzzled, but stood up anyway and followed Gus from the room.

"I have left this a bit late Jack, I should have spoken to you earlier and now I am sorry that I didn't. The thing is I am totally in love with Sally and I want her to be my wife."

Jack laughed aloud and slapped him on the back, "We already know that son, and it's as plain as the nose on your face. We will be delighted to welcome you into our family. You know we thought that Sally would never let anyone into her life, and that would have been a terrible shame. Liz and I can see how happy you make her."

Together they walked back into the room grinning at each other. Sally had no idea what that had been about, but when her Father leaned over and kissed her cheek, whispering in her ear, "I'm very proud and happy for you," she knew that Gus had told him. She looked at him sitting beside her and she had a lump in her throat and tears in her eyes.

"Now?" Ronnie said looking at Gus, and he replied nodding nervously, "Now."

Ronnie tapped his glass again and said, "I would like to announce the engagement of Sally and Gus."

Everyone clapped and cheered as Sally and Gus stood to accept hugs and kisses from everyone. Liz, Sally's Mum, was crying happily and everyone wanted to see Sally's ring.

Jack stood up and toasted them welcoming Gus into the family, and addressing Angus and Cathy, Gus's parent's, he said "And you too, now we will be family as well as neighbours."

When everything had calmed down Sally asked Gus, "Where you asking my Dad's permission?"

"Yeah, I left it a bit late didn't I?"

She threw her arms around him and kissed him, "I love you so much Gus. I didn't think that I would ever feel this way and I must be the happiest person ever."

Someone from the other side of the lounge began a cheer and everyone joined in and everyone laughed, as they kissed each other. Later, when they had all sat down to enjoy coffee someone asked when they were getting married and Sally answered, "We haven't actually talked about that."

Nessie suddenly said, "Why don't you have your handfasting on the same day as Alina and Ronnie?"

"That's a brilliant idea," said Alina, "Why don't we Sally?"

Sally stood up and went over to Alina who stood as her friend approached her. Sally put her arms around Alina and hugged her. "You are the best friend anyone could ever have Alina. That would make me very happy." They stood there together watched by everyone and wiped their tears, laughing and crying at the same time.

Ronnie and Gus looked at each other and Ronnie laughed as he said "Women," and they bumped fists together. "Looks like you are getting married at Beltane."

"The sooner the better Ronnie, the sooner the better," replied Gus.

The new year celebrations had come and gone; Sally and Gus had settled well into Lancefield Quay, Ronnie and Gus were kept busy looking at, purchasing and renovating homes to let or sell on, and Alina and Sally found time to organise their joint handfasting, but always, in the back of Alina's mind was Mary's curse. Had she done enough, did she do enough to make amends? Was it even in her power to break the curse? The first thing she did each day was her private morning ritual, and she always performed her ritual Esbat at the full moon, but the dark moon was the time that she thought would be the best time to break Mary's curse. She had a special blend of herbs that she created to help her intention; Chamomile for forgiveness, a little Rosemary to remember those who had been affected by it, and a mixture of peppers and spices, sharp in flavour or scent to dispel the negative energy. She performed these rituals alone for she believed the responsibility rested on her shoulders and still she worried. Ronnie always gave her space to do these things herself, they never discussed this, and such was the closeness of their relationship that he just understood her needs. She stood alone, the sky dark, wearing the sheer sapphire blue gown that she kept for this occasion and she recited her verse.

"A curse was sent some time ago and many did it harm

In angry words the curse was made knowing it would return

But, anger blinded common sense and warnings heeded not

For in her rage the Mither's words sadly were forgot.

With all my might and all my will those words I wish to break

And end the pain and suffering that the angry one did make

Time has passed and will again, as new days come and go

Lady hear my plea, break the curse, please make it so.

I make amends for words that should never have been sent

Ever shall I try to help others with good intent

Lady listen, hear my call, hear my honest plea

And grant my wish, please make it so, this curse no longer be.

And it harm none so mote it be"

Chapter 53

Everything was ready for the handfasting; Ronnie and Alina had already moved into Myrtle Cottage and Sally and Gus were staying in the annex until after the wedding the next day. They were having tea together when Sally asked, "Are we doing a circle tonight, can we join you?"

"Yes and of course you can join us, we'll go out into the garden later when the moon is out," replied Alina.

They choose an old tree that grew at the back of the garden. Ronnie had inlayed granite slabs at the four quarters and Alina unearthed one of the treasures that she had picked up when she toured with the Psychic Fair, it was a heavy stump of burr oak and it made a perfect altar. At the edge of each slab stood a cast iron candle holder and on each candle holder stood a pillar candle. All the tools were on the altar; incense, altar candle, a carved wooden chalice which was studded with crystals, pitcher of water, salt dish and some tapers.

They had cast the circle and each stood in their own positions, East, South, West, and North.

Alina spoke first,

"I call upon the Lord and Lady to hear our thanks and grant our blessings."

Ronnie recited his verse,

"With futures bright our love runs deep

And always in our hearts we keep

Our faith in those with whom we share

All our love and all our care"

Everyone said together, *"So mote it be.*

Sally spoke next,

"Lord and Lady high above

You have blessed our lives with light and love,

For these gifts my thanks I give

And on this path my life I'll live,"

They said together, *"So mote it be."*

Gus took a breath then,

"I've travelled over land and sea,

And home I find in front of me

My cherished love and friendships true

For that I give my thanks to you

Lord and Lady up above

I offer you my truth and love"

The others responded with *"So mote it be."*

Alina was to speak next but her head was down and tears were running down her face. All she could think about was Mary's curse and her marriage to Ronnie the next day. Would they have children? Would the curse harm her children? In her heart, she prayed, but she couldn't form the words to utter them out aloud.

No one moved; they watched her with sadness in their hearts, understanding what was in her mind without anyone speaking of it. A chill breeze moved the air and a cloud passed over the moon and still they stood, and still they waited. The cloud cleared and in the middle of the circle stood Mary. Alina looked up and gasped and Mary spoke,

A curse Ah made when Ah' should'ha known better

An' it has lived down tae the letter

Families suffered far an' wide

Includin' ours wi' whom we bide

Good deeds yi've done wi' them that care

An' noo Ah' can tell yi' the curse is nae mair

The bairns are safe an' yours will be tae

Stop worryin' lass enjoy yir day

Shut yir eyes Ah'll show yi mair

For awe yi've done tae show Ah care

Here's yer weans, Aye there be three

Jist a wee picture only yi can see

Noo dry yer eyes an' dinnae fret

There's mair' tae come an' better yet,

Enjoy yer day enjoy yer life

It's blessed now there'll be nae mair strife."

With that she was gone. Alina looked around her wondering if she was the only one who had seen the Mary's apparition, was she the only one who heard her speak? She glanced first at Ronnie and then Sally and Gus and she could see that they were all moved, they had all seen Mary. Alina stepped forward and said,

"My thank thanks I give for the life I have

For the friends and family too

My thanks I give for future and past

And the love I share with you"

As she said those words she stepped towards Ronnie and took his hand in hers.

"I make this oath, I make it now

This love will last forever

And always in my heart you'll be

Husband, friend, and lover."

Together they all said, *"So mote it be."*

They closed the circle and went inside.

"I know everyone saw that, you did, didn't you?"

Gus shook his head, "I saw that, I saw Mary and yet I can still hardly believe it, and to be honest I feel quite emotional," he laughed, but he was clearly moved.

"Did everyone hear what she said?"

They all nodded and then Sally asked, "She told you to close your eyes and see something, did you?"

Alina smiled, "Yes I did, but I don't think I am supposed to tell anyone so it will have to be my secret. Come on now let's get to bed, we have a wedding tomorrow."

They had booked the services of a registrar to come and perform the official part of their wedding ceremony, but they were doing the rest of the Handfasting by themselves. The two men were staying overnight in the annex and the girls were staying in the main part of the cottage. They laughed as they all kissed each other goodnight and went to the bedrooms that they were using.

Unbeknown to them Davy and Nancy had been meeting up with Jack Liz, and Nessie, all organised by Joanna, they were planning a surprise for the handfasting, and they were wishing each other goodnight at the same time. Joanna had given them all a CD to listen to and they had all been practising their roll in the surprise.

"They will be amazed," said Nancy "and I know that this will mean a lot to Alina especially."

"We'll pick you up at eleven Nessie, will that be early enough?"

"Och Aye, that'll be plenty of time, the Handfasting will start at three thirty. When we're all done with 'Jumping the Broomstick' then we'll eat." She threw her head back and laughed.

Chapter 54

Alina and Sally got up at six o'clock in the morning and went outside to perform their morning ritual. Sally made coffee and while they drank it they multi-tasked, preparing the garden for the wedding ceremony which was being held on the back lawn. They scattered flowers around the circle line so that their guests would know where to stand. Fourteen guests were coming; Ronnie's Auntie Nessie, Davy and Nancy, Alina's surrogate parents, Sally's parents Jack and Liz along with Gus's parents, Angus and Cathy who were travelling from Largs together. Alina's Cousin Joanna, her husband John and their daughter Rosemary with her fiancé Jed would be there too and lastly Bob and Fabiana.

Two tall pillar candleholders stood in the centre of the circle each holding white candles, which they had draped with ivy and wild flowers that they had picked from the field behind the garden. A small table sat between them and it held a thick altar candle, a pentacle, a dish of water, a small dish of salt, an incense stick and a small dish of essential oil of Rose. The most important items were the two white cords that would tie both brides' hands to their groom during the handfasting. Inside the circle, on each of the four granite slabs, stood lantern style candleholders for the small candles to be lit and placed inside them. Sally and Alina cast the circle in preparation for the ceremony, leaving an opening for the guests to enter when the ceremony was about to begin and as they finished they laid a broomstick by the opening.

Auntie Nessie was narrating the ceremony for the benefit of those who had never witnessed a handfasting and the brides were under strict instructions to leave everything to her once the circle had been cast. Alina and Sally had no idea what she was up to, but they had always thought that she was a bit of a witch anyway, so they were happy to let her do whatever it was she had planned. All they wanted to do now was to go each to their own ensuite bedrooms, relax, bathe, prepare themselves and dress for their wedding.

Davy and Nancy picked Nessie up as arranged, and the three of them loaded containers of food that Nessie and Nancy had been preparing for the event.

"Now mind that box Davy, carry it carefully for the wedding cake is inside that one," instructed Nessie. Davy scratched his head and muttered to no one in particular, "What size is that cake? How much food are we going to eat for goodness sake? It's just as well I've got a big boot."

Nancy and Nessie were too happy and excited to be concerned about what Davy thought.

"I think you've got everything Nessie but where's your nice dress and hat?"

"Oh for the love of Nora, it's still hanging behind the bedroom door, just a minute," she said hurrying back into the apartment to retrieve her outfit. She came back a few minutes later carrying a suit bag.

They made their way to Myrtle Cottage and when they arrived, they unloaded the boot of Davy's car and carried everything through to the kitchen. The wedding cake was set out on the table and they gasped when they saw it.

"My that's a bonny cake Nessie; you've done a grand job there."

Nessie had made the cake, joining two rounds together to make the shape of the figure eight in entwined circles. Rune symbols decorated the sides, and these were chosen for the gifts that Nessie wanted the couples to be blessed with; Gefu for love, Inguz for fertility, Fehu for wealth, and Othel for the home, family and integrity. Their names were iced on the tops of both circles, and random edible pink rosebuds and ivy completed the picture.

Liz and Jack with Cathy and Angus arrived at the same time, and the men were chased off to go to the annex to wait with the two Bridegrooms. Nessie and Nancy knocked on Alina's door as Liz and Cathy were knocking on Sally's door. The question was the same at both doors, "Can we come in?" and the conversations mirrored each other too, "Can I get you anything? Are you nervous? Do you have everything that you need?"

The answers given were the same too, "I'm glad you're here. No thank you, I have everything. Yes I'm really nervous."

When they women went back to the kitchen Auntie Nessie fetched two glasses and poured a brand in each of them while Nancy and Liz looked on. "It's a bit early for me said Nancy."

"Wheesht, it's for the lassies, it'll settle their nerves, purely medicinal," she said and took the glasses through to each of them. She didn't say anything to either of them; she just put a glass down beside Alina and then went through to Sally's room and put a glass down beside her. She went back into the kitchen and stood quietly, thinking, mulling something over in her mind, and then she fetched another glass and poured herself a stiff brandy. "It'll settle my nerves too."

"Oh well if you're having one, we will too, Liz?" Nancy asked.

"Go on then," said Liz and the three of them laughed and toasted each other.

Nancy had been under orders to bring rose petals and she had picked up the box of them from the florists on the way. They all went outside to scatter a path of petals for the brides to walk on and more to be scattered within the circle. "Now mind, you can only go in and out of the circle at this wee space where there are no flowers, that's the opening," said Nessie.

The next step was to prepare the decked area with chairs for everyone and tables to lay out the food, which they would bring out when the ceremony was over. When they were finished, the three women surveyed their additions, and pleased with their efforts, decided that it was time for them to go and get dressed themselves. As always, Nessie had a final word, "I'll just tell the girls that they are not to come out until we tell them."

Chapter 55

Sally finished getting ready and stood gazing at herself in the full-length mirror. The gown she had bought with Alina, originally intended as her Maid of Honour gown was now her wedding gown. The crushed velvet green gown brought out the depth of colour in her green eyes and as she turned this way and that, looking at her reflection, the colour of her dress shimmered as the light caught it. She wore her silver triple Goddess band that she used when she was performing her rituals. The silver orb depicting the moon with its two crescent moons on either side sat on her forehead and she had woven ivy and some tiny sprigs of wild flowers through the Celtic band. Her long blonde hair shone like glass as it cascaded down over her shoulders almost concealing the open back of her dress. The only other jewellery she wore was her silver pentacle necklace and her emerald ring, which she had placed on her right hand leaving her left bare for the ceremony. She tiptoed next door to Alina's room, knocked quietly and entered.

"Oh My Goddess, you are beautiful Alina."

Alina turned and looked at Sally and she smiled at her good friend, "And so are you Sally, you look radiant."

Sally walked around Alina, taking in every aspect of her, looking at the way her dress draped over her figure and how her long dark hair cascaded in luxurious waves down her back.

"No wonder Ronnie calls you his Gypsy Girl, you really are exotic and I love how you have done your eyes. He will fall over when he sees you."

"Don't make me cry, it took me ages to get my eyes right and I don't want mascara running down my face," laughed Alina, tearing up at the same time and hugging Sally close to her.

Dark blue eye shadow shimmered on Alina's eyes and faint black liner edged her eyes and tipped up at the outer corners. She was wearing ruby red lipstick and a similar silver triple Goddess headband as Sally's, but Alina had pleated two fine sections at either side of her head and she had attached ivy and small flowers to the pleats. A knock on the door announced the arrival of Liz, Nancy and Nessie and the room filled with ooh's and aah's as the women embraced and admired the two brides.

"Now I'm off out to get into position and in a bit your Father will come for you Sally, and Davy will come for you Alina, so the pair of you wait here till they do. Come on ladies, we've a handfasting to go to." All three of them left the room after kissing the brides.

A short while later Jack and Dave knocked on the bedroom door and entered. Both men stood and looked at the brides in wonder at their beauty. They each held out their arms and Alina and Sally moved into them for an emotional embrace.

"Your Mother and Father would be so proud of you Alina and my heart breaks for you that they are not here to see this day, but I'll tell you this lass, there has never been a prouder moment in my life than the moment I am in now," said Davy, his eyes full of tears.

Jack was holding Sally at arms' length, his arms on her shoulder, admiring every aspect of her, "My wee girl, my wee girl. You just take my breath away. I am so very proud of you and so is your Mother."

Davy and Alina led the way from the bedroom, down the hall and through to the double doors of the conservatory. Someone had draped a sheet over the open doors so that Alina and Sally, standing side by side, could not see what the women had planned for them. Someone drew the sheet away and both brides gasped in surprise. Their guests had lined up either side of a path of rose petals, women at one side and men at the other, leading the way to the opening of their circle where their grooms stood waiting.

Suddenly Alina's cousin John began singing in his beautiful baritone voice, Alina's heart jumped in her chest and her tears began to fall as she listened to him sing, because Joanna had told her many of the family stories and this was a song with a special significance to her Gypsy family.

"Johnny was born in a mansion doon in the County o' Clare

Rosie was born by a roadside somewhere in County Kildare

Destiny brought them together on the road to Killorglan one day

'Neath her bright tasty shawl, she was singing and she stole his young heart away.

And as he reached the chorus, everyone joined in and sang.

Meet me tonight by the campfire; come with me over the hill.

Let us be married tomorrow, please let me whisper 'I will'

What if the neighbours are talkin', who cares if yer friends stop and stare?

Ye'll be proud to be married to Rosie, Who was reared on the roads of Kildare.

As John started the second verse the guests all hummed quietly accompanying him.

Think of the parents who reared ye, think of the family name

How can ye marry a gypsy? Oh whit a terrible shame

Parents and friends stop yer pleading. Don't worry aboot my affair

For Ah've fallen in love wi' a gypsy, who was reared on the roads of Kildare?

This time around Alina and Sally knew what to expect, but it didn't stop them shedding a few more tears as everyone joined in again.

Meet me tonight by the campfire, come with me over the hill.

Let us be married tomorrow, please let me whisper 'I will'

What if the neighbours are talkin', who cares if yer friends stop and stare?

Ye'll be proud to be married to Rosie, Who was reared on the roads of Kildare.

The guests stilled their voices as John picked up the next verse

Johnny went down from his mansion, just as the sun had gone doon.

Turning his back on his kinfolk, likewise, his dear native toon

Facing the roads of old Ireland, wi' a gypsy he loved so sincere

When he came to the light of the campfire, these are the words he did hear

Then they all joined in for a resounding chorus

Meet me tonight by the campfire, come with me over the hill.

Let us be married tomorrow, please let me whisper 'I will'

What if the neighbours are talkin', who cares if yer friends stop and stare?

Ye'll be proud to be married to Rosie, Who was reared on the roads of Kildare.

As they sang the last chorus, Davy led Alina down the path followed by Sally and Jack. The guests all followed, entering the circle, forming a ring around the couples. Nessie stood behind the altar wearing a long flowing white robe, belted at the waist with a gold cord, her white hair, normally pinned up and coifed was flowing down over her shoulders. Alina was so surprised that she gasped, and looked back at Sally, who equally was wearing a surprised if not stunned look like Alina's.

Nessie looked like a High Priestess, like Mother Earth herself and she was smiling broadly, knowing by the bride's expressions that she had pleased them.

Chapter 56

The two brides stood in front of the altar, facing Nessie, their grooms stood by their brides' sides. Nessie picked up a crystal bell and rang it three times to announce the beginning of the ceremony. After a moment of silence Nessie said, "We are gathered together in this sacred space, in perfect truth, and perfect love. Let none be here except of their own free will." She turned to Alina and Ronnie and said, "It is our wish that Alina and Ronnie be blessed with a healthy life, filled with love, joy, stability and abundance for as long as they shall live."

She turned to Sally and Gus and said, "It is our wish that Sally and Gus be blessed with a healthy life, filled with love, joy, stability and abundance for as long as they shall live."

Nancy appeared at Alina's side and handed her a stick of Rose scented incense as Liz did the same to Sally and then they returned to their places.

Nessie announced, "Will the brides and grooms bless each other with the sacred element of air."

Alina and Ronnie, followed by Sally and Gus moved, to the East quarter and then Alina and Sally waved the smoke from the incense around their grooms and when they were done the men returned the blessing by waving the smoking incense stick over their brides.

As they were blessing each other, Nessie spoke saying, "Blessed be the sacred element of air. It will inspire you, motivate you and give you the breath of life."

Davy and Jack approached the men, handed them each a lit white candle, and took the incense sticks from them before laying them on the ground.

Nessie announced, "Will the grooms and brides bless each other with the sacred element of fire."

Both couples moved to the South and the grooms passed the lit candle up and down in front of their brides before handing the candles to them to return the blessing. Nessie spoke again, "Blessed be the sacred element of Fire. It will empower you both, fill your life with passion for each other, and may your love burn as powerful as this flame."

Liz and Nancy approached the brides offering them each a small dish of water as Nessie announced, "Will the brides and grooms bless each other with the sacred element of water."

Both couples moved to the West and while they were splashing the water over the grooms, Nessie spoke once more, "Blessed be the sacred element of water. It will quench your thirst and sustain you, as water is life. May it cleanse you in mind, body, and soul."

Both couples placed their dishes on the ground and moved to the North to meet Davy and Angus approaching the grooms with a small bowl containing the essential oil of Rose. The grooms dipped an index finger into the oil and anointed their bride's foreheads and then their brides anointed them. Nessie spoke while they did this. "Blessed be the sacred element of earth. It will support your homes in which, it will steady the ground beneath your feet, and it nourishes the food we plant." She waited a moment until all was quiet and then she said, "Will the brides and grooms approach the altar."

The two couples approached Nessie and stood in front of the altar. Nessie took the cord and tied Ronnie and Alina's cord to Ronnie's left wrist, and then did the same for the others tying Gus and Sally's cord to Gus's wrist. "It is our wish that the knots in this cord unite you in love, may this sacred union be blessed with love, trust, and respect for each other and may all that is positive and good be with you always. Would the grooms take the cord and place it over your brides' right wrist," said Nessie. Ronnie and Gus did so and then Nessie asked Ronnie, "Do you have a vow to make?" Ronnie nodded, took a breath and said,

"You Alina are the air that I breathe, you make the fire burn in my soul, you are the water that runs in my veins, and you are the earth beneath my feet.

Without you, I would be less than I am, and with you I am more than I thought I could be. I promise to love honour and cherish you as long as we both shall live."

"Do you have a vow to make Alina?"

"Yes, Ronnie, with you I feel safe, with you I feel loved, with you I can face any challenge or overcome any obstacle. You give me courage when I am afraid and strength when I am weak. You make me laugh when I am sad and you let me be who I am without complaint. Without you Ronnie, I would be only part of who I am. I promise to love you, cherish you and care for you for the rest of my days and beyond."

Together they said, "This is our oath this is our vow, in front of our loved ones we make it now. So mote it be." Nessie repeated, "So mote it be." She took the cord, resting on Alina's wrist and wrapped it several times, in the shape of a figure eight, from Alina's hand to Ronnie's hand.

She turned to Sally and Gus and said, "Do you have a vow to make?"

"I do," said Gus and he began to speak, "Sally, my enchantress, you bewitch me with your smile, and beguile me with your wit. With you in my life, my heart beats in time with yours. You are what I have been waiting for to make my life complete."

"Do you have a vow to make Sally?"

Sally cried all the way through her vow, barely holding it together. "Gus, before you, there was nothing, before you there was fear, before you there was loneliness. With you there is no fear for you have taught me how to love and more, how to be loved. In this place of love that I share with you, there is no loneliness, only love".

Nessie prompted them and they said, "This is our oath this is our vow, in front of our loved ones we make it now. So mote it be." "So mote it be," said Nessie. She took the cord resting on Sally's wrist and wrapped it several times, in the shape of a figure eight, from Sally's hand to Gus's hand.

The wedding rings were on the altar, two on a blue satin pillow, and two on a green satin pillow, matching the bride's gowns. Nessie lifted the pillows one in each hand and said, "These rings, blessed with air, fire, water, and earth, are the rings that bind forever. Promises made in the presence of the God, Goddess and the four sacred elements should be kept." She nodded to the grooms and said, "You may place the rings on your bride's finger."

Then it was Alina and Sally's turn to place the rings on their grooms.

Nessie announced, "I now pronounce you husbands and wives for as long as ye all shall live. So mote it be. You may kiss your brides."

Nessie said, There was loud cheering as the couples kissed, and no one paid any heed to Nessie who rang the crystal bell three times to indicate that the ceremony was over.

Someone had placed the broomstick across the opening for the circle and Alina and Ronnie, followed by Sally and Gus, followed by everyone else including Nessie, jumped the broomstick. There was much hilarity, laughing, celebrating, kissing and chatting. Drinks were poured, music was put on, and everyone toasted the union of the two couples. Nancy and Liz brought food out and everyone heaped food on their plates.

Much, much later, after a day of celebration, Alina and Ronnie were lying in their bed. Nessie, Nancy, Cathy, and Liz, had cleared everything away without Alina or Sally even noticing. Both couples had decided that they did not want to go away on honeymoon, instead opting to stay in their own homes. Sally and Gus had already left to loud cheers, covered in confetti and all the guest showered Ronnie and Alina with confetti before they left them in peace.

"It was a lovely day," said Alina.

Ronnie kissed her lips, "It was a wonderful day."

"I can't believe you and Gus managed to arrange all these things, the wedding script, arranging the men and the women to be the bearers of the elements at the quarters, and Nessie, she looked like Mother Earth. I was stunned and I think everyone else was too. When on earth did you have the time?" Ronnie just laughed aloud. For a while, they lay there, pensive, gazing at the moon through their dormer window, and then Ronnie said,

"So Mary let you see our children."

"I don't think I can tell you, I'm sure she said just for my eyes."

"Hmm, three of them."

"You saw them too?" said Alina, excited, and leaning on her elbow to gaze at her husband.

"Yes, she let me see our children and they are beautiful, a son and two daughters who look just like their Mother; rest in peace Mary."

"Rest in peace," responded Alina and they lay there, the room illuminated by the moon, and pictured their future together.

----)O(----

Other Books by Soraya

Before the Rose

The Wooden Rose

Reiki Training Manual

Psychic Guidance

Best Names & Numerology

Magickal Rune Vibrations

The Witches Companion

The Kitchen Witch

Book of Spells

Psychic Powers

Book of Tarot

Book of Runes

Little Book of Spells

Little Book of Cord and Candle Magick

Dedication

With thanks to my artist husband Martin, who helped with finding locations, creating my timeline and family tree, which 1 found impossible to do, checked grammar and spelling without laughing at my dyslexic mistakes, and coped with my inability to focus on anything except 'the book'. He has put up with an untidy house and the back of my head as I sit at my PC when I am "in the zone" writing.

The Rune images are illustrations which were done by Martin for my book of Runes and the significance of the images in this story has surprised even me. The images reflect my storyline so perfectly even though they were created several years ago.

To Rosey my best friend; there would be no novels if it wasn't for her encouragement and inspiration. She motivates me when I am lethargic, inspires me when I am discouraged, and makes me laugh when I am down. Thanks also go to Rosie's sister Joanne, whose hobby is genealogy, who plied me with relevant information that helped me to bring this story to life.

With special thanks to the following people who helped to make this story and for their kind permission in allowing their names to be used. I have to admit that for the songs, I used artistic licence because some of them did not exist until much later than the period that The Wooden Rose, and Before the Rose was set in.

The Tinkers Wedding was written by William Watt of Peeblesshire and first published in 1835.

The Yellow on the Broom was written by Adam McNaughton, a Glasgow songwriter and published in 1979.

John Duggan, who was a presenter on MID West Radio, wrote the Road to Kildare.

Thanks also to Jim Patterson, the director of Clyde Commercial Diving who took time out of his busy schedule to explain the procedures concerning the recovery of remains in the Clyde.

To my good friend Mel, or for those who are members of The Witches Web, Moonwolf, whom I have never met, but feel as though I know her very well. She patiently reads my first drafts and submits a weekly feature in my Witches Web Newsletter. You can subscribe to it on my website. www.soraya.co.uk With thanks to my readers whose kind words have encouraged me to keep writing novels.

Coincidences

The story began in my head with the image of a young woman gazing from her window, puzzling over the old woman who was staring up at her. Later, while chatting to my friend Rosie, she asked me what the book was going to be about, and when I began to tell her about the old woman Rosie suggested that she should be a gypsy. We laughed together as I said I would use her name and her daughter's name, Rosemarie, in the book.

Rosie phoned her sister Joanne, whom I had met once or twice, to tell her about the story that I was writing. Joanne, who is interested in genealogy, offered to help me with any research information, and of course, I had to name one of the characters Joanne. The details Joanne plied me with were invaluable.

A few days later, the story was taking shape and racing along and the first coincidence occurred. I break the news to my friend Rosie that the character Rosie disappears, never to be seen again.

"You're frightening me now," she says, "because that really happened."

"What happened?" I asked.

"In the 1920's a travelling girl from the Midlands disappeared and was never found again."

I had goose bumps and so did Rosie.

I continued to write, still racing through the story as though I was on a deadline. I reached part two of the story and had to think about a name for my heroine. People always say 'write about what you know' and I know Tarot, so my heroine had to be a psychic, and she had to have a name that would lend itself to that profession. I doodled, jotted down names, and even Googled, them to make sure that I wasn't using another psychic's name. Finally, I came up with Alina and thought no more about it.

Once I had put the bones of my story together, I went back to part one of the story to add character names and descriptions, and I began to email Joanne with research questions such as typical surnames, and where people would be married or buried. Joanne was a great help and promptly sent me the information that I was looking for. I began to develop my characters, and suddenly realised that Joanne had sent me Christian names and one of them was Coralina. I had named my Psychic Alina, which is found in Coralina! I must admit seeing that gave me a bit of a jolt and I wondered if I was channeling my story instead of creating it.

When I reached the part of the story where Alina begins to work with Runes, I knew in my mind exactly what Runes I would feature. On my bookshelf, I have several Rune books including one that I wrote. I turned and picked up the nearest to hand, just to check that I was using the right symbol. The book I picked is one I had used before I wrote my own version.

The last time I had looked at this book was when I was discussing with my husband Martin the illustrations that I wanted him to do for my Rune book, written in 2001. I opened the book at the Rune I wanted to use, and there, written in pencil was the word Gypsy Caravan. I had made this notation for my husband in 2001 as a brief hint at what I wanted him to use for the illustration. That astounded me and gave me goose bumps.

Later, I picked up the Rune book that I had written, and I was taken aback when I realised that one of the Runes that I planned to use had a rose in the illustration. So many coincidences, but it didn't stop there, one of my short stories in my book of Runes is about a travelling family!

Later in the story I realised that I would need logistical information concerning the recovery of a body from the Clyde, and Google came in handy again. I found the phone number for Clyde Commercial Diving and called to ask if anyone could help me. I was told that Jim Patterson was the director and I would need to speak to him, but he was in the Highlands inspecting a Cal Mac ferry that needed a repair. I laughed when I heard that, because the previous night I had been talking to my son Ian who is a purser on a Cal Mac ferry and he was part of the crew taking that same ferry in for the repair. Small world!

You will remember that in the beginning of the story Coralina runs away to marry a miller's son. In those days, it was common to have a surname that reflected your trade, so Coralina became Coralina Miller.

I told my friend Rosie that as a courtesy to her sister I was going to use her name, Joanne, as Alina's relative in the story. Rosie was delighted, and told me that Joanne would be thrilled. Much later in the book, when the character Joanne is located, I had to give her a surname, and I said to my hubby Martin that her surname would be Miller. "You can't use that," he said, "Coralina was a Miller."

"I know, but that was a hundred years ago, it has to be Miller, full circle." When it was done, I went to Rosie's house for coffee, my usual retreat, and told her the last part of the story and about Joanne's appearance in the book. She jumped out of her chair.

"You're kidding me, you're kidding me. I must phone Joanne."

I thought she was excited because Joanne was included in the story, but Rosie knew that, so I was puzzled when she put the phone on loudspeaker. She told Joanne that I was there, and she asked Joanne to guess what surname I had used. Joanne was as mystified as I was and admitted that she didn't know.

"MILLER!" exclaimed Rosie. "She's called her Joanne Miller, and she has called her husband John."

It turns out that Joanne's surname is Miller and her husband's name is John. I should point out that at that time I had only known Rosie for two years, and I did not know Joanne's family name. So for me, the question remains; did I write this book, or did I channel it?

I could never have written this story without the old woman that often appeared in my thoughts. I don't know who she was, but I am sure she had a hand in the creation of "The Wooden Rose." I remember telling my best friend Rosey about her and she suggested that I should write a story about it. I began that story; "The Wooden Rose" without really knowing what it was about or where it was going, but it flowed like a predestined plan. When it was finished, readers told me that they would love to know more about the earlier years, and so "Before the Rose" was born and here I am having put the finishing touches to "After the Rose," a trilogy that for me is a gift from above, "The Mystery of the Wooden Rose"

I hope my readers will enjoy all three books and be kind enough to review them on Amazon.

Love and Blessings as always, Soraya.

Printed in Poland
by Amazon Fulfillment
Poland Sp. z o.o., Wrocław